KT-474-969

READER'S DIGEST
SELECT EDITIONS

READER'S DIGEST
SELECT EDITIONS

The names, characters and incidents portrayed in the novels in this volume are the work of the authors' imaginations. Any resemblance to actual persons, living or dead, events or localities is entirely coincidental.

www.readersdigest.co.uk

The Reader's Digest Association Limited
11 Westferry Circus Canary Wharf London E14 4HE

For information as to ownership of copyright in the material of this book, and acknowledgments, see last page.

Printed in Germany
ISBN 978 0 276 44217 9

SELECTED AND CONDENSED
BY READER'S DIGEST

THE READER'S DIGEST ASSOCIATION LIMITED, LONDON

CONTENTS

Jason Steadman is a successful salesman who lacks the killer instinct that would take him to the top of the company he works for. But everything changes when he befriends former Special Forces officer Kurt Semko and suddenly his career takes off. Coincidence? Or has Jason chosen the kind of buddy you wouldn't wish on anyone? Joseph Finder, author of *Paranoia* and *Company Man*, weaves a high-voltage story of twisted loyalty, ambition and corporate machismo.

KILLER INSTINCT

JOSEPH FINDER

9

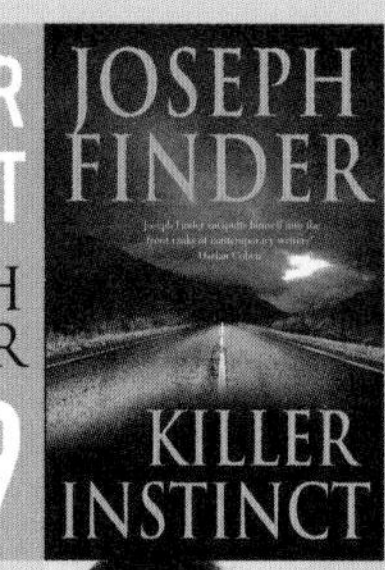

Living in a Queen Anne manor house on the banks of the River Itchen, and surrounded by a garden that's his pride and joy, Dr Christopher Devon just lacks one thing: someone to share his life with. But how can the lonely GP meet the woman of his dreams? His daughter has bags of advice; his son just wants his mum back; his mates Tiger and Gary are having some women problems of their own. Being in your fifties, it seems, is tricky. A light-hearted look at the trials and tribulations of middle age.

LOVE & DR DEVON

ALAN TITCHMARSH

155

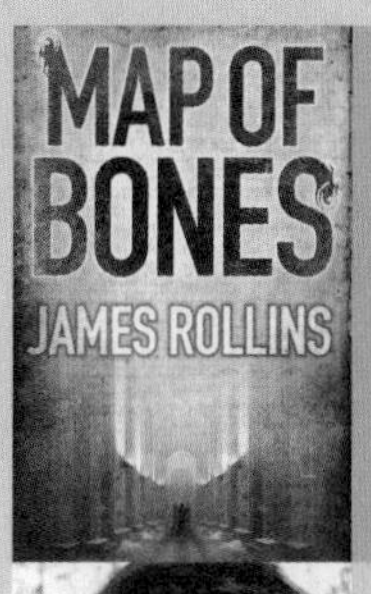

MAP OF BONES

JAMES ROLLINS

277

When a violent attack on the congregation in Cologne Cathedral culminates in the disappearance of a number of precious holy relics, the Vatican is in turmoil. Cardinal Spera drafts in the help of his art-investigator niece, Rachel Verona, as well as that of Gray Pierce from Sigma, an elite American crime-fighting force. It rapidly becomes apparent that this bizarre theft is part of an audacious attempt by an ancient secret fraternity to change the course of history itself.

Stella Rimington, former Director General of MI5, draws on her considerable experience of spycraft in this compelling novel. Agent Liz Carlyle is frustrated when her boss pulls her off a terrorist investigation and asks her to look into a tip-off that the IRA planted a sleeper in British Intelligence some years ago. The danger seems minimal to Liz, but she is soon proved wrong. The mole has been biding his time and is now ready to take his revenge on the British establishment that he has hated for so long.

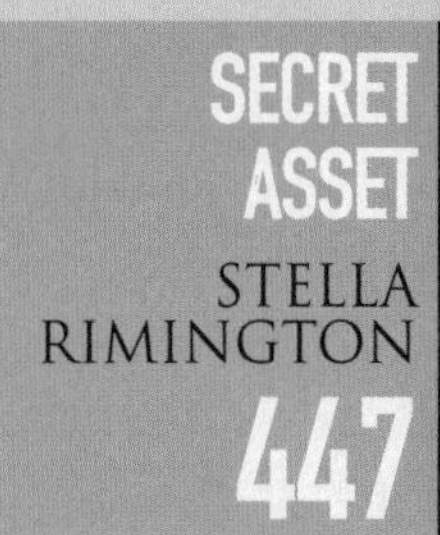

SECRET ASSET

STELLA RIMINGTON

447

KILLER INSTINCT

JOSEPH FINDER

Business is war,

or so they say.

But it's never a good

idea to take that

dictum too seriously—as

Jason Steadman is

about to find out.

PART ONE

CHAPTER 1

OK, so I'm an idiot.

The Acura went into a ditch because I was trying to do too many things at once. Radiohead's 'The Bends' was playing, loud, while I was driving home, too fast, since I was late as usual. Left hand on the wheel, while with my right hand I was thumbing my BlackBerry for emails, hoping I'd finally nailed a deal with a huge new customer.

When my cellphone rang, I dropped the BlackBerry on the car seat and grabbed the cell. I knew from the ring that it was my wife, Kate, so I didn't bother to turn down the music—I figured she was just calling to find out when I'd be home from work so she could get dinner ready. She'd been on a tofu-and-brown-rice kick the last few months. It had to be really good for you, since it tasted so bad. But I'd never tell her so.

That wasn't why she was calling, though. I could tell from Kate's voice that she'd been crying, and even before she said anything I knew why.

'DiMarco called,' she said. DiMarco was our doctor at Boston IVF who'd been trying to get Kate pregnant for the last two years or so. Personally, I was dubious about the whole process. I figured high-tech should be for flat-screen plasma monitors, not making babies. Even so, it felt like I'd been punched in the stomach.

But the worst thing was what it would do to Kate. She was crazy enough these days from the hormone injections. This would send her over the edge.

'I'm really sorry,' I said.

'They're not going to let us keep trying forever, you know,' she said. 'All they care about is their numbers, and we're bringing them down.'

'Kate, it's only our third try with the IVF stuff. It's like a ten per cent chance per cycle anyway, right? We'll keep at it, babe. That's all.'

'What are we going to do if it doesn't work?' Kate's voice got all choked. 'Go to California, do the donor egg thing? I can't go through that. Adopt?'

Adoption was fine with me. Or not. I focused on turning down the music. There's some little button on the steering wheel that I've never figured out how to use, so with the thumb of my driving hand I started pushing buttons, but instead the volume increased until Radiohead was blaring.

'Kate,' I said, but just then I realised that the car had veered onto the shoulder and then off the road. I dropped the phone, grabbed the wheel with both hands, cut it hard, but too late. I slammed on the brakes.

There was a sickening metallic crunch. I was jolted forward, thrown against the wheel, then back. Suddenly the car was canting all the way down to one side. The engine was racing, the wheels spinning in midair.

I knew I wasn't hurt seriously, but I might have bruised a couple of ribs. I turned the key, shut off the music, and sat there for a couple of seconds in silence before I picked the cellphone off the floor of the car to call Triple A.

But the line was still open, and I could hear Kate screaming.

'Jason, are you all right?' She was freaking out. 'What *happened*?'

'I'm fine, babe.'

'Jason, my God, did you get in an *accident*?'

'I'm fine sweetheart. Everything's cool. Don't worry about it.'

FORTY-FIVE MINUTES LATER a tow truck pulled up, a bright red truck, M.E. WALSH TOW painted on the side panel. The driver walked over to me. He was a tall, broad-shouldered guy with a scruffy goatee, wearing a bandana on his head knotted at the back, and long grey-flecked brown hair. He was wearing a black leather Harley-Davidson jacket.

'Let me guess,' the dude said. 'You were talking on your cellphone.'

I blinked for a microsecond before I said sheepishly, 'Yeah.'

'Damn things are a menace.'

'Yeah, totally.' I said. Like I could survive without my cellphone.

'You OK?' Harley said.

'Yeah, I'm good.'

He backed the truck around to my car, hooked the winch up to the Acura, switched on the electric pulley thing and started hauling my car out of the ditch. I noticed the truck had a yellow 'Support Our Troops' ribbon sticker on one side and one of those black-and-white POW/MIA stickers on the windshield. I made a mental note to myself not to criticise the war in Iraq.

'Climb in,' he said.

The cab of the truck smelled like stale cigar smoke and gasoline.

'You got a body shop you like?' he said.

I had a serious gearhead friend who'd know, but I couldn't tell a carburettor from a caribou. 'I don't get into accidents too often,' I said.

'Well, you don't look like the kinda guy who changes the oil himself,' Harley said. 'There's a body shop I know, not too far from here.'

We mostly sat there in silence while he drove. I made a couple of attempts to get a conversation started, but it was like striking a wet match.

Normally I could talk to anyone about anything—you name it, sports, kids, dogs, TV shows. I was a sales manager for one of the biggest electronics companies in the world, up there with Sony and Panasonic. The division I work for makes those big beautiful flat-panel LCD and plasma TVs and monitors that so many people lust after. And the really good sales reps, the ones who have the juice, can start a conversation with anybody. That's me.

But this guy didn't want to talk, and after a while I gave up. I was kind of uncomfortable being chauffeured around by a Hells Angel. I found myself staring at the collection of stickers on the dashboard—a 'These Colours Don't Run' flag decal, another one that said 'Special Forces—I'm the Man Your Mother Warned You About.' After a while, I said, 'This your truck?'

'Nah, my buddy owns the towing company and I help out.'

Guy was getting chatty. I said, 'He Special Forces?'

A long silence. I was about to repeat the question when he said, 'We both were.'

'Huh,' I said, and we both went quiet again. He switched on the ball game. The Red Sox were playing the Seattle Mariners at Fenway Park, and it was a tight, hard-fought, low-scoring game, pretty exciting. I love listening to baseball on the radio. I have a huge flat-panel TV at home, but there's nothing like a ball game on the radio—the crack of the bat, the rustling crowd, even the stupid ads for auto glass. The announcers sound exactly the way they did when I was a kid. Their flat, nasal voices use all the well-worn phrases like 'high—fly—ball!' and 'swing and a miss.'

One of the announcers was commenting about the Sox pitcher, saying, '. . . but even at the top of his game, he's never going to come close to the fastest recorded pitch speed of 100.9 miles an hour, thrown by . . . ? Jerry, you must know that one.'

And the other guy said, 'Nolan Ryan.'

'Nolan Ryan,' the first guy said, 'Very good. Clocked at Anaheim Stadium, August the 20th, 1974.'

I said, 'Wrong.'

The driver turned to me. 'Huh?'

I said, 'The fastest recorded pitch was Mark Wholers.'

'Very good,' Harley said. 'Mark Wholers. Hundred and three.'

'Right,' I said, surprised. 'Hundred and three miles per hour, in 1995.'

'Atlanta Braves spring training.' Then he smiled, an easy grin.

'So were you a baseball geek when you were a kid, too?' I said. 'Collection of thousands of baseball cards?'

He smiled again. 'You got it. Those Topps gum packs with that crappy stale bubble gum inside.'

'Your dad take you to Fenway a lot?' I said.

'My dad wasn't around,' he said. 'We couldn't afford to go to games.'

'We couldn't either,' I said. 'So I listened to games on the radio.'

'Same here.'

'Played baseball in the backyard?' I said. 'Break a lot of windows?'

'We didn't have a backyard.'

'Me neither. My friends and I played in a park down the street.'

I felt like I knew the guy. We came from the same background, probably—no money, no backyard, the whole deal. Only I went to college and was sitting here in a suit, and he'd gone into the army like a lot of my high school buddies did.

We listened to the game for a bit. Seattle's designated hitter was up. He swung at the first pitch. You could hear the crack of the bat. 'And there's a *high* fly ball hit *deep* to left field!' one of the announcers crowed. It was headed right for the glove of a great Red Sox slugger, who also happened to be a famously clumsy outfielder.

'He's got it,' said the announcer. 'It's headed right for his glove.'

'He's going to drop it,' I said.

Harley laughed. 'You said it.'

A roar of disappointment in the ballpark. 'The ball hit the *back* of the glove,' said the announcer. 'This is a *major*-league error right here.'

We groaned simultaneously.

Harley switched it off. 'I can't take it anymore,' he said.

'Thank you,' I said, as we pulled into the auto body shop parking lot.

IT WAS A KIND of scuzzy place that looked like a converted gas station. WILLKIE AUTO BODY, the sign said. The manager on duty was named Abdul. Harley came into the waiting room and watched him take down my insurance information. I noticed another 'Support Our Troops' sticker on the wall in here, too.

Harley said, 'Jeremiah at home?'

'Oh, yeah,' said Abdul. 'Sure. Home with the kids.'

'This is a friend of mine,' Harley said. 'Make sure you take care of him.'

I looked around and realised the tow-truck driver was talking about me.

'Of course, Kurt,' Abdul said.

I read an old copy of *Maxim* while the tow-truck driver and Abdul walked back to the shop. They returned a couple of minutes later.

'Abdul's going to put his best master tech on your car,' Harley said. 'They do good work here. Why don't you guys finish up the paperwork, and I'll get the car in the service bay.'

'Thanks, man,' I said.

I came out a few minutes later and saw Harley sitting in his tow truck, engine idling, listening to the game.

'Hey,' he said, 'where do you live? I'll drop you off.'

'It's pretty far. Belmont.'

'Grab your stuff out of the car and jump in.'

I got my CDs off the floor of the car and my briefcase and baseball glove off the back seat.

'You worked in a body shop?' I said when I'd got back into the truck.

'I've done everything.'

'How do you like towing?'

He turned and gave me an *Are you out of your mind?* look. 'I take whatever work I can get.'

'People don't like to hire soldiers anymore?'

'People love to hire soldiers,' he said. 'Just not ones with DDs.'

'What's a DD?'

'Dishonourable discharge. You gotta put it down on the application.'

'Oh,' I said. 'Sorry I asked. None of my business.'

'No big deal. It just pisses me off. You get a DD, you don't get any VA benefits or pension. Sucks big-time.'

'How'd it happen?' I said. 'If you don't mind my asking.'

Another long silence. Then he said: 'The CO of my Special Forces A-team ordered half of us to go on this suicide reconnaissance mission in Tikrit. I told him there was a ninety-nine per cent chance they'd get ambushed, and guess what? The guys got ambushed. Attacked with rocket-propelled grenades. And my buddy Jimmy Donadio was killed.'

He fell silent. Stared straight ahead at the road as he drove. Then: 'A good kid, just about finished with his tour, had a baby he'd never even seen. I loved the guy. So I just lost it. Went after the CO—headbutted the bastard. Broke his nose.'

'Wow,' I said. 'I can't blame you. So you got court-martialled?'

He shrugged. 'I'm lucky they didn't send me to Leavenworth. But nobody in the command wanted to draw any attention to what went down that night. Bad PR. So the deal was, dishonourable discharge, no time.'

'Wow,' I said again.

'So are you, like, a lawyer or something?'

'Entronics salesman. In Framingham.'

'Cool. Can you get me a deal on a plasma TV?'

I hesitated. 'I don't sell the consumer line, but I might be able to do something.'

He smiled. 'I'm kidding. I couldn't afford one of those anyway, even wholesale. So, I noticed the glove you got back there. Rawlings Gold Glove, same as the pros use. Looks brand-new. You play?'

'Not much. Mostly on my company's team. Softball, not baseball.' Our team sucked. We were on a losing streak that resembled the Baltimore Orioles' historically pathetic 1988 season. 'You play?'

He shrugged. 'Used to.' A long beat of silence. 'Got drafted by the Detroit Tigers, but never signed.'

'Seriously?'

'My pitch speed was clocked at ninety-four, ninety-five miles an hour.'

'No way!' I turned to look at him.

'But that wasn't where my head was, at that point. Enlisted instead. I'm Kurt, by the way.' He took his right hand off the wheel and gave me a firm handshake. 'Kurt Semko.'

'Jason Steadman.'

There was another long silence, and then I had an idea.

'We've got a game tomorrow night, and we sure could use a decent pitcher,' I said. 'How would you like to play on our team?'

'Don't you have to work for the company?'

'Guys we play have no idea who works for us and who doesn't.'

Kurt went quiet again.

After a minute, I said, 'So what do you think?'

He shrugged. 'I don't know, I'll think about it.'

At the time it seemed like a fun idea.

I LOVE MY WIFE.

Sometimes I can't believe that a woman as intelligent and sophisticated and, oh yeah, unbelievably beautiful, settled for a guy like me. She likes to joke that our courtship was the greatest job of salesmanship I ever pulled off. I don't disagree. I did close the deal, after all.

When I walked in, Kate was sitting on the couch watching TV. There was a bowl of popcorn in her lap and a glass of white wine on the coffee table. She was wearing faded gym shorts from her prep school, which nicely set off her long, toned legs. As soon as she saw me come in, she got up, ran over to hug me. 'Oh, my God,' she said. 'I've been so worried.'

'I'm fine, I told you. Though the tow-truck driver thought I was an idiot.'

'You're totally OK, Jase?' She pulled back to look at me. Her eyes were a great shade of hazel brown, her hair was full and black, and she had a sharp jaw line and high cheekbones. She reminded me of a young, dark-haired Katharine Hepburn. Tonight, though, her eyes were bloodshot and puffy. She'd obviously been crying a lot.

'The car just went off the side of the road,' I said. 'I'm fine, but the car got messed up.'

'The car,' she said with an airy wave, as if my Acura TL were a wad of toilet paper. I assume she inherited these aristocratic gestures from her parents. Kate's family was once very rich, but the money never made it to her generation. The Spencer fortune took a hit in 1929 and got finished off by her father, an alcoholic who only knew how to spend money, not manage it.

All Kate got was part of an expensive education, a cultivated voice, and a pile of antiques, many of which she'd jammed into our three-bedroom colonial house on a quarter-acre in Belmont.

'How'd you get back?' she said.

'Tow-truck driver. Interesting guy—ex-Special Forces.'

'Hmm,' she said, that not-interested-but-faking-it noise I knew so well.

'Is that dinner?' I said, pointing to the bowl of popcorn.

'Sweetie, I'm sorry. I just didn't feel like cooking tonight. You want me to make you something?'

I could visualise the brick of tofu lurking in the refrigerator, and I almost shuddered. 'Don't worry about it. I'll just grab something. Come here.' I hugged her again. 'I'm worried about you.'

All of a sudden she kind of crumpled. I felt her chest heave and her hot tears dampen my shirt. I squeezed her tight. 'It's just that I really thought this one was going to work,' she said.

'Next time, maybe. We just have to be patient, huh?'

'Do you not worry about *anything*?'

'Just stuff I can do something about,' I said.

AFTER A WHILE, we sat down together on the couch, which was an uncomfortable but no doubt valuable English antique as hard as a church pew, and watched a documentary on the Discovery channel about bonobos, a species of monkey apparently smarter and more highly evolved than us.

I took a handful of popcorn. It was air-popped and lightly spritzed with I Can't Believe It's Not Butter. It tasted like Styrofoam. I went to the kitchen and served myself a big bowl of ice cream. I didn't ask Kate if she wanted any. She never ate ice cream. She never ate anything remotely fattening.

I sat back down and dug into the ice cream.

Kate watched me tuck into it. 'Sweetheart, you might want to lay off the ice cream at night.'

'I never feel like it at breakfast.'

'You know what I'm saying,' she said, and touched her perfectly flat belly. I, on the other hand, was already developing a pot-belly at thirty.

'Can we watch something else?' I said. 'This is getting too boring.'

Kate grabbed the remote and began flipping through the hundreds of channels until she stopped at a show that looked familiar. I recognised that Fox show *S.B.,* about beautiful rich high-school kids and their broken families in Santa Barbara. It had become the hottest TV show of the season.

And it was created by my brother-in-law, Craig Glazer, the hotshot TV producer who was married to Kate's older sister, Susie. Craig and I pretended to get along.

'How can you watch that crap?' I said, grabbing the remote and switching the channel to some old *National Geographic*-style show about a primitive Amazonian tribe called the Yanomamo.

'You'd better deal with that hostility before Craig and Susie come next week.'

'They have no idea how I feel about him.'

Kate cocked a brow provocatively but said nothing.

We watched some more of the nature show, sort of listlessly. The narrator said in a plummy British accent that the Yanomami were the most violent, aggressive society in the world. They were always breaking out into wars, usually over women, who were scarce.

'I'll bet you like that, huh?' I said. 'Fighting over women?'

She shook her head. 'I studied the Yanomami in one of my feminism classes. The men beat their wives too. The women think the more machete scars they have, the more their husbands must love them.'

Kate had got interested in obscure African and South American cultures in the last few years because of her job, I think. She worked for the Mayer Foundation for Folk and Outsider Art in Boston, which gave money to poor and homeless people who made paintings and sculptures that looked like they could have been done by my eight-year-old nephew.

The narrator said that Yanomami boys proved their manhood by 'blooding their spear,' or killing someone. They used axes and spears and bows and arrows. And blowpipes carved from bamboo that shot poison darts.

When the show was over I gave her the latest news. The divisional vice-president, Crawford, had just left the company for Sony and taken six of his top guys with him. Which left a huge, gaping hole in my department. 'It sucks,' I said. 'Huge mess.'

'What are you talking about?' Kate said. 'It's terrific.'

'You don't get it. Entronics just announced they're acquiring the US business of this Dutch company called Meister.' Royal Meister Electronics N.V. is an immense electronics conglomerate, one of our biggest competitors. They had a unit based in Dallas that sold the same things we did—the LCDs and the plasma screens and the projectors and all that. 'So Crawford's getting the hell out. He must know something.'

Kate sat up, drew her knees to her chest. 'Listen, Jase, don't you realise what this means? You've been stuck at the level of district sales manager for *years*. If Crawford's gone, along with six of his top guys, the sales division has no choice but to back-fill some of those slots from inside, right? This is your chance to really start climbing the ladder.'

'Greasy pole, more like it. Katie, I like my job. I don't want to be a VP.'

'But your salary's basically capped out right now, right? You're never going to make much more than you do now.'

'What do you mean? I'm doing pretty good. Remember how much I made three years ago?'

She nodded, her eyes fixed on mine, like she was weighing whether to say more. Then she said, 'Honey, three years ago was a freak. Plasma screens were just coming out, and Entronics owned the market, right? That's never going to happen again. But if you get into management, baby, that's when you start making the real money.'

'Those guys in upper management never leave the office,' I said. 'They turn fishbelly white from being in meetings all the time. Too much sucking up, too much politics. It's not for me. Why are we talking about this?'

'Look. You become the area manager and then a DVP and then a VP and general manager and in a couple of years, you could be making a *fortune*.'

I took a deep breath, wanting to argue with her. When she got like this, she was like a terrier that wouldn't let go of its Nylabone.

The fact was, Kate and I had very different ideas of what a 'fortune' was. My dad was a sheet-metal worker. He rose as high as shop foreman, and he was active in the Sheet Metal Workers Local 63. He wasn't very ambitious but worked really hard, did overtime whenever possible. He arrived home at the end of the day wiped out, unable to do more than sit in front of the TV and drink Budweiser. Dad was missing the tips of two fingers, a silent reminder to me of how nasty his job was. When he told me he wanted me to go to college so I didn't have to do what he did, he really meant it.

We lived on one floor of a three-decker in Worcester that had asbestos siding and a concrete backyard. To go from that to owning my own colonial house in Belmont—well, that was pretty damned good, I thought.

Whereas the house Kate had grown up in, in Wellesley, was an immense stone mansion with a high wrought-iron fence. Even after her boozer father had finally killed off what remained of the family fortune and they'd had to sell it, as well as their summer house on Cape Cod, the place they moved to was about twice as big as the house she and I lived in now.

She pouted. 'Jason, you don't want to end up like Cal Taylor, do you?'

'That's a low blow.'

Cal Taylor was around sixty and had been a salesman with Entronics forever, since the days when they sold transistor radios and second-rate colour TVs. With his white hair and nicotine-yellowed moustache, his Jack Daniel's breath and his smoker's hack and his never-ending stock of stale jokes, he was a human cautionary tale. He managed to hang on because of a few tenuous relationships he'd built over the years. He was divorced, lived alone, and spent almost every night at a neighbourhood bar.

Then her face softened and she tipped her head. 'Honey,' she said softly, almost wheedling, 'look at this house.'

'What about it?'

'We don't want to bring up kids in a place like this,' she said. She suddenly looked sad. 'There's no room to play. There's barely a yard.'

'I hate mowing the lawn. Anyway, I didn't have a yard growing up.'

She paused, looked away. I wondered what she was thinking.

'Come on, Jason. When I met you, you were this totally fired-up, sky's-the-limit kind of guy. Remember?'

'That was just to get you to marry me.'

'I know you're kidding. You've got the drive, you *know* you do. You've just gotten'—she was about to say 'fat and happy', I'll bet, but instead she said, 'too comfortable. This is it. This is the time to go for it.'

I kept thinking about the Yanomami documentary. When Kate married me, she must have thought I was some warrior she could groom into a chieftain.

But I said, 'I'll talk to Gordy.' Kent Gordon was the senior VP who ran the entire sales division.

'Good,' she said. 'Tell him you demand a promotion.'

' "Demand" isn't exactly my style.'

'Well, surprise him. Show him some aggression. He'll love it. It's kill or be killed. You've got to show him you're a killer.'

'Yeah, right,' I said. 'You think I can get one of those Yanomami blowpipes on eBay?'

CHAPTER 2

'We're screwed, man,' said Ricky Festino. 'We are so screwed.'

Ricky Festino was a member of what we called the Band of Brothers, a fellow salesman for Entronics USA's Visual Systems unit. Salesmen are supposed to all be outgoing and affable, back-slappers, hail-fellows-well-met, but not Ricky Festino. He was dour, cynical, bitingly sarcastic.

As far as I could tell, he hated his job and didn't much like his wife and two little kids either. He chauffeured his younger boy to some private school every morning and coached his older boy's Little League team, which would theoretically make him a good dad, except for the fact that he was always complaining about it.

'Why's that?' I asked.

'The acquisition, what do you think?' he muttered, as he squeezed out a glistening dollop of antibacterial hand cleaner from a tiny bottle he carried with him everywhere. Ricky was an out-of-control germophobe. 'I just shook hands with that guy from CompuMax, and he kept sneezing on me.'

CompuMax was a 'system-builder', a company that assembled and sold low-end computers for corporations. They were a lousy client, because they didn't spend money on name-brand components, and Entronics was too name-brand for them. Ricky was trying to sell them a bunch of LCD monitors but my guess was that he didn't know how to pitch it.

'I'm starting to get why the Japs think we Westerners are so unclean,' he went on. 'He was, like, sneezing into his hands over and over, then he wanted to shake. Guy was a human petri dish. Want some?' He offered me the tiny plastic bottle.

'No, thanks, I'm good.'

He sank back in the visitor chair of my office. 'Let me tell you something about this deal. The Japanese always have a long-range master plan. We're just those little round game pieces—what's that strategy game the Japanese play?'

'Go?'

'"Go", right. "Go." Go take a leap. Go screw yourself.' I could see sweat stains under the arms of Ricky's blue button-down shirt. He was a couple of years older than me and was going to seed. He had a pot-belly more advanced than mine hanging over his belt, a roll of neck fat spilling over his collar. He'd started colouring his hair a couple of years ago.

I sneaked a glance at the time. I'd told the guy at Lockwood Hotel and Resorts that I'd call him before noon, and it was 12.05. 'Hey, uh, Ricky . . .'

'See, you don't get it. You're too *nice*.' He said it with a nasty curl to his lips. 'Entronics acquires Royal Meister's US operations, right? But why? You think their plasma screens are better than ours?'

'Nope,' I said, trying not to encourage him.

I'd tell the guy at Lockwood that I was closing a huge deal and couldn't call him earlier. I'd hint about a rival five-star luxury hotel chain I couldn't name that was also putting plasma-screen TVs in all their guest rooms.

'It's their *sales force*.' Ricky said. 'The boys in Tokyo are rubbing their hands at the prospect of buying a sales force that's more high-test than we are. So they get rid of all but the top ten per cent, and move them to Dallas. It's obvious, Jason. Why do you think Crawford went to Sony, man?'

Ricky was so proud of his Machiavellian genius that I didn't want to let him know I'd already come up with the same theory. So I nodded.

I noticed a slender Japanese man passing by my office, and gave a casual wave. 'Hey, Yoshi,' I said. Yoshi Tanaka, a personality-free guy with aviator-frame glasses, was a *funin-sha*, an expatriate Japanese, transferred to the

US to learn the ropes. His title was Manager for Business Planning, but everyone knew he was Tokyo's eyes and ears here. He spoke just about no English, though, which couldn't have been good for his spying.

Yoshi scared the shit out of everyone, but I felt bad for him. Being posted in a country where you didn't speak the language, without family—at least, I assumed he had family back in Tokyo—couldn't be easy. He was isolated, ostracised by his colleagues, all of them distrusted him. Not an easy gig. I never joined the others in Yoshi-bashing.

Ricky turned, gave Yoshi a smile and a wave, and as soon as Yoshi was out of range, muttered, 'Goddamned spy.'

'You think he heard you?' I said.

'Nah. Even if he did, he wouldn't understand.'

'Listen, Ricky, I'm late calling Lockwood.'

'They still dicking you around? Forget it, man. Stop pursuing them.'

'A forty-million-dollar deal, and you're telling me to forget it?'

'The guy just wants Super Bowl tickets. Any deal that takes this long is dead in the water.'

I sighed. Festino was an expert on deals that were dead in the water.

I stood up to encourage him to do the same. 'You playing tonight?'

He got up. 'Yeah, sure. Who're we playing tonight, Charles River?'

I nodded.

'Gonna be another ignominious defeat for the Band of Brothers. We got no pitching. Trevor sucks.'

I smiled, remembering the tow-truck driver. 'I got a pitcher. A guy who almost went pro.'

'What are you talking about?'

I filled him in quickly.

Ricky's eyes narrowed, and for the first time this morning, he smiled. 'We tell the Charles River boys he's the new stockboy.'

I nodded.

He cocked his head to one side, gave me an appraising look. 'You know, Jason, under that simpleton façade, you've got hidden reserves of craftiness. Never would have expected it. I'm impressed.'

THE LOCKWOOD HOTEL and Resort Group was one of the largest chains of luxury hotels in the world. Part of management's plan to compete with the Four Seasons and the Ritz-Carlton was to put Bose Wave Radios and forty-two-inch flat-panel plasma TVs in every room. I knew they were talking to

NEC and Toshiba too. I knew our product performed at least as well as the others, but the Vice-President for Property Management at Lockwood, Brian Borque, couldn't make a decision.

I wondered whether Ricky Festino was right, that Borque was stringing me along just for the Super Bowl tickets.

'Hey, Brian,' I said into the headset.

'There he is,' Brian said. He always sounded happy to hear from me.

'I should have called you earlier.' I almost gave him the lie about the other hotel chain, but I didn't have the heart. 'Meeting ran long.'

'No worries, man. Hey, I read something about you guys in the *Journal* this morning. You getting acquired by Meister?'

'Other way around. Entronics is acquiring Meister US.'

'Interesting. We've been talking to them too, you know.'

I hadn't known. Great, another player in this endless negotiation.

'Well, that'll mean one less competitor,' I said, keeping the tone light. 'How was Martha's birthday? You take her to Vienna, like she wanted?'

'Vienna, Virginia, more like. Hey, I've got to be in Boston next week—you feel like catching a Sox game? You guys still get those amazing seats?'

'I'll do what I can.' I hesitated. 'So, listen, Bri.'

He heard the change in my tone and cut me off. 'I wish I had an answer for you, buddy, but I don't.'

'Thing is, Brian, I'm getting a lot of pressure from senior management on this thing. Gordy wants me to set up a meeting with your CEO.'

'Gordy,' Brian said in disgust. Kent Gordon was ruthless, conniving and relentless, and my entire career lay in his hands. Gordy was in fact leaning on me hard to do this deal, since he leaned on everybody hard to do every deal. But Gordy hadn't asked for a meeting—yet. It was a bluff.

'I know,' I said, 'but, you know, I can't control what he does.'

'I don't recommend you do that. Jason, when I was on your side of the desk I tried that old trick plenty of times,' Brian said, not unkindly. 'Look, I wish I could tell you what's going on with this deal, but I'm out of the loop. Obviously there's stuff going on upstairs that I'm not privy to.'

'Someone up there's got a favourite or something?'

'Jason, I know you've worked your ass off on this deal, and if the product didn't measure up, I'd be straight with you. Or if the numbers didn't work. But it's not that. I don't know what it is.'

A beat of silence. 'I appreciate your honesty, Brian,' I said. 'What day next week you coming up?'

MY IMMEDIATE BOSS was a woman, which, in this business, is unusual. Her name was Joan Tureck, and she was an area manager in charge of all New England. I didn't know much about her. I'd heard she was gay and lived with a woman in Cambridge. She was a little dull, but we liked each other, and she'd always supported me, in her low-key way.

She was on the phone when I came by. She was always on the phone. All the Entronics offices have narrow windows on either side of the doors so everyone can always see inside. There's really no privacy.

Joan finally noticed me standing outside her office, and she held up a finger, then beckoned me in with a flick of her left hand.

'You talked to Lockwood Hotels this morning?' Joan said. She had short, curly, mousy brown hair with wisps of grey near the temple. She never wore any make-up. 'Nothing yet?'

'Nothing.'

'You think maybe it's time to call in some reinforcements? If there's anything I can do.' I noticed she looked unusually weary, almost beaten down. 'Is that what you wanted to talk about?'

'No, something else,' I said. 'You have a couple of minutes now?'

She glanced at her tiny wristwatch. 'I've got a lunch any minute, but we could talk until my lunch date shows up.'

'Thanks. So, Crawford's out of here,' I said.

She blinked, not helping me at all.

'And his whole posse,' I went on. 'You're probably moving up to the DVP job, right?'

She blinked, hesitated. 'Bear in mind that, with the Meister acquisition, we're going to be cutting back. Anyone who isn't a top performer.'

'Should I start packing up my desk?'

'You don't have to worry. You've made club four years in a row.' 'Club', or Club 101, was made up of those reps who'd outperformed, made 101 per cent of their revenue numbers. 'You had a bad fourth quarter. Everyone misses a quarter now and then. Bottom line is, people buy from people they like, and everyone likes you. But that's not what you came in to talk about.'

'Joan, do I have a chance at the area manager slot?'

She looked at me with surprise. 'Trevor's already put in for that, you know. And he's lobbying pretty hard.'

Some of the guys called oily Trevor Allard 'Teflon Trevor', because he always got away with everything.

'Trevor would be good. But so would I. Do I have your support?'

'I—I don't take sides, Jason,' she said unhappily. 'If you want me to put in a word for you with Gordy, I'm happy to do so; but I don't know how much he listens to my recommendations.'

'That's all I ask. Just put in a word. Tell him I want to be interviewed.'

'I will. But Trevor is—maybe more Gordy's type. He's what Gordy calls a meat-eater.'

Some people called him other things that weren't so nice. 'I eat steak.'

'I'll put in a word for you. But I'm not going to take sides.'

There was a knock at her door. She made her little beckoning sign.

The door opened, and a tall, handsome guy with tousled brown hair and sleepy brown eyes stood there and flashed her a perfect grin. Trevor Allard was long and lean and muscled and arrogant. 'Ready for lunch, Joan?' he said. 'Oh, hey, Jason. I didn't see you.'

YOU COULD HARDLY collect a more competitive bunch of guys than the sales team of Entronics USA. The company liked to hire athletes, figuring that jocks were persistent and thrived on competition. Those of us who weren't jocks were outgoing, naturally affable types, the social chairman in college, frat guys. That was me. Guilty on all counts.

So you'd think that, for all the jocks on the sales force, our softball team would be formidable.

Actually, we sucked.

Most of us were in lousy shape. We took clients out to lunch all the time, ate well, drank a lot of beer, and didn't have time to exercise. The only guys who'd stayed in shape were Trevor Allard, our pitcher, and Brett Gleason, our shortstop, your classic big dumb jock.

It was considered uncool to be too serious about our softball games. We had no uniforms, unless you count the ENTRONICS—BAND OF BROTHERS T-shirts that someone had made and that hardly anyone wore. We all chipped in to pay an umpire fifty bucks, whenever he was available.

Still, no one likes to lose, especially dog-eat-dog types like us.

Tonight's game was against the reigning champions of our corporate league, Charles River Financial. Their team was almost all traders, right out of college, and they were all twenty-two years old and over six feet tall.

The question wasn't whether we'd lose. It was how badly they'd mop the floor with us.

We played every week at the carefully maintained Stonington College field. The outfield grass was turquoise and lush, perfectly mowed; the red infield dirt was well raked; the foul lines were crisp and white.

The young studs from Charles River arrived all at the same time, driving Porsches and BMWs. They wore real uniforms, white jerseys with pin-stripes, with CHARLES RIVER FINANCIAL stitched across the front, and they each had numbers on their backs. They looked like pros.

By the time the game got under way, I'd forgotten all about the tow-truck driver. Apparently he'd forgotten too.

It got ugly fast. Allard allowed seven runs—four of them a grand slam by Charles River's team captain. Our guys were visibly uptight, trying too hard, so instead of aiming for base hits they kept swinging for home runs and inevitably got pop-ups instead. At the end of the third inning, the Charles River studs were ahead, 10-0. We were discouraged and pissed off.

Our manager, Cal Taylor, sat there drinking from a small flask of Jack Daniel's, poorly concealed in a well-used paper bag, and smoking Marlboros and shaking his head. There was the roar of a motorcycle nearby, coming closer, but I didn't pay much attention to it.

Then I noticed, in the waning light, a tall guy in a leather jacket walk onto the field. It took me a few seconds to recognise the tow-truck driver from last night. He stood there for a few minutes, watching us lose, and then during the break I went up to him.

'Hey, Kurt,' I said. 'You here to play?'

'Looks like you guys could use another player.'

EVERYONE WAS COOL with it except, of course, Trevor Allard. We called a time-out, and we all huddled around Cal Taylor.

'He's not an Entronics employee,' Trevor said. 'You can't play if you don't have a valid employee number. That's the rule.' I wasn't sure whether Trevor was just being his usual priggish self, or he'd heard that I'd put in for the promotion that he probably figured had his name on it.

Ricky Festino, who enjoyed twitting Trevor, said, 'So? If they challenge him, he says he's a contract employee and didn't know he wasn't eligible.'

'A contract employee?' Trevor said with disgust. 'Him?' As if a bum had just wandered onto the field from the street, reeking of cheap booze. Trevor wore long cargo shorts and a faded Red Sox cap, which he wore backwards, of course, and a T-shirt that said LIFE IS GOOD.

'You ever ask the Charles River guys for IDs?' said Ricky. 'How do we know they don't have their own ringers, from the Yankees farm team?'

'Or some guy named Vinny from the mailroom,' said Taminek, a tall, scrawny guy who did inside sales. 'Anyway, Hewlett-Packard uses ringers all the time.'

'Yo, Trevor, you're not objecting because this guy's a pitcher, are you, dude?' Gleason razzed. He was an overdeveloped lunk with Dumbo ears, a lantern jaw, a blond crew cut, and bright white choppers.

Trevor scowled and shook his head, but before he could say anything further, Cal Taylor said, 'Put him in. Trevor, you go to second.' And he took a swig from his paper bag.

ALL ANYONE had to say was 'new hire', and there were no questions asked.

Kurt was assigned to bat third in the line-up. Taminek was on first, and there was one out, when it was Kurt's turn at bat. I noticed he hadn't been warming up but had instead been standing there quietly, watching the Charles River pitcher and captain, Mike Welch, pitch.

He stepped up to the plate, took a few practice swings with his battered old aluminium bat, and hammered a shot to left-centre. The ball sailed over the back fence. As Taminek, and then Kurt, ran home, the guys cheered.

Kurt's homer was like an electric shock from those ER paddles. All of a sudden we started scoring. By the top of the fourth, we had five runs. Kurt took the mound to pitch to a big, beefy Charles River guy named Jarvis who was one of their sluggers. Kurt let loose with a wicked, blistering fastball, an amazing rise ball, then a change up, and Jarvis had struck out.

Ricky Festino caught my eye. He was grinning.

Kurt proceeded to strike out two more guys with a bewildering and unhittable assortment of drop curves and rise balls.

In the fifth inning, we managed to load the bases, and then it was Kurt's turn at bat. He swung lefty this time, and once again drove the ball somewhere into the next town, trimming the Charles River lead to one.

Kurt struck them out, one two three, in the sixth. I noticed that Trevor was no longer complaining about our ringer. Our turn at bat, he hit a double, Ricky singled, and by the time I struck out, we were up by two. Finally, in the bottom of the seventh, Kurt had struck out their first batter. A double play, and we'd actually won our first game since prehistoric times.

All the guys thronged around Kurt, who shrugged modestly and gave his easy smile. Everyone was talking and laughing loudly, narrating instant replays, reliving the double play that ended the game.

The inviolable tradition after each game was for our opponents to join us for food and beer and tequila shots at a nearby bar or restaurant. But the young studs from Charles River were heading sullenly for their cars.

'I think they're bummed out,' said Taminek.

I looked around and saw Kurt slipping out to the parking lot. I chased up to him and invited him to join us.

'Nah, you guys probably want to hang by yourselves,' he said. I could see Trevor, standing at his silver Porsche, talking to Brett Gleason.

'It's not like that,' I said. 'It's totally loose. Believe me, the guys would love to have a drink with you.'

'I don't drink anymore, man. Sorry.'

'Well, Diet Coke, whatever. Come on.'

He shrugged again. 'Sure you guys aren't going to mind?'

I FELT LIKE I'd brought Julia Roberts to audition for the high-school play. All of a sudden I was Mr Popular, basking in the reflected glory. We gathered round a long table at the Outback Steakhouse, a five-minute drive away, everyone jazzed from our comeback-from-oblivion victory. Some ordered beers, and Trevor asked for a single-malt Scotch called Talisker, but the waitress didn't know what he was talking about, so he settled for a Dewar's.

Kurt ordered iced water. I hesitated, then did the same. Brett Gleason hoisted his mug of Foster's and proposed a toast to Kurt saying, 'You don't have to buy another drink in this town again.'

Taminek said, 'Where'd you come from?'

'Michigan,' Kurt said, with a sly grin.

'I mean, like—you play in college or something?'

'Never went to college,' Kurt said. 'Joined the army instead, and they don't play much softball. Not in Iraq, anyway.'

'You were in Iraq?' said one of our top dogs, Doug Forsythe, a tall, slender guy with a thatch of brown hair and a cowlick.

'Yeah,' Kurt said, nodding. 'And Afghanistan. All the hot tourist spots. In Special Forces.' He looked down at his glass of water and fell silent.

Trevor was checking his BlackBerry for messages as he sipped his Dewar's. He looked up and said, 'So how do you guys know each other?'

I flinched. The cellphone, the Acura wiping out in a ditch.

Kurt said, 'Mutual interest in cars.'

I liked this guy more and more.

'Why are you guys the Band of Brothers?' Kurt said. 'Are you vets?'

'Vets?' I said. 'Us? Are you kidding? No, it's just a nickname. Not a very imaginative one, either. I don't even remember who thought of it.'

'All you guys in sales?'

'Yep.'

'You good?'

'I'm OK,' I said. I shrugged modestly, the way he seemed to shrug without saying anything. I tend to unconsciously imitate whoever I'm around.

Then I heard Trevor say, 'Steadman's fine. He's just not much of a closer anymore.' He sat back down at the table. 'Right, Steadman? How's that Lockwood deal going? Are we in the third year yet?'

'It's looking good,' I lied. 'How's it going with the Pavilion Group?'

The Pavilion Group owned a chain of movie theatres that wanted to put LCDs in their lobbies to run trailers and ads for concessions.

Trevor smiled with satisfaction. 'Textbook,' he said. 'I did an ROI test for them that showed a seventeen per cent increase in sales of Lemon Slushies. Tomorrow I've got a meet-and-greet with the CEO. He wants to shake my hand before he inks the deal. But it's in the bag.'

'Nice,' I said.

Trevor turned to Kurt. 'So, Kurt, you guys skydive and all that?'

'Skydive?' Kurt repeated with what sounded like a little twist of sarcasm. 'I guess you could call it that. We did jumps, sure.'

'How awesome is that?' said Trevor. 'I've gone skydiving a bunch of times. It was such a rush.'

'A rush.' Kurt said the word like it tasted bad. 'When you're dropped from a C-141 Starlifter at 35,000 feet to do a dump deep inside enemy territory, it's not exactly a *rush*. You're carrying 175 pounds of gear and weapons and you've got an oxygen mask blinding you and your stomach's in your throat and you're falling 150 miles an hour.' He took a sip of water. 'It's so cold at that altitude your goggles can freeze and shatter. Your eyeballs can freeze shut. You can get hypoxia and lose consciousness. Maybe your chute malfunctions. Even really experienced soldiers break their necks and die. You're scared shitless, and anyone who says they're not is lying.'

Trevor blushed, looked as if he'd just been slapped. Ricky Festino gave me a sidelong look of immense pleasure.

KURT WAS a huge hit.

Forsythe said, 'Hey, can you come back next week?'

'I don't know,' Kurt said. 'I work nights a lot.'

'Doing what?' Forsythe asked.

I braced myself—the tow truck, the Acura in the ditch . . .

But he said, 'I drive for a buddy of mine who owns an auto body shop.'

'We got to get this guy a job in Entronics,' Taminek said.

Kurt chuckled, and said, 'Yeah, right.'

The rest of the guys eventually went home, leaving just me and Kurt.

'So,' he said. 'Band of Brothers.'

I nodded.

'Pretty competitive bunch, looks like. That pretty-boy who sat across from me—what's his name, Trevor?—seems like a real dickhead.'

'I guess.'

'He's competing against you.'

'Yeah, well, it's complicated. We're both up for the same promotion.' I explained to him about the recent turmoil at Entronics and the AM job that had just opened up and the trouble I was having with the Lockwood Hotels deal. He listened without saying anything.

When I was done, he said, 'Not easy to have unit cohesion when you're all battling each other.'

'Unit cohesion?'

'See, in Special Forces, we'd work in twelve-man teams. Everyone's got his job—mine was demolitions expert. And we all had to work together, respect each other, or we'd never be battle-ready.'

'Battle-ready, huh?' I smiled, thinking of the corporation as a battlefield.

'You know the real reason soldiers are willing to die in war? You think it's about patriotism? Family? Country? No way, bro. It's all about your team. We all stand together. You get my point?'

I wasn't sure I did.

He looked like he was ready to leave. 'Mind if I ask *you* something?'

'Go for it.'

'So when we were in country, our most important weapon by far was always our intel. The intelligence we had on the enemy, right? Strength of their units, location of their encampments, all that. So what kind of intel do you guys collect on your potential customers?'

This guy was smart. 'They're not the enemy,' I said, amused.

'OK.' A bashful smile. 'But you know what I mean.'

'I guess. To be honest, not much. We sort of fly by the seat of our pants.'

He nodded. 'Wouldn't it help if you drilled down? Like the way you're getting dicked around by Lockwood Hotels—what's really going on there?'

'Would it help? Sure. But we don't have any way of knowing.'

Kurt kept nodding, staring straight ahead. 'I know a guy used to work in security for the Lockwood chain. He might still be there.'

'A security guard?'

Kurt smiled. 'Pretty high up in corporate security, at their headquarters. Lot of Special Forces guys go into corporate security. Give me some background. I'll see if I can find anything out for you. A little intel, right?'

Kurt Semko had already surprised me a couple of times, so maybe it wasn't so far-fetched. It made sense that there'd be a network of ex-Special Forces officers who now worked in the private sector. Why the hell not? I gave him a bit of background and scribbled Brian Borque's name on a napkin. I wrote down Kurt's email address.

'All right, man,' Kurt said, getting up and putting a big hand on my shoulder. 'No worries. I'll give you a call if I find anything out.'

IT WAS PRETTY LATE by the time I got home, driving the Geo Metro that Enterprise Rent-A-Car had brought over that morning. Kate was asleep.

I sat down at the computer in the little home office we shared to check my office email, as I always did before I went to bed. I found the workup I'd done on Lockwood, and forwarded it to Kurt. Then I scrolled quickly through the junk—health-plan notices, job listings, endless personnel notices—and found an email from Gordy that he'd sent after hours.

He wanted me to 'drop by' his office at eight o'clock tomorrow morning.

CHAPTER 3

The alarm went off at 5 a.m. Kate groaned and rolled over. I got up quietly, went downstairs and made coffee, and while it was brewing I took a quick shower. I wanted to get into the office before I met with Gordy so I could go over my accounts and get all the numbers in order.

When I got out of the shower, Kate was downstairs at the kitchen table in her pink bathrobe, drinking coffee.

'You're up early,' she said.

I gave her a kiss. 'You too. Sorry if I woke you.'

'You were out late.'

'The softball game, remember? We won, believe it or not.'

'Hey, that's a first.'

'Yeah, well, that guy Kurt played for us. He blew everyone away.'

'Kurt?'

'Remember, I told you about this guy who gave me a ride home after the Acura wiped out?'

'Navy SEALs.'

'Special Forces, but yeah. He's, like, the real thing. He's everything Gordy and all these other phony tough guys *pretend* to be, talking about "killing the competition". Only he's for real. He's actually killed people.'

I realised I was telling her everything except the one thing I was most anxious about: my interview with Gordy in a couple of hours. I wasn't sure I wanted to tell her. She'd probably just make me more nervous.

'Don't forget, Craig and Susie are going to be here tonight.'

I let out a half groan, half sigh. 'How long are they staying?'

'Just two nights.'

'Why are they coming to Boston? I thought LA was God's country.'

'He was just elected to the Harvard Board of Overseers, and his first meeting is tomorrow.'

'How could he be on the Harvard Board of Overseers? He's a Hollywood guy now. He probably doesn't even own a tie anymore.'

'He's not only a prominent alum but also a major contributor.'

When Susie met Craig, he was just a poor starving writer who taught expository writing at Harvard. He was kind of snooty, and Susie probably liked that, but she sure as hell wasn't going to live in genteel poverty, and I think he figured out pretty quickly that he was never going to make it in the literature business. So they moved to LA, where Craig started writing sitcoms. Eventually he got a gig writing for *Everybody Loves Raymond*. Then, somehow, he created this hit show and overnight became unbelievably rich.

Now, he, Susie and their son, Ethan, vacationed on St Bart's with Brad and Angelina. They had a big house in Holmby Hills and were always out to dinner with all the celebrities. And he never let me forget it.

She got up and poured herself another cup of coffee. 'Susie's going to take Ethan around Boston—the Freedom Trail, all that. All I ask is for you to be nice to them. And you and Ethan have some sort of great chemistry.'

'How come they're staying here anyway?' I said.

'Because she's my sister.'

'You know they're just going to complain the whole time about the bathroom and how we have the wrong coffeemaker and how come we don't have any Peet's Sumatra coffee beans—'

'You can't hold it against them, Jason. They're just accustomed to a higher standard of living.'

'Then maybe they should stay at the Four Seasons.'

'They want to stay with us,' she said firmly.

I went to the cereal cabinet and surveyed its depressing, low-cal, high-fibre contents of twigs and burlap strips in grim-looking boxes. I selected the least-disgusting-looking box—a tough choice—and reluctantly brought it to the table. In the refrigerator all we had now was skimmed milk. I hate skimmed milk. I brought the carton to the table, too.

Kate was stirring her coffee with a spoon, though she hadn't added anything to it. I felt bad for her. The plan wasn't for her to live in a 1,500-square-foot Colonial in the low-income part of Belmont. She must have expected more from me when she married me.

We met at a mutual friend's wedding. A guy I knew from my college frat was marrying a girl who went to Exeter with Kate. Kate had been forced to leave Exeter in her junior year when her family went broke. She went to Harvard, but on financial aid. There are buildings in Boston with her family name on it, and she had to suffer the humiliation of going to public school in Wellesley her last two years.

At the wedding, we were seated next to each other, and I immediately glommed on to this hot babe. She seemed a little pretentious: a comp lit major at Harvard, read all the French feminists—in French, of course. She definitely seemed out of my league. Later she told me she thought I was the best-looking guy there, and funny, and charming, too. She seemed amused by all my stories about my job—I'd just started as a sales rep at Entronics, and I wasn't yet burned-out. She liked the fact that I was so into my work. I probably went on too much about my master plan, how much money I'd be pulling down in five years, in ten years. But she was taken by it. She said she found me more 'real' than the guys she normally hung with.

Obviously Kate didn't marry me for my money—she knew plenty of rich guys in her social circles—but I think she expected me to take care of her. She could raise a family and do something vaguely artistic like landscape gardening or teaching literature. That was the deal. We'd have three kids and a big house in Newton or Brookline or Cambridge.

'Listen, Kate,' I finally said after a moment of silence. 'I've got an interview with Gordy this morning.'

Her face lit up. I hadn't seen her smile like that in weeks. 'Already? Oh, Jason. This is so great.'

'I think Trevor has it sewed up, though. He's been having his direct reports call Gordy and tell him how much they want Trevor to get the job.'

'But Gordy must see through all that.'

'Maybe. But he loves being sucked up to. Can't get enough of it.'

She nodded. 'You don't need to do that. Just show him how much you want the job. Want an omelette?'

'An omelette?' Was there such a thing as a tofu omelette?

'Yep. You need your protein. I'll put some Canadian bacon in it. Gordy likes his guys to be meat-eaters, right?'

ON THE WAY into work I popped a CD into the dashboard slot of the Geo Metro. It was one of my vast collection of motivational talks by the god worshipped by all salesmen, the great training guru Mark Simkins.

I'd probably listened to *Be A Winner* five hundred times. I could recite long stretches of it word for word. Simkins taught me never to use the word 'cost' or 'price' with a customer. It was 'total investment'. And never ask a prospect to 'sign' an agreement—you 'endorsed' the copies or 'OKed' the agreement. But most of all he taught that you had to believe in yourself.

Sometimes I listened to the discs just to get myself fired up. I needed all the confidence I could get for my interview with Gordy.

By the time I got to Framingham, I was swimming in caffeine—I'd brought the extra-large travel Thermos—and totally pumped. I walked from the parking lot reciting like a mantra a couple of my favourite Mark Simkins lines: 'Believe in yourself 100 per cent, and everyone else will have no choice but to follow you.' '*Expect* good things to happen.' 'The only thing that counts is how many times you succeed. For the more times you fail and keep trying, the more times you succeed.'

Gordy always kept people waiting. It was a power thing. I could see him through his office window, pacing back and forth with his headset on, gesticulating wildly. I sat at an empty cubicle next to his secretary, Melanie, a sweet, pretty woman with long brown hair. She apologised repeatedly, and offered to get me coffee. I said no. Any more caffeine and I'd go into orbit.

At close to eight-thirty, Gordy's door opened and he came barrelling through. Both of his stubby arms were extended in welcome, as if he wanted to give me a bear hug. Gordy, who looks sort of like a bear cub, only not cute, is a very huggy person.

'Steadman,' he said. 'How're you doing there, buddy?'

'Hey, Gordy,' I said.

'Melanie, get my buddy Steadman here some coffee, could you?'

'Already offered, Kent,' said Melanie. She was the only one in the office who called him by his first name.

'Water?' he said. 'Coke? Scotch?' He threw his head back and brayed, a sort of open-mouth cackle. He put his arm around my shoulder, and pulled me into the vast expanse of his office where he sank into his ergonomic desk chair and leaned back. I sat in the chair across from him. His desk was a ridiculously large oblong of black marble, which he kept fanatically neat. The only thing on it was a giant, thirty-inch Entronics flat-panel LCD monitor and a blue folder, which I assumed was my personnel file.

'So, man,' he said with a long, contented sigh, 'you want a promotion.'

'I do,' I said, 'and I think I'd kick ass.'

Believe in yourself 100 per cent, and everyone else will have no choice but to follow you, I chanted silently.

'I'll bet you would,' he said, no irony in his voice. He fixed me with his small brown eyes. Some of the Band of Brothers referred to Gordy's eyes as 'beady' or 'ferret-like', but right now they seemed warm and sincere. His eyes were set deeply beneath a low, Cro-Magnon brow. He had a large head, a double chin, a ruddy face that reminded me of a glazed ham, with deep acne pits. His obviously dyed dark brown hair was cut in a pompadour.

Now he hunched forward and studied my file. His lips moved a tiny bit as he read. As he flipped the pages, you could see a flash of monogrammed cuff link. Everything he wore was monogrammed with a big script KG.

I looked around the office. In one corner he had a golf putter in a mahogany stand next to an artificial-turf putting mat. On a shelf in his credenza was a bottle of Talisker eighteen-year-old single-malt Scotch, which he liked to brag was the only Scotch he drank. If so, he must have made a real dent in the world supply of it because he drank a lot.

'Your annual reviews aren't bad at all,' he said.

From Gordy, this was a rave. 'Thanks,' I said.

'You were Salesman of the Year three years ago,' he said. 'Club four years running.' He gave a low whistle. 'You like Grand Cayman?'

The Cayman Islands was one of the trips the company sent the Salesman of the Year on. 'Great diving,' I said.

'I'm impressed you were able to sell UPS those self-keystoning projectors. They wanted compression technology, which we don't do.'

'I sold them on future compatibility.'

'Booya,' he said, nodding.

That was Gordy's way of congratulating people. He was being too nice, which made me nervous. I was expecting his usual frontal assault.

'Morgan Stanley?' he said.

'They've got an RFP on the street, but they won't talk to me. Got to be an inside job. I'm just column fodder.'

'Sounds right,' he said. 'They're just specking the competition.'

'I'm not going to make it easy for them,' I said.

'And it looks like FedEx hasn't delivered yet, huh?'

'FedEx wants a bunch of LCD projectors for their logistics centre, to display the weather. I demo'd it for them in Memphis.'

'And?'

'They're looking at Sony, NEC and us. Doing a side-by-side shoot-out.'

'Deciding on price point, no doubt.'

'I'm trying to sell them on quality and reliability. I'd say we've got a thirty per cent chance of winning it.' That was a complete hallucination.

'That high, huh?'

'That's my take. I wouldn't forecast it, though.'

'Albertson's fell through,' he said, with a sad shake of the head. Albertson's is the second-largest chain in the country. They own thousands of supermarkets, drugstores and gas stations, and they wanted to put in fifteen-inch flat-panel LCD screens to run ads at every checkout lane. A 'network' that was going to be installed by this middleman, a company called SignNetwork that bought and installed all this stuff in stores. I'd been dealing with both Albertson's and SignNetwork, trying to sell them on the advantages of paying a bit more for quality and all that. No dice.

'They went with NEC,' I said.

'Why?'

'Jim Letasky is NEC's top sales guy, and they don't want to deal with any other company. They love the guy.'

'I know Letasky.'

'Nice guy,' I said. Unfortunately, I wished I could hate the guy, since he was stealing so much of our business, but I'd met him at the Consumer Electronics show a couple of years back. After we had a drink, *I* was almost ready to buy a bunch of NEC plasmas from Jim Letasky.

He fell silent again. 'And Lockwood drags on like a case of the clap. 'You're not giving up on this one, though, right?'

'Give up? Me?'

He smiled. 'Let me ask you something. Hope you don't mind if I get personal. You got problems in your marriage? Your wife sick or something?'

'She's fine.' Like: What the hell?

'You have cancer, maybe?'

I half smiled, said quietly, 'I'm in good health, Gordy.'

'Then what the hell's your problem?'

I pondered the best way to answer that wouldn't get me fired.

'Four years in a row you're Club 101. Then you're Festino.'

'What do you mean?'

'Can't close.'

'That's not the case, Gordy. I was Salesman of the Year.'

'In a great market. Rising tide floats all boats. Your boat still seaworthy? That's the question. Look at the last year. See, I'm starting to wonder whether you're losing that spark. You still have the fire in the belly?'

It's called acid reflux, and I was feeling it right now.

'It's still there,' I said. 'You know, like they say the only thing that counts is how many times you succeed. The more times you fail and keep trying, the more times you succeed.'

'I don't want to hear any of that Mark Simkins crapola,' he said. Busted. 'He's full of it. The more times you fail, the more accounts you lose, you get me? Now, you and Trevor Allard and Brett Gleason want to do a side-by-side? See who's up-and-coming and who's history?'

History. 'Trevor got lucky last year. Hyatt started buying big.'

'Steadman, listen to me, and listen good: you make your own luck.'

'Gordy, you assigned him the better accounts this year, OK?'

He looked up at me abruptly, those ferret eyes glittering. 'You got any *other* excuses while you're at it?' His voice got steadily louder until he was shouting. 'Let me tell you something. There is shit about to rain down on us from Tokyo, and we don't even know what kind of shit it is! And if I promote the wrong guy, it's *my* ass on the line!'

I wanted to say, Hey, I don't want this stupid promotion anyway. But I realised that, damn it, I wanted the job. Maybe I didn't want the job so much, as I wanted to *get* it. I said, 'You won't be making a mistake.'

He smiled again, and I was really starting to despise his evil little smiles. 'It's survival of the fittest around here, but sometimes evolution needs a little help. That's my job. I promote the fittest. Kill off the weak. And if you get this job, you've got to be able to fire people. Could you fire Festino?'

'I'd put him on a plan first.' A performance plan was the way the company told you to shape up or beat it.

'He's on a plan already, Steadman. He's dead wood, and you know it. If you get the job, could you fire his ass?'

'If I had to,' I said.

'Any member of your team doesn't perform, one weak link, we all suffer. Remember: There's no "I" in "team".'

I thought: *Yeah, well, there's an 'I' in 'idiot'. And a 'U' in 'stupid'.*

'See, Steadman, you can't be sentimental. You've got to be willing to push your grandmother under a bus to make your nums. Allard would. Allard's got that. So does Gleason. How about you?'

I said, 'My grandmother's dead.'

'You know what I'm saying. Motivating people to climb the hill for you isn't the same as carrying a bag.' That was insider-speak for selling.

'I know.'

'Do you? You got the fire in the belly? The killer instinct? Can you level-set? Can you incent your team?'

'I know how to do what it takes,' I said.

'What kind of car did you drive to work today, Steadman?'

'A Geo Metro, but that's because—'

'A Geo Metro,' he said. 'A Geo. Metro. I want you to say that loudly, Steadman. Say, "I drove a Geo Metro to work today".'

I exhaled noisily. 'I drove a Geo Metro to work today because—'

'Good. Now say, "And Gordy drove a Hummer". Got it?'

'Gordy drove a Hummer.'

'Correct. Is anything sinking in? Show me your watch, Steadman.'

I held out my left hand reluctantly. It was a decent-looking Fossil, about a hundred bucks at the kiosk in the Prudential Mall.

'Take a look at mine, Steadman.' He flicked his left wrist, shot his cuff, revealed a huge, gaudy Rolex, gold and diamond-encrusted.

'I think I get your point, Gordy.'

I noticed he was looking up at his door. He flashed a thumbs-up at whoever was outside. I turned round to see Trevor walking by.

'I'm not sure you do get my point,' he said. 'The top sixty per cent of the sales force hit their OTEs.' OTE was on-target earnings. 'Then there's the overachievers, OK? The Club. And *then* there's the high-octane, the best-in-breed. The meat-eaters. Like Trevor Allard. Like Brett Gleason. Are you a meat-eater, Steadman?'

'Medium rare,' I said.

'Do you have the killer instinct?'

'You have to ask?'

He stared at me. 'Show me,' he said. 'Next time I see you, I want to hear about how you closed one of your big accounts.'

I nodded.

He stood up to signal that our meeting was over. I stood up too. He came round the desk and put his arm round my shoulder. 'You're a good guy, Jason. A really good guy. But are you good enough to be on the G Team?'

It took me a few seconds to realise that G stood for Gordy. 'You know I am,' I said.

'Show me that killer instinct,' he said. 'Kill, baby, kill.'

Melanie gave me a sympathetic smile as I stumbled out of Gordy's office. I switched my cellphone back on as I walked towards mine. My cell started making that fast, urgent-sounding alarm tone that indicated I had a message. I called voicemail and heard a message from someone whose voice I didn't at first recognise. 'Yo, Jason,' a gravelly voice said. 'I got some information for you on that guy at Lockwood Hotels.'

Kurt Semko.

When I got to my office, I called him back.

'GUY'S NAME IS BRIAN BORQUE, right?' Kurt said.

'Yeah?' I was still feeling kind of numb from being beaten about the head and neck with Gordy's psychic rubber truncheon.

'My buddy at Lockwood did some poking around for me,' Kurt said. 'So dig this: Brian Borque and his fiancée just came back from Aruba, right?'

'Yeah? He said he took her to Vienna, Virginia.'

'First-class return tickets to Aruba, five-star hotel, all expenses paid, and by guess who?'

'Who?'

'Hitachi.'

I was silent for a few seconds as it dawned on me. 'Shit,' I said.

Kurt's reply was a slow, husky chuckle.

'He's been jerking me around for a year. Boy, that pisses me off.'

'Greedhead, huh?'

'I should have known. He was stringing me along for Super Bowl tickets and all the while he's in bed with Hitachi. All right. Thanks, man. At least now I know.'

'No worries. So . . . what are you going to do about it?'

'Close it or kill it, that's the rule around here. I kill it and move on.'

'I don't think so. See, there's something else you may not know.'

'Like what?'

'Seems Lockwood Hotels has a policy on not accepting gifts greater than a hundred bucks from a customer or vendor. That little trip to Aruba was worth a good five or six thousand bucks. I'd say that's a violation of company policy, wouldn't you?'

'What am I supposed to do with that? Blackmail the guy?'

'Naw, man. You help him out of his ethical dilemma. Lead him away from temptation. You . . . torque Borque.' He chuckled again. 'Then you're good to go.'

I CALLED Brian Borque but got his voicemail and asked him to call me back as soon as he could.

In the meantime I checked my email and ploughed through the usual meaningless company crap, but one subject header caught my eye. I normally ignore all the job listings—after all, I already have a job. But this one was a notice for a Corporate Security officer that had been posted today.

I skimmed it quickly. 'Perform various duties such as ensuring the physical security of the facility as well as acting as first response to all emergencies including security, medical, bomb and fire.' It went on to say, 'Prefer: recent military experience such as Military Police . . . Demonstrated leadership and experience with handguns a plus.'

I remembered what Taminek said at the Outback: 'We got to get this guy a job at Entronics.'

I saved the job listing as new in my email inbox, just as my phone rang. Lockwood Hotels came up on the caller ID.

'Hey, Brian,' I said.

'There he is,' Brian said, sounding typically buoyant. 'You got the Sox tickets, right?'

'That's not why I called,' I said. 'I wanted to circle back to you on the proposal.'

'You know I'm doing what I can,' he said, his voice suddenly flat. 'There's all kinds of factors in play here that are beyond my control.'

'I totally understand,' I said. My heart started beating fast. 'I know you're doing everything you can to work the system for me.'

'You know it,' Brian said.

'And Entronics will price-compete on any reasonable proposal.'

'No doubt.'

My mouth was dry. I grabbed a Poland Spring water bottle and drained it. 'Of course, some things we can't match and won't try,' I went on. 'Like the trip you and Martha just took to Aruba.'

He was silent. So I continued. 'Hard to compete with free, you know?'

He was still silent. I thought for a moment that the phone had gone dead.

Then Brian said, 'FedEx me a fresh set of docs, will you? I'll have 'em inked and on your desk by close of business Friday.'

I was stunned. 'Hey, thanks, Bri—that's great. You rock.'

'Don't mention it,' he said quietly, a note of hostility entering his voice. 'I mean it. Don't mention it.'

THE PHONE RANG again. It was a private caller and I picked it up.

'These are the voyages of the Starship *Enterprise*,' said a voice I immediately recognised.

'Graham,' I said, 'how's it going?'

'J-man. Where you been?'

Graham Runkel was a world-class stoner who lived in Cambridge. We went to high school together, and when I was younger and irresponsible, I'd from time to time buy a nickel bag of marijuana from him. Less often in recent years, though, but once in a while I'd stop by his apartment—the Den of Iniquity, he called it—and smoke a joint with him.

Graham was a man of many talents. He was always rebuilding engines, working on his 1971 VW Beetle in the backyard of his apartment building. He worked in a record store that sold only vinyl. He was also a 'Trekker', a fan of the original *Star Trek* TV series, which to him was the height of culture. He went to a lot of *Star Trek* conventions, and he'd built a scale model of the Starship *Enterprise*.

Graham had also done jail time, not unlike some of my other buddies from the old neighbourhood. In his early twenties he broke into a couple of houses, trying to pay back a marijuana deal.

Basically, Graham had ended up where I might have ended up if my parents hadn't been so insistent I go to college. His parents considered college a waste of money and refused to pay for it.

'Sorry, man,' I said. 'It's been real crazy at work.'

'Haven't heard from you in weeks, man. Weeks. Come on over to the Den of Iniquity—we'll do a spliff.'

'I'm awful sorry, Graham,' I said. 'Another time, OK?'

Around noon, Ricky Festino appeared in my office door. 'You hear about

Teflon Trevor?' There was a look of unmistakable glee on his face.

'What?'

He snickered. 'He had an appointment with the CEO of the Pavilion Group, a handshake kind of thing, and ink the deal. CEO's the kind of guy you don't keep waiting five seconds, you know? So what happens? One of the tyres on Trevor's Porsche blows out on the Pike. He missed the meeting, and the CEO was totally pissed.'

'So? He calls Pavilion on his cell and they reschedule. Big deal.'

'That's the beauty part. His cellphone died too. Couldn't make a call. So basically the CEO and everyone else is sitting around waiting for Trevor and he never shows up.' He squeezed out a dab of hand cleaner and looked up at me with a smile.

'Hate when that happens,' I said.

After Ricky left, I called Kurt. 'Listen,' I said. 'A job just opened up here. Corporate Security officer. It says they prefer recent military experience. Pay's not bad. Better than driving a tow truck, I'll bet.'

'What does it say about background checks?'

I looked at the screen. 'It says, "Must be able to pass full criminal, drug and employment background check".'

'There you go,' he said. 'They see the DD and they stop reading the application.'

'Not if you explain the circumstances.'

'You don't get that chance,' Kurt said. 'But I appreciate the thought.'

'I know the Director of Corporate Security,' I said. 'Dennis Scanlon. Good guy. He likes me. I could tell him about you.'

'Not that easy, buddy.'

'Worth a try, don't you think? Wait till I tell him about the softball game. We need to make you a legal Entronics employee. He'll get it.'

'He's looking for a Corporate Security officer, not a pitcher.'

'Let me make a call for you,' I said. 'I'll do it right now.'

I picked up the phone and called Dennis Scanlon and told him briefly about Kurt. How he was in Special Forces, got a dishonourable discharge, but not for any bad reason.

Scanlon was immediately interested. He said he loved military types.

I HAD NOTHING against my smarmy brother-in-law and his social-climbing wife, but my heart really squeezed for their poor, brilliant, maladjusted eight-year-old son, Ethan.

When I got home, Susie, Craig and Kate were gathered in our cramped kitchen, and young Ethan was nowhere to be found. They were laughing loudly and drinking from grotesquely large martini glasses, having such a good time that they didn't notice me entering the house. Though Susie was older, she and Katie looked exactly alike. Susie's eyelids were a bit heavier, and her mouth tilted down just a bit. Her hair also looked like it was cut and highlighted once a week at some $800-a-visit Beverly Hills salon.

'Hey, Jason,' Susie said, giving me a sisterly peck on the cheek as I walked into the kitchen. 'Ethan's so excited to see you I think he's going to jump out of his skin.'

'Jason!' exclaimed Craig like we were old buddies. He threw his bony arms around me. He seemed to get skinnier every time I saw him. I also noticed he'd shaved his head. He used to have a big mop of curly hair that was thinning on top and made him look like Bozo the Clown.

'Let me get you a martini,' said Kate as she hoisted a silver martini shaker and poured into one of the giant glasses.

'I didn't even know we had martini glasses,' I said.

'From Craig and Susie,' Kate said. 'Aren't they special?'

'Special,' I agreed.

'Careful,' Kate said, handing me a glass. 'Hundred dollars a stem.'

'Oh, there's plenty more where they came from,' said Craig. He looked at me with kindly condescension, as if I were some Fresh Air Fund kid. 'How's the corporate world?'

'It's OK,' I said, nodding. 'Gets crazy sometimes, but it's OK.'

'Hey, your boss, Dick Hardy, invited me to the Entronics Invitational last year at Pebble Beach. Nice guy. Man, I got to play golf with Tiger Woods and Vijay Singh—that was a blast.'

I got his point. He was a buddy of the CEO of my company, whom I'd never even met. 'Neat' was all I said.

'I could put in a word for you with Dick,' Craig said.

'Don't waste your time. He doesn't even know who I am.'

'It's cool. I'll just tell him to make sure you're taken care of.'

'Thanks, but no thanks, Craig. I appreciate the thought, though.'

'So, I want to hear about your work life,' Craig said.

'Oh, it's boring,' I said. 'No celebs.'

'I want to hear about it. I'm serious. I need to know what regular people's work life is like. I consider it research.'

I looked at him and mentally went through about a dozen really nasty and sarcastic replies, but luckily my cellphone went off. I forgot I'd still had it clipped onto my belt.

'There you go,' Craig said. 'That's got to be the office, right?' He looked from his wife to Kate. 'His boss or something. God, I love the way they crack the whip in the corporate world.'

I got up and went into the living room and answered the cell. 'Hey,' a voice said. I immediately recognised Kurt.

'How's it going?' I said, happy to be yanked away from Craig.

'I catch you during dinner?'

'Not at all,' I said.

'Thanks for talking to the Corporate Security guy. He called, and wants me to come in for an interview tomorrow.'

'You're good to go,' I said. 'He must be seriously interested in you.'

'Or desperate, I figure. Hey, so maybe I can grab you for a few minutes in the morning, talk on the phone. Get your take on Entronics and what the security problems are, all that. I like to be prepared.'

'How's right now?' I said.

WE MET at Charlie's Kitchen in Harvard Square. I hadn't eaten. Kate didn't look too happy at first about my abandoning her little dinner party, but I told her a work crisis had arisen, and that seemed to satisfy her.

I didn't recognise him at first—his goatee was gone and he'd had a haircut. He was a good-looking guy, I realised, and now he looked like a successful business executive, only he was wearing jeans and a sweatshirt.

Kurt just ordered his regular, a glass of iced water. He said he'd already eaten. When my plate arrived—a big old double cheeseburger and a mountain of fries with a plastic tankard of watery beer—Kurt took one look and scowled. 'You shouldn't eat that shit,' he said.

'You sound like my wife.'

'Don't take this the wrong way, but you might want to think about losing a little weight, do some cardio and free weights. You belong to a gym?'

'Yeah,' I said, 'I pay like a hundred bucks a month for a membership at CorpFit, so I figure I don't actually have to go there.'

'CorpFit? That's one of those smoothie-bar Evian-water places, right? I got to take you to a real gym. Where I go.'

'Sure,' I said, hoping he'd forget we ever talked about working out, but he didn't seem like the kind of guy who forgot anything.

'You have your Entronics ID with you?' Kurt asked.

I took it out and put it on the table. He examined it closely. 'Man, do you know how easy it is to counterfeit one of these babies?'

'Never thought about it.'

'I wonder if your security chief ever thought about it.'

'You have a résumé?' I asked, tucking into the burger.

'I can throw one together.'

'Tell you what. email me what you've got, and I'll go over it.'

'Hey, that would be awesome.'

'No problem. Now, if I had to predict, I'd say that Scanlon is a tough interview. Though he'll probably ask you the standards, like, "What's your greatest weakness?" or, "Tell me about a time when you took the initiative to solve a problem". Like that. How you work in a team.'

'Sounds like I can handle that,' he said.

'Make sure you get there on time. Early, in fact.'

'I'm a military guy, remember? We're all about punctuality. But I want to know some details about your access control system.'

'All I know is, you wave this card at one of the boxes and you go in.'

He asked me a bunch more questions, and I told him what little I knew. 'Your wife doesn't mind you staying out late?' he asked.

'I think she was glad to get rid of me.' I told him.

'You still duking it out with that guy Trevor for the promotion?'

'Yeah.' I told him about my 'interview' with Gordy. 'He's not going to give it to me, though. I can tell. He says I don't have the killer instinct. And Trevor's a superstar. His numbers are especially good this year. There's also Brett Gleason. He's kind of a lunk, but he has that animal aggressiveness that Gordy likes. I'd put money on Trevor. He's got a big demonstration at Fidelity Investments on Monday, and if our monitors win the shoot-out—which they will—then he lands Fidelity. Means he wins. And I'm screwed.'

'Look, I've been in my share of situations that looked hopeless. And the one thing I do know for sure is you often can't believe what you see, and you can never be certain about your enemy's plans and capabilities.'

'What does that have to do with getting a promotion?'

'I'm saying the only way to guarantee a loss is if you don't fight.' He took a long swig of iced water. 'Make sense?'

In the morning I slipped out of bed quietly at six, before the alarm went off. I could hear Kate's laboured breathing, from too much booze last night.

Downstairs, the kitchen and dining room were littered with the detritus of the dinner, dishes, wine and martini glasses, and I couldn't find the coffee-maker. Finally, I located it and put some coffee on to brew.

I heard a clinking sound, and I turned around. There at the kitchen table, concealed behind a stack of pots and pans, was little Ethan. He looked small and frail. He was eating Froot Loops from a giant soup tureen he must have found in the china cabinet.

'Morning, Ethan,' I said, quietly so as not to wake the slumbering party animals upstairs.

Ethan didn't reply.

'Hey there, buddy,' I said, a bit louder.

'Sorry, Uncle Jason,' Ethan replied. 'I'm not really a morning person.'

'Yeah, well, me neither.' I went up to him, about to muss his hair, but stopped myself when I remembered how much he disliked people mussing his hair. Instead I gave him a pat on the back.

I went out to the porch to get the morning papers. When I returned to the kitchen, Ethan said: 'Mummy said you went out last night to avoid Daddy.'

I laughed hollowly. 'I had to go out on business.'

He nodded as if he saw right through me. 'Daddy can be annoying,' he said. 'If I could drive, I wouldn't be home very much either.'

THE DAY WAS LONG and exhausting. The 'merger integration team' had just come from Royal Meister headquarters in Dallas. Rumours of impending disaster had begun to run through the halls.

At the end of the day, as I rode the elevator down to the lobby, the other passengers and I watched the flat-screen monitor mounted on the wall. It showed sports news, headlines and selected stock quotes. (Entronics was down a buck). A lot of the guys find the elevator TV thing really annoying, but I don't mind it. It takes my mind off the fact that I'm in a sealed coffin dangling from cables that might snap at any moment.

When the doors opened at the lobby, I was surprised to see Kurt talking to Dennis Scanlon. Kurt was wearing a navy blue suit, white shirt, and striped silver rep tie, and he looked like a vice-president. Clipped to his lapel was a blue temporary Entronics badge.

'Hey man,' I said. 'Why are you still here? I thought your interview was this morning.'

'It was.' He smiled.

'Meet our new Corporate Security officer,' said Scanlon. He was a small, frog-like man with no neck and a squat body.

'Really?' I said. 'That's great. Smart hire.'

'Kurt's already made some very shrewd suggestions for security improvements—he really knows the technology.' Scanlon said.

Kurt shrugged modestly.

Scanlon excused himself, and Kurt and I stood there for a few seconds. 'So that was fast work,' I said.

'I start Monday. Listen, man, thank you.'

'For what?'

'I mean it. I owe you one. You don't know me very well, but one thing you'll learn is, I never forget a favour.'

CHAPTER 4

The next morning I popped *Be A Winner* into the CD player in the Geo Metro. By the time I got to the office, I was so pumped, I was ready to barge into Gordy's office and just demand the promotion.

I was on my way to see him when I noticed Trevor leaving Joan Tureck's office. He looked uncharacteristically grim.

'How's it going there, Trevor?' I said.

'Great,' he said in a flat voice. 'Just great.'

Before I had a chance to express my condolences over his standing up the CEO of one of America's largest movie-theatre chains, he was gone, and Joan was beckoning me into her office with a flick of her left hand.

I was immediately on alert. Trevor had looked like he'd been kicked in the family jewels. I suspected Joan had been the bearer of bad news.

'Sit down, Jason,' she said. 'Congratulations on the Lockwood deal. I never thought you were going to close it, but I guess we should never underestimate you.'

I nodded, smiled modestly. 'Sometimes you just have to say the right words, and it all falls into place,' I said. 'I figure that ought to demonstrate my meat-eating credentials to Gordy.'

Joan got up and closed her office door, then heaved a long, loud sigh. The circles under her eyes were darker than I'd ever seen them. She went back to her desk. 'Gordy's not going to move me into Crawford's position,' she said.

'What do you mean?'

'There's something about me Gordy doesn't like. And, it's an age-old tradition, using consolidation as an excuse to shed employees you don't like.'

'He can't be that blatant.'

'Of course not. Gordy's smart. There's always a way to justify laying someone off. I didn't make my number because you guys didn't make yours last quarter. The merger team thinks I'm an unnecessary layer of management anyway. They've decided to get rid of the AM job. So Gordy's just going to fill Crawford's DVP slot. You or Trevor or Brett.'

'He wants to lay you off?' Now I felt really bad. Here I was, angling for a promotion, and she was losing her job. 'I'm so sorry.'

'It's fine,' she said. 'I've been in talks with FoodMark for a while.'

'That's the company that runs food courts in shopping malls?' I tried to say it neutrally, but I guess I didn't succeed at hiding what I thought.

Her smile was wan and a little embarrassed. 'Plasma displays or burritos, what's the difference?'

I didn't want to express my condolences, but congratulations didn't seem in order either. 'I guess it's all good, then.'

'Whatever,' she said with a rueful smile. 'You might want to go easy on Trevor Allard today. He just lost the biggest deal of his life.'

'You're talking about Pavilion?'

She nodded, compressed her lips.

'All for missing one appointment because of a flat tyre?'

'Once would have been acceptable. But not twice. This morning he was on his way to the rescheduled meeting with Watkins, the CEO of Pavilion. Well, guess what? His Porsche died on the road again.'

'You're kidding.'

'I wish. Electrical system malfunctioned. A real freak coincidence. He hasn't even had a chance to get his cellphone replaced, so he couldn't call Watkins's office in time. They've signed with Toshiba.'

'Jesus!' I said. 'Just like that?'

'The deal was already factored into next quarter's numbers as committed business. Which is a disaster, especially with the integration team poking around. The tables seem to have turned. Now it looks like you drive a bigger piece of the number than either Trevor of Brett.'

'Temporarily, yeah.'

'Gordy's all about momentum, and right now it's on your side. I know how much you want this job. But be careful what you ask for. You never know what you might be stepping into.'

TEN MINUTES LATER I was checking my email, still feeling dazed, when I noticed Brett Gleason standing in my office doorway.

'Hey Brett,' I said. 'I thought you had a presentation at Bank of America.'

'I lost the directions,' he said.

'To Bank of America? They're on Federal Street, you know that.'

'Guy's new and he's not listed on their website, and besides, I don't remember his last name.'

'You don't have his number?' Why, I wondered, was he in my office?

'That's gone too.'

'What do you mean, gone?'

'The Blue Screen of Death.'

'You had a disk crash or something?'

'Someone screwed with my computer.' He gave me a sidelong look. 'Which also wiped out my Palm Pilot. All my contacts, all my records—the IT dweebs say it's unrecoverable. Some prank, huh?' He turned to leave.

I thought, but didn't say, that if Brett had printed out his schedule, he wouldn't have had this problem. 'You don't seriously think someone did this to you, Brett, do you?' I said to Gleason's back.

But he kept going.

An instant message popped up on my computer screen. It was Gordy, and he wanted to see me immediately.

GORDY WAS WEARING a crisp white button-down shirt with a big blue KG monogram on the pocket. He didn't shake my hand as I entered.

'You locked in Lockwood,' he said.

'That's right.'

'Don't know how you finally got 'em to sign on the dotted line, but I'm impressed. We needed the deal. Bad. Especially the way Allard and Gleason've been dropping balls lately.'

'Have they? I'm sorry to hear that.'

'Please,' Gordy said. 'Practise your bullshit on someone who doesn't know better. Gleason blew off a presentation at Bank of America. Gave them some excuse about his computer getting wiped out. And now Trevor.' He shook his head. 'I like golf as much as the next guy—but you don't blow off a seventy-million-dollar client for nine holes at the Myopia Hunt Club.'

'You're kidding,' I said, truly surprised. That didn't sound like Trevor at all. 'Trevor was playing *golf*?'

'I got the lowdown from Watkins. Stood him up two days in a row claiming car trouble. Both days he says his cellphone isn't working.'

'Yeah, but all that really happened,' I said.

'Uh-uh. And you know where the idiot calls Watkins's office from? Right from the links. Number came up on the secretary's caller ID.' He shook his head, disgusted. 'Well, anyway, I'm inclined to give Allard another chance. He's a true meat-eater. But I got something for you.'

'Tell me.'

'Who's that guy from NEC that everyone likes?'

'Jim Letasky? The guy who owns the SignNetwork account?'

'Yeah, him. I want to land SignNetwork. The only way is to get Letasky on our team. Think you're high-test enough to recruit him?'

'From NEC? He lives in Chicago, got a wife and kids, plus he probably already makes good money.'

'Sounds like you're giving up before you even start,' Gordy said. 'I thought you wanted Crawford's job.'

'No, it's just—that won't be easy. But I'll try.'

'Try? How about, "Done, Gordy"?'

'Done, Gordy,' I said.

AFTER WORK, I drove to Willkie Auto Body to pick up my Acura. There's one upside to getting into an accident: when you get your car back from the shop it looks brand new. The Acura looked like I'd just driven it off the lot.

I called Kurt on the cellphone and told him I was maybe five miles from his house—he'd told me he rented a house in Holliston. He said come on, stop by.

I found it easily. He lived in a small raised ranch, red brick, white clapboard, black shutters, like you'd see in every single suburb in America. It was very small, and it was well cared for, recently painted.

I parked in the driveway, which was jet-black and obviously recently sealed, and rang Kurt's doorbell.

'Welcome to the Fortress of Solitude.' He said as he opened the screen door. 'I'm upgrading the electrical service.'

'You're doing it yourself?'

He nodded. 'It's a rental, but I got tired of the circuit breakers tripping all the time. Hundred amps just doesn't cut it. Plus the wiring's old. So I'm putting in a 400-amp service panel.'

'Cool. Hey, so, listen. I need a favour.'

'Name it. Come on in. I'll get you a drink. Show you some war trophies.'

His house was just as neat inside as it was outside. His refrigerator had nothing in it except bottles of water, Gatorade and protein shakes.

'Gatorade?'

'Water's fine,' I said.

He tossed me a bottle, took one for himself, and we went to his bare living room—a couch, a recliner, an old TV—and sat down.

I told him about the race for the divisional vice-president job, how Gleason had blown off Bank of America and Trevor had lost the Pavilion deal. But Trevor was doing a demo at Fidelity on Monday, I said. That would seal the deal. He'd be back in Gordy's good graces.

Then I told him about how Gordy wanted me to recruit Jim Letasky from NEC. 'It's an impossible assignment. He's setting me up to fail. So he can give the promotion to Trevor.'

'Why're you so sure you're gonna fail?'

'Because the guy lives in Chicago with his wife and kids, and he has no reason to move to Boston and start a new job with Entronics.'

'Know him well?'

'No, that's the thing. I've done the usual research, made a bunch of calls, but I haven't come up with anything I can sink my teeth into. You don't happen to know anyone in NEC corporate security, do you?'

'Sorry.' He smiled. 'Why, you want a backgrounder on him?'

'Is that even something you can do?'

'All you gotta know is where to look.'

'Could you find out what his exact compensation package is?'

'Betcha I can do a lot more than that.'

'That would be awesome.'

'Give me a couple days. I'll see what I can throw together.'

'Thanks, man.'

He shrugged. 'No thanks required. You put it on the line for me, bro, with Scanlon. You vouched for me.'

'That? That's nothing.'

'It's not nothing, Jason,' he said. 'It's not nothing.'

'Well, happy to do it. So what kind of war trophies do you have?'

He got up and opened the door to what looked like a spare bedroom. It smelled of gunpowder and other things, acrid and musty. Arranged on a bench in neat rows were some strange-looking weapons. He picked up an old rifle with a smooth wooden stock. 'Check this out. A World War Two vintage Mauser K98. Standard-issue infantry weapon in the Wehrmacht. Bought it off an Iraqi farmer who claimed he shot down one of our Apache helicopters with it.' He chuckled. 'Chopper didn't have a scratch.'

'Does it work?'

'No idea. I wouldn't want to try it.' He picked up a pistol, showed it to me. He seemed to want me to handle it, but I just looked.

He picked up a black rectangle with a bullet hole in the middle of it. 'Check this out. This is a SAPI plate. Small arms protection insert.'

'Either it's used or it's defective.'

'Saved my life. I'm standing in a tank turret on Highway One in Iraq, and suddenly I'm thrown forward. Sniper got me. Luckily I'd put this in my flak vest. Gave me a nasty bruise.'

'You were allowed to take all this stuff back with you?'

'Lot of guys did.'

'Legally?'

He gave a throaty laugh. 'Most of them are replicas. Fakes. Not reliable.'

I noticed a tray of tubes, like artist's oil paints. I picked one of the tubes up. It was labelled LIQUID METAL EMBRITTLEMENT AGENT (LME)—MERCURY/INDIUM AMALGAM. I asked him what it was.

'Very cool stuff. Classified technology. A mix of some liquid metal, like mercury, with some other metal. Paint it on steel, and it forms a chemical reaction. Turns steel as brittle as a cracker.'

'Neat.'

'You know how to use a gun?'

'Not my thing.'

'You should, you know. Every guy should learn how to use a gun. This day and age. You've got a wife to protect.'

'No, thanks. Not interested. I'm kinda scared of guns. No offence.'

'None taken.'

'Why do I get a feeling you miss being in the Special Forces?'

'Changed my life, bro.'

'How so?'

'Lousy home life.'

'Where'd you grow up?'

'Grand Rapids. Michigan. Wrong side of the tracks.'

'Sounds like my neighbourhood in Worcester.'

He nodded. 'But I was always in trouble. Never thought I'd amount to anything. Even when I got drafted by the Tigers, I figured I'd never make the majors. Not good enough. Then I joined the army, and I'm finally good at something. Then, if you're lucky, you get to go to one of the assholes of the universe like Afghanistan or Iraq. Or if you're really lucky, like me, both.'

'Fun.'

'Yep. You're in Iraq, in the middle of a sandstorm that just won't end, the desert's frickin' *cold* at night, your hands are so numb you can't make coffee. Or you're in some damned camp in Basra, with sand fleas crawling all over you and biting, and you're getting red welts all over.'

I nodded, silent for a while. 'Man,' I finally said. 'You're going to find your job kind of boring.'

He shrugged. 'Hey, it's nice to have a real job, finally. Make some money. I can buy a car now. Save up to buy a house. And maybe someday I'll meet some chick and decide to get married again.'

'Didn't work out last time, huh?'

'Didn't even last a year. Not sure I'm cut out for marriage. Most of the guys in SF are divorced. You want a family, Special Forces isn't for you. So what do *you* want?'

'What do I want?'

'I mean, in life. At work.'

'Red Sox season tickets. Peace on Earth.'

'You want kids?'

'Sure.' I shrugged, half smiled.

'Ah,' he said. 'Big issue for you.'

'Not an issue.'

'Yeah, it is. You and your wife are struggling with it. Or you're trying, and it's not happening. I can tell from your face.'

'You got a crystal ball in here too?'

'Seriously. You don't want to talk about it—that's cool—but I can read it in your face. You know what a "tell" is?'

'Poker, right? Little signals that tell you if someone's bluffing.'

'Most people aren't comfortable with lying. So when they're bluffing, they smile. Or they get stone-faced. Or they scratch their noses. Some of us in SF took classes in facial expression and threat assessment with this famous psychologist. To learn how to detect deception.'

'I can always tell when Gordy's lying,' I said.

'Oh yeah?'

'Yep. He moves his lips.'

'Yeah, yeah.' He didn't laugh. 'So you want kids. You want a bigger house, a fancier car. More toys. You want to run Entronics?'

'Last I looked, I wasn't Japanese.'

'You want to run some company, though. You're an ambitious guy.'

'My wife thinks I'm about as ambitious as a box turtle.'

'She underestimates you.'

'Maybe.'

'Well, I don't, man. Said it before and I'll say it again. I never forget a favour. You'll see.'

SATURDAY MORNING I called Jim Letasky at home.

He was surprised to hear from me. We talked a bit. I congratulated him on snagging the Albertson's deal away from us, then I got to the point.

'Gordy put you up to this?' Letasky said.

'We've had our eye on you for a while,' I said.

'I'm flattered,' he said. 'Really. But I already turned down a job offer from Gordy twice already. No offence, but I love it here. I love my job.'

'You ever get up to Boston on business?' I said.

'All the time,' he said. 'Once a week. It's part of my territory.'

We agreed to meet for breakfast at his Boston hotel in a few days.

EARLY MONDAY MORNING, Kurt took me to his gym in Somerville. No beautiful women in Lycra bodysuits working out here. This was a serious weightlifter's gym that stank of sweat and leather and adrenaline. The floor was ancient splintered planks. There were medicine balls and heavy bags and double-end bags, and a boxing ring in the centre of the room. Guys were jumping rope. They all seemed to know Kurt and like him.

I loved it. It was real, far more real than any of the other 'fitness clubs' I'd belonged to and almost never gone to.

We were both on the bikes warming up, Kurt and I, at five-thirty. Ten or fifteen minutes of hard pedalling to get our blood pumping, Kurt insisted, before the floor workout. Kurt was wearing a black muscle T. The guy had huge biceps, and delts that bulged out of his sleeveless shirt like grapefruit.

After we showered and changed, Kurt handed me a folder. I stood on the street in the early-morning sunlight and read through it. He'd managed to get the exact dollar figure of Jim Letasky's take-home for the last four years—salary, commission and bonuses. He had the amount of Letasky's mortgage, the monthly payment, the rate and the balance remaining, plus what he'd paid for his house and what it was worth now. His car payments.

The name of his wife and three kids. Kurt had noted that his kids were in private school, and what it cost. His bank account and credit-card balances. It was scary how much Kurt had found out.

'How'd you get all this?' I said as we walked to his motorcycle.

Kurt smiled. 'That's NTK, man.'

'Huh?'

'Need-to-know basis. And all *you* need to know is, you always wanna have better intel than the enemy.'

TREVOR ALLARD returned to the office from Fidelity around noon—earlier than I'd expected. I strolled over to his cubicle, and said, as casually as I could, 'How'd it go?'

He looked at me blankly.

'The demo,' I reminded him. 'This morning. At Fidelity. You were demo'ing the sixty-one-inch, right?'

His nostrils flared. 'The demo flopped. The monitor wouldn't even turn on. Total dud. No one wants to spend $10,000 per unit on a bunch of plasmas that are questionable. So I lost 'em.'

'Crap. And you forecast Fidelity as a "commit", right?' That meant as close to a sure thing as you could get in this world.

He compressed his lips. 'So here's the thing, Jason. My car gets a flat tyre, then some kind of electrical problem. Brett's computer gets wiped out. Now I somehow get a bad monitor. Both of us lose major deals as a result.'

'Yeah?'

'What do Brett and I have in common? We're both in the running for Crawford's job. Against you. And nothing happens to you.'

'You're looking for an explanation? I mean, it sucks, and I'm sorry about it, but you guys have both been unlucky lately. That's all.'

Maybe it wasn't just a matter of bad luck. Two competitive guys, Gleason and Allard. Rivals for a job that paid a lot more and put them on the management track. Was it possible that they'd been sabotaging each other? Stranger things happened in high-pressure companies like ours.

'Unlucky,' he repeated. His nostrils flared again. 'See, I've always been the kind of guy who has great luck.'

MY MUSCLES WERE BURNING, but Kurt wouldn't let me stop. First thing in the morning, and the guy had me running up and down the steps of Harvard Stadium.

'Time for a rest,' I said.

'Nope. Keep going. Body relaxed. Swing those arms all the way back, right up to your shoulders.'

'I'm dying here. My muscles feel like they're on fire.'

'Lactic acid. Outstanding. Keep moving.'

'You're not even winded.'

'It takes a lot to get me winded. Two more.'

When we were done, we fast-walked along the banks of the Charles River to cool down. We were walking for a few minutes before I was able to talk almost normally. 'Trevor thinks I'm trying to wrong-foot him. You know that big Fidelity demonstration he had? One of our sixty-one-inch plasmas was dead when he switched it on. Of course he lost the account.'

'Bad for him, good for you.'

'Maybe. But he thinks I sabotaged the monitor.'

'Did you?'

'Come on. Not exactly my style. Plus, I wouldn't know how to do it even if I wanted to.'

'Couldn't the monitor have gone bad on the truck?'

'Sure. There's all kinds of ways a plasma monitor can go out of whack.'

'All you can do is ignore the guy. He's just trying to make excuses.'

I nodded. Walked for a bit. 'I'm going to have to miss our workout Thursday morning,' I said. 'I'm having breakfast with Letasky.'

'Gonna make him an offer he can't refuse, huh?'

'Do my best. Thanks to you. That intel is going to be a huge help. Huge.'

He shrugged modestly.

'And I really appreciate all the work you did to get it for me. But you need to be really careful with that stuff. Some of that crosses the line. And if either of us is caught with it, we could get in some serious trouble.'

He was silent. A minute went by, then another minute. There was a flock of geese waddling along the riverbank by the Lars Anderson Bridge.

'You're the one who asked me to get a backgrounder on Letasky,' he said, sounding almost defensive.

'You're right. But I shouldn't have. I'm uncomfortable with this.'

Another minute's silence. A car roared by along Storrow Drive.

'So I guess you're not interested in another titbit about James Letasky that just came in.' He went on, without waiting for a reply. 'Last couple of years the Letasky family's spent their vacations camping. But the place James and his wife really love is Martha's Vineyard. That's where they honeymooned.

They keep wanting to go back, but it's too far from Chicago.'

'Interesting,' I said. Martha's Vineyard was a lot closer to Boston than to Chicago.

Kurt looked at his watch. 'We both got to get to work,' he said.

'You playing softball tonight?'

'Wouldn't miss it,' Kurt said.

JIM LETASKY WAS A PLUMP, round-faced guy in his mid-thirties with blond hair cut in a pudding-basin haircut. He had a ready smile and couldn't have been more charismatic and winning. He was blunt and straightforward and I liked that. He knew we wanted to hire him, and he made no secret of the fact that he wasn't much interested. Still, he hadn't slammed the door shut, since he was sitting here at breakfast with me at the Hyatt Regency.

We exchanged the usual business chitchat and I congratulated him again on the Albertson's deal, and he was suitably modest about it. I pried a little about his connection at that middleman company, SignNetwork, but he got a little evasive. Trade secrets and all that.

When he'd finished his third cup of coffee, Letasky said, 'Jason, it's always great to see you, but frankly Entronics can't afford me.'

'Top talent costs,' I said.

'You don't know what I make.'

I tried not to smile. 'Your comp package is only one small part of what we can offer you,' I said.

He laughed. 'Not too small a part, I hope,' he said.

I told him what we'd offer. It was exactly twenty-five per cent higher than he made at NEC, and it didn't require him to bust his balls as much. I knew from his private complaints to his boss—Kurt's dossier even included some of Letasky's emails—that he was trying to cut back on the travel, spend more time with his kids.

'See, we want our salesguys to have a life,' I said. That was so bogus, I couldn't believe the words were tumbling out of my mouth. 'The way the package is structured, you can make a lot more than you make now by working significantly fewer hours. You get to watch your kids grow up. You get to go to Kenny's hockey practice and the twins' ballet recitals.'

'How do you know—?' he began.

'I've done my homework.'

He blinked, momentarily silenced.

'These are precious years in your kids' lives,' I said. Just about the exact words he'd emailed his boss, in fact. 'And they go fast. I want you to think about what you're missing.'

'I've thought about it,' he conceded in a small voice.

'And why should you spend forty-five minutes commuting to work? That's time you could be spending with your kids.'

'We've got a great house.'

'For what you could get for your house in Evanston, you could be living in this house.' I took out a photo that I'd printed out from a Wellesley real estate website that morning. 'Over 200 years old. An old farmhouse that's been added to over the years.'

He stared at the photo. 'Man.'

'Cliff Road is the most exclusive neighbourhood in Wellesley. There's a great Montessori school not too far away—don't the twins go to a Montessori school?' I slid another piece of paper across the table at him. 'This is the relocation and signing bonus we're prepared to offer you.'

He read the number and blinked. 'It says the offer expires today.'

'I want you to have time to talk this over with Gail. But I don't want you using this as leverage within NEC to negotiate a better package.'

'They'd never match this,' he said. His honesty was refreshing. 'I have until five o'clock today to decide?'

'Boston time,' I said. 'That's four o'clock Chicago time.'

'Wow, man. I don't—this is so sudden.'

'You've thought about it for quite a while,' I said. 'Sometimes you just have to close your eyes and jump.' I could see he was thinking hard. 'Plus, do you know how close we are to the Vineyard?' I said. 'A hop, skip, and a jump. Ever been there? Your family would love it.'

I suggested he go back up to his hotel room and call his wife. I told him I'd wait down in the lobby, doing email on my BlackBerry.

Forty-five minutes later he returned to the lobby.

GORDY'S JAW DROPPED and for a few seconds he was speechless.

'Holy shit,' he said. 'How the hell did you do that?'

'You approved the package,' I said.

'I've offered him damn good packages before. What did you promise him?' he said suspiciously.

'Nothing you don't know about.'

'Well,' he said, 'good job. I don't know how you did it, but I'm impressed.'

He did not look happy.

WHEN I GOT BACK to my office after lunch on Friday, there was a voicemail from Gordy. He wanted me to come by his office at three o'clock.

At a few minutes before three I walked down the hall to his office.

Gordy actually stood when I entered. Next to him stood Yoshi Tanaka, eyes dead behind thick lenses.

'The better man won,' said Gordy. 'Our new Vice-President of Sales. Congratulations.' He extended a hand and gave what seemed to me a pretty damned grudging shake. Yoshi didn't shake my hand. He bowed, ever so slightly. Neither man smiled. Gordy struck me as unusually subdued, as if someone had a gun to his back.

'Thank you,' I said.

'Sit down,' Gordy said. We all took our places.

'I wish I could say this is a tribute to your own success,' Gordy said, 'but that's only part of it. You've had some good wins. Some *big* wins. Getting Letasky was a major coup, and I frankly didn't think you could pull it off. But the main thing is, I can't have a bumbler in the job. I need someone totally reliable. Not like Gleason, spacing out on appointments. Even Trevor, dropping the ball on Fidelity and Pavilion.'

'Well, I look forward to the challenge,' I said, which, when I heard the words come out of my mouth, almost made me barf.

'And a challenge it will be,' said Gordy. 'I think Yoshi-san wants to say a few words.'

Tanaka bowed his head solemnly. 'My most congratulation—to you.'

'Thank you.'

'You have very—imposu—impo—sent—job to do.'

'Important, yes.'

'Very—hard time for our—business.'

'I understand.'

'I think you not know how hard time,' Tanaka said quietly.

'Thank you, Yoshi-san,' said Gordy. 'Now I'd like to discuss salary specifics with Steadman. Could you give us a little privacy?'

Tanaka rose, tipped his head in a parting bow, and walked out.

I was determined not to let Gordy see me as a wimp. 'I have a pretty good sense of what my salary requirements are—' I began.

'Your *requirements*,' Gordy spit out. 'Your package is take-it-or-leave-it. I just said that to get the Jap out of the room.'

He told me what it was, and I tried not to smile. It was more than I'd expected. A lot more.

'You weren't my top choice, I think you know that,' Gordy said.

Now I understood why Yoshi was there. He was the enforcer, making sure Tokyo's will was done. Gordy must have hated that.

'I hope to prove you wrong,' I said.

He stared malevolently. 'I already told you there's shit raining down on us from the Mega Tower in Tokyo. Well, let me tell you who's doing the shitting. You know the name Hideo Nakamura, I assume.'

'Sure.' A couple of weeks ago a press release was emailed around that the chairman of the board of the Entronics Corporation, a guy named something-Ikehara, had been 'promoted' and was being replaced by this guy Nakamura.

'I flew down to headquarters in Santa Clara to meet Nakamura, and he's real polished. Speaks good English. Loves golf and Scotch. But this guy's an executioner. They put him in because the very top guys in the Mega Tower are real unhappy. They don't like our numbers. That's why they bought Royal Meister's US business—to extend their reach into the US market.'

'I see.'

'So we gotta show Nakamura what we're made of. Can you do that?'

'I can.'

'Can you pull a rabbit out of your hat?'

I almost said, *I'll sure as hell try*. But I said, 'You know it.'

'I'm going to expect a lot out of you.' He stuck out his hand. 'I hope I haven't made a mistake,' he said.

I tried not to smile. 'You haven't,' I said.

I SMILED all the way to my office. There I shut the door and pumped my fists into the air.

I called Kate's cell. 'Hey, babe,' I said. 'You at work?'

'I'm just sitting here at Starbucks, having a coffee with Claudia.' Claudia had gone to prep school and college with Kate, had an immense trust fund, and did nothing but go out with her friends. She didn't understand why Kate insisted on working at the foundation.

'I just saw Gordy.' I kept my voice neutral, a blank.

'And? You don't sound so good. You didn't get it?'

'I got it. You're talking to a vice-president. I want some deference.'

She let out a loud squeal. 'Oh, my God. Jason! That's so wonderful!'

'This means a huge boost in salary. *Serious* bonus.'

'We've got to celebrate. I'll make reservations at Hamersley's.'

'I'm kind of wiped out,' I said. 'It's been a long day.'

'All right, baby. We'll do something at home.'

BY THE TIME I got home I was feeling pretty good about life.

Kate ran to meet me at the door. She was wearing a white T-shirt and jeans, looked and smelled great. She threw her arms around me, kissed me right on the lips, and I kissed her back, and kept going.

When you've been married for a while, that kind of spontaneous combustion doesn't happen all that often, but I felt this surge of testosterone. I felt like Cro-Magnon man, returning to his woman in the cave, having speared a woolly mammoth.

I dropped my briefcase and slipped my hands under the waistband of her jeans. I felt her silky-smooth warm skin and began kneading her butt.

She gave a throaty giggle. 'What's the special occasion?' she said.

'Every day I'm married to you is a special occasion,' I said, and I went back to kissing her.

I moved up into the living room, pushed her back onto Grammy Spencer's rock-hard, chintz-covered couch.

'Jase,' she said. 'Wow.'

'We're allowed to do this without a plastic specimen cup, you know,' I said as I started to peel off her T-shirt. 'You're a beautiful woman, anyone ever tell you that?' I continued, as I unzipped her jeans.

'STAY THERE,' she said afterwards.

She went into the kitchen, where I could hear the refrigerator being opened and glasses clinking, and a couple of minutes later she emerged with a tray. She carried it to the couch, naked, and set it down on the coffee table. It was a bottle of Krug champagne, two champagne flutes and a mound of black caviar in a silver bowl.

I hate caviar, but it's not like we had it very often. I said, with all the excitement I could muster, 'Caviar!'

'Could you do the honours?' She handed me the cold champagne.

I stripped off the lead foil and twisted off the wire cage, and the cork came out with a quiet burp. I poured it into the flutes slowly and let the bubbles settle, then I handed her a glass and we clinked.

'Wait,' she said as I put my flute to my lips. 'A toast.'

'To the classics,' I said. 'Champagne and caviar and sex.'

'No,' she said with a laugh. 'To love and desire—the spirit's wings to great deeds. Goethe. Honey, do you realise what you've accomplished? How you've turned your whole career around?'

I nodded, couldn't look at her. My dad had a job. I have a *career*.

And if she only knew what kind of help I was getting.

'Vice-president. I'm so proud of you.'

'Aw, shucks,' I said.

'You really kick ass when you put your mind to it.'

'Well, you're the one who gave me the push. The jump start.'

'Sweetie.' She reached under the sofa and pulled out a large box.

'*Moi?*' I said. 'Wait, I know what it is.'

'You do not.'

'I do. It's one of those Yanomami blowpipes. With the poison darts.'

She gave me her great, sexy knowing smile. I loved that smile.

I unwrapped the box. It was a beautiful briefcase in chestnut leather with brass fittings. It had to cost a fortune. 'Jesus,' I said. 'Amazing.'

'It's made by Swaine Adeney Briggs and Sons. Claudia helped me pick it out. She says it's the Rolls-Royce of attaché cases.'

'And maybe someday a Rolls-Royce to put it in,' I said. 'Babe, this is incredibly sweet of you.'

Her eyes shone, wide with excitement. She took a sip of champagne and then turned back to the coffee table. She spread some of the vile, oily black eggs on a cracker and offered it to me with a sweet smile. 'Sevruga?'

PART TWO

CHAPTER 5

We found out Kate was pregnant two weeks later. She'd gone to the IVF clinic to start the gruesome process all over again. They gave her the usual blood work and the next day Dr DiMarco called Kate to tell her that an interesting complication had arisen, and there might not be a need for an IVF cycle after all. He seemed a little miffed, Kate told me. We'd gotten pregnant the old-fashioned way.

I had a secret theory. I think Kate got pregnant because things had started to break my way. Call me crazy, but you know how some people try for years to have a baby, then as soon as they adopt, boom, they get pregnant? Their biological roadblock gets blown away just by the decision to adopt.

Then again, it's possible that she got pregnant just because we'd finally had real sex, after months of my doing it into a plastic cup in a lab.

Whatever the reason, we were both elated.

The pregnancy was the biggest thing to happen to us in the first couple of months after my promotion, but it wasn't the only big thing. We moved out of the little house in Belmont and into a beautiful Victorian town house on Hilliard Street in Cambridge.

In the driveway—no garages in this fancy part of Cambridge, believe it or not—sat our two brand-new cars. I'd traded in my totally rebuilt Acura for a new Mercedes SLK 55 AMG Roadster, and Kate reluctantly traded in her tired old Nissan Maxima for a Lexus SUV hybrid.

It was all happening fast—maybe too fast.

JUST ABOUT every morning I worked out with Kurt, at his gym or at Harvard Stadium or running along the Charles River. Kurt had become my personal trainer. He told me I had to lose the paunch, had to become lean and mean.

After a couple of months I was down thirty pounds. I had to buy new clothes, which delighted Kate. She saw it as an opportunity to upgrade my wardrobe, get me into some Italian designer suits.

Kurt had me eating high-protein and low-fat and only 'good' carbs. He insisted I take the stairs at work at least once a week. *Twenty floors?* I squawked. *You're out of your mind!* One morning I tried it, and I had to change my shirt as soon as I got to my office. But after a while climbing twenty flights wasn't all that brutal. When you have an elevator phobia, you'll put up with a lot of pain to avoid being trapped in the vertical coffin.

Kate was thrilled. She'd never met this guy Kurt, but she liked what he was doing for me.

She didn't know the half of it, of course.

AT WORK, THINGS just started clicking into place for me. It was as if every pitch I swung at was a home run. One good thing led to another.

One day, when a new deal I was working on seemed to be far enough along, I stopped in to see Gordy and tell him the good news. He nodded, asked a few questions, didn't seem all that interested. He handed me the monthly expense reports and told me to go over them.

I glimpsed at the report, and said, 'Jesus, the Band of Brothers spends a lot on T&E, huh?' That's Travel & Entertainment—hotel, travel, meals.

'See?' he said. 'It's crazy. I've been meaning to crack down on abuses of corporate credit cards for some time. But now that I've got one throat to choke, I want *you* to come up with a new T&E policy.'

He wanted me to be the bad guy.

'Got it,' I said.

'One more thing. Time to rank 'n' yank.'

I knew what he meant—stack-rank everybody and fire the underperformers—but was he saying he wanted *me* to do it?

'You're kidding.'

'No one said it was gonna be easy. You and I rate our guys on a five-point scale, and then you get rid of the underperformers.'

'The underperformers?' I said, wanting to hear him say it aloud.

'The C players get fired.'

'Bottom ten per cent?'

'No,' he said with a fierce stare. 'Bottom third. This is a Darwinian struggle. Only the toughest survive. I want Tokyo to see an immediate change in our numbers.'

'How immediate are we talking about?'

He stared at me for a few seconds, then got up and shut his office door. He sat back down, folded his arms.

'Don't you breathe a *word* of this to any of your Band of Brothers. By the end of the second quarter Dick Hardy and the boys in the Mega Tower are making a decision. It's gonna be either us or the Royal Meister sales force. Framingham or Dallas. The one with the best numbers survives. The other office gets shut down. We have another quarter like this one and everyone in this building gets their walking papers. Now, ready for the bad news?'

'That was the good news?'

'It's all riding on you, buddy. You've got to pull a goddamned rabbit out of your hat in the next couple of months or everyone in the Framingham office, including you and your Band of Brothers, gets shot.'

'Don't you think we should let everyone know the stakes?' I said.

'No way, Steadman. Scared salesmen can't sell. Clients can see the flop sweat. They smell the panic. So this is our little secret. You and me. And if you screw up, I'm gonna have to get my résumé printed up too. The difference is, I'm eminently employable. You, on the other hand, will be blackballed from here to Tokyo. I will personally see to it.'

I wanted to say something about how the flop sweat wasn't good for managers either, but I stayed silent.

'You know,' Gordy said, 'I didn't want to give you this job at first. But now I'm glad I did. You know why?'

I tried to swallow, but my mouth had gone dry. 'Why's that, Gordy?'

'Because I like Trevor a lot more than I like you, and I wouldn't wish this on him.'

FOR THE REST of the morning, I went over the T&E expenses and began to devise the tough new policy that Gordy wanted. I thought of this as my 'no more Mister Nice Guy' memo. No more flying business class: economy all the way. No more fancy hotels: now the limit was $175 a night. I lowered the per diem to $50 a day. You couldn't write off any meals beyond that unless you were taking a customer.

I did some number-crunching and figured out how much this new policy would save the company, and I emailed the memo to Gordy.

Right after lunch, he called and said, 'I love it.'

I read over the memo again. Tried to soften the language a bit. Then I emailed it to Franny to double-check for typos and such.

Franny—Frances Barber—was the secretary I'd been assigned. She'd been with the company for over twenty years, and her only flaw was that she went out for a cigarette break every half hour. Franny had a real no-nonsense look, a tight mouth with vertical lines above her upper lip. She was forty-five but looked ten years older.

She buzzed me on the intercom and said, 'A Mister Sulu for you?' She sounded uncertain. 'Though he doesn't exactly *sound* Japanese.'

Obviously she didn't know Classic *Trek*. 'Graham,' I said as I picked up. 'Long time.'

'You sound kinda spun out.'

'Insane around here.'

'You been avoiding me, J-man? I'm starting to feel like a Klingon.'

'I'm sorry, Graham. I'm—well, I'm on this new regimen now.'

'*Regimen?* It's Kate, isn't it? She finally won.'

'It's a lot of things. Kate's pregnant, did you hear?'

'Hey, congratulations! A baby Steadman. Blows my mind. Lemme cut to the chase. I've got some stellar shit here. Some killer White Widow.'

'That some kind of heroin?'

He answered in a Jamaican accent: 'Ganja, mon.'

'I don't think so.'

'Come on, I'll roll us a doobie and we'll go for a ride in the Love Bug.'

'I told you, Graham,' I said firmly. 'I don't do that anymore.'

His voice got small. 'OK, man, I think I get it. You're a vice-president, now, right? Says that on your company's website. You got your own secretary, and a big fancy house. Guess you got to put a little distance between where you come from and where you are now, that it?'

'Cut me a little slack, will you? I'm over my head at work. As soon as I can, we'll go out. Dinner's on me. OK?'

'Yeah,' Graham said sullenly. 'I'll wait for your call.' He hung up.

Franny came into my office. 'Uh, Jason,' she said, standing at the door awkwardly. 'You sure you really want to send this out?'

'Why not?'

'Because I was just starting to like you, and I don't know if I'll like the next guy as much.'

I smiled. 'Gordy approved it,' I said.

'Sure he did,' Franny said, and she gave a little nervous laugh. 'Had you put it in your name so you'd catch the flak, not him.'

'It's a dirty job, but someone's got to do it,' I said. I looked the memo over one more time. It was harsh. It was guaranteed to be unpopular, which meant it would make its author unpopular. It was something Gordy should have done himself, not me. I clicked SEND.

Then the shit hit the fan.

RICKY FESTINO came flying into my office maybe five minutes later. 'What the hell's this?' he said. He wasn't holding or pointing to anything.

'What's what?' I said blandly.

'You know damned well what. This T&E shit.'

'Come on, Ricky. Everyone's abusing the system, and we're trying to cut costs—'

'Jason. Hello? It's me you're talking to. You don't have to bullshit me. Did Gordy make you put your name on this?'

I shook my head. 'He approved it, but it was my work.'

'You think Trevor and Gleason and all those guys are going to put up with staying at Motel Six and taking their clients to Applebee's?'

'I didn't say anything about Motel Six or Applebee's. Come on.' He was exaggerating, but not by much.

'The guys aren't going to put up with this.'

'They're not going to have a choice.'

'Don't be so sure, kid,' Festino said.

I WAS GETTING READY to leave for the day—Kate wanted to go shopping for baby stuff, which was the last thing I felt like doing—when Trevor Allard stopped by.

'Nice memo,' he said.

I nodded.

'Brilliant strategy. That's the way to hang on to your top talent.'

'You planning to take another job?' I said.

'I don't need to. I just have to wait for you to fall on your face.'

'There's no "I" in team, Trevor,' I said.

'Yeah. But there's a "Me" in Messiah.'

BABY WORLD WAS SUPREMELY annoying. It was a giant fluorescent-lit warehouse stocked with only baby things, from low-end to high.

Kate rolled through the departments like a tank, picking out a changing table, a contoured changing pad and a mobile that played classical music, to help develop the baby's cognitive skills.

Meanwhile, I kept furtively checking my BlackBerry and my cellphone. My cellphone said no service—another reason to hate Baby World—while my BlackBerry kept receiving messages complaining about my memo.

Kate was showing me a Bellini crib. 'Sally Wynter bought this one for Anderson,' she said. She heard my BlackBerry buzz, and she threw me an exasperated look. 'Are you here, or are you at work?'

I'd have rather been anywhere else. 'Sorry,' I said. I switched the BlackBerry alert mode to silent, so she wouldn't hear it anymore.

We moved on to small electronics. She grabbed a box off the shelf and dropped it into our shopping cart. 'This is so genius,' she said. 'It's a back-seat baby monitor. You plug it into the cigarette lighter, and the camera goes on the back of the headrest, and the monitor goes on the dashboard. So you can keep a watch on baby without turning around.'

That's what I need, I thought. More distractions while I'm driving. 'Cool,' I said.

'Oh, here we are,' Kate said. 'The best part of all.'

I followed her into the baby carriage department, where she immediately glommed on to a big, scary, black carriage with big wheels, antique-looking and forbidding. It seemed like something out of *Rosemary's Baby*.

'God, Jason, will you look at this Silver Cross Balmoral pram?' she said. 'It's so unbelievably elegant, isn't it?'

I took a look at the price tag. 'Does that say $2,800?'

'Is that how much it is? Forget it,' Kate said. 'That's crazy. Sorry.'

'Whatever you want, Kate.'

'For way less money, there's the Stokke Xplory,' she said. 'The baby rides higher off the ground. It encourages parent-child bonding. Not much storage space underneath, though.' I saw her cast a longing glance at the Silver Cross Balmoral pram when she thought I wasn't looking.

I glanced at my BlackBerry and saw an email from Gordy. Its subject line was URGENT! The message read, 'Call me IMMEDIATELY.'

'I've been hearing a lot about the Bebe Confort Lite Chassis,' Kate said. 'It's a fraction of the price of the Silver Cross.'

'I've got to make a call,' I said.

'Can't it wait?'

'Gordy's trying to reach me, and he says it's urgent. I'm sorry.'

I turned and hurried through the aisles to the parking lot, where I picked up a cellphone signal. I punched out Gordy's cell number.

'What the hell are you doing?' Gordy barked when he picked up.

'Shopping for baby stuff.'

'This goddamned memo of yours. What the hell's that all about?'

'Gordy, you approved it before I sent it out. Is there a problem?'

'Is there a *problem*? Trevor just came into my office and told me how the entire sales force is on the verge of revolt.'

'Trevor?' I said. 'Trevor doesn't speak for the "entire sales force".'

'Well, I got news for you. We just lost Forsythe over this.'

'What do you mean, we "lost" Forsythe?'

'It was the last straw for the guy. Apparently he had a standing offer from Crawford at Sony, and guess what? Late this afternoon he called and accepted their offer. Why? Because of your damned crackdown.'

My crackdown?

'What do you want me to do?'

'I've taken care of it,' Gordy said. 'I just sent out an email revoking your new policy. Told them there was a miscommunication.'

I gritted my teeth. 'So is Forsythe still leaving?' I said.

But Gordy had hung up.

I walked back across Baby World. Kate was staring at me as I approached.

'You look like you just got kicked in the stomach,' she said.

'The balls, more like. There's all kinds of shit going down at work.'

'Well, I'm ready to check out anyway. But you shouldn't have come tonight. You should have stayed at work.'

'What's that supposed to mean?'

'You're totally distracted with your job. You're not required to go shopping with me, Jase.'

'We're buying baby stuff. I think it's important for us to do it together.'

'Yeah, but your head is back at the office.'

She pushed the cart towards the checkout line, and I followed her. Both of us were silent, stewing. We stood there in line. Finally, I said, 'Why don't you go get the tag for the *Rosemary's Baby* carriage.'

'The Silver Cross Balmoral pram? But that's crazy expensive.'

'It's the one you want. It's the one we'll get. It would be downright irresponsible to put our baby in a carriage that doesn't have shock absorbers and side-impact bars. Baby Steadman's going to travel in style.'

When the cashier rang everything up, I stared at the bill in disbelief. If my father had seen how much we were spending on baby stuff, he'd have had a heart attack in his Barcalounger right in front of the TV set.

AS SOON AS Doug Forsythe got in the next morning, I strolled by his cubicle and tapped him on the shoulder.

'Got a minute?' I said.

He looked up at me and said, 'Sure thing boss.' He knew what this was about and didn't bother to hide it. He followed me to my office.

'Doug, did you just accept an offer from Sony?'

He paused, but only for a second. 'Verbally, yeah.' he said. 'I won't lie to you. Crawford made me a killer offer.'

Verbally, he was careful to say. Maybe there was some wiggle room.

'You've been here eight years. Are you unhappy?'

'Unhappy? No, not at all. God, no.'

'Then why've you been talking to Crawford?'

He shrugged and opened his palms. 'He made an offer. Look, Jason, I don't even know if I'm going to be here a year from now.'

'You're crazy, Doug. You're bulletproof. With numbers like yours, you don't have a worry in the world.'

'I'm not talking about me personally. I mean all of us.'

'I don't follow.'

'Well, that expenses memo—that really put the fear of God into a lot of us guys. Like, Entronics must really be in rough shape.'

'We're not in rough shape,' I said. 'We just need to be more competitive. Cut costs. Anyway, Gordy overruled me on that.'

'I know,' Forsythe said. 'But I get a feeling that's just the tip of the old iceberg. I've heard Entronics plans to get rid of its entire Visual Systems sales force. Now that they have Royal Meister's, they don't need us.'

'That's ridiculous.'

'It's not true?' He looked right at me now.

I shook my head. Lying like a kid caught with his hand stuck in the cookie jar. 'Totally not true,' I said.

'Really?' He sounded genuinely perplexed.

'We'll match any offer Sony makes you,' I said. 'We don't want to lose you, you know that.'

'I do.'

'Come on, Doug. We need you here. Entronics is your home,' I said.

He didn't reply.

'So forget those rumours,' I said. 'I'll see you at the game tonight.'

WHEN I GOT HOME before the game I noticed an almost-new-looking black Mustang parked in our narrow brick-topped driveway. Kurt's. He'd bought it from his friend who owned the auto body shop.

I hurried into the house, wondering why he was here.

Kurt was sitting in our living room, talking to Kate. The two of them were laughing about something. Kate had set out a tray with butter cookies.

'Well, hello. Sorry I'm late,' I said to Kate. 'Lot happening at the office.'

'Jason,' Kate said, 'you never told me Kurt's a handyman too.'

'Hey, Kurt. What a surprise, huh?'

'Hey, bro. I had to meet with a vendor in Cambridge. I finally got approval for the biometric fingerprint verification system, and I had to finalise some details. I figured since I was in your neck of the woods, I'd give you a lift to the softball game.'

'OK, sure,' I said.

'Will you take a look at what Kurt did to the stairs?' Kate said to me.

'Come on,' Kurt said. 'It's no big deal.'

I followed her to the staircase that led to the first floor. The junky oatmeal-coloured carpet had been removed, exposing handsome wood. The old carpet lay in a neat pile, cut up into rectangular sections.

'Can you believe how beautiful that wood is?' Kate said. 'You'd never know it, with that gross carpet covering it up.'

'Wasn't safe,' Kurt said. 'You could break your neck. With Kate pregnant and all, you've really got to take care of stuff like that.'

'Very kind of you,' I said.

'You should install a runner,' Kurt said. 'Safer that way.'

'And how about brass carpet rods?' Kate said, excited.

'Easy,' Kurt said.

'Speak for yourself,' I said, a little peevish. 'I had no idea you knew how to do this. You can kill people *and* remove old carpeting.'

Kurt ignored the dig. Or maybe it wasn't a dig to him.

'Could you do that, do you think?' Kate said. 'The runner and the carpet rods and everything? We'd pay you, of course. We insist.'

'Don't worry about it,' Kurt said. 'Your husband here got me my job. I owe him.'

'You don't owe me anything,' I said.

'Kurt thinks we have way too many things plugged into that power strip thingy in the living room.'

'Electrical hazard,' Kurt said. 'You need another outlet on that wall. Easy to put in.'

'You're an electrician too?' Kate said.

'He just rewired his entire house,' I said, 'and it's not even his house.'

'God,' Kate said to Kurt, 'is there anything you *can't* do?'

KURT DROVE his Mustang fast and skillfully. I was impressed. Most drivers who haven't grown up around Boston get intimidated by the aggressiveness of the native Boston driver. Kurt handled the traffic like a native.

We sat in silence for a good ten minutes, and then Kurt said, 'Hey, man, did I piss you off?'

'Piss me off? Why do you say that?'

'Like you were ticked off I was at your house when you got home.'

'No,' I said in that terse, male way where the tone says it all.

'Just trying to help you there, bud. With the stairs. I figured, I know how to fix stuff, and you're a busy executive.'

'I appreciate it.' I said. 'Kate did too. You were right—she's pregnant, and we've got to be careful about stuff like that.'

'All right. Just so long as we're cool.'

'Yeah, sure. I just had a bad day at work.'

THAT NIGHT we played EMC, a giant computer-storage company, and once again we won, though we were short one player. Doug Forsythe never showed up.

My own softball game had improved, for some reason. When I stepped up to the plate, I swung harder and with greater confidence. I began hitting them deep. My fielding was better too.

But a couple of times, Trevor Allard threw the ball by me and around me, deliberately cutting me off, as if I couldn't be trusted with the ball. The one time he threw the ball to me was when I wasn't prepared—I was half turned away—and he almost took off my ear.

After the game, Kurt and I walked to the parking lot. Trevor was in his Porsche, blasting that Kanye West song, 'Gold Digger'—*He got that ambition, baby, look in his eyes*—and it didn't seem to be a coincidence.

I told Kurt I wanted to head right home if he didn't mind giving me a lift. 'I told Kate I'd be home. These days she doesn't like me staying out as late.'

'Pregnant women need to feel protected,' Kurt said. 'Primitive instinct. Listen to me—like I know. She's a nice chick. Pretty, too.'

'And mine.'

'Things OK on the home front?'

'Not bad,' I said.

'Important to take care of the home front,' he said. 'If the home front isn't in good shape, everything else suffers.'

'Yeah.'

'Hey, so what happened to Doug Forsythe tonight?' Kurt said.

'I think we're about to lose him to Sony.'

'Because of your hard-ass memo?'

'That may have been the last straw. I pleaded with him, but the guy obviously wants to leave. And I can't blame him. Gordy's no fun to work for.'

'Listen,' Kurt said. 'It's none of my business, but you can't let Trevor disrespect you. If he thinks he can get away with that kind of disrespect on the ball field, it's just going to carry over to the workplace.'

'It's no big deal.'

'Yes, it is,' Kurt said. 'It's a big deal. And it's unsat.'

IT WAS SEVEN-THIRTY in the morning, and Gordy was on his third giant mug of coffee. He was bouncing off the walls.

'Rank 'n' yank time,' he said. 'Gotta tell ya, your performance reviews of some of these guys were awful generous.'

I said nothing. He was right. I'd been generous in my assessments. I'd also given a boost to some of the outliers, like Ricky Festino and Cal Taylor. I didn't want to give Gordy any ammunition he didn't need.

'Time for Taylor and Festino to hit the road,' he said.

So what was the point of the 'performance review' exercise he'd just put me through?

'Cal Taylor's two years from retirement,' I said.

'He retired years ago. He just didn't tell anyone.'

'Festino just needs some more hands-on guidance. What about moving him to Inside Sales?'

'So he can botch that too? Taminek handles Inside Sales just fine. Festino's been on life support for too long. Time to yank the feeding tube.'

'Gordy,' I said, 'the guy's a family man with a mortgage and a kid in private school.'

'You don't understand. I wasn't asking your advice.'

'I can't do this, Gordy.'

He stared at me. 'Why does that not surprise me? Why do I get the feeling you're not cut out for the G Team?'

I'D NEVER FIRED anyone before, and I had to start with a sixty-three-year-old man.

Cal Taylor cried in my office.

I pushed a box of Kleenex across the desk and assured him this was nothing personal. Though in one sense it was entirely personal. It was all about his inability to crawl out of the Jack Daniel's bottle, get on the phone and deal with the constant rejection that salespeople face every day.

He sat there in front of me wearing his cheap grey summer-weight suit that he wore year-round. His shirt collar was frayed. His white hair was Brylcreemed back, his nicotine-yellowed moustache neatly trimmed.

And he wept.

Entronics had a 'termination script' you had to use whenever you fired anyone. No ad-libbing allowed. After me, he'd have to go to HR and then outplacement counselling. They'd tell him about his health benefits and how long he'd continue to get his salary. Then a Corporate Security officer would escort him out of the building. Forty years with the company, and they shooed you out like you were a shoplifter.

When the deed was done, he stood up, and looked at me with injured eyes. 'You happy? Being Gordy's hatchet man? His chief executioner?'

That didn't require an answer, so I didn't give him one. I felt as if I'd been kicked in the balls. I could only imagine how he felt. I closed my office door and sank down in my desk chair and watched him walk, slope-shouldered, across the expanse of the cube farm to his cubicle.

Through the gaps in the venetian blinds, I could see him talking to Forsythe and Harnett. Someone brought him a stack of white cardboard boxes and began setting them up for him. A few people gathered round his cubicle as he began putting his belongings in them. Trevor was shooting baleful glances in my direction.

Word spread like ripples on the surface of a pond. People came up to Taylor and said brief, consoling things, then walked away. Others passed by making broad gestures but not slowing their stride. It's funny the way people act around someone who's been fired. Getting terminated is sort of like having a contagious disease; for every person who stopped to share his sadness there were two who didn't want to get too close and catch it.

As I picked up my phone to ask Ricky Festino to come in, there was a knock at the door.

It was Ricky.

'Ricky,' I said.

'Steadman,' Festino said. 'Tell me you didn't just shoot Cal Taylor. Is it the merger integration team? That who gave the orders?'

I wanted to say, *It wasn't my idea*, but that was too weaselly. I said, 'Have a seat, Ricky.'

He did. 'I gotta tell you, as your friend, that I don't like what's happening to you. You've gone over to the dark side.'

'Ricky,' I tried to interrupt.

'So Taylor's the first guy voted off the island? Who's next, me?'

I looked at him for a couple of seconds before looking away.

'You're kidding, right? Don't kid a kidder, Jason.'

'The lower thirty per cent are being let go, Ricky.' I said softly.

I could see the blood drain from his face.

'I'm really sorry.'

'Jason,' he said, a note of wheedling entering his voice, 'I've got a family to feed. Entronics covers my wife's and kids' health plans.'

'You won't just be cut off, Ricky. Your benefits will be continued for up to eighteen months.'

'I've got *tuition* to pay, Jason. It's like $30,000 a *year*.'

'The public schools are great where you live, Ricky.'

'Not for a kid with Down's syndrome, Steadman.' His eyes were fierce, and they were moist.

I couldn't talk for a couple of seconds. 'I had no idea, Ricky.'

'Is this your decision, Jason?'

'Gordy's,' I said at last, feeling like the coward I was.

'Can I talk to Gordy?'

'It won't help, Ricky. He's made up his mind.'

'You can talk to him for me, then. Right? Jason, please.'

I was silent. I was dying inside.

'You of all people,' he said. He stood up slowly and went to the door.

'Ricky,' I said. He stopped, his back to me, his hand on the knob.

'Let me talk to Gordy,' I said.

MELANIE STOPPED ME outside Gordy's office. 'He's on the phone.'

'I'll come back.'

She glanced through Gordy's venetian blinds. 'His body language tells me he's almost off.'

Melanie and I talked for a bit. Finally, Gordy was off the phone, and I went in. 'I need to talk to you about Festino,' I said.

'Guy freaks out on you, you call Security. He could do that, you know.'

'No, it's not that.' I told him about Festino's child.

Gordy's eyes grew beady. I stared at his pompadour, because I couldn't look into his eyes. It seemed puffier than usual. He looked like he'd had his hair coloured recently. 'I really don't give a shit,' he said.

'I won't do it,' I said. 'I won't fire Festino. I can't do it to the guy.'

He tipped his head to one side, looked curious. 'You're *refusing?*'

I swallowed and hoped it wasn't audible. I had the feeling I was about to cross some kind of office Rubicon. 'Yeah,' I said.

A long, long silence. Then he said, slowly and deliberately, 'OK. For now. But after TechComm, you and me are going to have a talk.'

TechComm was the huge trade show, where we always threw a swanky dinner for our biggest customers. Gordy was always the master of ceremonies at the dinner, and he liked to keep the theme a secret until we got there. 'I don't want any disruptions before TechComm.'

'Sure,' I said.

'You know something? I don't think you have what it takes.'

For once I didn't answer.

CHAPTER 6

I wanted to get out of the office on time today. Kurt had Red Sox tickets. I had to get home and change out of my suit and kiss Kate and get over to Fenway Park by seven.

I was packing up my fancy leather briefcase when I saw Doug Forsythe standing at my office door. 'Got a sec?' he asked.

'Of course,' I said. 'Come on in.'

He sat down, with a tentative look about him. 'You know, what you said before? I've been thinking. And—you're right. Entronics is my home.'

I was stunned. 'Really? Hey, that's great.'

I noticed an instant message pop up on my computer screen. It was from Gordy. CALL ME NOW, it said.

'Doug, I'm so happy to hear that.'

Another IM. WHERE THE HELL ARE YOU? GET OVER HERE!

'Yeah, well,' he said. He didn't sound happy, that was the strange thing. 'I guess it's for the best.'

'You want us to match Sony's offer,' I said, taking a stab at it. 'And I told you we would.'

He inhaled slowly, deeply. 'No need,' he said. 'I don't want to hold you guys up for more money.'

No salesguy in the history of Western civilisation has ever said that. Or at least said it and meant it. I was immediately on alert.

'Doug,' I said, 'I gave you a promise. Now, don't make me beg.'

Forsythe stood up. 'Really, it's fine,' he said. 'Here I am, and here I'll stay. I'm fine with it. I'm cool, I really am.'

He left, and I sat there for a few seconds, baffled. I turned back to the screen and saw another IM from Gordy. NOW! it said.

I IM'd back: ON MY WAY.

GORDY WAS LEANING all the way back in his office chair, arms folded behind his back, beaming like a lunatic.

'What took you so long?' he said.

'Doug Forsythe just came into my office,' I said. 'He's staying.'

'Oh, is *that* right?' he said. 'What in the world would make a high-test guy like Doug Forsythe back out of a job offer that's at least thirty per cent better than what he's doing here? Did he ask you to match Sony's offer?'

'No, in fact.'

'You didn't think that was bizarre?'

'Yeah, it was.'

Gordy tipped his chair forward, planted his elbows on his desk, and said triumphantly, '*The goddamned offer dried up*. Sony pulled it.'

'That's impossible.'

'I kid you not. I just got a call from a buddy of mine at Sony. Somewhere way up in the hierarchy, someone got cold feet about Doug Forsythe. He was notified early this afternoon that they were revoking the offer.'

'But why?'

He shook his head. 'No idea. No one knows. Something must have come up. I have no idea what. But it's over and done with. Forsythe returns to the mother ship.' He cackled. 'Love it when shit like this happens.'

THERE WAS the usual crowd around Fenway Park, the scalpers, the guys hawking Italian sausages and hot dogs and programmes. I found Kurt standing at the turnstiles near Gate A, as we'd arranged. I was surprised to see that he had his arm round a woman's waist.

She had brassy red hair, a cascade of frizzy curls, and she wore a peach tank top that was tight on her enormous boobs. She had a tiny waist and a great ass, which was well displayed by a pair of short shorts.

This was not the sort of woman I expected Kurt to be going out with. He'd never mentioned any girlfriend, and you don't bring just anybody to a Red Sox game. The tickets are too hard to get.

'Hey, chief,' he said, reaching out for me with his left hand, touching my shoulder. 'Jason, I'd like you to meet Leslie.'

'Hi, Leslie,' I said. We shook hands. She had long red fingernails.

'Let's rock 'n' roll,' Kurt said.

I walked alongside them through the cavernous underbelly of the ballpark, looking for our section. I felt like a third wheel.

When we got to the stairs at our section, Leslie announced she had to use the little girls' room. That's what she called it.

'She's cute,' I said, when Leslie had gone off to the little girls' room. 'How long have you been going out with her?'

He glanced at his watch. 'Eighteen hours. Met her in a bar last night.'

'I think I'm going to get a steak-and-cheese sub. You want one?'

'You don't want to eat that shit,' Kurt said. 'Look at all the progress you're making. You don't want that crap in your body.'

I'd lost my appetite. 'How's work going?'

'Good,' he said. 'Been doing some background investigations and some badge-replacement. Routine stuff. And the biometric fingerprint readers are in, so everyone's going to have to stop down at Corporate Security over the next couple of days and give us a fingerprint.' He looked at me. 'You're not sleeping. What's up? Problems on the home front?'

'Not really,' I said. 'It's Gordy.'

'Guy has it in for you,' he said. 'Gotta do something about that.'

'What do you mean, he has it in for me? You know something?'

He paused. 'One of my responsibilities is to monitor email.'

'You guys do that?'

'Have to. Scan for key words and stuff.'

'But you're looking at his email for other reasons,' I said.

He blinked. 'Part of my job.'

'What does he say about me?'

'You're obviously a threat. See, what Gordy doesn't understand is that his job isn't quite so secure as he thinks.'

'What does that mean?'

'The Japanese don't like his style. His profanity. His crudeness.'

'I don't know about that,' I said. 'He gets results.'

He shook his head. 'He's a racist. Hates the Japanese. I've been doing some reading. The Japanese admire the strong-willed American manager style. But the second he shows anti-Japanese racism in public, he's gone.'

'He's too smart for that.'

'Maybe,' Kurt said.

Then Leslie walked up in a toxic cloud of cheap perfume. She put her arm round Kurt, grabbing his butt.

'Let's find our seats,' he said.

I'VE BEEN TO Fenway scores of times, maybe a hundred times, but I never fail to feel a thrill when I walk up the steps and the field appears before me suddenly, brilliant green glittering in the sun or the lights.

We had amazing seats, right behind the Red Sox dugout, two rows from the field. Leslie didn't know too much about baseball and Kurt had to explain the game to her. We missed a great play, so we looked up at the enormous electronic scoreboard, where they run the video instant replays.

'I can't even see what happened,' Kurt said.

'It's a lousy screen,' I said.

'We must have something better than that.' He meant Entronics.

'Oh, God, yeah. That's an old RGB LED large-format video display. We've got a large-format HD video screen that's crystal-clear.'

'I know the assistant equipment manager. He'll know who to talk to.'

'About replacing the scoreboard? Great idea, man.'

'I've got a million of 'em.'

Suddenly the Sox hit a grand slam, and everyone jumped to their feet.

'What just happened?' Leslie asked. 'Was that good or bad?'

I GOT TO THE OFFICE at seven the next morning, feeling invigorated and a little mellow after a particularly tough workout at Kurt's gym. I ploughed through paperwork and reports, played a little dodgeball by leaving phone messages for people I didn't want to talk to. Of the thirty or so sales cycles I was involved in, the two biggest by far were the Chicago Presbyterian Hospital project and, giant among giants, the Atlanta airport. I sent off some emails on those.

The Red Sox scoreboard thing had really got under my skin. The more I looked into it, the more intrigued I got. The scoreboard at Fenway was basically a twenty-four-foot-by-thirty-one-foot video screen that used light-emitting diode technology—that's LEDs to you. From a distance it looks great, like a giant TV screen. From a distance.

They've got these electronic digital signs all over the world by now. What's cool about them is that, with a few keystrokes of a computer, you can change the display entirely. Not like the old billboard days when guys had to go up there and tear down the old poster.

They're cool, but they're also kind of grainy, kind of coarse. The technology was developed a decade ago.

But now Entronics had something even brighter, even better. We had the new flexible OLED PictureScreen in prototype. It was high-definition, low-glare, weather-safe, and it was way better than anything else out there.

Once I got an Entronics PictureScreen above centre field at Fenway Park in Boston, I could start getting them in other baseball parks, then football stadiums. Then Times Square and Las Vegas and Piccadilly Circus. The Tour de France. Formula One. The Cannes Film Festival.

The *Vatican*. They had those huge projection TVs around St Peter's Square so people could watch the Pope celebrate mass.

How come, I wondered, no one at the top of Entronics in Tokyo had thought of this? It was a true brainstorm. It was *huge*.

So in a state of total delirium, I wrote up a business plan of how Entronics PictureScreens could take over the world. I did quick-and-dirty research into the drawbacks of the existing technologies and by nine o'clock, I'd finished a draft of a memo that, I was convinced, would transform Entronics, save our division, and catapult me to the top of the company.

Now what? Now what should I do with it? Give it to Gordy so he could swipe it and claim credit?

I looked up as someone passed my office, a scrawny Japanese man with aviator glasses. Yoshi Tanaka. The conduit to Tokyo.

I waved at him, beckoned him into my office.

'Jason-san,' he said. 'Hello.'

'Say, Yoshi, I've got this killer idea I want to run by you.'

He furrowed his brow. I told him about the memo I'd written. How much revenue I thought this concept could generate for the company. We'd already developed the technology—the sunk costs were already budgeted. There'd be no additional R&D. The more I talked, the better it sounded.

Then I saw Yoshi's blank stare of utter incomprehension. The man hadn't understood a word I was saying.

I might as well have been speaking . . . well, English.

I'D REALISED I was going to have to get Gordy's sign-off on my big electronic billboard idea, like it or not. Without his endorsement, the concept wasn't going anywhere.

He leaned back in his chair, arms folded behind his back.

I told him. I handed him a hard copy of my business plan.

'So now you're going into marketing,' he said. 'Don't waste your time. That idea's so old it's got whiskers and liver spots. It came up at the last planning meeting in Tokyo, and the Jap engineers said it wouldn't fly.'

'Why not?'

'Not enough candelas or something to use outside.'

'I've been over the technical specs, and it's as bright as an LED.'

'Look, Jason. Forget it, OK? It's not going to work. I want your mind on TechComm. From the second we all arrive in Miami, a couple of days from now, I want you schmoozing our resellers and channel partners. And remember, first night is the dinner for our biggest customers, and I'm the MC. So I want you in full battle mode. We got a division to save.'

KURT'S BLACK MUSTANG was parked in my driveway.

I entered quietly. Kate and Kurt were sitting in the living room talking. They didn't hear me come in.

'It's too much,' she was saying. 'It's eating him up. It's all he wants to talk about, Gordy and the Band of Brothers.'

Kurt mumbled something, and Kate said, 'But Gordy's just going to stand in his way, don't you think?'

'My ears are burning,' I said.

That jolted the two of them. 'Jason!' Kate said.

'Sorry to interrupt your conversation.'

'Notice anything?' Kate said.

'Besides the fact that my wife and my friend seem to be conducting an affair?'

'The walls, silly.'

I looked at the walls, and all I saw were the framed paintings Kate had collected over the years from artists the Mayer Foundation funded.

'You got a new painting?' They all looked the same to me.

'You don't notice they're all hanging straight, finally?'

'Oh, right. Yes, very straight.'

'Kurt,' she announced.

Kurt shook his head modestly. 'I always like to use two hangers on each frame—that brass kind with the three brads.'

'Me, too,' I said.

'And Kurt fixed that dripping faucet in the bathroom that's always driving us crazy,' Kate said.

'Just needed a new washer and O-ring,' Kurt said. 'A little plumber's grease and an adjustable wrench.'

'Very kind of you, Kurt,' I said. 'You had to see a vendor in Cambridge again?'

He nodded. 'Figured I'd stop by and say hi, and Kate put me to work.'

I shot Kate a dirty look. 'Are we still going to the movies tonight, Kate?'

Kurt got the message and said good-bye. Then Kate began the incredibly long and involved process of getting ready to go out. I sat in the bedroom, impatiently watching her do her make-up. 'Hey, Kate,' I said.

'Mm?' She was lining her lips with that pencil-looking thing.

'I don't want you to exploit Kurt anymore.'

'*Exploit* him? What are you talking about?' She turned around.

'Every time he comes over here, you put him to work fixing something.'

'Oh, come on, Jason, he *volunteers*. I think it makes him feel useful.'

'Uh-huh. Well, it strikes me as a little—I don't know, entitled.'

'Do I detect a note of jealousy?'

'Jesus, Kate. Of what?'

'I don't know. Maybe the fact that he's so handy, such a regular *guy*.'

'A regular guy,' I repeated. 'And I'm—what? Thurston Howell the Third? My dad worked in a sheet-metal plant, for God's sake.'

She shook her head, snorted softly. 'When you told me he was Special Forces, I was expecting crude, rough around the edges. But he's awfully considerate.' She let out a low giggle. 'Plus, he's not unattractive.'

'Not unattractive? What's that supposed to mean?'

'Oh, you know what I mean. Not—not what I expected, that's all. Don't be jealous, sweetie. *You're* my husband.'

'Yeah, and he's, what? Now he's like your—your Yohimbe warrior with the blowgun and the machete?'

'Yanomami.'

'Whatever.'

'Well, sometimes a machete is just the tool you need,' she said.

I HAD A MID-MORNING flight to Miami out of Logan for TechComm, so I didn't go in to work. I decided to sleep late. Late being relative, of course. Kate snuggled right up against me in bed, which was nice, until I suddenly noticed the time. It was almost eight. I bolted out of bed to finish packing.

'Hey, Kate,' I said, 'aren't you going to work?'

She mumbled into the pillow. 'I don't feel well.'

'What's the matter?'

'Cramps.'

Alarmed, I went to her side of the bed. 'Down—there?'

'Yeah.'

'Call Dr DiMarco.'

'It's not a big deal.'

'Call him anyway.'

She paged him while I nervously bustled about packing, took a shower, shaved. When I came out of the bathroom, she was asleep.

'Did he call back?'

She turned over. 'He said not to worry. Said call him if there's bleeding.'

'Will you call me on my cell?'

'Don't worry about it, sweetie. I'll call if there's anything.'

JUST ABOUT ALL of the Band of Brothers was aboard the Delta flight to Miami. Everyone but Gordy sat in economy. Gordy was in business class. Not sitting in first class was his money-saving gesture.

I had an aisle seat, several rows away from the other guys, and I was enjoying the fact that there were empty seats on either side. Until a woman sidled past me, holding a screaming baby. She started speaking Spanish to the infant, who wouldn't stop crying. Then she began changing the wriggling creature, right there. The smell of baby poop was overpowering.

I thought: Good God almighty, is this what's in store for me? Changing diapers on airplanes?

Behind me, some of the Entronics guys were getting a little rowdy, like frat boys. I turned round for a quick look. They were laughing loudly as some guy, whose face I couldn't see, was showing them something in a magazine. Trevor waved the guy over, said something, and both of them exploded in guffaws. The guy punched Trevor lightly on the shoulder and turned round and I could see it was Kurt.

At that moment he saw me and walked down the aisle. 'This seat taken?' he asked.

'Hey, Kurt,' I said warily. 'What are you doing here?'

'Booth security. Mind if I sit down?' he said, squeezing past me. He turned to the woman with the baby. '*Buenos días, señora*,' he said in an awfully good Spanish accent. He sniffed the air, caught the diaper aroma. 'That you?' He was trying to defuse the tension by cracking a joke.

I smiled to say I got it but it wasn't funny.

'So, you still don't want my help?'

I nodded.

'That include information I came across that concerns you?'

I hesitated. I couldn't let him keep doing this. It was wrong, and I knew it. But the lure was overpowering.

'All right,' I said. 'Let's hear it.'

He unzipped a nylon portfolio and took out a brown file folder and handed it to me.

'You know that big idea you came up with at Fenway?'

'The billboard thing?'

'Take a look.'

I hesitated, then opened the folder. It held printouts of emails between Gordy and Dick Hardy, the CEO of Entronics USA.

'I guess our CEO is coming to TechComm.'

'He never misses it.' I read through the emails. Gordy was all excited about a 'major idea' he'd come up with, a 'disruptive' application of existing technology that could transform Entronics's position in the global market. Digital signage! He used some of the exact phrases I'd used: 'The sunk costs are already budgeted.' And 'It will put Entronics on the map in the digital signage industry.'

'This pisses me off,' I said.

'I thought it might. That broke dick's not going to get away with screwing you over again.'

'What are you talking about?'

'I'm not talking.'

'What are you *thinking* about?'

'Nothing. When you're in combat, you don't think. You just act.'

'No,' I said. 'No favours.'

He was silent.

'I mean it,' I said. 'Come on, Kurt. No more. Please.'

THE HOTEL was a big fancy Westin attached to the convention centre. Our rooms all had balconies overlooking Miami and Biscayne Bay. I worked out in the hotel fitness centre and had a late room-service lunch while I did email and returned calls. I checked in with Kate at home and she said the cramps had gone away.

At five, I dressed and went down to the big opening reception. When I got there, I saw the whole Band of Brothers, plus Gordy. There was bad music and decent hors d'oeuvres and drinks. People were getting their badges and programme guides and figuring out which seminars and panel discussions they wanted to go to when they weren't on booth duty.

Snatches of conversation wafted by me: '. . . native resolution of nineteen-twenty-by-ten-eighty . . . totally seamless playback . . .' Ricky Festino told me that NEC was giving away a Corvette and wondered whether we could enter the draw. Then he said, 'Hey, look. It's Mister Big.'

Dick Hardy entered the party like he was Jay Gatsby. He was a big, trim man with a big head, a ruddy face, a strong jaw. He looked like a CEO out of Central Casting, which is probably why our Japanese overlords named him to the job. He wore a blue blazer over some kind of white linen T-shirt.

Gordy spotted him and rushed over, gave him a bear hug. Since Hardy was a lot taller than Gordy, the hug was comic—Gordy's arms grabbed Hardy round the belly.

TechComm is pretty damned cool. Everywhere the next morning you could see huge screens and displays, multimedia shows of light and sound. Video walls twelve feet high playing movie trailers and commercials. One booth was a virtual-reality simulation of a Renaissance palace you could walk into, all done by hologram. It was magic.

We had our biggest and best plasma and LCD screens and our six newest, lightest, and brightest LCD projectors for schools and businesses on display. I manned the booth a little, greeting walk-bys, but most of the time I was in meetings with big customers.

Later on, I did the booth crawl, checking out the competitors. I stopped at the booth of one company that did rotating video displays and weather-proof, 360-degree outdoor LED displays. I'd removed my badge so they'd think I was just another end user. At the booth of a company that sold huge indoor/outdoor LED video screens, assembled from modular panels, I dug deep, asking a bunch of questions about pixel pitch and colour correction. I really wanted to know what the competition was up to. They told me their screens had been used in Sting and Metallica concerts.

I checked out the booth of a company called AirView Systems, which sold flight information display systems to airports. They were one of our biggest competitors for the Atlanta airport contract, so I wanted to see what they did. I shook hands with the CFO, Steve Bingham, a handsome guy in his fifties with silver anchorman hair, a lean face and deep-set eyes.

Then I stopped at the Royal Meister booth. The young guy who was manning it was all over me, since he thought I was a potential customer. He handed me his business card, wanted to show us the latest and greatest. He asked for mine, and I patted my pockets and told him I must have left them back at my hotel room and turned to get the hell out of there, hoping he wouldn't see me at the Entronics booth when *he* did his booth crawl.

'Let me introduce you to our new Senior VP of Sales,' he said.

'Thanks, but I've got to get to a seminar.'

'Are you sure?' a woman said. 'I always like to say hello to prospects.'

I didn't recognise her at first. Her mousy brown hair was the colour of honey, with highlights too. She was wearing make-up for the first time.

'Joan,' I said, startled. 'Fancy meeting you here.'

'Jason,' Joan Tureck said, extending her hand. 'I don't see an exhibitor badge—you're no longer with Entronics?'

'No, I—I think I misplaced the badge,' I said. 'I thought you had gone to FoodMark.'

'This position opened up. Being a carnivore wasn't a requirement.'

It made perfect sense that Royal Meister had hired Joan Tureck. In the big battle between divisions, duking it out over which sales force lived and which died, she was a huge asset. She knew where all our fault lines were, all our weaknesses and soft spots.

'You look great,' I said. 'So you've got the equivalent of Gordy's job.'

'I wish that were all there was to it. Most of my job these days is taken up with planning for the integration.'

'Meaning what's going to happen to your sales force?'

She smiled. 'More like what's going to happen to *your* sales force.'

'I thought you hated Dallas.'

'Sheila grew up in Austin, you know. So it's not so bad. They've invented something called air-conditioning.' She drew closer and walked with me out of the booth. 'Jason, can I give you some unsolicited advice?'

'Of course.'

'Get out now, while you can. It's much easier to look for a job when you already have one.'

'It's not a sure thing, Joan,' I said weakly.

'I'm telling you as a friend, Jason. Call me a rat, but I know a sinking ship when I see one.'

I CALLED KATE, took a shower, and changed into a suit and tie for dinner. Entronics had taken over one of the Westin ballrooms. Gordy had, as usual, kept the theme of the dinner a secret.

His TechComm dinners were always blowout extravaganzas. The year before, the theme had been *The Apprentice*, and he got to be Donald Trump, of course. He always gave an over-the-top talk, a cross between that self-help guru Tony Robbins and Mr Pink from *Reservoir Dogs*.

We were all wondering what it would be this year.

When I walked in I saw that the whole place had been decorated, at what had to be enormous expense, to look like a boxing arena. Projected on the walls were all sorts of vintage fight posters. In the middle of the room was a boxing ring—steel frame and corner posts, covered ropes, canvas floor, even the stools in opposite corners. It sat there in the middle of the banquet hall, surrounded by dining tables.

It looked incredibly stupid.

Kurt came up to me. 'This must have cost a couple of bucks, huh?'

'Where's Gordy?'

'Probably backstage having a last hit of courage. He asked me to go get his Scotch bottle.'

Each of the Band of Brothers was seated with important customers. I found my assigned seat, at a table close to the boxing ring.

I just had time to introduce myself to a guy from SignNetwork before the lights went down and a pair of spotlights swung around and stopped at the blue velvet stage curtains at the front of the room. A loud trumpet fanfare blared from loudspeakers: the theme from *Rocky*.

The curtains parted and two burly guys burst through carrying a throne. On it sat Gordy, wearing a shiny red boxing robe with gold trim and hood, and shiny red boxing gloves. The throne was labelled 'CHAMP'. In front of them scurried a young woman, flinging rose petals from a basket. Gordy was beaming and punching the air.

There was tittering, and some outright laughter, from the tables.

The guys set the throne down next to the boxing ring, and Gordy rose to his feet, gloves way up in the air, as the music faded.

'Yo, Adrian!' he shouted. There was laughter. People were starting to roll with it. I still couldn't believe Gordy was doing this, but he was known to do strange routines at our annual kickoffs.

He turned round to show off the back of his robe. It said ITALIAN STALLION in gold block letters. He turned back round and lifted his robe coquettishly to give us a peek of his stars-and-stripes boxing trunks.

'Wrong movie,' Trevor shouted from his table over to one side. 'That's *Rocky III*!'

'Yeah, yeah,' Gordy said, beaming. He found his bottle of Talisker 18 on a little table next to the ring, glugged some into a glass, and took a swig before stepping into the ring. He bowed, and there was applause.

'We at Entronics are going to go the distance for you,' he shouted. He pulled down the hood but left the robe on—probably a wise decision, given his physique. There was a high-pitched squeal of feedback.

'Yeah!' Trevor shouted back, and he was joined by a bunch of the other guys. I clapped and tried not to roll my eyes.

'We're going all fifteen rounds!' Gordy shouted.

The rose-petal woman was standing at a long table next to the ring, cracking eggs into glasses. There was a pile of egg cartons on the table. I knew what was coming. There were probably twenty-eight glasses lined up, and she was cracking three eggs into each glass.

Gordy took another gulp of his Scotch. 'When your back is to the wall and it's do or die, you look within yourself to find the spirit of a hero,' he said. 'Like Rocky Balboa, we think of ourselves as the underdog. Rocky had Apollo Creed. Well, we have NEC and Panasonic.'

Raucous cheers from the Band of Brothers.

'We're here to make your dreams a reality!' Gordy said. 'Now, I'm not going to get down and do one-arm press-ups for you.'

'Come on, Gordy!' Trevor shouted.

'I'll spare you,' he said. 'Because this is not about Gordy. It's about the *team.*' His words seemed to be a little slurred. 'The G Team! We're all team players. Jason, where are you?'

'Right here,' I said, my stomach sinking.

'Get up here, sparring partner!'

I stood up. Get me the hell out of here. 'Hey, Gordy,' I said.

I approached the ring, and the rose-petal girl came up to me with a glass.

'Drink it down, Jason,' Gordy said.

I could hear cheering and laughter.

I held the glass of eggs, looked at it, smiled like a good sport. I shook my head. 'I've got high cholesterol,' I said.

'Drink up,' Gordy commanded.

I lifted the glass to my mouth and began swallowing. The eggs slid down in a gooey, viscous string. I felt sick, but I kept going. When I handed the empty glass to the girl, a cheer arose.

'All *right*!' Gordy said. He tapped my head with a glove. 'Who's next? Where's Forsythe? Where's Festino?'

I returned to my table, looking around for the nearest restroom in case I had to hurl.

Gordy began weaving around the canvas like a real punch-drunk fighter, and I could tell he wasn't faking it. He was drunk. 'Thing is, wanna know why we invited you all?' he slurred. 'Think we invited you because we like spending time with you? Hell, no. We want every frickin' last one of you to standardise on Entronics,' Gordy said. 'Know why?' He held up his gloves, punched the air. 'Because I want the whole G Team to be as rich as me.'

Some of the Band of Brothers guffawed loudly.

'You know what kind of car Gordy drives?' he said. 'A Hummer. Not a goddamned Toyota. Not a Japmobile. Know what kind of watch Gordy wears? A Rolex. Not a stinking Seiko. Where's Yoshi Tanaka?'

'Not here,' someone said.

'Yoshi-*san*,' Gordy said with a sarcastic twist. 'Not here. Good. Fact, I *b'lieve* none of our Japanese expatriates are here. Prob'ly too busy filing their secret informant reports on us. Goddamned spies.'

There was laughter, but now it was the nervous kind.

'Japs don't trust us,' Gordy went on, 'but we show them, don' we?'

There was rustling, forks clinking as the guests quietly ate their salads.

'They're slow-kill, those Japs,' he said. 'Passive-aggressive. Never tell you what the hell they're thinking, those Japs. Inscrutable assholes.'

'Gordy,' Trevor called out. 'Take a seat.'

Gordy was leaning on the ropes now. 'Think it's easy working for a bunch of slant eyes who want you to fail just because you're a white guy?' he said. His words were more and more slurred.

Trevor got up, and I did too. 'Come on, Gordy,' he called out. We walked over to the ring, and so did Kurt and Forsythe. Gordy was leaning against the ropes. He looked up and saw us approaching. His eyes were bleary and bloodshot. 'The hell away from me,' he said.

We grabbed him, and I heard him mumble, 'Wha' happens in Miami stays in . . . Miami . . .' before he passed out.

As we carried Gordy out of the banquet room, I saw Dick Hardy standing against a wall, his arms folded, his face a dark mask of fury.

PART THREE

CHAPTER 7

Everything Gordy used to do I wanted to do the opposite. After all, I was the anti-Gordy. That's why Dick Hardy had named me the new VP of Sales. That and the fact that Entronics was desperate to fill the slot as fast as possible. They wanted to put the Gordy debacle behind them.

Gordy's drunken rampage was all over the Internet the next day, stories of the *Rocky* show, the glasses of raw eggs, the Rolex and the Hummer, and especially the anti-Japanese slurs.

The Entronics Public Relations Manager at US headquarters in Santa Clara put out a press release saying that 'Kent Gordon has left Entronics for personal and family reasons.'

I got a slew of congratulatory phone calls and emails—from friends I hadn't heard from in years, from people who were probably positioning themselves for a job with Entronics. Joan Tureck sent me a very nice email congratulating me and adding, ominously, 'Good luck. You'll need it.'

The first thing I did was to call in Yoshi Tanaka and let him know that unlike my predecessor, I wanted to work with him. I wanted his input. I spoke slowly, used simple words.

I won't say Yoshi smiled at me but he nodded solemnly and thanked me. I think he understood what I was saying, though I couldn't be sure.

The second thing I did was ask Dick Hardy to make a stopover in Boston on his way to Santa Clara. I called all my troops together to meet Mister Big and give a rousing, inspirational speech. I told them my door was always open. I told them they should feel free to come to me with any complaints, that although I expected nothing but the best efforts from them, I wasn't going to ream them out for telling me something wasn't going right. I announced a small increase in incentive pay and bonuses.

Dick Hardy stood next to me in the front of the room, wearing a navy blue suit and crisp white shirt, looking very much the CEO. He shook everyone's hand as they filed in. He told them they were the 'lifeblood' of Entronics Visual Systems and that he had 'complete confidence' in me.

Hardy clapped me on both shoulders when we had a few private moments after the staff rally. 'It's been a rough ride,' he said soulfully. 'But if anyone can steady the keel, it's you.' He loved sailing metaphors. He looked directly into my eyes, and said, 'Remember: you can't control the wind. You can only control the sail.'

'Yes, sir.'

The third thing I did was to promote Trevor Allard to my old job. Why? I think partly it was to make amends. If it hadn't been for Kurt, Trevor would probably have been in Gordy's office, not me. Partly it was because I knew he'd be good at the job. And partly, I admit, it was that old saying, 'Keep your friends close and your enemies closer.'

And, finally, I told Kurt I didn't want his inside information anymore.

Kurt's reaction was muted. It was clear that his feelings were hurt.

I broke it to him early one morning at the gym while I was lifting and he was spotting. 'I can't risk it,' I said. On the third set, I wimped out on the sixth rep, my arms trembling, going into muscle failure, and for the first time he didn't help me finish the set. He just watched me struggle to raise the bar high enough to replace it in the stand.

I didn't make it, and the bar came crashing down on my chest. I groaned. Then he lifted it up and out of my way.

'You're afraid you're going to get caught?' he asked. 'That it?'

'No,' I said. 'Because it's wrong. It creeps me out.'

'Look who's suddenly got religion. Now's when you need me more than ever. You're running the sales force of a major division of Entronics. You need to know everything that's going on. IFF, we call it.'

'IFF?'

'Identify Friend from Foe. So you shoot your enemies and not your friends. Like, for example, you need to know what Yoshi Tanaka's really up to. He's incredibly powerful. You want to stay on his good side.'

'His loyalty lies in Tokyo. As long as I keep that in mind, I'm fine.'

'What if I told you I'd captured a couple of emails he's sent to Tokyo in the last couple of days? Written in Japanese, but I know a Japanese chick. Tell me you don't want to know what he's saying about you.' He smiled.

I hesitated, but only for a second. 'No,' I said. 'I don't.'

'And your buddy Trevor?'

I shook my head.

'No,' I said. 'No more.'

His smile looked a little sardonic now. 'Up to you, boss.'

I WAS IN THE RESTROOM taking a pee when Trevor Allard came in. He nodded at me and went to the urinal at the far end of the row.

He waited for me to talk first, and I waited for him. I was perfectly willing to be civil to the guy, but I wasn't going to extend myself. Let him suck up a little.

When I'd finished, I went to the sink to wash my hands, and after I'd dried them and wadded up the paper towel, Trevor spoke.

'How's it going, Jason?' His voice echoed.

'Good, Trevor,' I said. 'You?'

'Fine.' He zipped up, washed his hands, dried them. Then he turned to face me. He spoke softly, quickly. 'Brett Gleason went to Security to ask for copies of the surveillance tapes for the day before his computer got wiped out. And guess what? They're all gone. Erased.'

I shrugged. 'I don't know anything about it.'

'Would you like to guess who the last person was to access those files? Whose name do you think was on the log?'

I said nothing.

'A guy named Kurt Semko. Our pitcher. Your asshole buddy.'

I shrugged, shook my head.

'So you know what it looks like to me? It looks like you're using this guy to get revenge on people you don't like, Jason. If you think you can get away with using Corporate Security as your personal goon squad, you've got your head up your ass.'

'That's ridiculous. You're full of it.'

'A lot of the guys are taken in by you. Your whole Easy Ed act. But I see right through you. Like when I had car trouble two days in a row, made me lose the Pavilion deal. You think I didn't call and apologise and tell them what happened? And you know what they told me?'

I said nothing.

'They said I called them from a golf club. Like I was playing golf, blowing them off. Well, I asked around. And the lady who runs the pro shop there told me some guy in a leather Harley jacket came in that morning and asked to use the phone. Right around the time Pavilion got that call. She remembers because he didn't look like a member.'

'Trevor, I don't know what you're talking about.'

'Of course not. What do they call that—plausible deniability? Well, stay tuned, Jason. There's more to come. A lot more.'

I THOUGHT ABOUT the conversation. The 'backgrounders'—the inside information Kurt had given me on Brian Borque and Jim Letasky; that was borderline acceptable, as far as I was concerned. But what he'd done to the Fidelity Investment monitor, that was some kind of lunacy. Kurt had a strange violent streak, a brazenness. He was dangerous.

And what about Gordy's drunken tirade? Gordy had asked Kurt to get him the Talisker bottle. Did Kurt spike it with something?

Kurt had boosted me up the corporate ladder. But now he was out of control. He had to be stopped. Trevor was digging, and in time he'd unearth proof that Kurt had done some stuff he shouldn't do. And I'd be implicated too. I'd go down. It would end my career.

And that I couldn't afford. Not with a mortgage, car payments, and a baby on the way.

I'd made a terrible mistake getting him a job in the first place. Now I'd have to make things right. I'd have to talk to Dennis Scanlon, Kurt's boss, and lay it all out.

Kurt had to be fired. There really was no choice.

In the morning I flew to Chicago with one of our junior sales reps, Wayne Fallon, for a quick morning meeting to try to nail down the big hospital contract. I met in a conference room of Chicago Presbyterian with the Assistant Vice-President for Communications, a guy named Barry Ulasewicz. We'd been going back and forth on prices and delivery dates for months now. He wanted 100 fifty-inch plasmas for their operating rooms, plasmas and projectors for more than 100 conference rooms, and a bunch more for their waiting rooms and lobbies.

I didn't like Ulasewicz, but that wasn't important. Just so long as he liked me. And he seemed to. We started at ten in the morning and met with a parade of administrators and techies. He even brought in the CEO of the hospital for a grip-and-grin.

Around one in the afternoon, when I was feeling squeezed out like a lemon, Ulasewicz, with a theatrical flourish, suddenly pulled out a proposal from Royal Meister that was identical in every way except for the prices, which were about ten per cent lower. I'd given him the lowest price I could get away with, and this pissed me off.

He expected me to cave. Because I'd put in months and months, and flown to Chicago, and I thought it was a lock. Ulasewicz figured that at this point I'd do anything to save the deal.

But he didn't realise that I had flow. I once read an article on the Internet about something called 'flow'. It's the way a painter gets so absorbed in his canvas that he loses track of time. Happens to athletes and surgeons and chess players. You're in this state of ecstasy where everything comes together, you've got the juice, you're in the zone.

That's what had happened to me. I was in the zone. I had flow.

And I was doing it on my own, without Kurt's poisoned candy.

I calmly looked over the Royal Meister proposal. It was full of tangled clauses, all kinds of smoke and mirrors. The delivery dates were estimates. The prices could change due to fluctuations in the euro. I pointed this out to Ulasewicz, and he began to argue.

And then I stood up, shook his hand, and packed up my leather portfolio.

'Barry,' I said, 'we won't waste any more of your time. Obviously you prefer the uncertainty of Meister's terms, and you don't mind their higher failure rate, or the fact that you'll probably end up paying more for an inferior product that you won't get when you want it. And that's OK. So I want to thank you for considering Entronics, and I wish you the best of luck.'

And I picked up our contracts and left the room. I was able to sneak a glimpse of Ulasewicz's stunned expression, which almost made it all worth it. Wayne grabbed me in the elevator, panic-stricken, and said, 'We just lost it, Jason. Don't you think you should have negotiated?'

I shook my head. 'Just be patient,' I said.

By the time we got down to the parking garage, my cellphone was ringing. I looked at Wayne and smiled. His look of panic had changed to wide-eyed admiration.

I flew back home with executed copies of the agreement.

I WENT STRAIGHT from the airport to the office.

There was a Hardygram waiting for me in my email—'Great job in Chicago!' Dick Hardy wrote. Joan Tureck congratulated me, too, which was gracious of her, considering that I'd outsold her.

I considered, then rejected, emailing Dennis Scanlon. I knew Kurt was able to read my email. Instead, I called Scanlon. Got him on the second try. I asked him to come to my office.

DENNIS SCANLON always reminded me of Mr Toad of Toad Hall. He was sweaty and eager to please and had a funny sort of speech impediment.

I told him I wanted to speak in absolute confidence, and then I told him that I had some concerns about one of his employees, Kurt Semko.

'But—weren't you the one who recommended him?' he said.

'I think frankly I may have made a mistake,' I said.

He ran a hand over his damp face. 'Can you give me any specifics? Has he been causing problems of any sort?'

I folded my hands and hunched forward. 'I've been hearing complaints about Kurt from some of my employees. Harassment.'

'Can you give me specifics?'

I could give him all sorts of specifics. But how far did I want to go with this? Should I tell Scanlon about all the emails Kurt had accessed? No. It could come back to bite me in the ass. Kurt might even say that I'd asked him to get me information.

'I don't know all the details,' I said. 'But it's my strong feeling—and, again, it's of the utmost importance that this conversation remain strictly confidential—that Kurt should be let go.'

Scanlon nodded. 'Are you willing to file a complaint report?'

I hesitated, but only for a second. 'Not with my name on it, no. I think that would get too complicated.'

He nodded some more. 'I can't just let him go for no reason. Would any of your employees be willing to file complaints with me, then?'

'I'd rather not ask them. Plus, I don't think anyone would want to stick their necks out. You understand, I'm sure.'

'Listen, Jason. Kurt is one of the best hires I've ever made. The fellow can do anything.'

'I understand.'

'I don't want to lose him. But I also don't want any of my employees causing trouble up here. So I'll look into this.'

'That's all I ask,' I said.

I CALLED KATE at work and was told she'd taken the day off. I called her at home, and woke her up.

'You still have cramps?' I said.

'Yeah. DiMarco said it's normal, just lie down until they pass.'

'Good idea. I have a business dinner tonight.'

'Oh, right. The hospital people?'

'Airport. Atlanta airport. But whatever.'

'Atlanta airport in Boston? I don't understand.'

'It's boring,' I said. 'Trade show.'

It was the big Information Display trade show at the Bayside Expo Center. When I heard the Atlanta folks were going to be in town for it, I invited them for dinner, told them it would be a great opportunity to 'celebrate' our agreement. Translation: I wanted to try to nail down the deal.

'Where are you taking them?'

'I don't know the name of it. Some fancy restaurant in the South End that Franny likes. But if you need to reach me, I'll have my cell with me.'

I hung up the phone, and then I noticed that Kurt was standing in the doorway to my office.

'MISSED YOU at the gym this morning,' Kurt said.

'Had to fly to Chicago early.'

'So, you were talking to Scanlon.'

I nodded. 'A background check that HR doesn't seem to be able to do.'

'If you have a problem with my work, you should take it up with me,' he said, closing the door. 'Not with my boss.'

I swallowed. 'I don't have a problem with your work.'

'Really? Then why're you trying to get me fired?'

I looked at him for a few seconds. 'What makes you say that?'

He advanced into my office. Stood directly in front of my desk. 'My suggestion to you—my *strong feeling*'—his eyebrows shot up, and he began speaking archly—'and, again, it's of the *utmost importance that this conversation remain strictly confidential* . . .' He smiled. ' . . . Is that if you have issues with me, you take them up with me. Don't go behind my back. Because I will find out. And you will regret it.'

I WAS FREAKED OUT: he knew what I'd said to Scanlon, word for word. It had to be some surveillance device he'd placed in my office.

Now that he knew I was trying to have him terminated, there was going to be trouble. Things could never go back to the way they used to be.

In the car on the way to South End, my phone rang. It was Dick Hardy. 'What's your take on the Atlanta airport?' he said.

'I'm feeling good about it.'

'If this comes through, it may save the division.'

'All I can do is my best.'

'I'm counting on it, Jason. Everything's riding on this. Everything.'

I handed my keys to the valet and entered the restaurant with a nonchalant grin plastered on my face. Jim Letasky was already at the table, studying a file. We were fifteen minutes early. I'd invited Jim to join me at dinner. I wanted to bring him in on the biggest deal I had going. I needed his wattage. I had an ulterior motive, too, but he'd figured it out.

'I know why you wanted me here,' he said. 'You're afraid that our main competition is NEC. I've just spent nine years telling the world how much better NEC's products are than anyone else's, and now—'

'Now you've found God,' I said, looking over the wine list. My memo had instructed all Entronics salespeople to make sure they always ordered the wine at a customer dinner and not leave it to the customer.

'But listen, Jason. I think you're wrong about NEC.' He squeezed lime into his Pellegrino water. 'I dug deep into the airport's website. There's a company called AirView Systems, based in Atlanta.'

I nodded. 'I met the CFO at TechComm. Guy named Steve Bingham.' I remembered the silver anchorman hair, the deep-set eyes.

'Biggest provider of flight information display systems. They put in the system for Atlanta last time. So why change horses in midstream?'

'Maybe that horse was too expensive.'

'You've been negotiating directly with Duffy, right?'

'You do your homework,' I said. Tom Duffy was the Aviation General Manager of the airport. Mister Big. Lorna Evers, our other dinner guest, was the Deputy Procurement Officer for the City of Atlanta.

'They're not just in this for a free dinner, right?'

'I think they want to close the deal. Let's knock 'em dead, Letasky.'

LORNA EVERS was a buxom blonde of that indeterminate age that could have been early fifties or maybe hard-living forties. She'd also obviously had cosmetic work done: when she smiled, only her overstuffed lips moved. Someone had overdone the Botox and the collagen injections.

'So you're the new Gordy,' she said, adjusting her gold silk scarf.

'You could say that.'

'Don't let this man have any Scotch,' she said, and she threw back her head and gave a raucous, open-mouthed laugh. Her eyes didn't move.

Tom Duffy was an affable, moon-faced, burly man with a grey crew cut. He wore a bow tie and a loose navy blazer. He laughed quietly.

'Nice to meet you,' she said, extending a hand with long pink fingernails to Letasky. 'So there's been a hell of a lot of turnover at Entronics, I hear.'

'I just joined Entronics from NEC,' he replied. 'I figured it was time to join the championship team.'

Score one for Letasky. Give this man a raise.

'I need a glass of wine,' she said, settling into her chair.

'Let's order,' I said, reaching for the long leather wine list.

But Lorna was quicker. She grabbed the menu and flipped it open.

'Warm evening like this, I like to get a nice crisp white,' Duffy said.

Lorna was peering at the list through black reading glasses. 'And I was thinking of a Pauillac. How about the Lafite Rothschild?'

I almost gulped. Four hundred dollars a bottle.

'Great idea,' Letasky said, giving me a quick look that said, for the millions we're going to make on this deal, forget about the wine bill.

Lorna waved the waiter over and ordered the Pauillac and a couple of bottles of Pellegrino.

'So, Atlanta airport is one of the busiest in the country,' Letasky said.

'The busiest in the world, in fact,' Duffy said.

Lorna's cell rang, and she picked it up and began talking loudly. A waiter came over and whispered in her ear, and she glared at him, then snapped it closed with visible annoyance.

'They insist all guests turn off their phones,' she announced. 'As if anyone can hear a cellphone ring in this place. I'm going positively *deaf*.'

I reached down and turned mine off, trying to be subtle about it.

After dinner—Lorna ordered a lobster dish with truffles, the most expensive thing on the menu—I excused myself to go to the john.

Letasky joined me in there a minute or so later.

'At the risk of stating the obvious,' he said, standing at the other urinal. 'I think Tom Duffy has been deballed.'

'She's the decision maker,' I said. 'Every move she makes, he mirrors.'

'You think she has another candidate?'

'I'll tell you this much—she didn't listen to a word I said.'

'She nodded a lot when you were talking.'

'Women do that. They nod to show they're listening.'

'You're right. You think it's time for a little brinksmanship?' I'd told him about Chicago.

'No,' I said. 'She's not ours. We get up from the table, and the deal goes to Hitachi or whatever.'

'AirView Systems.'

BY THE TIME dinner was over, the conversation had rambled everywhere but flight information display systems. We'd gone through three bottles of the Pauillac, and Lorna had had a great time.

We said good night, and I got my car from the valet and popped my phone into the hands-free cradle and turned it on.

There were six voicemail messages.

Kate's voice was weak. 'Jason, I'm—I'm bleeding.'

I went cold all over.

The next four messages were from Kate, too. She was sounding weaker and more desperate. There was a lot of blood, she said.

'Where are you?' she said. 'Will you call me back? Please?'

The sixth message was a male voice. Kurt's.

'Jason,' he said. 'I'm with Kate at the Children's Hospital emergency room. Get over here. Now.'

I RUSHED INTO the emergency room area, saw Kurt sitting in the waiting room, his face stony.

'Where is she?' I said.

'Trauma room.' He pointed. 'She's OK. Lost a lot of blood.'

'Did we lose the baby?' I couldn't believe I was saying the words.

He shook his head. 'Talk to the nurse. I think it's OK. Why the hell didn't you tell her where you were?'

'I—' I began. What, I didn't know the name of the restaurant? 'She has my cellphone number.'

'You should have left it on. You've got a pregnant wife, for Christ's sake. You're out at dinner and you turn off your phone because you don't want to screw up a *sale*? That's messed up, man. You're lucky I was there.'

'She called you?'

'I called the house. Good thing too.'

'Mr Steadman?' An ER nurse in blue scrubs approached Kurt. 'Your wife is fine. She came in anaemic, but we're replacing the lost blood.'

'I'm the husband,' I said.

'Sorry,' the nurse said, turning to me. 'She's sixteen weeks pregnant?'

'Right.' I noticed she hadn't used the past tense.

'Would you prefer to speak in private, Mr Steadman?'

'No, it's all right.' I glanced at Kurt. 'He's a friend.'

'OK. She has something called placenta previa, where the placenta covers the cervix. Do you need me to explain?' She spoke in a calm, almost hypnotic voice.

'I think I get it,' I said.

'Her pregnancy is considered high-risk. She's going to have to stay in the hospital for a couple of days, then stay in bed lying on her side as much as possible for the remainder of her pregnancy. After a while she'll be able to sit up and take the occasional car ride. But she can't exert herself.'

'What's the risk to my wife?'

'There's a pretty good chance the placenta will start to move away from the cervix on its own. She should be fine.' The nurse crossed her fingers.

KURT STAYED OUT in the waiting room while I went in to see Kate.

She looked pale, sad, circles under her eyes. She was hooked up to a couple of IVs, one with blood and one with clear fluid.

'Baby,' I said. I put a hand on her forehead, stroked her face, her hair. 'How are you feeling?'

'Tired. I almost passed out. There was blood everywhere.'

'They said you're going to be OK. The baby's going to be OK.'

'I'm going to have to stay in bed until I deliver. I guess that means I'm taking an early pregnancy leave.'

'The foundation will get by without you.'

'That's what I'm afraid of.' She smiled a little, an attempt at a joke.

'I'm sorry I had my cellphone turned off. The restaurant made me do it, but I should have left it on anyway.'

'It's OK. I was about to call an ambulance, then Kurt called, thank God.'

'Thank God.'

'What a good friend that guy is, huh?'

I nodded but didn't reply.

I SPENT THE NIGHT in Kate's hospital room on a couch. In the morning, aching all over, I drove home, retrieved some things she wanted, and brought them to the hospital. Not until noon did I get to work.

I found a message on my cellphone from Jim Letasky, but when I called him back, there was no answer on his cell or at his office. I called Ricky Festino and asked him to locate Letasky for me.

I went on the Internet and researched placenta previa. Some of the websites made it seem like not a big deal. Some of them made it sound awfully dire. I didn't know which one to believe.

Letasky appeared in my doorway, dressed in a suit and tie.

'You have your browser open?'

'Yeah?'

'Go to the City of Atlanta website.'

I typed in the web address.

'You see "Aviation RFPs/Bids"?'

It came up on the screen: the deal I'd hoped would be ours. In red letters it said, APPARENT LOW BIDDER AIRVIEW SYSTEMS CORPORATION and CONTRACT AWARD PENDING. The contact name was Lorna Evers.

My stomach sank. 'Crap. You mean those bastards let us take them to dinner, and all the while this was up on their website?'

'We didn't have a chance,' Letasky said.

An email popped up in my inbox from Dick Hardy. The subject line was: ATLANTA. The message contained one word: 'Well?'

I emailed back, 'Still working it. Not optimistic.'

On his way out of the office, Letasky stopped for a few seconds and turned back. 'Oh, listen. Trevor invited me to play basketball with him on Thursday nights, and if Gail lets me, I'll probably do it.'

'OK,' I said, not sure what he was getting at.

'I just wanted you to know. It's not like I'm choosing up sides.'

'Sides? Trevor's my second-line manager. We're not on opposite sides.'

'OK.' Letasky nodded, humouring me. 'It's just that—well, you know, maybe it's none of my business, but, well, did anyone ever tell you that Trevor sometimes . . . bad-mouths you.'

'I'm sorry to hear that.'

'He says you can be ruthless—that you do stuff to your rivals.'

I shook my head, smiled sadly. 'I appreciate your telling me.'

After Letasky had left, I stared for a long time at the City of Atlanta website. Then I picked up the phone and called Kurt.

'I need your help,' I said. 'Just one more time.'

AT THE HOSPITAL that night we got the word that Kate was OK to go home in the morning. I told her I wanted to hire a private nurse to help her out at home, but she told me I was being ridiculous, she didn't need a nurse.

'Susie wants to visit. You know, make sure I'm OK.'

I nodded. 'Good. I don't want you home alone.'

'She's flying over from Nantucket.' Craig and Susie had taken a house in Nantucket for August and September, as usual. 'She's bringing Ethan.'

'I'm glad she's coming.' Without Craig.

In the morning, they did an amnio to make sure everything was OK. The nurse asked if we wanted to know the sex of the baby, and Kate quickly said no, so the nurse said they'd send the results without mentioning sex.

I drove Kate home, and spent a few hours getting her set up in bed with a commode right next to her. I made sure the phone and the TV remote were within reach on the bedside table. I put a tall stack of books on the table too. For Christmas last year I'd bought her a hardcover set of Russian novels in a 'hot new translation', as Kate put it. Her idea, obviously; to me, that's worse than getting socks for Christmas. She often talked about how she wished she had time to read all of Dostoyevsky. Now was her chance. She grabbed *The Brothers Karamazov* and dived right in.

I arrived at the office late, and among my many voicemail messages was one from Kurt inviting me to lunch. I called him back and said, 'Thanks, man, but I'm just going to grab a sandwich.'

'I've made reservations at a really nice Japanese restaurant in Boston,' Kurt interrupted. 'One o'clock.'

I didn't know Kurt liked Japanese food, and I didn't quite get his insistence. 'Another time would be great.'

'This is not optional,' Kurt said. 'We've had a lucky break. Meet me at Kansai at one.'

I'D WORKED FOR a Japanese-owned company for years, but I'd never really gotten into Japanese food. Too healthy, maybe. Too minimalist.

We were shown to a low black-lacquered table where we had to remove our shoes and sit on tatami mats on the floor. There was a hot plate on the table with a hunk of kelp boiling away in a big bowl of murky water.

'Need to use the bathroom?' he said.

'No, thanks, Dad.'

'Why don't you anyway? Men's room is down the hall on the left. But you might want to keep going down the row to the last booth on your right.'

'And?'

'Go ahead.'

I shrugged and went down the hall to the last booth on the right. A rice-paper screen provided privacy, but by shifting over a few inches I was able to see in at an angle.

What I saw in there almost took the top of my head off.

Lorna Evers, the Deputy Procurement Officer for the City of Atlanta, was enjoying a romantic luncheon with a man with silver anchorman hair and deep-set eyes. Steve Bingham, the CFO of AirView Systems.

The company that had just won the Atlanta airport contract.

They were sitting next to each other on one side of the table, sucking face, and Lorna's hand was expertly kneading the man's crotch. On the table, untouched, was a platter of paper-thin slices of raw beef.

I went back to our table. Kurt watched me approach, eyebrows raised.

'How'd you know?' I asked, stony.

'I know a PI in Atlanta who deals a lot with the city. So I did a little prep work in Lorna's hotel room.'

'God*dammit*. She's the goddamned deputy procurement officer. The city's got to have all kinds of laws against this.'

'Code of ethics, sections 2-812 and 2-813,' Kurt said. 'Miss Lorna can not only lose her job but also get locked up for six months. I also don't think her husband would be too happy about it.'

'She's married.'

'So is Steve Bingham. He has five kids too.'

I stood up. 'Excuse me. I want to say hi to Lorna.'

I made my way back to her booth and barged right in to the gap between the rice-paper screens. The two looked up, embarrassed.

'Oh, hey, Lorna,' I said. 'Great place, huh?'

'J-Jason?'

'I hear the hand roll's excellent. Aren't you going to introduce me to your friend?' I said. 'Steve, right? Steve Bingham, from AirView? I think we met at TechComm.'

Steve Bingham's deep crimson blush contrasted interestingly with his silver hair. 'We've met?' he said, and cleared his throat.

'TechComm can be a zoo,' I said. 'You meet so many people. But you two are obviously well acquainted.'

'Jason—' Lorna said in a pleading tone.

'Awful sorry to interrupt,' I said. 'I'll call you on your cell later on.'

AS IT TURNED OUT, I didn't have to call Lorna. She called me an hour or so later. She'd found some 'discrepancies' in AirView's bid, she said, and had decided to award the contract to me.

I should have been elated, but instead I felt sullied. This was not how I'd hoped to win the biggest deal in my career.

Hardy called a few minutes after I emailed him the good news, almost giddy with excitement, to tell me that he was almost certain I'd saved our division from the chopping block.

'Great,' I said. 'I'm glad.'

'Boy, are you low-key about this,' Hardy said, his voice booming. 'The press release is going out over the Internet any minute now. Hedge fund managers are starting to look at Entronics stock differently now. They know what a big deal this is. Even if you don't.'

THAT NIGHT we had a game against Metadyne, a semi-conductor company, and Kurt was pitching lights out. But what was really amazing was how many long balls Trevor hit. Every time he stepped up to the plate, the balls just exploded off his bat, each flying easily 300 feet. Trevor himself seemed amazed at how well he was playing.

The Metadyne guys weren't great, weren't terrible, but they weren't enjoying this game. In the fourth inning, Trevor slugged another one, and his bat went flying out of his hands, slamming against the dirt with a loud metallic ping. And then something bizarre happened.

The end of his bat had popped off. The end cap had separated from the barrel and rolled a good distance away into the infield. One of the Metadyne players picked up the end cap as Trevor ran the bases.

He looked at it curiously, weighed it in his hand. 'Man,' he said. 'Heavy. Look at this!'

He took it over to another one of the Metadyne players, who I remembered was an electrical engineer. The engineer weighed it in his palm just like the other guy had done.

'Oh, man, someone put, like, lead fishing weights and hot melt inside this cap. Unbelievable.' Then he walked over to the decapitated metal bat and picked it up. He looked inside the bat, then waved some of his teammates over.

'Hey,' one of them shouted. 'This bat is juiced!'

Trevor, running triumphantly home, nowhere near out of breath, loped over to see what the commotion was.

'You doctored the bat,' another one of the Metadyne guys shouted.

'The inside's been machined, or lathed, or something,' the engineer was saying. 'You can even see the shavings—graphite or resin, I think.'

'Hey, I didn't do that!' Trevor protested. 'I wouldn't even know how.'

'Nah, he sent it to one of those bat doctors,' said another Metadyne guy.

'No way!' Trevor shouted.

'The game gets forfeited,' the engineer said. 'That's the rules. These Entronics guys are cheating.'

But Trevor was not going down without a fight. He stood there in his cargo shorts and his LIFE IS GOOD T-shirt and protested that he'd never in his life cheated at sports, that he'd never do such a thing.

'Either the thing came that way,' Trevor said, 'or . . .'

He looked at Kurt. 'This bastard did it.' His voice rose. 'He set me up again.' Now he pointed to me, then to Kurt. 'Both of these guys. It's like a goddamned reign of terror around here.'

Kurt gave him a puzzled look, shrugged, then headed off towards the parking lot. I followed him.

'How come?' I said when we were out of earshot of our teammates.

'You don't think I did that, do you?'

'Yes. I do.'

But Trevor had caught up, walking alongside us. 'You're an interesting guy,' he said, addressing Kurt. 'A man of many secrets.'

'That right?' Kurt said blandly, not letting up his pace.

'I did a little research,' Trevor said. 'I found this Special Forces website, and I posted a notice. I asked if anyone knew a Kurt Semko. Someone posted an answer the next day. I didn't know you had a dishonourable discharge, Kurt. Did you know that, Jason? You recommended him.'

'Trevor, that's enough,' I said.

'How much do you know about the—what's the term they used?—"sick shit" Kurt got into in Iraq, Jason?'

I shook my head.

'Now I see why your friend is so willing to do your dirty work. Because you got him a job he never would have gotten.' He looked at Kurt. 'You can try to sabotage me. But in the end, both of you are going down.'

Kurt stopped, grabbed Trevor by the T-shirt and pulled him close.

Trevor drew breath. 'Go ahead, hit me. I'll see to it you don't have a job to go to tomorrow morning.'

'Kurt,' I said.

Kurt let go of Trevor's T-shirt abruptly. Trevor's shoulders slumped.

'Trevor,' Kurt said, 'are you sure?'

'Am I sure of what?'

'Your shirt, I mean.' He pointed at Trevor's T-shirt. His index finger circled the LIFE IS GOOD logo. 'Are you sure life is good, Trevor? Because I wouldn't be so sure if I were you.'

CHAPTER 8

When I got home, Kate was still awake. She was clicking away on her laptop, surfing a tsunami of trivia on the Internet, digging deep into movie adaptations of Jane Austen novels.

'Aren't you the one who said that watching movie versions of Jane Austen's novels was like hearing a Beethoven symphony played on a harmonica?' I said.

She glared at me. 'The cable's not working. I asked Kurt to take a look at it,' she said.

'That's nice.'

'He's coming over tomorrow. I invited him to stay for dinner.'

'For dinner?'

'Yeah, is that a big deal? You're always saying I exploit him—I thought it was only right to invite him to break bread with us.'

'I thought your sister's coming tomorrow.'

'She and Kurt might enjoy meeting each other.' I couldn't see Kurt and St Bart's Susie having a whole lot to talk about.

'Um, Kate, I think we need to talk.'

'Isn't that my line?'

'It's about Kurt.'

I told her what I should have told her before.

'How come you never said anything?' she said.

'I don't know,' I said after a long pause. 'Maybe because I was embarrassed. If it wasn't for him I wouldn't be here.'

'I don't believe that. Maybe he gave you a leg up, but it's you who's doing the job so incredibly well.'

'I think maybe I was afraid that if I told you, you'd want me to just—shut up and go along. Put up with it.'

'Why in the world would I want that?'

'Because of *this*.' I waved around the room, indicating the whole house. 'I know how much this house means to you. And I knew that as soon as I went up against him, I'd be putting all this in jeopardy.'

She bowed her head, and a few tears dripped to the bedsheets. 'So what?' she said, her voice muffled. 'You think that's what I care about?'

I was silent.

She looked up. Her eyes were red. 'Look, I grew up in a huge house with servants and a pool and tennis court and horseback-riding and winters in Bermuda and summers on the beach . . . It was hard to lose all that. But I didn't marry you because I thought you'd make me rich again. I married you because you were *real*. No pretence, and I loved it. I loved your energy, your drive, your ambition. But then you started to lose it.'

I nodded.

'You can see how you've changed, can't you? The confidence? You're not settling anymore. I admire you so much, you know that?'

Tears were running down her cheeks. I felt like a jerk.

'Because you know something? When I was born, I was handed the keys. You had to earn them. And look at where you've come from. What you've achieved on your own.'

'With the help—'

'*No*,' she said fiercely. '*Without* Kurt. *That's* what makes me happy. But what am I going to do about tomorrow? I can't uninvite Kurt, can I?'

I shook my head. 'Better not to, I think.'

'I think it's better for him to think everything's normal until you do whatever you do about him—and you need to do *something*—I just think it's better to stay on his good side.'

NEXT AFTERNOON Kate called me to ask me to pick up some Thai food for dinner. 'Susie loves Thai food,' she said.

'Oh, right. Is Kurt there now?'

'He fixed the cable box, but he's coming back around seven.'

'I'll be home at six forty-five,' I said.

On the way home I stopped at a cellphone store and bought a new cellphone, keeping the same number. I had no idea if it was even possible to bug a cellphone, but if so, I'd have to assume that Kurt had bugged mine.

I kissed and hugged Susie, who was making herbal tea for Kate in the kitchen. She was so deeply tanned she looked like she'd applied walnut stain. 'You've really been out in the sun,' I said.

'Me? Please. Clarins self-tanner. I hate the sun.'

Ethan appeared in the kitchen doorway. I went over and gave him a hug.

'Who's this friend who's coming for dinner?' Susie asked.

'He's an interesting guy,' I said. I looked at my watch. 'He's late.'

'Is that dinner?' Ethan asked, pointing at the oil-stained paper bags I'd just brought in.

'Yep,' I said. 'Thai food.'

'I hate Thai food. Is there any sushi?'

'No sushi,' I said. 'Sorry.'

'Mom, can I have Froot Loops for dinner?'

I set up the Thai food in a kind of buffet on a table in the dining room. Kate was lying on the couch. She was now allowed to sit up, even get out of bed, so long as she lay down as much as possible.

'Kurt's late,' I said to Kate. 'Should we just start eating?'

'Let's wait a bit longer.'

At seven forty-five I tried Kurt's cell, but there was no answer. I looked in the phone book for his home number. No Kurt Semko listed.

By eight, Susie and Kate and I started in on the skewers of chicken satay. At eight-thirty, the doorbell rang.

Kurt's hair was wet, and he looked like he'd just gotten out of a shower. 'Sorry, man,' he said. 'I must have fallen asleep.'

'Turned off your cell? After giving me all that grief?'

'Didn't have it with me. Sorry.'

'I hope you don't mind we ate already.'

'No worries. Can I join you anyway?'

'Of course.'

Kurt followed me into the living room, where he kissed Kate on the cheek. I didn't know they were on kissing terms already, but I didn't say anything. He shook Susie's hand. 'How's the cable TV?' he asked Kate.

'You know,' Kate said, 'the reception is better than it used to be. I mean, it's digital cable, and it's supposed to be perfect, but the analog channels were always a little fuzzy. Now they're as good as the digital ones.'

I thought I heard my cellphone ringing upstairs, but I ignored it.

Kurt took a paper plate and shovelled on pad thai, vegetables in garlic sauce, fried rice, beef salad. 'I don't know who wired the cable for you, but I changed the RF connection to S-video, and it's way better. Now you're taking advantage of the plasma.'

'I see,' Kate said. 'Thank you.'

It definitely was my cellphone, and it was ringing again, a second or third attempt.

'He doesn't have anything to drink,' Kate said. 'Jason, could you go to the kitchen and get him a beer? We have Sam Adams, do you like that?'

'Just water. Tap's fine.'

I went down the hall to the kitchen, and the wall phone rang.

'Jason? Jason—it's Jim Letasky.' He sounded out of breath.

'Oh, hey, Jim' I said, a little surprised that he was calling me at home. 'Was that you on my cell just now?'

'Jason—oh, Jesus. Oh, my God.' He was breathing hard.

'What *is* it, Jim? You OK?'

'I was at this—this high-school gym in Waltham, I guess? Where Trevor and Brett play basketball? And—and—'

'And *what*? Something happen? Everything all right?'

'There was an accident.' He was crying. 'Car accident. They're—dead.'

'Dead? Who's dead?'

'Trevor and Brett. He—Trevor was driving his Porsche real hard, and I guess he lost control—oh, man. This guy saw it happen. They went into the median strip and hit a guardrail and flipped over.'

I felt unsteady. My knees buckled, and I sank to the kitchen floor, the phone receiver flying out of my hand, dangling on its cord.

After a minute or so sitting there, in a state of shock, I got up unsteadily and hung up the phone. I sat on a kitchen chair staring into space, my mind racing. Then I was jolted by Kurt's voice. He stood in the kitchen doorway. 'Hey, bro,' he said. 'You OK?'

I looked up at him. 'Trevor and Gleason were in a car accident,' I said. 'Trevor's car went out of control.' I paused. 'They were both killed.'

Kurt seemed to take this in for a couple of seconds. Then his eyes widened. 'You're kidding me. This just happen?'

'They were on their way to basketball. Trevor was driving his Porsche. Car hit a guardrail and rolled over.'

'Oh, shit. Unbelievable.' His eyes were on mine. He didn't glance away, nothing like that. But it was the delay in his reaction, a quick tightening of the muscles around the eyes. A couple of rapid blinks.

He already knew.

I smiled. A forced smile, but still a smile. 'Couldn't happen to a nicer couple of guys.'

Kurt watched my face, didn't react.

I breathed in, breathed out. Kept the smile on. 'Sometimes fate just lends a hand,' I said. 'Kicks in when you need a little cosmic help.'

Kurt didn't react.

'Couldn't ask for a more convenient car accident.'

Kurt was watching my face, I could see that. Watching closely. He was reading me. Trying to determine whether I was trying to manipulate him.

'They could have caused me some serious problems,' I said.

After a pause, Kurt said, 'Might have.'

'You watch out for me,' I said. 'I appreciate that.'

'I don't get what you're saying,' Kurt said.

'Are you positive,' I said very quietly, 'that no one can ever find out?'

I didn't look at him. I looked down, studied the tile. Waited.

'Find out what?' he said.

I looked up, saw the set of his mouth, a glint in his eyes. Not quite a smile, not a smirk. But something. An unspoken satisfaction.

'How'd you do it?' I said, even more quietly.

Five, ten seconds.

'You did something to his car, didn't you?' I said. My stomach was flooded with something sour. A bitter taste in my mouth.

'I don't know what you're talking about,' Kurt said.

I lunged for the kitchen sink and vomited. Heaved until nothing was left in my stomach, and then kept going. I felt as if I was going to pass out.

I could see Kurt standing beside me, his face looming grotesquely large. 'You OK?'

I gripped the edge of the counter, the tile cold in my hands. Slowly I turned to face him, my face hot.

'You killed them,' I said. 'You goddamn *killed* them. You knew they'd both be in Trevor's Porsche on their basketball night. My God.'

Something hardened in Kurt's expression and his eyes went flat, dead. 'That's enough,' he said. 'You've crossed the line there, buddy. Throwing wild accusations around like that.'

'Are you *denying* it?' I shouted.

'Will you chill, please? You're going to have to stop the crazy shit. I don't like to be accused of something I didn't do. Get hold of yourself. Because you don't want to be talking to me like that. I really don't like it.'

I just looked at him, didn't know what to say.

'Friends don't talk to me like that,' he said, an opaque look in his eyes. 'And believe me, you don't want me as an enemy.'

Then he turned round slowly, and without saying another word he walked out of the house.

SHOULD I HAVE TOLD Kate right then and there?

Maybe so. But I knew how upset she'd be when I told her my suspicions.

Kurt had denied it, of course. But I knew.

At some point soon I'd have to tell her. Or she'd find it out. But I wanted to get myself together, tell her calmly. Sounding in control, a protector.

'Where's Kurt?' Kate asked when I went back into the dining room.

'He had to take off.'

'Did you guys have a fight or something? I thought I heard an argument.' She looked at me closely.

'No big deal. Yeah, we sort of had it out on something at work. Nothing important. Can I put the food away?'

'Jason, you look really upset. What happened? Who was on the phone?'

'Really,' I said. 'Nothing important.'

THE GUYS STARTED gathering in my office around nine the next morning—first Jim Letasky, then Ricky Festino and Doug Forsythe, until I had a small crowd. They were all in shock. They spoke quietly, trying to puzzle out what had happened. Letasky told them what he'd heard from the basketball team member who'd been driving behind the Porsche—how the highway curved to the right but the Porsche drove straight into the guardrail and then a concrete bridge-support column, and then the car had flipped over. The emergency medical technicians had who arrived and realised that no ambulance was needed: both men were dead.

'I know Trevor drove fast,' Forsythe said. 'But he knew how to drive.

How could he lose control of the car? It didn't rain last night, right?'

Letasky shook his head.

'An oil slick or something?' Forsythe asked.

'I took 95,' Letasky said, 'and there wasn't any kind of oil slick.'

'Mechanical defect or something?' said Festino.

Letasky inhaled. 'I suppose anything's possible.'

'Mrs Allard's going to have one hell of a lawsuit against Porsche,' Festino said.

NEWS TRAVELS FAST in the age of email. Just before lunch I got an email from Joan Tureck in Dallas:

> I'm so sorry to hear about Trevor Allard and Brett Gleason. I can scarcely believe it. If I were at all superstitious, I'd say Entronics is cursed.

Maybe she had a point.

At lunchtime, I found a pay phone in the employee cafeteria. I'd decided to call the cops.

On the Massachusetts State Police website I'd found a press release about the accident and I called the trooper whose name was on it. Trooper Sean McAfee was in charge of investigating the collision, though I doubted he was doing anything but the most pro forma investigation.

I didn't want this call tracked back to me, though. The police, I assumed, can trace just about any call these days, including cellphones. If they were going to trace the call, at least they'd get no further than a pay phone in the employee cafeteria of the Entronics building.

'This is Sergeant McAfee,' said a rough voice. Southie vowels.

No one was anywhere nearby—this was an alcove off the cafeteria—but I still didn't dare speak loudly. 'Sergeant McAfee,' I said in my best cold-calling voice, 'you're investigating a collision that took place last night on I-95 in Waltham? The Porsche?'

Suspicious: 'Yeah?'

'I have some information about it. I'm a friend of the driver's.'

'Name?'

My name? Name of the driver? 'I'm afraid I can't give my name.'

'What's your information?'

'I think something might have been done to the Porsche.'

Long pause. 'Why do you think that?'

'Because the driver had an enemy.'

'Then you think someone monkeyed around with the car?'

'That's what I think.'

'Sir, if you have information material to this investigation, you should do yourself, and the deceased, a favour and come in to talk to me.'

'I can't do that.'

'I'm happy to come out to Framingham,' he said.

He knew where the call was coming from.

'I can't meet with you.'

The cop raised his voice. 'Sir, without more information, like a name of this "enemy" you're talking about, I don't have enough to work with. The crime scene techs did a whole investigation of the scene. There's no tyre marks, nothing that tells us anything except the driver drove straight into the guardrail. Far as we're concerned, it's a single-car fatal, driver error.'

'I just think,' I said very quietly, 'that you should have your guys look very closely at the car. I'll bet you find evidence of sabotage.'

'Sir, the car was totalled, and then it caught fire.' The cop shot back. 'There's not a hell of a lot left of it, OK?'

'His name's Kurt Semko,' I said quickly, and I hung up the phone.

THE INTERCOM BUZZED, and Franny said, 'It's Mr Hardy.'

'Jason,' came the mellifluous voice, 'forgive this short notice, but I need you to fly out here tomorrow. I've set up a meeting, and I want you there.'

He paused. I groaned inwardly, said, 'Gotcha.'

'With Nakamura-san,' he added.

'Nakamura-san? Hideo Nakamura?' Hideo Nakamura was the chairman of the board of the Entronics Corporation. He was like the great Oz. No one had ever seen him.

'He's flying in from New York, en route to Tokyo. I persuaded him to make a quick stopover in Santa Clara, see for himself how you've turned around sales. I want to knock his socks off.'

'Yes, sir,' I said. 'Can do.'

'I had to do a good deal of arm-twisting to get him to make a stop. He comes to the US once or twice a year, if that, you know.'

'Should I prepare an agenda?'

'Of course. Nakamura-san loves PowerPoint. Do a brief PowerPoint presentation. Five or six bullet points, no more. Performance of your division, key achievements, key struggles.'

'Gotcha.'

'Arrive by ten-thirty at the boardroom here at Santa Clara. Nakamura-san and his entourage will arrive at precisely eleven o'clock, and will leave at precisely twelve o'clock. It is imperative that you be on time. *Imperative*. Nakamura-san is extraordinarily punctual.'

'Gotcha. It's too late to make an evening flight, but I'm sure there are plenty of early-morning ones. I'll be there.'

'On time. And afterwards, if you have time, come out for a sail with me on my new eighty-foot Lazzara. It's a real beauty. You'll love it.'

WHILE FRANNY worked on getting me a flight, I cancelled my next day's appointments, then called Kate to tell her. Then I started crunching numbers and composing a draft of my PowerPoint slides for Franny to make up.

A little while later she stopped in. 'There's only one flight that'll get you there with enough time. US Air's six-thirty into San Francisco. Arrives nine fifty-two. It'll be close. I'll rent you a car.'

She went back to her cubicle to call our corporate travel company, while I went out, the corporate hunter-gatherer, in search of numbers to crunch.

WHEN I GOT BACK, twenty minutes later, Franny said, 'Kurt was here. Put something on your desk. He said he'll stop by later.'

I felt a prickle of tension. Kurt had no business-related reason to come by. It couldn't be good.

There was nothing on my desk.

My cellphone rang. I looked around my desk for it, couldn't find it. It rang again, sounding muffled and distant. It was coming from my fancy English briefcase, although I didn't remember leaving it there.

I lifted the briefcase from the floor next to my desk, opened it—

And something exploded.

There was a loud pop, a great whoosh, and whole scattering of something hit my face, momentarily blinding me. I leapt back.

'Jesus!' I shouted.

I swept small, hard particles off my face, out of my eyes. Confetti. My desk was covered with the stuff.

I heard low, hoarse laughter. Kurt was standing there, laughing helplessly. Franny had run in, her hands to her face, terrified.

'Happy birthday,' Kurt said. 'Excuse me.'

He nudged Franny out of the door and closed it behind her.

'It's not my birthday,' I said. 'What the hell was that?'

'Hobby store stuff. Model rocket motor, electrically initiated. A microswitch from Radio Shack. A clothespin, a couple of thumbtacks, some rosin-core solder, and a nine-volt battery. Fortunately for you, the rocket motor was stuck in a bag of confetti. But let's say instead of a rocket motor, I used an electric blasting cap. And let's say instead of a bag of confetti I used some C-4 plastic explosive.' He winked. 'My point getting through here? One day you open the trunk of your car, maybe. Kablooey.'

'What do you want, Kurt?'

'I got a heads-up from a buddy of mine on the state police. Said someone called in with an anonymous tip. About the death of Trevor Allard. From a pay phone. The one off the cafeteria.'

Jesus. I blinked, shrugged.

'The caller mentioned my name.'

I prayed nothing in my face gave me away. 'What are you talking to me for?'

Kurt drew close. 'Let me tell you something,' he said, almost under his breath. 'Anyone you talk to in the cops, guaranteed I'll hear about it within a couple hours. Who the *hell* you think you're playing with?'

I tried to look right into his eyes, but they were too menacing.

'You don't want to be my enemy, bro. Haven't you figured that out yet?'

'Because you kill your enemies. Right? Why haven't you killed me yet? I don't understand.'

'You're not my enemy, Jason. If you were, you wouldn't be here.'

'So I guess that makes me your friend.'

'Has anyone ever done more for you than me? I hope you don't think you got where you are today on your own. We both know I changed your life.'

'You were just willing to play dirty, Kurt. I should have cut you off long ago, but I was weak. And you were out of control,' I said.

'And you don't know what a pawn you are. You have no idea. "Save the division"? That's a laugh. Gordy was just waiting for the right opportunity to get rid of you, you know. You were a threat to him.'

'So you got him drunk, that it?'

'Drunk? That wasn't just booze, friend. A cocktail. A drop of DMT—Dimethyltryptamine, a psychedelic. Plus a little upper. And he lost his inhibitions. Showed his true colours.'

'You're a goddamned lunatic.'

'Don't tell me you didn't know what I was doing. You *wanted* me to do what I did. You just didn't want to acknowledge it.'

'You didn't kill Trevor and Gleason because of me. You killed them because they were uncovering what you'd done. They could have landed you in serious trouble.'

'I could have handled it,' Kurt said. 'Everything I did, I did for you. So my advice to you is to keep your goddamned mouth shut. Because everything you do, I'm watching. Everywhere you go. There is *nothing*'—he bared his lower teeth like some sort of rabid animal—'nothing you can do that I won't find out about. You've got a lot to lose.'

The bottom of my stomach dropped. I knew he meant Kate.

'After all I've done for you,' he said, and turned. 'You disappoint me.'

I DIDN'T GET OUT of the office until nine, but before I left I did a quick search for the Special Forces website Trevor had mentioned.

The search didn't take long. I just put 'Kurt Semko' and 'Special Forces' in Google and immediately found it. In one area of the site was the 'guest book', where Trevor had posted his question, and I found the reply, from someone named Scolaro with a Hotmail address.

I clicked on the address and wrote Scolaro an email. 'What kind of "sick shit" did he get into?' I wrote. 'Guy lives next door and I want to know.' I put down an AOL address I rarely used. No name.

I GOT TO THE AIRPORT at 4.45 a.m., almost two hours before my flight was supposed to leave. The terminal was dark, almost deserted. I found the one open coffee place, got a large coffee and a bagel and sat down on a plastic bucket seat. I took my laptop out of my old nylon briefcase—I'd left the English briefcase, the one Kurt had tampered with, back in my office—ponied up the eight bucks for WiFi Internet access, and checked my email. Went over the PowerPoint presentation, rehearsing it silently.

I tried to keep my mind on my presentation, not on Kurt's threats.

You've got a lot to lose.

When I'd arrived home last night, Kate was asleep. She was still asleep, naturally, when I left the house at four-thirty in the morning. That was just as well: I might have been tempted to talk to her, tell her about Kurt's threats. Which I most definitely didn't want to do.

Because I had no doubt that Kurt had somehow rigged Trevor's car. He was an extremely dangerous man. Who was no longer my friend.

An hour later I got into the security line. I took my laptop out of my briefcase and put it on the conveyor belt, put my briefcase and overnight bag on the belt after it, slipped off my shoes and put them in the grey Rubbermaid tray. I put my keys and coins in the little coin tray, and shuffled through the metal detector. A woman asked me to turn my computer on, which I did.

I padded over to the next portal, one of the new explosives detectors they'd just installed. Stood there while I was hit with a blast of air. An electronic voice told me to move on.

And then, a few seconds later, a high-pitched alarm went off.

One of the airport security agents grabbed my overnight bag as it emerged from the explosives detector. Another one took me by the elbow, and said, 'Sir, please come with us.'

I was no longer half-awake. The adrenaline had kicked in. 'What's going on?' I said. 'There some kind of problem here?'

'This way, sir.'

People in line stared as I was pulled off to the side, behind a tall panel. 'Hands in front of you, sir,' one of them said.

I put my hands out. 'What is it?' I asked.

No one answered. The other agent passed a metal-detector wand up and down my chest, up the inside of my legs and back down the other leg. When he was done, a third guy—a supervisor, I guessed, said, 'Follow me, sir.'

'I have a flight to catch,' I said.

He led me to a small, hardly lit, glassed-in room. 'Sit here, please.'

He asked for my ticket and boarding pass. He wanted to know why I was flying to California and back in one day.

'Am I on some kind of no-fly list?' I said.

'Did you pack your bags yourself? the man asked, not exactly answering my question.

'No, my valet did. Yes, of course I did.'

'Was your suitcase out of your possession at any time?'

'I keep it in my office. I travel a lot. Sometimes I leave my office to go home. What's the problem? Was there something in it?'

He didn't answer. I looked at my watch. 'I'm going to miss my flight,' I said. 'Where's my cellphone?'

'I wouldn't worry about it,' the security guy said. 'You're not going to be on that flight.'

'Look, I have a really important business meeting. With the chairman of the board of my corporation. I need my cellphone.'

'Not possible, sir. All the contents of your briefcase are being swabbed and inspected.'

'Swabbed? Swabbed for what?'

He didn't answer.

'Are you at least going to get me on the next flight out?'

'We don't have anything to do with the airlines, sir.'

'Then the least you can do is let me use a phone so I can get myself on the next flight out.'

'I don't think you're going to be on the next flight out, sir.'

'What's *that* supposed to mean?' I said raising my voice.

'Sir, if you don't keep your voice down, I can have you arrested.' He stood up and walked out. Closed the door behind him. I heard it lock.

I'd definitely missed my flight. I wondered if another airline had a flight that would get me there close to eleven. Maybe I could floor it and still get to Santa Clara on time.

I kept looking at my watch. Twenty minutes later, a couple of Boston police officers, a man and a woman, came in and showed their badges.

'What's the problem, Officers?'

'Where are you travelling, Mr Steadman?' the man said.

'Santa Clara. I just went through all this with the security guy.'

'A one-day trip to California?' said the woman.

'My wife's pregnant,' I said. 'I wanted to get back home so she's not left alone. She's confined to bed. A high-risk pregnancy.'

Get it? I wanted to say. Corporate executive, family man, married. Not exactly the standard profile of an al-Qaeda terrorist.

'Mr Steadman,' the woman said, 'your suitcase tested positive for the presence of C-4. Plastic explosives.'

'*What?* That's obviously a mistake. Your machine's screwed up.'

'No, sir,' the male officer said. 'The screeners confirmed it by running another test.'

'Well, it's a false positive,' I said. 'I've never touched C-4 in my life. Look, I'm a senior vice-president at a major corporation. I'm flying to Santa Clara for a meeting with the chairman of the board. One simple phone call, and you'll be able to confirm what I'm saying.'

The cops remained stony-faced.

'I think we all know there's been some kind of a mistake. Can we all be reasonable here? You have my name and my address and phone number. If you need to reach me for anything, you know where I live. I own a house in Cambridge. With a pregnant wife and a mortgage.'

'Thank you, sir,' the man said, sounding like he was concluding the interview. They both got up and left me to cool my heels for another half an hour or so before the security supervisor came in and told me I was free to go.

It was just after eight in the morning. I ran to the departure gate and asked the agent when the next flight to San Francisco was.

There was an American Airlines flight at 9.10, she said. Arriving at 12.23. I could be in Santa Clara at 1 p.m. When the extremely punctual Nakamura-san would be sitting in first class on his way to Tokyo.

I called Dick Hardy. In California it was a little after five in the morning. 'Steadman,' he said, his voice thick.

'Sorry to wake you, sir,' I said. 'But I'm not on the flight to San Francisco. I was detained for questioning. Some sort of screw-up.'

'Well, get on the next one, for God's sake.'

'The next one gets me in just after noon.'

'After noon? That's too late. Got to be an earlier flight.'

'I know, I know. But there's nothing else.'

Now he was fully awake. 'You're standing up Hideo Nakamura?'

'I don't know what else to do. Unless you can reschedule him—'

'Reschedule *Nakamura-san*? '

'Sir, I'm terribly sorry. But all these terrorist precautions—'

'God*damn* you, Steadman,' he said, and he hung up.

I walked back to the parking garage, dazed. I'd just blown off my boss and the chairman of the board.

It was unreal, an out-of-body experience.

I kept flashing on the security supervisor.

'*Was your suitcase out of your possession at any time?*'

Franny saying, '*Kurt was here. Put something on your desk.*'

He knew I was flying to Santa Clara, and he'd been in my office recently, rigging up my briefcase with his little toy confetti bomb. I kept my overnight bag in my office closet.

He'd set me up. The way he'd set the other guys up.

Trevor Allard and Brett Gleason were dead.

And now Kurt had turned on me.

MY DAY'S APPOINTMENTS had been cancelled, so I drove straight home, steaming mad. Kate was surprised to see me. She seemed sombre, remote. She told me that her sister had taken Ethan to the Museum of Fine Arts and I gave her the short version of how airport security had detained me for almost two hours on a bogus suspicion that I was carrying a bomb.

She was barely listening, and normally this was the sort of thing that really got her going. Instead she made little pro forma clucks of sympathy, her mind somewhere else far away. She looked haggard. Her eyes were bloodshot. While I was telling her how Dick Hardy had basically exploded, she cut me off. 'You must be so unhappy with me.'

'What in the world makes you say that?'

Her face crumpled and tears began flowing. 'I sit here all day like—like an invalid—and I know how sexually—frustrated you must be.'

'Kate,' I said, 'where's all this coming from? You're pregnant. High-risk pregnancy. We both understand that. We're in this together.'

She was crying even harder. She could barely speak. 'You're a big shot now. Women are probably coming on to you all the time.'

I leaned over next to her, took her head in my hands, stroked her hair. The pregnancy, the crazy hormones, all this time in bed. She was going out of her mind. 'Not even in my wet dreams,' I tried to joke.

But she reached over to her nightstand and picked something up, held it out to me without looking. 'Why, Jason? How could you?'

I looked. It was a condom, still in its packet. A Durex condom.

'That's not mine,' I said.

She shook her head slowly. 'You dropped your suit on the bed this morning when you were packing. And when I got up, I felt something in your pocket.' Her breathing was uneven. 'And I—oh, God, I can't believe you.'

'Baby, it's not mine.'

She twisted her head to look up at me. 'Please don't lie to me. Don't tell me you're carrying someone else's condom around.'

'I didn't put it there, Kate. Believe me. It's not mine.'

She pushed my hands away. 'How could you *do* this?' she said.

Furious, I grabbed my BlackBerry from my suit's coat pocket and hurled it towards her. 'There you go,' I shouted. 'That's my personal scheduler. Go ahead, look through it. Maybe you can figure out when the hell I'd even have *time* to have an affair, huh? Huh?'

She stared at me, taken aback.

'Let's see,' I said. 'Ah, yes. How about some nookie between my eight forty-five supply-chain management call and the nine o'clock staff meeting? Slip in a little horizontal mamba between the ten o'clock end of the staff meeting and the ten-fifteen sales call with Detwiler?'

'Jason.'

'For you to accuse me of something like this just pisses me off.'

'He told me, you know. He told me he was worried for us.'

'Who?'

'Kurt. He said—said he probably shouldn't say anything—but he wondered if maybe you were having an affair.'

'Kurt,' I said. '*Kurt* said this. When did he say this to you?'

'I don't know. A couple of weeks ago.'

'Don't you understand what he's doing? That just fits right in to the pattern of everything else.'

She glanced at me, shaking her head. 'This isn't about Kurt, whatever his flaws,' she said. 'We have bigger problems than Kurt.'

'No, Kate. You don't know Kurt. You don't know what he did.'

'You told me.'

'No,' I said. 'There's more.'

I TOLD HER everything now. Her disbelief slowly melted. Maybe it's more accurate to say it turned into disbelief of another kind.

'Are you leaving anything out?'

'Nothing.'

'Jason, you've got to talk to the police. No anonymous calls. Openly. You have nothing to hide. Tell them everything you know.'

'He'll find out. He knows people all over the place.' I paused. 'And—he threatened me. He said he'll do something to you.'

'He wouldn't. He likes me.'

'We were friends, too, him and me—remember? But he's totally ruthless. He'll do anything to protect himself.'

'That's why you've got to call the police. He's got to be arrested.'

I FRIED SOME EGGS, toasted an English muffin, brought a breakfast tray up to her. Then I went to my study and booted up my laptop. I pulled up that Special Forces website I'd bookmarked and went to the 'Guestbook' where Trevor had posted his question about Kurt. No other replies had gone up.

I signed on to AOL, the account I hardly ever used. There was an email from a Hotmail address. Scolaro. The guy who'd replied to Trevor, said he knew something about Kurt. I opened it.

> I don't know this guy Semko personally. One of my SF brothers does and I asked him. He said Semko got a DD for fragging a team member.

DD, I remembered, meant 'dishonourable discharge.'

I hit REPLY and typed:

Thanks. Where can I get proof of his DD?

I hit SEND, and was about to sign off, when the little blue AOL triangle started bouncing. New mail from Scolaro.

If he got DD he was court-martialled. Army court documents are public record. Go to the Army Court of Criminal Appeals website.

Quickly I typed a reply:

What's your tel#? I'd like to give you a call.

I waited a minute. email is strange—sometimes it goes through in a couple of seconds; other times the mail won't get through for an hour.

Or maybe he just didn't want to answer.

While I waited, I did a Google search for the Army Court of Criminal Appeals. The browser popped up with a website.

I scanned it. On the menu bar on the left, one of the items was 'Published Army Opinions', and I clicked on 'By Name'.

A list came right up. Each line began with a last name. Then ARMY and a seven- or eight-digit number—a court case number, maybe?—and the 'United States v.' and the rank and name of a soldier.

The names were listed in alphabetical order. I scrolled down, so fast that the list became a blur, then slowed down a bit.

And came to SEMKO. 'United States vs. Sergeant KURT M. SEMKO.'

My heart raced.

The blue AOL triangle was bouncing. Another email from Scolaro. I double-clicked on it.

No way. Not talking about Semko. Said too much already. I got a wife and kids. Sorry. You're on your own.

I clicked on SEMKO and a PDF document opened.

UNITED STATES ARMY COURT OF CRIMINAL APPEALS
UNITED STATES, Appellee
v.
Sergeant First Class KURT M. SEMKO
United States Army Special Forces, Appellant

A lot of names and numbers and legalese. I skimmed it quickly. Kurt had been charged with the murder of a fellow soldier—a 'fragging', they called it—named Sergeant First Class James F. Donadio. Donadio was described as 'formerly a close friend of the appellant'. A 'protégé', some of Kurt's teammates testified. Until Donadio had reported Kurt for stealing war trophies—'retained illegal weapons'—which was against regulations.

Kurt had turned on his protégé. Donadio had found a cartridge jammed into the barrel of his M4 rifle. The weapon would have blown up if he hadn't noticed it. Then a 'flash-bang' grenade, normally used to clear a room, had been rigged up to Donadio's bed so it exploded one night. Flash-bang grenades made a loud explosion but caused no injuries. Another time, a jumpmaster noticed Donadio's static-line parachute had been sabotaged.

Kurt was suspected of all these acts, but there was no evidence. Then one morning, Donadio had opened the door to the Ground Mobility Vehicle he always drove and maintained, and an M-67 fragmentation grenade exploded. Donadio was killed.

All but one of the twelve team members testified against Kurt. His only defender was named Jeremiah Willkie.

I remembered the night I'd met Kurt, when he took me to that autobody shop owned by an SF buddy of his. He'd asked after the owner, whose name was Jeremiah. Willkie Auto Body had repaired my Acura. Kurt once mentioned he kept a storage unit there for his tools and such.

The defence argued that Kurt Semko was a highly decorated soldier of documented bravery in combat. He'd won three Purple Hearts.

The evidence was lacking. Kurt was found not guilty of premeditated murder, but found guilty of making false statements to the criminal investigator. He was given a dishonourable discharge but not sentenced to any time.

So that story he'd told about confronting his commanding officer over a 'suicide mission' that killed Jimmy Donadio—he'd made it up. The truth was he'd fragged a protégé who'd turned against him.

This was exactly what I needed. The state police would see who they were dealing with. There'd be no doubt that Kurt was capable of disabling Trevor's car, killing him and Gleason. No doubt at all.

I printed five copies.

WHEN KATE read it over she said, 'Is this enough to get Kurt arrested?'

'I doubt it. It's obviously enough to get him fired, but that's only the first step. What do I do until I can convince the police to arrest him?'

She nodded. 'He's totally charming and seductive. Narcissists like to feel superior. He needs your adulation.'

'He got yours, let me remind you.'

'We were both taken in.'

'Well, that's over, and he knows it. It's all out in the open between us now. He knows how I feel.'

'Well, turn the tap back on. The adulation. Let him think there's more hero worship in the tank, that you've got an endless supply.'

'Why?'

'To neutralise him. Until you get the cops in to arrest him.'

'You make it sound easy,' I said. 'It's not going to be easy at all.'

'Do you have a choice?' she said.

I HEADED RIGHT to Corporate Security to look for Scanlon.

I was mad, and in a hurry, and I didn't have my badge out, so I used the biometric fingerprint reader to get in. As the reader beeped to admit me, I suddenly realised how Kurt always knew where I went in the building. My access badge, the fingerprint reader—every time I accessed another part of the building, he probably knew right away.

I found the door with the plaque that said DIRECTOR OF CORPORATE SECURITY. It was closed. I walked up, grabbed the knob, but I was stopped by Scanlon's secretary.

'He's on the phone,' she said.

'Good,' I said, and I turned the knob and barged right into Scanlon's office. Against the sun streaming in, the security director was only a silhouette. He was on the phone, looking out of the window.

'Hey,' I said. In one hand I held a printout of Kurt's court-martial record.

He swivelled round slowly. 'You're looking for the director?' Kurt said, putting the phone down.

I stared in shock.

'Scanlon opted for early retirement,' Kurt said. 'I'm the new Director of Corporate Security. Can I help you?'

WHEN I GOT to my office, I saw a man sitting at the cubicle near Franny's cube that I used as a waiting room for my visitors. He was a black man, maybe fifty, with small ears and a large bullet head. He wore khaki slacks and a blue blazer, a blue shirt and solid navy blue tie.

'Jason,' Franny said, turning round in her chair.

'Mr Steadman,' said the man, rising quickly. I noticed handcuffs on his belt, and a gun. 'Sergeant Ray Kenyon, Massachusetts State Police.'

CHAPTER 9

He wanted to talk in my office, but I led him instead to a conference room. 'I'm investigating a collision involving two of your employees, Trevor Allard and Brett Gleason.'

I nodded. 'A terrible tragedy. Anything I can do to help.'

He smiled. His skin was very dark, and his teeth were incredibly white. His head was so shiny it looked waxed. He spoke slowly, like he wasn't the sharpest knife in the drawer, but I could see that his eyes missed nothing.

'How well did you know these two men?'

'Fairly well. They worked for me. I can't say they were close friends, but I saw them every day.'

'There was no animosity between you?'

'Animosity?' I wondered who he'd talked to and what he knew. 'Sergeant Kenyon, I thought Trevor and Brett died in a car crash.'

'They did. We want to find out why that happened.'

'Are you saying it wasn't just an accident?'

He peered at me for a few seconds. 'What do you think?'

I stared right back, but squinted as if I didn't quite understand.

I knew that whatever I said next would change everything.

Obviously I wanted the police to investigate the crash—but for me to accuse Kurt openly . . . Well, there was no putting that toothpaste back in the tube. Kurt would find out.

'I've wondered about it.' I said. 'How it could have happened, you know? *Was* there something done to Trevor's car?'

'That's not my department. That's Accident Recon. I just do the background investigation. Help them out.'

'They must have found something,' I said. 'If you're here.'

'Well, now,' he said, and I thought he looked pretty darned evasive, 'we work separately. They look at the brake lines and such, and I look at the people. Which brings me back to my question. Which you didn't answer. Whether there was any tension, any bad feeling, between you and them.'

I shook my head. 'Not that I can recall.'

He nodded, exhaling loudly through his nostrils. 'Mr Steadman, what you're saying doesn't quite dovetail with this.'

He pulled out of his pocket a folded piece of paper. He unfolded it, put it on the conference table in front of me. It was a photocopy of an email.

From me to Trevor. Dated about a week ago.

I won't put up with your disrespect & your undermining of me anymore. There are ways to get rid of you that don't involve HR.

'I'd never make a threat like that. And I'd sure never put it in an email.'

'You wouldn't want a record out there, that it?'

I closed my eyes in frustration. 'I didn't write it. Look, I—'

'Mr Steadman, have you ever been to Mr Allard's home?'

'No, he never invited me over. We weren't really personal friends.'

'You know where he lives?'

'I know he lives—*lived*—in Wellesley.'

'I see. And his garage—connected to his house. Were you ever there?'

'No. I just told you, I've never been to his house.'

He nodded, appeared to be thinking. 'So I'm wondering, why your fingerprints might have been found in his garage.'

'My fingerprints? That's impossible.'

'Your right index finger, anyway.'

'Come *on*,' I said. 'You don't have fingerprints to compare them against.'

He looked puzzled. 'You didn't give the print of your index finger to your Corporate Security department? For the new biometric reader?'

'Yes. Right. I forgot. I did—we all did. Our forefinger or our thumb. But I never went to Trevor Allard's house or garage.'

His eyes watched me steadily. 'See, the problem with fingerprints,' he said quietly, 'is that they don't lie.'

'Doesn't it strike you as maybe a little too convenient?'

'What's too convenient, Mr Steadman?'

'The one fingerprint you found in Trevor's garage is my right index finger, the one print that Corporate Security has in their biometric reader?'

'So?'

'So you tell me—aren't there ways to copy and transfer a fingerprint? You guys believe in coincidence? A print from the same finger as the one print I gave Corporate Security. An email I didn't write—'

'There's all kinds of headers and paths and directories on every email, Mr Steadman—'

'Which can be forged. It's easy if you work in Corporate Security.'

That shut him up. 'See,' I said, 'we have an employee who's done this sort of thing before.' I leaned forward, my eyes on his. 'I want to show you a document,' I said. 'That should give you a sense of who we're dealing with.'

I handed him the court-martial printout. When he'd finished, he said, 'Jesus Christ, your company hired this guy?'

I nodded.

'Don't you do background checks?'

'It's my fault. I vouched for him. I didn't know him well at the time.'

He shook his head, looking disgusted. But I could tell that he was looking at me differently. Something in him had shifted.

'This guy Semko,' he said. 'What reason would he have to set you up?'

'It's a long story. Complicated. He and I were friends. He did some things to help me out. Some things he shouldn't have done.'

'Like?'

'Underhanded things. But . . . Look, Sergeant. He's already threatened me. He told me if I said anything to the cops, he'd kill my wife. He knows lots of clever ways to kill people. I have to trust you. Can I?'

'Trust me how?'

'He knows people in the state police. A lot of people. He has contacts who tell him what's going on.'

Kenyon smiled cryptically, nodded.

'What?' I said. 'You look sceptical.'

'No. But I'm not going to lie. The truth is—we leak like a sieve. Military guys like your friend, sometimes they know a lot of people on the force.'

'Great,' I said darkly. 'If he finds out I've even talked to you, he'll do something to my wife. He works in Corporate Security—he knows the names of everyone who comes and goes here. You probably signed in at the front desk, right? To see Jason Steadman?'

'It's not like that. I'm here to talk to a lot of people.'

'OK.'

'I'm going to need to get specifics from you. Like some of the "underhanded things" this Semko person did.'

He turned a page of his notebook. He asked me questions. I talked, and he took a lot of notes.

'Maybe we can help each other,' he said. He handed me his card. He wrote down another number on the back. 'My cell. Sometimes my partner, Sanchez, answers my line. You can trust him.'

I shook my head. 'If I call you, how about if I use a fake name. I'll use—' I thought a moment. 'Josh Gibson.'

His big white smile took over his face. 'Josh Gibson? You're thinking *the* Josh Gibson? Negro Leagues?'

'One of the greatest power hitters of all time,' I said.

'I'll remember,' Kenyon said.

I WENT OUT for some lunch, and when I pulled back into the Entronics parking lot afterwards a black Mustang pulled in beside me with a loud squealing of brakes, and Kurt jumped out.

I sat in the car, waited for him to keep going. But he pulled open my passenger-side door and got in.

'How goes the battle?' he said. 'I thought you were going to California.'

'Missed the flight,' I said. 'So, congratulations on your promotion.'

He nodded, smiled. 'It's good to be king.'

'I'm impressed. Dick Hardy must think highly of you.'

'Dick Hardy wants me to be happy. He's decided I'm invaluable.'

'You got something on him, huh?' I smiled, nodding, as if I appreciated his cleverness.

'He even invited me on his yacht. Ever been on his yacht?'

'He invited me,' I said. 'But I couldn't make it.'

'It's an eighty-foot Lazzara. A bargain at 2.3 million. But it sure seemed out of his league, so I did a little digging. Turns out Hardy has been doing stock trading on the side. Set up a Channel Island trust in the name of the Samurai Trust. Samurai being the name of his yacht. And the Samurai Trust has been buying and selling out-of-the-money options on Entronics stock on the Australian Stock Exchange. Every time an Entronics press release goes out, every time there's another blip of good news, the Samurai Trust cashes in. If there's bad news, he makes money, too, on shorts. Very clever—just about impossible to get caught. And all to pay for his yacht.'

Finally, I understood. Dick Hardy was lighting a fire under us, getting us to sign deals all over the place so we could save our jobs, but that wasn't his sole motive. He was lining his own pockets at the same time.

'He's a clever guy,' I said.

'Clever enough to do his personal banking business using an encrypted Hushmail account. Not clever enough to realise that I could access his emails on the company computer.'

'Wow. Very cool.'

'So there you are, you and your Band of Brothers, working your butts off to try to save your division. When all you're really doing is paying off his yacht. Or his new house in the Highland Park section of Dallas.'

'Dallas?'

'Choke on that, buddy. Wonder why he's moving to Dallas.'

My shoulders sagged. I looked up, shaking my head regretfully. 'You're right. I was a pawn. You were just trying to help me out. While Gordy and Hardy were moving me around like a chess piece. You're my only ally.'

He turned to look at me. I couldn't read his face.

'I mean it,' I said. 'I really don't give a shit what you did to Trevor and Brett. I freaked out, I admit it. I called the cops—I'm not going to lie to you. That was a stupid thing to do.' I sounded genuinely contrite.

He was staring straight ahead out of the windshield. God, I hoped Kate's theory was right, that Kurt was a sucker for adulation.

Kurt's eyes flicked towards me, then back towards the windshield. 'You talked to that cop,' he said. His voice was softer. 'Kenyon. Did I not warn you to keep your mouth shut?'

'You did. And I did. But the guy showed up at my office. He said he's talking to everyone who worked with Trevor and Brett. He asked about you, and I told him that as far as I knew you had a good relationship with those two. That they really admired you.'

Kurt nodded. 'That's good,' he said.

It was working. Thank God. Relief flooded my body.

'That's very good,' he continued. 'Very smooth. I see why you're so good at closing deals.' He turned, his face a few inches from mine. 'Because you're a goddamned *liar*,' he shouted. 'I know every goddamned word you said to that cop. "He knows lots of clever ways to kill people", you said.'

No. Had Kenyon talked to somebody on the force who knew Kurt?

'"I have to trust you",' he went on. '"Can I?" No, asshole, you *can't* trust anyone. You think you can talk anywhere in the building without my knowing? I'm not going to say this again. Go behind my back one more time—I will find out. And if you step over the line—one millimetre over the line . . .

'You think you live in a safe neighbourhood. But break-ins happen all the time in that part of town. Sometimes they even kill innocent people. You've got a wife and unborn child, Jason. You want to be real careful.'

GRAHAM RUNKEL'S apartment still smelled like a bong, and his 1971 VW Bug was still in his backyard. It looked like he was working on it.

'How's the Love Bug?' I said.

'I'm hot-rodding it. Turbo rebuild. Wait right here.'

He came back with a Ziploc bag of marijuana buds. 'The last of the White Widow. A peace offering. Welcome back.'

'Not for me, thanks. I told you, I don't do that anymore.' I handed him a wrapped package.

'What's this?'

'A guilt offering. Because I'm a jerk.'

He tore it open. 'A complete set of *The Prisoner* on DVD? Unfreakingbelievable, Steadman.' Back in Worcester, Graham used to come over to my house when my parents were at work, and we'd get high and watch old reruns of the classic British spy show.

'I'm here to ask for your help, and I feel like such an asshole just showing up after all these months that I figured this might make you feel a little less pissed off at me.'

'It certainly goes a long way,' he said. 'But what you really need is the comfort of the White Widow. You're wound tighter than a . . . whatever's wound really tight.' Graham's brown hair was shoulder length and looked dirty. He was wearing an old red T-shirt with yellow McDonald's golden arches on it.

I came straight out with it. 'If you wanted to do something to someone's car so it wiped out while he drove it, what would you do?'

He looked at me funny. 'Cut the brake lines?'

'If you cut the brake lines, wouldn't the brakes feel all mushy as soon as you start driving it?'

'What's this about, J-man?'

I gave him a quick overview, told him about Kurt and what I thought he'd done. Graham listened with his bloodshot eyes wide open.

'It was a Porsche?' he said.

I nodded. 'Carrera 911. Brand-new. At most, a year old.'

'Was the driver wasted?'

I shook my head. 'Just lost control.'

'Hmm. Well, yeah, you wouldn't cut the brake lines. The driver would know right away. You wouldn't loosen the lug nuts on the wheels either—the car would start wobbling as soon as it hit the road. Of course, if somebody screwed with the ball joints . . . *man*.'

'What?'

'The driver would just lose control.'

'Screwed with the ball joints? How? Like, cut it?'

'Shaved down or filed away. Weakened somehow. So when the car—'

'Weakened?' I said. 'How do you weaken metal?'

'Shit, I don't know. Lots of ways, I figure.'

'Weaken metal,' I said aloud. 'I think I know.'

'OK, man, so why don't we celebrate?' He reached for the bag of marijuana. 'Last call,' he said.

I GOT HOME around seven-thirty. Susie and Ethan were finishing dinner in the kitchen and Kate was in bed, clicking away in cyberspace.

'Kate, you look like you could use a little fresh air.'

'Fresh air?' Then she saw me putting my index finger over my lips. She nodded. 'Good idea,' she said.

She slipped out of bed, and I lifted her up. It was surprisingly easy, probably because of all of Kurt's strength conditioning. I carried her down the stairs and out of the house to the backyard. 'I'm sorry, but I have to assume that Kurt has our bedroom bugged.'

Her eyes widened. 'No way!'

'Listen, how long does Susie have that rental in Nantucket?'

She cocked her head. 'Till the end of September, probably. Why?'

'Do you think it's safe for you to fly over there?'

'Flying's fine. As long as I don't exert myself. But what's this all about?'

'I want Susie and Ethan to go back to Nantucket and take you with them. As soon as possible. Tomorrow morning, first thing.'

She looked at me. A series of expressions played on her face: confusion, scepticism, amusement.

Then realisation. 'It's about Kurt, isn't it?' she said.

KATE AND SUSIE and Ethan got in a cab the next morning for Logan Airport and a flight to Nantucket. I went to the office, and at nine o'clock I grabbed a few minutes between meetings. I left the Entronics building, drove a few blocks away, took out Sergeant Kenyon's card, and called him from my cell.

The phone was answered in a gruff voice, a Spanish accent: 'State police, Trooper Sanchez.'

'Sergeant Kenyon, please.'

'Who's calling?'

I paused just a second. 'Josh Gibson.'

In a minute, Kenyon picked up. 'Mr Gibson,' he said. 'I was going to call you, give you the news.'

'News?'

'Accident Recon found nothing. No evidence of a crime. No evidence of a crime means no investigation. Means I get assigned to something else.'

'But I know that Kurt—I *know* he did something to the car. Did anyone check the ball joints?'

'I don't know what they checked,' Kenyon said. 'All I know is, they didn't find anything.'

'Where's the wreck?'

'Scrapped, I bet. Normally they ask the deceased's family if they want it, and when it's totalled like this, the family always says no, so they sell it off for scrap. Why?'

'Which tow yard?'

A pause. Kenyon laughed. 'Uh-uh. Forget it.'

I tried another approach. 'If you search Kurt Semko's house, I'll bet you find some tubes of something called LME. Liquid Metal Embrittlement agent. Issued to the US Army Special Forces.'

'LME, huh? Well, here's the problem, see. There's not going to be any search. No evidence means no investigation means no search warrant. As far as the state police goes, there *is* no case anymore. I'm sorry.'

'So Kurt's just going to get away with this?'

'I'm sorry, Mr Steadman.'

I CALLED directory assistance, got the number for J & A Towing—the company that had towed away Trevor's car—and gave them a call.

'You have my brother's Porsche,' I said to the woman who answered the phone. 'Name is Trevor Allard.'

'Hold on.'

When she got back on, she said. 'Hey, looks like your brother's widow gave us the go-ahead to sell it for scrap.'

'Shit,' I said. 'That was my brother's car. Can you find out if it's been picked up yet? I'm sorry to bother you—it's just that—well, there's, like, a sentimental value. He really cared about that car.'

'Hold on.'

A man picked up. 'This is Ed. We followed all the proper procedures, sir. We notified the next of kin, and she authorised us to scrap it. The wreck's scheduled to be picked up this afternoon by Kuzma Auto Salvage—'

'Listen, this is really important to me. What do you get from the salvage company for it?'

'Could be a hundred, two hundred bucks.'

'I'll give you three.'

'You really want this wreck, huh?'

'Tow it to my yard in Cambridge, and you'll get $300 in cash. Unless that Porsche's made of titanium, you're getting a pretty damned good deal.'

He chortled. 'I'll have one of the guys tow it out to you tomorrow.'

'Today,' I said. 'By two o'clock this afternoon.'

TREVOR ALLARD'S wrecked Porsche was a terrible sight. The front end was so badly crumpled it was almost unrecognisable. The hood stuck way up, the driver's door was just about off its hinges, both front tyres were flat. The undercarriage had been ripped apart.

Graham and I stood there, looking at it solemnly.

'My landlord's going to have a cow,' Graham said.

'As soon as you find the damaged part, I'll have it towed away.'

Graham got out his toolbox and began dismantling the wreck. He removed the front left wheel and poked around in the dark innards of the wheel well.

'This one's fine,' he said. 'No ball joint damage here.'

Then he went around to the other wheel and did the same. A few minutes later, he announced, 'This one's fine too.'

'What else could it be?'

I made work phone calls in his backyard while he searched under the front hood. There seemed to be nothing there either.

'Damn, this is frustrating,' Graham said.

He opened the driver's side door and wriggled into the collapsed front seat. He sat there for a moment. 'Speedometer's stuck at sixty-five,' he said. 'They weren't speeding.'

He pumped the brakes with his foot. 'They work fine.'

He turned the steering wheel. 'Oh, baby,' he said.

'What?'

'Turns a little too easy. Are the wheels turning?'

I stepped back and looked. 'No.'

'This could be the problem. You're driving on the turnpike at sixty-five and the road bends, so you steer, but your wheels keep going straight.'

'What causes that?'

'Could be a couple of things.' He bent down and messed with the wires under the dashboard. He removed some screws, and lifted the airbag unit from the steering wheel, then the airbag connector.

'Air bags didn't deploy,' he said. Now, with a wrench, he removed the steering wheel nut and bolt. He yanked at the steering wheel, but it didn't move. Then he grabbed a rubber mallet from his toolbox and hammered at it from behind a few times, then lifted the wheel straight out.

A minute later, I heard him say, 'This is weird.' He pulled out a thin rod about a foot long that had a U-joint at one end. The other end was jagged.

'What's that?'

'Steering shaft. Actually, half the steering shaft. This'—he pulled out a matching piece—'is the other half.'

'Broke?'

'These things are made to withstand a hell of a lot of torque. I've never seen anything like it. The steel didn't snap. It looks like it ripped. Like a piece of liquorice or something.'

'You should have been a cop,' I said.

SERGEANT KENYON had left a message on my cell. As I drove back to work, I returned his call.

'I asked around about LME,' Kenyon said. 'You may have something there. Liquid Metal Embrittlement is scary stuff. I don't know where you'd buy the chemical—a welding supply house, maybe?'

'Or take it from an army supply depot. I have a question for you. Let's say I somehow managed to get a piece from Trevor Allard's car that proved some kind of sabotage. Would that be evidence you could use in court?'

'What kind of piece?'

I hesitated. 'The steering shaft.'

'Well, in isolation, all that would tell me is that the car was tampered with. But I've still got a problem. A major problem.'

'Which is?'

'Connecting it to Kurt Semko. So you've got to establish that he had the means to do this—this LME. That he has or had access to it.'

'He *has* the stuff in his house,' I said. 'I've seen it. All you have to do is search his house.'

'I told you before,' Kenyon said. 'We're not going to have probable cause to search. So how the hell can you prove he has it?'

'Maybe there's a way,' I said.

There was, of course. Graham Runkel was working on it.

'Like what?'

'I'll have to get back to you on that,' I said.

KURT GREETED ME with a wave, from a distance, and a friendly smile. I smiled back, just as friendly, said, 'Hey.'

He was on the mound already, warming up. The ballpark lights were on. The opposing team, a motley crew from the Bear Stearns retail group, was already inspecting our bats. The word had got around.

My cellphone rang. I knew who it was, so I walked off a good distance before I answered it, on the third ring.

'I'm in,' Runkel said. He had broken into Kurt's place.

'Not a problem?' I asked.

'The doors were double-locked, but the overhead garage door was open. The door to the house from the garage is always the weak link.'

'You know where to look?'

'You told me.' His voice was sort of jiggling as he walked through the house. 'The spare bedroom off the family room, right?'

'Right.'

'You care what I use to set off the smoke alarm? Like a doobie?'

Kurt was waving to me again, and so was Ricky Festino.

I held up an index finger.

Once Graham found Kurt's cache of stolen weapons and explosives, he was going to leave open the door to the room where it was kept. When the fire department came, summoned by the smoke alarm, and broke in, they'd see the illegal armaments, and they would call in the police.

And then we'd have Kurt nailed. No arrest warrant needed, and all perfectly legal.

'Find it?' I said.

'No,' said Runkel. 'There's nothing here.'

'OK,' I said, 'if you're looking at the fireplace in the family room, it's the door on your right. The only one on that wall.'

'I'm there. I see the door, but there's no stash here.'

'It's there,' I said, desperation rising. Kurt was walking towards me. I lowered my voice. 'I've *seen* it.'

'I'm in the room,' Runkel said. 'There's a single bed. The room smells a little like gunpowder, maybe. But there's *nothing here*.'

'Then he moved it. Look in the basement. It has to be there.'

'Let's go, Jason,' Kurt said, maybe ten feet away. 'You're keeping everyone waiting.'

'Don't give up,' I said, and hung up.

'You're a busy guy,' Kurt said. 'Who was that?'

'It's a contract,' I said. 'Guy misplaced it.'

'That's annoying. So you're playing first base. Can you handle that?'

'Sure,' I said. 'Kurt. About all that—all that stuff I threw at you. About the car and everything.'

He shook his head. 'Not now.'

'No, I just want to apologise. I was out of line.'

'Don't worry about it,' he said. 'Come on, let's get to the field.'

He put his arm round me, like a fellow soldier, the way he used to.

But something about him had changed. He was hard and distant.

He didn't believe me.

KURT HAD MOVED his cache of stolen armaments and war trophies.

That made sense. The heat was on, and he didn't want to risk a search.

So where had he moved it?

The answer came to me while I stood at first base, and it was so obvious I couldn't believe I hadn't thought of it before. Willkie Auto Body. The shop owned by Kurt's friend and SF buddy, Jeremiah Willkie, where Kurt had taken my car the night I met him. Where he stored all his tools and stuff in the warehouse out back.

That's where I had to go.

THE MINUTE THE GAME was over, I took Ricky Festino aside and asked him to invite Kurt out for drinks with the rest of the Band of Brothers. Make sure of it, I said. I didn't give him an explanation, and he didn't demand one.

Then, in the car on the way to Cambridge, I tried Graham's cell, then his home number. No answer, which freaked me out a little. It wasn't like him to fall out of contact. He was a stoner, but he was basically responsible.

So why wasn't he answering the phone? I didn't want to let myself think the worst—besides, I knew Kurt couldn't have done anything to Graham, since I'd been with him the whole time.

I HAD NO IDEA what I was going to do once I got to Willkie Auto Body. I was pretty sure Kurt's storage locker was in the back building, which was a warehouse for auto parts and paint. The front building, which looked like an old gas station that had been retrofitted, was where the customer waiting area was, and the small office, and the work bays.

Willkie Auto Body was a desolate place. It was surrounded by a tall chain-link fence, but its front gate was open. Most of the red-brick front building was dark, too, except for the reception area.

As I turned into the lot, I shut off my headlights, slowed way down, and stayed all the way to the right side of the parking lot, where I hoped I wouldn't be seen from inside. A few feet beyond the front building the asphalt pavement ended, giving way to hard-packed dirt.

The rear building was about a half storey taller than the front one. It had corrugated steel walls, and it looked like an ice-skating rink. The only illumination came from the almost-full moon. I killed the engine and coasted to a stop next to a Dumpster between the two buildings.

I waited in the car and just listened for a few minutes. No noise back here. I took my gym bag from the front seat and got out of the car quietly. Pushed the door shut.

Then I just stood there and listened a little more. No footsteps. No sounds except, every ten seconds or so, a car driving past.

Now I walked slowly to the rear building. There were no windows, just some steel doors, each marked with a sign—PARTS and PAINT MIXING. A loading dock to the side, marked RECEIVING. I walked up close to it. A concrete pier about four feet off the ground, a rusted iron stepladder.

The loading-dock door was an overhead, folding-type door, probably steel. It was padlocked. I climbed the stepladder to the concrete pier and unzipped my gym bag. Inside were some basic tools I'd picked up at Home Depot on the way over, including a fourteen-inch pair of tungsten-carbide bolt cutters, which the salesman had assured me would cut through just about any padlock like butter.

I bent over to take a closer look at the padlock, and suddenly I was blinded by a bright light.

I looked up.

A high-powered flashlight was pointing at me from about twenty feet away. I felt a jolt of fear, a shot of adrenaline.

I was dead meat.

Shielding my eyes with a hand, I got to my feet. Something had kicked in, some hindbrain survival instinct. 'Hey, where were you?' I shouted.

'Who are you?' A man's voice, a Middle Eastern accent. The voice sounded familiar.

'Didn't you guys hear me?' I went on. 'Didn't you get the message? Are you Abdul or something?'

'Yes. Who are you?'

I sauntered down the stepladder, the gym bag on my shoulder. 'Kurt didn't tell you Kenny was coming by to get stuff from his storage locker?'

I thought quickly, tried to remember Willkie's first name. It came to me immediately—how could I forget 'Jeremiah'?

'Christ,' I said, 'I thought Kurt and Jeremiah had this all worked out.'

'Had what worked out?' He came closer.

'Shit, let me use your phone. And your john, if you don't mind. I got way too many beers in me tonight.'

'Bathroom's out front,' Abdul said. 'Did Kurt talk to Jeremiah?'

'Yeah, yeah,' I said. 'Show me to the john first.'

He led the way over to the front building, took out a ring of keys, and unlocked the back door. 'Down the hall, on your right.'

I used the urinal, then took out a pen and Kurt's business card from my wallet. On the back of Kurt's card I wrote, imitating Kurt's precise handwriting, all capital letters, 'WILLKIE AUTO BODY' and the address. Then, 'Abdul will meet you out back.'

I put the card in my pocket, flushed the urinal, and came out.

'OK, now I can think straight,' I said. 'I forgot I have my cell on me—I don't need your phone. Hold on.' I reached into my pocket, took out Kurt's business card, and handed it to Abdul. 'Is this you?' I asked. 'On the back?'

He flipped it over. Read the handwriting. 'You should have just gone to the front office,' he said.

ALONG THE BACK WALL of the warehouse was a row of storage units, ten feet wide and high and twenty feet deep. Abdul took out his key ring again and unlocked one of the padlocks.

'If you need anything, come get me,' he said, and he left me alone.

I pulled the door open and saw everything there, in neat stacks, in cartons and crates. Much more than I'd seen that day in his house. More than just his antique rifles and replica handguns. An entire pilfered armoury.

Colourful spools labelled PRIMACORD DETONATING CORD, in festive orange and yellow, the colour of kids' soft-drink mix. A box of M60 fuse igniters. A pile of blocks wrapped in olive drab Mylar film. Each one had printing on the top that said, CHARGE DEMOLITION M112 (1.25 LBS COMP C4).

I knew what that was. C-4 plastic explosive.

Kurt's auto tools were there too, in two tool chests, but I ignored them.

I found a tray containing several small tubes labelled LIQUID METAL EMBRITTLEMENT AGENT (LME)—MERCURY/INDIUM AMALGAM.

I took one of the tubes. My evidence.

Then I stopped and looked over the whole stash and realised there were some other things I could take.

WHEN I WAS more than halfway to Boston, I pulled over to the shoulder of the highway and called Sergeant Kenyon on his cell.

'I have all the evidence you need to arrest him,' I said after filling him in. 'Enough to tie him to the murders of Allard and Gleason.'

'Maybe,' he said.

'For Christ's sake,' I said. 'Why don't you send some guys over to Willkie Auto Body right now? There's a locker out back where Kurt's got enough explosives to take down the John Hancock Building.'

'Your hearsay isn't enough.'

'Kenyon, maybe you'd prefer me to just call the FBI, tell them the Massachusetts State Police weren't interested in following up on my report of stolen army munitions?'

Kenyon paused. I heard a rush of static on the line. 'I can send some guys over there,' he said.

My cellphone beeped. Call-waiting. I glanced at the read-out, saw it wasn't Graham; it said KURT.

'Let me call you back,' I said.

I clicked over to Kurt's call, said, 'Yeah?'

Raucous bar noise in the background. Loud voices and laughter.

'Hey there, bro. I just got a call from Abdul. You know Abdul.'

My stomach seized up. I didn't reply.

'And the funniest thing happened tonight during the game. Some guy broke into my house.'

'Oh yeah?'

'Friend of yours. Graham something. Runkel?' Casual, almost airy. 'Had your phone number programmed into his cell. Gotta be a friend.'

I felt a chill. He knew Graham's name, knew about the connection.

'Nosy bastard. Made the mistake of looking in my footlocker. Hundred and ten volts wired to the lock on that baby, my little security measure. Knocked him right out.'

Tears sprang to my eyes.

I bit my lip. 'Where is he?'

'He's resting comfortably in an undisclosed location, Jason, ol' buddy. Tied up and locked inside a big old trunk I had lying around. Well, maybe not so comfortably. Not a lot of air in there, and you know how panic makes you breathe harder, right?'

'I've got something you want,' I said abruptly.

'Oh yeah?'

'A damaged steering shaft from a Porsche Carrera. Let Graham go, and I'll give you the part. An even trade. My friend for a guarantee you won't be going to prison for life. Sounds like a pretty good deal to me.'

He hesitated. Everything, anything might be a trick. I needed to sell him on the fact that I really wanted to make a deal. And I needed to sell him on the fact that I was trying to sell him. This was a mirror reflecting a mirror.

'Sure,' he finally said. 'I got no problem with that.'

I thrust back. 'Sure, *you've* got no problem with that. I hand it over, you hand over Graham, and then you head over to Hilliard Street and kill my wife and then me.'

'You saying my word's not good enough for you?'

I laughed. 'It was, once. Not anymore. This steering shaft, it's a key piece of physical evidence. Without it, the police have no probable cause for arrest. You're good to go. But what about me?'

'Well, think about it,' he said. 'Without your evidence, you're powerless. Means you're no longer a threat.'

'But I know things,' I said. 'Facts about you. In my head. How do you know I'm not going to go to the cops again?'

'How do you know I'm not going to head over to Hilliard Street? Pay the wifey a visit? So we've got ourselves a situation here. It's called mutual assured destruction. Military doctrine throughout the entire Cold War.'

'You have a point,' I said. 'All right. So?'

'So we meet.'

'Where? It has to be someplace neutral. Someplace safe. Not public. Not your house. Not my house.'

'Work,' he said. 'The Entronics building.'

Where he felt comfortable. Where he controlled the situation.

'One hour,' I said. 'With Graham.'

'Two. And you're not exactly in a position to negotiate. You give me the scrap of metal, and I'll tell you where he is. Think it over. Take your time. I've got all the time in the world. Oh—that's right. Your friend doesn't. He has three or four hours' worth of air. If he calms down and breathes normal.'

'All right.'

CHAPTER 10

I called Kenyon back.

'I've just made a deal with Kurt Semko,' I said, and I explained.

'Are you out of your goddamned mind?' he said.

'You have a better idea?'

'Hell, yeah. I'll send a unit over to this auto body shop. Once they find the explosives, we'll easily have enough to arrest Semko.'

'How long are we talking?'

'Six hours, I'd say, if we get a judge out of bed.'

'No,' I said. 'My friend won't make it. So I'm meeting Kurt whether you like it or not, and I want you to wire me up. I'll get him to talk.'

'Stop right there,' Kenyon said. 'Our Special Services staff don't work at midnight. We're talking quick-and-dirty.'

'That'll do.'

More static. A long silence. 'I don't know about this. I'd be putting you in serious danger. It's extremely irregular.'

'Serious danger? You want to talk serious danger? A friend of mine is slowly suffocating in a trunk somewhere. I'm going to meet with Kurt.'

'Are you certain you can get him to talk?'

'I'm a salesman,' I said. 'That's what I do.'

I MET KENYON about a half-hour later at an all-night Dunkin' Donuts near the Entronics building. It was shortly after eleven. There were a couple of drunk young guys in low-hanging shorts, and a bum who'd surrounded his table with shopping bags full of junk.

Kenyon was wearing a navy sweatshirt and chinos and looked tired. We both got large coffees, and then he took me out back to a new-looking white van. He opened the rear doors and we climbed inside.

'This is the best I can do on short notice,' he said, handing me a coil of wire. 'Take off your shirt.'

I did. He taped the transmitter to the small of my back.

'Is he going to spot your back-up team? Don't forget, he's a pro.'

'So are they.'

I took in a lungful of air and let it out slowly. 'Is this going to work?'

'The transmitter's going to work fine. Everything else—well, that depends on you. We'll be monitoring the transmission. If you need us, just say something. Some phrase we agree on. And we'll come running.'

'A phrase. How about, "I'm not getting a good feeling about this"?'

'Works for me,' he said. 'OK, then. We're good to go.'

FIFTEEN MINUTES after midnight.

I arrived at my office a quarter of an hour before the time we'd agreed to meet. I set down my gym bag and my briefcase as I entered. The lights were already on. So was my computer.

Kurt had been using it, I assumed, but for what?

I went behind the desk to look at the monitor, and I heard Kurt's voice from the doorway. 'You have something for me.'

I looked up. Nodded.

'Let's make this fast.'

I stood still, looked in his eyes. 'What's my guarantee Graham's going to be where you say he is?'

'I guess you'll just have to take me at my word.' Kurt said.

'What good is this thing to you anyway?' I asked. 'It's just a piece of scrap metal.'

'It's worth nothing to me.'

'So why are you willing to deal?'

Last-minute hesitation. Happened all the time in my business.

'Why? Because I'd rather keep it out of the cops' hands. Not that my buddies on the force might not happen to 'lose' a piece of evidence against me. But I'm a thorough guy.'

'Who says the cops are even going to know it's from a Porsche?'

'All it takes is one smart forensic guy to find traces of mercury or whatever's on there. Or the pattern of breakage—I really don't know. But why take the chance? When you and I can come to terms.'

I nodded.

Got it. That was enough to incriminate him.

'I'm taking a huge chance,' I said.

'Life's a risk. Hand it over.'

I was silent for a long time.

True sales champions, Mark Simkins said, *can sit there quietly all day if they have to. You want to say something. But don't! Keep your mouth shut.*

When enough time had passed, I picked up the gym bag, unzipped it.

Pulled out the piece, which I'd wrapped in plastic and duct-taped up.

Handed it to him.

'Good,' he said. He unravelled the layers of plastic from the steering shaft, held up the twisted thick steel rod with a U-shaped joint at one end. Weighed it in his hand, admiring it. It was heavy.

'All right,' I said. 'Where's Graham?'

'You know where the old General Motors assembly plant is?'

'On Western Avenue, a mile or so from here?'

'Right. That vacant lot there.' He handed me a small key. To the trunk, I guessed. 'Funny how your life can depend on a little piece of metal,' he said. He walked slowly to the big glass window. 'Like a round of ammunition. It can save your life.' Now he was looking out of the window. He swivelled round. 'Or it can kill you.'

With that, he swung the steering shaft at the window.

The glass exploded with a loud pop, a million shards showering all over the carpet. 'Cheap-ass tempered glass,' he said.

'I'm not getting a good feeling about this,' I said.

Cold wind whipped into the office.

'OK,' he said. 'You've been under a lot of stress. All sorts of pressures on you to save the division. Mega Tower planned all along to shut it down. You found out the truth, and it was too much. So you do the only thing that makes sense. You're going to jump. It's a good day to die, don't you think?'

The wind was sluicing through the office, blowing papers around.

'Speak for yourself,' I said.

I reached into the gym bag, pulled out Kurt's Colt pistol. An army-issue semiautomatic .45.

Kurt saw it, smiled. 'You've left a suicide note,' he said calmly. 'On your computer. Happens more and more often these days.'

The gun felt heavy in my right hand, awkward. The cold blue-black steel, the rough grip. My heart was knocking so hard my hand was twitching.

'The cops can hear every word we're saying,' I said. 'I'm wired, my friend. Your suicide ruse isn't going to work. Sorry.'

'One-handed grip?' Kurt said, surprised. 'That's not easy.'

I brought my other hand up so I was holding the gun with both hands.

'You've apologised to your wife and your unborn daughter. That's what the amnio results said, by the way. A girl. Congratulations.'

For a second he almost stopped me. I froze for an instant.

'Did you load it, Jason? Do you even know how?'

Kurt grinned. There was something almost paternal in his expression.

Where was Kenyon? Couldn't he hear me?

'Good choice of firearms, Jason,' he said. He took a few steps towards me. 'Model 1911 A1 Series 70. Outstanding weapon.'

He came closer.

'Freeze, Kurt.'

He came even closer. Maybe ten feet away. Very close.

'*Stop right there or I'll blow you away!*' I shouted.

I curled my finger round the trigger. It felt surprisingly insubstantial.

Where the hell were they?

'You're not going to kill me, Jason. You've never killed a man before, and you're not going to start now.' He spoke quietly, steadily. Almost lulling. 'Close range like this, you get sprayed with blood and brain tissue, fragments of bone. It'll haunt you for the rest of your life.'

'Watch me,' I said, and I squeezed the trigger.

The strange thing was, he didn't move. He stood there, arms at his side.

The gun didn't fire. I pulled the trigger again, all the way back. Nothing.

Suddenly his right hand shot out, pushed the gun to the side as he grabbed it, wrenched it out of my hands in one smooth motion.

'Friggin' amateur,' he said. He turned the gun round, pointed it at me. 'You loaded it, but you didn't squeeze the grip safety.'

I spun round, ran.

As fast as I could. Like racing up the steps of Harvard Stadium, but with every fibre of my being engaged in a desperate attempt to save my life.

Out of the office, through the maze of cubicles.

The elevators just ahead. I leapt towards the panel, pressed all the buttons.

'Nowhere to run,' came Kurt's voice, sounding closer.

The bing of an elevator arriving. The elevator doors slid open and I jumped inside, heard Kurt's footsteps, punched the LOBBY button, punched and punched at it until the doors, so agonisingly slow, finally closed.

The elevator wasn't moving. Then, a little jolt and it began to descend.

Floor buttons began to light up one after another, slowly: 19 . . . 18 . . . The flat-panel screen was dark, and the lights in the elevator cabin seemed dim. I stared at the numbers, willing them to move faster.

Where the hell was Kenyon?

The elevator shuddered to a stop. The orange 9 button frozen.

I punched the LOBBY button again, but nothing moved.

Then everything went dark. I could see nothing. Pitch-black.

He'd turned off the power. I reached out in the darkness, flailing at the buttons. Ran my fingers over them, punched each one. Nothing.

I remembered the emergency switch was at the bottom of the control panel. I slid my hands down to the toggle switch. I grabbed it, flipped it up.

Nothing. No alarm, no sound, nothing.

A wave of panic hit me. I felt the cold smooth steel doors until I found the crack where the two doors met. A tiny gap, not enough to get my fingertips into. Sweat prickled at the back of my neck. In frustration, I pounded the door. Kicked at it. The steel was cold and unmoving.

Found my cellphone, opened it so the screen illuminated. Punched 911.

That little chirp tone that told me the call had failed.

No reception in here.

My heart was racing. The sweat was trickling down my cheeks and neck. I backed up, swung my arms around, felt for the walls of the elevator.

Closing in on me.

I flung my hands up, felt for the ceiling, had to jump to reach it. Felt something round, a hole. Remembered that the ceiling in here had little recessed downlights in it. There had to be an emergency escape. Wasn't that required by code?

The sweat was pouring now. I had to get out of here. I tried to swing my foot up onto the handrail, to boost myself up, but it was too high.

I was trapped.

The ceiling lights suddenly came on.

Then the panel lit up blue, then white, then . . . Kurt's face appeared.

A close-up of his face, slightly out of focus. A big smile.

'Boy, you are drenched,' he said. 'Hot in there, huh?'

How the hell was he doing this? I looked up, saw the silvery black dome in one corner of the ceiling. The CCTV camera lens.

'Yep, that's right,' Kurt said. 'That's me. And you look like a drowned rat. No need to hit the emergency call button. I disabled it.'

'What are you going to do, Kurt? Leave me in here overnight?'

'No, I thought I'd entertain you with a little live video feed. Watch.'

The image of his face blinked, and the screen went dark. Then another image came up, fuzzy and indistinct. My bedroom. The image slowly zoomed in on the bed. Kate lying there. Blue light flickering over her face.

'There's the wifey,' Kurt said. 'Couple of nights ago. Guess she fell asleep watching TV while you were out somewhere.'

My heart was going ka-thunk, ka-thunk, ka-thunk.

'Lots of opportunities to install that camera. She was always inviting me in. Maybe she was attracted to a real man. Not a pathetic fake like you.'

Another scene appeared. Kate and me in bed. Making love.

The image had a greenish, night-vision cast.

'No comment on your sexual technique, bro,' Kurt said.

'I guess you don't want the other half then,' I said.

'The other half?' The image of Kate switched to Kurt's face. Big, looming close-up. A curious look.

'The steering shaft in the Porsche Carrera is eighteen inches long,' I said. 'The piece I gave you was, what—maybe ten inches?'

'Ah,' he said, chuckling. 'Maybe you did learn something after all.'

'I learned from the master,' I said. 'You want it, you bring me back up to my office. I get it from the hiding place, hand it to you. And then you let me go. I retrieve Graham. And it's over.'

Kurt's big face stared at me. Blinked a few times.

'Do we have a deal?' I said.

He smiled. His face pulled back, and I could see my office. He'd been sitting at my computer. Maybe a camera hooked up to it.

The elevator made another jolt, and it started to move.

I watched the buttons on the control panels light up orange: 12 . . . 13 . . .

Hit redial on the cellphone. This time the call went through.

'Police emergency.' A man's voice, clipped.

'I'm in an elevator in the Entronics building in Framingham,' I said. 'My name is Jason Steadman. My life is in danger. There's a guy on the twentieth floor who's trying to kill me.'

'Hold on, please.'

'*Just send someone!*' I shouted.

The orange 20 button lit up. A ding. The elevator doors opened.

On the phone, another voice came on. 'Trooper Sanchez.'

I didn't understand. 'Sanchez? Where's Kenyon?' I could see a figure in the shadows in the twentieth-floor lobby. Kurt, it had to be.

I whispered. 'I'm Jason Steadman. I'm in the Entronics building—you've got to radio Kenyon, send someone over here *now*.'

'Steadman?' Sanchez said. 'That scum-sucking piece of shit?' His Hispanic accent was even thicker now.

Two figures emerged from the shadows. Kurt was holding a cellphone to his ear. 'Would you like Sergeant Kenyon's voicemail?' Kurt said in his Sanchez voice, leering.

Another man, holding a cellphone.

Ray Kenyon.

In his other hand was a pistol. Kenyon waved it at me. 'Let's go,' he said. 'Go, go, go. Hand me the other half.'

I stared in shock. I'd pressed 911. I was *sure* of it.

'Jerry,' came Kurt's voice. 'Hand me the weapon. I'll take over.'

Jerry. Jeremiah. Jeremiah Willkie. His Special Forces brother. The one who wouldn't testify against him. Who owned the auto body shop. Who was 'Ray Kenyon'.

Jeremiah Willkie handed Kurt the weapon. It looked like the Colt I'd stolen from Kurt's storage locker, but I couldn't be sure.

'The guys are never going to believe this one,' said Willkie/Kenyon.

'No, they won't,' said Kurt, and he pointed the barrel at Jeremiah Willkie and fired. 'Because they're not going to hear about it.'

Willkie collapsed to the floor. His left temple was bloodied. His eyes remained open.

I stared at Kurt.

'Jeremiah has a drinking problem,' Kurt said. 'Get a couple vodkas in him, and he talks too much. But he made a convincing cop, didn't he?'

'I called 911.'

'It's called cellphone phreaking. Cloned your phone so I could listen to all your calls. And pick up on outgoing calls too.' He pointed the gun at me. 'Sounds like you hid the part in your office. You tricky guy. Let's go.'

I entered the office and he followed. The wind howled. Papers covered the carpet, and piles of whitish glass fragments.

'Well, I know it's not in your desk,' Kurt said. 'Or in your bookcase. Or any of the usual hiding places.'

My eyes flicked towards the briefcase, then away. It was still there.

'Ceiling panel,' I said.

He'd seen my eyes.

'I don't think so,' Kurt said. 'Hand the piece over, and you're free to go.'

'I'm not going out that window,' I said.

'Hand me the rest of the shaft.'

My eyes darted again, almost involuntarily, towards the briefcase.

I said, 'I need a ladder or something so I can reach the ceiling panel.'

'A ladder? I sure don't think you need a ladder.' He stepped towards my desk, grabbed the English leather briefcase. 'Didn't I teach you about the "tell"? Those little giveaway signs in a person's face?'

I tried to grab the briefcase back from him, but of course he was much stronger, and he wrested it from my grip. As he fiddled with the latches, I took advantage of his momentary distraction, backed away from him.

'Nowhere to run, Jason,' Kurt said, loud but matter-of-fact. I backed away slowly as he flipped open one of the brass latches, then the other, and then my back was against the doorframe.

A tiny scraping sound.

I saw the realisation dawn on Kurt's face, an expression of fury combined with something I'd never seen in his face before.

Fear.

But only for a fraction of a second, before the blast swallowed him, blew him apart, limbs flying, horrific carnage like something you might see in a war movie. The immense explosion threw me backwards and as I tumbled I felt fragments of wood and plaster spray against my face.

I struggled to my feet, ears ringing, my face stinging.

A block of Kurt's own C-4 plastic explosive connected to the confetti-bomb apparatus he'd put in my briefcase that day. I'd left it in my briefcase and gone back to using my old one.

And he was right that a little C-4 was enough. There was no chance of him surviving.

Reached the elevator banks, then stopped. Wasn't going to try that again. The stairs. Twenty flights was nothing. I was in great condition now.

Well, not exactly. My back ached, and a couple of my ribs were sore, probably bruised if not broken. But I was flooded with adrenaline.

Opened the door to the stairs and started down the twenty flights. I was limping, and I grimaced from the pain, but I knew I'd make it just fine.

EPILOGUE

Kurt was right, of course.

It was a girl. Nine pounds, twelve ounces. A beautiful, healthy, big girl. She looked sort of like Jack Nicholson, with the straggly black hair and the bad comb-over. And I'd always hoped that, if we got a girl, she'd look like Katharine Hepburn. Oh, well.

The baby—Josephine, we named her; Josie—was so big that Kate had to deliver by C-section. So the delivery was scheduled a couple of days in advance, which was, unfortunately, plenty of notice for my brother-in-law to fly in from LA to join his wife and Kate and me.

I was so happy I barely minded having Craig there.

The police business took a few days to straighten out. Graham Runkel and I spent long hours at state police headquarters. Graham told them about how Kurt had locked him into a trunk, where he might have suffocated had I not released him, barely in time.

They wanted to know how I'd learned to make a bomb. I told them Kurt had done most of the work for me, and the rest I'd gotten online. It's amazing what you can find on the Internet.

Now that Kurt was dead, it was easy to get his Special Forces teammates to come forward. The picture that emerged wasn't pretty. Just about every one of the cops who interviewed me said I was 'lucky' I hadn't been killed.

Lucky. Yeah, right.

Not long after Yoshi had passed on to Tokyo the information about how the CEO of Entronics USA, Dick Hardy, had been able to afford his yacht and his house in Dallas, Hardy was jettisoned. Soon he was facing what Gordy used to call a 'gangbang' of civil, criminal and tax fraud charges.

I was flown to New York to meet with our chairman of the board, Hideo Nakamura, and about a dozen other honchos, to interview for Dick Hardy's job. It was me versus a bunch of other internal candidates, all of them older and much more qualified. Instead of just sitting there on the hot seat being grilled by Nakamura-san, I decided to go out on a limb and make a PowerPoint presentation to my interviewers.

My presentation made a business case for shutting down Entronics headquarters in Santa Clara, selling off its valuable Silicon Valley real estate, and moving headquarters to lovely Framingham, where Entronics already had a building. All it needed was some repair work on the twentieth floor.

The kicker was my slide showing how Royal Meister's Dallas offices could be sold at an immense profit. The Dallas Cowboys, see, wanted a new stadium, and they were willing to pay handsomely for the land.

This impressed them, I think.

The interviews seemed to go well, if facial expressions are any indication. Yoshi Tanaka sat by my side the entire time, as if he were my attorney.

In the last interview there seemed to be a really heated exchange between Yoshi, Nakamura-san and another board member in rapid Japanese. Yoshi said something, and they all nodded.

Yoshi turned to me and said, 'Please forgive me, I'm being terribly rude.'

I looked at him in astonishment. He was speaking in a plummy British accent. He sounded like Laurence Olivier.

'It's just that they keep referring to you as *nonki*, which I suppose I'd translate as "easy-going", and a *gokurakutonbo*, which you might say means "happy-go-lucky fellow". But I'm afraid neither is a compliment. I had to explain to them that your people speak of you with a certain trepidation. I told them that's what I like about you. You have that killer instinct.'

LATER ON, as Yoshi and I waited for the hiring committee to finish their deliberations, I blurted out, 'Your English is amazing. I had no idea.'

'*My* English? My dear boy, you're too kind. I did my master's thesis at Trinity College, Cambridge, on the late novels of Henry James. Now there's a *true* master of the language.'

Of course. How else could he get people to talk so freely in his presence?

'So when I told you all about my big idea for the PictureScreen, and you just stared blankly—'

'In stunned admiration, Jason-san. That was when I realised you were a bloody visionary. I immediately told Nakamura-san, and he insisted on meeting you in Santa Clara. But alas, it was not to be.'

In the end, I was tapped for Dick Hardy's job, and they approved my suggestion to move US headquarters to Framingham. Now Joan Tureck was working for me, and she and her partner were happy to be back in Boston.

SO, WHERE WAS I?

Oh, yes. At the hospital, Craig treated me with newfound respect. He kept talking about the Entronics Invitational, what a blast he had last year when Dick Hardy had invited him, how cool it was playing a few holes with Tiger Woods. It took me a while to figure out that Craig was angling for an invitation again this year. Now that I was the CEO of Entronics.

'We're trying to keep the head count down this year,' I said, 'but I'm sure we can work something out. Just contact my assistant, Franny Barber.'

I have to say that I enjoyed that.

We all sat in Kate's room watching Baby Josie clamp on to Kate's boobs and suck away like a champ. Finally, she fell asleep.

I gave Kate a smooch, and said, 'I'm married to the greatest woman, and I have the greatest baby, and I just feel like the luckiest man in the world.' I was almost overcome by emotion.

'I thought you said a man makes his own luck,' she said, arching her brows.

'I don't think I believe that anymore,' I said slowly. 'Sometimes the luck makes the man.'

Kate and Susie started discussing nannies. Kate said she'd found several promising candidates on the *Irish Echo* newspaper's website. Susie told her that the only nannies to hire were Filipinas. They went back and forth on this, and Craig joined in. I didn't care one way or another, of course.

But when they started arguing about which was better, a live-in or a live-out nanny, I jumped in. 'I really don't want a stranger living under the same roof,' I said.

'She wouldn't be a stranger once we got to know her,' Kate pointed out.

'You really want to be able to leave the baby with the nanny when you two go out,' Craig said. 'That's what was so great about Corazon. We were able to leave Ethan with her all the time. We barely saw him.'

'That's wonderful,' I said. Kate and I exchanged a look.

'I expressed my breast milk and put it in the Sub-Zero,' Susie said, nodding. 'But there's really only one kind of breast pump to buy.'

'I know,' Kate said. 'I've been on every baby website.'

'Can we not talk about breast pumps?' I said. 'I want to go back to the live-in/live-out thing.'

'Why?' Kate said. 'It's decided.'

'The hell it is. Don't even bother.'

Kate saw the resolve in my face. 'Oh, I've only just begun,' she said with that knowing smile that she knew always turned me to mulch.

'Uh-oh,' I said. 'Now it's war.'

JOSEPH FINDER

Home: Boston, USA
Likes: gadgets and technology
Website: www.josephfinder.com

RD: Your last three books have all dealt with the darker side of the business world. What first led you to pick on that particular theme?

JF: It's funny. I didn't set out to take on that world, but when a CIA friend of mine suggested I write about corporate espionage, I thought that would be fresh and different, something that hadn't been done in fiction. As soon as I started doing research into companies like Apple and Hewlett Packard, I became fascinated by the culture of modern corporations. There's a great sense of community; and yet there's also backstabbing and visciousness and terrible politics. Most of us spend most of our day at work—why shouldn't novels deal with this world we know and have such ambivalent feelings about?

RD: And was there a starting point for the plot of Killer Instinct?

JF: I guess it came from that notion you hear so often, that 'Business is war'. When I interview CEOs and other corporate execs, I often see leadership books on their shelves with titles like *The Navy SEALS Guide to Success At Work*. I've always found that ironic, because most company men are nothing like soldiers. They just love the macho, military language, the aggressive approach and the warrior ethic. They like to talk about 'killing the competition'. So the premise occurred to me—what would happen if I put a highly trained Special Forces officer, with a ruthless bent, into a corporation and had him go up against some of the faux warriors? What if 'killing the competition' became no longer just a buzz phrase?

RD: What do you think of the whole 'Business is war' ethos?

JF: I think it's basically ridiculous, a way to fire up the troops. The truth is—and it's sort of the point of the novel—that untrammelled ruthlessness in business inevitably backfires. It's not a good way to live your llife or conduct your business.

RD: Is the character of Kurt based on anyone that you've met?

JF: He's loosely based on a couple of cases I've heard about, Special Forces officers who came back from war, having been trained to kill, and were then unconstrained by societal conventions. These guys were the bad apples. So the basic type exists. I just turned that type into a charismatic, sociopathic, and utterly winning guy.

RD: How did you set about creating your main character, Jason?

JF: I decided he had to be a salesman, because that's a culture that breeds aggressiveness and ruthlessness. A guy like Jason, who's not really aggressive, would naturally feel inadequate in such company and would reach out for the help of someone like Kurt, who's ruthless. So I interviewed a lot of sales people to get a sense of what their daily lives are like, their homes, their family lives, their victories and defeats at work.

RD: What do you find hardest about writing a novel?

JF: Starting. I love the research and I spend too much time 'clearing my throat' and planning the book before I summon up the nerve to actually dive in. A writer friend of mine compares starting a novel to digging a tunnel with a spoon. It's a fairly daunting undertaking. Once it's underway, it's OK.

RD: And, finally, what's your biggest indulgence?

JF: If pressed, I'd say food. I love good food, and I love cooking. In the summer, especially, when we spend three months on Cape Cod, I love freshly caught fish—particularly the bass. And I love to gather oysters and clams with my wife and daughter—we eat a lot of shellfish that we collect ourselves. And I have a couple of big gardens where I grow heirloom tomatoes. If I ever worked out the numbers, it would be a whole lot cheaper to just buy them. But it wouldn't be as enjoyable.

BEHIND THE MASK

Over the years, the character of the ruthless psychopath, consumed by envy, hatred or jealousy, has provided a feast of story-lines for numerous writers and film-makers. One classic example is Shakespeare's Iago, who orchestrates a malicious campaign against his friend and general, Othello, culminating in his own destruction. In the cinema, the award-winning 1950s film, *All About Eve*, starring Bette Davis, features an ambitious young actress's fall from grace after her calculated betrayal of an idolised movie star, and *Cape Fear* (1962, 1991), tracks the relentless progress of a psychopath's mission of revenge, which leads to his downfall. *Right*: the 1962 poster for *Cape Fear*.

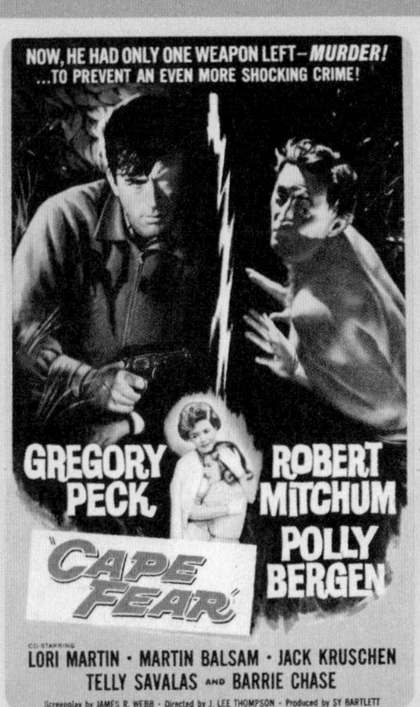

ALAN TITCHMARSH

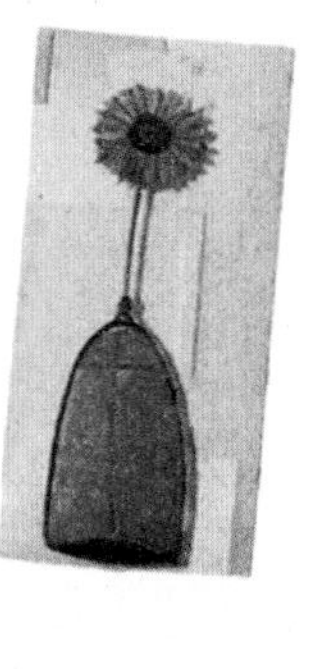

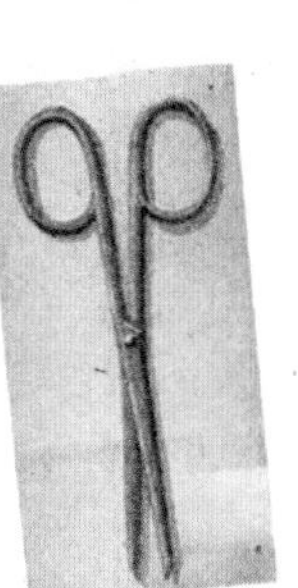

LOVE & DR DEVON

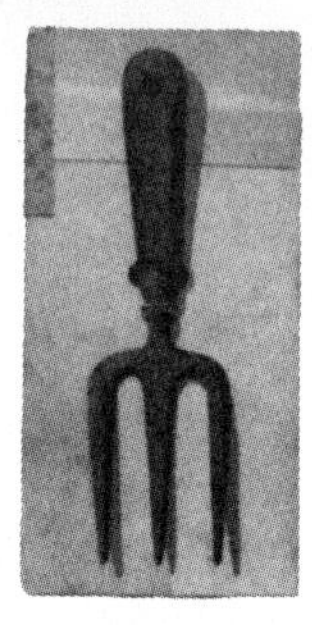

Watching your wife walk out on you and then losing your job . . . it's a double whammy that has left Dr Christopher Devon down in the doldrums. Now that the high spot of his week is a Friday night game of dominoes in the Hare and Hounds, with his pals Gary Flynn and Tiger Wilson, he reckons it's high time a bit of excitement came his way . . .

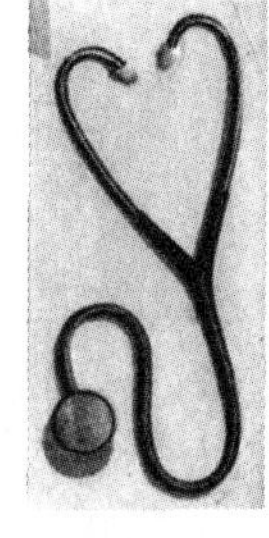

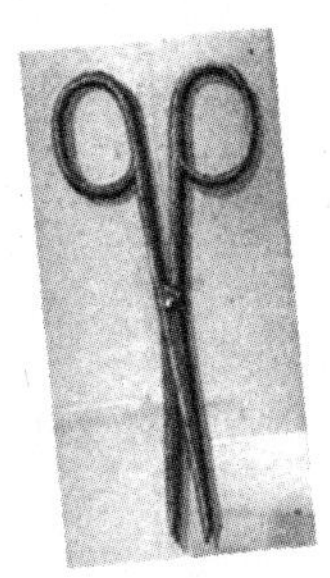

Chapter One

Years ago we discovered the exact point, the dead centre of middle age. It comes when you are too young to take up golf and too old to rush up to the net.

Nods and Becks, Franklin P. Adams (1881–1960)

There were just the three of them to start with—Tiger Wilson, Dr Christopher Devon and Gary Flynn—and they met on Friday nights in the Hare and Hounds. Well, not every Friday night, because sometimes Tiger's wife wanted to be taken out to dinner, and sometimes Christopher Devon was on call, and sometimes Gary Flynn had a better offer. But not very often. Which is why, at least three weeks out of four, they played dominoes in the Hare and Hounds on a Friday night.

They would like to have played squash. It would have been better for their self-esteem. Dominoes was a game for old men. And they were not old. They were in their fifties. The prime of life. At their peak. Established in their professions. Until recently at any rate.

They met . . . well, they dispute this. Tiger thinks it was at a drinks party, Christopher says they were his patients long before that and Gary claims to have no recollection, which most likely pins it down to the drinks party.

Like most men in their fifties they were at a crossroads. They had accomplished what they set out to do. Reached the top of the tree. Well, the higher branches anyway.

Sorted, eh? At fifty. In their prime. With just one niggling little question: Is that it?

Not that in the early days of the domino club this had ever been alluded to in so many words. It was more of an undercurrent. A frustration that occasionally erupted, thanks to a newspaper article that highlighted the folly of government, or some local injustice.

Then one day Dr Christopher Devon said, '*We* should do something about it.'

'What sort of something?' asked Gary.

And Tiger said, 'We should form a sort of secret society.'

HE HAD BEEN called 'Tiger' from the very beginning. 'Andrew', bestowed at the font, had never been used by anyone except his mother in moments of impatience. She had died when he was fifteen and from then on to his father he was always 'Tiger'. He had gone off the rails a bit after her death. Nothing disastrous, but one or two run-ins with the law.

When he left school and refused any form of higher education the paternal foot had been put down. Old man Wilson pushed Tiger in the direction of the only career he had ever known himself—the RAF. At first Tiger had rebelled. The services with their structured lifestyle were the last thing he wanted. But then he discovered flying. The feeling of liberation, when he penetrated the cloud layer for the first time in an aircraft under his own control, would never leave him. It was the ultimate independence.

He came home with a light in his eyes and told his father of the moment when he knew that a life in the air was for him.

His father smiled knowingly. 'I'm glad you found it. Found yourself.'

Tiger never received the acclaim his father enjoyed—high-ranking and decorated for his wartime exploits—but he was a respected helicopter pilot and left the service with the rank of squadron leader.

Not that he wanted to leave. But the RAF ground their pilots at fifty, and rather than take up a desk job, Tiger had settled for a pension and the chance of staying in the pilot's seat. He now flew for a civilian helicopter company—executives to and from Battersea Heliport, well-to-do passengers to Ascot and Goodwood, bits of filming for TV companies, that sort of thing.

Wing Commander Wilson died the year after his son married, so he never saw his grandchildren. While Tiger's nickname had been bestowed as a mark of his father's fondness for the Tiger Moth, Tiger's own children's names—Aisling and Kirsty—were the product of his wife Erica's Scottish and Irish parentage.

So here he was. Sitting pretty with two pretty daughters away at uni. Still married, still flying helicopters, and quite comfortably off. And yet he knew that his best days were behind him. The days of high achievement. The days of excitement and hunger.

Maybe this was how it was supposed to be. Maybe you just had to get used to a gradual winding down. It was a thought that left him sometimes frightened and more often dispirited.

And that's why he had mentioned the secret society. Though, if he were honest, the moment he had done so he felt a bit of a fool.

'SO WHAT EXACTLY do you mean by a secret society?' Christopher Devon laid down a three and a two against Tiger's double three.

'I don't really know,' said Tiger, opening a packet of peanuts. 'It's just that it might be a bit of fun to try and make a difference, have a bit of excitement, instead of just whinging about things the whole time.'

Christopher looked at him sideways. 'I'd have thought you'd get enough excitement flying helicopters.'

'But that's just what I *do*. I want . . . something more out of life.'

Gary put down a five and two, then folded his arms. 'All right, then. We form a secret society. To do what exactly?'

Tiger frowned. 'I haven't quite worked that out yet.'

'I see,' said Christopher. 'We meet in secret and do secret things that we haven't quite worked out yet.'

'Look,' said Tiger, 'is it just me or is this a funny time of life?'

Christopher took a deep breath. 'I can tell you that medically it's not funny at all. It's very critical. When a man hits his fifties, all kinds of things start to happen. His sperm count goes down . . . his libido slackens . . . and things start to malfunction or drop off.'

'Not much to look forward to then!' said Tiger.

'Depends how you look at it,' replied Christopher.

Tiger asked, 'But all those years of experience, surely there must be some advantage to those?' There was a genuine note of concern in his voice. 'Other bits of us might be falling off but our minds are sharp as a razor, aren't they?' He tipped some peanuts into his hand and popped them into his mouth.

'In some ways, yes. Our reactions and reflexes are not quite what they were but our powers of reasoning are, in many cases, more well developed.'

'There you are then.'

'There I am what?' asked Christopher.

'Three men at the peak of their mental powers and all sidelined by society in favour of younger models.'

'Hey, watch who you're calling sidelined,' said Gary. 'You two might consider yourselves past it but as far as I'm concerned I haven't got there yet.'

'I hate to disabuse you of that conceit,' said Christopher, 'but clinically you are every bit as over the hill as we are.'

Gary raised his voice. 'Is it something in the beer or are you two on a right downer tonight?'

Christopher shrugged. 'Just offering you the benefit of my medical advice, that's all.'

Tiger laid down a double five and crumpled up the empty packet of nuts. 'Chips.'

'Jammy devil,' said Gary.

'Another one, gentlemen?' asked Christopher.

'Nah,' said Gary. 'I think I'll be off. All this talk about age has worn me out. And I've someone to meet tomorrow. Someone considerably younger than I am, who thinks that I'm pretty hot, actually.'

'Lucky you,' said Tiger.

'Yes, I am, aren't I?' Gary grinned. 'Dinner at that little restaurant down by the river, then, with any luck, back to my place. Or hers. I'm not fussy.'

'We know that,' said Christopher under his breath.

'Beats being married,' said Gary.

'How would you know?' asked Tiger.

'Yes, how would you know?' repeated Christopher, getting up from his seat and avoiding Gary's eye.

'Oh, sorry. You know what I mean. Sorry . . .'

TUCKED AWAY down the lane in a sleepy Hampshire village is a small, pleasantly proportioned Queen Anne manor house. The River Itchen runs past the end of its walled garden, which is peppered with ancient fruit trees that have romantic-sounding names like 'Devonshire Quarrenden' and 'Beauty of Bath', and in early summer the air is filled with the fragrance of old-fashioned roses, clove pinks and lavender. Idyllic.

Christopher Devon was left the house by a wealthy aunt. She knew he would appreciate the garden and the fact that it needed new life breathed into it, rather than being allowed to stagnate. He was a doctor. He understood about life. About renewal. And he was a gardener. He enjoyed the respite that tending plants gave him in between tending patients.

Daunted at first, Christopher had soon begun to relish the challenge that the garden presented. At weekends he would battle with brambles and briars and barrow in loads of manure from a nearby farm.

For twenty-six years Kate, his wife, was happy to do her bit of battling, too—with patients who made excessive demands, and with two children who had their own needs. They grew up all too fast and, at almost twenty-three, the girl went to Africa to do voluntary work, while the boy, a year younger, went to the States where he landed a job in publishing.

Ellie was her dad's girl. The one with the social conscience. Money and designer labels meant nothing to her. A simple soul with a skinny body and long blonde hair, she turned heads in a baggy T-shirt and combats, much to her father's amusement. Walking down the street with her on his arm he felt a million dollars. Always.

Matt was a different kettle of fish. Shy and diffident as a child, he had grown into a confident youth; confident, that is, in everything except his sexuality. Discovering your son is gay is never an easy thing for a father. Christopher tried to hide his disappointment and asked himself why he should be disappointed. Matt was creative, energetic, thoughtful and sensitive. Would being heterosexual have made him a better person?

Kate seemed to find it easier to cope. There was always a slight unease between father and son and Christopher felt it was his fault. Perhaps he should have offered more help—not that Matt ever asked for it. But they rubbed along and kept talking, and their respect for one another survived.

He missed both his children when they left. Always the first to rise in the mornings, he would walk into their rooms and open the curtains, then turn and see the empty beds, always with a stab of wistfulness.

The marriage to Kate had outlasted those of most of his friends—except Tiger. It had its quiet moments after close on thirty years, and there were days when it seemed routine, but the fact that they actually liked one another made up for the dissipation of that once magical attraction. Didn't it?

With her children off her hands and a husband who seemed to be married in turns to his surgery and his garden, Kate walked out. She was sorry, she said. She was still fond of him, but wanted more out of life than he seemed able or willing to give. And she wanted it while there was still time.

It came like a bolt from the blue. Christopher had no inkling at all of her unhappiness, and blamed himself for that. Offered to change. To spend more time with her. Asked what he could do to make amends. But to no avail. It never occurred to him that Kate might have found someone else.

There was no denying that her leaving affected his work, made him less tolerant. From being courteous and unflappable he had become irascible and tetchy. Those around him tried to make allowances, but Randall Cummings, the senior partner in the practice, felt obliged to have a word with him. And things seemed to be improving, until one day, out of nowhere, Cummings said that it would probably be best for everybody if Christopher left the practice.

Other colleagues were surprised not only at the senior partner's precipitate action, but also at Christopher's tacit acceptance of the decision. There was no farewell party. He just slipped quietly away. Preoccupied. Troubled.

Having devoted himself to medicine for the better part of his life he began to wonder what difference he had made. The raw energy that drove him on in his early days as a GP had gone. At the end he had found himself to be drowning in a sea of forms and regulations. That and loneliness. He tried not to wallow in it, but it had grown ever more enveloping since Kate's departure.

He could feel no bitterness towards her. Just profound sadness at his own myopic self-absorption that had forced her to leave—the long hours, the putting of patients' interests first, the weekends on call, the Christmas dinners interrupted. It had been all his fault. It must have been. Kate seemed apologetic when she left, but she had not kept in touch. He began to wonder if perhaps she had someone else to care about.

He had stayed on in the house—it was his only anchor—and decided to set about finding another position. But he was in his fifties. He had been scanning the *British Medical Journal* for six months and doing a bit of locum work, but nothing permanent had come along.

Ellie had suggested that he should try to get out more. Said that he should try to find female company. The idea appalled him. He had been a one-woman man. Never imagined that he would ever be 'on the market' again. And, anyway, where did you look if you wanted to find someone? He didn't want to join a club or a dating agency.

And so the blanket of loneliness enfolded him still further until one night, seated in front of his laptop and surfing the net, he typed in the word 'soulmate' to see what would come up.

The results surprised him, as did his actions. He had had three assignations. The first was with a voluptuous widow from Winchester who looked upon him as a personal physician. The second was with a timid librarian with an interest in gardening, and the third, and most unsettling, was with a nymphomaniac from Southampton who, having discovered the relative warmth of his house, began to divest herself of more than her opinion on the state of the nation. Next time he would heed the warning that first meetings should be on neutral ground.

Friday nights in the Hare and Hounds were not the sort of high spot that he had had in mind for his social life. But at least they were undemanding and pleasant. Tiger had enough enthusiasm to lift him out of the mire when he was feeling low and self-absorbed, and Gary was always good for a laugh.

As for himself, he was content for the moment to look after the orchids in his conservatory, and to try to put the worries of the past behind him. Spring was approaching, and a new year would, he hoped, bring a new lease of life. Maybe even someone to share it with. Someone normal, pleasant, loving. That above all. At fifty-five he could do with a bit of love.

FEW PEOPLE REALLY KNEW Gary Flynn. He made sure of that. He let people speculate on the nature of his employment without ever putting them straight. But that makes sense when you're in the intelligence service.

It would not have taken a first-rate sleuth to discover what this civil servant really did. Some days he went to the MI5 building on Millbank, and some days he did not. When he did go there he varied his route, just to be on the safe side. He was not an 'M' or a 'Q', or even a '007', but the fact that he worked where he worked, and that he saw what he saw, made him naturally cautious when it came to making friends.

And that included women. He had never had a lasting relationship. Had never really wanted one. He was frequently away, and often on business that had risky consequences, and you couldn't expect a woman to settle for that. Better to be a free agent.

His current operation involved monitoring the activities of a Chinese diplomat suspected of smuggling illegally acquired currency out of the country. At the moment any definite proof of such activity was lacking and the source of the illicit funding was uncertain, but the next time Tan Lao Sok tried to leave the UK, Gary would be standing in his way.

In the gym, in the basement of the MI5 building, Gary mused on the likely events of the next few days. Sweat poured off his brow as he pulled at the oars on the rowing machine. The prospect of catching his quarry with the currency did give him a frisson of excitement. Most smuggling operations today involved Internet banking fraud, and it was the Serious Fraud Office and Customs and Excise who took charge. But the diplomatic post held by Mr Tan meant MI5 involvement, which was why Gary was on the case.

He showered and changed, then went back upstairs to his desk and flicked through the *Independent*. His mind drifted back to the Friday-night dominoes and Tiger's suggestion that they form a secret society. He could not help but smile. If only they knew. Then his eye lighted on an article in the business section about the performance of an ever-expanding chain of Chinese restaurants. They were celebrating the opening of yet another of their successful eateries under the banner of the 'Red Dragon'. Gary looked at the caption below the photo and felt a dart of tension. The new restaurant was in Winchester, and standing next to the owner of this particular franchise, smiling at the camera, was Mr Tan. The devil on his doorstep.

Chapter Two

My wife, who, poor wretch, is troubled with her lonely life.
Diary, December 19, 1662, Samuel Pepys (1633–1703)

The roar of the engines intensified as the helicopter rose gently into the hover. At fifteen feet Tiger eased the stick forward and powered away into the blue. His passenger, a dyspeptic-looking businessman en route for City Airport, grabbed at a handle above his head as the helicopter surged forward with its nose tipping downwards.

At 200 feet the Hampshire countryside opened out beneath them. On this clear, still day the tributaries of the River Test glittered in the early-morning sunlight like silver ribbons. Fresh green fields of youthful wheat were spread like emerald velvet between the hedgerows, and everywhere there were great sprawling cushions of purple-grey woodland. The businessman had settled down to enjoy the view and, apart from keeping in contact with air traffic control, Tiger said little, happy to start the day quietly.

It took just forty minutes to get to City Airport, and having put down on the Tarmac, Tiger escorted his passenger to the small departure lounge and said goodbye. Today was a rarity. A neat dovetailing. Instead of flying back empty he was to return with another passenger. A woman. Glancing around the lounge he spotted only three likely candidates: a City type with an attaché case, a power-dressed businesswoman, and Kate Devon.

'Hello, Tiger.' She looked at him apologetically.

'Kate! What are you doing here?'

'Waiting for you, I suppose. Waiting for a helicopter anyway.'

'Where are you expecting to go?'

'Southampton Airport.'

'Well, yes, I'm your man then.' Tiger picked up her smart Mulberry holdall and gestured towards the door. 'How are you?'

'Oh, you know. Battling on.'

Her lack of enthusiasm surprised him. Her customary fizz was absent and she seemed weary as they walked across the Tarmac. Eventually Tiger asked, 'How long has it been now?'

'Eighteen months.'

'As long as that?'

Kate nodded.

'And how are . . . things?'

'OK. Good days and bad days. Up and down. It's never easy, is it? After such a long time. But I made my bed and now . . .' She shrugged.

'Oh dear.'

'No. Not really oh dear.'

'No regrets, then?'

'Of course I have regrets. Regrets that my children have split loyalties. Regrets that I couldn't be content with what I had.'

Tiger stowed her bag in the locker at the side of the aircraft, then opened the door and helped her into the passenger seat. She was smartly dressed in a dark brown trouser suit, her hair cut into a neat bob.

She and Christopher had always been an attractive couple: Kate with her ravishing blonde hair and designer clothes, and Christopher, tall and fair with a smile that made women go weak at the knees.

Tiger closed the door and went round to the other side to climb into his own seat. As he did so he noticed her hands. They were as neatly manicured as ever, but there was more jewellery about her now. He glanced at the large diamond ring on Kate's third finger.

'It's on my right hand,' she said.

Tiger was momentarily embarrassed.

'You can ask, you know,' said Kate.

'I didn't like to.'

'He's a businessman. Quite well off. Very attentive. We travel a lot—LA, New York, Frankfurt.'

'Goodness.'

Tiger checked his instruments and started up the engine. He handed Kate a pair of earphones and then asked for clearance to take off.

While they waited he asked, 'So what does he do?'

'Howie? He's in real estate.'

'An estate agent?'

'He's American. A realtor. Buys and sells commercial properties. We met at a singles club.' She looked across at Tiger. 'It wasn't planned. It just gradually sort of grew.'

'*Windjammer Three* cleared for take off,' came the message over the radio, and Tiger turned his attention to the controls in front of him. As the helicopter rose from the Tarmac, he manoeuvred it into a neat pirouette. They lifted higher still and then cut a graceful arc out towards the west.

His flight adjustments completed, he asked, 'Where are you living now?'

'Rome, mostly. It's a wonderful city.'

'Romantic,' said Tiger.

Kate did not reply, but gazed out across the grey London skyline.

'So where are you off to now?' He asked it more as a way of filling the uneasy silence than anything else.

'Back to Rome. Howie's meeting me at Southampton. He likes to fly from there. Quieter.'

'I know what he means.'

Kate's melancholy mood was not what Tiger would have expected. When she was married to Christopher she was vibrant and lively, always exuding an air of bright capability.

He and Erica had seen it coming. The break up. But what could you do? It would be easy to say that Christopher had been selfish about his career, but when that career was concerned with the welfare of the rest of the human race it made a mockery of the usual 'self-centred' accusations levelled at workaholics.

Kate Devon and Erica Wilson had been good friends. They'd opened a small bookshop in Winchester, specialising in topography and travel. Now Erica ran the shop alone, with a bit of part-time help.

It was as though she read his mind. 'Funny, isn't it?' she asked through the microphone linked to Tiger's headset. 'All those books packed full of dreams and now I'm realising them.' Kate turned away to look out of the window and he saw her brush at her cheek with the back of her hand.

They spoke little for the next half-hour and then Tiger began to circle the airport before finally lowering the craft gently onto the apron.

'It's been good to see you again,' Kate said, as they walked across to the terminal building. 'Give my love to Erica. Tell her I miss her.' Then she kissed him lightly on the cheek, smiled, and was gone.

'DR DEVON, YOUR LUNCH is ready!'

'Coming! I won't be a minute.' From the top of the house he could hear the call from the kitchen. He addressed the envelope, peeled a stamp from the book and stuck it on the letter ready for posting.

'It's going cold, Dr Devon!' The tone was more insistent.

'I'm on my way.' He tramped downstairs with the letter, wishing that he could be allowed to get his own lunch. Luisa was sixty-odd, Italian and irritable, and he really only wanted her to do a bit of cleaning, but she insisted on preparing him a plate of pasta on the days he was at home. Always pasta, with something in it. He was never quite sure what. It was glutinous and uninspiring. Food with a flavour bypass.

With any luck she would go before he had finished it and he could consign it to the bin and get a mini pork pie from the fridge and an apple from the bowl. That would do nicely.

He sat down at the table and managed a weak smile. 'Thank you, Mrs Bassani. Pasta. How nice.'

'Your favourite!' she beamed, handing him a spoon and fork.

'Now, Dr Devon'—she pronounced his name with a rolling 'r' at the end of the doctor bit—'I have some bad news for you.'

He looked up. 'Oh dear.'

'I am going away.'

He tried his best to look crestfallen. 'Oh?'

'Yes. I am going away for two weeks.'

'Oh dear.'

'But I make, how you say . . . provision?'

'Now, Mrs Bassani, there really is no need . . . I'm sure I can manage without any . . . provision.'

'Oh yes? And who will wash and who will iron and who will make sure you are well fed?'

She stood with her hands on her broad hips, a white apron over her black cardigan and skirt, a caricature of the archetypal Italian mamma.

'Mrs Bassani, if I can't manage for two weeks . . .'

'It may be more. I not sure.'

Christopher knew that this was his last hope of freedom. 'You mustn't worry yourself, Mrs Bassani. I've been thinking about things and—'

'Is all sorted.' Mrs Bassani made it clear that there was no room for further negotiation.

'Sorry?'

'My daughter Maria. She start on Monday.'

'But, Mrs Bassani, that really won't be necessary. I—'

'You no want my daughter?'

'Well, it's not that I don't want her, I—'

'Good. That's all sorted then. Maria start on Monday. She clean and wash and she make you lunch when you are here. Her cooking is—how you say?—no great shakes . . . but she very willing and happy to learn.'

Christopher felt himself drowning in the futility of it all. He thought the mother's cooking was bad enough, but if the daughter's was worse . . .

Mrs Bassani was taking off her apron. 'Don't worry about my wages. You just give to Maria. She use them for food. And as she not such good cook, she only charge five pound an hour instead of eight. OK?'

With a mouth full of pasta Christopher Devon could only nod and move his eyes in mute agreement.

'Good. I have changed bedding and ironed shirts. Milk in fridge and food for weekend. Be good, Dr Devon!'

And with that she pulled on her thick black coat and walked out of the kitchen towards her car. As the little Fiat with the round lady at the helm pulled out of the drive, the good doctor put down the fork and spoon and got up from the table in search of the pork pie and the apple.

GARY WAS LOOKING out of the window at the River Thames. His boss was sitting behind a large desk, his head resting on his hands.

'So what now?'

Gary turned round. 'Steady nerves. I don't want to rush it. We know from experience that he doesn't rush things himself. He won't be going back to China straight away if previous trips are anything to go by.'

'Well, he wasn't due back in the UK until next week, so supposing he's changed his system?'

Gary considered the question and tapped lightly on the window ledge with his fingertips. 'Unlikely. He can offload quickly at the other end, but he still needs the time to gather funds at this end. I can't see him leaving us again for a while. The important thing is that he mustn't get even a whiff of the fact that we're on to him. The moment that happens he'll go to ground.'

'So why didn't we get him before he made the last trip?'

'We weren't confident he was in possession and we're still not sure where the funds come from. I want to be certain of both. If we mess it up we're back to square one.'

His boss straightened up in his chair then asked, 'You do think it's worth all this trouble for the amount of money he's smuggling out?'

'Oh, yes. The money is something concrete that we can get him on. But I'm pretty sure there's more to it than currency smuggling. We need him to lead us to others before we jump on him. There are all kinds of strange things going on now, with the Chinese economy ballooning like it is.'

'Do you need more help?' his boss asked wearily.

'Not for now. I'll carry on with Sarah and I've got Ben Atkinson doing the foot slogging. I might need some more muscle later on, but I think we can manage.'

'I've heard you say that before. Just make sure that as soon as you think you're getting out of your depth you call for reinforcements. No heroics.'

'OK.' Gary walked towards the door.

'And keep me informed.'

'I will.' He closed the door behind him and murmured, 'Most of the time.'

'So?' Sarah Perry sat on the edge of her desk, dangling her legs.

'I've made sure he knows we can't rush it,' said Gary. 'I think I've bought us a bit more time.'

'And more help?'

'No. I've said we we're fine for now. If Ben can keep providing us with intelligence I thought you and I could manage.'

Sarah frowned. 'As long as you think we can cope.'

Gary grinned at her and looked at the long legs, encased in their black-patterned tights, the short skirt, the tight black sweater and the shiny dark brown hair. 'Oh, I think I can cope.'

Sarah grinned back. 'Oh, you wish, Mr Flynn! You wish!'

Gary sighed. 'Yes, well, it's not for want of trying. Anyway, as long as you keep fending me off at least our working relationship isn't compromised. Though why that should be an advantage I can't think.'

Sarah slipped down off the desk and moved across to the water machine. He watched her sinuous walk with a stab of pleasure.

'So what's next?'

'Mmm?' He was miles away. On some beach. Lying next to her.

'I said, what's next?'

'Right. Yes. We need to find out where the money's coming from and when and how it's leaving the country. And to do that we need some sort of strategy.'

'Meaning?'

Gary smiled. 'Meaning we shall have to see rather a lot of each other over the next few days.'

Sarah screwed up her face. 'Oh, lucky me.'

'DO YOU WANT this bath or not?'

Erica Wilson was sitting on the edge of the tub. She was swathed in a white towel, her long brown hair combed back from her face.

'If you like.' Tiger put his head round the bathroom door. 'I remember when we used to share them.'

'Oh, don't start that. You can share them with me now if you want except that you're always too busy doing something else.' She wiped a trickle of water from her forehead with the edge of the towel.

Tiger eyed her up proprietorially. She played tennis three times a week in between running the shop, and the regular exercise kept her in good trim.

'You look very tantalising sitting there,' Tiger said as he pulled his shirt over his head.

'Bet you say that to all the girls.'

'Nope. Just the one.' He slipped off the rest of his clothes and slid into the tub.

'Well, you're not in such bad shape yourself, Mr Wilson.' She surveyed him over the rim of the bath. 'You've still got all your hair and your body's in a tolerable state. Not bad for a man of advancing years.'

'Do you mind! I'm a bit sensitive about my advancing years.'

'Why's that? Feeling your age?'

Tiger frowned. 'A bit.'

'Aches and pains?'

'No. Just . . . in other ways.'

A look of concern flickered across her face. 'Is it me?'

He lifted his hand and laid it on her arm. 'No. It's not you.'

'What then?'

'Oh, I was just thinking. You get married because you want to be together, because you just want each other. And then children come along and it all changes. You try your best to make sure that you still care for each other, that you give each other time, and yet it all gets a bit diluted. You're so busy sorting the kids out, worrying about them, ferrying them here and there—they become the entire focus of your life. Then they go and suddenly you're on your own again. You still worry about them—more if anything—but you can't really do anything constructive. So you have to pick up the pieces and start all over again with each other.'

'Is that what it feels like?' she asked. 'Starting all over again?'

'Not completely. You're sort of starting from a different place. Can you see what I mean?'

'I suppose it happens to every couple with kids.'

'Those that are still together. By the way, I saw Kate Devon today.'

The introspective mood was broken. Probably, thought Tiger, for the better. 'What?' Erica was surprised. 'Where?'

'I had to fly her from the City Airport to Southampton.'

'Well . . . what did she say? What did she look like? Was she with a man?'

'Er, answering those one at a time, she said very little, looked stunning—dripping with gold—and was on her way to meet her man, who's called Howie and who's clearly not without a bob or two.'

'Oh, poor Christopher. I'd always hoped they'd get back together.'

'Yes.' Tiger paused. 'I wonder if I should tell Christopher about Howie.'

'He probably knows.'

'He never says anything. Never mentions Kate at all. It's as if she didn't exist.' Tiger handed her the bar of soap. 'Do my back?'

'Go on!' She pushed him forward and began to soap his shoulders.

'I was talking to Christopher and Gary at the pub. About . . . this feeling. Well, that you can't make much of a difference any more.'

'Is that how they feel as well?'

'I think so. They won't admit it—but I'm pretty sure they do.'

'And?'

'Well, I had this daft idea.'

'How daft?'

'You'll laugh.'

'Try me.'

'I said we should form a secret society. You know, to right wrongs and generally make a difference.'

Erica carried on washing his back. 'Like Robin Hood?'

'A bit. But without anybody knowing. I haven't really thought it through. Do you think I'm crackers?'

'Oh, yes. But then I've always thought you were crackers.'

'So it's a daft idea?'

'Yes.'

'And I shouldn't pursue it?'

'I didn't say that.' She looked at him; picking up on the earlier part of the conversation. 'You *are* still happy, aren't you? I mean, with us?'

He hesitated for the tiniest split second. 'Of course I am. Like you said, it must be just my time of life, that's all. It makes you take stock.'

Chapter Three

I have always depended on the kindness of strangers.
A Streetcar Named Desire, Tennessee Williams (1911–1983)

The city of Winchester lies in the valley of the River Itchen. It is handsome and airy, as cities go, and more of a town in terms of its size. Approaching from the east, you can see it lying peacefully in the valley below, snoozing in the summer sun, or hunkered down to avoid the bitter winter winds. The pale buff-grey Norman cathedral dominates not just the green close that surrounds it, but this entire section of the broad valley through which the trout-rich Itchen snakes its way.

The Adventure Bookshop was tucked away down an alleyway that ran off the cathedral close—a small double-fronted shop with Georgian windows. Erica rented the ground floor—there were flats above—and there was just enough room for a kitchenette and loo at the back of the shop, and a small stockroom, though most of the stock resided on floor-to-ceiling shelves.

Today was unlikely to be busy. There were a few new titles to unpack, but Erica was looking forward to a quiet time. Her tennis match was booked in at three and she could be well sorted by then, leaving Brian, the rather wet but willing student, to hold the fort for the rest of the afternoon.

It was at around 11 a.m. that an insignificant-looking man in a black anorak, and carrying a black holdall, entered the shop. He wandered up and down the shelves, clearly preoccupied.

Erica nodded at Brian to keep an eye. The man was shoplifter material.

The only other customer in the shop came to the counter with a copy of James Morris's *Venice*. 'You'll enjoy that,' said Erica, slipping it into a bag but barely taking her eyes off the man in black.

The customer thanked her and left. Then, as if he had been waiting to have the shop to himself, the man came up to the counter. Erica didn't like the look of him much. He was quite neat, scrubbed even, but there was something about him that seemed shifty. She asked pointedly, 'Can I help you?'

'Well, it's more how I can help you,' replied the man. 'I represent the local cooperative business venture.'

Erica looked puzzled. 'I don't think I've ever heard of it.' She glanced sideways at Brian who shrugged.

Unabashed, the man continued. 'We are a consortium of local businesses who pool resources, such as business expertise, contacts and insurance, for mutual benefit. We have quite a lot of traders on board now and they all know that it makes sense to pull together.'

Erica didn't want to appear obstructive. 'Is it something to do with the local Chamber of Commerce?'

'Not exactly. Sort of affiliated but not a part of, if you see what I mean.'

'Well, what does it involve? I'm not sure I have the time for any more commitments, you see.' Erica was hopeful of getting rid of him.

'Oh, it will take none of your time at all. Just a contribution once a month.' He turned and looked around the shop. 'In your case I should think we'd be talking in terms of around one hundred pounds a month.'

'A hundred pounds a month!' Erica laughed. 'I'm afraid that in my case I don't have the sort of profits that would enable me to pay that.'

'I'm sure we could come to some arrangement,' said the man.

'I really don't think—'

They were interrupted by the pinging of the door bell, and a mother with two small children clattered into the shop. The man stepped back from the counter. 'I'll let you think about it. I'll pop back in a day or two.'

'No. Really, there's no need. I don't think it's for me.'

The man edged round the mother and children, as if afraid to touch them, and backed out of the door, smiling nervously.

'Well,' said Erica to Brian, 'what do you make of that?'

Brian shrugged. Some days it seemed that all Brian ever did was shrug. Asking him to hold the fort for a few minutes, Erica went out, turned left and pushed open the door of the Belgian chocolate shop.

Isobel, the jolly, spherical lady who presided over the stacked counters of rose and violet creams, bitter chocolate orange-peel sticks and bespoke bonbons was busy, as usual, arranging her handmade sweetmeats in small gold boxes to be tied with scarlet ribbon.

She looked up from the lacy frills of her apron straps and said, 'Hello, Erica. Can we tempt you?'

'Not today, Isobel. I'm playing tennis this afternoon. I came to ask if you'd just had that man in?'

'What man, dear?' Isobel went back to putting her chocolates into their little boxes.

'The one in the black anorak. To do with some cooperative or other.'

'Oh, him. Yes.' Isobel stopped what she was doing. 'Didn't like him at all.' Isobel looked serious. 'He asked me about joining his cooperative. It was quite ridiculous. He wanted a hundred and fifty pounds a month! Well, I mean that's just silly isn't it, dear? I couldn't possibly afford that.'

'So what did you say?'

'I sent him packing with a flea in his ear, I'm afraid. I don't like to be rude but he was so persistent, and to be perfectly honest, Erica, I was getting a bit rattled. He didn't seem to take no for an answer.'

'Yes, I know.'

Isobel asked, 'Did you join his cooperative, then?'

'No,' replied Erica, distractedly. 'No, I didn't. But he said he'd come back, so I don't think he's given up on me.'

'Oh dear! Well, good luck. And if you take my advice you'll do what I did and tell him where to get off next time.'

'Yes. Yes, I will. I'll tell him where to get off.'

CHRISTOPHER DEVON had one last patient to see at the surgery before making his house calls. He was doing some locum work in a practice in Romsey and was surprised when a young mother he'd known from his Winchester surgery walked in with her five-year-old daughter.

'Mrs Fraser. How lovely to see you. But what are you doing down here?'

The mother looked slightly embarrassed. 'Oh, we moved, Doctor.'

'Hello, Daisy. How are you?' asked Christopher.

Daisy managed a smile before attempting to hide behind her mother.

'Well, how nice to see you both. What can I do for you, Mrs Fraser?'

'Nothing really, Doctor. I spoke to reception and they said I could just pop in after surgery to say thank you.'

'Oh?'

'About Richard.'

'But . . .'

'I know it all went wrong in the end, but I know you did your best. You made his life as comfortable as you could. We just wanted to say thank you for all you did. And we never got a chance to, what with you leaving.'

'No. No, I'm sorry about that.'

Mrs Fraser was a good-looking woman in her early thirties. Her husband had been a strapping farmer who had developed kidney trouble. They had been unable to procure him a new kidney and, two years later, Richard Fraser had died, leaving a widow and three children under the age of seven.

Christopher was back there for a moment, back in the bleakness of it all. Remembering the frustration and the anger he felt with himself for not being able to make a difference. For not getting Richard Fraser a kidney and for not taking more of a stand against those who were unwilling to help. If he had done, wouldn't Richard Fraser be alive now? Mrs Fraser cleared her throat, and he came back to the present with a start. 'But are things looking up now that you've moved down here?'

'Yes, thank you, Doctor.'

'So where are you living now?'

'In Wellow. One of the little villages.' She looked reflective for a moment, then gathered her thoughts. 'Anyway, Dr Devon, I don't want to take up any more of your time. But thank you so much. You made it all more bearable.'

'Oh, Mrs Fraser . . .'

'No, really, you did. I don't know how we'd have coped without you. Anyway, Daisy's brought you a thank-you letter, haven't you Daisy?'

The child nodded, then reached into her mother's basket and pulled out an envelope that was addressed in a childish scrawl: *To Docter Deven.*

'Thank you, Daisy. That's very kind.' He laid the envelope on his desk.

'We'll be going now then. Come on Daisy.' Christopher stood up as Mrs Fraser took Daisy's hand and walked her towards the door. Then she turned. 'I do hope everything turns out all right for you, Doctor.'

'Thank you, Mrs Fraser.'

With more murmured words, the mother and daughter left the surgery and closed the door behind them.

Christopher sat down heavily in his chair, considering the twists of fate that could deprive a thirty-year-old mother of her husband and three young children of their father. He picked up the envelope and turned it over in his hand. It had been decorated with brightly coloured flowers. He used a knife to slit open the flap and pulled out the homemade card. It showed a man in brown trousers and a white shirt holding a bucket. He was standing next to a black and white cow in a green meadow dotted with yellow flowers. Above them, in the middle of a blue sky decorated with fluffy white clouds made of stuck-on bits of cotton wool was an angel with golden wings.

He opened the card and read the simple legend inside: *Docter Deven—My Hero—Love Daisy xxx.*

He laid the card on the desk, leaned forward on his arms and wept.

'SO, HAVE WE any idea where they get the money from?' Sarah Perry was leaning forward on a small sofa in a corner of the office at MI5.

'Not yet, no,' said Gary. 'I mean, this could just be some bit of diplomatic PR.' He pointed at the newspaper picture of Mr Tan. 'You know, doing his bit for Anglo-Chinese relations. I can't think it's from restaurant tips.'

'What do we know about Red Dragon?' asked Sarah.

'They opened their first restaurant in Canterbury in 2001, then around half a dozen others every year since then. They now have twenty-eight of them across the south. I've run a check and the business seems to be above board—no dodgy accounts or anything like that.'

She raised her head. 'Have you ever eaten in one?'

'No. But this one's just round the corner from me,' he said, tapping the paper.

'Could we risk going for a meal there?' she asked. 'It might be useful to get the feel of the place.'

Gary beamed at her. 'Are you asking me out to dinner?'

'Yes, but not in the way you think. This is purely a business arrangement.'

'So when's our date, then?'

'If you start calling it that there won't be one. Tomorrow night? I can't manage tonight because Max is taking me to see some art-house movie.'

'His choice or yours?'

'Oh, his. I'm not into Japanese stuff. Give me Katharine Hepburn any day.' She got up and walked to the hat stand to collect her coat.

Gary watched her as she reached up for her scarf. She really did have a figure to die for. He cleared his throat. 'Right.'

She turned, putting on her coat. 'So if we go straight from here tomorrow evening, then?'

'Yes. Fine. I'll ring up and book. What time shall I say?'

'Well, if we said a table for eight thirty? We could take our time then and just see if there are any comings and goings during the evening.'

'Yes. OK, then.'

'Take care. See you tomorrow morning.' She lifted her black satchel onto her shoulder and glided out of the office.

He shook his head, wondering if he stood the remotest chance of getting anywhere with her. He caught sight of his reflection in the dark glass of the office next door. It quite surprised him. He looked younger than usual. And he was only just fifty. And she was nearly forty. He laughed out loud; a lone, solitary laugh. Then he grabbed his leather jacket and turned out the lights.

IT WAS ONLY because Tiger had no work that morning that he walked Erica to the bookshop. Otherwise she would have made the discovery on her own.

It was a warm, clear morning. Unseasonably mild. They crossed the cathedral close holding hands, looking up at the grey building as a bell struck the quarter, and Tiger looked at his watch. 'It's a minute fast.'

'If it's all the same to you I'd rather live by cathedral time than Omega time.'

'Yes, well you can't run an airline on cathedral time.'

The conversation stopped when they rounded the corner of the alley and saw Isobel sweeping up broken glass. Erica broke away from Tiger and dashed up to her. 'Isobel, whatever's happened? Have you had an accident?'

'No, dear,' Isobel was close to tears, 'not an accident at all. Quite intentional. Look . . .' Shards of glass lay on the pavement and among the display boxes of artificial chocolates that were piled up in the window.

'Vandals. Ruddy vandals.' Tiger stepped forward to assess the damage. In the middle of the display was a single brick. He turned to Isobel. 'Have you called the police?'

'Oh, they've been and gone, dear. I asked them if they wanted to take fingerprints but they didn't seem interested. So much of it going on at the moment, apparently. Unless they catch the culprits red-handed there's little chance of them ever finding out who did it.'

Tiger shook his head, then turned to take the brush from Isobel. 'You go and have a coffee with Erica, I'll finish clearing this up and then we'd better see about getting your window replaced. I'll give the glaziers a call.'

'Thank you, Tiger. Thank you so much.' Then Isobel burst into tears.

The distraught Isobel was taken into the kitchen of Erica's shop while Tiger assessed the damage. The glass was gone, and the window dressing destroyed, but the carved wooden uprights were intact. Poor Isobel. Why did they always have to do it to the nicest people? People whose lives would be turned upside down by one mindless act.

CHRISTOPHER DEVON PUT ON old clothes, wolfed down a bowl of porridge and went out into the garden. He had the day off. He would work out there for as long as he could. Put aside his worries and fill his mind with rose pruning, snowdrop dividing, revitalising borders and tidying flowerbeds.

He was bent double between 'Madame Pierre Oger' and 'Madame Alfred Carrière' when he heard the voice calling him.

'Dr Devon! Excuse me! Dr Devon!'

He stood up, unhooked the sleeve of his sweater from a thorn, picked his way out of the border and walked across the lawn to where she stood.

She was a small, good-looking woman in her forties, with short dark hair and delicate, expressive features. She was wearing fitted jeans and a baggy sweater and didn't seem to have the manner of most people who came to the door—ladies conducting market research.

'I'm afraid I don't do surveys or anything like that,' said Christopher.

A look of amusement crossed her face. 'I'm glad to hear it. Neither do I.'

She spoke perfect English, but something about her helped him make the connection. 'Oh goodness! Are you Maria?'

'Yes. I'm sorry. I didn't mean to disturb you. I've come to sort you out.' The words were innocently prophetic.

'No. That's all right. Only you don't . . . I mean . . .'

'I don't look like my mother? No!'

He considered whether it was a good idea to try and ingratiate himself further, but thought better of it. 'Well . . . hello.' He offered his hand, and for the first time in many years experienced a faint feeling of shyness.

She shook his hand firmly and smiled. 'I'll try not to get in your way.'

'Oh, don't worry about that. Do you . . . would you like a coffee?'

She seemed very relaxed, which surprised him. It was not an accusation that could ever be levelled at her mother. He reproached himself for wondering how such a plain mother could have given birth to such a beautiful daughter, and put the uncharitable thought out of his head.

'I was saying to Luisa—er . . . your mum—that I don't really need quite the looking after she seems to think I do.'

'Oh? She just told me to keep the house clean, to do the washing and ironing and to make sure you had lunch when you were at home.'

'I see.'

He made the coffee and polite conversation. He should have told her he didn't want lunch, but somehow he didn't get round to it.

'Shall we start upstairs?' he asked. Then realised the *double entendre*. 'I mean . . .'

'Yes, then we can work our way down,' she said, with a smile.

He showed her the bedrooms and bathrooms, then his own study on the top floor. 'Far too messy. You won't be able to do much in here.'

Maria looked around at the pale, book-lined shelves that lined the wall. 'You like opera?' she asked, pointing at the fat volume of Kobbé.

'Some. Not all. Puccini and Verdi. Some Mozart. One Wagner.'

'Which one?'

'*Meistersingers*.'

Maria nodded. 'That's the only one I can take, too.'

Christopher laughed, and a ray of sunlight beamed in at the window. Maria looked out over the garden. 'Wow! Who does that?'

'Er . . . I do, actually.'

'I see.' She looked out again, at the lawns and the beds, but said nothing.

'Shall we go downstairs, then?' Christopher gestured towards the door.

They toured the ground floor—sitting room, dining room, hallway and utility room, and quite before he knew where he was they were sitting down having lunch together. Not pasta. Not a pork pie and an apple. Instead slices of melon and Parma ham, roasted peppers, olives and ciabatta.

She listened quietly while he explained his modest requirements—a bit of dusting, but not in the study; vacuuming the floors, turfing out the old newspapers, doing a spot of washing and ironing and keeping fresh flowers on the hall table. He felt embarrassed about this last request; especially when she smiled and looked at him with her head cocked at a slight angle.

'Sorry. Is that a bit much?'

She shook her head. 'Not at all. I think it's rather fine.'

Rather fine. He liked that turn of phrase. Not 'OK', but 'rather fine'.

'And lunch when you are at home?' she asked.

He hesitated. 'That would be very nice. If it's not too much trouble.'

'Oh, it's no trouble,' said Maria. 'No trouble at all.'

THREE MEALS were enjoyed that night. Christopher Devon ate at home, and Tiger and Erica dined, unexpectedly, in the company of Gary and Sarah.

The Wilsons arrived a little before the MI5 contingent, having promised themselves that after their recent excitement they would treat themselves and try the new Chinese restaurant. They were shown to a corner table by a waitress in a gold-edged black silk dress with a generous slit up the side.

Erica noticed the sparkle in Tiger's eye and dug him in the ribs. 'Do you mind not being quite so obvious.'

'Well, I haven't seen anything like that since I flew Singapore Airlines. And that was before I met you.'

'Well, you've met me now, so be careful. Anyway, what do you think?'

Tiger looked around at the interior of the Red Dragon. 'It's smarter than your usual Chinese,' he said.

The walls and ceiling were painted black, the picture and dado rails of the old Georgian building were gilded, and black paper lanterns hung from the ceiling, each one emblazoned with a rampant red dragon. The walls were hung with black-and-white photographs of modern Chinese cities.

'Very classy,' confirmed Erica.

'As long as we don't have to use chopsticks,' muttered Tiger.

'Dr Cummings isn't,' offered Erica, tilting her head in the direction of the fat, grey-haired man sitting in the far corner of the restaurant. A Chinese gentleman sat opposite him, nodding as the doctor spoke softly.

'Adding this lot to his list of patients, is he?' asked Tiger with an edge to his voice.

'You don't like him, do you?'

'Not much. Not since he gave Christopher the push. He should have been more understanding. As if Christopher hadn't been through enough.'

Their conversation was curtailed by the return of the waitress bearing a small lacquer tray on which were unidentifiable Chinese canapés. She laid it down on their table with a bow, and asked what they would like to drink.

Tiger was about to suggest two halves of lager when Erica cut in and asked for a bottle of chilled Sancerre. The waitress bowed once more, and went off in the direction of the kitchen, returning only moments later with the bottle, pleasingly coated with condensation, and two shapely glasses.

Only four tables were occupied, out of a total of about twenty. 'It's a bit quiet,' said Tiger, looking around.

'Oh, it's early yet. I expect most folk come at around half past eight.'

Erica was not wrong. Within ten minutes a steady trickle of diners had arrived and the restaurant began to fill up. At eight thirty-five Tiger said, 'Good God! Look over there.'

Erica turned in the direction of Tiger's gaze and saw Gary Flynn being shown to a table, along with a slim, dark-haired girl.

Tiger said, with a little too much interest for Erica's liking, 'Who on earth is that with Gary?'

'You could always go and ask him,' said Erica, popping one of the hors d'oeuvres into her mouth and giving Tiger a withering look.

'Yes. I'd better say hello, or he'll only tell me off later.'

Before Erica could waylay him with a restraining arm, Tiger had risen from the table. He walked across to where Gary and Sarah were seated and said, 'Are you trying it out as well, then?'

He was rather disappointed at Gary's reaction. If he hadn't known better he'd have said that Gary wasn't pleased to see him.

'Hi. Yes. Thought we'd give it a try.' He spoke softly and without any apparent enthusiasm.

Tiger turned to Sarah. 'Hi! I'm Tiger, Gary's mate.' He offered his hand.

Sarah shook it and smiled, darting a look across at Gary as she did so.

Tiger read the signals. 'Sorry. Didn't want to muscle in. Just thought I'd better say hello. You know.'

Gary did his best to make amends. 'Sure. Sarah's from . . . Sarah's a friend. We just thought we'd try it out. New place and all that.'

'Yes. Right. Well, enjoy your evening.' Tiger nodded, hesitated, smiled apologetically and then made his way back across the restaurant. He sat down opposite Erica and picked up his napkin. 'That was a bit frosty.'

'I'm not surprised.'

'What do you mean?'

'Here's Gary, come for a romantic night out *à deux*, and one of his beer-drinking dominoes partners lurches over and introduces himself.'

'I didn't lurch over.'

'You know what I mean.' Erica glanced in Gary's direction. 'Anyway, she does look rather nice. Very classy.'

'Yes,' said Tiger wistfully. 'I was never sure whether he was bullshitting us with all this talk about his sex life. Perhaps it wasn't made up after all.'

'A meal in a restaurant with a pretty girl doesn't necessarily mean he's . . .'

Tiger grinned at her. 'No?'

'SORRY ABOUT THAT.' Gary filled Sarah in on the identity of their visitor and explained that they had known each other for a few years. Did a bit of sport together. He didn't say what. Then he changed the subject. 'Looks a cut above your usual Chinese takeaway.'

'Yes. Very smart,' confirmed Sarah.

Gary looked across at her, beautiful and shining in her cream sweater and black trousers. But she was preoccupied. Not her usual bouncy self.

'Are you all right?' he asked, after the waitress had brought the wine.

'Yes, fine,' she answered, avoiding his eye.

'No, you're not. I know when you're not right. What's wrong?'

Sarah shook her head and turned away, and he saw her eyes fill with tears.

'Is it me? Is it something I've said?'

She shook her head again and tried to smile. 'No, it's not you. It's just . . .'

He offered her a napkin, and she dabbed at her tears.

'Is it Max?'

Sarah nodded, and turned away again. 'Silly. Not worth it. Told me last night. Someone else. Not me any more.'

Gary murmured platitudes of the 'better off without him' variety, and did his best not to be too hard in his criticism of a man who clearly did not know a goddess when she came up and bit him. He tried to jolly her out of it, and she seemed to respond. 'Are you hungry?' he asked eventually.

'Not really, but it seems rude not to eat.'

'Anything special, or do you want me to order?' he asked helpfully.

'Oh, anything. I don't really mind.' She began to pull herself together. 'I'm sorry. Didn't mean to bring my private life to work.'

'It's not work exactly, is it?' he asked with just a note of hope in his voice.

She gave him a look that put him in his place. Firm enough but, he hoped, with just a hint of kindness.

He beckoned the waitress to their table, gave the order and then leaned back and looked around. 'They've not stinted themselves, have they?'

'No. Boat certainly pushed out. And they have thirty-odd like this?'

'Apparently. Same sort of livery for each one. Not done on a shoestring.'

'And there's nobody here you recognise?' Sarah asked.

'Well, not apart from Tiger and Erica, no.'

'Hardly surprising, I suppose. I should think Mr Tan makes a point of not dining in the same place twice. But what about any associates?' Sarah scanned the room unobtrusively.

'Doesn't look like there are any here.'

'No. Maybe we're wasting our time.'

'Oh, I don't think so,' said Gary. 'Time spent doing things like this is never wasted.' He was pleased she didn't see what he was getting at.

'WOW! IT'S HIM!'

'What?' Tiger was dealing with a particularly crisp spring roll that required all his concentration, and so he did not look up at first.

'That man over there in the corner. He's the one who came to the shop.'

Tiger looked up. 'I'd like to say I understood what you were talking about, but as quite a lot of men come into your shop I can't say that I do.'

'Didn't I tell you? We had a man round the other day, trying to get us to join some sort of shopkeepers' cooperative. He said it was for mutual benefit. Self-help. That kind of thing.'

'What exactly did he want you to do?' asked Tiger.

'Well, basically pay a hundred quid a month.'

'For what?'

'For all the benefits it would offer.' Erica shrugged. 'It wasn't clear really. I went round to ask Isobel if he'd approached her and she said that he'd been in and she'd sent him away with a flea in his ear. She said he wanted a hundred and fifty quid from her. She told him she couldn't afford it.'

Tiger put down his fork. 'This was before Isobel's window was broken?'

'Yes,' confirmed Erica. 'The day before . . . What? Do you think there might be a connection between that man asking for money and Isobel's shop window being smashed?'

Tiger shrugged and picked up his fork again. 'Probably just a coincidence. But if it wasn't, I'd say it could be some sort of protection racket. Then again, maybe I've got a vivid imagination.'

Now it was Erica's turn to lay down her fork. 'What do you mean?'

'Well, you know what a protection racket is?'

'The sort of thing that happened in America, in the Prohibition.'

'Yes. I've never heard of it happening round here, but you do hear of gangs who go round and ask for money for "insurance purposes". To make sure that your property stays safe. Veiled threats.'

'But he wasn't threatening,' said Erica. 'It was almost as though he were selling insurance . . .'

'Which, of course, he was,' said Tiger. 'Maybe you've hit on it.' Then, softly and quite deliberately he said, 'Bloody hell! Who'd have thought it? I mean, here in Hampshire.'

'But he looks so mild,' said Erica. 'I mean . . . well, look at him.'

They turned to where the man had been sitting, but his chair was no longer occupied. Neither of them had seen him leave.

AT A QUARTER TO ELEVEN Gary and Sarah decided to call it a day.

'I suppose it was a long shot,' admitted Sarah. 'Nothing exciting at the kitchen table? You could see it better than me.'

The kitchen table—the one nearest the kitchen door—was the one used by 'management', who could then slip in and out of the restaurant.

'Not really. A few comings and goings. The odd shifty character, but since when has being shifty been a criminal offence?'

'In your case it's borderline,' quipped Sarah.

'You're perking up.'

'Yes. Just a bit. Thanks for tonight.'

'That sounds as though you're bringing the meeting to a close.'

'Yes. Well, I suppose I am.' Sarah reached down for her bag. 'If I get my skates on I can catch the last train home.'

Gary sighed. 'If you must, but I can offer you a bed if you want one.'

Sarah looked at him levelly. 'Oh, I'm sure you can, Mr Flynn. It's probably got notches carved on the end of it.'

'Ow!' he said.

Sarah looked apologetic. 'Sorry. Below the belt. I feel a bit sensitive at the moment, a bit bruised. Two years is a long time to be in a relationship and then have it crumble around you.'

'I wouldn't know,' said Gary. 'The most I've managed is three weeks.'

'Really? And I thought you had staying power.'

'Not where love is concerned.'

'Love? So we're talking love, are we?' asked Sarah looking startled. 'Not just a bit on the side.'

'Slip of the tongue,' said Gary. He took a card from his wallet and settled the bill.

CHRISTOPHER DEVON WAS EATING ALONE that evening, with a tray on his lap. It wasn't as good as his lunch, but that didn't matter. Normally he would have sat in front of the television, but tonight he didn't want the distraction. Instead, he ate his salmon fish cakes in front of a roaring log fire to the strains of Puccini. As Katia Ricciarelli soared through 'Vissi d'arte' he felt himself transported to another world.

And when it finished, and the room was quiet, except for the occasional crackling of a log, he could not remember feeling quite so emotional since Kate left. But then he was, he told himself, going through a bit of a phase at the moment. The reappearance of Mrs Fraser and young Daisy had quite thrown him off-balance.

Mrs Fraser and Miss Bassani. Except that he didn't know if it was Miss Bassani. Maybe she was married. Bound to be. She was probably Mrs Whatever. He was surprised that the thought had not struck him before. They had talked about opera and about food but never got round to her private life. He had no idea if she was married. Or had children. Luisa had never said. Never mentioned her family at all until the morning she left.

And she wasn't the sort of woman he felt he could ask.

Anyway, what did it matter? Maria was just coming in to clean for him. And she was being paid, after all.

He took the tray into the kitchen and went up to bed.

Chapter Four

> In planning for battle I have always found that plans are useless, but planning is indispensable.
>
> Dwight D. Eisenhower (1890–1969)

The domino club met on Thursday that week. Christopher rang them to say that he would be unable to make their usual date thanks to being on call, so Tiger and Gary had agreed to meet a day earlier rather than postpone.

Settled round their table in one corner of the Hare and Hounds the conversation turned, as it inevitably did in Gary's case, to women. Except that on this occasion it was not Gary who brought the subject up.

'Go well did it? Your night out?' Tiger asked mischievously.

Gary didn't look up, but laid down a double six. 'Yes, thank you.'

Christopher laid down a six and a three and raised an enquiring eyebrow.

'We both turned up on the same night at that new Chinese in Winchester,' confided Tiger, setting a double three on the table. 'I was with Erica, Gary was with Sarah.' He grinned. 'Very tall. Very classy. Very young.'

'Do you mind!' Gary put down another domino. 'I wish you'd remember that I'm younger than you two.'

'Not much,' said Christopher and Tiger in unison.

'Enough.' And then, 'Can we just finish this game, please?'

'Oh, serious stuff,' said Tiger, and then, obligingly, carried on playing without further reference to Gary's conquest.

It was a couple of games later when the subject returned to the evening at the restaurant. Tiger said, 'I've got a project for our secret society.'

Christopher said, 'I thought that had gone away.'

'No,' said Tiger. 'I was just waiting for the right thing to come along. It might not amount to anything, but unless I'm barking up the wrong tree I think there's some kind of protection racket going on.'

Gary tried to sound offhand. 'What sort of protection racket?'

Tiger filled the two of them in on the breaking of Isobel's window, and the man in black who had asked both Isobel and Erica to contribute to the funds for 'mutual benefit'. The very man who had been sitting in the Red Dragon the same night that he and Gary had dined there.

'It does sound a bit of a strange coincidence,' agreed Christopher. 'But what are you suggesting we do?'

'Make enquiries,' said Tiger. 'Ask other shopkeepers if they've been approached.'

'The police have probably got someone on the case already,' said Gary. 'You can't just start sticking your oar in. They'll get narked.'

'But they're not interested,' Tiger explained. 'Isobel tried to get them involved and they couldn't care less.'

Christopher frowned. 'I didn't really imagine your secret society was going to be doing things quite so . . . well . . . potentially dangerous.'

'It's not *my* secret society, it's *our* secret society, and anyway there's nothing dangerous about making enquiries,' said Tiger irritably.

'If I were you,' said Gary, 'I'd stay well out of it.'

'So you don't want to help?'

'It's not that I don't *want* to help,' said Gary. 'I don't think I *can* help.'

'How do you know until you try? Honestly. You civil servants, you live such sedentary lives, and then when something comes along that might be a bit interesting you stick your heads in the sand and hope it will go away.'

'Look,' said Christopher, 'I don't see how, as a local doctor, I can go around asking questions like that. What does Erica think? Is she happy for you to take the law into your own hands?'

'I haven't necessarily told her yet.'

Christopher looked thoughtful. 'I can imagine what Kate's reaction would have been.'

'Kate would probably have chased them out of the shop with a meat axe!' said Gary, grinning.

'I saw her the other day,' said Tiger. The words came out before he could stop them.

'Saw Kate?' asked Christopher. 'Where?'

'At City Airport. Briefly.' Tiger tried to play it down. 'She was flying to Southampton.'

'With Howie?'

'To meet him . . . so you know about him, then?'

'Yes.' His voice was steady. 'American high-flier. Everything I'm not.'

'I wasn't sure whether to mention it or not. Didn't know if you knew . . .'

'Yes, I knew. But not from Kate. Patients are always happy to keep you up to date on gossip. Apparently she's been with Howie for about six months now. They met salsa dancing. At an executive singles club.'

'Salsa dancing?' asked Gary incredulously.

'They tell me it's huge fun,' said Christopher. Then he looked suddenly sad. 'And full of sexual tension.'

'Well, if it's any consolation she didn't look as if she was having much fun the other day,' Tiger confided.

Christopher drained his glass and sat back in his chair. 'That's a shame. I'd like at least to think that she was happy.'

'But that's daft,' Gary spluttered. 'She dumped you.'

'Thank you for reminding me. But after twenty-odd years of marriage,' said Christopher, 'I can't wish her ill.'

'What you need to do is get yourself someone else. Someone young. That'll show her.'

Christopher looked reflective. 'Maybe. One day. I don't really want to carry on living alone.' Then he turned to Gary. 'Do you?'

Gary shrugged. 'Who knows.'

'That's not an answer.' It was Christopher's turn to pursue his quarry.

'I'm not short of a woman, if that's what you mean.'

'Oh, we know that. But so far you've not shown much in the way of loyalty, have you?'

'That's a bit unfair. Maybe I just haven't found the right person yet.'

'What about Sarah?' asked Tiger.

Gary felt himself colouring up.

'Oh, I think we might have touched a nerve there,' said Christopher.

'Dream on,' said Gary.

'Us or you?' said Tiger.

'Both. For all you know I might be turning over a new leaf.'

'Can a leopard change its spots?' asked Tiger.

'That's rich, coming from a man with your name,' said Gary, relieved to break the mood. 'Another pint, then?'

But none of them seemed to have the appetite for it, and Tiger didn't think it was the right time to pursue the matter of the protection racket. He went home to Erica more than a little crestfallen. He didn't tell her what he had suggested. He didn't want to be shot down in flames yet again.

CHRISTOPHER HADN'T WANTED to let Tiger down, but he knew there was no way he could involve himself in his harebrained scheme.

Gary, on the other hand, was now convinced that the Red Dragon restaurants figured somewhere in Mr Tan's bigger scheme. He had to find out more about this potential protection racket before Tiger started thrashing around and clouding the water. What he needed to do was to get Tiger out of the way for a few days so that he and Sarah could get stuck in.

The solution he found was relatively straightforward.

TIGER SAT AT THE DESK in his home in Winchester and looked out over the cathedral close. Thick grey clouds were looming behind the cathedral, far darker than the pale grey stones of its towers and flying buttresses. It seemed perverse to be looking over something so majestic and musing on something so sordid: the manipulation of ordinary people. How could he ignore it as Gary seemed prepared to do? He could understand Christopher's reluctance, being the local doctor, but he had hoped Gary would come on board.

Beyond the close-cropped grass and the old irregular walls were the streets of shops where he would have to ask his questions. He would make a list of the shops in the main streets, then ask the manager of each whether he or she had been approached by the man in black. Those who said that they had not seen the man would either have paid the money or had not yet been visited. Any shops that had been vandalised would go on the list of managers who had been visited and had declined 'protection'. And if any denied they had been approached, but said they had been vandalised? Well, that was tricky. They would probably have been the victims of drunken yobs. And what about those who had been approached by the man in black, agreed to pay, but would tell Tiger they had declined protection? How would he know whether they were telling the truth?

He leaned back in his chair. The more he thought about it, the less certain he was of what it would achieve . . .

The phone rang. It was the helicopter company. A job had come up. An urgent job. Could he be at Southampton Airport in a couple of hours? With an overnight bag. Well, rather larger than that, actually. He would be away for the best part of a week.

'A PROTECTION RACKET?' Sarah was looking out of the window across the Thames towards Lambeth Palace. She turned to face Gary.

'Sounds like it.'

'But could he raise the sort of money we're talking about with a protection racket?'

'Depends on how many clients he has.'

'Well, it would explain why the money's in cash.'

Gary drummed his fingers on the desk. 'We need to get cracking before other parties start interfering.' He walked across to the window to join her.

'Other parties?' Sarah look quizzical.

'Yes. You're not going to believe this, but Tiger—my mate who came over the other night in the Red Dragon—was the one who woke me up to it. His wife runs a bookshop in Winchester. She had an approach. So did the woman who runs the chocolate shop next door. She had a brick through her window the day after she declined to join "the club".'

'And that's why you think there's something in it?'

'Well, it's worth following up. Apparently the guy who had been asking them both for money was in the Red Dragon the night we were there.'

'Right.' Sarah sat down at her desk. 'Could we take your friend Tiger through a few Photofits, or get a detailed description of the guy?'

'We could. If Tiger had any idea what I did for a living. He thinks I'm a civil servant.'

'Which, of course, you are.'

'Yes. Just not the sort of civil servant he thinks I am.'

Sarah looked thoughtful. 'We could get one of our other guys to go and ask him some questions.'

'Well, it's a bit tricky at the moment,' said Gary. 'Right now he's ferrying men from the Ordnance Survey around the Isles of Scilly.'

ERICA DIDN'T KNOW what made her go to see Christopher Devon. Perhaps it was a combination of Tiger meeting Kate at the airport, and the two of them seeing Dr Cummings in the Chinese restaurant. She just felt that it was time to catch up.

When he and Kate had been together, the four of them had dined out, even shared the odd weekend away. But since Kate's departure it had been difficult. Tiger met Christopher regularly on Friday nights, but Erica had hardly encountered him at all, except on the rare occasions when he had dropped Tiger off after their domino sessions.

She parked in the bumpy lane outside his house and peered over the low flint wall. It was just as she remembered it. Evenly mown lawns lay to right and left, and beyond them, on the far side of the house, paths were mown among apple trees which grew in the daffodil-dappled grass that sloped down to the river. Such a picture. Such a sadness that it was no longer a happy house.

Erica pushed open the gate and walked up the path to the front door. Before she could ring the bell the door was opened, not by Christopher, but by a petite woman in her forties.

'Maria! What are you doing here?'

'Oh, a bit of this and that. Cleaning mostly. Mum does it usually. Only she's away and asked me if I'd hold the fort. So here I am. Fort-holding.'

Erica heard footsteps coming down the stairs, further back in the hall.

'Who is it?' enquired Christopher's voice. And then he saw her. 'Erica! What a nice surprise.' He came forward and kissed her, then realised that he had interrupted a conversation. 'Do you two know one another?'

Maria laughed. 'Just a little. Our children were at playgroup together.'

Over coffee the story unfolded. Maria, not wanting to intrude on Erica and Christopher's catching up, had gone upstairs to continue her cleaning.

'My two are a bit older than Maria's but they were good friends for a while when they were little. Then as soon as they went to different schools they drifted apart. I bump into Maria occasionally at the supermarket.'

'So she's married?' asked Christopher, doing his best to sound polite rather than curious.

'Divorced.'

'Oh?'

Erica read the question mark. 'Bit of a naughty boy really, Charlie Spicer. A long-distance lorry driver.'

'Oh, I see. A girl in every port?'

'Well, not *every* port. But certainly a few of them. The divorce must have been four or five years ago now.'

'And is . . .' Christopher got no further with his question.

'No. There's nobody else from what I can gather. Or did I guess the wrong question?'

Christopher looked embarrassed and Erica felt that she had overstepped the mark. 'Sorry. I just came round to see how you were. I haven't seen you for ages and wondered how you were getting on.'

'Oh, I'm managing.' Christopher smiled rather wanly. 'I shall be glad when summer comes, and the better weather. Then I can get outside a bit more. Do lots of gardening.' He looked out of the window. 'This sunny spell's a rarity. I should really be out there now.'

Erica made to get up.

'No. That wasn't an invitation for you to leave. Do stay for some lunch. Maria is a much better cook than her mum. Luisa makes the most dreadful pasta you have ever tasted. It would stick wallpaper to anything.'

Erica laughed. 'So Maria's offerings are more palatable?'

'She keeps it simple—Parma ham and melon, salami and Italian bread. And that's all I want for lunch.'

'You could prepare that yourself, you know.'

'I could. And I was perfectly happy to. It was Luisa who insisted that I be cooked for—helpless single chap and all that.'

'Have you told Maria?'

'Well, no. I tried to. But, anyway . . .'

Erica looked at him with her head on one side.

Christopher drew a large breath. 'Well, I enjoy her company.'

ON THE ISLAND of Tresco, Tiger wasn't enjoying anyone's company. Why this job had suddenly come up he couldn't for the life of him imagine. He looked at the sky. It was grey, and the cloud base was low. The guys were out surveying whatever they needed to survey, and he was waiting for them to return. He thought about Erica working in the bookshop and wondered, just for a moment, if she was thinking about him.

Tiger had dropped the two-man Ordnance Survey team on St Agnes and been instructed by his base to fly to St Marys and pick up a copilot. The firm had been a pilot short for a month now, without any sign of a replacement for old Eric, who had finally retired. The new pilot would be billeted with him for the rest of the week, sitting in the left-hand seat so that Tiger could ensure the new recruit was up to scratch.

He scrutinised the passengers as they came off the Penzance helicopter. He had a name and a description. Sam Ross. Red hair. About thirty-five. Medium height. He wondered if his expected contact had missed the flight.

'Are you Tiger?'

He turned round to see a redheaded thirty-five-year-old of medium height. 'I'm Sam Ross,' she said.

Tiger covered his embarrassment at making the obvious false assumption and shook her hand. 'Hi! Tiger Wilson. Can I take your bag?'

She shook her head. 'No, thanks. I can manage. Where do we go?'

Tiger indicated the small café. 'Coffee first?'

'Yeah. Thanks.'

Had Tiger been expecting a woman, Sam Ross was not the sort of woman he would have been looking for. She seemed too slight to be a helicopter pilot, but her slender figure presumably belied her strength. Her bright eyes were light blue and her skin pale except for gently flushed cheeks.

Inside the café they sat down at a table, and Tiger was surprised at how relaxed Sam seemed to be. 'So you know the Jet Ranger?' he asked.

'Pretty well. I've flown them for two years now, along with Squirrels.'

'And how long have you been flying altogether?' Tiger asked.

'Oh, since I was eighteen. Got my private pilot's licence in my twenties. But I never thought I'd be able to fly for a living.'

'We do have female airline pilots,' Tiger said gently.

'Yes, but it's hard. And there are lots of men who wish we weren't there.'

'Oh dear.' Tiger pulled a face.

'Sorry. Didn't mean to be heavy. But you do get looked up and down a bit.' Sam paused. 'I think a lot of guys think you must be . . . you know . . . the other way.'

'And you're not?' teased Tiger.

Sam frowned in mock admonishment. 'Please!' Then she grinned. 'No. Far too interested in . . . well . . . Just ordinary, that's all.'

Asked to choose a word that would describe Sam Ross, 'ordinary' was not the one that Tiger would have picked.

CHRISTOPHER DEVON took the phone call in the surgery in Romsey where he was working as a locum. It was from one of his former partners.

'I only called to see how you were doing,' said Dr Reggie Silverwood.

'Oh, I'm surviving, Reggie. How about you?'

Christopher had got on well with Dr Silverwood since he had first arrived at the practice. By then, Randall Cummings had taken the role of senior partner, but Reggie had been determined to remain on a part-time basis for as long as he could. He was a GP of the old school, greatly respected by his patients and with a bedside manner that inspired confidence. He was the practice's grand old man, and as long as he just about pulled his weight, Randall Cummings was prepared to let him stay.

Christopher was fond of Reggie. He used to see him regularly at the surgery, and very occasionally for a drink after 'office hours'. He was a small, birdlike man, with wire-framed glasses and a slight stoop.

He sounded, today, a little more weary than usual. 'Oh, just about surviving, too, but I don't know for how much longer. Maybe the time's come for me to pack it in.'

Christopher made his surprise clearly audible. 'Pack it in?'

'I think so.'

'Oh, it'll just be a temporary blip, Reggie. You'll have had a few cases that have got you down. You know how it is.'

'Mmm. I'd like to think so. But it's a bit more than that.' Dr Silverwood cleared his throat. 'Not at all sure I understand, Christopher. Things going on. Things I can't really believe. Perhaps I'm mistaken. Confused.'

Christopher spoke seriously. 'Reggie, do you want to talk?'

'I'm not sure I should . . .'

'Why don't you come round for a drink tonight? It would be nice to see you.' Christopher played a card that he thought might work on a man who had devoted his life to the well-being of others. 'The evenings are rather long for me now, being on my own.'

Reggie took the bait. 'Well, I suppose I could drop in for a quick one. See how you are. What time would suit?'

Christopher looked at his watch. 'Say half past seven? I finish here at six and that will give me time to get home and light a fire. Stay for supper, if you like.' He knew the offer would be declined, but he wanted to make the offer all the same.

'Oh, no. I won't put you to all that trouble. A glass of Scotch will do nicely. Then I'll be off home to Betty.'

'OK, Reggie. I'll see you at half past seven.'

Chapter Five

> An office party is not, as is sometimes supposed, the Managing Director's chance to kiss the tea-girl. It is the tea-girl's chance to kiss the Managing Director.
>
> *Roundabout*, Katharine Whitehorn (born 1926)

'Did you call the police?' Tiger asked. Why was it that family disasters invariably happened when one of you was away from home? Erica assured him that the police had been and gone, convinced that it was drunken yobs who had put a brick through her shop window.

'But didn't the alarm go off?' he asked.

Erica spoke softly. 'I left Brian to lock up and he forgot to set it.'

'Oh God! Didn't you drill it into him?' Tiger was angry. Not only at Brian's apparent stupidity, but because he was unable to help.

'There's no need to have a go at me,' Erica said, wounded by his tone.

'I just can't see how Brian could have been so daft, that's all.'

'Yes, well, it won't do any good to keep going on about it. The glazier's coming to fit new glass this afternoon and so we should be safe by tonight.'

'And what about the man in black? Any sign of him?'

'No. None. And if he does come back you can be sure he won't be going anywhere until I've asked him a few questions. If it *is* him who's responsible I don't want him thinking he can intimidate me by lobbing a brick through my window.'

'Erica, you don't know what he'll do next. I don't want you getting involved.'

'I think it's a bit late for that. I *am* involved. More than you at the moment. And it'll take us all afternoon to clear the broken glass out of the window.'

He felt deflated. Detached from it all. Unable to connect with Erica.

'Look, I'm sorry I'm not there. Just don't do anything hasty.'

'So when *are* you back?'

'Friday afternoon. These guys finish here on Friday lunchtime and I'll fly them back then.'

'Right. It'll be good to see you.'

'The only thing is . . .'

'Yes?'

'Would you mind if I went to play dominoes? Only I want to talk through all this with the guys and see if they have any ideas.'

'No. Fine. If that's what you want to do.'

He could hear the disappointment in her voice. 'I won't be late back. And, anyway, I'll see you for an hour or so before I go.'

'It's up to you.'

SAM ROSS WAS A NATURAL. She handled the Jet Ranger with practised precision, and Tiger commented, at the end of their second flight, 'I don't know why I'm here. You don't need me at all.'

'I should hope not,' she replied with a grin. 'Far too independent.'

'Well, next week you'll be on your own. The second helicopter's being serviced now and she'll be ready on Monday.'

Tiger sat back in the left-hand seat as Sam circled the tiny island of Samson. The weather had cleared. The early-morning sun had turned the sky a soft shade of forget-me-not blue, and the water beneath them was pure turquoise.

'Wonderful, isn't it?' asked Sam.

'Blissful.'

'I've always wanted to live here,' she said.

'Idling?' he asked.

'I'd find enough to keep me occupied. Taking pleasure flights, probably.'

Tiger chuckled. 'I think you'd get bored of that.'

'S'pose so. But it's nice to dream.'

The Ordnance Survey men were put down on St Martins, the long, bone-shaped island at the northeastern corner of the group. They asked to be picked up in two hours, so Sam lifted up the aircraft and headed south towards St Marys.

'Do you dream a lot?' asked Tiger, idly.

'A bit.'

'Not happy with what you're doing, then?'

'Perfectly happy. It'd be nice to have somebody to share it with, that's all.' She banked the helicopter to the left of Hugh Town and tilted over towards St Agnes, lining up with the white lighthouse. 'You share yours, then?'

'Thirty years now.'

'God, that's impressive.'

Tiger looked out of the window at the white stump of the lighthouse, its lantern glinting in the sun as they wheeled round a couple of hundred feet above it. He watched as the foaming water broke over the rocks and sprayed into the air. Sam was right, it was blissful out here. A different world.

GARY FLYNN was deep in thought, poring over papers at his desk. With a pen he traced down the sheet of paper line by line, noting times and locations. Before him lay the weekly life of Mr Tan. Thanks to the assiduousness of Ben Atkinson, Gary even knew what Mr Tan had for lunch at the Savoy Grill and who he ate it with.

'Doesn't stint himself, does he?' murmured Gary, noticing that Mr Tan had spent £4,400 on two pairs of handmade shoes.

'So he's not just doing it for his country, then?' asked Sarah.

'I should think that's the last thing he's doing it for. I think Mr Tan's main concern is Mr Tan—and family. Gary looked up. 'You've seen this?'

'Of course.' Sarah looked impassive.

'Notice any patterns? Anything odd?'

'Only one thing. Do we know if Mr Tan is fit and well?'

'He's in his forties, smokes like a chimney, but I think he's as healthy as your average Chinese male city dweller. Why do you ask?'

Sarah came over to Gary's desk and leaned over his shoulder. He could feel her warmth. Smell her scent. She pointed to several entries. 'Look at these. Harley Street. But two different addresses.'

'Odd. Do we know who he was seeing?'

'No. There are several consultancies in each building but Harley Street being Harley Street—and a model of discretion—we couldn't tell who he saw when he was inside.'

'Could have been getting a second opinion.'

'Yes,' agreed Sarah. 'I'd thought of that. Or flogging them cheap drugs.'

'But what's his source?' Gary said. 'We've no record of him visiting any suppliers, have we?'

'No. But they could be knocked off. I've got the guys checking records.'

Gary closed the file and got up from his desk. 'There's something there. Something I'm not seeing.'

'I can't see it either,' admitted Sarah. 'I've thought of drugs, money laundering, protection rackets. I just can't make the connection.'

'We need more time to work this out.' Gary walked to the window, then turned back to her. 'And how are you doing? After your . . . difficulties.'

She was surprised by his concern. 'I'm fine, thank you. Why do you ask?'

'Oh, just like to make sure that my staff are all right. Don't like to think that they might be suffering in silence.'

'Suffering?' Sarah gave a laugh. 'I suppose that might be pushing it. I have my moments. You know . . . on evenings where there's nothing on the box and I've run out of stuff to read.'

'Funny,' said Gary. 'I always thought of you as having a mad social life.'

Sarah smiled ruefully. 'Me? No. Home bird really.' Then she said briskly, 'Anyway . . . what about Mr Tan?'

'I'd rather talk about you, to be honest.'

'Steady on, Mr Flynn, or I might begin to think you really care.' She walked across to her desk and dropped down into the chair.

Would that be such a terrible thing? Gary thought.

THE FIRE WAS CRACKLING in the grate at the Manor House. Christopher had broken open a new bottle of Laphroaig and had poured a tot for himself while waiting for Reggie Silverwood to arrive.

Half past seven came and went. Eight o'clock. At 8.15 Christopher phoned Reggie's home. Betty answered. 'No. I thought he was coming for a drink with you.'

At 8.30 he phoned the hospital, and at 8.32 he learned that Reggie Silverwood had been involved in a road accident. He was lying unconscious in the Hampshire Royal Infirmary. No other cars involved, confirmed the houseman. From the condition of the driver when they had found him it looked as though Dr Silverwood had had a heart attack at the wheel, and had then plunged down a ditch off the main road just before the turning to Christopher's house. His condition was stable, but the next twenty-four hours would be critical.

Reggie's accident was a blow. He had been a kind and generous colleague and a good, if reserved, friend. Now, gnawing away inside, was the regret that they had not had a chance to talk, and for Reggie to share whatever it was that was troubling him. All Christopher could do was wait.

'SO WHAT HAPPENED?' There was an edge in Tiger's voice.

Erica could tell he was not happy. She had just told him that the man in the black anorak had paid her another call at the shop. This time she had called the police and they had taken him in for questioning, but she knew that the information she was about to give would not improve things. 'They had to let him go.'

'What?!'

Erica held the telephone away from her ear for a moment, then continued, 'They said they were sorry but that they had no reason to hold him. He had nothing on him that gave them any cause to suspect that he had anything to do with the broken windows.'

'But what about the demand for money?'

'They said he denied that he had asked for anything. Then they asked me if he had threatened me and I had to admit that he hadn't. They were sympathetic but said there was nothing else they could do.'

'Did they take his fingerprints?'

'I don't know. They might have done. They took him down to the police station but then came back and said they'd had to let him go. They seem to think he was pretty harmless.'

'But that's ludicrous,' Tiger fumed. 'Oh, bugger. Why did this have to happen while I was away?'

Impatience showed in Erica's voice. 'I'm sorry. If I'd thought, I could have asked him to delay his return until you'd come back. Sometimes things happen and I have to tell you about them, even if you don't want to hear.'

He felt guilty now. Guilty at having a go at her. Guilty at not being there when she needed him. 'I'm sorry. I'll be back soon.'

'And when are you next away? Do you know?'

'No. 'Fraid not. I don't know what I've got on next week.'

Erica became aware that she was sounding like a whinging wife. She tried to make amends. 'Well, we'll just have to make sure we have some time together this weekend.'

'Yes.'

They both hung up with an overall feeling of dissatisfaction.

THE KITCHEN TABLE was laid with the now customary antipasti—olives and salami, rocket leaves with Parmesan shavings and other Italian delicacies.

'I'm getting rather used to this,' said Christopher.

Maria looked troubled. 'Oh! Would you rather have something else?'

He grinned. 'That's not what I meant at all. I meant it's very nice. Are you sure you won't join me?'

She smiled. 'I can't have lunch with you every day. I'm supposed to be cleaning. Mum would tell me to "looka after the doctorr".'

Christopher laughed. 'That was scarily accurate.'

'Yes. It is a worry, isn't it? I might grow into her with age.'

'No. Highly unlikely.' He put on a mock-serious voice. 'As a doctor I can tell you that the measurements of your bones and your general demeanour indicate that it is more than probable that you will retain your slender figure into old age, regardless of your genetic background.'

'Is that so?'

'No. I just made it up, but it sounded very plausible, don't you think?'

She held him with a measured look. 'You know, I thought you'd be such a serious man.'

Christopher sat back in his chair. 'Why?'

'Well, you're a respected doctor.'

'I don't know about "respected". And I'm a bit worried about "serious".'

'So you're not serious, then?' she asked.

'Oh, I can be very serious. But I've had rather enough of being that. I really do think I should snap out of it. Get myself out more.'

'Where to?' she asked, breaking off from cleaning the cooker.

'I haven't been to the opera for ages. A bit of Puccini, or Verdi, that's what I need.' He stood up and went to fill the kettle. 'Do you want to come?'

'What?'

'To the opera. You said you liked Italian rather than German.'

'Oh, I couldn't possibly. My mother—'

'Your mother's not in charge of my social life. There's no reason why you shouldn't come with me.' Then it occurred to him that she might not actually want to go with him. 'But, of course, you probably have other things . . . someone else to . . .'

Maria butted in. 'No. I just . . . well . . . if you're sure . . . ?'

'Quite sure. I'll get hold of the programme for Covent Garden. We'll have a look and see what we fancy. If that's OK?'

'Fine. Lovely.'

ON THURSDAY NIGHT the men from the Ordnance Survey decided that they would go out under their own steam. Tiger and Sam had dined with them in the hotel every other evening, so he was not sorry when they said that on their last night they'd go off on their own.

'There's a seafood restaurant down by the harbour. Lobster and crab, that sort of thing,' Sam suggested. 'Shall we go and eat there?'

No matter how long a man has been married, and however loyal he is to his wife, there are moments, when he finds himself in the company of an attractive woman, when he can forget for a while that he is spoken for. No harm comes of it, in most cases, and it is extremely good for morale. It shows him that he can still be good company, still court an admiring glance from someone who is not bound by loyalty or family ties.

Tiger looked at Sam sitting across the table from him and saw how the candlelight played in her eyes. Saw the coppery tints of her hair, the delicate curve of her chin and the warm smile, and for a while at least he remembered what it was like to be young and in love. Not that he was in love with her. But she had the knack that some women do of listening as though you are the only person in the room, and he did find her very attractive. For one evening at least, he could be single again. And desirable. Not disloyal, but just happy in his own imaginings. Somewhere else. With someone else. Dreaming a little. Indulging his fantasies.

'I do like it here,' she said.

'Yes. A good find.' He came back from his reverie and topped up her wine glass.

'So do you know what you'll be doing next week?' she asked.

'Not until Saturday morning. The usual flexible life.'

'Some people couldn't cope with that.'

'What about you?'

'Got used to it,' she said, and took a sip of wine. 'Makes for a nomadic life. Maybe that's why I'm still single.'

'Do you mind that?'

'Oh, sometimes. Other times it's OK. Depends where the job takes me. If it's coming to places like this, then I can hack it. But if I'm stuck in some seedy B&B or motel, I'd happily swap it.'

They were interrupted by the arrival of their food. Tiger had steak, Sam a grilled lemon sole. The young waitress laid them down and did a little bob before leaving them to eat.

'*Bon appétit*,' said Tiger.

They talked easily over the meal. Tiger telling about his father, then about his time in the Air Force—the countries where he had flown and stories of narrow escapes—then he became aware that he was doing all the talking.

'I'm sorry. All these *Boy's Own* stories. Boring the pants off you.'

Sam shook her head. 'No, you're not. It's good to hear someone who's keen on their job.'

'Yes, but I can talk about other things.'

'OK, then.' She smiled. 'What do you know about the Scilly Isles?'

'I know that if you call them that the inhabitants will shoot you. They're called "Scilly"—a bit like the Scots hating to be called Scotch.'

'Anything else?'

Tiger took a deep breath. 'I know that the island of Samson was inhabited until eighteen fifty-five and that Harold Wilson used to have a holiday home on St Marys. I know that the gardens on Tresco hardly ever have a frost and that means they have the finest collection of Mediterranean plants in Britain. Will that do for starters?'

'What a mine of information you are.'

'I know. Deadly, isn't it?'

She shook her head. 'Oh, I don't think so. You can make people laugh and that's what's important.'

Tiger looked reflective. 'Yes. Only I don't seem to have done that a lot lately,' he murmured, and ordered another glass of red wine to accompany what was left of his steak.

Finally, at a quarter to midnight, Sam said, 'I think we'd better be going.'

They walked along the harbour wall and looked out across the calm water, where pleasure boats and fishing smacks bobbed on their moorings, and the halyards of yachts chimed gently against their masts in the evening breeze. The moon was almost full, and casting its light in silvery shards across the rippling water.

'Perfect,' murmured Tiger. 'Just perfect.'

'Yes,' she agreed. 'Perfect.' Then she turned and kissed him on the lips.

Chapter Six

> Thy wife shall be as a fruitful vine by the sides of thine house:
> thy children like olive plants: round about thy table.
>
> Psalm 128:3

Christopher had explained to the Romsey practice that he would be unable to cover for them that day. He did not feel a need to explain why. It was his birthday. Nobody else needed to know, but he wanted to be at home.

Maria did not work on Fridays, and he had not told her of the day's significance. He got up at half past seven to a clear blue sky and the sound of blackbirds and thrushes singing their hearts out. He sipped his morning coffee and looked out over the frosted grass, sparkling in the early slant of amber sunlight that filtered through the branches of the yew tree. The cobwebs that stretched across the topiary box bushes glinted like diamonds. A good day to be up early. A good day to have a birthday.

But then his thoughts turned to Reggie Silverwood. He would call later for an update, and to see if his old friend was up to seeing visitors. And then he thought about Kate. He tried not to think of her too often. To do so was to be overtaken by a deep sadness born of guilt and errors of omission.

He showered and changed into his gardening clothes—jeans and an ancient fleece—then wandered outside, down the flagstone path that led to the greenhouse. He turned the key in the lock, opened the door and inhaled. That aroma of leaf and flower, of compost and dampness, was every bit as uplifting and full of pleasure as the first mouthful of champagne.

He picked up the long-spouted watering can and moved among the plants, dispensing liquid refreshment where needed. He pulled off a browning leaf here, a faded flower there, murmuring to his charges as he did so.

He left the greenhouse and walked along the side of the house, past borders where daffodils were bursting their buds, and walls were festooned with jasmine and japonica. As he turned the corner he saw two people walking up the path to the front door.

'Ellie? Matt? What on earth?'

They stood before him on the path, smiling broadly.

'But you're in America and you're . . . but you're here!'

Ellie walked up and wrapped her arms round him, laying her head on his chest. 'Happy birthday, Dad.'

Matt hung back for a moment, then came forward and kissed his father softly on the cheek. 'Happy birthday, Pa.'

Christopher stepped back and surveyed them both. He shook his head. 'I'm sorry. But why . . . ? I mean, it's not a special birthday or anything . . .'

'Yes, it is,' confirmed Ellie. 'It's yours.'

'I tell you what, Dad,' said Matt, 'it's bloody cold out here.'

With Christopher's arms round each of their shoulders they walked up the path to the front door.

Matt was on his way to a meeting in London and Ellie had a week off between changing locations with her charity in Africa. They had not planned ahead much, but when each had realised they would be free during the same week, they had decided on a surprise visit.

He looked at them sitting on either side of the kitchen table—Ellie looking as elegant as only she could in a pair of combat trousers and a sweat shirt emblazoned with the words 'Feed Africa', lest anyone should be in any doubt as to her intentions. Matt wore a charcoal-grey sweater that had been revealed, along with the scarf around his neck, when he took off his thick overcoat. He had turned into a youth every bit as handsome, in his father's eyes, as Michelangelo's *David*. You could have cracked an egg on his cheekbones and his hair was dark and curly.

Ellie talked avidly about her work—laying on water, teaching people how to grow things, helping them to help themselves. Matt was more reticent. 'Oh, it's fine, you know. Busy. Company shake-ups.'

'And have you heard from your mum?' asked Christopher.

They both nodded, but seemed reticent. 'Now and again,' said Ellie.

'Mmm,' said Matt.

'Think she's pretty busy,' offered Ellie. 'Travelling a lot.'

Matt asked 'You've not . . . ?'

'No,' cut in Christopher. 'No, I've not seen her for quite a while now.'

He made to brighten the mood. 'So, how long are you staying? Shall we go out to dinner?'

'Well, I can stay for a few days,' said Ellie, 'but Matt's got to go in a couple of hours.'

'You've come all this way and you can only stay a couple of hours?' asked Christopher.

'Sorry, Dad. It was that or nothing.'

Christopher was anxious not to appear ungrateful. 'Oh, I'm not nagging or anything. It's just that . . . well . . . you'll stay for lunch?'

'Of course. In fact'—he reached down for the holdall that he had brought with him and put it on the table—'everything you need for a birthday lunch.' He unzipped the bag and lifted out cheeses and pâté, a bottle of champagne, crackers and pickle and, finally, a hand of bananas.

'Bananas!'

'And . . .' said Ellie, with theatrical finality dipping into the bag and pulling out a plastic tub, 'Marks and Spencer's custard!'

Christopher threw back his head and laughed. Bananas and custard had been their father's favourite since his children could remember.

Christopher turned to Matt. 'So, it's all going well with you?'

'Sort of. A bit up and down, but I'm managing. The job's a bit tricky, to be honest. I just wish we could get on with it, but the money men keep getting in the way. The world seems to be run by accountants now. They call the shots, I guess.'

Christopher chuckled.

'What?' asked Matt.

'*I guess*. Sorry. You suddenly sounded very American.'

'Oh dear. *I suppose*, then. Is that better?'

Christopher shook his head. 'It doesn't really matter. Just glad to have you here.'

'Well, you can blame Matt,' said Ellie. 'He said we should come.'

'I was coming anyway,' mumbled Matt. 'And I just thought it would be nice if we were both here, and Ellie managed to engineer a break and . . . well, here we are.'

'Thank you,' said Christopher. 'Thank you very much. You've really made my day.'

'So, are you getting out, Dad?' Ellie asked. 'Are you meeting people?'

'Of course I am. I meet people every day.'

'I don't mean patients. I mean . . . special people.'

'I've always maintained that everybody is special,' said Christopher, prevaricating.

'When you want to you can be so irritating,' moaned Ellie.

Matt sat quietly, munching on a cracker.

'I play dominoes every Friday . . .'

'Oh, that's great. You'll meet just the right sort of people down the pub!'

'And,' he countered, with increased volume, 'I have just invited someone to the opera.'

'Good!' cried Ellie positively. 'Are we allowed to know who?'

'Her name's Maria.'

'And? What does she do?'

Christopher smiled weakly. 'She cleans for me.'

'Oh.'

Matt looked doubtful.

'There's no need to look like that. She knows about opera and . . . things. She's part Italian, but she speaks perfect English. Anyway, it's just an evening out. But she's very pleasant and I enjoy her company and . . .' He became aware that they were both trying not to smirk. 'Are you teasing me?'

'No, Dad,' said Matt. 'If you want to go out with a cleaner then that's fine. But just make sure she's not after your money.'

Christopher was not sure whether he was serious or not.

'Well I think it's lovely,' offered Ellie. 'At least it's a start.'

'What?' asked Christopher. 'You think I can work my way up from a cleaner and probably end up with a real lady?'

Ellie got up from the table and walked behind her father, draping her arms over his shoulders and putting her head next to his. 'I don't care who you go out with as long as it makes you happy.'

Christopher shot a look at Matt, who shrugged. 'Up to you, Dad. Just be aware that there are gold-diggers everywhere.'

'Oh, shut up, Matt!' cried Ellie. 'Don't listen to him, Dad.'

Christopher had heard enough. 'What about you two?' he asked. 'Any men on the horizon?' He realised that he only needed to enquire about the one sex.

Ellie flopped down in her chair again. 'I've got one guy trying it on, but I'm not very keen. He's a doctor.'

Christopher raised an eyebrow.

'Yes, but unfortunately he's not like you. Got an ego the size of a house. Thinks he's God's gift. Trouble is, he is rather.'

He turned to Matt. 'How about you?'

Matt avoided his eye. 'Yes. There is a guy. We share an apartment. We've been together for six months.'

'Good. I'm glad,' said Christopher. And then, 'Anyone like coffee?'

MATT GAVE HIS FATHER a farewell hug and strolled down the garden path with the empty holdall under his arm. Christopher returned to Ellie, who was still sitting at the kitchen table. 'Do you think he's all right?'

Ellie nodded. 'Yes, he's all right. Big shake-ups at work. Came to London for a big meeting.'

'And what about—you know—his private life?'

'Still finds it difficult to talk about it, but I think he's happy.'

'What he was saying about . . . gold-diggers. Is he really worried?'

'I think he's worried that you might be taken advantage of. Doesn't want you to get hurt.'

Christopher sighed. 'I don't want to get hurt myself. Again. Anyway, I'm starting off gently. I'm not committing myself to anything. You'll like Maria. She's very nice. And fun. You'll meet her on Monday.'

GARY LOOKED PLEASED with himself. He was leafing through a report and making satisfied little grunts as he did so.

'What are you looking at?' asked Sarah.

'A police file on our friend who was trying to sell protection.'

'How have you got that?'

'Well, I tipped the wink to the Hampshire Constabulary and asked them to keep an eye open. Said that if they managed to collar him to be gentle and let him off lightly. But that I wanted chapter and verse on who he was.'

'And you've got it?'

Gary tapped the file. 'It seems that he went back to see Erica again and she called the police. Fortunately someone was sharp enough to stop them from being too heavy and our man in black—Kevin Whittier—has been released. No clues though. He's got no previous form.'

'But it's unlikely he'll go back to demanding money, isn't it?'

'For a while, I should think. But he might lead us to someone bigger. We're keeping tabs on him.'

'Oh, well,' said Sarah, with a hint of disappointment in her voice. 'I'd been hoping I might be able to come with you to the domino club tonight, to ask Tiger some innocent questions and maybe progress this case. But now the man in black has been identified . . .'

'Come anyway. I don't mind.' Gary wondered whether he should have invited her. It was nothing more than vanity really. But Tiger and Christopher had given him such stick for not being able to hang on to women that he wanted to show them the sort of woman he could get if he put his mind to it. Not that he had got her just yet. But given time . . . and if she really did want to come . . .

'Fine. I will.'

So it was done. And there was no way he could backtrack.

TIGER WISHED THERE was some way *he* could backtrack. It had been nothing more than a kiss, but he would be fooling himself if he tried to believe he had not enjoyed it. And it was definitely more than a peck.

The following morning nothing was mentioned, but Sam seemed to have an extra sparkle in her eye. An extra spring in her step. And Tiger's mind was racing. Should he say anything? Best not. Best let it lie.

But as they flew back to Southampton he would glance at her occasionally when she wasn't looking, and enjoy her close proximity. He felt exhilarated. Alive. Invigorated. Twenty years younger. The warning bells should have been ringing loudly, but they were not. Or if they were, he was blocking them out.

ELLIE TOOK THE PHONE CALL at four o'clock in the afternoon. 'Dad? It's for you. The Royal Infirmary.'

He took the handset from her. 'Dr Devon? This is Mark Armstrong, the houseman at the Royal.'

'Hello. Yes?'

'I'm afraid it's bad news. Dr Silverwood took a sudden turn for the worse and died an hour ago. I'm so sorry. His next of kin have been informed, but I thought you'd like to know.'

'Right. Thank you.' Christopher put down the phone.

'Is it serious?' asked Ellie.

'Yes, sweetheart. It's very serious.'

GARY WAS NOT disappointed by the reactions of Tiger and Christopher that evening. Their jaws could scarcely have been lower as Sarah sat down next to him at the table in the Hare and Hounds. They had commandeered their usual table in the far corner to the right of the fireplace where they could see the comings and goings as well as the spots on the dominoes.

Christopher had nearly rung to cancel, but Ellie said that she wanted an evening to pamper herself, and he knew that would mean at least three hours in the bathroom.

Erica had said she didn't mind that Tiger wanted a couple of hours with his mates, but privately she wondered why he seemed so distracted. Perhaps he was just preoccupied with the break-in.

Gary went through the introductions, then asked, 'Well, are we playing?'

Tiger and Christopher pulled themselves together. Tiger went for the drinks while Christopher emptied out the dominoes onto the table. It wasn't until they had played a couple of games, both of which Sarah managed to win, that the conversation began to flow.

'So how did you two meet?' Tiger asked.

Gary seemed lost for words so Sarah replied. 'At a club.'

'So you saw him across a crowded room?' asked Christopher.

'Something like that.'

'He has a terrible reputation, you know.'

Gary cut in. 'Do you mind not running me down? I brought Sarah here for a pleasant evening out, not for a bit of character assassination.'

'Sorry,' said Christopher. 'We'll try to be on our best behaviour.' And then, to Sarah, 'It's just that we've never been allowed to meet any of the others.'

Sarah smiled mischievously. 'Oh, so there have been others, have there?'

'Well,' said Tiger, 'he's not a young man. He's very experienced.'

'No. I'm sorry. This conversation has got to stop,' said Gary.

Christopher looked contrite. 'Yes. How very rude.' He turned to Sarah, 'It's just nice to see him suffer for a change. He's so much younger than we are, you see, and he usually reminds us of that.'

'Really?' countered Sarah. 'He doesn't look it.'

Gary shot her a look, then got up and went over to the bar.

Geoff, the barman, grinned at him. 'Wishing you'd not brought her now? Giving you a bit of stick, are they?'

'Just a bit,' murmured Gary. 'Just a bit.'

At the table, Sarah turned to Tiger. 'I'm sorry to hear about the shop.'

'Yes, bit of a shock,' confirmed Tiger.

'Gary says you think it's some sort of protection racket?'

Tiger looked alarmed.

'Oh, it's all right. Gary told me not to tell anyone.'

Tiger relaxed. 'Yes. Well, we've no proof as yet, but I want to question the shopkeepers in the High Street to see if I can make any sense of it.'

'You've no idea where the man in the black anorak came from? No clue as to who's behind it?'

'No. But I think it's too much of a coincidence that our shop window and the one next door were broken so soon after his visits.'

Sarah nodded, then decided to let the subject go as Gary returned with the drinks and handed them round. She turned her attention to Christopher. 'So how long have you been a GP?'

'Oh, nearly thirty years now.'

Sarah sipped at her glass of white wine. 'Never thought of going private? Harley Street or anything like that?'

Christopher laughed. 'No. I'm not a specialist. Just a general practitioner.'

Gary watched Sarah warily. He knew where she was leading.

'How does it work then, Harley Street? If you need a specialist how do you find one? Could you shop around? You know, go to several specialists and get different quotes?'

'Certainly. Years ago your doctor would probably have recommended you to someone, but it's rather different now. Harley Street has become competitive, just like anywhere else.'

'Is it all specialist medicine there, then? Rather than aches and pains?'

'It tends to be. Things like cosmetic surgery. Transplants. And simple operations, too, for private patients. People who can afford not to wait.'

'I see.' Sarah paused and considered the facts.

Taking advantage of the lull, Gary butted in, nervous of the fact that Sarah had slipped into interrogation mode. 'Er, look, if we want to make that restaurant for dinner I think we'll have to be getting along.'

'Not the Red Dragon, by any chance?' asked Tiger.

'No. Not tonight.'

'Good.' He sipped his pint then added, 'I'm not sure about that place. Not since we saw our "protection man" there. It's rather put me off it.'

Christopher chipped in: 'I've not been there yet. Was the food any good?'

'Not bad at all,' confirmed Tiger. 'But I'm not sure you'd want to go. I saw Randall Cummings sitting in a corner. Talking to the owner. At least I take it that he was the owner. He was Chinese. Looked very proprietorial.'

'I've never met him,' said Gary. 'What does he look like?'

And then they noticed Christopher.

'Are you all right?' enquired Tiger.

'Sorry?' replied Christopher absently.

'Only you suddenly look a bit pale.'

LATER THAT NIGHT, after dinner at a gastropub on the banks of the River Itchen, Sarah did not catch her train from Winchester to London. Instead she became, as she would have put it, another notch on Gary's bedpost. They made love looking up at the stars in Gary's penthouse—which is what he called his top-floor flat with a Velux window. Sarah slept peacefully in his arms as Gary gazed at the outline of Orion through the darkened glass. There was a certain satisfaction in the conquest, but also a slight nervousness that he could not pin down. Normally it would not have troubled him. He wondered why it should do so now.

Not so many miles away, Erica lay awake for a long time. She rolled over at one point and put her arms around Tiger. He did not respond. He acted as though he were asleep, but she was sure he was still awake. Eventually she drew away from him, turned over and moved to her own side of the bed. She heard the clock of the cathedral strike one. Then two. Then three. Then she fell into a fitful, uncomfortable sleep.

Back home at the Manor House, Christopher sat up until midnight talking to Ellie, learning more about her African exploits and asking about Matt. Most of the information he gleaned about Matt came from Ellie.

'I do worry,' confided Christopher.

'So do we,' said Ellie.

'What do you mean?'

'About you. We worry about you.'

Christopher laughed it off. 'But I'm far too old to be worried about.'

'That's so typical. Just because you're a parent you think that all the worry is one way. Matt and I worry about you every bit as much.'

'But why?'

She came and sat on the arm of his chair. 'Because we love you.'

Christopher looked up at her. 'That's very kind,' he said softly, and stroked her arm. 'And mum?'

'Yes. We love her too,' murmured Ellie. 'In spite of it all.'

'You mustn't blame her. If I thought that you did, I'd be very upset.'

'Dad, she went off and left you.'

'Yes. But it was my fault. I didn't pay her enough attention.'

'But you're a doctor, you're bound to be preoccupied. At least you were here. It wasn't as if you were away for weeks on end.' Ellie spoke more softly. 'You did your best, Dad. Sometimes things don't work out the way they should. But that's no reason to feel you've failed.'

'Listen to you. You're not supposed to talk like that. I'm the one with all the experience. I should be the one making value judgments.'

She leaned into him. 'I'm sorry. I just hate to see both of you unhappy.'

'You think your mother is unhappy?' There was surprise in his voice.

'She doesn't say, but I know it's not what she thought it would be.'

'With Howie?'

Ellie nodded. 'I don't think the grass is as green as she imagined.'

'Mmm. It seldom is,' he murmured absent-mindedly.

'Dad, are you sure you're all right?'

Christopher broke out of his reverie and smiled gently. 'Yes. I'm fine.'

'Is it something to do with this afternoon? That phone call?'

'Yes. You remember Dr Silverwood?'

'Yes. The little doctor with the beaky nose and the glasses.'

'Well, he died earlier today.'

'Oh, I'm sorry. You were rather fond of him, weren't you?'

'Yes. I was rather. And . . . well . . .' He paused. 'Ellie, if you knew someone had done something that you thought was wrong, and yet to mention it might cause even greater problems, would you mention the thing that was wrong, whatever the circumstances, or would you keep quiet?'

Ellie thought for a moment, then said carefully, 'I think it depends on whether you thought that the person might do the wrong thing again.'

Chapter Seven

One would be in less danger
From the wiles of a stranger
If one's own kin and kith
Were more fun to be with.
'Family Court', Ogden Nash (1902–1971)

At half past nine on Saturday morning, while Ellie was still asleep, Christopher rang Randall Cummings at his home. The phone was answered in the abrupt manner he had become used to.

'Randall, it's Christopher Devon. May I come round?'

'It's not very convenient. I've got a golf match in an hour.'

'It won't take long. I can be with you in fifteen minutes.'

'You'll have to take your chance. I might be here, I might have gone.'

There was a click as Cummings put the phone down.

Christopher took a deep breath to calm himself and went outside to his car.

Cummings's house was in a neighbouring village, within a stone's throw of the Itchen Valley Golf Club. Christopher pulled up alongside the high brick wall that surrounded the property. To enter the premises any caller had to press a button in the brick pillar beside the electronically controlled wrought-iron gates. There were gilded spears at the top of each black upright, which seemed to Christopher an appropriate indication of the owner's character.

He got out of his car and pressed the call button. After a few seconds a low hum indicated that the gates were opening. He got back into the car and drove up to the front door, where he parked alongside a silver Mercedes. The boot was open and contained a red leather golf bag filled with clubs.

As Christopher approached the pillared portico the front door opened, and a large, grey-haired man in plus fours and a lemon-yellow cashmere sweater walked out onto the broad apron of steps.

'Hello, Randall,' offered Christopher.

'You'll have to be quick,' growled Cummings, looking at his watch. 'I have to leave in ten minutes.'

'Right. Can I come inside?'

Cummings shrugged, turned on his heel and walked back into the house, with Christopher following. Once inside the cream-coloured marble hallway, Cummings rounded on him. 'I don't like being bothered at home. Especially at weekends.'

'Randall, I don't relish having to come and see you whatever day of the week, but I wanted to talk to you. Nobody knows why I really left the practice. And I don't want to have to tell them.'

'Are you trying to blackmail me?'

'Don't be ridiculous.'

'What then?'

'You've got to start being more even-handed. You can't go on reserving the best treatment for the people who can pay most.'

'That's a slanderous allegation.'

'It would be slanderous if it weren't true.'

'So what's brought all this on? Why the pricking of conscience now?'

'You know perfectly well that my conscience was pricked the moment I knew what was going on. I said so at the time.'

'So?'

'Mrs Fraser came to see me the other day.'

'Which Mrs Fraser?'

'The Mrs Fraser whose husband died because he couldn't get a kidney transplant.'

Cummings pushed his hands deep into the pockets of his plus fours. 'Lots of people die because they can't get a transplant.'

'But Mr Fraser could have had one, if you'd not decided that money was more important than ethics.'

Cummings's face began to turn red. 'If you're telling me that I made an error of judgment—'

'Of course I am. Of course you did. You gave a kidney to someone who could pay for it. You bumped them to the top of the list and ignored those who were already there and it's got to stop.'

Cummings glowered, his face now a deep shade of crimson. 'If you're threatening me . . .'

'I'm telling you how I feel, that's all. I'm a doctor, like you, but I didn't become a doctor to make a fortune.'

Cummings threw back his head and laughed. 'Ha! That's rich, coming from you. Left a manor house by your auntie. When have you ever had to struggle, eh? You with your Cambridge education and your flowery bedside manner. You never could stomach the fact that I was the senior member of the practice—apart from Reggie Silverwood—and much good he was.'

'Reggie Silverwood was a good doctor who cared for his patients.'

'And are you saying that I don't?'

'I'm saying that you're not even-handed. And while we're on the subject of Reggie, what happened on Thursday?'

Cummings was caught off guard. 'What do you mean?'

'Reggie rang me. There was something wrong. Had he rumbled you, Randall?'

'Don't be ridiculous. Anyway, there's not much point in talking about it now, is there? Not after his accident. Bloody bad luck. But there we are.'

'You're sure it was just bad luck?'

'Of course I am. Had a heart attack and lost control.'

'Well, the post-mortem will confirm whether it really was an accident.'

'Post-mortem? What post-mortem? Just exactly what are you implying?'

'I don't know, Randall. I just want an easy conscience, that's all. I want to be able to sleep at night knowing that I've done all I can.'

'All you can to what?'

'Save lives.'

'You sanctimonious bugger. Get out!'

'I'm sorry that I'm not prepared to put my head in the sand, Randall. It might suit your *modus operandi*. It might make for a quieter life for me. But I can't do it.' Christopher turned and walked out of the door and down the steps to his car.

TIGER TRIED TO AVOID working on Saturdays, especially when he had been away for much of the preceding week. But today he had to call in at the helicopter hangar to check his workload for the following week and to tell the mechanic about a couple of things that needed attending to.

He was sitting in the office going over paperwork when Sam walked in.

He looked up and saw it was her. Then he noticed her expression. 'Are you OK?'

'Not really, no. It's my aircraft. There's a problem with the engine and they can't fix it until the end of next week.'

'But we're supposed to have an express delivery system so that we're not out of the sky for any longer than we have to be.'

'I know. But the particular part they need doesn't exist in this country, can you believe? They have to get it from the States and that's going to take three days and then they have to fit it.' Sam flopped down in the chair at the desk that butted on to the front of the one Tiger sat at. 'So I'm sorry. It means you'll have company next week.'

'Oh?' he tried to sound level.

'Yes. The boss says he thinks it would be good if I kept you company, then at least I won't be completely wasting my time.' She paused. Then said, 'If it's all right with you?'

'Yes. Yes, of course. No problem at all.'

GARY PROPPED HIMSELF up on his elbow and looked at Sarah sleeping on the pillow next to him, her long dark hair spread out like some raven wave, her expression calm and relaxed.

Carefully he stroked a few stray strands from the side of her face and she murmured something so softly that he could not hear. Then she opened her eyes, looked startled for a moment, then relaxed again.

'Do you want some coffee?'

Sarah shook her head. 'No. Tea. Please.'

Gary bent down and kissed her on the cheek, then slid out of bed and walked down the few steps that led into the living area. He crossed to the kitchen in the far corner.

Sarah watched him go. 'Nice bum.'

'Thank you.'

'For someone your age.'

He turned and looked at her.

'Nice other things as well.'

Gary picked up a towel from a pile of washing in the kitchen and wrapped it round himself.

'Well, well . . .' said Sarah.

'What?' asked Gary, filling the kettle at the tap.

'That's not a word I would ever have associated with you.'

'What isn't?'

'Embarrassment.'

He put the kettle on the hob and walked back towards the bed. 'How do you know I'm embarrassed?'

'Because you've gone just a tiny bit pink.'

Gary pulled the sheet away from her and gazed at her body. 'And you're quite a lot pink,' he said, bending down and kissing her stomach.

They had their tea and coffee later, when they could no longer stand the insistent whistling of the kettle.

CHRISTOPHER WAS SHAKING by the time he drank his coffee in the kitchen at the Manor House. But at least he had done it. Cleared his conscience. Up to a point. Whether it would make any difference only time would tell.

He had thought long and hard about it. Wondered whether he was being cowardly in not taking the matter to a higher authority. But the warning he had given Cummings was as far as he would go, for now. If he discovered the merest suggestion that Cummings was still on the make then he would have to go further.

Ellie came down, bleary and tousled, at around half past ten. 'Mmm . . . hello,' she murmured, opening the fridge and hauling out a pint of milk.

'Hello, you. Sleep well?'

Ellie smiled a beatific smile without opening her eyes. 'Yup.'

Christopher grinned. 'So are you ready for a shopping trip?'

'Do I look ready?'

'Well, if you get your skates on I'll drop you in town.'

Ellie snapped awake. 'Give me twenty minutes and I'm yours.'

True to her word she appeared at the bottom of the stairs at the appointed time. 'Anyway, Dad, what are you doing going into town on a Saturday? I'd have thought you'd be happier in the garden.'

'Er . . . I'm just dropping in on Maria. She asked if I'd look at her roses. It sounds as though they might have a bit of canker.'

'And you being a good doctor she thought you'd be able to sort her out?'

'No. Me being a good *gardener* she thought I'd be able to sort *them* out.'

As they walked to the car, Christopher said, 'I don't know why you're grinning like that. There is absolutely nothing funny about canker on roses.'

HE HAD EXPECTED a small garden with a few forlorn rose bushes within it. What met his eye on that spring Saturday morning was an altogether different sight.

Maria's house was a small Georgian terraced cottage a few streets away from the cathedral close. The house fronts were stucco, and painted in different colours—soft yellow, pale blue, warm cream and even blush pink. All the front gardens had retained their low-pillared walls and contained either modern minimalist gardens, traditional cottage-garden plants or tiny squares of lawn bordered by daffodils.

Number 34 was the gem among them. Christopher cast his eye over the mixture of plants that jostled for position in the small tapestry that was Maria's front garden. It was a plantswoman's garden, put together with skill and good taste, and Christopher was taken aback.

His reverie was broken by the sound of her voice. He looked up to see her standing in the doorway. 'Don't look too close. It's a bit early in the year.'

Christopher raised his hands in amazement. 'It's perfect.' He opened the gate and walked down the path to greet her. 'I thought it would just be a bit of a rose bed with a few tired old bushes in it.'

She smiled. 'It was when I came here five years ago.'

Christopher looked around. 'So where's the rose you mentioned?'

'It's in the back garden.'

Maria led him through the house to the kitchen at the back—a sleek, modern room with pale wooden worktops and a pair of French doors that opened onto the tiny back garden. It was a simple creation, centred by a rectangular box-edged bed sliced into four triangles. On the wall at the end, a lion's head fountain spurted into a lead cistern, and everywhere the same skilful mixture of plants that had been evident in the front garden.

Christopher shook his head. 'I had no idea that you were such a good gardener. I saw the way you looked at mine, when I took you round on that first day, and I thought it was because you couldn't understand it.'

'Oh, no. It was envy. I'd never seen so much garden!'

'Well, you've made the most of this patch.' He brought his eyes to focus on his immediate surroundings now. The kitchen was fresh and painted white with floor-to-ceiling bookshelves down one wall. He glanced at some of the titles—gardening mixed up with cookery and with fiction.

She made coffee while he sat at the table.

Maria pointed out of the window. 'That's the rose with the canker. The one over there in the corner. "Souvenir de la Malmaison". It's a lovely pale pink but it doesn't seem very happy.'

'No,' confirmed Christopher. 'I gave up with mine years ago. I think you'd be better off planting something with a stronger constitution.'

'Any suggestions?'

'Try "Jacques Cartier". It never seems to get diseased and it flowers for most of the summer, too. It is a bit bigger, though.'

'Thank you, Doctor.'

'That'll be five guineas.'

She laughed. 'Very reasonable.'

'Or I'll settle for a cup of coffee.'

Maria joined him at the kitchen table and for the next half hour they talked easily about gardens and plants, about books and cooking.

There was a moment where he came close to confiding in her. Wanted to tell her where he had been early that morning. Wanted her opinion on what he should do, whether he should take it any further. He would have liked to hear her point of view. He opened his mouth to broach the subject but instead found himself saying: 'I've made enquiries about the opera. There's a performance of *Tosca* at Covent Garden next Wednesday.'

'Perfect.'

'You don't need to look in your diary?'

Maria shook her head. 'It's not exactly packed with social engagements.'

Christopher made to get up. 'Right. Well, I'd better be going. I'll see you on Monday.'

'You're about then? Not on call?'

'No. Not next week. They've given me a week off.'

He tried not to sound worried, and Maria did not like to pursue the subject. Instead, she said brightly, 'I'll make sure you have some lunch, then.'

TIGER WAS NOT getting on too well. Having finished his paperwork at the airport he had gone into Winchester and begun his inventory of shops, thinking that if nothing else it would take his mind off Sam. He battled with himself over her. Half the time he wallowed in the pleasurable thought of being next to her for another week. Wondering where it might lead. Then his conscience would get the better of him.

The shopkeepers he questioned did not exactly welcome him with open arms on a busy Saturday morning, neither were they forthcoming with much information. After an hour of futile questioning he realised he was getting nowhere. He walked to the bookshop where Erica was working the morning shift, Brian having gone to see his mother in Bournemouth.

'You look a bit down in the mouth,' said Erica. 'No luck?'

Tiger leaned against one of the towering bookshelves. 'Bloody useless.'

'I'm glad.'

'What do you mean?'

'Well, if you'd found something you'd have gone at it like a dog with a bone, and I don't know that I want you getting mixed up in this.'

Tiger looked disappointed. 'But you said yourself that the police weren't doing anything about it.'

'I know, but I'd just like to see if that warning they gave him has frightened him off. Then you won't need to get involved.'

Not get involved. Something about the words echoed around his head.

'Are you all right?'

'Mmm?'

'Only your mind's been somewhere else since you came back.'

CHRISTOPHER HAD THREATENED Randall Cummings with a post-mortem to warn him off. If he was to carry out his threat he could not put off ringing the coroner any longer. He'd known Monty Loveday for many years. Perhaps he could arrange a post-mortem with the minimum of fuss.

Old cars were Monty's thing, and Christopher was fairly confident of catching him at home on a Saturday. He was a fifty-year-old man with the the tall, gangling body of an adolescent, all the better for reaching the inner recesses of his 1938 Wolseley, which rejoiced in the name of Veronica.

'Monty, I'm sorry to bother you on a Saturday.'

'Christopher, the car's in bits so to be honest I'm glad of the break.'

'Bit of advice, Monty. I've got a death that I'm a bit suspicious about. I was wondering if you could authorise a PM.'

'How suspicious?'

'Well, the cause of death was thought to be accidental, but I'm not sure.'

Monty sounded serious. 'Christopher, if you think that death was in suspicious circumstances then you should be talking to the police.'

'I know. But I don't want to make ripples if there's no need. I just want to satisfy myself that his death was due to an accident, nothing else.'

'I'd like to help. But I really don't see how I can.'

'Of course. No.'

'Is it anybody I know?'

'Reggie Silverwood.'

'Ah, poor Reggie. Very sad. But you don't really think his death was suspicious, do you? From what I've heard he had a heart attack and ended up in a ditch. Open-and-shut case.'

'Perhaps you're right . . .'

'I'm getting the feeling you're not telling me everything, Christopher.' Monty sounded puzzled.

'Oh, it's just a thought. Look, never mind, Monty. I'll get back to you if I need to. I'm sorry to bother you on your day off.'

Christopher put down the phone and reasoned with himself. Randall Cummings might be lining his pockets more than he should, but there was no way he would actually have brought about Reggie's death. It was time he stopped overreacting.

He decided to telephone Betty Silverwood to offer his condolences. That way he could be both personal and brief, without the distance of a letter or the imposition of a house call. He had met her on a number of occasions over the years—when the practice had organised a dinner, or occasionally when she had come to pick Reggie up from the surgery.

'It was a bit of a shock,' she admitted. Reggie's capacity for understatement and calmness in the face of all difficulties was clearly a characteristic shared by his wife. 'He'd seemed fine,' she continued. 'A bit preoccupied, perhaps. But you're all like that from time to time, aren't you?'

Christopher voiced his agreement, then asked, 'But he'd not said that he was worried about anything in particular?'

'No. Not at all. No more than usual.'

'So have you set a date for the funeral?'

'No. Not yet. Anyway, it'll be a service of thanksgiving rather than a funeral. Reggie left his body to science, you see. Once his organs had been donated. He was very keen on that.'

'I REALLY CAN get myself onto a train, you know,' said Sarah.

'Yes, but I want to make sure.'

'Why? Can't wait to get me out of your hair?' She looked at the top of his head. 'Not that there is much of it.'

'Are you complaining?'

'No,' she said. 'No, I'm not.'

Gary walked her up to the platform of Winchester Station. They were not holding hands. She had hers on the strap of the satchel that hung from her shoulder. His were plunged deep into the pockets of his leather jacket.

'Why me, Sarah?' he asked, matter-of-factly. 'You've fended me off for months. Why the change of heart?'

'Who knows?'

'You can tell me if it was just a one-night stand.'

'Is that what you'd prefer? Is that what you're used to?'

'Used to, yes. But not what I'd prefer.'

They stood back as the train thundered alongside the platform and drew to a halt.

'You could stay if you want,' he said, as the electric doors slid open. 'You don't have to go back.'

'No clothes,' she said. 'Can't wear these all weekend.'

'But you could come back when you've got them.'

She stepped up onto the train and turned to face him. 'Maybe next time.' She leaned forward and kissed him on the cheek, then the doors slid closed and the train pulled slowly out of the station.

Gary watched until the train was a tiny dot at the end of the track and then decided to walk into town and pay a visit to Erica's bookshop.

'We don't see you here very often,' said Erica. 'Going on holiday?'

'I wish,' said Gary. 'Too much on. Just thought I'd come and pick up a bit of reading. Could you point me in the direction of China?'

'You'll find China down the third alleyway somewhere between Borneo and Denmark. Anything in particular?'

'Well, not so much a travel guide as a book on Chinese culture.'

Erica led the way to the third aisle. 'I think something came in a couple of weeks ago.' She scrutinised the shelves in the section marked CHINA. 'There you are . . . up there. The one with the dreary cover.'

Gary stretched up and pulled down the book. '*Modern China: Its Economy and Changing Culture*. I see what you mean about the cover.'

'The title's not very exciting either, is it? I'm sure we can find something more inspiring. Wouldn't you rather have something with more photographs?'

'No, this'll be perfect.'

'If you're sure.'

Gary paid for the book, took it home, and for the rest of the afternoon immersed himself in the culture of the East. It took his mind off Sarah for a while, and it was not a wasted exercise. He had never met Mr Tan, but now he could picture him a little more clearly.

Chapter Eight

Who shall decide, when doctors disagree?
'Epistles to Several Persons', Alexander Pope (1688–1744)

Monday morning dawned cold and damp. Christopher greeted Maria warmly, but she could see that he was preoccupied.

'I'm just nipping out to the hospital for a while,' he told her.

'Fine. Lunch at about one? I can do some soup to warm you up.'

Her kindness pricked his conscience. 'Thanks. That will be lovely.' He looked at her, unsure what to say, then smiled hesitantly and turned to go. He stopped at the door. 'I really am grateful, you know. I do appreciate it.'

She looked down. 'Oh . . . it's nothing.'

There were no more words between them, just a glance. To Christopher, in that split second, it seemed that something had touched him—reached out and reassured him. He hoped he wasn't convincing himself there was more to it than there was. In spite of his worries about Randall Cummings and Reggie Silverwood, the existence of Maria in his life, and the return of Ellie, had cheered him up more than he could have imagined. Ellie. He must talk to her more, make time for her. Tonight he would cook her something special for supper.

AT THE HOSPITAL, Dr Armstrong was apologetic. 'I'm sorry you didn't know. It didn't occur to me to say at the time.'

Christopher was standing in front of the young doctor in his office at the end of one of the wards. 'So the organs were removed straight away?'

'Almost immediately, yes. The kidneys, the other useful bits.'

'And the rest of the body?'

'Off to a teaching hospital.' Then he looked a little apprehensive. 'It was all done quite properly. All the forms were signed.'

'Yes, yes, I'm sure. I should have realised. Reggie was always so keen on his patients carrying donor cards it would have been surprising if he hadn't carried one himself.'

Christopher made to go, then he turned at the door. 'How long have you been working here, Mark?'

'Oh, about eighteen months. Why?'

'Do you have many dealings with Dr Cummings?'

'Not if I can help it. Scares the pants off me. Gruff old bugger.'

'Not popular, then?'

'No. The patients are terrified of him and most of the nurses are wary. He's not very friendly, not very chatty. A bit hard to get to know. But then with a bark like that no one really wants to make the effort.'

Christopher nodded thoughtfully. 'I gather he signed Dr Silverwood's death certificate?'

'Yes. He happened to be on the ward when he died.'

'And did he know about Reggie's organ donor card?'

'Yes. In fact, I think he alerted us to it. Yes, that's right. He said he would put in a call to someone. But we have our own procedure for organ donation and so it was taken in hand here.'

Christopher sighed with relief.

'Is something wrong, Dr Devon?'

'No. Not this time, thank God.'

THIS PARTICULAR MONDAY morning found Tiger apprehensive. He'd been unable to settle to anything over the weekend, with the events of the previous Thursday evening playing over and over in his mind. He tried to rationalise. It had been a kiss, for God's sake, a simple, single kiss. But then his mind went into that peculiar self-destruct overdrive: did he want it to be that simple? Had he enjoyed it? Yes. Would he like to do it again? Yes. No! But yes. Would he like it to go further? Yes. No! Definitely not. But if it did, what would it be like? It was, he knew, a dangerous brew.

He checked in at the helicopter base at Southampton Airport and found himself scheduled for a flight to Leeds Bradford Airport with two executives and Sam. The flight was uneventful and the two gents were dropped off midmorning.

It was a wait and return job. Tiger and Sam had three hours to kill. They refuelled, then went to the waiting room. He wondered how they would pass the time. He did not have long to wait.

'Let's hire a taxi,' said Sam. 'We could run up to the moors. Take in the view. Have a cup of tea.'

Tiger laughed. 'Nice thought. But if they finish their meeting early and come back to find we're up on the moors, I can't see they'll be best pleased.'

'No. I suppose not.'

He wondered if she had forgotten what had happened. Maybe he was making too much of it. Then she broke the tension.

'The other night . . .' she said.

So there it was. 'Yes.'

'I'm sorry if what I did upset you. I didn't mean to.'

'Didn't mean to do it?'

'No. Didn't mean to upset you.'

'Well, you didn't upset me.'

'So you don't mind?'

'No.'

She turned to him and smiled. 'That's all right, then.'

WHEN SARAH ARRIVED at work that morning she found Gary sitting behind his desk looking particularly smug.

'Hello. You look pleased with yourself. Something you'd like to share?'

'I thought we'd already done that,' he said.

'Oh, very clever. So is that look the sort of look I'm going to get every morning from now on?'

'Probably not.'

She hung up her coat and turned round. He flattered himself that he detected a look of disappointment. 'Oh?'

'Had a bit of a breakthrough at the weekend.'

'Go on.' She came over and perched on the edge of his desk.

'Well, what did we notice about Mr Tan last week? Where did he go?' asked Gary.

'To the Chinese restaurant . . . the Red Dragon . . . and to Harley Street.'

'Exactly.'

'So it's Harley Street that's important. I was right,' she said triumphantly. 'Don't tell me. Mr Tan's into dodgy cosmetic surgery. He leaves all his patients looking like the Bride of Wildenstein and then does a runner with the money?'

'He could do, but I think it's unlikely.'

'So what's left?'

'Transplants. He's selling people's organs.'

'How could he do that?'

Gary was warming to his subject. 'Well, if you've been reading the newspapers you might have seen pieces about corpses being relieved of their organs before they were released for burial.'

'Yes.'

'It seems there's a massive illegal market out there. Criminal gangs work out deals with undertakers—or even dodgy hospital staff—and arrange for the removal of body parts for sale to transplant companies.'

'Transplant *companies*?'

'Yes. If you need a transplant and have enough money they'll find you a heart or a kidney or whatever you want, and arrange it.'

'You make it sound like buying a car.'

'A very expensive car.'

'So you think Mr Tan is involved with dodgy undertakers?' asked Sarah, sliding off Gary's desk and walking round to her own.

'Not necessarily. The National Health Service waiting lists are still far too long and more people are going private so they can skip queues. But that still presupposes, where transplants are concerned, that there are enough organs to go round.'

'Which there aren't,' chipped in Sarah.

'Correct. So, another private market develops, where the very rich can book themselves into a Harley Street clinic, for instance, which specialises in transplants.'

'So if you're rolling in dosh, but need a new kidney, you can get one straight away?'

'Exactly. But where do these organs come from?'

'Corpses?'

'Not always.'

'No. I remember reading about poor people in some country or other who will sell a kidney to earn money.'

'That's right. In Moldova, for instance—desperately poor country, sandwiched between Romania and the Ukraine—people actually mortgage their bodies. They'll sell one of their kidneys for a few thousand quid. And what does it sell for to a prospective patient? Go on, guess.'

'Ten grand?'

'As much as ninety-five thousand pounds.'

'Bloody hell!' Sarah sat back in her chair. 'But what makes you think Mr Tan is involved? He's never been to Moldova—at least not since we've been tracking him.'

'No. But Moldova's only one of the countries involved. Israeli patients fly to Turkey and get most of the Moldovan kidneys. There are brokers in New York who work with Russian immigrants; rich Palestinians go to Iraq . . .'

Sarah whistled. 'So it's a worldwide trade?'

'You bet. But in the UK it's illegal to profit from trading in body parts. That means all such trading is driven underground. And there are new restrictive laws in India now, which means it's recently been overtaken in the transplant export market by which country?'

'China?'

'Got it in one, Miss Perry.' Gary leaned back in his chair and folded his arms behind his head. 'The organs you can buy in India come mainly from live donors, but China's do not.' He paused.

Sarah leaned forward in her chair. 'Go on.'

'Well, it's not very nice. Condemned prisoners in China are shot through the head to avoid damaging their organs, which are then sold.'

'That's gross.'

'It's a fact.' Gary rifled through the papers on his desk. 'Here. These are figures from Amnesty International. In 1996 they reported that ninety per cent of transplanted kidneys in China came from executed prisoners.'

Sarah stood up and walked to the window. 'How depressing.'

'Depressing but unbelievably lucrative. If you're rich and your life depends on a new kidney, you'll spend whatever it takes to get one.'

'And Mr Tan can oblige?'

'Probably. Of course, I don't know for certain. But since we haven't been able to link him with drugs, and if he's not visiting Harley Street for private medical reasons, it would make sense of everything we've seen.'

Sarah shook her head. 'It's one heck of an assumption.'

CHRISTOPHER COULDN'T REMEMBER when he had last lit a candle. He thought he'd make an effort. Ellie would be with him until the end of the week, she had said, but he reckoned that most evenings she'd be out catching up with her mates and so he'd make the most of tonight.

'Are we dressing for dinner?' she'd asked. With tongue in cheek he'd replied, 'Of course,' but he was surprised when she came down in a sparkly top with her long fair hair cascading over her shoulders.

'You know, when you make an effort it's quite amazing what you can look like,' he teased.

'Yes. Well, it's just a shame you didn't do the same.'

'OK. Point taken. Would you like me to go and change?'

'Don't be daft. Only kidding. Anyway, this is probably the last chance I'll get to wear anything decent before I go back to Africa.'

'I thought you'd be out on the town.'

'Not out. In. It's better to see my friends at home, then we can talk properly instead of shouting over all that loud music.'

Christopher smiled. 'I thought I was supposed to think like that, not you.'

'Oh, I don't know, Dad. I can't take the racket like I used to.'

'At twenty-three?'

'And three-quarters.'

Christopher poured her a glass of wine and they sat down at either side of the kitchen table. 'I don't remember when I last did this,' he said.

'That's sad,' said Ellie. 'Maybe you'll be doing more of it soon. Have you asked Maria round to dinner?'

'No. Not yet. Don't want her to think I'm pushing things. We're going to the opera on Wednesday, though. *Tosca*. At Covent Garden.'

'Safe.'

'What do you mean?'

'Well, not much time to talk. Except in the interval. Not much time to get to know one another.'

'We're getting to know one another quite well, I think. I told you—I've been to look at her rose bush—and she joins me for lunch some days.'

Ellie giggled. 'How romantic! You've been to look at her rose bush . . .'

Christopher sounded hurt. 'Well, it's all right for you. I mean people of your age are expected to go on dates. People of my age are usually fixed up, but when you're not, you don't seem to be able to do anything without it having . . . great significance.'

Ellie took a sip of her wine. 'Would you like this one to have great significance?'

Christopher thought for a moment. 'Yes. I think I probably would. But it's early days.'

'Are you still worrying about mum?'

'Of course.' He took a gulp of the wine. 'Never stop.'

'Dad, I know I shouldn't really say this . . .'

Christopher looked up from his glass.

'You're going to have to get a life of your own.'

He sighed. 'Fancy you having to tell me that. How very grown-up.'

'No. Not grown-up. Just realistic. I know it might seem disloyal, and I don't want to be disloyal to either of you but . . . well . . . mum's made her own life now. You're not that old and you're still quite dishy.'

'Me? Dishy?'

'Yes! Some of my friends' mums go quite weak at the knees whenever your name is mentioned.'

'Don't be silly.'

'They do! You're a good catch.'

'For a gold-digger?'

'That's just Matt being protective.'

'Of me or your mother?'

'Both. I think really he'd like you back together—'

Christopher interrupted, 'I don't think that's being realistic . . .'

'But I know he wants you to be happy, too.' Ellie shook her head. 'You haven't exactly made an effort to find a new partner have you?'

Christopher took a deep breath. 'I did go on the Internet.'

'What?'

'I just typed in "soulmate" to see what would come up.'

Ellie's eyes lit up. She leaned across the table. 'What happened?'

'Disastrous. One hypochondriac, one rather dull librarian and one who was . . . how shall I put it? . . . rather keen on the physical side of things.'

'Dad! You didn't . . . ?'

'No, I did not. I got her out of here before her feet could touch the ground.'

'You invited her here?'

'Well, I thought it might be more private. I didn't want to do my . . . courting . . . in public. In front of patients, with them all nudging and winking.'

'I'd never thought of that.'

'No. Most people don't. There's no anonymity when you're the local doctor. They all mutter and give each other knowing glances. Well, they would if given half a chance. So I thought I'd be safer here.'

'But Maria. She seems very nice.'

Ellie noticed that her father's whole demeanour changed at the mention of her name. The hunted look disappeared. His face relaxed.

'Yes. She is. And she likes gardening. And opera. Your mum never . . .'

'No,' said Ellie softly.

'And we talk. A lot. About all kinds of things.'

'And there's no other man in her life?'

'Not as far as I can make out. I mean, there's no sign of a man round at the house. Her children have left home. Apparently she's divorced.'

'Well, I think it's lovely.'

'Do you now?' Christopher got up and walked over to the Aga. 'I hope you think the same about your dinner. What would you say to a little fish?'

'Hello, little fish,' she said.

TIGER AND ERICA were finishing a meal when the call came at half past ten that evening.

'Mr Wilson?'

'Yes?'

'Do you think you could come down to the police station? We've caught someone trying to break into your shop.'

They went down together. Tiger drove.

'Do you think it's him?' asked Erica. 'If they've got him, it would be such a result.'

'Yes. I'd like to punch his lights out.'

Erica seemed surprised. 'That's not like you.'

'Well, we've never been done over like this before. I didn't realise how I'd feel about it, I suppose. I mean, we're not that well off, and whatever we've got, we've earned. It just pisses me off that somebody else thinks they can have it by lobbing a brick through your window. It's as if they're saying, "Why waste your time working for it, mate, when all you need is a bit of muscle?" It makes me angry.'

Erica sat quietly for the rest of the journey. The police station was only a few minutes away. They parked outside and walked up the steps.

Tiger spoke to the young policeman behind the desk. 'The name's Wilson. You caught someone trying to break into our shop.'

'Oh yes, sir. Would you come this way?'

He led them down the corridor and tapped on one of the doors.

'Come in.'

The policeman showed them in to a small room. 'Mr and Mrs Wilson, sir. The shop owners.'

'Ah, yes.' An overweight man in his forties with an open-necked shirt and brown jacket nodded at them and shook their hands. 'Detective Sergeant

Evans. They didn't manage to get into your shop. Our lads caught them in the act of trying. Bashed the lock a bit, but the shop is still secure. I know you had a bit of bother last week, and just wondered if you've seen any of these before.' He gestured at a large window in one of the walls, with a view through to another room. 'They can't see you. It's special glass.'

Tiger and Erica looked through the window at the three teenage youths slumped round a table. Then they looked at each other. Erica shook her head. Tiger sighed. 'No, Sergeant. No, we've not seen any of them before.'

The sergeant registered their disappointment. 'It would have been neat if it had been the man you complained about last week, I know. But we wondered if there was any way you could associate him with these three?'

'No, I'm afraid not.'

'Well, they've had a go at one or two other shops as well. Maybe we've found our men. With any luck the two things won't be related and hopefully you won't hear any more from your caller.'

Tiger nodded. 'Well, thanks very much. What will happen to the lads?'

'They'll probably be sent to a detention centre for a bit. It might help. It might not. But hopefully this will be an end to your troubles.'

If only it were that easy, thought Tiger.

Chapter Nine

> A kiss can be a comma, a question mark or an exclamation point.
> That's basic spelling that every woman ought to know.
>
> Mistinguette (1875–1956)

After a short burst of frenetic activity, the Adventure Bookshop had calmed down. Now it was more like the usual Wednesday morning. Erica could have done with a game of tennis to get her endorphins going, but Brian's mother in Bournemouth had had a funny turn and he said he'd have to stay with her for a few days, if that was all right. How could she refuse?

The shop was empty now, with only the soft sounds of a Mozart tape to break the silence. Erica wandered through to the back to make herself a coffee. At least she had a few minutes to herself. Not that she felt very comfortable about that. She didn't much relish being alone on the premises after the events of the previous few days, and aside from her worries about security, she was unsettled in her mind about other things.

Something wasn't right. She could not define it, and Tiger certainly never said anything, but he remained disconnected from her. She could have a conversation with him and he'd give her his full attention, but then he'd drift off again. He didn't spend much time in the same room as her, and in bed he seldom came over to her side; spent most of the time facing in the opposite direction. She tried to tell herself it was just a passing phase, and yet sadness gnawed at her.

Her train of thought was broken by the sound of the shop bell. She took a deep breath and came out of the back room to find Kate Devon standing in front of the counter.

'Kate!' She put her arms round her and kissed her on both cheeks, and when she stepped back she noticed that Kate's eyes were filled with tears.

'Are you all right? What is it?'

'Oh, I'm sorry. I'm fine. It's just that I haven't seen you for ages.' Her eyes scanned the shelves of books. 'Haven't seen this place for ages.'

'We're still here.'

'I'm glad. I wouldn't like to think the old world had all disappeared.'

Erica smiled ruefully. 'No. The old world is still here. Limping on. Look, do you want to go out for a coffee? I'll close the shop for half an hour.'

'Are you sure? Only I don't want to . . .'

'Of course I'm sure. I want to hear all your news.' Erica pulled down the blind on the shop door, hastily scribbled '*Open again at noon*' on a piece of card and placed it in the side window. 'Come on.'

She took Kate to a small café further down the alley, and they sat down at a corner table where they could talk without being overheard.

'So tell me all about him. Howie, is it?'

Kate replied without enthusiasm. 'Yes. Howie. He's in Barcelona.'

'And you're not with him? How can you resist Barcelona? All that architecture . . .' Erica's enthusiasm was in marked contrast to Kate's responses.

'Well, when you've done it three times it doesn't have quite the appeal.'

Erica could see that the first bloom of love was beginning to wear off. 'So where are you living?'

'Rome mostly, but I thought I'd come here for a few days. On my own.'

'To Winchester?'

'No. To London. I thought I'd pamper myself in the Ritz for a while.' She looked at Erica. 'Though to be honest I'd rather be in a B&B in Winchester.'

'Well, stay the night then.'

'Oh, Erica, I couldn't. I've nothing to wear.'

Erica looked at Kate, with her blonde hair, her well-cut trouser suit and her brown crocodile boots, then glanced down at her own nondescript working clothes. She said drily, 'Well, you could make do with the rags you've got on. And we do have clothes shops in Winchester.'

Kate smiled apologetically. 'Oh, I couldn't.'

'Yes, you could. And anyway, Tiger's out tonight and I could do with a bit of company. How do you fancy a girl's night in?'

Kate's face relaxed. 'To tell you the truth, I'd love one.'

'YOU WANT TO DO WHAT?' Sarah was looking at Gary as though he'd just lost the plot.

'Christopher's the only doctor I know. I'm not going to give anything away. Just sound him out a bit. See what he knows about the transplant trade in Britain. He might not know anything, of course, but he must have patients in need of transplants. I've asked Ben Atkinson to make enquiries in Harley Street but I'm not that hopeful. They're a tightly knit bunch.'

He just needed to get a better feel for the lie of the land. But how to broach the subject without making Christopher suspicious? Maybe he could give the impression that he was taking Tiger up on his 'secret society' idea. It was a bit risky, and a bit far-fetched, but just supposing the domino club secret society took an interest in finding out more about illegal transplants . . . He could make sure the topic was dropped before they ever got close to actually *doing* anything.

Sarah dropped a file on his desk. 'Here you are. Mr Tan's latest movements. Three more visits to Harley Street. One on Monday, two yesterday.'

'In which case he's either very ill or very greedy.'

'He doesn't look especially poorly,' said Sarah briskly.

'But we don't know yet that it's organs he's selling, not drugs. And there's still the possibility of the protection racket, even though all the police have come up with so far is a group of layabouts looking for a bit of excitement. We can't go much further until we have a positive lead. I really don't see how there can be any danger in just talking to my mates Christopher and Tiger about what I've been reading about the trade in organs.'

Sarah sighed. 'I suppose you're right. But just be careful. Don't let anything slip about what you do.'

Christopher had taken ages to choose his tie, checked three times to make sure that he had the tickets, and set off for London in his car allowing two hours for the journey. Maria had said she would already be in London that day. She was meeting her daughter to go around the Wallace Collection. Something to do with her fine-arts degree.

Now he stood on the pavement outside the Floral Hall as a cold north wind whipped down Bow Street and away towards the river. The Opera House foyer was crowded already. Had he told her the right time?

Then, out of the melee of pedestrians, came a small figure. At first he was not sure that it really was Maria. She was dressed in a fitted cream coat and her eyes seemed more defined, her whole face more glowing than before.

'Goodness,' Christopher beamed at her. 'You look lovely.' He glanced at his watch. 'Time for a glass of champagne?'

'You're in charge,' she said. And then, quite naturally and with no fuss at all, she slipped her arm into his and they walked into the Floral Hall.

Later, in the huge expanse of the auditorium, Puccini's music filled the air and saturated their senses. Christopher turned to look at Maria. Simply to sit next to someone who was enjoying watching what you were watching, and who was hopefully enjoying the fact that they were watching it with you, was enough. 'Do we have to go?' Maria asked at the end.

Christopher laughed. 'I don't think there's any more.'

'No. It's such a sad ending but, oh, that music!'

'Blame your mother,' said Christopher as he guided Maria out of the Opera House towards his car. 'It's probably because you're half Italian that it touches you so much.'

'You're not Italian, and it touches you.'

'Yes, but I'm a romantic.'

'Ah, I see.'

They talked animatedly on the way home, about the opera, about Maria's afternoon with her daughter, about Fragonard's painting of the girl on the swing in the Wallace Collection, and when Christopher dropped her off Maria invited him in for a coffee. He was hesitant. 'If you're sure?'

'Of course I'm sure. Come on.'

She got out of the car before he could walk round to open the door, then led him into the house. They talked easily while she put the kettle on and gathered cups and saucers in the kitchen, then she motioned him through to the small sitting room at the front of the house where they sat and drank their coffee.

'Perhaps we could do it again?' Christopher asked tentatively. 'Only next time we'll go out to eat. Then we'll have more time to talk.'

'I might run out of conversation,' she said.

'Do you really think so?'

She paused for a moment, then said, 'No. No, I don't. Not with you.'

Eventually Christopher stood up to leave. Maria stood up too, and walked towards him. 'Thank you so much,' she said. 'For such a great time.'

'No. Thank *you*. It made such a change.'

It all seemed so desperately polite, thought Christopher. Like two people testing the water. Afraid to overstep the mark.

Maria smiled. 'Are you out of practice as much as I am?'

Christopher nodded. 'I guess.' He laid his arms on her shoulders and bent to kiss her gently on the lips.

'What a day,' she said. 'What a lovely day.'

ERICA GAVE KATE SUPPER on her lap.

'It's nothing special, I'm afraid. Marks and Sparks' best.'

Kate, wrapped up in a white towelling robe and sitting in front of a crackling log fire, dipped into the moussaka with a fork and almost purred. 'If you knew how much I've longed to do this . . .'

Finally, Erica asked, 'Is it not how you thought it would be?'

Kate was defensive at first. 'I knew what I was doing, Erica. How could I not be happy? I have everything. A guy who makes a fuss of me, the chance to travel all over the world, and plenty of money. I can indulge myself. That's all a girl needs, isn't it?'

Erica took her time over her mouthful of food. Then she said, 'Is it?'

Kate spoke softly. 'Not really, no.' She put down the plate and picked up her glass of wine, taking a large gulp. 'I don't know why.' She gazed into the flames. 'I used to be so annoyed that he never seemed to be able to give me any time. He was always so busy with his patients,' she half laughed, 'or his garden. But the time we did spend together was somehow . . . whole.' She turned to Erica. 'Does that make sense?'

'Yes.'

'The trouble was, it just wasn't enough. I wasn't completely satisfied.'

'Maybe it's not possible to be completely satisfied,' Erica said, softly.

'You don't think I'm someone who thinks the grass is always greener on the other side of the fence?'

'A bit. You did go, Kate. You did have the choice.'

'Yes. I'm just not sure I made the right one.'

'Does Howie know you're not happy?'

'I think he suspects. I've not been the best of company lately.'

Erica leaned forward and rested her hand on Kate's. 'Do you think you made a mistake? Looking back, I mean?'

'Yes. Yes, I do. And I wish I could undo it all and start again.' She picked up the plate of food and forked a little more of it into her mouth. Eventually she asked, 'If I went to see Christopher, do you think he'd take me back?'

'Oh, Kate, I don't know. Only Christopher knows the answer to that one.' As she said the words she remembered her meeting with Christopher and the look in his eyes when he had talked about Maria.

Kate pulled her feet up under her body and sat back in the chair. 'What about you and Tiger? You've lasted the course.'

'So far . . .'

'That doesn't sound very hopeful.'

'We're just going through a tricky patch. Nothing serious. At least I don't think so. Tiger seems preoccupied. Somewhere else altogether.'

'There's nobody else is there? With Tiger I mean?'

'Good God, no! I think I'd know if there was! It's just our age, I suppose, and the fact that we've been together so long. It does make you take one another for granted.'

'It's probably something to do with work. It usually is. Where's Tiger tonight? Off playing dominoes?'

'No. That's Friday nights. He's away on business tonight. Has to stop over in Jersey or Guernsey, I think. He's coming back tomorrow.'

'Does he go away a lot?'

'It varies. Sometimes not for a couple of weeks, then he'll have the odd week when he's away all the time. Like last week.'

'And you don't mind?'

'Part of the job. You've just got to get on with it really, haven't you?'

THE JERSEY HOTEL where Tiger and Sam were staying overlooked the sea. The little restaurant served excellent seafood, but Tiger was happier with the steak and kidney pudding. They had a bottle of Spanish red with their meal and retired for the night at around half past eleven. Tiger said good night to Sam outside the door of her room.

She looked up at him. 'Why don't you come in? Then we can say good night properly.'

Chapter Ten

And life is given to none freehold, but it is leasehold for all.

Lucretius (*c.* 94–55 BC)

Tiger did not appear at breakfast the following morning. Sam tapped on his door at 8.30 but he didn't answer. She rang him on the internal telephone. No reply. Eventually she asked the manager if he could let himself into Tiger's room to make sure everything was all right. The manager was reluctant. He suggested that Tiger might have gone out for a walk. The thought had occurred to Sam as well, but she had expected to see him at breakfast. At nine o'clock the manager telephoned Tiger's room. Still no reply. When, at last, Sam persuaded him to take his pass key and let himself in, she wished that she had acted sooner.

SAM FLEW WITH HIM in the air ambulance, her face ashen, her body shaking. A stroke, the doctor said. It was a pity they had not discovered him earlier. A pity that no one had been with him at the time. Sam considered the irony and injustice of it all. If he had agreed to come to her room she *would* have been with him and would have been able to act quickly. But then the very fact that she had been there would have raised other questions.

Would Tiger's unwillingness to be unfaithful cost him his life? She could not believe it had happened the way it had. Here she was, sitting next to his bed, stroking the back of his hand, waiting for his wife to arrive.

Sam looked at his prone body, at the wires and the tubes and the drips. How could a man who was flying helicopters in the sky yesterday be so grounded and fettered to a bed just hours later?

The doctor came back into the room. 'Miss Ross?'

She heard her name echoing. She looked up at him with a vacant stare.

'The gentlemen you brought over here—from Southampton—I think they need to be taken back.'

'But what about . . . ?'

'Mr Wilson's wife is on her way. We'll take care of him until she arrives.'

The reality of the situation bit into her. His wife would be coming. She could get back to her job. She was no longer needed here. 'Yes. Of course.'

She got up from her chair and looked down at Tiger, half covered by the crisp white sheet. Softly she traced her index finger down the back of his hand, then turned and left the room.

GARY FLYNN had two mobile phones. One was a work number, known only to his colleagues, the other was a personal phone, which he left switched off most of the time. This was why it was not until the evening that he discovered what had happened to Tiger.

Christopher's message was short and to the point: 'Gary, it's Christopher. Bad news, I'm afraid. Tiger's had a stroke and is in hospital in Jersey. Erica's over there with him. Can't tell you much more. He's comfortable but still in intensive care. Give me a ring this evening, will you?'

Gary did not ring Christopher. Instead he called round at about eight o'clock. Ellie let him in.

'Hello, Gary. Rotten news, isn't it?'

'The worst,' said Gary. 'But don't look so worried. I'm sure Tiger will pull through.' He gave Ellie a light kiss on her cheek. 'Nice to see you again. Are you here for long?'

'No. Going back tomorrow.'

'Your dad will miss you.'

'I think he'll be OK. Got another woman in his life now.' She registered Gary's look of surprise. 'Oh dear. Hasn't he told you?'

Gary shook his head.

'Oh, God! Please don't say a word, Gary.'

'It's OK.' He put his arm round her shoulder. 'Your secret's safe with me.'

'Thanks.' She gestured towards the sitting room. 'Dad's in there. I'm going out in a bit and I expect you'll be gone by the time I get back. I'll see you next time I'm over.'

'Well, you take care of yourself. Africa's a dangerous place.'

'Oh, Gary, you have such a jaundiced outlook on life. You should get out more. The world's not nearly so frightening as you think, you know.'

Gary found Christopher beside the fire in the sitting room. He was crouched over a glass of malt.

'So, how bad is it?'

Christopher indicated that Gary should help himself to a malt. 'Pretty bad.'

'Ironic, isn't it?' Gary said, pouring whisky into a glass. 'There he was, saying how we should all put a bit of excitement into our lives and now this.'

'Not the kind of excitement he had in mind.' Christopher looked thoughtful. 'The next twenty-four hours will be critical. God! I've heard that said a few times in the last couple of days.'

Gary looked quizzical.

'Oh, lost a colleague this week and I'm still smarting.'

'It's no easier, then, when you're a doctor?'

'I wish it was. I'm sure people think it must be.'

Gary took a sip of whisky, then asked, 'When will we know about Tiger?'

'We should have a better idea of how he's progressing tomorrow.'

Gary looked into the flames again. 'Fragile, isn't it?'

'Sorry?'

'Life. As solid and as strong as a rock one minute, then hanging by a thread the next.'

''Fraid so.'

'Like relationships.'

'That sounds ominous. Has Sarah given up on you? Or you on her?'

'Neither, actually.'

'Oh?'

Gary turned from the fire and faced Christopher across his glass. 'I'm fifty. Been happily bonking everything in sight for a good thirty-odd of those years and now . . .' He sighed heavily and shook his head.

'Oh dear. You poor chap. Is this the one, then? You've finally realised the error of your ways?'

'Not the error. It was fine before. I was very happy to shop around.'

'But not any more?'

'It's a weird feeling. It's like . . . well . . . a worry. A kind of fear. And at the same time a thrill. Excitement . . . and sadness . . . all rolled into one. A sort of ache.' He took a large gulp from his glass. 'Maybe I should see a doctor. Bloody stupid! At my time of life.'

Christopher spoke softly. 'If you want a doctor's opinion I'd say that you're exhibiting the symptoms of the most virulent of all afflictions.'

Gary turned to him. 'Is there any cure?'

'Time, in some cases, will effect a cure. But only in some cases. In others, the symptoms seem to last a lifetime with varying degrees of severity.'

'And you?' asked Gary.

'Well, I was affected by it once, but it went away. Without warning.'

'So you're cured?'

'I thought I was. But I think I might be contracting it again.' Christopher looked into the embers. 'And there's absolutely nothing I can do about it.'

SARAH GAZED OUT over the rooftops from the window of her mansion flat in Wimbledon. They were shining. The rain on the slates was caught in the glimmer of a hundred street lamps. It was not a particularly beautiful view, but tonight it seemed almost like fairyland. She pulled the curtains and slid into bed. Her mind ran over the events of the past few weeks.

Was it too soon to get into another relationship? Was this another relationship? She knew that he wanted it to be. But for how long?

She switched off the light and turned over, but she could not ignore the shimmering glow of the street lamps beyond her curtains and the gentle sound of spring rain on her windowpane.

IN THE SOFT POOL of light cast by the hospital lamp, Erica watched Tiger breathing slowly beneath the oxygen mask. The worries of the past few days were gone now. Light years away. They had been replaced with deeper concerns. With matters of life and death.

There was nothing she could do but wait. She stared hard at his expressionless face. It had been so troubled the last time she had seen it. It didn't matter. Not now. She reached over and stroked the dark hair above his forehead, and thought about the girls, who would be coming back from university to see their father like this. And suddenly she was engulfed by panic at the possibility of losing him. She did not want it to end like this, here in some darkened hospital room, miles away from home.

She felt her eyes stinging, found it difficult to focus on his face, as the tears welled up and streamed down her cheeks.

'YOU MUST ENJOY yourself. You must let go. Have a bit of fun,' Ellie urged, pushing more T-shirts and shorts into the already overstuffed holdall.

'Yes,' he responded meekly.

'And don't let Matt persuade you otherwise.'

'No.' He stood up and walked to the window of her bedroom. 'What do you think?' he asked, as he looked out over the garden.

'About Maria?'

'Yes. Do you like her?'

'Does it matter?'

He turned round to face her. 'Yes, it does. Very much.'

Ellie's face broke into a sympathetic smile. 'I think she's lovely. We had a chat about you. This week. In the kitchen.'

Christopher looked anxious.

'It's all right. I didn't pry. We just talked about her being here, and how she liked the garden and opera. Nothing too personal. She's'—Ellie struggled to find the right words—'very sensitive. And, well, nice. And I think you should get to know her better.' She looked apologetic. 'Am I being bossy?'

'Just a bit.' Then he smiled. 'But it's kind of you to mind.'

Ellie came up to face him, and lifted her arms until they were round his neck. 'I do mind. Desperately. And I think we all need to move on.'

'That's a very brave thing to say.'

Ellie flopped down onto her bed. 'Probably just fighting talk.'

Christopher flopped down next to her. 'Is this a front? To help you cope?'

Ellie looked pensive. 'It was once. But I'm coming through now, Dad. It was really awful, you know? Like the worst thing that had ever happened to me. I thought I'd die.'

He felt as though he'd been cut by a knife. 'Don't say that.'

'I'm only saying it now because I feel I can. I'm more on top of it. It's the reason I went to Africa. To have bigger things to think about. Bigger cares and concerns. And they helped me put my own problems into perspective.' She put her hand on top of his. 'And you are not to worry about me any more. Or to feel guilty, or anything like that.'

Christopher shook his head. 'What will I do without you?'

Ellie got up from the bed and began to zip up her holdall. 'You'll cope, Dad. Even if you do sometimes need a rocket up your bum.'

'That's no way to talk to your father!'

'No, Dad—sometimes it's the *only* way to talk to your father.'

THE LAST WEEK had brought rather too many surprises for Christopher's liking. No sooner had he waved Ellie off than a dark figure walked up the path to the Manor House. A figure that he had seen only a few days before.

'Hello, Dad.'

'Matt? I thought you were only here for a day. You said you were going back to the States after your meeting.'

'Change of plan.' And then, under his breath, 'Change of life.'

Christopher ushered his son through the front door and stood back as he hurried past and climbed the stairs to his room.

It was evening before Matt was ready to talk. The meeting in London had not been a good one. He had known there were going to be shake-ups; what had not been made clear to him was that he was a dispensable part of them. His job had disappeared due to a merging of posts. They were sorry, they said. He had done well for them and they would make sure he had a good reference, but they would prefer him to leave without working his notice.

'Why?' Christopher had asked. 'Why, if you're so good, do they not even want you to work out your notice?'

'Dad, big business is like that. They want you every waking hour of every day, and then when they've done with you they just want you out from under their feet. In case you make life uncomfortable for them.'

'And would you have?'

'No. Of course not. But they may think that my relationship would have made it difficult. The guy I live with works there too.'

'So why would that have made matters difficult?'

'He got my job.'

'Oh. I see.' Christopher offered Matt a drink. He refused, but Christopher poured one for himself. 'And where does that leave you now?'

Matt smiled ruefully. 'Without a job and without a partner.'

'Your decision or his?'

'Mutual. He came over here, too. We've been staying in London. He's gone back to the States. I'll go back in a couple of days. Tie up loose ends.'

'I am sorry, Matt.'

'Yeah. Me too. I really thought I'd cracked it this time, Dad. The job was good, I had plenty of freedom, you know, artistically, and I had someone who wanted to live with me.'

'And he doesn't any more?'

Matt looked at him. 'Would you? It's not going to work now, is it?'

'No. I suppose not. God, what a week.' Christopher took a gulp of Scotch.

'Yes. I'm sorry to add to it. And sorry to hear about Tiger.'

Christopher raised an eyebrow.

'Ellie phoned me.'

'Ah, I see.' Christopher started to apologise. 'Sorry. I should have called you, only . . . well, you get used to being on your own. Silly really. Your world shrinks. Then this week it's suddenly expanded again.'

'Thanks to me and Ellie?'

'A bit.'

'And Maria?'

Christopher looked across at him. 'Yes.' Then he asked, 'Do you mind?'

'What's it to do with me?'

'A lot. You're my son. I'd like—'

'My approval? Matt flopped into a chair. 'I don't know her, so I can't approve or disapprove.'

'You'll meet her. She's here from Monday to Thursday in the mornings.'

Matt didn't answer, so Christopher carried on. 'It's been eighteen months now. I've hardly seen your mother in that time.'

'Have you tried to get in touch?'

'How can I? She's made a life with a new man. What would I look like if I kept ringing her up? Anyway, as it happens she has a new mobile phone and she hasn't given me the number.'

His son did not reply.

'I have to make a new life, Matt. If not I'll just turn into a lonely and grumpy old man and no one will want to be anywhere near me—not even you and Ellie.'

Christopher moved over to the chair where Matt was slumped. 'You two are all I've got now. You'll always have me, but I won't always have you. Ellie will go and get married, and you'll do the same.'

Matt made to protest, but Christopher interrupted. 'Oh, I know you probably think that's it; that you'll never bother again. That nobody will ever want you. That's how I felt. Totally alone. And miserable. You can get quite used to it. And you don't have to make any effort to stay there, believe me. But then, when someone does come along and you find yourself thinking that they're more than just good company, that there's something else there—a spark of joy, of hope—just remind yourself of this conversation. It doesn't matter one jot whether you're a man with a woman or a man with a man, or a woman with a woman, when you've been battling on your own and somebody comes along who enjoys being with you, you'll find yourself actually wanting to get up in the morning.'

It wasn't until he heard himself speaking, heard himself putting his own thoughts into words that he saw how he had begun to change. That Maria had affected him more than he had realised. He began to smile. 'You notice things—colours, smells. Things you've always taken for granted. It might be a cliché, but it's true. It sharpens your senses. Brings you to life.' He stopped, wondering if, to his son, this all sounded rather foolish.

Matt sat quietly for a moment, then stood up. 'I'm going to bed,' he said.

TIGER REGAINED CONSCIOUSNESS the following day. Erica was with him when he opened his eyes. He appeared to have difficulty focusing at first, but then he seemed to be able to make her out and smiled weakly.

In a sudden rush of relief Erica lay her head on the bed and sobbed. Then she felt his hand stroking her hair, and she lifted her head to look at him, though she could barely see through the veil of tears.

'Where've you been?' she asked. 'Where've you been?'

CHRISTOPHER WAS BEGINNING TO WONDER if he would ever practice again. The locum work at Romsey had dried up—the missing partner had returned from holiday just in time to deal with the onset of a flu epidemic—and nothing else had materialised. He tried not to think about it too much. Tried not to get down.

In the meantime he found solace in the fact that his garden had never looked better at this time of year. He was forking over a flowerbed by the wall when a voice assailed him. 'So this is how you spend your time off. Digging up the daisies.' It was Gary.

Christopher *was* surprised. He could not recall when Gary had ever been to the Manor House during the day. Come to think of it, he didn't think he'd ever seen Gary during the hours of daylight, except on the rare occasions when he had visited the surgery, and even then it would most likely have been in the evening.

'I thought you only came out at night!' he said. 'You *must* be lovesick!'

Gary grinned apologetically. 'No. It's not that. It's something else.'

The day was mild, so Gary and Christopher sat on the bench beneath the yew tree.

'So, what are you doing round here, during the day?' asked Christopher.

'Oh, I've got the day off,' Gary lied. 'Thought I'd come round and take you out for a pub lunch.'

'Very thoughtful. But I'm not sure I could stomach lunch at the Hare and Hounds—all that cholesterol. And with Tiger . . . well, you know.'

'Any news?'

'Out of danger. He's still in hospital in Jersey, but Erica called to say he's regained consciousness. They don't want to move him yet.'

'Thank God! That's worth a celebration on its own. Anyway, there are other pubs around here, aren't there? The Seahorse, that's a good one.'

'Oh, well, if you're going upmarket then I'll join you.'

'I tell you what, though,' said Gary, doing his best to sound offhand. 'I was reading something in the paper that you might know about . . .'

'What's that?'

'Well, it was about illegal trading in body parts. For transplants and stuff.'

Christopher looked startled for a moment. 'Oh yes?'

'I mean, I know it goes on in the States. But does it go on here as well?'

Christopher cleared his throat. 'I have heard rumours . . . no, rather more than rumours. It does go on here. Shamefully. Strictly illegal, of course.'

'So what happens?'

Christopher relaxed. 'We have around ten thousand bone transplants a year, so there is a demand for good bones. Seven thousand people are waiting for kidneys but there are only three thousand kidney transplants a year. It's harder to get a kidney than it used to be. Our records have improved. Safer roads mean fewer deaths, fewer deaths mean fewer kidneys.'

'So where do we get them from?'

'Abroad, in the main.'

'Right. Now I was reading about that.'

'Yes. Most of them come from India. Well, they did until new laws were passed. There was a time, not so long ago, when India was known as the Great Organs Bazaar, but not any more.'

'I was reading about other countries that do it, though. Moldova, for instance.'

'Yes. It makes my blood boil.'

Gary nodded in agreement, then asked, 'Do you have much involvement with transplants?'

Christopher looked uneasy again. 'A little. I've had patients who've needed them. But I don't have any involvement in locating body parts. That's down to the hospitals.'

'So everyone stands an equal chance of getting one, then?'

'They should do.' Christopher sighed. 'Money talks, I'm afraid. Even in medicine, it saddens me to say. I know people who have helped others to jump the queue. Because they can pay.'

'You don't know people who trade in body parts, do you?' Gary asked.

'Good God, no!'

Gary moved the conversation along. 'Of course, you know where the majority of illegal organs come from nowadays?'

'Nigeria?' offered Christopher.

'No,' said Gary, pausing before playing his trump card. 'China.'

Chapter Eleven

The truth is rarely pure, and never simple.
The Importance of Being Earnest, Oscar Wilde (1854–1900)

'So, did you learn much?' asked Sarah.

'Well, I learned that there's enough illegal trading going on over here to make it a very profitable business,' confirmed Gary.

'Did Christopher know anybody involved?'

'No. Not that he would have told me if he had. But I know Christopher won't have any personal experience of it. Far too upright.'

'You make him sound dull.'

'Do I? I didn't mean to.'

They were walking along the Thames Embankment, taking a lunchtime stroll. The weather was set fair. Sarah stopped and leaned on the granite wall of the riverbank.

'I think he's rather lonely. Such a waste.'

Gary leaned on the wall next to her. 'I reckon you've got rather a soft spot for the good doctor.'

'Oh, I wouldn't say that. I just thought he was too good to be on his own.'

'Like me.'

She glanced at him. 'Are you fishing, Mr Flynn?' She looked down at the river. 'Because you won't catch much in this water.'

'Just because it looks a bit murky doesn't mean it's not full of hidden treasure, you know. You can't always go on appearances.'

Sarah turned to look at him. 'What, exactly, are you trying to say?'

Gary remained staring at the water. 'This river used to be one of the dirtiest in Europe. It couldn't support a single fish. Now it's one of the cleanest, but you wouldn't necessarily know that by looking at it. Sometimes things change almost without you noticing.'

'I see. So you think a leopard can change its spots?'

'I wouldn't go that far. But spots can fade, can't they?'

'I'd like to believe that, but I'm not sure I can.'

He turned to her. 'Come home with me tonight.'

'No, Gary. Not tonight. I'm not saying "no" full stop. I'm just saying . . . don't rush me.'

CHRISTOPHER HAD THOUGHT that he would take Maria to the Hotel du Vin in Winchester. It was smart in that shabby-chic sort of way, with a warm atmosphere. Instead, he found himself being taken out by Maria. 'You took me to the opera, so it's only fair that I should take you out to supper.'

Which is how they came to be ordering a bottle of wine in the Red Dragon.

'You do like Chinese food, don't you?' asked Maria after the waitress had brought the bottle and a menu to their table. There was a worried note in her voice. Christopher seemed to be uneasy.

'Yes. Love it. It's just that . . .'

'You don't like it here.'

Christopher snapped out of his reverie and smiled at her. 'Of course I do.' He laid his hand on hers. 'It's fine. Don't worry. I've heard a lot about the place and it'll be good to try it out.'

After a glass of wine Maria began to relax. 'I don't remember the last time I came out to dinner.' She smiled. 'It's not something Charlie and I did.'

'Tell me about Charlie.'

Maria's smile faded.

'Unless you don't want to?'

'No, it's all right. Not much to tell, really. We married quite young, then had two children. Charlie was away a lot. Driving lorries on the Continent. I suppose I realised something was wrong when his trips got longer and longer. It's funny how men think you won't notice things.'

'What sort of things?'

'Oh, the fact that their mind is somewhere else. I mean, we're not clairvoyant, but we can tell when something's not right. By all those little things—telephone calls that you interrupt; when they go out for a paper at a strange time of day. That sort of thing.'

'Yes.'

Then she said lightly, 'I'm sorry. I'm not really the suspicious type. Quite happy really. Quite straightforward. On an even keel. Most of the time.'

'Do you miss the company?' he asked.

'Yes. Yes, I do. Not that I had very much of it.' Then she stopped herself. 'Listen to me . . . What about you?'

'Oh, married to the job for thirty-odd years, married to a wife for most of them. Job stayed, wife went, then job went. All a bit of a disaster really.'

'How did the children take it?'

'Badly at first. They were older—I mean, at least they weren't in their teens. But I don't think it's easy when your parents split up, whatever your age. Ellie coped with it better than Matt. He always got on better with his mother than with me. Not that we got on badly.'

'Father and son rivalry?' asked Maria.

'A bit, I suppose. But it wasn't just that. He's gay. I think he feels that he's been a disappointment to me.'

'And has he?' Maria asked gently.

'No. Not at all. It was a bit of a shock, if I'm honest, but it doesn't embarrass me. I'd be lying, though, if I said it hadn't made things more difficult; hadn't made the break-up harder. I always felt that Matt would rather have been living with his mum.'

'You must feel very bitter.'

Christopher sighed. 'No. Not bitter. Sad. Guilty. But not bitter.' Then his face relaxed and broke into a smile. 'And right now I'm happier than I can remember.'

Maria looked self-conscious, as though she had been caught searching for a compliment. Her discomfort was relieved by the arrival of the food.

'How about you?' asked Christopher. 'Are you happy?'

'Yes. More than happy. Content.'

'Perhaps that's the secret. Perhaps what people should really ask is, "Are you content?" It's about getting in touch with reality. About balancing aspirations and actuality.'

'That sounds very deep.'

Christopher brightened. 'And very boring.'

'Not at all. Thoughtful. Accurate. Just what a doctor should be.'

Christopher was silent for a moment, then he said, 'I think it's a mistake always to rely on your head. I think sometimes you need to let your heart have a bit of a free rein.'

She smiled at him. 'I do so like being with you,' she said.

'And you,' he murmured. 'And you.'

At that moment the waitress came and asked them if everything was all right. Christopher looked up to assure her that it was, and as he did so he noticed a movement in the far corner of the restaurant. A Chinese gentleman in a suit had stood up to greet another man who had just come in. The greeting was quite muted, but Christopher gazed at the two men transfixed, as they sat down opposite one another and a waitress poured them each a glass of Scotch.

Maria noticed the change in his mood and laid down her chopsticks. 'You know what I was saying about men not realising that women notice things?'

'Mmm?'

'Christopher!'

He came back to earth. 'Sorry. Yes.'

'What is it? What's wrong?'

He took a deep breath. 'Do you ever do those puzzles in newspapers?'

She looked at him with a bewildered expression. 'What sort of puzzles?'

'Connections, I think they're called. You have to decide how one person who has apparently nothing to do with two or three other people is in fact connected to them.'

Maria looked worried. 'Are you sure you're feeling well?'

'Yes. Yes I am. But I've just had what I believe they call an epiphany.'

'I thought that came after Christmas.'

'It does. But in my case I think Christmas has come early this year.'

HAVING WORKED LATE the previous night, Gary was in no rush to turn up at the office. At eleven o'clock he was walking across Lambeth Bridge, bending forward to slice through the wind. The dull brown Thames below was being whipped into frenzied wavelets, and a barge slowly butted upstream. It was the sort of day that made him grateful he worked in an office.

Sarah would be sitting at her desk. He could see her in his mind's eye and his heart leapt. There was a difference in the way she affected him now. Before she had been a distraction. She had become so much more.

As he walked through the door she looked up and smiled at him. 'Good morning!'

'I wish,' he replied.

'Mr Tan's on the move, Gary. Went to the Red Dragon in Winchester last night, apparently.'

'Damn!'

'Yes. We picked the wrong night. The boss thinks it's time we moved in.'

'I thought I was in charge of this op?' Gary sounded irritated.

Sarah handed a file to Gary. 'You would have been if you'd turned up early enough. We were just about to send out a search party.'

Gary opened the file and read the first page. 'So we've got him?'

'Yup. And it is transplants. We managed to get some intelligence on one of the firms he's been dealing with—after a long process of elimination.'

'Yes!' He punched the air. 'So we're setting the trap?'

'As we speak. And you're a Harley Street specialist.'

'I am? I thought we were sending Ben Atkinson in when we got this far?'

'Ben called in sick and we don't want to cancel the appointment.'

'Which is when?'

'Mr Tan is expecting you at three o'clock tomorrow afternoon at the lounge in the Savoy.'

'Bloody hell! Couldn't we have made it any later?'

'Well, we could have made it next week,' Sarah said with a hint of sarcasm, 'but we thought that Mr T. might have pushed off back to Beijing.' She handed him a passport and a wallet. 'Documentation.'

Gary opened the passport and read out loud, 'Dr Andrew Wilson. Ha! They could have chosen a better name.'

'What's wrong with Andrew Wilson?'

'Oh, it's just that it's Tiger's real name. Perhaps that's an omen.' He closed the passport and looked through the wallet, muttering. 'What am I meant to do, then? Go up to Mr Tan and say, "Got any organs for sale, guv?"'

Sarah frowned. 'Don't be ridiculous. All Mr Tan's interested in is your credentials and your money. You know the form. Proof of identity and a case full of cash. It's all been arranged.'

'But do I look like a surgeon?'

'No.' Sarah nodded in the direction of the coat stand. 'There you are.'

Gary walked over and took down the suit carrier. He laid it on his desk and unzipped it, then looked at the label above the inside pocket. 'Henry Poole. Savile Row. How do you know it'll fit?'

'Luckily you and Ben are the same build.'

'Are we?'

'Yes. Almost identical,' said Sarah, archly.

'I won't ask you how you know that,' grumbled Gary.

'It's not what you think. Women just notice these things. Anyway, as Mr Tan knows a good suit when he sees one he wouldn't be too keen to deal with a Harley Street specialist who was dressed by Top Man.'

'I can't believe that all Harley Street specialists have their suits made in Savile Row. What about the shoes?'

Sarah bent down and picked up a box. She removed the lid and took out a highly polished black brogue. 'Before you ask, no, they're not new. They need to look as though you've worn them before.'

'OK. I know the ropes.' He sighed and sat on the edge of his desk. 'I just wish that I'd had a bit more notice, that's all.'

CHRISTOPHER WAS SITTING at his study desk. Maria was cleaning the bathrooms. He'd greeted her with a kiss on the cheek, but she had seemed distant. Not her usual bright-eyed self. Perhaps she had had some family upset. He would ask her as soon as he had a moment. Maybe when they had a coffee. He'd been trying to sort out in his mind his precise plan of action when the phone rang. It was Monty Loveday, the coroner.

'About our conversation the other day,' he said.

'Oh, I decided not to proceed, Monty. I didn't do anything about it.'

'No. I know you didn't. But I did. I thought that if you had your suspicions, maybe I should, too. I tracked Reggie's body down. Some of the organs had already been removed, but the pathologist examined what was left. No traces of anything untoward. No marks—other than the bruising you'd expect from a car accident. I thought you'd like to know.'

'Right. Thank you, Monty.' Christopher put down the phone, thought for a few minutes, then picked it up again and dialled a number.

After a few seconds, a woman's voice answered, 'Dr Silverwood's practice.'

'Hello, Stella, it's Christopher Devon.'

'Dr Devon! How nice to hear from you.'

'Thank you. Stella, I'm so sorry about the news. About Reggie.'

'Yes. Terrible shock. It's so difficult having to answer the phone with his name, but then not every patient knows yet, so I have to.'

Stella Walters had been Reggie's secretary for ten years or more. She was a stalwart of the health centre. Christopher listened as she explained how sad they all were, then he asked, 'Reggie wasn't a diabetic, was he?'

'No. Why do you ask?'

'Oh, it's just that he'd donated his organs and I knew that if he were a diabetic that wouldn't be the case. Then I thought that the condition might have developed after he decided to donate them, and I was wondering if it might have caused him to have had a blackout while he was driving.'

'No. Dr Silverwood was very healthy, for his age. He was a bit worried about the flu that's going round, but he had the flu injection the day he died. He said he thought he'd better. So that he could stay well enough to keep treating his patients . . .' Her voice tailed off, overwhelmed by emotion.

'I'm sorry to ask questions, Stella. There's just one more. Can you tell me who gave him the flu injection?'

'I saw him just before he went in. It was Dr Cummings.'

Chapter Twelve

> Men's souls are naturally inclined to covetousness; but if ye be kind towards women and fear to wrong them, God is well acquainted with what ye do.
>
> Koran

So there it was. All neatly laid out in front of him. The things he had not wanted to believe. The things he could hardly believe. But there was now no doubt in his mind. Christopher picked up the telephone to make his final call.

'Dr Silverwood's surgery. Can I help you?'

'Stella, it's Christopher Devon. Sorry to bother you again, but I wonder if you could put me through to Dr Cummings?'

'I'm sorry, Dr Devon, but he's finished surgery and gone. In fact, he's gone off for a couple of days. Can I give him a message when he gets back?'

'No. Don't worry, Stella.'

And then the front doorbell rang. He got up from his desk and went downstairs. In a week of unexpected callers, this one was the most surprising. Standing in front of him on the doorstep, her hands plunged into the pockets of her long red coat, was Kate.

'How have you been?' she asked. She was standing in the kitchen while he busied himself making coffee.

Where did he begin? He thought it best to regard it as a rhetorical question and shrugged.

'I meant to call more. To check on how things were but . . . well . . . it never seemed to be the right time.' Kate sat down at the kitchen table and undid the gold buttons on her coat to reveal a smart black polo-neck dress.

'No,' said Christopher softly. And then, 'How is . . . er . . . Howie?' He tried to ask the question in a level tone.

'Fine. In Barcelona at the moment. Clinching some deal or other.'

Kate looked around the kitchen, at the familiar furniture, the plates on the wall, the vase of daffodils by the sink. It was hard to bear.

Christopher did his best to keep the conversation going. 'So, how long are you here for?'

'Oh, just a few days. Not long. I go back the day after tomorrow.'

'I see.'

'But I don't have to.'

Christopher was not quite sure what she meant. 'I'm sorry?'

'I don't have to go back. I could stay.'

He still did not grasp her meaning. Thought that she must mean she could extend her stay to see friends or something.

He put a cup of coffee in front of her and sat down opposite. 'You know about Tiger?' he asked.

'Yes. Dreadful. But at least he's pulling through. I've been speaking to Erica. The girls are with him now as well.'

It surprised him that she had been in touch with their friends. Hurt him a little that she had wanted to talk to them, but not to him. He continued, 'They should be able to bring him home soon. Well, back to Hampshire anyway. I think they're hopeful of a complete recovery.'

'Yes.'

He sipped his coffee.

'I meant . . . I mean . . .' Kate hesitated. 'I could come back to you.'

At first he was not sure he had heard correctly. The words reverberated in his head, then he lowered his cup and set it carefully on the saucer. 'I see.'

Kate's words tumbled out in a jumble. 'I think I made a mistake. I shouldn't have gone. We should have talked more. I didn't really think it through.'

'No.'

'What do you think?'

Christopher took a deep breath. 'I don't know what to think.'

'Could we try again?' Kate asked. 'Give it another go?'

Of all the things he thought might happen when he saw Kate standing on his doorstep, this one had not crossed his mind. He tried to formulate words to respond, but could only say, 'I don't know, Kate. I don't know.'

'But you were happy, weren't you? With the way things were?'

'I *was* happy with the way things were. But that was almost two years ago. I don't know whether I can pick up where we left off. Not just like that.'

'But you would have me back . . . if it could be like it was?'

'But how can it be like it was? I can't just discount what has happened.'

'You could if you forgave me.'

The words bit into him. They were designed to. And the truth of what she said sank home. Wasn't she right? He had longed for her to come back; to be able to make a fresh start. Now she was offering the one thing he'd almost given up hoping for. Was it only his lack of forgiveness standing in the way?

'Yes. If I could forgive you. But that would mean I thought it was all your fault. And it wasn't. It was mine.'

Kate reached out for his hand, but he picked up his cup before she could reach it. 'It doesn't matter whose fault it was. The important thing is that we can carry on. Make sure it doesn't happen again.'

'Do you think we could be certain?'

Kate sighed. 'Nothing's certain. But wouldn't you like to give it a go?'

Christopher got up from the table. 'I don't know. I need time to get my head round this. It's so completely unexpected . . .'

Kate rose to her feet and began buttoning up her coat. 'Think about it. Please. I'm staying at the Hotel du Vin. I'll call you.'

'No. No, let me call you. I just need time . . .'

He walked Kate down the path from the front door to the garden gate. She kissed him lightly on the cheek and squeezed his hand, then got into her taxi and was driven away.

From an upstairs window, Maria watched her go.

'So LET'S GET THIS straight, shall we?' Gary was pacing the office. 'We know Mr Tan is going back to China the day after tomorrow, yes?'

Sarah ran her finger down a sheet of paper that lay in front of her on her desk. 'Yes, he's booked on the British Airways eighteen-forty flight from Heathrow, Terminal Four. Flight number zero three nine.'

'Except that he won't get on it.'

'Not if everything goes according to plan,' confirmed Sarah.

'He's expecting me at three p.m. at the Savoy.'

'Where he's agreed to meet Dr Wilson, a Harley Street specialist, to discuss a regular supply of organs for his clinic.'

'And he wants money there and then?'

'It's his way of making sure that the doctor is serious. Otherwise he could end up supplying organs and not getting his money.'

'So what does Mr Tan know about me—I mean about Dr Wilson?'

'He knows that Dr Wilson is a respected practitioner who's forty-nine, accomplished in his job and runs a thriving clinic. He hasn't met him, but he has met one of his colleagues.'

'When was this?' asked Gary.

'Yesterday. Ben managed to get a guy into one of the clinics. They'd had an approach from organ vendors before and declined any involvement, but we managed to persuade them to call Mr Tan and arrange an appointment.'

'He's good, Ben, isn't he? Shame about his health.'

'Don't be unkind.'

Gary looked suitably chastened. 'So I just go in and meet Mr Tan and strike up a conversation?'

Sarah pushed a piece of paper towards him. 'Here are some notes on things you can ask. You'll be wired for sound, and we have the numbers of all the bank notes. Not that we should need them. Mr Tan will be intercepted as he leaves the hotel and by then we should have all we want.'

'OK. Well, I suppose I'd better do my swotting. Make sure that I sound as though I know what I'm doing.' He paused, then asked, 'I don't suppose there's any point in asking you . . .'

'Not tonight,' said Sarah. 'Maybe tomorrow. When we've got something to celebrate. *If* we've got something to celebrate.'

CHRISTOPHER SAT at the desk in his study for more than an hour. He wasn't any further forward. The two dilemmas shimmied around in his head but he seemed unable to resolve either of them. He jolted himself into full consciousness and looked at his watch. One o'clock. He would go downstairs and find Maria. Her presence would improve his frame of mind.

The kitchen table was laid out with cheeses and fresh bread, jars of pickle and some freshly cut ham. Propped against the jar of mango chutney was a letter, addressed simply to 'C'. He pushed his finger underneath the flap and opened the envelope, sliding out the folded piece of paper inside.

Dear Christopher,

I'm sorry not to see you before I go, but I just wanted to say thank you for your company over the past couple of weeks. It has been such fun being with you and I shall treasure my visit to the opera always. My mother will be back with you next week and I will explain that you prefer a light lunch to pasta. I do hope we can meet again sometime.

With love and thanks, Maria

He sat down at the table and put the letter down in front of him. He had forgotten that Luisa would be back on Monday. He had been so bound up in his own little world that it had never occurred to him that Maria must have seen Kate come into the house. And leave. What must she have thought?

He reached out for the phone and rang her number. There was no answer.

TIGER WAS SITTING UP in the hospital bed. He was feeling sorry for himself and was not in the sunniest frame of mind.

Erica sat beside him on the uncomfortable chair and did her best to cheer him up. 'They say you can come home in a few days.'

Tiger spoke with care, enunciating the words as clearly as he could, 'Bloody pain. Just want to fly.'

Erica squeezed his hand. 'Hey! You've been lucky. So lucky. It could have been much worse. Let's just be grateful for that, shall we? You'll fly again one day, you know that. You'll fly.'

Tiger shook his head. 'I don't think so. Sorry. Not very good company.'

'That doesn't matter. You're here. Still here. That's what matters.'

'And what about the shop? And the man in black?'

'Oh, that seems to have died down. Nobody's seen him since. I don't think he can have had much success. They reckon he was a one-man band, and not a very good one at that. And there have been no more bricks through windows. It looks as though it was those yobs after all.'

'So much for my secret society. Didn't really do much good, did I?'

Erica stroked his cheek. 'You did your best.'

Tiger inclined his head to one side and gazed into her eyes. 'Do you still love me?' he murmured. 'Even after all this?'

'Of course I still love you. I'm afraid you're stuck with me.' Then she frowned with mock seriousness. 'As long as you want to be stuck with me?'

Tiger forced his unwilling mouth into a smile. 'Yes, please,' he said. Then his eyes closed and he drifted off to sleep.

MARIA WISHED she did not have to sleep at her mother's. But her mother had said that her mind would be at rest if Maria could spend a few nights there, to keep the cat company, while she was on her annual holiday with her brother in Italy. Company for a cat, maybe that was her lot now. She lay awake on the narrow bed in the spare room feeling lower than she could remember.

It was her own fault. She should have been more assertive. Should have made her feelings better known. But that was not her style. He must have guessed, mustn't he? That it wasn't just a friendship?

But if she were honest with herself, that's all it was. So far. How could she claim it was more? There seemed to be a bond between them but it remained, as yet, largely unexplored. And now his wife had come back. She had left again soon afterwards, but probably only to go and get her things. If that were not the case he would have explained it to her, wouldn't he? Especially on her last day.

GARY DID NOT SLEEP MUCH that night. He lay awake thinking about the proposed meeting with Mr Tan the following day, and about Sarah. Was she cooling towards him? Why had he let her get to him? What if she told him it would be better if they kept to a working relationship, nothing more?

At half past six in the morning he was up and sitting at the desk in his flat, running over the likely events of the day in front of him. He felt unusually nervous. He went to the bathroom and had a shower, a long one, then towelled himself down and sat in his robe watching as dawn broke over the cathedral city. He looked at the suit hanging on the wardrobe door, at the shoes on the floor beneath it and at the shirt and tie on the back of the chair. It occurred to him at that moment, for the first time in his life, that he was getting too old for dressing up.

CHRISTOPHER HAD ARRANGED to meet Monty Loveday on the cathedral close in Winchester. The day was cold and the sky the colour of parchment, with dove-grey clouds rolling in from the west. As they met the weather broke and a heavy shower forced them to seek shelter in the cathedral.

'Not the best place to talk, is it?' muttered Monty as they strolled quietly down the north aisle.

'Well, we can walk in the rain if you'd rather,' said Christopher.

'No, thanks. I don't want to order my own post-mortem.' Monty chuckled. 'What is it then? Why the cloak and dagger?'

Christopher spoke softly. 'It's about Reggie Silverwood. I don't want this to sound like the ravings of an embittered doctor who is out for retribution, but it's to do with Randall Cummings.'

Monty stopped walking. 'Has he been up to something?'

'I think it's almost certain. It's only a theory, but I just have a feeling that it's an accurate one.' Monty walked on slowly and Christopher moved with him. 'I've known for some time that Randall has been encouraging some of his patients to go private. Telling them he could offer them better care that way.'

'Disagreeable but not illegal.'

'Not as such, no. But I know for a fact that in the case of at least one kidney transplant patient the organ was withheld and given to someone who could afford to pay for it.'

Monty stopped walking again. 'Are you certain?'

'Perfectly. I'd checked that a kidney was available and had the patient lined up for it. At the last minute, Cummings diverted the kidney to another patient, known only to him, and as a result my patient was unable to receive the transplant and died before another kidney became available.'

'Did you challenge him about this?'

'Did I? I raised merry hell. Within a week I'd been given the push.'

'And Reggie Silverwood? Did he know about it?'

'Not at the time. Nobody did. They must have thought it odd that I went so quietly, but that's all I could do—pack my bags and go. I knew that if I said anything it would undermine the confidence in the practice.'

Monty looked at him questioningly. 'So you put your head in the sand?'

'Yes. I know it was wrong, but on balance it seemed to me to be the right course of action at the time. I see now that it wasn't.'

'And what's brought about the change of mind?' asked Monty evenly.

'Reggie rang me the night he died. Said that he'd discovered something that he was unhappy about. I suggested he come round for a talk. He was on his way to meet me when he had the accident.'

'And you think he'd discovered Cummings's'—he searched for a suitable phrase—'lack of fairness?'

'I'm pretty certain so, yes.'

Monty leaned against a pillar, his hands still in his pockets. 'But he never got a chance to tell you?'

'No.'

'And you think his accident was suspicious?'

'Yes, I do. Reggie might have looked frail but he was as strong as an ox. Always had regular health checks. I asked his secretary, Stella Walters, if he'd developed diabetes lately, which might have resulted in a blackout, but apparently he was as sound as a bell.' Christopher lowered his voice to a whisper, 'Then I discovered that just before he left to see me he'd been given a flu injection by Randall Cummings.'

'So?'

'If Randall Cummings had given him an overdose of insulin instead, the symptoms would be just like those of a heart attack. And there would be no trace of anything untoward at a post-mortem because by then the insulin would have been broken down by the body's metabolism.'

Monty Loveday's expression changed to one of incredulity. 'It's a bit fanciful, isn't it? Do you really think Cummings would have resorted to murder just to stop Reggie blowing the whistle on a bit of unethical medicine?'

'Not just unethical. Illegal.' Christopher explained about his sighting of Randall Cummings at the Red Dragon, sitting down with the Chinese man. He confided, also, that it had not been the first time that Cummings had been seen there in such company. 'And do you know where the majority of organs for transplant come from nowadays?' he asked Monty.

'India?'

'China.'

'So you think Reggie had rumbled Cummings and was about to blow the gaff?'

'Yes. And in doing so he would not only have ruined Cummings's career, but also stopped him from earning hundreds of thousands a year in backhanders. The illegal organs market runs into millions.'

'You can't prove that Cummings injected Reggie with insulin, though.'

'No, I can't.'

'So where's Cummings now?'

'He's gone away for two days and the surgery has no way of contacting him.'

Monty thought for a moment. 'Sounds like something from a novel. Only much more squalid. Come on. We're going to the police station.'

THEY BROUGHT TIGER HOME that afternoon. He was not the easiest of patients, but Erica had said she could manage. She worried about the shop, about whether Brian would be able to cope, but decided that he would have to rise to the challenge. It was more important that she was here.

Mercifully, Tiger's stroke had not been as severe as they first thought and his recovery was steady. If no great strides were made each day, he was still moving forward slowly. He could walk quite well thanks to ongoing physiotherapy, but his face was still a little numb and his speech not clear.

Erica put an armchair by the window so that he could sit and watch what was going on in the cathedral close.

'I'm not a bloody invalid,' he insisted.

'No. Just a pain in the neck,' Erica had remarked. 'Here you are. A cup of coffee. And try not to dribble.'

He gave her a withering glance and muttered, 'I don't know why they couldn't send me home with one of those nice nurses.'

Erica shot him a glance. 'You're improving.'

Tiger took a sip of coffee and grinned. 'Daren't do otherwise. Not with you on my back.'

She came and crouched by his chair. 'Are you going to be nice to me?'

He lifted his hand up and stroked her cheek. 'Sorry, love. Hate being like this. Just want to get back to normal.'

'You will. But you'll need rest as well as exercise.' She stood up and walked across the room. 'By the way,' she asked, 'what happened to the girl who was with you? Sam, wasn't it? She didn't come to visit you in hospital, did she? Only I wanted to say thank you.'

GARY WAS STANDING by the office window dressed in his suit. His nervousness manifested itself in its usual way—he was drumming his fingers on the windowsill.

Sarah examined the sky. 'I wonder if you ought to take a mac?'

Gary sighed heavily. 'I'm on my way to meet a man who'd probably bump me off as soon as look at me and all you can worry about is whether I should take a raincoat?'

'Well, we don't want you going down with flu like Ben Atkinson. If we lose two of you then we really are up shit creek.'

Gary smiled sarcastically. 'Don't worry. I'll take my paddle. Talking of which, has the money come?'

'Fifty grand is on its way.'

'Oh, that'll do nicely.'

Sarah sat at her desk. 'That's about a month's salary for you, isn't it?'

'I wish. Mind you, it would be worth running away with, wouldn't it? Come on. Let's sneak off to the Caribbean and lie on a sun-soaked beach.'

'No,' she said. 'I've got to have my hair cut tomorrow.'

'Oh. Shame. Perhaps I could take somebody else.'

'You do and I'll break your legs,' she murmured.

'What?' he spun round to face her. At that moment the door opened and a man came in with a suitcase.

'Is there someone who can sign for this?'

Gary walked forward. 'That'll be me.'

'Check it first please, sir.'

Gary laid the case on the desk and pressed the catches to release the locks. He lifted the lid and gazed on the neat bundles of money.

'There's five hundred in each bundle, sir, and there should be a hundred bundles. Will you count them, please?'

Gary went through the process of counting the money, then signed the form on the clipboard.

'Thank you, sir.' The man took his clipboard and left the room.

'Well, it's make-your-mind-up time. Either you elope with me now or your chance has gone for ever.'

Sarah pushed her chair back and lifted her legs up onto her desk.

Gary watched the long limbs unfurl. 'I do wish you wouldn't do that.'

'Does it unnerve you?' she asked.

'Hugely.'

'Good.' She paused. 'You won't do anything stupid, will you?'

''Fraid I can't promise that,' he replied. 'I've been doing stupid things all my life. Too late to stop now.'

Chapter Thirteen

> Rule 1 on page 1 of the book of war is: 'Do not march on Moscow . . .'
> Rule 2 is: 'Do not go fighting with your land armies in China.'
>
> Lord Montgomery of Alamein (1887–1976)

Monty Loveday had been quite impressive at the police station. He knew the chief inspector—another old-car enthusiast—and that had, to use an appropriate metaphor, oiled the wheels. The chief inspector accepted that Christopher's theory involved a good deal of conjecture, but felt that at least they had enough reason to bring in Randall Cummings for questioning. He made it clear, though, that there was little concrete evidence of malpractice.

Coming out of the police station the two were in less than high spirits.

'He didn't look totally convinced, did he?' mused Christopher.

'Oh, I wouldn't worry on that score,' said Monty. 'Tom knows that I wouldn't bother him without good reason. But he can't do anything until Cummings bowls up again. Where he is now is anybody's guess.'

THE UNMARKED CAR took Gary from the basement garages of MI5 into the centre of London. It dropped him off in Park Crescent, just a short walk from Harley Street, where he hailed a taxi. The cabby dropped him off opposite Savoy Court, and he crossed the road and walked down the short cul-de-sac that led to the entrance of the hotel.

The lobby was reasonably busy, which made him feel better. He looked at his watch: forty minutes early. He checked that the microphone was in position and that the equipment was switched on, then walked past reception and down the steps into the lounge. He would sit in a corner, where he could watch any comings and goings. As he crossed the lounge, he took in the four members of MI5 who were there. One was sitting on his own reading a newspaper. Two others, a man and a woman, were having tea. A fourth was tucking into a plate of pastries.

Mr Tan was seated halfway down the lounge on the far side, and with him were two men. One of them, Gary could see, was fat with grey hair. The other a sparely built man. Both wore grey suits. Doctors? Or dealers? They were all three crouched over a low table set with cups and saucers. Mr Tan appeared to be talking, while the other two listened intently. After a few minutes he sat back while the two men spoke to one another.

Gary leaned on his right hand and spoke softly to his wrist. 'Hope you've clocked the two guys.'

After another twenty minutes of intense conversation the two men nodded to each other as if they were in agreement, at which point Mr Tan reached into his briefcase and pulled out an envelope which he handed to the fatter of the two men. After a few more pleasantries the two men got up to leave. They shook Mr Tan by the hand and walked across the lounge, up the stairs and out into the lobby.

Gary looked at his watch. Ten minutes to go. He got up and walked across the lounge to the gentlemen's cloakroom, where he went into a cubicle, locked the door and once more checked the contents of the case. He sat down on the closed lid of the lavatory and thought through his approach once more, then checked his watch again. One minute to go. He stood up, flushed the lavatory, then unlocked the door and walked out.

It was exactly three o'clock.

CHRISTOPHER NEEDED AIR. He pushed the wheelbarrow across the garden and down to the bottom of the orchard. There, on the banks of the river, he sat on the wooden bench and watched the water trickling by. It had been a dry winter and the stream was shallow and playful in its notes, not the deep and tumbling torrent that it could be. He tossed a twig into the water and watched it slowly pirouetting out of sight. How different it used to be, when they played here with the children. Where was she now? he wondered. She was still not answering her phone. He had called her twice at lunchtime. He would call again this evening. And if she were not there? What then? Could he still turn back the clock?

His mind was a miasma of disorganised thoughts. At least he had done what he could about Randall Cummings. Now he would have to await developments. And repercussions. Would it affect his own employment prospects? More than likely. He looked around at the garden. The fruit trees were on the verge of bursting their buds and the first glossy tufts of bluebell leaves sprang from the banks of the stream.

Maybe he would pack it all in and just be a gardener. He didn't need much. He turned to look back at the mellow bricks and the white-framed windows, the old moss-encrusted tiles on the roof. It was the house he was married to now. The house and the garden. It would be nice, though, if that did not have to be the beginning and the end of it.

MR TAN STOOD UP with an outstretched hand as Gary approached. He was taller than he had appeared in the photographs, and more heavily built. He gave a curt bow as he shook Gary's hand and said, 'Dr Wilson, I presume. How good to see you.' His smile was broad and Gary saw that among the even row of teeth there was one large, gold crown.

'Mr Tan.' Gary inclined his head in a gentle nod.

Mr Tan motioned Gary to sit and then said to a passing waitress, 'May we have some tea, please. China. And some scones, with jam and cream.'

Gary thought that he had better get down to business. 'So you think you can help me, Mr Tan?'

'That rather depends, Dr Wilson, on what you have in mind.'

Gary slipped into what he hoped would sound like surgeon mode. 'We have a busy clinic, Mr Tan. We perform, on average, three kidney transplants a month and we could perform many more if we could get hold of the organs.' Mr Tan remained impassive and so he continued. 'We also carry out bone transplants and liver and heart transplants, though these are not so frequent as the operations for kidney replacement.'

'So what exactly would you be requiring from me?'Mr Tan asked.

'We could use another three kidneys a month, certainly, but we would like a flexible arrangement that would allow us to use more or less than this according to patient demand.'

'That could be arranged.'

'What I do need, Mr Tan, is assurance that the kidneys are in perfect health and that they will arrive in good condition.'

'You need have no worries on that account, Dr Wilson. Our kidneys are all from healthy people.' Mr Tan hesitated. 'Well, people who were healthy before they were . . . before they gave their kidneys up for transplantation.'

Gary was warming to his role. 'Which leaves us with the subject of cost.'

At this point the waitress came with the tea tray. Gary wished she had not. He was just getting into his stride.

'Ah, tea. A great British institution is it not, Dr Wilson?'

Gary muttered to the affirmative.

'And a great Chinese institution, too,' confirmed Mr Tan.

The waitress took what seemed to be an inordinate length of time setting out the cups and saucers, the milk jug and sugar basin, the plate of scones and the jam and the cream. By the time she was laying their butter knives neatly on the side of the plates Gary had almost reached breaking point.

When the waitress departed, Mr Tan rubbed his hands together. 'Shall I be mother?' he asked, smiling broadly. The gold crown glinted in the light from a chandelier as he began rearranging the cups.

Gary tried again. 'So, as I was saying, Mr Tan, we just have to sort out the financial arrangements.'

'Yes. Yes, of course. But first the tea.'

Mr Tan bowed gently, then silently set to work. First he poured a little of the tea into a cup. then he emptied the contents of that cup into a small bowl the waitress had provided. Then he poured the tea into two more cups, bowed again to Gary and pushed one of the cups towards him. His next question was not one normally associated with the Chinese tea ceremony.

'Would you like a scone?'

'No. No, thank you.'

'They really are very good, Dr Wilson. The Savoy Hotel makes a very good scone.'

For the sake of appeasing Mr Tan, Gary took a scone, wondering when, if ever, this elaborate ceremony would end.

'Help yourself to cream and jam.'

'Thank you.' Gary tried to look interested in the scone and spooned on the strawberry jam and then the cream.

Mr Tan did the same. All outside influences faded into insignificance as he concentrated intently on the matter in hand. The construction work completed, he raised the embellished scone to his mouth and took a large bite. The expression on his face was one of rapt delight.

Gary sipped his tea.

When Mr Tan's scone had disappeared, he wiped his hands on his napkin and leaned forward. 'Have you brought the first instalment with you?'

Gary tapped the case. 'Fifty thousand. That was what we agreed, wasn't it?'

Mr Tan bowed his head. 'To seal the agreement. In future, you will let us know your needs through the agreed channels and we will supply exactly what you want, when you need it.'

'As simple as that?'

'As simple as that, Dr Wilson.'

'And what sort of notice do you need? How quickly can you get the organs to us?'

'Generally within a week. Ten days at most, but that would be in unusual circumstances.' Mr Tan drained his cup. 'Would you like a refill, Dr Wilson?'

'No, I'm fine, thank you.'

Gary was anxious to move the meeting to a close. He had all he needed now. The recording would be sufficient to incriminate Mr Tan. He just had to be seen leaving the hotel with the money.

'So, there is just the question of contacts, then,' confirmed Gary. 'The "agreed channels" you mentioned.'

Mr Tan reached into the inside pocket of his jacket and pulled out a large black leather wallet. He opened it and took a visiting card from one of the compartments, which he slipped it into the top pocket of Gary's jacket.

'If you just ring that number with the details of what you need, Dr Wilson, you will find that everything will fall neatly into place.'

'Thank you. I'm very grateful.' Gary made to get up.

Mr Tan rose with him. 'I look forward to a long and continued association, Dr Wilson. I am sure you will not be disappointed.'

'I am sure I will not, Mr Tan,' replied Gary.

The two men shook hands and bowed, and Gary walked across the lounge and up the stairs into the lobby. He looked over his shoulder and saw, behind him, Mr Tan slipping a bank note underneath the plate of scones and picking up the attaché case and his own briefcase.

Gary walked smartly through the swing doors at the front of the hotel and turned left into the corner of the taxi rank, pressing himself against the wall. Mr Tan came through the door twenty seconds later and hailed a taxi. But he did not reach the door of the cab. As he approached it, two burly men—one dressed as a businessman, the other as a hall porter—converged on him from either side. One of them took the briefcase and pushed his left arm up behind his back, the other eased the attaché case from his right hand, but before he could pin back Mr Tan's other arm, the Chinaman struck out at his assailant and knocked him off-balance, then slammed his elbow into the face of the other man. In that split second he broke free and ran past the row of taxis in the courtyard and on towards the Strand, his arms flailing.

But as he rounded the corner a third agent, who had supposedly been selling newspapers, performed a neat flying tackle and brought Mr Tan to the ground with a heavy thud. Winded himself, he stood up and leaned over his captive, ready to prevent any further attempts at escape. At that moment, before anyone could reach out and stop him, Mr Tan slipped his hand into his pocket and then into his mouth. Gary ran to give assistance, but by the time he had covered the twenty yards that lay between them, he could see Mr Tan's body being convulsed with heaving spasms.

He knew that it was too late. Mr Tan's mouth was contorted in agony and Gary could see the gold crown glistening in the sunlight.

THERE WAS SOMETHING THERAPEUTIC about tedious manual labour, thought Christopher as he emptied the final load from the grass box into the wheelbarrow and put the mower away in the shed. He smiled to himself. Why it should surprise him after all these years he did not know, but a little work in his garden went a long way towards making him feel whole.

He glanced up as he walked across the lawns that flanked the house, and saw Matt walking towards him.

'Hi!' His son's greeting was brief.

'Hi! Are you off or just back?'

'I'm out for a couple of hours, then back, if that's OK?'

'Sure. Whatever.' Christopher tried to sound easy-going.

Matt looked hesitant. Then he said, 'I gather mum came round.'

'Yes. Who told you?'

'She did. She rang me.'

'I see.'

'She said she offered to come back.'

Christopher knew where the conversation was going. 'Yes, she did,' he confirmed. 'And I said that I wasn't sure.'

Christopher saw the look of incredulity on Matt's face.

'But I thought you always wanted her back. You said you still loved her.'

'I did still love her. I do still love her, but I don't know that it would work out. And please don't use that phrase "wanted her back". It makes it sound as though she's some kind of possession. Lost and found.'

'Well, she is, isn't she? In a way? You were married. You belong to each other. You agreed that when you signed the marriage certificate.'

Christopher was irritated now. 'Look, Matt, I really don't want to have this conversation with my son about his mother.'

Matt kicked at some grass. 'I just don't understand why, when she offers to come back, you turn her down.'

'I haven't turned her down. I just said that it isn't an easy decision.'

'So you will have her back?'

Christopher seldom raised his voice. He did so now. 'I don't know, Matt. I can't just sweep everything that's happened under the carpet. I need to consider whether it really could work out. Can you see that?'

His son shook his head as though the person he were trying to communicate with was being deliberately obtuse. Then he turned on his heels and walked back across the lawn. Christopher opened his mouth to shout after him, but he thought better of it and just watched his son go.

GARY DID NOT ENJOY the debriefing. He did not enjoy being involved in any operation that resulted in a person's death. He was angry that one of his colleagues had been too slow to prevent Mr Tan from slipping a cyanide capsule into his mouth. It was unjust anger, he knew. His colleague was pretty devastated, too.

He pulled off his tie and slipped off his jacket then sat down at his desk and leaned forward with his head in his hands.

Sarah came back into the office with two mugs of coffee. 'Do you want anything in this?'

Gary looked up. 'No, thanks. Want to keep a clear head.'

'Don't blame yourself,' she said. 'You know it's counterproductive.'

'That sounds very matter of fact. Very calculating.'

'Hey!'

He looked at her apologetically. 'Sorry. Thought we'd got it all sorted and then . . .'

'Well, you've got the two guys downstairs.'

Gary took a sip of his coffee and said, 'Yes, there is that. Do you want to come and have a look?'

'Yes. Yes, I do.'

GARY AND SARAH walked into the room next door to the one in which the two men were being interrogated. They looked down on the scene through one-way glass. The conversation was audible through speakers.

Two MI5 agents were questioning the men and didn't seem to be getting very far. One of them was leaning on the far wall and saying, 'We saw Mr Tan give you the envelope full of money. What was it for?'

Neither of the two men spoke.

Sarah whispered, 'Wasn't the fat one in the Red Dragon that night?'

Gary looked at the large man in the grey suit. 'I don't know. I can't say that I remember him.' He turned and spoke to a woman who was taking notes behind him. 'Do you have the names of the two men?' he asked.

'Yes,' she said, and flipped back the pages on her pad. 'The fat one's name is Randall Cummings and the thin one . . . Montagu Loveday.'

CHRISTOPHER SHOWERED and changed. His mind was clearer now. He would not rush things. He would take his time and do it properly. Matt was right in one respect at least. He did still love Kate.

He poured a large Scotch for himself and took it into the sitting room. Then he ran his finger along the shelf of CDs behind the sofa. *La Bohème?* No. Too tragic. *Tosca?* Too many recent memories. He settled on *The Barber of Seville*. Rossini would lift his spirits. He took a slug of Scotch and heard the opening bars of the overture. Then he heard the doorbell. Matt must have forgotten his key. He walked across the hall to open the front door.

It was not Matt. It was Kate.

'Hello,' she said.

He had not expected her to come back so soon. She looked radiant, her hair and make-up fresh, as though she were about to go out.

'Oh! Hello!' Then, by way of breaking the ice, 'You look smart. You must be going somewhere.'

Kate shrugged. 'Only here.'

Christopher was taken aback. 'Oh, I see. Well, come in.'

He took her coat, then gestured towards the sitting room. It seemed odd, doing that to your own wife in her own home. Well, what *was* her own home.

'Drink?' he asked.

'Thanks.'

Christopher did not have to ask what she wanted. He left her for a moment and went to the fridge in the kitchen to get her a glass of chilled white wine. When he came back she was sitting at one end of the sofa, with the music playing behind her.

'I'm sorry. I'll turn it down . . .'

'No, really. It's fine.'

'No. I know you don't like it.' He adjusted the volume so that the music was barely audible.

'I didn't expect you back so soon.' He sat down opposite her in an armchair.

'No. Only I didn't want to wait any longer. To see what you thought.'

He looked at her sitting on the sofa. Her blonde hair was immaculate, her face seemed to be shining and she wore a little black dress and black tights, her legs crossed at an angle. She looked almost like a model and astonishing for her age. He had been lucky to catch her all those years ago. The envy of all his friends.

'Yes,' he said quietly.

'What do you think?'

'I still love you, Kate.'

'I still love you, too,' she said eagerly.

'I don't know how I've managed without you. But I just don't think . . . I can't see how we can pick up where we left off.'

'No?' She looked crestfallen.

'Please don't think I haven't thought hard about this. So hard. I do know that I still love you.'

'But not enough?'

He paused, wanting to explain clearly what he thought. 'When you left . . . I didn't know whether I could carry on. I was so . . . well . . . bereft is the only word I can think of. We were such a part of each others' lives. Life without you was not something I'd ever contemplated. We'd been through such a lot together—all those years without money, then the children, and bringing them up. Going through all those traumas with Ellie and her boyfriends. And with Matt. You were so good with Matt and I was so . . . clueless.'

'No,' she protested.

'Oh, I was. I got there in the end, but it was harder for me than it should have been. I didn't do as much for him as I could have or should have. I'll always regret that.'

'But it's all right now.'

'It's better. I love him very much, but I do find it hard to tell him . . . But, Kate, you can't build a marriage solely on a love of children. Especially not when they've left home.'

'But you've said you still love me.' She was leaning forward on the sofa now, willing him to agree.

'I do. But I can't go through it all again . . . because I can't feel the same as I did.' Christopher put down his glass and clasped his hands together, almost as if he were trying to channel his emotions. 'When you went my world fell apart. I wanted to call you. I was desperate to get in touch, but you didn't leave an address and you even changed your mobile number.'

Kate looked down, embarrassed. 'I'm sorry. I shouldn't have done that.'

'I know it was my own fault. I didn't let you know how much I loved you, how much I needed you. I don't know how I got through the months after you left. It sounds dramatic, but I do know what living hell is now, and I wouldn't wish it on my worst enemy. I did come close to giving up. I had the means. But then I got so angry with myself. What would my children think of a father who took the easy way out?'

Christopher took a sip of his whisky. 'And then, to crown it all, I got the push. Not that that was anything to do with us. Not really. Though I suppose there were some who thought it was. No wife, no job, no prospects.'

Kate sat quite still, the tears welling up in her eyes.

'But the anger helped. It made me bloody-minded enough to get through. If you'd have come back at any time then, I'd have had you back, in an instant. But you didn't. There was no call. No message. Nothing. So I had to carry on. The guys were kind—Tiger and Gary—tried to take me out of myself. And then I thought that if I didn't do something soon it would just be a waste of a life. And so I've tried. And nothing has really happened yet. But something might.'

'I see,' said Kate, softly.

'I can't go back there, Kate. I'd love to say yes, let's give it another go, but I really don't have the appetite for it. I'm so very sorry.'

The room was silent, apart from the faintest strains of an operatic aria that seemed miles away. Kate sat quite still, gazing into the middle distance. Then she got up and moved to the door. 'I'd better be going.'

'Where? Where will you go?' he asked.

'Oh, back to my hotel. Then on to . . . wherever it is this week.'

He looked at her standing there. The woman with whom he had shared nearly half of his life, knowing that if he said the word she would stay. But he could not bring himself to say it, and she slipped on her coat and walked out of the front door, closing it quietly behind her.

Christopher stood there for a few moments, listening to the echoes of moments past, then turned, and saw Matt standing in front of him.

His son stared at him without speaking and then, very softly, murmured, 'Oh, Dad!' He walked forward and put his arms round his father's shoulders, burying his head in his neck. Christopher could not speak, but he could feel his son's tears running down his skin.

MATT TOOK a large gulp of whisky. He had almost stopped shaking now. 'I had no idea you were there,' Christopher said. 'I'm sorry you had to hear. They weren't really for your ears, you know. The things I said. They were between your mother and me.'

'I know. I came in and heard voices and I just couldn't go.'

'I wouldn't want Ellie to know.'

'Of course not.'

After a few moments Matt said, 'Those things I said to you. I had no right to. I had no idea. I mean . . .'

'Well, there we are,' Christopher said with finality.

'I'm sorry I was a complete bastard, Dad.'

Christopher half laughed. 'Oh, I don't know. Not a complete one. Just a bit of one. And you have got a few things on your mind.'

'I guess.'

Christopher perched on the arm of a chair. 'Funny, isn't it?'

'What?' asked Matt. 'How we all seem to just miss sometimes? I try to understand you and don't quite get there, and you try to understand me . . .'

'And don't get there either. Yes.'

'At least we try, Dad. At least we try.'

Christopher nodded, then drained his glass and got up.

'Another one?' Matt asked.

'No. I can drive on one, but not on two. And I have to go out for a while.' He turned in the doorway. 'We'll get there, Matt. In the end. Both of us.'

Chapter Fourteen

A woman's friendship ever ends in love.

Dione, John Gay (1685–1732)

'Bloody hell!' Gary could think of nothing else to say.

'How come you didn't know what Randall Cummings looks like?' asked Sarah. 'He's from your neck of the woods.'

'Because I have my own doctor—Christopher—and although I know *of* Randall Cummings I've never met him. Tiger knows him because he used to be Erica's GP, until he gave Christopher the push.'

'What about the other one?' she asked. 'Montagu Loveday.'

'Not met him either. Apparently he's our local coroner.'

'And they were in it together?' Sarah was scrutinising the two men.

'It looks like it, though neither of them is giving anything away.'

Cummings had taken off his jacket now. It was on the back of his chair. He was mopping his brow with a handkerchief. Monty Loveday, on the other hand, was coolness personified.

'We have the envelope, gentlemen. We know you were dealing with Mr Tan, and we know what Mr Tan was dealing in. It is illegal in this country to profit from the sale of body parts.'

Cummings cleared his throat. 'We don't know anything about that. We were just being paid for some medical advice we had offered him. Consultancy work. That's what consultants do—provide advice.'

'Advice and clients. You were lining up clients for Mr Tan and taking a cut of the proceeds. There was five thousand pounds in the envelope.'

Monty Loveday spoke without looking at his interrogator, 'We really have nothing more to say. We admit we met Mr Tan and we've told you why—he wasn't a well man and we were offering him medical advice. Admittedly we should have been more careful about the way in which we were paid, but I can't believe you put us through all this just because we were avoiding VAT.'

Gary looked at Sarah. 'Cool customers, aren't they?'

'Is he right?' asked Sarah. 'Have they really got no more to go on?'

'No. We didn't tape the conversation so we can't get them on that.' Then his mood changed. 'Hang on a minute.' He left the room. Sarah half expected him to appear in the interview room to see if he could do any better. Instead, a few minutes later, another figure came through the interview-room door. It was a woman with a tray containing the possessions of the two men. She whispered to one of the agents, who then put it down on the table.

'You can have these back now,' he said.

The relief on the faces of Cummings and Loveday was plain to see. Each man leaned forward and scooped up his belongings, put them into his pockets and then stood up in readiness to leave.

Sarah heard the door open behind her. Gary came in, carrying his mobile phone and a visiting card. He held up the card. 'Mr Tan gave me this. This was to be my—Dr Wilson's—contact whenever I needed body parts.'

The card had nothing on it except a mobile telephone number. Gary punched in the numbers. Through the loudspeaker they could hear the ringing of another mobile phone, and through the glass they saw Randall Cummings put his hand into his jacket pocket.

TIGER WAS SITTING in his chair by the window, and Gary was looking out over the cathedral close.

'Have you told Christopher yet?' asked Tiger.

'No. I thought I'd nip over there after I'd called on you.'

'He'll be a bit shocked. I think Monty Loveday was a friend of his.'

'I have a feeling that he won't be surprised about Randall Cummings.'

Tiger looked up. 'You think he knew?'

'I think he had an inkling. Don't know why I say that. Just a feeling.'

'Do you think they'll give Christopher his job back?'

'Can't see how they could refuse. Not after all this.'

'How did you come to hear about it all, then?' asked Tiger.

'Oh . . . er . . . I heard it from Sarah. She has a friend who was involved in nabbing them.'

'God, I bet that was a bit of a case. Think how much undercover work they must have had to do. Must have taken them ages.'

'Yes, it did . . . er . . . apparently . . .'

The sparkle had come back into Tiger's eye. 'So this Sarah . . .'

'Mmm?'

'Is she involved in police work? Investigations?'

Gary feigned ignorance. 'Oh, I don't think so. She's a civil servant like me. Leads a very sedentary life.'

'Yes.' Tiger looked at him sideways. 'You know, I've always thought you were a bit of a dark horse, Gary.'

Gary turned to face him 'Me? Nah. What you see is what you get.'

'Oh. Really?'

'Yup.' Gary spread his arms wide. 'An open book, that's me.'

Tiger grinned. 'Ha! If you're an open book, Gary Flynn, then there's one thing that anybody can see.'

'What's that?'

'You've never been so besotted with a girl in all your life.'

'Well,' said Gary, 'you might just have something there. Perhaps leopards can change their spots.' He knelt down by Tiger's chair and looked up at him. 'And what about Tigers? Can they change their stripes?'

Tiger looked serious. 'I might have to. Not sure if they'll let me fly again. Bloody determined to try, though. Nothing else like it.'

'Haven't you had enough excitement for a bit?'

A look of something that even Gary could not quite identify flickered across Tiger's face. 'For the time being, yes. I thought it would be a bit of fun. But in the end it turned out that it wasn't worth the candle.'

Gary could not quite understand. 'So if you can't fly, what will you do instead?'

'Well, there's a lot to be said for running a bookshop.'

At that moment Erica walked into the room with two mugs of tea. Tiger turned to acknowledge her, then looked back at Gary. 'Especially if you're in love with the owner,' he said.

'Soft bugger,' said Gary.

'Yeah. Suppose I am really.'

THE SURGERY was as busy as ever. Christopher managed to find a parking space round the back and walked in the side door, hoping to have a word with Stella Walters about Randall Cummings. He did not manage it. Instead Stella's office was occupied by the chief inspector that he had visited that morning with Monty Loveday.

'Hello, Dr Devon. Have you got a minute?'

THE TEA HAD SUGAR in it, but Christopher couldn't taste it. 'Monty Loveday?'

'I'm afraid so,' confirmed the chief inspector. 'It was as big a shock to me as it is to you.'

'But we were with him only this morning.'

'After which he shot off to London to meet Cummings.'

'So they were in it together?'

'Apparently so. As a coroner I suppose Monty was a handy accomplice.'

'But why? I thought he couldn't stand Randall Cummings.'

'It was all a front, clearly.'

Christopher was finding it difficult to take in. 'But why did he come with me to see you?'

'A calculated risk. He'd know that the evidence you had was circumstantial, nothing more. He'd know that we wouldn't have enough to go on.'

'And then he went off to London. To meet Cummings.'

'Another risk. But the meeting must already have been planned by then, and they wouldn't want to risk losing their money.'

'All for the money . . . And to think I worked with him all those years.'

'Yes, sir. We never really know people as well as we think we do, do we?'

'Apparently not.'

'But I have to say I'm a great believer in instinct. Gut reaction. It let me down this time, but it doesn't often,' mused the policeman.

Christopher pushed away the cup of tea and stood up. 'Oh, I don't think that the occasional mistake like this one should get in the way of your true inner feelings. They don't let you down very often, and sometimes, officer, you just have to take risks, don't you?'

CHRISTOPHER TAPPED on the door. There was no reply. Then he heard a lot of muttering and the door opened to reveal Luisa Bassani.

'Dr Devon! What you doing here? I back on Monday.'

'Hello, Mrs Bassani. Yes, I know. I was just wondering if Maria was in?'

'No. She not in. She out. She go to cathedral to do flowers.'

'She . . . ? Oh! I had no idea she did the flowers.'

Luisa looked at her watch. 'She always good at—how you say—arranging? If you go you maybe catch her.'

'Fine. Yes. Yes, I'll do that.'

He was crossing the cathedral close when he saw a familiar figure walking towards him. Maria did not notice him at first. She seemed to be in a world of her own. She had almost walked right into him when he said, 'Hello!'

She looked up, squinting in the late shafts of spring sunshine and shielding her eyes in order to see. 'Oh! Christopher. Hello!' She hesitated. 'What are you doing here?'

'I came looking for you.'

'But my mother is back. I left a note.'

'Yes, you did. But I wanted to give you this, anyway.' He pulled an envelope from his pocket and handed it to her.

Maria looked confused, but she tore at the flap and pulled out the letter inside.

Dear Maria,

It is with great regret that I have to terminate your employment as of today. However, I was wondering if there would be the faintest possibility that our relationship might continue on a less businesslike footing. Should you be able to see your way to carrying on being in my company even more frequently than you have been to date, with a view to a more permanent relationship, I would be most grateful. This is not something I ask without a great deal of forethought. Neither is it something that I take lightly. Unless, of course, you would prefer that I did so.

I hope this letter finds you well, and I have to say that an early reply would be appreciated.

I remain, madam, your humble and obedient servant,
Christopher Devon

Maria folded up the letter and slipped it back in the envelope.

'How early would you like your reply?' she asked.

Christopher thought for a moment. 'Now?' he said.

'As soon as that?'

He nodded silently.

'Well, then, Dr Devon, you'd better come home and meet my mother.'

ALAN TITCHMARSH

Homes: Hampshire, the Isle of Wight
Dislikes: bad manners and rudeness
Website: www.alantitchmarsh.co.uk

RD: In *Love & Dr Devon* you write glowingly about what it's like to look down on the land and sea from the air. Are you tempted by the thought of having a pilot's licence?

AT: I haven't got the time at the moment, but, yes, I wouldn't mind learning to fly helicopters. When we made the BBC television series *British Isles: A Natural History*, we flew all over the country in them. It was an astonishing experience that definitely inspired the character of Tiger in the book. You're between a hundred and a thousand feet up and get such a detailed view. Landscape is what my life's all about and it was a great chance to become intimate with it.

RD: *Rosie* was set in the Isle of Wight and the Isles of Scilly feature in your latest novel. Are the islands round Britain particular favourites of yours?

AT: I think they are really. I do love Scilly and I have a flat on the Isle of Wight. We're an island race, we live on a big island and it's part of our psyche. Going to a smaller island kind of emphasises that. We can be as sociable as we like when we're there, but we can also cut ourselves off. That's the appeal for me. It's a bit like pulling up a drawbridge.

RD: Christopher, Tiger and Gary are each facing different kinds of midlife crisis. Have you drawn these characters from observations of people around you?

AT: Well, I always wonder how much of *yourself* there is in the characters you create, although P.D. James has never, to my knowledge, murdered anybody! But, you know, a huge part of it has to have something of yourself, because to write a character you have to get into the mind of that person. For me, at least, when I am writing about Christopher, Tiger or Gary, I become chameleon-like; I become the mouthpiece of each individual and have to feel like he is feeling. You have to try to interpret those feelings, melt them down and distill them. If you try to write about something you haven't experienced at all, then it's much harder. I think that the greatest compliment you can be paid in your writing life is that your characters ring true.

RD: Was it difficult to write about middle age, and particularly from the female perspective as well as from the male?

AT: I think that the so-called midlife crisis, the feeling that time is running out, is a kind of anxiety that society forces on you. You might not be worried about it, but you are constantly being made aware that perhaps you ought to be! I don't write maudlin books, I write affecting books. I think you write to get things out of your system. You want to find a common bond, a touchstone, between yourself and your readers. It doesn't have to be enormously erudite. Feelings are quite basic, and it's rewarding to be able to put them over in a way that makes people write and say, 'Yes, that's how it is, that's how it feels, but how did you know?' People have been kind and said that I write women quite well, which I'm pleased about.

RD: What gave you the idea to feature the trade in body parts in your book?

AT: I came across a story in *The Week*. It was called 'The Body Snatchers' and it was one of those little damascene moments when I thought, 'That's it!' The article was all about body parts being sold on the web. I'd started with the idea of a protection racket, but I wasn't comfortable that it would be of sufficient magnitude and it became the red herring. I needed something that would be difficult for Gary to work out.

RD: When you chose to leave two popular television gardening series, and sold your house, you made two big decisions. Are you pleased that you did?

RT: Yes, I am. I didn't plan to do both together, it just happened. And then my mother died at the same time, so it was an enormous upheaval for me. But, yes, after two and a half years the new house and garden are lovely now. Back then I was looking for a new challenge, so when *British Isles: A Natural History* came up, I jumped at it.

RD: Do you still enjoy gardening at home?

AT: Just as much. Someone came round to my house the other day and found me pottering on my knees in the garden. He said, 'You do that for a living, you don't have to do that for pleasure.' I said, 'Yes, I do.'

RD: You're a Yorkshireman by birth, but you've lived much of your adult life in the south of England. What do you miss most about Yorkshire?

AT: I like going back to the Moors and Dales. I'm a Dalesman. I need to go back there and breathe deeply. It's literally a breath of fresh air for me. The nice thing is that it's always there and I do go back often. It was life and work that brought me south.

RD: If you could choose to do something completely new, what would it be?

AT: Oh gosh! Maybe something to do with music, or with art. I'd love to paint better.

RD: What has been your proudest moment or achievement to date?

AT: Apart from producing two smashing daughters . . . I was chuffed to get the MBE and bowled over to receive the Victoria Medal of Honour, the Royal Horticultural Society's highest honour. If you are congratulated by your peers it's a vindication in a way. It's a big thing. When I left school at fifteen with only an O level in Art, most people thought, 'Well, that's him done.' I didn't try to become a success to prove a point, but it kind of pleases you when you think, 'I didn't do bad really, did I?'

James Rollins

MAP OF BONES

For centuries there have been rumours of a clandestine fraternity of alchemists working within the Catholic Church. Called the Dragon Court, its aim has long been to establish a new world order, using arcane scientific knowledge. Their day, it seems, has now come, and it's up to Commander Gray Pierce, together with the powers of the Vatican, to discover the key to the plan before its deadly power can be unleashed.

The race is on . . .

PROLOGUE

March 1162 AD

The archbishop's men fled into the shadows of the valley. Behind them, atop the winter pass, horses screamed, arrow-bit and cleaved. Men shouted, cried and roared. The clash of steel rang as silvery as a chapel's bells. But it was not God's work being done here.

The rearguard must hold.

Friar Joachim clutched the reins of his horse as it slid on its haunches down the steep slope. The loaded wagon had reached the valley floor safely. But true escape still lay another league away. If only they could reach it.

At the bottom of the valley, Joachim risked a glance behind him.

Though spring beckoned, winter still ruled the heights. The peaks shone in the setting sun. Snow reflected the light, while a billow of rime-frost flagged off the mountains' razored tips. But here in the shadowed gorges snowmelt had turned the forest floor into a muddy bog. The horses slogged up to their fetlocks, and ahead the wagon was mired just shy of its axles.

'Ey-ya!' yelled the wagon master, snapping a whip.

The lead horse threw its head back, then heaved against the yoke. Chains strained, horses chuffed white into the cold air, and men swore foully.

Slowly, too slowly, the wagon dragged free of the mud with a sucking sound, then it continued, climbing again. The three large stone sarcophagi in the open wagon bed slid against the ropes that lashed them in place.

If any should break . . .

Friar Joachim kicked his mare to join the soldiers at the wagon.

His fellow brother, Franz, moved closer. 'The trail ahead scouts clear.'

'The relics cannot be taken to Rome. We must reach the German border.'

Franz nodded, understanding. The relics were no longer safe on Italian soil, not with the true pope exiled and the false pope residing in Rome.

Joachim gazed back at the far ridge, staring over his mount's rump. The sounds of battle had settled to groans and sobbing, echoing eerily across the valley. The ring of swords had died, signalling the defeat of the rearguard.

Then Joachim spotted a flash of silver.

A lone figure appeared, limned in a patch of sunlight, armour glinting.

Joachim did not need to see the red dragon sigil on the man's chestplate to recognise the false pope's lieutenant. The Saracen, who had taken the Christian name Fierabras, stood a full head taller than all his men. A true giant. More Christian blood stained his hands than any other man's. But baptised this past year, the Saracen now stood beside Cardinal Octavius, the black pope who took the name Victor IV.

The wagon crested the ridge at last and reached the rutted, dry trail atop it. They would make good speed now. The Saracen knew he was too late; his ambush had failed.

Movement drew Joachim's attention.

Fierabras drew a great bow from over a shoulder, black as the shadows. He slowly set arrow to string, notched it, then drew a full pull.

Joachim frowned. What did he hope to win with one feathered bolt?

The bow sprang and the arrow flew, arching over the valley, lost for a moment in the sunlight above the ridge line. Then, as silent as a diving falcon, the arrow dropped towards the centre casket.

As the bolt struck, the sarcophagus's lid cracked with the sound of a thunderbolt. Ropes broke free as the crate split, scattering open. Loosed now, all three crates slid towards the open rear of the wagon.

Men ran forward, hands reached, the wagon was halted. Still, one of the crates tilted too far. It toppled to the ground and crushed a soldier beneath, breaking leg and pelvis. His screams christened the air.

Franz hurried, dropping from his saddle. He joined the men who were attempting to lift the stone crate off the soldier and back into the wagon.

The sarcophagus was lifted, the man dragged free, but one of the bearers slipped. The sarcophagus fell again, on its side. Its stone lid fell open.

The sound of hoof beats rose behind them. Joachim turned. Horses, lathered and shining in the sun, bore down on them. Though a quarter league off, it was plain all the riders were dressed in black. A second ambush.

Joachim merely sat on his horse. There would be no escape.

Franz gasped—not at their predicament, but at the contents of the spilled sarcophagus. *Or rather the lack thereof.*

'Empty!' the young friar exclaimed. 'It's empty.'

Shock drove Franz back to his feet. He climbed on to the wagon's bed and stared into the crate shattered by the Saracen's arrow.

'Nothing again.' Franz fell to his knees. 'The relics? What ruin is this?' The young friar found Joachim's eyes and read the lack of surprise. 'You knew.'

Their caravan had been a ruse, a ploy to draw off the black pope's men. The true courier had left a day ahead, with a mule team, bearing the true relics wrapped in rough-spun cloth and hidden inside a hay bundle.

Joachim turned to stare across the vale at Fierabras. The Saracen might have his blood this day, but the black pope would never have the relics.

Present Day

July 26

As midnight approached, Jason passed his iPod to Mandy. 'Listen. It's Godsmack's new single. It's not even released in the States yet.'

Mandy took the proffered earphones, brushed back the pink tips of her black hair and settled the phones to her ears. The movement opened her jacket enough to reveal the press of her breasts against her black T-shirt.

The two were seated on a thin grass sward that surrounded Cologne's massive Gothic cathedral, the Kölner Dom. They were on summer holiday from Boston College, backpacking through Germany with two friends, but the other two were more interested in the local pubs than attending tonight's Midnight Mass. Mandy, though, had been raised a Roman Catholic. Midnight Masses at the cathedral were limited to a few select holidays, each attended by the Archbishop of Cologne himself, like tonight's Feast of the Three Kings, and she had not wanted to miss it. Jason had agreed to accompany her.

The song ended. Mandy removed the earphones.

'We should be getting inside,' she whispered, and nodded towards the line of people flowing through the open door of the cathedral.

They threw their empty Coke cans into a bin, and crossed the square. Ahead, candlelight flowed through the cathedral's open doorway, flickering down the stone steps. It enhanced the feeling of ancientness.

In the foyer Mandy dabbed holy water from a basin and made the sign of the cross. 'Follow me,' she said. 'I want to get a good seat, but not too close.'

As Jason stepped after her into the church, he was struck by the simple majesty of the space. The central nave stretched 400 feet ahead of him, bisected by a 300-foot transept, forming a cross with the altar at the centre. A thousand candles trailed thin spirals of smoke up to the vaulted roof.

Mandy led him towards the altar. The transept areas to either side had been roped off, but there were plenty of empty seats in the central nave.

'How about here?' she said, stopping midway up the aisle.

He nodded. Mandy took his hand and pulled him down to the end of the pew, by the wall. He settled to his seat, glad she had kept her hand in his.

Finally, a bell sounded and a choir started to sing. The Mass was beginning. Jason took his cues from Mandy: standing, kneeling and sitting in an elaborate ballet of faith. He found himself becoming lost in the pageantry: the robed priests swinging smoking globes of incense, the processional that accompanied the arrival of the archbishop with his tall mitre hat and gold-trimmed vestments, the songs, the lighting of the Feast candles.

And everywhere the art as much part of the ceremony as the participants. A wooden sculpture of Mary and baby Jesus, the Milan Madonna, glowed with age and grace. Across the way, a marble statue of St Christopher bore a child in his arms with a beatific smile. And overlooking all were the massive stained-glass windows, dark now, but still resplendent with reflected candlelight, creating jewels out of ordinary glass.

But no piece of art was more spectacular than the golden sarcophagus behind the altar, locked inside glass and metal. While only the size of a large trunk and constructed in the shape of a miniature church, the reliquary was the centrepiece of the cathedral, the reason for the construction of such a massive house of worship, the focal point of faith and art. It protected the church's most holy relics. Constructed of solid gold, the reliquary had been forged before the cathedral had even broken ground. Designed by Nicolas of Verdun in the late twelfth century, the sarcophagus was considered to be the best example of medieval goldwork in existence.

At last, it was time for Communion. Parishioners slowly filed from their pews to accept the body and blood of Jesus Christ.

When her time came, Mandy rose along with the others in her pew, slipping her hand from his. 'I'll be right back,' she whispered.

The pew emptied and Jason rose to stretch his legs. He used the moment to study the statuary that flanked a confessional booth. He regretted drinking that third can of Coke. There was a public restroom outside the nave.

Glancing back longingly towards the vestibule, Jason spotted a group of monks entering the rear of the cathedral through the back doors. They were in long black robes, hooded and belted at the waist, but something struck Jason as odd. They moved too quickly, with an assured military precision, slipping into shadows.

A glance around the cathedral revealed more cloaked figures at other doors, even beyond the roped transept beside the altar. While keeping their heads bowed piously down, they also seemed to be standing guard.

The Communion finished and the last parishioners returned to their seats. Jason waved Mandy into the pew, then sat next to her as she knelt down.

'What's with all the monks?' he asked, leaning forward.

Her head was bowed, her only answer a shushing sound. He sat back.

Suddenly, the monks on either side of the altar pulled weapons from beneath folds of cloth. Gunmetal shone with oil in the candlelight, snub-nosed Uzis, mounted with long, black silencers.

A chatter of gunfire, no louder than a chain-smoker's staccato cough, spat across the altar. Heads rose along the pews. Behind the altar the priest, garbed in white, danced with the impacts, as if he were being pelted with paintballs—crimson paintballs. He fell atop the altar.

After a stunned silence, cries rose from the parishioners. People sprang up. The elderly archbishop stumbled from his dais.

Monks swept up the aisles from the rear and sides. Orders were shouted and barked in German, French and English. *Stay seated or die!*

Mandy sat back with Jason. Her hand reached for his. He clutched her fingers and glanced around. All the doors were closed, guarded.

From the pack of armed monks near the main entrance, a figure appeared, dressed like the others, only taller. His cloak was more like a cape. Clearly the leader, he strode boldly down the central aisle.

He met the archbishop at the altar. A heated argument ensued.

The archbishop suddenly fell back in horror. The leader stepped aside. Two men came forward and fired upon the faceplate that sealed the golden reliquary. Glass etched and pocked, but held. Bulletproof.

'Thieves . . .' Jason mumbled. This was all an elaborate robbery.

The leader waved another two monks to the front. They flanked the sealed vault and lifted large metal disks to either side of the casement.

The effect was instantaneous. The weakened bulletproof glass exploded outwards as if shoved by some unseen wind. In the flickering candlelight, the sarcophagus shimmered. Jason felt a sudden pressure, an internal popping of his ears, as if the walls of the cathedral had suddenly pushed inwards, squashing all. The pressure deafened his ears; his vision squeezed.

He turned to Mandy. Her hand was still clasped tightly to his, but her neck was arched back, her mouth stretched open.

'Mandy . . .'

From the corner of his eye, he saw other parishioners fixed in the same wracked poses. Mandy's hand began to tremble in his. Tears ran down her face, turning bloody as he watched. She did not breathe. Her body then jerked and stiffened, knocking his hand free, but not before he felt the bite of an electrical shock arc from her fingertips to his.

He stood up, too horrified to sit.

A thin trail of smoke rose from Mandy's open mouth. Her eyes had rolled back to white, but already they were smouldering black at the corners.

Dead.

Jason, muted by terror, searched the cathedral. The same was happening everywhere. Only a few were unscathed: a pair of young children, pinned between their parents, cried and wailed. Jason recognised the unaffected. Those who had not partaken of the Communion bread. Like him.

He fell back into the shadows by the wall. His motion had gone unnoticed. His back found a door, one unguarded by the monks. Not a true door.

Jason pulled it open enough to slip inside the confessional booth.

He crouched down, hugging himself. Prayers came to his lips.

Then, just as suddenly, it ended. He felt it in his head. A pop. A release of pressure. The walls of the cathedral sighing back.

He risked peeking out through a hole in the confessional door.

The air reeked of burnt hair. Cries and wails still echoed, but now the chorus came from only a handful of throats. Those still living. One figure stumbled out of the pew and ran down a side aisle. He was shot in the back of the head. One shot. His body sprawled.

Biting back sobs, Jason kept his eyes focused towards the altar.

Four monks lifted the golden sarcophagus from its shattered case. The priest's body was kicked from the altar and replaced by the reliquary. The leader slipped a sack from beneath his cloak. The monks opened the reliquary's lid and upended the contents into the bag. Once empty, the priceless sarcophagus was pushed to the floor and abandoned with a crash.

The leader shouldered his burden and headed back down the central aisle with the stolen relics. The archbishop called out to him in Latin. It sounded like a curse. The only response was a wave of the man's arm.

Another of the monks stepped behind the archbishop and raised a pistol to the back of the man's head. Jason slunk down, wanting to see no more.

He closed his eyes. Other shots rang out across the cathedral. Sporadic. Cries suddenly silenced as the monks slaughtered the remaining survivors.

Jason kept his eyes closed and prayed.

A moment before, he had spotted the coat of arms on the leader's surcoat. The man's cloak had parted as he'd lifted his arm, revealing a crimson sigil beneath: a coiled dragon, the tail wrapped round its neck.

Jason squeezed his eyes tight, against the horror, against the sacrilege.

All for a sack of bones.

And though the cathedral had been built around those bones—this very Mass was a feast to those long-dead kings—a question rose in Jason's mind.

Why steal the bones of the Magi?

July 24

1

Grayson Pierce edged his motorcycle between the dark buildings that made up the heart of Fort Detrick, in Frederick, Maryland. The bike's electric engine purred no louder than a refrigerator motor.

A courtyard opened ahead, a dark chasm framed by the brick-and-mortar buildings that composed the National Cancer Institute, an adjunct to USAMRIID, the US Army Medical Research Institute of Infectious Diseases. Here the country's war on bioterrorism was waged across 60,000 square feet of maximum-containment labs.

Staying in the alley, Gray cut the engine. His left knee rested against the satchel. It held the $70,000. He subvocalised into his throat mike. 'Mule to Eagle, I've reached the rendezvous. Proceeding on foot.'

'Roger that. We've got you on satellite.'

Gray shouldered the money bag. Warily, he walked his bike to a shadowed alcove, parked it, then walked down the alley.

He glanced at the glowing dial on his Breitling diver's watch: 4.45 a.m. The meeting was set for fifteen minutes from now.

He reached his destination, Building 470. It was deserted at this hour. Due for demolition next month and poorly secured, the building was perfect for the rendezvous, yet the choice of venue was also oddly ironic. In the sixties, spores of anthrax had been brewed inside, until the toxic brewery had been decommissioned in 1971. Since then, the building had become a giant storage closet for the National Cancer Institute.

But once again the business of anthrax would be conducted under this roof. He glanced up. He was to meet the seller on the fourth floor.

Reaching the side door, he swiped the lock with an electronic keycard supplied by his contact at the base. He carried the second half of the payment over his shoulder, having wired the first half a month before. Gray also bore a plastic, carbonised dagger in a concealed wrist sheath. His only weapon. He couldn't risk bringing anything else through the security gate.

Gray closed the door and crossed to the stairwell, which was lit only by the red EXIT sign. He reached up to his motorcycle helmet and toggled on the night-vision mode. The world brightened in tones of green and silver.

He climbed the stairs to the fourth floor. He had no idea where he was supposed to meet his contact. Only that he was to await the man's signal. At the top of the stairs a corridor stretched ahead. Frosted-glass office doors lined the inner walls; windows slitted the other. He proceeded warily.

Light flooded through one of the external windows, washing over him.

Had he been spotted? He rolled against a wall, back into darkness. The light pierced the other windows, one after the other, ahead of him.

Leaning forward, he peered through a window. It faced the wide courtyard that fronted the building. Across the way, he watched a Humvee trundle slowly down the street. Its searchlight swept the courtyard.

The patrol vanished momentarily behind a hulking structure in the middle of the courtyard. Looking like some rusting spaceship, it was a million-litre steel containment sphere, three storeys tall, mounted on a dozen pedestal legs. Ladders and scaffolding surrounded the structure, a former Cold War research facility, which was undergoing renovation.

Gray knew the giant globe's nickname at the base. The Eight Ball.

The patrol finally reappeared beyond the structure and rolled away.

Gray continued to the end of the corridor. Swinging double doors blocked the passage, but their narrow windows revealed a larger room beyond. He spotted a few tall metal and glass tanks. One of the old labs.

A new light flared inside, incandescent, bright enough to require Gray to flick off his night-vision. A flashlight. It blinked three times.

His approach must have been noted.

He stepped to the door and used a toe to push open one of the swinging sides. He slid through the narrow opening.

'Over here,' a voice said calmly. It was the first time Gray had heard his contact's voice. Prior to this, it had always been electronically muffled.

It was a *woman's* voice. The revelation piqued his wariness.

He followed the sound across a maze of tables with chairs stacked on top. The woman sat at one of the tables. Its other chairs were still stacked on top of it. Except for one. On the opposite side of the table.

She kicked one of its legs. 'Sit.'

Gray had expected to find a nervous scientist, someone out for an extra pay cheque. Treason for hire was becoming more and more commonplace at the top research facilities. USAMRIID was no exception . . . only much more deadly. Each vial for sale had the capability to kill thousands. And she was selling fifteen of them.

He settled into his seat, placing the satchel of money on the table.

The woman was Asian . . . no, *Eur*asian. Her skin was deeply tanned to a handsome bronze. She wore a black turtleneck body suit, not unlike the one he wore, hugging a slim, lithe frame. A silver pendant dangled from her neck, bright against her suit, bearing a tiny curled-dragon charm. Gray studied her face. The Dragon Lady looked bored.

Of course, the 9mm Sig Sauer pointed at his chest and equipped with a silencer might be the source of her confidence.

'Good evening, Commander Pierce.'

He was startled to hear his name. *If she knew that . . .*

He was already moving . . . and already too late.

The gun fired at near-point-blank range.

The impact kicked his body backwards, taking the chair with him. He landed on his back, tangled in the chair legs. Pain flattened his chest, making it impossible to breathe.

She stepped round the table and leaned over him, gun still pointing. 'I suspect you're recording all this through your helmet, Commander Pierce. Perhaps even transmitting to Washington . . . to Sigma. You won't mind if I borrow a little air time, will you?'

He was in no position to object.

The woman leaned closer. 'In the next ten minutes, the Guild will shut down all of Fort Detrick. Contaminate the entire base with anthrax. Payback for Sigma's interference with our operation in Oman. But I owe your director, Painter Crowe, something more. Something personal. This is for my sister in the field, Cassandra Sanchez.'

The gun shifted to his visor.

'Blood for blood.' She pulled the trigger.

FORTY-TWO MILES away, in Washington, DC, the satellite feed went dead.

'Where's his back-up?' Painter Crowe kept his voice firm, biting back a litany of curses. Panic would not serve them.

'Still ten minutes out.'

'Can you re-establish the link?'

The technician shook his head. 'We've lost main feed from his helmet cam. But we still have the bird's-eye of the base from the NRO sat.' The young man indicated another monitor. It showed a black-and-white overshot of Fort Detrick, centred on a courtyard of buildings.

Painter paced before the array of monitors. It had been a trap, directed at Sigma and aimed at him personally. 'Alert Fort Detrick's security.'

'Sir?' The question rose from his second-in-command, Logan Gregory.

Painter understood Logan's hesitation. Only a handful of those in power knew of Sigma and the agents it employed: the President, the Joint Chiefs, and his immediate supervisors over at DARPA. After last year's shake-up among the top brass, the organisation was under intense scrutiny.

'I won't risk an agent,' Painter said. 'Call in their security.'

'Yes, sir.' Logan crossed to a phone.

The man appeared more a California surfer than a leading strategist: blond hair, tanned, fit but going a bit soft in the belly. Painter was his darker shadow, half Native American, black hair, blue eyes. But no tan. He didn't know the last time he had seen the sun.

Painter had assumed control of the organisation eight months ago. And most of that time had been spent restructuring and shoring up security after the infiltration of the group by an international cartel known as the Guild. Everything had to be purged and rebuilt from scratch. Even their central command had been pulled out of Arlington and moved to a subterranean warren here in Washington.

Painter knew what the Guild was doing. Four weeks ago, he had begun to put operatives into the field again, the first in a year. It was a test. Two teams. One in Los Alamos investigating the loss of a nuclear data base . . . and the other at Fort Detrick, only one hour from Washington.

The Guild's attack sought to prove that they still had the knowledge to undermine Sigma. It was a feint to force Sigma to pull back again, to regroup, possibly to disband. As long as Painter's group was out of commission, the Guild could operate with impunity.

'I keep getting cut off,' Logan said, nodding to the earpiece. 'They're having intermittent communication blackouts throughout the base.'

Certainly the handiwork of the Guild too . . .

Frustrated, Painter leaned on the console and stared at the mission's dossier. Imprinted on the front of the manila file was a single Greek letter: Σ.

In mathematics, the letter *sigma* represented 'the sum of all parts', the unification of disparate sets into a whole. It was also emblematic of the organisation Painter directed: Sigma Force.

Operating under the auspices of DARPA—the Department of Defense's research and development wing—Sigma served as the agency's covert arm out in the world, sent forth to safeguard, acquire or neutralise technologies vital to US security. Its team members were a secret cadre of ex-Special Forces soldiers who had been handpicked and placed into rigorous fast-track doctoral programs, covering a wide range of scientific disciplines.

Or in plain language, killer scientists.

Painter opened the dossier before him. The team leader's file fronted the record. Dr and Commander Grayson Pierce.

The agent's photograph stared up at him from the corner. It was the man's mugshot from his year of incarceration at Leavenworth Penitentiary. Dark hair shaved to a stubble, blue eyes still angry. His Welsh heritage was evident in the sharp cheekbones, wide eyes and strong jaw. But his complexion was all Texan, burnt by the sun over the dry hills of Brown County.

Painter didn't bother glancing over the inch-thick file. He knew the details. Gray Pierce had joined the army at eighteen, the Rangers at twenty-one, and served to distinction off and on the field. Then, at twenty-three, he was court-martialled for striking a superior officer. Painter knew the details and the back history of the two soldiers involved. And considering the events, Painter might have done the same. Still, rules were codified in granite among the armed forces. Pierce spent one year in Leavenworth.

But the decorated soldier was too valuable to be cast aside for ever. His training and skill could not be wasted.

Sigma had recruited him three years ago, right out of prison.

'I've got base security!' Logan said, relief ringing in his voice.

'Get them over—'

'Sir!' The technician leapt to his feet, still tethered to his console by the headset's cord. 'Director Crowe, I'm picking up a trace audio feed.'

'What—?' Painter raised a hand to hold off Logan.

The technician turned up the feed on the speakers.

A tinny voice reached them, though the video feed remained fritzed.

One word formed. '*Goddamnpieceofshit* . . .'

GRAY KICKED OUT, catching the woman in the midriff. He felt a satisfying thud of flesh, but heard nothing. His ears rang from the concussion of the slug against his Kevlar helmet. The shot had spiderwebbed his visor. His left ear burned as the electronic bay shorted with a burst of static.

Rolling to his feet, he slipped the carbonised dagger from its wrist sheath and dived under a row of tables. Another shot, sounding like a loud cough, penetrated the ringing in his ears. Wood splintered from the table's edge.

He cleared the far side of the table and kept a wary crouch while searching the room. His kick had caused the woman to drop her flashlight, which rolled on the floor, skittering shadows everywhere. He touched his chest. The body blow of the assassin's first shot still burned and ached. But no blood.

The woman called to him from the shadows. 'Liquid body armour.'

Gray dropped lower, attempting to pinpoint the woman's location. The dive under the table had jarred his helmet's internal heads-up display. Its holographic images flickered incoherently across the inside of his face shield, interfering with his sight lines, but he dared not abandon the helmet. It was protecting him against the weapon in the woman's hand.

That and his body suit. The assassin was right. *Liquid body armour.* Developed by US Army Research Laboratory in 2003. The fabric of his body suit had been soaked in a fluid comprising hard microparticles of silica suspended in a polyethylene glycol solution. During normal movement, it acted like a liquid, but once a bullet struck, the material in that area solidified into a rigid shield, preventing penetration.

The woman spoke again, coldly calm, as she slowly circled towards the door. 'I rigged the building with C4 and TNT. Easy enough since the structure's already scheduled for demolition. The army was nice enough to have it all prewired. It just took a minor detonator modification to change the building's implosion to one that will cause an explosive *updraft*.'

Gray pictured the resulting plume of smoke and debris riding high into the early morning sky. 'The vials of anthrax . . .' he murmured. She had turned the building into a biological bomb. Not only was the base at risk, but so was the nearby town of Frederick.

She had to be stopped.

Gray edged towards the door, wary of her gun. He tried flicking on his night-vision mode, earning another snap of flame by his ear. The heads-up display continued its erratic flashing, dazzling and confusing to the eye.

He thumbed the catch and yanked the helmet off. Staying low, he carried it in one hand, the dagger in the other. He spotted a shift of shadows near the door. The woman was crouching three feet from the door, shielded by a table, and would have to expose herself to escape.

Gray threw his helmet towards the opposite side of the lab. It landed with a crash and tinkle of glass. He ran towards her. He had only seconds.

She popped from her hiding place, swivelling to fire in the direction of the noise. At the same time, she leaped gracefully towards the door, seeming to use the recoil from her gun to propel herself.

Arm already cocked, Gray whipped his dagger through the air. Balanced to perfection, the carbonised blade flew with unerring accuracy.

It struck the woman square in the hollow of her throat.

Gray continued his headlong rush. Only then did he realise his mistake.

The dagger bounced harmlessly away and clattered to the floor.

Liquid body armour. No wonder the Dragon Lady knew about his body suit. She was wearing the same.

The attack, though, threw her off her leap, and as she landed she turned a knee. But ever the skilled assassin, she never lost sight of her target. She aimed the Sig Sauer at his face and fired.

The shot whistled past Gray's ear.

He was lucky. The assassin had shot too fast, before being properly set.

Gray tackled the woman and pinned her gun between them. She fired again. The slug sucker-punched into his gut. Pounded all the way to his spine, his breath blew out of him.

The Sig Sauer had a fifteen-round magazine. He needed to end this.

He lifted his head back and slammed his forehead into her face. But she was no novice to brawling. She turned her head, taking the blow to the side of her skull. Still, it bought him time to kick out at a flex trailing from the nearby table. The library lamp attached to it came crashing to the floor. Its green glass shade shattered.

Bear-hugging the woman, he rolled her over the lamp. He heard the pop of the lamp's bulb under their combined weight.

Good enough. Frogging his legs under him, Gray leaped outwards. It was a gamble. He flew towards the light switch beside the swinging door.

A cough of a pistol accompanied a slam into his lower back.

His body struck the wall. As he bounded off, his hand palmed the electrical box and flipped the switch. Lights flickered across the lab.

He hoped whoever had last used the desk had left the lamp switched *on*.

The Dragon Lady sat atop the broken lamp, arm outstretched towards him, gun pointing. She pulled the trigger, but her aim was off.

Gray stepped round to the side, moving out of range. For the woman could not track him. She was frozen rigidly in place.

'Liquid body armour,' he said, repeating her earlier words. He stalked up to her side and relieved her of her gun. 'It has one disadvantage. Propylene glycol is a good conductor of electricity. Even a small charge, like from a broken light bulb, will flow over a suit in seconds. And the suit reacts.'

He kicked her in the shin. The suit was as hard as a rock.

Gray searched her rapidly as she strained to move.

'You won't find any detonator,' she said, her face reddening from the effort. 'It's all on a timer. Set for—' Her eyes glanced down to a wristwatch. 'Two minutes from now. You'll never deactivate all the charges.'

He noted the digits on her watch drop below 02:00.

'Where did you stash the vials?'

He knew she wouldn't tell him. But he watched her eyes. For a moment, the pupils shifted slightly up, then centred on him.

The roof.

It made sense. Anthrax was sensitive to heat. If she wanted the bloom of toxic spores to spread out from the blast, the vials would have to be up high, away from the heat of the explosion, and jettisoned skyward by the blast.

He straightened and ran for the door.

'You'll never make it!' she called as he headed for the stairwell.

He pounded up the two flights to reach the roof door. A panic bar gated the door, made for quick evacuation in case of a fire. He struck the bar, initiating an alarm Klaxon, and pushed out into the dark grey of early dawn.

He scanned the area. There were too many places to hide the vials: vents, pipes, satellite dishes. His eyes returned to a hooded exhaust vent.

Of course. The exhaust flume would serve as the perfect chimney to expel the spores as the lower building imploded, creating a toxic blowgun.

He didn't have time to check for booby traps. Kneeling, he yanked the vent off with a grunt.

The bomb rested inside the duct. The fifteen glass vials were arrayed in a starburst round a central pellet of C4 explosive, just enough to shatter the containers. He reached down and carefully removed the bomb. A timer counted down: 00:54, 00:53, 00:52.

Gray did a fast check of the bomb. It was rigged against tampering. He had no time to decipher the wires and electronics. He had to get it away from the building, away from the blast zone, preferably away from him.

As the timer clicked to 00:41, he tucked the bomb into a nylon ditty pouch over one shoulder and sprinted to the front of the building. He had no choice. He had to get it clear.

He took a deep breath and leapt over the brick parapet.

Two storeys below and twenty yards out, the spherical roof of the Eight Ball rose up to meet him. The steel sphere glistened with morning dew.

His booted feet hit the million-litre containment globe. The liquid body armour cemented round his ankles, protecting against a break. Momentum slammed him forward, face down, spread-eagled. Fingers scrabbled, but there was no traction. His body slid down the dew-slicked steel. He spread his legs, toes dragging for friction. Then he was past the point of no return, free-falling down the sheer side.

He didn't see the catwalk until he struck it. He landed on hands and knees atop the scaffolding that had been built round the equator of the steel globe. He shoved to his feet, legs wobbling from the strain and the terror.

Gray searched the curve of the sphere while freeing the bio-bomb from his ditty bag. He glanced at the timer: 00:18.

He clomped around the catwalk. He felt like he was running in ski boots, his ankles still cemented in his body suit.

An entry hatch appeared ahead. A steel door with a porthole.

'YOU! HOLD RIGHT THERE!'

Base security, drawn by the alarm. The boom of the bullhorn almost made him obey. Almost. But he kept running. A spotlight splayed over him.

'STOP OR WE'LL FIRE!'

Gray had no time to negotiate. A rattle of gunfire pelted the side of the sphere, a few rounds pinging off the catwalk. None was near. Warning shots.

He reached the hatch, grabbed the handle, twisted and tugged.

It stuck for a breath, then popped open. A sob of relief escaped him.

He pitched the device into the hollow interior of the sphere, slammed the door secure, and leaned his back against it.

'YOU THERE! STAY WHERE YOU ARE!'

He felt a small jolt on his back. The sphere rang like a struck bell. The device had blown inside, safely contained.

But it was only the primer cord of greater things to come.

A series of explosions rocked the ground. *Boom . . . boom . . . boom . . .*

It was the wired demolitions of Building 470.

Even insulated on the far side of the sphere, Gray felt the slight suck of air, then a mighty whoosh of displacement. A dense wall of dust and debris washed outwards as the building collapsed. Gray glanced up in time to see a mighty plume of smoke and dust bloom upwards, seeding high and spreading out with the wind. But no death rode this breeze.

A final explosion thundered from the dying building. Gray ran several steps along the catwalk until he found a ladder.

The line of security trucks had retreated from the explosion. But they would not stay gone. And he must not get caught.

Gray felt the tarmac of the courtyard beneath his feet and stumbled back into the pall of smoke from the collapsed building. He hurried to the alley where he had left his motorcycle, shedding the body suit as he ran.

He found the bike intact. Throwing a leg over the seat, he keyed the ignition. The engine purred happily to life. He reached for the throttle, then paused. Something had been hooked round his handlebar. He freed it, stared at it for a moment, then shoved it in a pocket.

He hunched down, gunned the engine and sped off towards the more rural section of the base, a parkland of rolling hills and hardwood forest.

He would wait out the worst of the commotion, then slip away. For now, he was safe. Still, he felt the weight of the object in his pocket, left as decoration on his bike. A silver chain . . . with a dangling dragon pendant.

PAINTER CROWE stepped back from the satellite console, having watched Grayson's escape. Logan was still on the phone to base security. The trouble at the base would be blamed on faulty wiring, decomposing munitions. Sigma Force would not be mentioned.

'Sir, I have a call from the director of DARPA,' the technician announced.

Painter plucked up the receiver. 'Director McKnight?' he said, suspecting the man was calling to get a mission debrief.

His suspicion proved wrong. He heard the stress in the other's voice.

'I just received some intel out of Germany, Painter. Strange deaths at a cathedral. We need a team on the ground there by nightfall and your best agent to head the team.'

Painter turned back to the satellite monitor. He watched the motorcycle skim through the hills. 'I have just the man. What's the urgency?'

'A call came in early this morning. Sigma has been specifically summoned to investigate this matter.'

'Summoned? By whom?'

To have Dr McKnight this rattled, it had to be someone as high up as the President. But once again, Painter's supposition proved wrong.

The director explained, 'By the Vatican.'

2

It was already noon. So much for making her lunch date.

Lieutenant Rachel Verona climbed down the narrow stairs that led deep under Rome's Basilica di San Clemente. The excavation was being overseen by a team of archaeologists from the University of Naples.

'*Lasciate ogni speranza . . .*' Rachel muttered.

Her guide, Professor Lena Giovanna, the project leader, glanced back at her. She was a tall woman, mid-fifties, but the permanent crook in her back made her seem older. She offered Rachel a tired smile. 'So you know your Dante. "Abandon all hope, ye who enter here."'

Rachel felt a twinge of embarrassment. According to Dante, those words were written on the gates of Hell. She had not meant her words to be heard, but the acoustics here left little privacy. 'No offence intended, *Professore.*'

A chuckle answered her. 'None taken, Lieutenant. I was just surprised to find someone in the military police with such fluency. Even someone working for the Tutela Patrimonio Culturale.'

Rachel understood the misconception. It was typical to paint all the Carabinieri Corps with the same brush. Most civilians only saw the uniformed men and women guarding streets and buildings, armed with rifles. But she had entered the Corps not as a soldier but with a postgraduate degree in art history, recruited to the TPC, the special unit involved with the investigation of art and antiquity thefts.

Reaching the bottom of the stairs, Rachel stepped into a pool of dank water. She was wearing a borrowed pair of rubber boots, and carried her new Ferragamo pumps, a birthday gift from her mother, in her left hand. If she lost them or got them soiled, she'd never hear the end of it.

Professor Giovanna wore a utilitarian overall, an attire more fitting for exploring waterlogged ruins than Rachel's navy slacks and silk flowered blouse. But when Rachel's pager had gone off a quarter of an hour ago, she had been heading over to a lunch date with her mother and sister and she'd had no time to return to her apartment and change into uniform.

In some regards, Rachel was glad of the temporary reprieve. She had put off letting her mother know that she and Gino had broken up more than a month ago. Rachel could already picture her mother's disappointment. And her older sister, three years married, would be pointedly twisting the wedding band on her finger and nodding sagely.

Neither had been pleased with Rachel's choice of profession.

'How are you to keep a husband, you crazy girl?' her mother had intoned, throwing her arms towards heaven. 'You cut your beautiful hair so short. You sleep with a gun. No man can compete with that.'

As a consequence, Rachel rarely left Rome to visit her family in rural Castel Gandolfo, where they had settled after World War II, in the shadow of the pope's summer residence. Only her grandmother understood her. The two shared a love of antiquities and firearms. While growing up, Rachel had listened avidly to her stories of the war: gruesome tales laced with graveyard humour. Her *nonna* even kept a Nazi P08 Luger in her bedside table, oiled and polished, a relic stolen from a border guard during her family's flight.

'It's just up ahead,' the professor said. She splashed forward towards a glowing doorway. 'My students are keeping watch on the site.'

Rachel followed her guide into a cavelike room. Illuminated by carbide lanterns, the vaulted roof arched overhead, constructed of hewn blocks of volcanic *tufa*. A man-made grotto. Plainly a Roman temple.

'These are my two students,' the professor said. 'Tia and Roberto.'

Rachel followed the professor's gaze and looked down, discovering the crouching forms of the young man and woman, both dark haired and attired in soiled overalls. They had been tagging bits of broken pottery and now rose to greet them. Rachel shook their hands.

'Over here,' Professor Giovanna said, and led Rachel to an alcove in the far wall. 'The thieves must have struck during last night's storm.'

She pointed her flashlight at a marble figure in a far niche. It stood a metre tall—or would have if the head weren't missing. All that remained was a torso, legs and a protruding phallus. A Roman fertility god.

Reaching out, Rachel ran her free hand over the stump of the statue's neck. Her fingers felt a familiar roughness. 'Hacksaw,' she mumbled.

'Why didn't the bastards just steal the whole statue?' asked Tia. 'At least it would have been preserved intact.'

Rachel tapped the statue's phallic protuberance with one of her shoes. 'Despite the convenient handle here, the artefact is too large. The thief must already have an international buyer. The bust alone would be easier to smuggle across the border.'

'Is there any hope of recovery?' Professor Giovanna asked.

Rachel did not offer any false promises. Of the 6,000 ancient artefacts stolen last year, only a handful had been recovered. 'I'll need photographs of the intact statue to post with Interpol.'

'We have a digital data base,' Professor Giovanna said. 'I can forward pictures by email.'

Rachel nodded and kept her focus on the beheaded statue. 'Or Roberto over there could just tell us what he did with the head.'

Roberto took a step back. 'Wh-what?' His gaze travelled around the room, settling on his teacher. '*Professore* . . . truly, I know nothing.'

Rachel had weighed the odds of playing her hand now or back at the station. But that would have meant interviewing everyone, taking statements, a mountain of paperwork. If she had any hope of recovering the piece, speed could prove essential.

'Did you know that sixty-four per cent of archaeological thefts are abetted by workers at the site?' she said turning to the trio. 'How many people knew the site would be unguarded during last night's storm?' Rachel kept her focus on one person. 'Roberto, do you have anything to say?'

His face was a frozen mask of disbelief. 'I had nothing to do with this.'

Rachel unsnapped her radio from her belt. 'Then you won't mind if we search your garret. Perhaps to turn up a hacksaw, something with enough traces of marble in its teeth to match the statue here.'

A wild look entered his eyes. 'I . . . I . . .'

'The minimum penalty is five years in prison,' she pressed.

In the lamplight, he visibly paled.

'That is, unless you cooperate. Leniency can be arranged.'

He shook his head, but it was unclear what he was denying.

'You had your chance.' She raised her radio to her lips.

'No!' Roberto raised his hand, stopping her. His gaze dropped to the floor. He finally let out a soft sob. 'I . . . had debts. I had no choice.'

Rachel lifted the radio to her lips. 'Carabiniere Gerard,' she said to the officer she had left waiting for her in the basilica. 'I'm heading up with someone who has additional information.'

She clicked the radio off. Roberto stood with his hands over his face.

'How did you know?' the professor asked.

'It's not only the head that sells well on the black market. There's a huge demand for ancient art of the *erotic* nature. I suspect neither of you women would have had any problem sawing off that prominent appendage, but for some reason, men are reluctant.' Rachel shook her head and crossed to the stairs leading up to the basilica. 'They take it so personally.'

RACHEL HURRIED across the piazza in front of the San Clemente Basilica to the Mini Cooper convertible parked at the edge of the square. The midday sun cast it in blinding silver. A smile formed. The car was another birthday present. To herself. You only turned thirty once.

She unlocked the door, but before she climbed inside, her cellphone chimed at her belt. Now what?

She squinted at the incoming phone number. She recognised the telephone prefix—a six—but not the number.

Why was someone from the Vatican calling her?

Rachel flipped her cellphone to her ear. 'Lieutenant Verona here.'

A familiar voice answered. 'How is my favourite niece doing today . . . besides aggravating her mother?'

'Uncle Vigor?' A smile formed. Her uncle, better known as Monsignor Vigor Verona, headed the Pontifical Institute of Christian Archaeology. But he was not calling from his university office.

'I called your mother, thinking you were with her. But it seems a Carabiniere's work follows no clock. A fact your mother does not appreciate.'

'I'm on my way to the restaurant right now.'

'Or you would be . . . if not for my call. Don't worry. I've already passed on your regrets to your mother. You will be meeting her for dinner instead.'

'What's this all about, Uncle?'

'I need you to join me here at the Vatican. Immediately. I'll have a pass waiting for you at the St Anne's Gate.'

She checked her watch. 'I'm supposed to meet with General Rende—'

'I've already spoken with your commander. He's approved your excursion here. I'll explain all when you get here. *Ciao, bambina mia*.'

Shaking her head, she climbed into her car.

When the Vatican spoke, even the military listened, it seemed. Then again, General Rende was a family friend, and it wasn't pure chance that Rachel had been recruited by the general from the University of Rome. Uncle Vigor had been watching over her since her father died fifteen years before. And while her uncle might have preferred that Rachel had entered a convent and followed in his footsteps, he had recognised she was too much of a hellion for such a pious profession and encouraged her to pursue her passion. He had also instilled in her a love and respect for history and art.

Slipping on a pair of Revo sunglasses, she pulled out onto via Labicana and headed towards the Coliseum. Traffic was congested around the landmark, but she crisscrossed through some narrow back streets, slipping through the gears with the skill of a Grand Prix racer, until she approached a roundabout where five streets converged in a mad circle. There she lunged between an overloaded flatbed and a boxy Mercedes SUV. She flicked round the Mercedes and filled the tiny space in front of it, earning the blare of a car horn, but she was already gone, heading towards the Tiber.

As she raced down the wider thoroughfare, she kept an eye fixed on the flow of traffic on all sides. To move safely through Roman streets required not so much caution as it did strategic planning. As a result of such particular attention, Rachel noted her tail.

The black BMW saloon swung into position, five cars back.

FIFTEEN MINUTES LATER, Rachel pulled into a parking space in an underground garage just outside the walls of the Vatican. She walked up the ramp, then headed towards St Peter's Square, keeping a watch on the nearby streets and alleys. The black BMW had vanished shortly after she had crossed the Tiber River. There was still no sign of it.

The car's occupants had probably just been tourists, surveying the city's landmarks in air-conditioned luxury rather than on foot in the midday heat. Summer was high season, and all visitors eventually headed to the Vatican, which was most likely why she thought she was being followed.

As she crossed St Peter's Square, voices all around babbled in French, Arabic, Polish, Hebrew, Dutch, Chinese. Tour groups congregated around guides; grinning sightseers stood as photographs were taken; a few pious supplicants stood in the sun, heads bowed in prayer; vendors worked the crowd, selling papal coins, scented rosaries and blessed crucifixes.

Rachel gratefully reached the far side of the square and approached one of the five entrances to the main complex, Porta Sant'Anna. She stepped up to one of the Swiss Guards. As was traditional for this gate, he was dressed in a blue uniform with a white collar, topped by a black beret. He took her name, checked her identification and directed her to the side, where one of the Vatican Police handed her a laminated pass.

Armed with the pass, she proceeded through the gate. Most of the city-state was off limits. But one section was truly forbidden to all but a few. The Apostolic Palace, the home of the pope. Her destination.

After showing her pass three times to Swiss Guards, she at last gained admission to the palace proper. A guide awaited her, an American seminary student named Jacob. He was a wiry man in his mid-twenties, dressed in black linen slacks and a white shirt, buttoned to the top.

'If you'll follow me, I've been directed to take you to Monsignor Verona.' He did a comical double take at her visitor's pass. 'Lieutenant . . . Verona?' he stuttered. 'Are . . . are you related to the monsignor?'

'He's my uncle.'

A rapid nod as he collected himself. 'I'm sorry. I was only told to expect a Carabinieri officer.' He waved her to follow him. 'I'm a student and aide for Monsignor Verona at the Greg.'

She nodded. Most of her uncle's students at the Gregorian University revered the man. He was devoted to the Church but maintained a strong scientific outlook. He even had a notice on the door to his university office, bearing the inscription that once graced the door of Plato's Academy: *Let no one enter who does not know geometry.*

Rachel was led through the entrance to the palace. She quickly lost her bearings. The place was gigantic, with 1,500 rooms, 1,000 staircases and twenty courtyards. But at last they reached a small, nondescript door.

Jacob opened it for her. She stepped through into an odd, Kafkaesque chamber. Sterilely lit, the chamber was long and narrow, but its ceilings were high. Against the walls, grey steel filing cabinets and drawers climbed from floor to ceiling. A tall library ladder leaned against one wall.

'Rachel!' her uncle called from a corner, where he was standing beside another priest seated at a desk. He waved her over. 'You made good time, my dear. Then again, I've driven with you before. Any casualties?'

She smiled and noted that her uncle was not wearing his usual outfit of jeans, T-shirt and cardigan, but was dressed more formally in a black cassock with purple piping and buttons. He'd even oiled the curls of his salt-and-pepper hair and trimmed his goatee tight to his face.

'This is Father Torres,' her uncle introduced. 'Keeper of the bones.'

The elderly man stood. He was short and stocky, dressed all in black with a Roman collar. He smiled. 'I prefer the title "rector of the *reliquiae*."'

Rachel studied the towering wall of filing cabinets. She had heard of this place, the Vatican's relic depository. Catalogued and stored in all the drawers and shelves were bits and pieces of saints and martyrs: finger bones, snips of hair, vials of ash, scraps of garments, mummified skin, nail clippings, blood. Few people know that, by canon law, each and every Catholic altar must contain a holy relic. And with new churches or chapels being erected worldwide regularly, this priest's job was to box and FedEx bits of bone or other earthly remains of various saints. Rachel had never understood the Church's obsession with relics. It gave her the creeps.

She found her voice. 'Was something stolen here?'

Uncle Vigor lifted an arm to his student. 'Jacob, perhaps you could fetch us some cappuccinos.'

'Certainly, Monsignor.' Jacob left, closing the door.

Vigor looked at Rachel. 'Have you heard of the massacre in Cologne?'

Rachel had been running all day long and had had little chance to watch the news, but there had been no way to avoid hearing about the midnight murders in Germany last night. The details remained sketchy.

'Only what's been reported on the radio,' she answered.

He nodded. 'The Curia here has been receiving intelligence in advance of what's being broadcast. Eighty-five people were killed, including the Archbishop of Cologne. But it is the manner of their deaths that is being kept from the public for the moment.

'What do you mean?'

'A handful were shot, but the majority seem to have been electrocuted.'

'Electrocuted? How . . . ?'

'That answer may have to wait. The cathedral is swarming with investigators, but as the crime took place in a Roman Catholic cathedral, sanctified territory, the Vatican has invoked its *omerta*.'

'Its code of silence.' Rachel shook her head. 'But what does all this have to do with you calling me here?'

'From the initial investigation, there seems to be only one motive. The golden reliquary at the cathedral was broken into.'

'They stole the reliquary?'

'No, that's just it. They left behind the gold box. A priceless artefact. They only stole its contents. Its relics.'

Father Torres interjected. 'The bones of the biblical Magi.'

'As in the Three Wise Men?' Rachel couldn't keep the incredulity out of her voice. 'They steal the bones, but leave the gold box. Surely the reliquary would fetch a better price on the black market than the bones.'

Uncle Vigor sighed. 'At the secretary of state's request, I came down here to evaluate the provenance of those relics. They have an illustrious past. The bones came to Europe through the relic-collecting verve of St Helena, the mother of Emperor Constantine. Helena returned from one of her pilgrimages with a large stone sarcophagus, claiming to have recovered the bodies of the Three Kings. The relics were in Constantinople, but following Constantine's death they were transferred to Milan. In the twelfth century, Emperor Frederick Barbarossa of Germany plundered Milan and stole the relics. The circumstances surrounding this are clouded with a mix of rumours. But all stories end with the relics in Cologne.'

'Until last night.' Rachel closed her eyes, thinking. She heard the door open to the depository. 'And the murders? Why not steal the bones when the church was empty? The act must have been meant also as an attack on the Church. The violence suggests a secondary motive—not just theft.'

'Very good.' A new voice spoke from the doorway.

Startled, Rachel opened her eyes. She immediately recognised the robes worn by the newcomer: the black cassock with shoulder cape, the wide sash worn high round the hips, scarlet to match the skullcap. She also recognised the man in the clothes. 'Cardinal Spera,' she said, bowing her head.

He waved her up, his gold ring flashing. The ring marked him as a cardinal, but he also wore a second ring, a twin of the first, on his other hand, representative of his station as the Vatican's secretary of state. He was Sicilian, dark haired and complexioned, not yet fifty years old.

He offered her a warm smile. 'I see, Monsignor Verona, that you were not wrong about your niece.'

'It would have been improper of me to lie to a cardinal, especially one who happens to be the pope's right-hand man.' Her uncle crossed over and, rather than chastely kissing either of the man's rings, gave him a firm hug.

'After we met this morning, I contacted His Eminence in St Petersburg,' said the cardinal. 'He's flying back tomorrow.'

Rachel felt overwhelmed. While the pope was the head of the Vatican, the true power of the state rested with this one man, its prime minister.

'And has your research turned up anything here?' the cardinal asked.

'It has,' Vigor said. 'The thieves don't possess all the bones.'

Rachel stirred. 'There are more?'

'That's what we came down her to ascertain. It seems the city of Milan, after the bones were plundered by Barbarossa, spent centuries clamouring for their return. To settle the matter, a few of the Magi bones were sent back to Milan in 1906, to the Basilica of St Eustorgio.'

'Thank the Lord,' Cardinal Spera said. 'So they aren't entirely lost.'

Father Torres spoke up. 'We should arrange for them to be sent here immediately. Safeguarded at the depository.'

'Until that can be arranged, I'll have security tightened at the basilica,' said the cardinal. He motioned to Vigor. 'On your return from Cologne, I'll have you stop off and collect the bones in Milan.'

Uncle Vigor nodded.

'Oh, I was also able to arrange an earlier flight,' the cardinal continued. 'The helicopter will take you both to the airfield in three hours.'

'All the better.' Uncle Vigor turned to Rachel. 'It looks like we must disappoint your mother once again. No family dinner.'

'I'm . . . we're going to Cologne?' she asked.

'As Vatican nuncios,' her uncle said.

Rachel looked puzzled. Nuncios were the Vatican's ambassadors abroad.

'Emergency nuncios,' Cardinal Spera corrected. 'You are to be passive observers, to represent Vatican interests and report back. I need keen eyes out there. Someone familiar with thefts of antiquities.' A nod to Rachel.

'That is our cover, anyway,' Uncle Vigor said.

Cardinal Spera frowned, a warning tone entering his voice. 'Vigor . . .'

Her uncle turned to the secretary of state. 'She has a right to know.'

The two men stared each other down. Finally, the cardinal sighed with a wave of an arm, relenting. Vigor turned back to Rachel.

'The nuncio assignation is just a smoke screen.'

'Then what are we—?'

He told her.

'WE'RE GOING IN as Vatican *spies*?' Rachel asked, when they were alone, outside the depository.

Uncle Vigor lifted his brows. 'Are you surprised? The Vatican, a sovereign country, has always had an intelligence service.'

'And we've just been recruited into this service?'

'*You've* been recruited. I've worked with the intelligence service for over fifteen years. What better cover than as a archaeologist in humble service to the Vatican?' He waved her out of the door. 'Come. Let's see about getting everything in order. You'll need to grab an overnight bag, your passport, and whatever else you might need for a day or two abroad.'

Rachel stumbled after her uncle, trying to see him with new eyes.

'We'll be meeting up with a party of American scientists. Like us, they'll be investigating the attack in secret, concentrating more on the deaths, leaving us to handle the theft of the relics.'

'I don't understand. Why all this subterfuge?'

Her uncle pulled her into a small side chapel, no larger than a closet.

'Only a handful of people know this,' he said. 'But there was a survivor of the attack. A boy. He is still in shock, at a hospital in Cologne, but he described the deaths. Most of them occurred in a single moment. The boy had no explanation, but he was adamant about who succumbed. Only those who took the Eucharist during the Communion.'

A chill passed through Rachel. 'Were the wafers poisoned?'

'That's still unknown. But the Vatican wants answers immediately. And the Holy See wants them first. I think this is an opening gambit in a much larger game. But what game is being played?'

Rachel nodded. 'And what do the bones of the Magi have to do with it?'

'Exactly. While you collect your things, I'm going off to the archives. I already have a team of scholars sifting through all references to the Magi. By the time the helicopter lifts off, I'll have a full dossier.'

Her uncle led her out of the Apostolic Palace, then they parted ways.

With barely any note of the passage of time, Rachel reached her Mini Cooper. She sped out of the underground car park and squealed round a tight corner into traffic. Then she raced over the Tiber River and headed for the centre of town.

With her mind on autopilot, she failed to note when she had regained her tail. Only that the black BMW was back there again.

She made a couple of fast turns, not enough to alert her tail that he had been spotted, just her usual controlled recklessness. The BMW kept pace.

Who had she pissed off? As a member of the TPC, she had enemies among the organised-crime families who trafficked in stolen antiquities.

As she pondered this thought, Rachel spotted a blur of black. The BMW whipped up alongside her Mini Cooper. A second car appeared on her other side. Identical, except this one was *white.* She'd had not one tail . . . but *two.*

The two cars slammed into her, pinning her between them. Their back windows were lowered. The blunt noses of submachine guns poked out.

3

In the gym locker room, Grayson Pierce pulled on a pair of black cycling shorts, then slipped a loose-fitting nylon soccer jersey over his head.

Behind him, the locker-room door swung open and Monk Kokkalis entered, a basketball under one arm. Standing only three inches over five feet, Monk looked like a pitbull terrier in sweats.

Monk eyeballed Gray. 'You wearing that to meet Commander Crowe?'

Gray stood. 'I'm heading over to my folks'.'

'I thought we were told to stick to campus?'

'Screw that.'

Monk raised an eyebrow. The bushy brows were the only hair on his shaved head. He stuck to the look drilled into him by the Green Berets. The other physical attributes from his former military life were three puckered bullet-wound scars—shoulder, thigh and chest. He had been the only one of his team to survive an ambush in Afghanistan. During his recovery, Sigma had recruited him because of his genius-level IQ, then retrained him through a doctoral program in forensic medicine.

Gray grabbed his backpack from the bench. 'I'll have my beeper with me. I'm only fifteen minutes away by Metro.'

'And you're going to leave the director waiting?'

Gray shrugged. He needed to get away for a while. He'd had enough: the debriefing, the medical, and now this mysterious summons by Director Crowe. He knew he was due for a dressing-down. He shouldn't have gone in alone to Fort Detrick. It had been a bad call. But now Gray couldn't sit idle and simply wait. Crowe had gone off to a meeting over at DARPA headquarters in Arlington. There was no telling when he would be back.

'Have you heard who else has been summoned to the meeting with the director?' Monk asked. 'Kat Bryant.'

Captain Kathryn Bryant had entered Sigma only ten months ago, but had already completed a geology programme and had moved on to engineering.

'Then it can't be a mission assignation,' Gray said. 'They wouldn't send someone so green out into the field.'

'She isn't *that* green.' Monk headed for the showers. 'She came out of the intelligence branch of the Navy. Black ops, they say.'

'*They* say a lot of things,' Gray mumbled. He pulled on his backpack and left the gym, striding through the labyrinth of hallways to the elevator bay.

The subterranean stronghold of Sigma central command was once an underground bunker and a fallout shelter, but it had long been abandoned and closed off. Few knew of its existence, buried beneath the campus of museums and laboratories that made up the Smithsonian Institution.

Now the underground warren had new tenants. To the world at large, it was just another think tank. Many of its members worked at laboratories throughout the institution, doing research and utilising the resources at hand. The Smithsonian became both a resource and a cover.

Gray climbed inside the elevator and pressed the button marked LOBBY.

The doors opened into a reception area manned by two armed guards and a receptionist. It could pass as a bank lobby. But the amount of surveillance and state-of-the-art countermeasures rivalled those at Fort Knox.

One of the guards opened the door and Gray headed for the Metro station. He had other responsibilities besides keeping America safe.

Something he had neglected for too long.

THE TWO BMWs continued to hem in the Mini Cooper. Rachel struggled, but she could not pull free. The guns in the back seats swung forward.

Before the assailants could fire, Rachel shoved the gear into park and yanked her handbrake. The car jolted with a scream of tearing metal, throwing off the gunmen's aim, but the BMWs still dragged the Mini forward.

Rachel dived for the footwell. Gunfire shattered the driver's side window. She hit the controls to her convertible roof. The windows began to lower and the cloth roof folded back.

She leapt off the centre console and used the lip of the passenger door to hurdle through the half-open roof. The white saloon was still crammed against the passenger side. She landed on its roof.

By now, their speed had slowed to less than twenty miles per hour.

Bullets blasted from below. She threw herself off the roof, aiming for a line of cars parked at the edge of the road. She struck the roof of a Jaguar and slid belly-first onto the pavement on the far side.

Dazed, she lay still. The parked cars shielded her from the road. Half a block away, unable to brake fast enough, the BMWs roared off.

In the distance, Rachel heard the *wha-wha* of police sirens.

She struggled up, knowing the assassins would not return. Already, multiple cars were stopping in the street, blocked by her Mini Cooper.

Rachel had a larger concern. Unlike the first time, she had caught a glimpse of the black BMW's licence plate: SCV 03681.

SCV stood for *Stato della Città del Vaticano*. Vatican City.

Rachel's heart was pounding. If she was attacked by someone with connections to the Vatican, another target was surely in danger.

'Uncle Vigor . . .'

'GRAY! IS THAT YOU?'

Grayson Pierce climbed the steps to the porch of his parents' bungalow in Takoma Park, Maryland, and called through the screen door. 'Yeah, Mom!'

He leaned the bike against the porch railing. He had phoned the house from the Metro station, giving his mother fair warning of his arrival. He kept a bike locked up at the local station for times like this.

'I have lunch almost ready.'

'What? You're cooking?' He swung open the screen door. It snapped closed behind him. 'Will wonders never cease?'

'Don't give me any of your lip, young man. I'm fully capable of making sandwiches. Ham and cheese.'

He crossed through the living room, noting the fine coating of dust. His mother had never been much of a homemaker, spending most of her time teaching biological sciences at George Washington University. His parents had moved out here three years ago. Gray had an apartment a couple of miles away. He had wanted to be close, to help out where he could.

'Where's Dad?' he asked as he entered the kitchen.

'Out in the garage. Working on another birdhouse. His therapist says it's good for him to have a hobby.' She crossed with two plates of sandwiches.

His mother had come straight from her university office. She still wore her blue blazer over a white blouse, her blonde-grey hair pulled back and bobby-pinned. Neat, professorial. But Gray noted the haggard edge to her eyes. She looked more drawn, thinner.

Gray took the plates. 'Dad's woodworking may help him, but does it always have to be birdhouses? There are only so many birds in Maryland.'

She smiled. 'Eat your sandwiches. Do you want any pickles?'

'No.' It was the way they always were. Small talk to avoid the larger matters. But some things couldn't be put off. 'Where did they find him?'

'Over by the 7-Eleven on Cedar. He got confused. Ended up heading the wrong way. He had enough presence of mind to call John and Suz.'

The neighbours must have then telephoned Gray's mother, and she had called Gray, worried, half panicked. Five minutes later she had called again. His father was home and fine. Still, Gray knew he had better stop by.

His father had been diagnosed with Alzheimer's shortly after moving out here. It had started with small bouts of forgetfulness: where he had placed his keys, telephone numbers, the names of neighbours. Then came spats of frustrated anger. Not that such a line was ever hard for his father to cross.

'Why don't you take his plate out to him?' his mother asked. 'I have to call in to the office.'

Gray reached and took the sandwiches, letting his hand rest on hers for a moment. 'Maybe we need to talk about that live-in nurse.'

She shook her head. Gray had hit this wall before. His father would not allow it, and his mother felt it was her responsibility to care for him. But it was wearing on her.

'How is everything at the lab?' she asked.

'Going fine,' he said. Neither of his folks knew of his role with Sigma. They thought he simply did low-level research for the military.

Plate in hand, Gray headed for the garage, where he found his father crouched over a vice-gripped piece of wood, hand-planing an edge.

'Pop,' he said.

His dad straightened and turned. He was as tall as Grayson, but built stocky, wider shoulders, broader back. He had worked the oil fields while putting himself through college, earning a good degree in petroleum engineering. He had done well until an industrial accident at a well sheared away his left leg at the knee. The settlement and disability allowed him to retire at forty-seven. That had been fifteen years ago.

Half of Grayson's life. The bad half.

His father turned towards him. 'Gray?' He wiped the sweat from his brow. A scowl formed. 'There was no need to come all the way out here.'

'How else would these sandwiches get to you?' He lifted the plate.

'Your mother made those?'

'You know Mom. She tried her best.'

'Then I'd better eat them. Can't discourage the habit.' He hobbled stiff-legged to a small fridge in the back. 'Beer?'

'I have to go back to work in a bit.'

'One beer won't kill you. I've some of that Sam Adams swill you like.'

His father was more of a Budweiser man. But stocking his fridge with Sam Adams was the equivalent of a pat on the back. He couldn't refuse.

Gray used the opener built into the worktable to pop it open. His father lifted his Budweiser in salute. 'It sucks to get old, but there's always beer.'

'So true.' Gray drank deeply. It had been a long, long morning.

His father stared at him. The silence threatened to become awkward.

'So,' Gray said, 'can't find your way home any longer.'

'Fuck you,' his father responded with false anger, weakened by a grin and a shake of his head. He appreciated honest talk. *Straight shooting,* as he used to say. 'At least I was no goddamn felon.'

'You can't let go of my stint in Leavenworth. *That* you remember!'

His father tipped his beer bottle at Gray. 'I will as long as I damn can.'

Their eyes met. He saw something glint behind his father's banter, something he had seldom seen before. Fear.

The two had never had an easy relationship. His father had taken to heavy drinking after the accident, accompanied by bouts of depression. It was hard for an oilman to suddenly become a housewife, raising two boys while his spouse went to work. To compensate, he had run the household like a boot camp. And Gray had always pushed the envelope, a born rebel.

Until, at eighteen, Gray had simply packed his bags and joined the army.

Afterwards the two did not speak for a full two years.

Slowly his mother had brought them back together. Still, it had remained an uncomfortable détente. She had once said, 'You two are more alike than you are different.' Grayson had not heard scarier words.

'This goddamn sucks . . .' his father said softly, breaking the silence.

Grayson lifted his beer bottle. 'That's why I only drink Sam Adams.'

His father grinned. 'You're an asshole.'

'You raised me.'

His father rolled his eyes. 'Why do you even bother coming over?'

Because I don't know how long you'll remember me, Gray thought, but dared not say aloud. There remained a tight spot behind his sternum, an old resentment that he could not let go. There were words he wanted to say, wanted to hear . . . and part of him knew he was running out of time.

'Where did you get these sandwiches?' his father asked, taking a bite and speaking around the mouthful. 'They're pretty good.'

Gray kept his face passive. 'Mom made 'em.'

A flicker of confusion followed. 'Oh . . . yeah.'

Their eyes met again. Fear flared brighter in his father's gaze . . . and shame.

'Pop . . . I . . .'

'Drink your beer.'

Gray heard an edge of familiar anger, and reflexively shied from it. His beeper went off at his waist. He grabbed it too quickly. 'That's the office,' he said when he saw the Sigma number. 'I . . . I have a meeting.'

His father nodded. 'I should get back to this damn birdhouse.'

They shook hands, two uneasy adversaries conceding no contest.

THE SEARCH for the truth behind the Three Magi had turned into a painstaking archaeological dig—but instead of hauling dirt and rock, Monsignor Vigor Verona and a crew of archivists were digging through crumbling books and parchments. The crew of *scrittori* had done the initial spadework in the main Vatican Library; now Vigor sifted for clues about the Magi in one of the most guarded areas of the Holy See: the Secret Archives.

His young student Jacob carried a laptop, maintaining a data base on their subject. 'So there were not just *three* Magi?' he said.

'The Gospels were never specific on the number of Magi,' Vigor replied. 'Only Matthew directly refers to them, and even then only vaguely. The common assumption of *three* comes from the number of gifts borne by the Magi: gold, frankincense and myrrh. In fact, they might not even have been kings. The word *magi* comes from the Greek word *magoi,* or "magician".'

'They were magicians?'

'Rather practitioners of hidden wisdom. Hence the "wise men" reference. Most scholars believe they were astrologers out of Persia or Babylon.'

Vigor had one more clue he wanted to investigate before he left for Germany. They crossed the Manuscript Depository to the elevator.

'Where are we headed now?' Jacob asked as they stepped into the cage.

'To the Tower of the Winds. There is an ancient document kept up there. A copy of Marco Polo's *Description of the World*. In it he relates myths out of Persia, concerning the Magi. They supposedly founded a fraternity of arcane wisdom. I'd like to trace that myth.'

The elevator shuddered to a stop. They exited down a long corridor, which ended at the tower. The room Vigor sought was at its very top. Cursing the lack of an elevator he entered the dark staircase.

At the end of the long climb was one of the Vatican's most unique historic chambers, the Meridian Room. The sixteenth-century solar observatory was where the Gregorian calendar had been established and where Galileo had tried to prove that the Earth revolved round the sun.

Vigor took a moment to slow his breathing after the climb. He wiped sweat from his brow and directed Jacob to a neighbouring chamber off the Meridian Room. A massive bookshelf covered its back wall.

'According to the index, the book we seek should be on the third shelf.'

Jacob stepped through, tripping the wire that ran across the threshold.

Vigor heard the twang. No time for warning.

The incendiary device exploded, blowing Jacob's body out the doorway and into Vigor. They fell backwards as a wall of flames roared outwards, rolling over them, like the brimstone breath of a dragon.

THE INTERCOM BUZZED on Painter Crowe's desk in Washington.

He hit the button. 'Go ahead.'

'Director Crowe, I have Doctors Kokkalis and Bryant here.'

'Send them in.'

A chime sounded at the door as the lock released. Monk Kokkalis pushed in first, but he held the door for Kathryn Bryant. The woman stood a head taller than the stocky former Green Beret. She moved with a leonine grace of constrained power. Her auburn hair, straight to the shoulder, was as conservative as her attire: navy blue suit, white blouse, leather pumps.

'Please take a seat,' Painter said, acknowledging them both with a nod. 'Where's Commander Pierce?'

Monk shifted in his seat. 'Gray . . . Commander Pierce had a family emergency. He just arrived back. He'll be up in a moment.'

Covering for him, Painter thought. Good. It was one of the reasons he had chosen Kokkalis for this mission, pairing him up with Grayson Pierce. They complemented each other's skills—but more importantly, they suited each other's personalities. Monk could be a tad staid, by-the-book, but Grayson listened to him more than to any other member of Sigma. He tempered the steel in Gray. Monk had a way of joking and humouring that was as convincing as any well-debated argument. They made a good pair.

On the other hand . . .

Painter noted how stiffly Kat Bryant sat, still at attention. He had decided to include her on this mission due to her intelligence background more than her current study of engineering. And she had previously worked with one of the Vatican operatives who would be jointly overseeing this investigation, Monsignor Vigor Verona.

'We might as well get the paperwork out of the way while we await Commander Pierce.' Painter passed out two thick dossiers in black file jackets, one each to Bryant and Kokkalis. A third waited for Pierce.

'That'll fill in all the finer details for this op.' Painter tapped the touch screen built into his desktop. The three flat-panel screens—one behind his shoulder, one to the left, and one to the right—changed from panoramic views of mountain landscapes to a silver Σ. 'I'll be doing the mission briefing myself, rather than the usual ops manager.'

'Compartmentalising the intel,' Kat said softly, her Southern accent softening the edges of her consonants. 'Due to the ambush at Fort Detrick.'

Painter nodded. 'Information is being restricted in advance of a system-wide check of our security protocols. Word from—'

The buzz of the intercom interrupted. Painter hit the button.

'Director Crowe,' his secretary announced, 'Dr Pierce has arrived.'

'Send him in.'

The door chimed open, and Grayson Pierce strode inside. He wore black

Levi's dressed up with black leather shoes and a starched white shirt. His hair was slicked down, still wet from a shower.

'Sorry,' Grayson said. A certain hardness in his eyes belied the apology. He kept a stiff posture, ready for reprimand.

And he deserved it. After the security breach, now was not the time to be thumbing his nose at command. However, a modicum of insubordination had always been tolerated at Sigma. These men and women were the best of the best. You couldn't ask them to act independently out in the field, then expect them to bend to totalitarian authority here.

Painter stared at Grayson for several seconds before waving him to a seat. 'Family is important,' he said. 'Just don't let tardiness become a habit.'

'No, sir.' Grayson crossed and sat. A crease formed between his brows. The lack of reprimand had unsettled him. Good.

Painter slid the third folder towards Grayson. 'We were just starting the mission briefing.' He tapped the screen on his desk.

A Gothic cathedral appeared on the left screen, an exterior shot. An interior view appeared on the right. Bodies lay sprawled. Behind his shoulder, Painter knew, was a picture of an altar, still bloodstained, chalk outlining the sprawl of a murdered priest. He watched the agents' gazes.

'The massacre in Cologne,' Kat Bryant said.

Painter nodded. 'Eighty-five people were killed. The motive appears to be robbery. The cathedral's priceless reliquary was broken into.' He flicked through images of the golden sarcophagus and the shattered remains of its security cage. 'The only items stolen were the shrine's contents. The supposed bones of the biblical Magi.'

'Bones?' Monk asked. 'They leave behind a crate of solid gold and take a bunch of bones? Who would do that?'

'Unknown. There was only one survivor of the massacre.' He brought up a photo of a young man in a hospital bed. 'Jason Pendleton. American. Age Twenty-one. He was found hiding in a confessional booth. Barely coherent when first discovered, but later he was able to describe how men robed and cloaked as monks stormed the cathedral armed with rifles. No faces were ID'd. Several people were shot, including the priest and the archbishop.'

'And how does this involve Sigma?' Kat asked.

'There were other deaths. To break into the security vault, the assailants employed a device that not only shattered the bulletproof cage, but also, according to the survivor, triggered a wave of death across the cathedral.'

Painter hit a key. Across all three screens, views of various corpses appeared. The bodies were contorted, heads thrown back. One image was a close-up of a face. Eyes were open, corneas gone opaque, while trails of bloody tears leached from the corners. Lips were stretched back, frozen in a rictus of agony. The tongue was swollen, blackened at the edges.

'Full autopsy reports are in your folders,' Painter said. 'The initial conclusion from the coroners is that the deaths were due to an epileptiform seizure. An extreme convulsive event coupled with severe hyperthermia, resulting in the complete liquefaction of the outer surfaces of the brain. All died with their hearts in a contracted state. One man's pacemaker had exploded in his chest. A woman with a metal pin in a femur was found with her leg still on fire, hours later.'

Gray was the first to speak. 'And we're sure the deaths are connected to the device employed by the thieves.'

'As sure as we can be. The survivor reported feeling an intense pressure in his head as the device was turned on. He described it like descending in an airplane. Felt in the ears. The deaths occurred at this time.'

'But Jason lived,' Kat said, taking a deep breath.

'Some others did, too. But the unaffected were shot by the perpetrators.'

Monk stirred. 'So some people succumbed, others did not. Why? Was there any commonality between the victims of the seizures?'

'Just one. The only ones to suffer seizures appear to be those who had partaken of the Communion. The Vatican fears repercussions if it becomes known that some group may be targeting the Communion service. Possibly poisoning its wafers. They want answers as soon as possible. Your team will be working with two intelligence agents representing the Holy See.'

'And our end goal?' Kat asked.

'To find out who perpetrated the crime and what device they employed. If it could kill in such a specific and targeted manner, we need to know what we're dealing with and who controls it.'

Grayson turned to Painter. 'Was any wine passed out during the service?'

'To a handful of parishioners. But they also took the Communion bread.'

'The bread *must* have been poisoned,' Grayson said. 'With something that made the victims susceptible to whatever force was generated by the device. Were the host wafers examined for any contamination?'

'Wafers left over from the service were sent to several independent labs for analysis. The results showed nothing but the usual bakery ingredients.'

The crease deepened between Grayson's brows. 'That's impossible.'

Painter heard the stubborn edge to his voice, almost belligerent.

Kat crossed her arms. 'Then there must be another explanation for—'

'Bullshit,' Grayson said, cutting her off. 'The labs were all wrong.'

Painter restrained a smile. 'You're right,' he finally said. 'The labs here did find something. They carbonised the sample down to its component parts and separated out all the organic components. After all trace elements were stripped away, they still had a quarter of the dry weight of the host remaining on their scales. A dry, whitish powder.'

'I don't understand,' Monk said.

Grayson explained. 'The remaining powder couldn't be detected by the analysing equipment.'

'It was sitting on the scales, but the machines were telling the technicians nothing was there,' Painter added.

'The powdery substance must be totally inert,' Grayson said.

Painter nodded. 'So the lab boys here tested it further. They heated it to its melting point, 1,160 degrees. It melted and formed a clear liquid, which, when the temperature dropped, hardened to form a clear amber glass. If you ground the glass in a mortar and pestle, it again formed the white powder. But in every stage it remained inert, undetectable by modern equipment.'

'What can do that?' Kat asked.

'Something we all know, but in a state that was only discovered in the last couple of decades.' Painter flicked to the next picture. It showed a carbon electrode in an inert gas chamber. 'One of the technicians worked at Cornell University, where this test was developed. Using an electroplating technique, they were able to get the powder back to its more common state.'

He tapped up the last picture. It was a close-up of the carbon electrode, only it was no longer *black*.

Grayson leaned forward in his seat. 'Gold.'

THE CAR'S SIREN wailed in Rachel's ears. She sat in the passenger seat of the Carabinieri patrol car, bruised, aching, head throbbing. But all she could feel was an icy certainty that Uncle Vigor was dead.

Rachel half heard the patrolman speaking into his radio. His vehicle had been the first on the scene after the ambush. She had refused medical care and ordered the man to take her to the Vatican. And now, as St Peter's came into view, what she saw rising behind the basilica lifted her from her seat.

A sooty column of smoke coiled into the indigo sky.

The closer they got to the Vatican, the worse the congestion became. The convergence of emergency vehicles had snarled all traffic in the area.

Rachel could not wait any longer. She yanked on the door handle.

'Tenente Verona,' the patrolman said. 'Here. You may need this.'

Rachel stared down at the black pistol, a Beretta 92, the man's service weapon. She took it with a nod of thanks and, shoving the pistol into her waistband, set off on foot.

Ahead she spotted a fire engine edging through St Anne's Gate. A contingent of Swiss Guards formed a barricade to either side, on high alert. No ceremonial halberds here. Each man had an assault rifle in hand.

Rachel pushed towards the guard line. 'Lieutenant Verona with the Carabinieri Corps!' she yelled, ID in hand. 'I must reach Cardinal Spera!'

Expressions remained hard, unbending. But from the back of the line, a single guard pushed forward, dressed in midnight blue. Rachel recognised him as the same guard to whom she had spoken earlier.

'Lieutenant Verona,' he said. 'I've been ordered to escort you inside. Come with me.' He turned on a heel and led her away.

She hurried to keep up. 'My uncle . . . Monsignor Verona . . .'

'I know nothing except to escort you to the *eliporto*.' He directed her to an electric groundskeeper's cart. 'Orders from Cardinal Spera.'

Rachel climbed inside and, skirting the emergency traffic jam, the cart headed for the gardens that covered the back half of the city-state. Finally, their destination appeared ahead: the Vatican heliport.

On the tarmac, a single helicopter's blades were beginning to spin. It was the pope's private helicopter, nicknamed the 'Holycopter'.

The motor cart braked. Rachel leapt out.

From the back of the helicopter, a figure stepped out and hurried towards her. She rushed to meet him and hugged him tight.

'Uncle Vigor . . .' Hot tears ran down her face.

He pulled back. 'You're late, child.'

'I was distracted,' she answered.

'So I heard. General Rende passed on word of your attack.'

Rachel smelt the smoke in his hair. His eyebrows were singed. 'It seems I wasn't the only one attacked. Thank God you're OK.'

Her uncle's face darkened, his voice tightened. 'Unfortunately, not all were so blessed. Jacob was killed in the blast. His body shielded mine, saved me.' She heard the anguish in his words. 'Come, we must get away.'

Rachel followed her uncle into the helicopter. They strapped themselves in as the door was shoved closed. The craft rose smoothly into the air.

'The attackers' vehicles had Vatican licence plates,' Rachel began.

Her uncle nodded, unsurprised. 'The Vatican not only has spies abroad, but, it seems, is also spied against within its own midst.' He reached into his jacket, removed a folded slip of paper and passed it to her. 'The survivor of the Cologne massacre described this for a sketch artist. He saw it embroidered on the chest of one of the attackers.'

Rachel unfolded the slip of paper. On it was drawn the coiled figure of a red dragon, wings blazed out, tail twisted, wrapped round its own neck.

'A symbol,' her uncle said, 'dating back to the fourteenth century, of the Dragon Court, a medieval alchemical cult created by a schism in the early Church, the schism that saw the rise of popes and antipopes.'

Rachel was familiar with antipopes, men who sat as head of the Catholic Church but whose election was later declared uncanonical. They arose for a variety of reasons, the most common being the usurpation and exile of the legitimately elected pope, usually by a militant faction backed by a king or emperor. During the fourteenth century, the legitimate papacy was driven out of Rome and popes reigned in exile in France.

'What does that have to do with the situation now?' she asked.

'The Dragon Court is still active today. And it openly admits to having members within the Catholic Church. Even here in the Vatican.'

Rachel felt her stomach lurch. She and her uncle had been targeted by someone inside the Vatican. 'What else do you know about the Court?'

'Not much. In the eighth century, Emperor Charlemagne conquered Europe in the name of the Holy Church, smashing pagan nature cults and replacing them with Catholicism. But the twelfth century saw a resurgence in mystical or Gnostic belief. It was taken up by many emperors. A schism formed as the Church moved towards the Catholicism we know today, while the emperors continued their Gnostic practices. It came to a head at the end of the fourteenth century, when the exiled papacy in France returned. To make peace, the Holy Roman Emperor Sigismund of Luxembourg backed the Vatican politically, while creating among the royal families of Europe a secret society dedicated to alchemical and mystical pursuits. The Ordinis Draconis. The Imperial Royal Dragon Court. It continues to this day. There are many sects in different countries, some benign, merely ceremonial, but others with leaders who believe that they and their members are the chosen rulers of mankind. That they were born to rule by the purity of their blood.'

'Hitler's master-race syndrome.'

A nod. 'But they seek more. Not just kingship. They seek all forms of ancient knowledge to further their cause of domination and apocalypse.

Mostly they've operated behind a screen of secrecy and ritual. But now someone is showing their hand, brazenly, bloodily.'

'What does it mean?'

Uncle Vigor shook his head. 'I fear this sect has discovered something of major importance, something that draws them out of hiding.'

'And the deaths?'

'A warning to the Church. This particular Court is flexing its muscles.'

'But to what end?'

Uncle Vigor sighed. 'To achieve the goal of all madmen. Armageddon.'

GRAY SHOOK his tumbler, clinking the ice.

Kat Bryant glanced across the plush cabin of the private jet. She didn't say anything, but her furrowed brow spoke volumes. She had been concentrating on the mission dossier—for the second time. Gray stood and crossed to the antique mahogany bar at the back of the cabin. He shook his head at the opulence: Waterford crystal, burled walnut, leather seating.

'Another Coke?' Monk asked from behind the bar.

Gray placed his glass on the counter. 'I think I've reached my limit.'

'Lightweight,' his friend muttered.

Gray turned and faced the cabin of the custom Citation X. 'OK, enough with hitting the books,' he said, drawing Kat's eyes. 'We have less than four hours of flight time, with an ETA of two a.m. local time. I suggest we try to get some sleep. But first let's compare notes. We've had a lot thrown at us.'

He pointed to the seats in the main cabin area. Monk dropped into one. Gray joined them, facing Kat across a table.

'OK, first, what do we know?'

Kat maintained a fixed expression. 'We know the perpetrators are somehow involved with the cult society known as the Royal Dragon Court.'

'That's as good as saying they're involved with Hari Krishnas,' Monk countered. 'The group is as shadowy and weedy as crabgrass. We don't have a clue who is truly behind all this.'

Gray nodded. They had been faxed this information while en route, along with the news of an attack upon their counterparts from the Vatican.

'What about that weird gold in the Communion bread?' Monk said.

They had been given reams of data in their dossier on this strange gold, culled from labs around the world. The powder had not been ordinary gold dust, it had been an entirely new elemental state of gold. Rather than its usual metallic matrix, the gold was broken down into individual atoms.

Monatomic, or m-state. Until recently, scientists had no idea that gold could transmute into an inert white powder form.

'OK,' Gray said, 'we've all read the files. Let's round-robin the topic.'

Monk spoke up. 'First, it's not just gold that does this. It seems any of the transitional metals on the periodic table—platinum, rhodium, iridium and others—can also transmute into a powder.'

Kat opened her dossier folder. 'What about this paper on superconductivity? While the powder appears inert, the atomic state is far from low-energy. It was as if each atom took all the energy it used to react to its neighbour and turned it *inwards* on itself. The energy deformed the atom's nucleus, stretching it out to an elongated shape, known as an asymmetrical high-spin state. Such high-spin atoms can pass energy from one atom to the next with no net energy loss.'

'Superconductivity,' Monk said.

'Energy passed into a superconductor would continue to flow through the material with no loss of power. A perfect superconductor would allow this energy to flow infinitely, until the end of time itself.'

Silence settled over them as they pondered the perplexities here.

Gray checked his watch, stifling a yawn. 'Let's grab some downtime.'

The others nodded. Monk grabbed pillows and blankets. Kat closed the shades on the windows. Gray accepted his pillow and sat down. He did not recline his seat. Despite his exhaustion, he did not expect to get much sleep.

CHÂTEAU SAUVAGE crouched in a mountain pass of the Savoy Alps like a stone giant. Constructed during the twelfth century on the ruins of a Roman fort, it overlooked Lake Geneva and the cliff-side city of Lausanne, and had belonged to the Sauvage family since the fifteenth century. The only access to its gates was over a stone bridge spanning the pass.

The castle's current master, Baron Raoul de Sauvage, descended the stairs that led below the castle. He had been summoned to an audience with the Sovereign Grand Imperator. Behind him, a huge Bernese mountain dog followed in his steps. Raoul also had a kennel of champion pit-fighting dogs, hundred-pound brutes from Gran Canaria, short-haired, thick-necked, tortured to a savage edge.

He passed the dungeon level. Four stone cells had been updated with stainless steel gates, electronic locks and video surveillance. Near the cells, one room still housed ancient torture devices . . . and a few modern ones. His family had helped several Nazi leaders escape out of Austria after

World War II. They had been hidden down here. As payment, Raoul's grandfather had taken his 'toll', as he called it, which had helped keep the castle within the family.

But now, at the age of thirty-three, Raoul was the only living male offspring. And among the Sauvage family, genetic ties were given precedence over those of marriage. He had even been conceived by arrangement. Another of Grandfather's tolls.

The Baron of Sauvage climbed deeper into the mountainside, to a cave in the rock that the Romans had converted into a temple to the god Mithras.

Raoul entered the wide grotto. The roof of the cave was a natural stone dome. An old Mithraic altar, where young bulls had been sacrificed, stood on the far side. Beyond it ran a deep, cold spring, a small river. Raoul imagined that the sacrificed bodies had been dumped into it to be carried away. He had disposed of a few of his own that way, too.

At the entrance, Raoul shed his leather smock. Beneath the coat, he wore an old rough-spun shirt embroidered with the coiled dragon, the symbol of the Ordinis Draconis, his birthright going back generations.

'Stay, Drakko,' he ordered the dog.

The Bernese mountain dog dropped to its haunches. It knew better than to disobey. As did the dog's master.

Raoul acknowledged the cave's occupant with a half bow.

The Sovereign Grand Imperator of the Court waited for him before the altar, dressed in the black leathers of a motorcycle outfit. Though he was two decades older than Raoul, the man matched his height and breadth of shoulder. He showed no withering of age, but remained stolid and firm of muscle. He kept his helmet in place, visor down. The leader had entered through the secret back entrance, and with him was a stranger.

It was forbidden for anyone outside the Court to view the Imperator's face. The stranger had been blindfolded as an extra precaution.

Raoul also noted the five bodyguards at the back of the cavern, all armed with automatic weapons, the elite guard of the Imperator. Raoul strode forward, right arm across his chest, and dropped to a knee. Raoul was head of the Court's military order. But all bowed to the Imperator. A mantle Raoul hoped one day to assume for himself.

'Stand,' he was ordered.

Raoul gained his feet.

'The Americans are under way,' the Imperator said. His voice, muffled by the helmet, was still heavy with command. 'Are your men ready?'

'Yes, sir. I handpicked a dozen men. We only await your order.'

'Very good. Our allies have lent us someone to assist on this operation. Someone who knows these American agents.'

Raoul grimaced. He did not need help from a stranger.

'A plane awaits you and your men at the Yverdon airfield. Failure will not be tolerated a second time.'

Raoul cringed inwardly. He had led the mission to steal the bones in Cologne, but had failed to purge the sanctuary. There had been one survivor. One who had pointed in their direction. Raoul had been disgraced. He now had to clear up the mess. It meant another trip to Germany.

He waited for the Imperator to leave. Drakko trotted after the men, as if the dog scented the true power here. Then again, the leader had visited the castle often during the last ten years, when the keys to damnation and salvation had fallen into his lap.

All due to a fortuitous discovery at the Cairo Museum . . .

With his leader gone, Raoul finally faced the stranger. What he saw, he found lacking, and he let his scowl show it. But at least the stranger's garb, all black, was fitting. As was the bit of silver decoration.

From the woman's pendant, a silver dragon dangled.

July 25

4

As his team crossed the square, Gray studied Cologne cathedral. Lit up by exterior spotlights, the structure exuded a palpable dread.

They were all dressed in inconspicuous dark civilian clothes. But beneath, each team member wore liquid body armour, and their black backpacks were stuffed with tools of the trade, including Glock pistols fitted with night sights, provided by the CIA agent who had met them at the airport. Monk also had a Scattergun-built shotgun, strapped to his left thigh, hidden under a long jacket. The weapon was snub-nosed and compact, like Monk himself. Kat went more low-tech. She managed to hide eight daggers on her body. A blade lay only a fingertip away, no matter her position.

Parked in front of the cathedral was a truck with the municipal *Polizei* logo on its side. It served as the base of operation for the forensic teams. Upon landing, Gray had been informed by Logan Gregory, the ops manager of this mission and Sigma's second-in-command, that the investigative teams had been pulled out at midnight but would be returning at 6 a.m. For four hours they had the church to themselves.

Well, not entirely. One of the flanking side doors to the cathedral opened as they neared. A tall, thin figure stood limned against the light inside.

'Monsignor Verona,' Kat whispered under her breath.

The priest crossed to one of the police guards that had been posted to keep the curious away from the crime scene, spoke quietly, then motioned the trio through the barricade. They followed him through the open doorway and into the front vestibule.

'Captain Bryant,' the monsignor said, smiling warmly. 'Despite the tragic circumstances, it's wonderful to see you again.'

'Thank you, Professor,' Kat said, returning an affectionate grin.

'Please call me Vigor.'

Gray scrutinised the monsignor. The man was nearly his height, but wirier. His salt-and-pepper hair had been combed back, curling in waves. He wore a trimmed goatee and was dressed in midnight-blue jeans and a black V-neck sweater, revealing the Roman collar of his station. But it was the steady fix of his gaze that most struck Gray. Despite his welcoming manner, there was a steely edge to the man.

The monsignor led the way through the doors to the nave and the heart of the church. A woman rose from a pew to greet them. She looked like a young Audrey Hepburn: snowy skin, short ebony hair parted and swept behind her ears, caramel-coloured eyes. Her gaze swept over the newcomers, settling a moment longer on Gray.

He recognised the familial resemblance between her and the monsignor, more from the intensity of her scrutiny than any physical features.

'My niece,' Vigor introduced. 'Lieutenant Rachel Verona.'

Once the introductions were finished, the monsignor led the way down the central aisle. 'We should get started,' he said.

Gray noted that sections of the pews had been marked off with masking tape. Place cards had been affixed to each with the names of the deceased. He stepped round the chalked outlines on the floor. Yellow plastic markers fixed the positions of shell casings, long gone to forensics.

They reached the altar. Vigor and his niece made the sign of the cross. Then Vigor led them through a gate in the chancel railing. The altar was also marked in chalk, the travertine marble stained. Crashed onto the floor, the golden sarcophagus lay on its side. Its top rested two steps down.

Gray shrugged off his backpack and donned a pair of latex gloves. 'This is where the bones were enshrined?'

Vigor nodded. 'Since the thirteenth century.'

The reliquary had been carved in the form of a miniature church, with arched windows and scenes from Christ's life etched in the gold with rubies and emeralds.

Kat joined Gray. 'I see they've already dusted it for prints.' She pointed to the fine white powder clinging to cracks and crevices in the reliefs.

'No prints were found,' Rachel said.

Monk glanced across the cathedral. 'And nothing else was taken?'

'A full inventory was conducted,' Rachel continued. 'We've already had a chance to interview the entire staff, including the priests.'

'I may want to speak to them myself,' Gray mumbled, studying the box.

'Their apartments are across a cloistered yard,' Rachel responded. 'No one heard or saw anything. But if you want to waste your time, feel free.'

Gray glanced up at her. 'I only said I *may* want to speak to them.'

She met his gaze without shrinking. 'And I was under the impression that this investigation was a *joint* effort. If we're going to recheck each other's work at every step, we'll get nowhere.'

Vigor placed a hand on his niece's shoulder. 'I assure you the interrogation was thorough. Among my colleagues, where prudence of tongue often surpasses good sense, I doubt you'd gain any further details, especially when being interviewed by someone not wearing a clerical collar.'

Monk spoke up. 'That's all well and good. But can we get back to me?' All eyes turned to him. He wore a crooked grin. 'I believe I was asking if anything else was taken.'

Rachel fixed Monk with her uncompromising gaze. 'As I said, nothing.'

'I was just curious if any other relics are kept here at the cathedral.

Rachel's face relaxed, contemplating this angle. The anger bled away.

The monsignor answered Monk. 'There's a treasure chamber off the nave. It holds the staff and chain of St Peter, and pieces of the cross.'

'And nothing was stolen from the treasure chamber.'

'It was all inventoried,' Rachel answered. 'Nothing else was stolen.'

Kat crouched down with Gray, but her eyes were on those still standing. 'So only the bones were taken. Why?'

Gray turned his attention to the open sarcophagus. He slipped a penlight from his backpack and examined the interior. He noted a bit of white powder sifted over the bottom surface. More latent powder? Bone ash?

There was only one way to find out. He pulled out a small battery-powered vacuum from his pack and sniffed up some powder into a test tube.

'We might be able to test the dust for age,' he said. 'Find out if the stolen bones were from someone who lived during Christ's time. Or not.'

Gray sealed the test tube and packed it away. From the corner of his eye, he had noted Kat's interest in the reliquary. She was all but ducking her head inside to investigate. Now she crouched on the marble floor, holding up a tiny brush. In her other hand, she held a small butane pistol-lighter. She squeezed the trigger and a tiny blue flame hissed from the end. She applied the flame to a pile of the white powder swept from the reliquary.

After a couple of seconds, the powder melted, bubbling and frothing into a translucent amber liquid. It dribbled over the cold marble and hardened into glass. The sheen against the white marble was unmistakable.

'Gold,' Monk said. All eyes had been drawn to the experiment.

Kat sat back, extinguishing her torch. 'The residual powder in the reliquary is the same as in the tainted wafers. Monatomic, or m-state, gold.'

Gray remembered Director Crowe's description of the lab tests, how the powder could be melted down to a slag glass. A glass made of solid gold.

'That's gold?' Rachel asked. 'Are you sure?'

Kat was already busy proving her assertion. She had an eyedropper in her hand and was dribbling its contents onto the glass. Gray knew what filled the eyedropper: a cyanide compound that had been supplied by the Sigma labs for just this purpose. For years, miners had been using this process to dissolve gold out of old tailings.

Where the drop touched, the glass etched as if burned by acid. But rather than frosting the glass, the cyanide carved a trail of pure gold.

Kat had been leaning over her sample with a magnifying lens and an ultraviolet lamp. 'I think there might be more than gold here. I can spot tiny silvery pools in the gold. It might be platinum. Remember that the monatomic state occurs not just in gold but *any* of the transitional metals on the periodic table. Maybe the device affected the gold in the reliquary and caused it to transmute. We have no idea by what mechanism—'

'I may have one clue,' Monk said, cutting her off. He stepped over to a bulky iron cross resting in a stanchion. 'It looks like one of our forensic experts missed a shell.' He reached out and plucked a hollow casing from beneath the feet of the crucified Christ figure. He took a step back again, held the casing out towards the cross and let it go. It flew through six inches of air, and with a *ping*, stuck again to the cross. 'It's magnetised,' Monk said.

Another *ping* sounded. Louder. Sharper. The cross spun half a turn in its stanchion. For half a second, Gray did not comprehend what had happened.

Monk dived for the altar. 'Down!' he screamed.

Other shots rang out.

Gray felt a kick to his shoulder, throwing him off kilter, but his body armour saved him from real injury. Rachel grabbed his arm and yanked him into a row of pews. Bullets chewed wood, sparked off marble and stone.

Kat ducked with the monsignor, shielding him with her body. She took a glancing shot to the thigh, but they fell together behind the altar with Monk.

Gray had only managed a quick glimpse of their attackers.

Men in hooded robes.

A sharp pop sounded. Gray glanced up to see a fist-sized black object arc across the breadth of the church.

'Grenade!' he screamed, and shoved Rachel down the pew.

They scrambled low and ran for the south wall.

The grenade hit the altar and exploded. Smoke rolled and billowed.

Half deafened by the blast, Monk hauled Kat and Vigor to their feet. 'Follow me!' he shouted.

As he ran towards the north wall, he spotted a wide wooden door. Shots came from all directions now. More of the hooded assailants had taken up positions deeper in the church, coming in other doors, surrounding them.

Monk yanked his snub-nosed shotgun from its straps, and took crude aim at the door handle. The blast punched a fist-sized hole through the door, taking the handle and lock with it. Still running, Monk struck the door with his shoulder. It banged open and he fell inside, followed by Kat and the monsignor. Kat turned, limping, and shoved the door closed.

The vaulted room was the size of a small garage. Monk stared at the glass cases crowded with old robes and insignia, bits of sculpture.

It was the cathedral's treasure chamber. There was no exit.

'WHAT NOW?' Rachel asked, crouching behind a giant pillar. She removed her pistol from a shoulder holster, the Beretta given to her by the Carabinieri driver back in Rome.

'This line of columns parallels the wall. We stick to cover,' Gray said.

'And our goal?'

'To get the hell out of this death trap.' The American must have noted Rachel's worried frown. 'We'll head for the street. Draw off as many of the bastards as we can.'

She nodded. They would play decoy for the others. 'Let's go.'

They proceeded briskly, staying low, using the pews in the nave as additional cover. The ploy worked. More gunfire concentrated on their position. But it slowed them down, putting them at risk of a second grenade attack. They had only made it halfway down the nave.

As Rachel paused for breath, the door to the confessional swung open behind her. Before she could move, an arm lashed out and wrapped round her neck. Her weapon was knocked from her fingers. The cold steel of a gun barrel pressed against her neck.

'Don't move,' a deep bass voice ordered. The attacker's arm felt like a tree trunk, strangling her. He was tall, a giant of a man, practically hauling her to her toes. 'Drop your weapons.'

'I'd do as he says,' a new voice said silkily, coming from the penitent's booth neighbouring the priest's confessional. The door opened and a second figure stepped out, dressed in black leather. A woman. Slender, Eurasian.

She lifted her pistol, a black Sig Sauer. She pointed it at Gray's face. '*Déjà vu*, Commander Pierce?'

THE DOOR was a problem. With the lock blown off, every strike of a bullet threatened to pop it open. And they dared not keep it shouldered closed. Most of the rounds were stopped by the wood planks, but a few still found weak spots and cracked through, making Swiss cheese out of the door.

Monk kept one boot against the frame, anchoring the door with his heel, while keeping his body off to the side. 'Hurry it up back there,' he urged.

He pointed his shotgun out through the hole in the door and fired blindly, keeping the assailants at a distance.

A rattle of keys drew his eye. Monsignor Verona had been struggling with a key ring, given to him by the cathedral's caretaker. He fought to get the third bulletproof case open. Finally, with a cry of relief, he found the right key, and the front of the case swung open like a gate.

Kat reached over his shoulder and grabbed a long sword from the case. A decorative weapon with a gold and jewelled hilt. She crossed the chamber and, keeping out of the line of fire, stabbed the sword between the door and its frame, jamming and securing the door.

Monk risked a fast glance out. One of the assailants lay sprawled on his back. One of his blind shots had found a target.

A black smooth pineapple bounced down the pew, aimed at their door.

Monk flung himself flat against the stone. 'Fire in the hole!'

THE EXPLOSION on the opposite side of the church drew all eyes, except Gray's. There was nothing he could do now for the others.

A grim smile creased the tall man's face. 'It seems your friends—'

With the momentary distraction, her captor must have loosened his grip, perhaps underestimating the slim woman. Rachel dropped her head and snapped it back, smacking the man's jaw hard enough to hear teeth crack.

Moving with surprising speed, she struck the encircling arm with the heel of her hand and dropped at the same time. She elbowed her assailant's midriff, then twisted and punched a fist into the man's crotch.

Gray swung his pistol towards the Dragon Lady. But she was quicker, stepping forward and placing her gun between his eyes, an inch away.

To the side, the tall man crumpled round his waist, falling to a knee. Rachel kicked his gun aside.

'Run!' Gray hissed at her, but he kept his eyes on the Dragon Lady.

The woman met his gaze—then did the oddest thing. She flicked the muzzle of her gun in the direction of the exit and motioned with her head.

She was letting him go.

Gray stepped back. She didn't fire, but she kept her gun focused on him, ready if he tried to make a move against her.

He grabbed Rachel by the arm and hauled ass towards the exit doors.

A shot sounded directly behind him. He was struck in the upper arm and spun slightly. The Dragon Lady's pistol smoked. She had shot Gray as she helped the tall man up, to cover her subterfuge. But she had purposely missed her target.

Gray risked a glance towards the gunfire at the back of the cathedral. Smoke billowed from the blasted doorway. The gunmen fired a barrage through the opening. Then one of the men tossed a second grenade—right through the blasted doorway. The other gunmen ducked as it blew.

Smoke and debris shattered outwards. Gray turned away.

Rachel had also witnessed the attack. Tears welled in her eyes. He felt her sag against him, legs weakening. Something deep inside him ached at her grief. He had lost teammates in the past. He was trained to mourn later.

But she had lost family.

'Keep moving,' he said gruffly. He had to get her to safety.

She glanced at him and seemed to gain strength from his hard countenance. It was what she needed. Not sympathy. Strength.

Together they ran and slammed through the rear doors.

A pair of assassins manned the vestibule, posted over the bodies of two men in German police uniforms. One of the monks fired, driving Rachel and Gray towards a doorway to their left.

With no choice, they dodged through it. The second man raised his weapon. A wall of fire cascaded towards them. He had a goddamn flamethrower. Gray slammed the door, but flames licked under the jamb.

He glanced behind him. Stairs spiralled up.

'The tower stair,' Rachel said.

Gunshots struck the door.

'Go,' he said.

He pushed Rachel ahead of him, and they fled up the stairs. Behind and below, the door crashed open. Footsteps pounded on the stone steps.

With the twist of the staircase, neither party had a clear shot at the other, though a fountain of flames chased Gray and Rachel as they climbed.

At last they reached the belfry of the tower. A massive free-swinging bell hung over the tower's steel-grated well. There was a deck round the bell.

'A public observation deck,' Rachel said. She kept a gun, one borrowed from Gray, fixed on the opening to the stairs.

Gray hurried round. There was no other way out. The city views opened around him. But there was no escape to the streets below.

Distantly he heard police sirens, a forlorn and eerily foreign wail.

Gray raised his eyes, calculating.

A shout rose from Rachel. Gray turned as a jet of flames erupted from the stairwell. Rachel fled back, joining him. They had run out of time.

'HELP THE MONSIGNOR,' Kat whispered to Monk. At least she hoped she whispered. She could not hear. Her head still rang from the grenade blast.

Monk stepped over to one of the glass display cases and manhandled the monsignor free. All of them had hidden inside a bulletproof case after the first grenade blast, knowing a second would follow.

It had. But the three security cases had done their job, protecting the most valuable treasure of all: their lives. The shrapnel had cut through the room, but shielded behind the bulletproof glass, they had survived.

'We should move,' Kat said now, motioning them out. Sticking to the wall, she led them to where the nave crossed with the transept and waved them round the corner.

Once out of the direct view of the gunmen, the monsignor pointed down the length of the transept. 'That way,' he whispered.

Another set of doors. Unguarded.

AS THE FLAMES faltered from the stairwell, Rachel aimed and squeezed the trigger. The pistol's slide locked open.

Out of bullets. She backed away and circled the bell to the far side.

Gray had his pack off and had tied a rope round a window bar. The other end was wrapped round his waist and the slack over one arm. He had used a hand jack in a tool kit to prise apart two of the window's bars.

'Hold the slack,' he said.

She took the nylon rope, about five metres in length.

Gray grabbed his pack and squeezed between the bars. Once out on the stone parapet, he donned the backpack and turned back to her. 'The rope.'

She passed it to him. 'Be careful.'

He stared down between his toes. Not a wise thing to do, Rachel thought. The hundred-metre drop would weaken anyone's knees.

Gray faced forward from the ledge of the cathedral's south spire. Four metres away, over a fatal drop, stood the north spire, a twin to this one. Off limits to the public, there were no bars across the far window. But there was also no hope of jumping from window to window, not from a standing position. Instead, Gray planned to dive straight out and grab whatever handhold he could on the decorated façade of the opposite tower.

He bent his knees. Rachel held her breath.

He leaned out and leapt, arching his body, flinging away the coil of slack rope. He flew across the gap and struck just below the window ledge. He lunged with both arms and grabbed the sill, miraculously catching it. But the impact bounced him back. He could not hold on. He began to fall.

'Your left foot!' she yelled to him.

He heard her. His left toe scrambled against the stone surface and found a gargoyle on the lower tier. He planted his foot on its head.

With his plummet stopped, he regained a handful of ledge above and found another toehold for his right leg, clinging like a fly to a wall. He took a deep breath, then climbed and manhandled himself through the window.

Rachel shimmied through the bars and grabbed the rope.

Across the gap, Gray had secured his end of the rope, forming a bridge. 'Hurry! I have you.'

She met his eyes across the gap and found firm assurance. Then she heard the bell ring behind her. Startled, she glanced back and watched a dumbbell-shaped silver cylinder bounce across the stone deck.

Needing no other encouragement, she swung out on the rope and scrambled across the bridge, legs kicking, hand over hand.

'Bomb,' she gasped, as Gray caught her round the midriff.

'What—?'

The blast cut off further words. Buffeted from behind, Rachel was shoved through the casement into Gray's chest. They fell in a tangle to the floor of the bell tower. A wall of flame rolled over them through the window, blast-furnace hot. Gray held her tight, shielding her with his body.

But the flames quickly dissipated in the gusty winds.

Gray rolled aside as Rachel elbowed up. She stared back at the south tower. The spire was aflame. Gray hauled in the rope. The knot on the far side had burned away, severing the bridge. The flames rippled in the strong winds, like a candle in the night. A final memorial to those killed, both last night and tonight. Rachel pictured the rakish smile of her uncle. Dead.

Grief welled through her. She stumbled back, but Gray caught her.

'We must go,' he said. 'They'll think we're dead. Let's keep it that way.'

She allowed herself to be led to the stairwell. They hurried down, winding round and round, and hit the vestibule at a run. One of the doors to the nave had been left ajar. Rachel glanced into the church—towards where her uncle had been killed. But something drew her eye, closer, on the floor.

Silver barbells. A dozen or more. Daisy-chained with red wires.

'Run!' she yelled, turning on a heel.

Together they hit the main doors and flew into the square.

Without a word, they fled towards the only shelter. The German Polizei truck on the square. They dived behind it just as the devices exploded.

A shatter of glass was loud enough to be heard above the popping explosions. Rachel looked up. The giant medieval stained-glass window blew out in a brilliant cascade of fire and jewelled glass.

Then a new noise intruded. Muffled voices, from inside the van.

They circled round the back of the van. Before they could touch the handle, the door popped open.

Rachel stared in disbelief as Gray's stocky team member stumbled out. He was followed by his female partner. And by a familiar, welcome figure.

'Uncle Vigor!' Rachel clasped him in a bear hug.

AN HOUR LATER, Gray paced the hotel room, still edgy, nerves stretched thin. They had gone to ground in a hotel less than half a mile from the cathedral, to regroup, establish a plan of action. But first they needed more intel.

A key scuffled in the door lock. Gray placed a palm on his pistol. But it was only Monsignor Verona returning from a scouting expedition.

Vigor pushed into the room, his expression grim. 'The boy's dead,' he said. 'Jason Pendleton. The boy who survived the massacre. It's just been reported on the BBC that he was found dead in his hospital room. Cause of death is still unknown, but foul play is suspected. Especially coinciding with the firebombing of the cathedral.'

Rachel shook her head sadly. It made a certain horrible sense. The cathedral attack had obviously been a whitewash operation, to erase any residual trail. And that would include silencing the only witness.

Kat was working on a laptop wired to a digital camera. 'The photos are uploading now,' she said.

Gray stepped to the desk. Monk and the others had sought not only a hiding place in the police van after their escape, but also a vantage to get some photos of the assailants. Thumbnail images filled the screen.

'There,' Rachel said, pointing to one. 'That's the guy who grabbed me.'

'The leader of the group,' Gray said.

Kat double-clicked the image and brought up a full-scale photo. He was frozen in midstride as he exited the cathedral. He had dark hair, cut long, almost to the shoulder. No facial hair. Aquiline features. Rocky and expressionless. Even in the photo, he gave off an air of superiority.

'Does anyone recognise him?' Gray asked.

Heads shook.

'I can uplink it to Sigma's facial-recognition software,' Kat said.

'Not yet,' Gray said. 'We need to stay incommunicado. Someone knew we were alone in the cathedral. Either they were already watching the church or they had prior intel.' Gray turned back to the laptop and pointed to another thumbnail picture. 'Bring that one up.'

Kat double-clicked. An image of a slender woman climbing into the back of a black van swelled across the monitor, her face in silhouette.

Gray glanced at the others. 'The woman who attacked me at Fort Detrick.'

Monk leaned closer. 'The Guild operative?'

Vigor and Rachel looked confused. Gray gave an overview of the organisation: its terrorist-cell structure, its interest in new technologies.

When he finished, Kat said, 'You think the leak might be at our end?'

Gray frowned. 'Who can tell? But the Guild is here, operating alongside the Dragon Court, and I can't help thinking they've been drawn in because of our involvement. But I think they're as late to the game as we are.'

'Why do you say that?' Rachel asked.

Gray pointed at the screen. 'The Dragon Lady let me escape.'

There was a stunned silence, then Rachel asked, 'Why would she do that?'

'Because she's playing the Dragon Court. Like I said, I think the only reason the Guild has been called into this venture is because Sigma became involved. The Court wanted the Guild's assistance to eliminate us.'

Kat nodded. 'And if we were dead, then the Guild would no longer be needed. The partnership would end, and the Guild would never find out what the Dragon Court knows.'

'But now the Court thinks we were killed,' Rachel said.

'Exactly. And that's another reason to keep that ruse going for as long as possible. If we're dead, the Court will sever its ties with the Guild.'

'What do we do next?' Kat asked.

Gray glanced over to his pack. 'The powder we recovered from the reliquary must hold a key to all this. But if we can't send it to Sigma to test . . .'

Vigor spoke up. 'Maybe we should be asking *how* the powder got there, rather than what it is. Once every few years, the bones are taken from the reliquary and the sarcophagus is cleaned. I'm sure they dust the interior.'

Kat sat up. 'Before the attack, we wondered if the device had altered the gold of the sarcophagus, transmuted the lining into the white powder. But the powder was not just gold. We spotted other elements. Maybe platinum. I think the powder came from the *bones*.'

Monk frowned. 'But we cannot test your hypothesis. They have the bones.'

Rachel and Vigor exchanged a sudden glance.

'What?' Gray asked, reading the excitement in their expressions.

'They don't have *all* the bones,' Rachel said.

Gray's brow furrowed. 'Where—?'

Vigor answered. 'In Milan.'

5

Gray and the others fell out of the rented Mercedes and stumbled onto the cobbled square of the Italian lakeside town of Como. It was 10.14 a.m. and they had driven all night. Across Germany to Switzerland, then over the Alps into Italy. They had travelled by car to maintain their anonymity, passing borders with false ID. They did not want to alert anyone that their group had survived the attack in Cologne.

Gray planned on contacting Sigma command after they had secured the bones from the basilica in Milan and had reached the Vatican. In the meantime, the plan was to rotate drivers while en route to Milan, to let everyone get a bit of shuteye. It hadn't worked out that way.

Monk stood at the edge of the road, bent over, hands on his knees, slightly green in the face. 'I've been on fighter planes,' he grumbled, 'doing goddamn loopty-loops. This . . . was worse.'

Rachel climbed out of the driver's seat and closed the car door. She had driven the entire way at breakneck speed, flying down the Autobahns and taking the hairpin turns of the Alpine roads at physics-defying velocities.

'You just need some breakfast,' she assured Monk. 'I know a nice bistro along the Piazza Cavour.'

Despite some reservations, Gray had agreed to stop for food. They needed gas, and the place was remote. They were road-weary and famished.

Rachel led the way across the square towards the restaurant. Gray followed her with his eyes. Despite the overnight drive, she moved with no sign of fatigue. If anything, she seemed enlivened by her Alpine racing.

'A drive-through would have been fine,' Gray said, checking his watch.

Vigor stepped next to him. 'We'll reach Milan in another hour.'

'But the bones—'

Vigor silenced him with a frown. 'Commander, the Vatican is well aware of the risk to the relics in the Basilica di Sant'Eustorgio. I was already under orders to stop in Milan to collect them on my way back to Rome. In the meantime, the bones have been secured in the basilica's safe.'

Though far from satisfied, Gray conceded the point. The group needed to refuel as much as their automobile.

Rachel opened a gate to a bougainvillea-adorned terrace overlooking the lake. 'The Imbarcadero serves the best local dishes. You should try the golden perch with risotto. But definitely have a small plate of agnolotti.'

Vigor nodded. 'A ravioli with aubergine and mozzarella,' he translated.

'So I take it you've eaten here a few times,' Monk said, dropping heavily into a seat. He eyed Gray. So much for anonymity.

Vigor patted Monk's shoulder. 'The owners are friends of our family. Rest assured, they know how to be discreet.' He waved to a rotund server. '*Ciao, Mario! Bianco Secco di Montecchia, per favore!*'

'Right away, *Padre*! I also have a nice Chiaretto from Bellagio.'

'*Perfetto!* A bottle of each then while we wait!'

'Antipasti?'

'Of course, Mario. We are not barbarians.'

Their order was placed with much bravado: salmon salad with apple vinegar, barley stew, breaded veal, tagliatelle with whitefish, pappardelle.

Mario brought out a large platter piled with olives and antipasti, along with two bottles of wine, one red, one white. '*Buon appetito!*' he said.

Wine flowed. Glasses lifted. Salami and cheese were passed round.

Monk leaned back, and failed to stifle a belch. 'That overfilled the tank.'

Kat had eaten just as much, but she was now studying the dessert menu with the same intensity with which she had read the mission dossier.

'*Signorina?*' Mario asked, noting her interest.

She pointed to the menu. '*Macedonia con panna.*'

Monk groaned.

'It's only fruit salad with cream.' She glanced at the others, eyes wide.

Gray sat back. He didn't suppress the bravado. He sensed they all needed this momentary respite. Once under way, the day would be a blur.

Vigor suddenly focused on Gray. He pushed back from the table. 'Commander Pierce, while we're waiting on the kitchen, I wonder if I might have a private word. Perhaps we could stretch our legs.'

Gray settled his glass and stood. The monsignor led him off the terrace and onto the promenade that bordered the lake.

'The Vatican's role in all this is centred on the theft of the relics,' Vigor said, keeping his eyes on the lake. 'And once we return to Rome, I suspect you plan on cutting ties and pursuing the Dragon Court on your own.'

Gray knew he could not risk further endangering this man and his niece. 'I think it's best,' he said. 'And I'm sure both our superiors will agree.'

'But I don't.' A bit of heat entered his words. 'If you're right about the bones being the source for the strange amalgam powder, then I believe our roles here are more deeply entwined than either organisation suspected.'

'I don't see how.'

Vigor looked at him again with a focused intensity that seemed to be a family trait. 'Then let me convince you. We know the Dragon Court is an aristocratic society involved in the search for secret or lost knowledge. They've concentrated on ancient Gnostic texts and other arcana.'

'What does this have to do with the massacre at Cologne?' Gray said.

The monsignor sighed. 'In some ways, the attack today could be traced back to a conflict between two apostles. Thomas and John.'

Gray shook his head. 'What are you talking about?'

'In the second century, the bishop of Lyons wrote five volumes under the title *Against Heresies*. It was the moment where all early Gnostic beliefs were sifted out of the Christian religion, creating the fourfold Gospel canon. Three of the Gospels—Matthew, Mark and Luke—tell the same story. But the Gospel of John relates a very different history; even events in Christ's life don't match the chronology in the others. But John was included in the Bible because of his fellow apostle, Thomas.'

'As in *Doubting* Thomas?'

Vigor nodded. 'But did you know that *only* the Gospel of John tells the story of Doubting Thomas? Only John portrays Thomas as this faithless disciple. The other gospels revere Thomas. John, with his disparaging account, sought to discredit Thomas, or more specifically, Thomas's followers, who were numerous at that time. In the early church, there was a fundamental schism between the gospels of Thomas and John. They were *so* different that only one gospel could survive.'

'What do you mean? How different could they be?'

'It goes back to the very beginning of the Bible, to the opening verses of Genesis. "Let there be light." Both John and Thomas identify Jesus with this primordial light, the light of creation. But from there, their interpretations widely diverge. According to Thomas, the light not only brought the universe into being but still exists within all things, especially within mankind, who was made in the image of God, and the light is hidden within each person, waiting to be found. John declared that *only* Christ held this light, and the rest of the world, including mankind, remained in darkness. And that the path back to this light, back to salvation and God, could only be found through the worship of the divine Christ.'

'A much narrower view.'

'And more pragmatic for the young church. John offered salvation through the worship of Christ. Contrarily Thomas suggested everyone had an innate ability to find God, by looking within, requiring no worship.'

Gray realised how far off track they had got. 'What does all this have to do with the massacre in Cologne?'

'First, I think this attack harks back to the age-old conflict between John's orthodox faith and Thomas's ancient Gnostic tradition.'

'With the Church on one side and the Dragon Court on the other?'

'No. The Dragon Court, while it seeks knowledge through Gnostic mysteries, does not seek God, only *power*. They want a new world order, a return to feudalism, with themselves at the helm. So I don't think the Dragon Court represents the Gnostic side of this ancient conflict. I think they are perverters of it. But they definitely have roots back to that tradition.'

Gray grudgingly conceded the point, but he was far from swayed.

'Point two,' Vigor continued. 'According to historical texts, Thomas went on to evangelise in the East, all the way to India. He baptised thousands of people, spread the faith, and was most famous for one act, one act of baptism. He baptised the Three Magi.'

Gray's eyes widened. His mind whirled with the threads here: St Thomas and his Gnostic tradition, tied to the Magi. Did the connection extend further, to the deaths in the cathedral?

'I think there is more to the murders in Cologne than technology,' Vigor said confidently. 'Whatever happened is entwined with the early Catholic Church. And I am certain I can be a continuing asset to this investigation.'

Gray bowed his head in thought, slowly won over.

'But not my niece,' Vigor finished, revealing at last why he had pulled Gray aside. He held out his hand. 'Once we return to Rome, I will send her back to the Carabinieri. I will not risk her again.'

Gray reached out and shook the monsignor's hand.

Finally something the two of them could agree on.

RACHEL HEARD A STEP behind her, expecting it to be Mario returning with their desserts. Glancing up, she almost fell out of her seat as she gazed at the elderly woman who stood there, leaning on a cane, dressed in a blue summer frock. Her white hair was curled, her eyes flashing in amusement.

Rachel gained her feet. '*Nonna?* What are you doing here?'

Her grandmother patted Rachel on a cheek, speaking in Italian. 'Your mother goes off to see you in Rome. Leaves me alone. So I come to our villa. I took the train. And then Mario calls me to tell me that you and Viggie are here. I tell him not to tell you. Who are your friends?'

Rachel introduced Gray's two partners. 'This is my grandmother.'

She shook each of their hands. 'Call me Camilla,' she said in English. She eyed Monk up and down. 'Why do you cut off all your hair? A shame. But you have nice eyes.' She turned to Kat. 'Is Signor Monk your boyfriend?'

Kat crinkled her brow in surprise. 'No,' she said, a tad too tartly.

'You make a nice couple,' Camilla declared.

Rachel spotted Gray and her uncle returning. She noted that her uncle would not meet her eye and immediately she knew why.

Uncle Vigor noticed the additional guest at their table. Shock shattered his grim expression. The surprise was again explained.

As Gray was introduced, Rachel's grandmother glanced askance at her, one eyebrow raised, before fixing her gaze on the American. She clearly liked what she saw: stubbled dark chin, storm-blue eyes, lanky black hair.

She leaned towards Rachel. 'I see beautiful babies,' she whispered. She raised her voice. 'Signore Pierce, are you *italiano*?'

'No, I'm afraid not.'

'Would you like to be? My granddaughter—'

Rachel cut her off. '*Nonna,* we don't have much time.' She made a show of checking her wristwatch. 'We have business in Milan.'

The grandmother brightened. 'Carabinieri work. Tracking stolen art? I read about the murders up in Germania. Terrible, just terrible.'

A waiter arrived laden with two heavy bags of food.

Uncle Vigor spoke, leaning forward to kiss both her cheeks. 'Mamma, we must go. We'll see you back home in Gandolfo in a couple of days.'

As Gray stepped past, Camilla took his hand and pulled him closer. 'You watch after my granddaughter.'

Gray looked at Rachel. 'I will, but she takes pretty good care of herself.'

The old woman patted his backside as he stepped away. '*Ragazzo buono.*'

As the others headed out, Camilla turned back the corner of Rachel's open vest, exposing the empty holster. 'You lost something, no?'

Rachel had forgotten she was still wearing the holster. She had left the borrowed Beretta back at the cathedral.

'A woman should never leave the house naked.' Her grandmother reached down and collected her handbag. She opened it to disclose her prized Nazi P08 Luger. 'You take mine.'

'*Nonna!* You shouldn't be carrying that around.'

Her grandmother dismissed her concern with a wave. 'The trains are not that safe for a woman alone. But I think you need this more than me.'

Rachel reached out and closed the handbag with a snap. '*Grazie, Nonna.* But I'll be fine.' She began to turn away, but her wrist was grabbed.

'He likes you,' her grandmother said. 'Signore Pierce.'

Rachel was saved by Mario arriving with the bill. She paid, leaving enough to cover her *nonna*'s lunch. She met her uncle and the others at the car.

She looked from Gray to the monsignor, fixing them with a poisonous stare. 'If you think you're going to kick me off this investigation, you can walk to Rome.' Keys in hand, she slid into the driver's seat, slammed her door and keyed the ignition.

'Rachel!' Her uncle knocked on the window.

She shifted into gear.

'*Va bene!*' her uncle yelled, agreeing. 'We stay together.'

Rachel twisted and locked eyes on Gray, his face hard. He looked ready to hot-wire a car and take off on his own. Had she overplayed her hand? At that moment, she felt how deeply she wanted to remain, down to the marrow of her bones. Maybe Gray understood. Ever so slowly he nodded, a barely perceptible movement. It was enough.

She unlocked the doors. The others climbed in.

Monk was last. 'I was fine with walking.'

BY NOON they had reached Milan. Now they stood on a shaded sidewalk bordering the unassuming façade of the Basilica of St Eustorgio, having searched the entire church's periphery from a distance. All seemed quiet. Gray had also used a set of telescoping lenses to peer through several windows. The side chapels and central nave appeared deserted.

'Let's do this,' Gray said, walking towards the side door. He turned to Kat and pointed to the lock. 'Can you get it open?'

Kat dropped to a knee. Monk and Gray shielded her with their bodies. With the meticulous skill of a surgeon she set to work on the door's lock.

A snick of a latch. The door opened an inch.

Gray waved the others back. 'Monk and I will go in alone.' He reached to his collar and secured an earpiece in place. 'Radio up while we have a chance. Kat, stay here with Rachel and Vigor.' He taped on a throat mike for subvocalisation.

Vigor stepped forward. 'Priests are more likely to speak to someone wearing a collar. I'll go with you.'

Gray hesitated—but the monsignor made sense. 'Stay behind us.'

He turned and opened the door enough to slip through. When they were all inside, Monk closed the outer door and flipped his long coat aside to rest a hand on his shotgun. Gray pushed open the central door of the inner nave with the palm of one hand. He had his Glock in the other. They entered the nave and moved down the centre aisle.

'The rectory is off to the left,' Vigor said. 'That's where the bones have been taken. It's connected through the sacristy.' He pointed.

As if responding to his signal, a door smacked open across the nave. Gray dropped to a knee. Monk yanked the monsignor behind a pillar.

A single figure strode out. It was a young man dressed in black with a clerical collar. He began lighting a set of candles on the far side of the altar.

Gray waited until the man was only two yards away. No others appeared. Slowly he gained his feet, coming into view.

The priest froze when he spotted Gray. His expression turned to shock when he spotted the pistol in Gray's hand. '*Chi sei?*'

Vigor stepped out of hiding. '*Padre* . . . I am Monsignor Verona.'

The man shook his head. 'You can't be Monsignor Verona.'

Vigor stepped forward and showed him his Vatican ID.

The man glanced from it back to Vigor. 'But a man came here this morning. A tall man. Very tall. With identification as Monsignor Verona. He bore papers with proper seals from the Vatican. To take the bones.'

Gray exchanged a look with the monsignor. They'd been outmanoeuvred. The Dragon Court must have known about Vigor's mission here to collect the relics.

His radio buzzed and Kat came on the line. 'Is it all clear, Commander?'

'Clear . . . and too late,' he answered back sourly.

Kat and Rachel joined them.

'So the bones are gone,' Rachel said.

The priest nodded. 'Monsignor Verona, if you'd like to see the paperwork, we have it in the safe in the sacristy. Maybe that would help.'

'We could check it for fingerprints,' Rachel said.

Gray nodded. 'You go and bag it up. We'll see what we can find here.'

Rachel and her uncle headed across the nave, and Gray strode over to the massive sarcophagus in the chapel nearest the altar. The only access to the interior was through a small barred window low in the front face.

'Any ideas?' Monk asked as the sacristy door closed.

Gray knelt down by the tiny window. 'We should vacuum the interior,' he said. 'See if we can confirm the presence of the amalgam powder here, too.'

He leaned closely, cocking his head, not sure what he was looking for. But he found it anyway. A mark on the silk-lined roof of the reliquary chamber. A red seal pressed into the white silk. A tiny curled dragon. The ink looked fresh . . . too fresh. But it was not ink. . . .

Blood. A warning left behind by the Dragon Lady.

Gray straightened, suddenly knowing the truth.

ONCE INSIDE, the priest closed the door to the sacristy, the chamber where the clergy and altar boys robed themselves prior to Mass.

Rachel heard the lock click behind her. She half turned and found a pistol levelled at her chest. Held in the hand of the priest.

The door on the opposite end of the sacristy opened.

A familiar bull of a man entered, filling the doorway. It was the man who had attacked her in Cologne. He wore street clothes—khakis, a black T-shirt and a dark jacket—and carried a long knife in one hand. He had a radio headset over one ear, and spoke into the mike at his throat. 'Clear the church.'

Behind her, Rachel heard doors slam open in the nave. Gray and the others would be caught off guard. She waited for a spate of gunfire or the blast of a grenade. But all she heard was the patter of boots on marble.

Their captor shoved forward, passing between Vigor and Rachel.

'Watch them,' he growled to the fake priest. A second gunman had taken up a post by the back exit to the sacristy.

The tall man yanked open the door to the nave. An armed figure strode over to him, accompanied by the Eurasian woman, holding her pistol.

'No one's here,' the man reported.

The giant's eyes settled on the Eurasian woman.

She shrugged. 'They might have found an open window.'

'Keep searching. Send three men outside. They can't have got far.'

As the giant turned, Rachel made her move. She snatched a ceremonial pole with a silver crucifix and rammed its butt end square into the man's solar plexus. He grunted and fell back into the priest. She yanked the pole back, and slammed the cross end into the gunman's face behind her.

He fell back through the rear exit. Rachel followed him, her uncle on her heels. She slammed the door and propped the pole against it, jamming it shut.

Beside her Vigor kicked the fallen gunman. His head bounced against the stone floor with a thud, then his form went slack.

Rachel bent down and grabbed his pistol.

The door rattled in its frame. The Bull was trying to break through.

She followed Vigor down the hall a few steps.

'I hear someone groaning,' he whispered. 'In here.'

They reached a door cracked open. Rachel shouldered in, gun ready.

The room had once been a dining hall. Now it was a slaughterhouse. One priest lay face down in a pool of blood. Another lay sprawled on one of the tables, spread-eagled, tied to the bench legs. An older priest. His chest was a pool of blood. His head was missing both ears. Tortured to death.

A sobbing moan sounded to the left. On the floor, tied hand and foot, was a man, stripped to boxer shorts, gagged.

'It's all right,' Vigor soothed. He cut the plastic ties with a knife.

Rachel fished out a cellphone and dialled the emergency number.

FOOTSTEPS APPROACHED Gray's hiding place. He held perfectly still, not breathing. The steps stopped nearby. He strained to listen.

A man spoke. A familiar voice, angry. It was the leader of the monks. 'The Milan authorities have been alerted.'

There was no reply, but Gray was certain two people had approached.

'Seichan?' the man asked. 'Did you hear me?'

A bored voice answered. It was equally recognisable. The Dragon Lady. But now she had a name. *Seichan*.

'They must have gone out through a window, Raoul,' she said. 'Sigma is slippery. I warned you. We should be gone before they return with reinforcements. The police may already be on their way.'

The footsteps departed. It sounded like the heavier of them was limping.

A door slammed on the far side of the church. As the sound echoed away, Gray strained his ears. He heard no more footsteps, no voices.

With the church silent, he nudged Monk, who lay spooned next to him. Kat lay scrunched on Monk's other side. They rolled over with a sickening crunch of desiccated bone and reached overhead. Together they shifted the stone lid to the sepulchre.

After spotting the Dragon Lady's warning in blood, Gray had known they'd been ensnared. All exit doors would be guarded. And with Rachel and her uncle in the sacristy, there was nothing he could do to help.

So Gray had led the others into the neighbouring chapel, to a massive marble sepulchre. They had shifted its lid enough to climb inside, then pulled the lid back over them just as the doors crashed open.

Now they climbed out and shook the bone dust from their clothes.

'Let's not do that again,' Monk grumbled, as he and Kat followed Gray across the nave towards the sacristy.

WHILE RACHEL kept guard, Vigor helped the young priest stand. 'What happened?' he asked.

'They came an hour ago. They had papal seals and papers, identification. But Father Belcarro had a faxed picture.' The priest's eyes widened. 'Of you. From the Vatican. Father Belcarro knew the lie immediately. They wanted the combination to the safe. They tortured him. He would not speak. But they made me watch. I couldn't let it continue. I . . . I told them.'

'And they took the bones from the safe?'

The priest nodded.

'Then all is lost,' Vigor said.

Mumbling to himself, the priest stumbled to the body of Father Belcarro. He folded back the older man's bloody robe, reached into a pocket and pulled out a pack of cigarettes. It seemed the elderly father had not shed all his vices . . . nor had the young priest. Fingers shaking, the man peeled back the top and shook out the contents. Six cigarettes—and a stub of chalk. The man dropped the cigarettes and held out the stub.

Vigor took it. Not chalk. Bone.

'Father Belcarro feared sending away all the holy relics,' the priest said. 'In case something happened. So he kept one back. For the church.'

The old priest had died a martyr. Tortured while hiding the holy relic on his own body.

A loud blast made them all jump. The priest fell back to the floor.

But Rachel recognised the gauge of weapon. 'Monk's shotgun . . .' she said, eyes widening with hope.

Then she heard Gray's voice. 'Rachel! Vigor!'

She opened the door and ran into the hallway. Gray was coming out of the sacristy. Monk followed him, shouldering his shotgun, which he'd just used to blow a hole through the sacristy door.

Monk grinned. 'I'm going to owe the Catholic Church a month's salary for carpentry repair.'

AN HOUR LATER, the team were on the fast train to Rome. They had booked two first-class cabins. One was a sleeping compartment to allow them to catnap in shifts. But no one was sleeping yet. Everyone had gathered in the other cabin, seated at the table. The window blinds had been drawn.

Gray had unboxed an assortment of compact analysing equipment from his backpack and wired it to a laptop. Other tools were neatly aligned in front of him. In the centre of the table, resting on a stainless-steel sample tray, was the relic from one of the Magi.

'Let's see if this can solve any mysteries for us,' said Gray. He slipped on a pair of glasses fitted with a jeweller's magnifying loupe and donned latex gloves. With a tiny trepanning drill, he cored a thin sliver through the centre of the bone, then used a mortar and pestle to grind the sample to a powder.

'With this mass spectrometer,' he said, 'we can determine if any of the m-state metal is in the bones, and therefore whether the Magi bones were the source of the powder found in the gold reliquary.'

Gray mixed the powder with distilled water, then sucked the silty liquid into a pipette and transferred it to a test tube. He inserted the sample tube into the compact spectrometer. Then he prepared a second tube of pure distilled water and placed it in another slot. He pressed a green button.

'This is a standard to calibrate,' he explained.

A graph appeared on the laptop screen with a flat line across it.

He switched a dial so that it pointed to the other slot. 'And now the pulverised bone.' He pressed the green button again.

The graph on the screen disappeared and refreshed with the new data.

It looked identical.

Monk frowned. 'Even if the Magi had osteoporosis, the calcium in the bone should be spiking through the roof. Not to mention carbon.'

Gray nodded. 'Kat, do you have some of that cyanide solution?'

She swung to her pack, fished through it, and came up with a tiny vial.

Gray soaked a cotton-tipped swab, then pinched the bone between his gloved fingers. He rubbed the wet swab back and forth across the bone.

Where he rubbed, the brownish-yellow bone turned a rich gold.

He glanced up at the group. 'This isn't bone.'

Rachel could not keep the awe from her voice. 'It's solid gold.'

GRAY SPENT HALF the train journey disproving Rachel's statement. There was more than just gold in these bones. Also it wasn't heavy *metallic* gold, but that strange gold glass again.

'The fake bone is a mixture of elements across the platinum group,' he explained when he had finished his analysis. 'Whoever crafted this mixed a powdery amalgam of various transitional metals and melted it down to glass. As it cooled, they moulded the glass and roughed up the surfaces to make it *appear* like bone. It's predominantly gold and platinum, with smaller amounts of iridium and rhodium, even osmium and palladium.'

'A regular potpourri,' Monk said with a yawn.

'But a potpourri whose exact recipe may be forever unknown,' Gray said. 'With the m-state powder's stubborn lack of reactivity, I don't think any analysing equipment could tell you the exact ratio of metals.'

'So if it can't be tested . . .' Monk's words were cut off by another yawn.

Gray patted Monk on the shoulder. 'We'll be in Rome in another hour. Why don't you catch some sleep in the next room? That's an order.'

Monk stood. 'Well, if it's an order . . .' He walked to the door, but paused in the doorway. 'You know,' he said bleary-eyed, 'maybe history misinterpreted the words *the Magi's bones*. Rather than referring to the skeleton of those guys, maybe it meant the bones were *made* by the Magi. Like it was their property.' Monk shrugged and half fell out the door. 'Hell, what do I know? I can hardly think straight.' The door closed.

'Your teammate might not be so far off base,' Vigor said.

He was using Monk's laptop. Like Kat, he was connected to the DSL line built into the train's first-class cabins. They were searching for more information. Kat concentrated on the science behind the white gold, while Vigor searched for more history connecting the Magi to this amalgam.

Rachel stretched one arm in the air. 'What do you mean?' she asked.

The monsignor's eyes remained on his screen. 'Somebody forged those fake bones. Somebody with a skill barely reproducible today. But who did it? And why hide them in the heart of a Catholic cathedral?'

'Could it be someone connected to the Dragon Court?' Rachel asked.

'Or someone within the Church itself?' Kat said.

'No,' Vigor said firmly. 'I think there is a third group involved here. A brotherhood that existed before either group.'

'How can you be certain?' Gray asked.

'In 1982, some of the Magi burial cloths were tested. They dated to the second century. Well before the Dragon Court was founded. Before even Constantine's mother, Helena, discovered the bones somewhere in the East.'

'And no one tested the bones?'

Vigor glanced at Gray. 'The Church forbade it.'

Rachel cut in. 'It wouldn't want its most precious treasures ruled fake.'

Vigor frowned at her. 'The Church places much weight on faith. The world certainly could use more of it.'

'So if not the Church or the Court, who forged the bones?' Gray asked.

'I think it was an ancient fraternity of mages. A group that may predate Christianity, going back to Egyptian times.' Vigor clicked the laptop's mouse, bringing up a file. 'Listen to this. In 1450 BC, Pharaoh Tuthmosis III united his best master craftsmen into a thirty-nine-member group called the Great White Brotherhood—named after the mysterious *white* powder they studied. The powder was described as forged from gold, but shaped into pyramidal cakes, called "white bread". The cakes were prepared only for the pharaohs. To be consumed. Supposedly to increase their powers of perception.'

Kat sat straighter. 'I've been reading some of the properties of high-spin-state metals. Specifically gold and platinum. Exposure through ingestion can stimulate endocrine systems, creating heightened senses of awareness. Remember the articles on superconductors?'

Gray nodded. High-spin atoms acted as perfect superconductors.

'The US Naval Research Facility has confirmed that communication between brain cells cannot be explained by pure chemical transmission across synapses. Brain cells communicate too quickly. They've concluded that some form of superconductivity is involved. I did a search for platinum-group metals and their uses. And I found an article about calf and pig brains. A metal analysis of mammalian brains shows that four to five per cent of the dry weight is rhodium and iridium in their monatomic state.'

'And you think these m-state elements might be the source of the brain's superconductivity? Its communication pathway?'

'Hard to say. The study of superconductivity is still in its infancy.'

'Yet the Egyptians knew about it,' Gray scoffed.

'No,' Vigor countered. 'But perhaps they learned some way of tapping into it by accident. However it came about, this interest in these white powders of gold appears throughout history. In Egypt it went by many names, including, as I said, "white bread". But its oldest name can be found in the Egyptian *Book of the Dead*. The substance is named hundreds of times, along with its amazing properties. It is simply called "what is it". In Hebrew, however, "what is it" translates to *Ma Na*.'

'Manna,' Kat said.

Vigor nodded. 'The Holy Bread of the Israelites. According to the Old Testament, it fell from the heavens to feed the starving refugees fleeing Egypt, led by Moses.' He let that sink in and fiddled with his gathered files. 'While in Egypt, Moses showed such wisdom and skill that he was considered a potential successor to the Egyptian throne. Such esteem would entitle him to participate in the deepest level of Egyptian mysticism.'

'Are you saying Moses stole the secret to make this powder?'

'In the Bible, it went by many names. Manna. Holy Bread. Shrewbread. Bread of Presence. It was so precious that it was stored in the Ark of the Covenant, alongside the tablets bearing the Ten Commandments. There are many things that have perplexed historians and theologians in regard to this mysterious manna. For instance, whom does Moses ask to make this Holy Bread, this manna from heaven? In the Bible, he doesn't ask a baker to prepare it. He asks Bezalel, the Israelites' *goldsmith*. Why ask a goldsmith to bake bread unless it was something other than bread? There are also texts from the Jewish Kabbalah that speak directly of a white powder of gold, declaring it magical, but a magic that could be used for good or evil.'

'So what became of this knowledge?' Gray asked. 'Where did it go?'

'To find hints of it, we skip forward two centuries, to another famous figure, who spent much of his life in Babylon, studying with scientists and mystics.' Vigor paused for emphasis. 'Alexander the Great. He conquered Egypt in 332 BC. The man was always interested in esoteric knowledge. He collected a series of scrolls, concerning Old Egypt's secret knowledge and magic. After his death, his successor, Ptolemy I, gathered these into the Library of Alexandria. One Alexandrian text tells a story about an object called the Paradise Stone. It was said to have mystical properties. When solid, it could surpass its own weight in gold, yet when crushed into a *powder*, it weighed less than a feather and could float.'

'Levitation in superconducting material is well documented,' said Kat, interrupting. 'Superconductors will float in strong magnetic fields. Even these m-state powders demonstrate superconducting levitation. In 1984, laboratory tests in both Arizona and Texas showed that rapid cooling of monatomic powders could raise their tested weight fourfold. Yet if heated again, the weight vanished to less than zero.'

'What do you mean, *less* than zero?'

'The pan weighed less *with* the substance on it, as if the pan were levitating.'

'The Paradise Stone rediscovered,' Vigor declared.

Gray began to sense the truth. A secret knowledge passed down through the generations. 'Where does the powdery trail lead next?'

'To the time of Christ,' Vigor answered. 'A tale related by Marco Polo tells the story of the Magi receiving a gift from the Christ child, a dull white stone. During their journey home, the stone burst forth with fire that could not be extinguished, an eternal flame that symbolises enlightenment. In Mesopotamia, the term for "fire-stone" is *manna*.'

Gray nodded. 'So we've come back to the Magi. Does it stop there?'

Vigor shook his head. 'I need to do more research, but I think it continues in an unbroken chain of research into purifying this process, conducted by a secret alchemical society through the ages. I think the mainstream scientific community is only now beginning to discover it.'

'The monsignor is right,' said Kat. 'There are incredible discoveries being made about these m-state superconductors. From levitation to the possibility of trans-dimensional shifting. But more practical applications are being explored. Cis-platinum and carbono-platinum are already being used to treat cancers. Bristol-Meyers Squibb has reported success with monatomic ruthenium to correct cancer cells. These atoms actually make the DNA strand correct itself without drugs or radiation. Iridium has been shown to stimulate the pineal gland and appears to fire up "junk DNA", leading to the possibility of increased longevity. Purdue University reports using rhodium to kill viruses with light from *inside* a body.'

Rachel finally spoke up. 'It makes one wonder.'

'What?' Gray turned to her.

'Scientists are talking about heightening awareness, levitation, miraculous healing, anti-ageing. It sounds like a list of miracles from biblical times. It makes me wonder why so many miracles happened back then, but not now. In the past few centuries, we're lucky to see an image of the Virgin Mary on a tortilla. Yet now, *science* is rediscovering these miracles. And much of it traces back to a white powder. Could such secret knowledge have been the source for the epidemic of miracles back in biblical times?'

Gray pondered this, meeting her gaze. 'And if these ancient Magi knew more than we know now,' he extrapolated, 'what has this lost fraternity of wise men done with this knowledge, to what level have they refined it?'

Rachel continued the thread. 'Maybe that's what the Dragon Court is after! Maybe they found some clue, something tied to the bones that could lead them to whatever this purified end product might be.'

'And along the way, the Court learned that murderous trick back in Cologne, a way to use the powder to kill.'

Rachel's face sobered. 'We've got to stop them. If they should gain access to the secret knowledge of these ancient wise men, they could change the world, remake it in their own sick image.'

Vigor nodded. 'We're going to have to search for clues to these ancient alchemists. That means following in the footsteps of the Dragon Court.'

Gray shook his head. 'I'm done with following the bastards. We need to *pass* them. Let them eat our dust for a change.'

SEICHAN SLIPPED ON a pair of Versace sunglasses. When in Rome . . .

She stepped out onto Piazza Pia from the express bus. She wore a breezy white summer dress and nothing else except for a pair of stiletto-heeled Harley Davidson boots with silver buckles.

The bus pulled away. Before her, a drum-shaped building filled the sky-line, a fortress overlooking the Tiber River. Castel Sant'Angelo.

Seichan crossed the gardens to the entrance and passed through the twenty-foot-thick walls to enter the first floor. This late in the day, tourists were dribbling out. She headed in, climbing up the wide Roman steps. She was going to the middle level, to a terrace restaurant that overlooked the

Tiber. She was to meet her contact there. After the firebombing, it was deemed too risky to meet in the Vatican itself.

Seichan checked her watch. Ten minutes early. Just as well. She had a call to make. She slipped out her cellphone, pressed the scramble feature, and tapped in the speed-dial code. A private, unlisted number. She leaned on a hip, phone to her ear, and waited for the international connection.

The line buzzed, clicked, and a firm, no-nonsense voice answered.

'Good afternoon. You've reached Sigma command.'

6

'I need pen and paper,' Gray said, his satellite phone in his hand.

The group waited at a sidewalk trattoria across from Rome's central train station. Upon arriving, Rachel had called for a pair of Carabinieri vehicles to collect and escort the team to the Vatican City. While they waited, Gray decided it was time to break his silence with central command.

After a short debriefing of events in Cologne and Milan, Director Crowe had his own surprising bit of news.

'Why would she call you?' Gray asked the director, as Monk fished in his pack for pad and pen.

'Seichan is playing our two groups off one another,' Painter answered. 'She's not even trying to hide it. The intel she passed us was stolen from the Dragon Court's field operative, a man named Raoul. She can't decipher it on her own, so she passed it to us—both to solve it for her and to keep you on the tail of the Court. But don't trust her. She'll eventually turn on you.'

'OK,' Gray said when he had pen and paper in hand. 'I'm ready.'

As Painter passed on the message, Gray wrote it down.

'And it's broken into stanzas, like a poem?' Gray asked.

'Exactly,' the director said, 'I have codebreakers working on it here.'

Gray frowned at the pad. 'I'll see if we can make anything of it.' With a few final clarifications, he signed off and stored the phone away.

'What was that all about?' Monk asked.

'The Dragon Lady called Sigma with a mystery for us to solve. It seems she has no idea what the Court is going to do next, and while they prepare, she wants us to be nipping at their heels. So she leaked some archaic passage, something discovered two months ago by the Dragon Court in Egypt. Whatever its content, she says it initiated the current operation.'

Vigor stood up from one of the trattoria's outdoor tables. He leaned over to read the passage along with the others.

When the full moon mates with the sun,
It is born eldest.
What is it?
Where it drowns,
It floats in darkness and stares at the lost king.
What is it?
The Twin waits for water,
But will be burned to bone by bone upon the altar.
What is it?

'I mentioned this on the train.' Vigor tapped a finger on the pad. 'A book also broken into lines of cryptic description, followed by the one line repeated many times: "What is it?"'

Kat remembered first. 'From the Egyptian *Book of the Dead*.'

Vigor nodded. 'The Papyrus of Ani, to be exact. But these passages aren't from the *Book of the Dead*,' he continued. 'I'm familiar enough with it to be certain of that.'

'Then where did they come from?' Rachel asked.

'I'm sure that as a member of the Carabinieri TPC you were informed of the recent chaos at the Egyptian Museum in Cairo. The museum sent out an alert through Interpol.'

Rachel nodded and explained to the others. 'Egypt's Supreme Council of Antiquities began a process in 2004 of emptying the basement of the Egyptian Museum, prior to renovation. But on opening the basement, they discovered over a hundred thousand pharaonic artefacts among its maze of corridors, an archaeological dumping ground that was all but forgotten.'

'They estimate it will take five years to catalogue,' Vigor said. 'But as a professor of archaeology, I've heard titbits of discoveries. There was a room of crumbling parchments that scholars suspect may have come from the lost Library of Alexandria, a major bastion of Gnostic study.'

Gray recalled Vigor's discussion about Gnosticism and the pursuit of secret knowledge. 'Such a discovery would attract the Dragon Court.'

'One of the items catalogued,' Vigor continued, 'came from a collection of Abd el-Latif, a fifteenth-century physician and explorer who lived in Cairo. It was a fourteenth-century illuminated copy of the Egyptian *Book of the Dead.*' Vigor stared hard at Gray. 'It was stolen four months ago.'

'But if the book is just a bootleg of the original,' Monk said, 'what's the significance?'

'The Papyrus of Ani has hundreds of stanzas. I wager someone forged this copy and hid *these* specific stanzas among the more ancient ones.'

'Our lost alchemists,' Kat said.

'Hiding needles in a haystack,' Monk said.

Gray nodded. 'Till some Dragon Court scholar was wise enough to pick them out, decipher the clues and act on it. But where does that leave us?'

Vigor smiled. 'You mentioned on the train a desire to catch up and pass the Dragon Court. We have the riddle. Now is our chance.'

'But it could take days to decipher it.'

Vigor glanced over his shoulder. 'Not if I've already solved it.' He waved for the pad of paper and flipped to a blank page. 'Let me show you.' He wet his finger in his espresso and dampened the bottom of his tiny cup. He pressed the cup upon the paper, leaving a perfect ring of coffee stain on the blank page. He repeated it again, applying a second ring below it, this one overlapping the first. 'The full moon mating with the sun.'

'*Vesica Pisces*,' Rachel said, her face dawning with understanding.

Vigor grinned at her. 'Did I ever tell you how proud I am of my niece?'

RACHEL FOLLOWED Gray's broad back down to the rear of the public bus. Vigor had insisted that they take alternate transportation to investigate the new lead. So, reluctantly, she had called in to the station and requested that the patrol cars be recalled.

The bus left the kerb and shouldered into traffic. Rachel climbed into a seat with Gray. Their row of seats faced Monk, Kat and Uncle Vigor.

'OK,' Gray said, 'I've taken you at your word that this side excursion is necessary. Now, how about a bit of elaboration?'

Vigor raised a palm, conceding. 'If I had gone into detail, we would have missed our bus. He opened the pad again. 'This shape of overlapping circles is called *Vesica Pisces*, or Vessel of the Fishes.' Vigor inked over a section of the two intersecting circles to reveal a fishlike shape.

Gray peered closer. 'It's the fish symbol that represents Christianity. But how does this lead us anywhere?'

The second line reads, "It is born *eldest*". It's directing us to the oldest representation of the fish symbol. That would be found in the Crypt of Lucina in the Catacombs of St Callistus. The other stanzas hint at it, too.

"Where it drowns, it floats in darkness." A fish can't drown, not in water, but it can in earth. And the mention of darkness. It all points to a crypt.'

When they got off the bus, Vigor guided them through Porta San Sebastiano, gateway to the parklands that surround the Appian Way, a preserved section of the famous ancient Roman road. Sheep dotted the hillsides, which were shaded by umbrella pines.

At seven thirty in the evening, with most of the attractions closed and the sun near to setting, they had the Appian Way to themselves. Vigor led the way through an area of vineyards. Ahead appeared the courtyard entrance to their destination: the Catacombs of St Callistus.

The subterranean cemetery had closed at five o'clock, but Vigor had called the caretaker and arranged this special 'tour'. A petite, snowy-maned gentleman in grey overalls stepped out of a sheltered doorway. He hobbled over, using a wooden shepherd's crook as a cane. Vigor knew him well. His family had been shepherds here for generations.

'Monsignor Verona,' he said. '*Come va?*'

'*Bene, grazie. E lei,* Giuseppe?'

'I'm fine, *Padre. Grazie.*' He waved towards the doorway. 'It is open.'

Vigor led them to the gateway to the catacombs. He pulled open the door and waved the others through, noting that Giuseppe had left the string of electric lights lit. The staircase descended ahead of them. Vigor closed the door behind him and took the lead again, heading down the stairs.

'This catacomb is one of Rome's oldest,' he said. 'It was once a private Christian cemetery, but it spread out when some of the popes chose to be buried at this site. It now covers ninety acres and descends in four levels.'

The air grew danker as they descended, rich with the smell of loam and seeping rainwater. At the foot of the stairs, they reached a vestibule with *loculi* cut into the walls, horizontal niches for bodies to be laid to rest.

The way narrowed. Ahead, a chamber opened. Its walls were pocked with larger *loculi* and elaborate arched gravesites.

'The Papal Crypt,' Vigor announced. 'Sixteen popes were laid to rest here, from Eutychianus to Zephyrinus. But when the outskirts of Rome were plundered by Goths, Vandals and Lombards in the fifth century, the bodies of many of the important persons buried here were moved to churches inside the city. By the twelfth century, the catacombs were abandoned and forgotten.'

'And the twelfth century was when the bones of the Magi were moved to Germany,' said Gray.

Vigor nodded. 'It was a tumultuous time, with the papacy run out of Rome by the end of the next century. The alchemists, driven into deeper hiding, may have sought to protect what they had learned, leaving behind clues in case of their demise, breadcrumbs for other Gnostic believers to follow.'

'Like this sect of the Dragon Court.'

'I don't think they imagined such a perverse group to be enlightened enough to seek higher truths. An unfortunate miscalculation. Either way, you may have pegged the time when these clues were placed.'

The monsignor piloted them through a series of galleries, crypts and *cubicoli* until their goal appeared. A modest crypt.

Vigor pointed to two neighbouring walls. 'Here is what we came to find.'

Gray approached the nearest wall. A fish had been painted against a green background. Above it was a basket of bread. He turned to the second wall. This fresco seemed a mirror image of the first, except the basket also bore a bottle of wine.

'It's all symbolic of the first Eucharistic meal,' Vigor said. 'Fish, bread and wine. It also represents the miracle of the fishes.'

'But where do we go from here?' Monk asked.

'Follow the riddle,' Gray answered. 'The second stanza reads, "Where it drowns, it floats in darkness and stares at the lost king". We found where it floats in darkness, so now we follow where it stares.' He pointed in the direction the first fish was facing: further into the galleries.

Gray strode off in that direction, searching around him. It did not take long to find a depiction of kings. They stopped before a fresco illustrating the adoration of the Magi. It was faded, but the details were plain enough. The Virgin Mary was sitting on a throne with the Christ child on her lap. Bowed before her were three robed figures offering gifts.

'We keep running into these guys,' said Monk.

'But did these ancient alchemists lead us here?' Gray said. 'To this particular depiction of the Magi?'

Rachel offered a possible avenue to pursue. 'The Dragon Court went after the Magi bones. Maybe we need to look at it from their perspective.'

Gray nodded. He should have thought of that. The Dragon Court had already solved the riddle. All they had to do was backtrack.

He considered this for a while. 'Maybe the fish is staring towards these particular kings because they are buried,' he said. 'In a graveyard. Under the earth, where a fish would drown. The answer to the clue is not living Magi, but dead and buried ones, in a crypt once filled with *bones*. I think the Dragon Court already knew the bones were not bones. They've had their nose to this trail for centuries. They must have known. Look what happened at the cathedral. They used the powder of white gold in some way to kill. They're well ahead of the game.'

Vigor's eyes narrowed in concentration. 'And if you're right, maybe the transfer of the bones to Germany was not plunder, as history attests, but was done by arrangement. To safeguard the amalgam.'

Gray nodded. 'And the Dragon Court let them remain in Cologne, knowing they were significant, but not knowing what to do with them.'

'Until now,' Monk said from a few paces away.

'We're forgetting,' Kat said. 'The stanza from the passage states the fish "stares at the lost *king*." Not "kings", plural. There are three kings here. I think we're missing another layer of meaning or symbolism.' She turned to the others. 'What "lost king" is the clue hinting about?'

Vigor had dropped his chin into his hand, concentrating. 'There is a fresco in a neighbouring catacomb. The Catacomb of Domatilla. The fresco is painted with not three Magi, but *four*. Because the Bible was never specific on the number of Magi, early Christian artists varied the number. The lost king could mean another Magi, the one missing here.' He nodded, raising his head. 'The second stanza's message hints that the Magi bones can be used to find this fourth Magi. Whoever he may be.'

Rachel shook her head. 'Don't forget this clue is buried in a crypt. I bet it's not the fourth Magi we're supposed to find, but his *tomb*. Possibly another cache of amalgam.'

'Or something greater. That would certainly excite the Dragon Court.'

Gray headed back to the Crypt of Lucina. 'The answer has to be in the *third* stanza.'

PAINTER CROWE woke to a knock on his door. He had fallen asleep in his chair, tilted back. He cleared the sleep from his throat. 'Come in.'

Logan Gregory entered. His hair was wet and he wore a fresh shirt. It looked like he'd just come in for the day, rather than being here twenty-four-seven.

Logan must have noted Painter's attention. He ran a hand down his starched shirt. 'I went for a run. I keep a second set of clothes in my locker.'

Painter had no reply. Youth. He didn't think he could climb out of his chair, let alone run. But then again, Logan was only five years his junior.

'Sir,' Logan continued, 'I received word from General Rende, our liaison with the Carabinieri Corps in Rome. Commander Pierce and the others have gone to ground again. After your call, they waved off the Carabinieri escort and took off on their own. Should we post an alert?'

'We'll wait for his next call. We'll give him room to run his own game.'

Logan did not seem satisfied. 'What do you want me to do, then?'

'I suggest, Logan, that you get some rest.'

'Yes, sir.' He headed for the door.

Painter leaned back in his chair and covered his eyes with his arm. Damn, but this chair was comfortable. He drifted away, but something troubled him, keeping him from sleep. Something nagged. Something Gray had said. Not trusting Sigma. A leak. Could it be?

There was only one person besides himself with full intel on this operation up until now. Not even the Director of DARPA, Sean McKnight, knew everything. He slowly tilted forward, eyes open.

It couldn't be.

BACK AT THE CRYPT of Lucina, Gray stood by the second fish fresco.

'The third stanza has the fish waiting for water,' he said. 'Like the first fish, we're supposed to follow where it's facing.' Gray motioned to the gallery the second fish pointed to.

But Vigor continued his study of the two fishes, looking at one, then the other. 'Whoever devised these riddles loved to layer them with symbolism. Referring to the second fish as "twin" cannot be insignificant.'

'I don't see the connection,' Gray said.

'You just don't know your Greek, Commander.'

Monk chimed in, proving that his Greek heritage extended beyond a fondness for ouzo and bad dancing. ' "Twin" translates to *didymus*.'

'Very good,' Vigor said. 'And in Hebrew, "twin" translates to *Thomas*. As in Didymus Thomas. One of the twelve apostles.'

Gray remembered the discussion at Lake Como with the monsignor. 'Thomas was the apostle in conflict with John.'

'And the one who baptised the Magi,' Vigor reminded them. 'Thomas represented Gnostic belief. I think using the words "twin" here is a tribute to the Gospel of Thomas. I wonder if these alchemists might not have been Thomas Christians themselves,churchgoers who followed Rome but still continued their Gnostic practices in secret. There were always whispers of such a church within the Church. This may be the proof.'

Gray followed this line of logic. It might be worth pursuing, but for now they had another riddle to solve. He pointed down the gallery. 'Whoever left these clues, they left us a third challenge.'

The Twin waits for water . . .

Gray led the way down the new gallery. He searched for a fresco with water in it. Vigor called behind him. He turned.

The others were gathered by one niche. He went back to them. He had looked at that fresco already. It showed a man in a robe striking a stone with a stick. Not a drop of water.

'This is an illustration of Moses in the desert,' Vigor said. 'According to the Bible, he struck a rock in the desert and a spring burst forth to quench the thirst of the fleeing Israelites. This must be the fresco indicated by the stanza. 'Remember, Moses knew about manna and these miraculous white powders. It would be appropriate to acknowledge him.'

'So what clue does this crumbling painting hold?' Gray asked.

'"The Twin waits for water, but will be burned to bone by bone upon the altar",' Vigor quoted. 'What did the Dragon Court do, in Cologne? The parishioners were burned somehow, a massive electrical storm in the brain. And it involved white gold. And possibly the amalgam in the Magi bones.'

'Is that the message?' Rachel asked, looking uneasy. 'To kill?'

'No,' Gray answered. 'The Dragon Court ignited the bones and seemingly learned nothing, since they continued in the same trail afterwards. Maybe Cologne was just a test or a trial run. Maybe the Dragon Court was not sure of their interpretation of the riddle. Either way, they were plainly aware of some of the white powder's capabilities. With their device, they proved they can activate the energy in these high-spin superconductors. They used it to kill. But I don't think that is what the alchemists originally intended.'

Gray considered all he had learned. The amalgam was composed of metals in the platinum group, its exact recipe impossible to determine. It was then shaped into bones and secured in a cathedral. Why?

He mulled over the indecipherable codex of chemicals, left behind as a series of clues to a possible storehouse of ancient power. An indecipherable codex . . . About to give up, the answer came to him, sudden and sharp, a pain behind the eyes. Not a codex.

'It's a *key*,' he exclaimed. 'The amalgam is an indecipherable chemical key, impossible to duplicate. Within its unique chemistry must be the power to unlock the location of the tomb of the fourth Magi. But where's the lock? Not in Cologne. The Dragon Court failed there. Here? In this fresco?' He turned and pointed to it. 'Are we supposed to search for Moses' stone?'

'No,' Vigor said. He touched the painted rock. 'Remember the layers of symbolism in the riddle. This is not *Moses*' stone. At least not his alone. The fresco is actually titled "Moses-Peter Striking the Rock". In the catacombs, St Peter's image was often superimposed upon Moses' acts. It was a way of glorifying the apostle. "Rock" in Greek is *petros*. This is why the apostle Simon Bar-Jona took the name Peter. From Christ's words, "You are Peter, and on this rock I will build my Church".'

Gray attempted to put this together. 'Are you suggesting that the altar named in the riddle is the altar inside St Peter's Basilica?'

Rachel suddenly twisted round. 'No. We've got the symbolism backwards. In the stanza, the word *altar* is used, but the painting replaces it with the word *rock*. It's not an altar we're looking for, it's a rock.' Her eyes shone with excitement. 'What site was St Peter's Basilica built on? What *rock* is buried under the foundations of the church?'

Gray answered, eyes widening. 'St Peter's tomb.' He sensed the truth. The bones were the key. The tomb was the lock.

Rachel nodded. 'That's where the Dragon Court will be heading next. We should contact Cardinal Spera immediately.'

'Oh no . . .' Vigor stiffened.

'What's wrong?" Gray asked.

'A memorial service for the tragedy in Cologne is scheduled for tonight, at sunset. Thousands will be in attendance, including the pope.'

DUSK WAS SETTLING over the Appian Way as they climbed out of the catacombs. The caretaker, Giuseppe, held the door for them, then locked it.

'Giuseppe, do you have a car?' Gray asked.

The old man nodded, noting the strain on their faces. 'Around back.'

He led the way. Behind his cottage stood a stone shack. It had no door. Through the opening, a shape filled the space, covered by a tarp.

Giuseppe waved. 'The keys are inside. I filled it with gas last week.'

Monk and Kat pulled the tarpaulin aside, revealing a classic '66 Maserati Sebring, black as obsidian.

They thanked Giuseppe and quickly climbed inside. Rachel slid into the driver's seat. She knew the streets of Rome the best.

'Monk,' she said as she turned the key and the engine roared. 'You'd better close your eyes.'

As Rachel pulled away, Vigor tried to call Cardinal Spera on Gray's cellphone. He was at the memorial service, already under way, as was General

Rende, who was overseeing the Carabinieri force that guarded St Peter's Square. Messages were left, the alarm raised. But would it be in time?

'With the memorial crowds, we'll never reach the front entrances,' Vigor warned. 'We should try for the railway entry. Go in the back way.'

Rachel nodded. The traffic was already congested as the flow bottlenecked towards the bridge over the Tiber River.

'Tell me about the excavations under the basilica, the necropolis where St Peter's tomb is located,' Gray said. 'Are there any other entrances to it?'

'No,' Vigor said. 'The Scavi is self-contained. Under St Peter's lie the Sacred Grottoes, accessed through the basilica. Many of the papal tombs reside there. But in 1939, workers were digging a tomb site for Pope Pius XI and discovered another layer beneath the grottoes, a necropolis of mausoleums dating back to the first century. It was named simply the *Scavi*, or Excavations. It's a vast maze of gravesites, shrines and stone streets.'

Rachel finally reached the bridge and fought her way across the Tiber. On the far side, she swung to the south. After a few serpentine turns, the Maserati arrived at the towering Leonine Walls of the Vatican. It was dark now, and there were few street lamps.

'Just ahead,' Vigor said, pointing an arm.

The railway spanned the road via a stone bridge. Here the Vatican's railway line exited the Holy See and joined Rome's system of tracks.

'Take that turn before the bridge,' Vigor said.

Rachel yanked the wheel, fishtailing off the main avenue and onto a steep service road. The road hit a dead end at the tracks.

'That way!' Vigor pointed to the left.

There was no street, only a narrow sward of grass, weeds and rocks that paralleled the railroad tracks. Rachel twisted the wheel and bumped off the service road towards the archway built into the Leonine Wall. Reaching the wall, she manhandled the Maserati through the opening.

Her headlights splashed across the side of a midnight-blue service van which blocked the way. A pair of Swiss Guards, in blue night uniforms, flanked the van. They had rifles out, pointing at the intruders.

Rachel braked, arm already out of the window, waving her Carabinieri ID. She yelled. 'Lieutenant Verona! With Monsignor Verona! Emergency!'

Her uncle showed his Vatican papers. 'We must reach Cardinal Spera.'

A flashlight searched the car, passing over the other occupants.

'I vouch for them,' Vigor said sternly. 'As will Cardinal Spera.'

The van was directed through, clearing the path into the Vatican.

Vigor leaned out and asked, 'Has word reached you of a possible attack?'

The guard's eyes widened. He shook his head. 'No, Monsignor.'

'Do not let anyone else through,' Vigor ordered. 'Lock this entry down.'

Rachel tore through a small parking lot, then turned right, passing between the Palazzo del Tribunale and the Palazzo San Carlo.

'Park here,' her uncle ordered. 'We'll have to continue on foot.'

Rachel pulled up at the kerb. The Sacristy of St Peter rose on her left, connected to the giant basilica. The entrance to the Scavi lay on the far side.

As they climbed out, muffled singing reached them—the Pontifical Choir singing 'Ave Maria'. The Mass was under way.

Vigor led the way through a covered archway into an open yard. It was deserted. All attention had turned to the basilica, to the pope.

On the far side of the sacristy, from beyond the Arch of Bells, a low sonorous noise joined the singing. It came from St Peter's Square. It was the murmur of a thousand voices, rising from the crowd in the piazza.

'Here,' Vigor said, pulling free a ring of keys. He led them to a nondescript steel door at the edge of the yard. 'This leads down to the Scavi.'

'No guards,' Gray noted.

The only security was a pair of Swiss Guards posted by the Arch of Bells. They were armed with rifles as they studied the crowd. They didn't even glance back towards the newcomers.

'It's locked,' Vigor said. 'Maybe we've beaten them here after all.'

'We can't count on that,' Gray warned. 'They may have keys.'

'Only a few people have these keys. As head of the Pontifical Institute of Archaeology, I have a set.' He turned to Rachel and held out two other keys. 'These open the lower door . . . and these open the tomb site of St Peter.'

Rachel refused to take them. 'What—?'

'You know the layout of the Scavi better than anyone. I must reach Cardinal Spera. The pope must be removed from harm's way, and the basilica emptied without creating panic.' He touched his clerical collar. 'No one else can get there as fast.'

Rachel nodded and took the keys. Even General Rende did not have jurisdiction on Vatican soil.

Vigor gave Gray a sharp stare before heading for the heart of the basilica. Rachel interpreted it. *Watch after my niece*.

Gray turned to the group and had them don their radios, securing an extra for Rachel, taping the microphone to her throat himself.

Monk cracked the door open. The way down to the basement was dark.

'There's a light switch just inside,' Rachel whispered.

'We go in the dark,' Gray said.

Monk and Kat pulled night-vision goggles over their eyes. Gray handed Rachel a pair. She donned them. The world brightened into shades of green.

Gray led the way; Rachel followed with Kat. Monk silently closed the door behind him. The way became dark, even with the goggles. Night vision required some light. Gray clicked on a handheld ultraviolet flashlight. It flared bright in the gloom, illuminating the anteroom. Displays and models dotted the space. One was a model of Constantine's first church, built here in 324 BC. Another was a model of an *aedicula*, a burial shrine shaped like a tiny two-level temple. Such a temple had marked St Peter's gravesite. According to historians, Constantine had constructed a cube of marble and porphyry to encase the *aedicula*, then built his original church around it.

When the necropolis was excavated, the cube was rediscovered, positioned directly under the main altar of St Peter's. A wall of the original temple remained, scratched and scrawled with Christian graffiti, including the Greek letters spelling out *Petros eni*, or 'Peter is within'.

And indeed, inside a cavity in that graffitied wall, bones and cloth were found that matched a man of St Peter's stature and age. Now they were sealed in bulletproof plastic boxes and secured back in the wall cavity.

That was their goal.

'This way.' Rachel pointed to a steep, circular stair that led below.

Gray took the lead. They wound down below the basement and deeper. At the bottom of the stairs, a small door blocked the way. Rachel unlocked the door and Gray pulled it open a few centimetres and stared through.

'All clear,' he said, and pulled open the door.

Rachel readied herself for some kind of attack, but found only silence.

As they pushed inside, Gray turned to the group. 'For once, we've got the jump on the Dragon Court. It's about time *we* set up the ambush.'

'What's the plan?' Monk asked.

'No chances. We set the trap and get the hell out of here.' Gray pointed to the door. 'Monk, stand guard at the door. It's the only way out or in.' He handed what looked like two small egg cartons to Kat. 'Sonic grenades and flash bombs. I expect they'll come in the dark like we did. Let's blind and deafen them. Distribute these as we cross to the tomb.'

Kat nodded.

Gray turned to Rachel. 'Show me St Peter's tomb.'

She headed into the necropolis. Family crypts and mausoleums lined the ancient Roman path, decorated with frescoes and mosaics. Rachel mapped out the route to the centre of the necropolis. A metal walkway led up to a platform and rectangular window. She pointed through it.

'The tomb of St Peter.'

Gray shone his UV flashlight in to the gravesite.

Ten feet beyond the window, a brick wall rose alongside a massive cube of marble. There was an opening near the base of the wall. Bending down, he aimed his light into the opening. Inside a clear box he could see a blob of white, claylike material. Bone. From St Peter.

Gray straightened. 'Can we get closer?' he asked Rachel.

She pulled out the second key her uncle had given her and unlocked a gate that led in to the inner sanctum.

Sensing that time was running short, Gray fixed a tiny video camera in a crevice in a neighbouring mausoleum and pointed it at the tomb. He positioned a second camera facing back through the window.

'What are you doing?' Rachel asked.

Gray waved her back out. 'I don't want to spring the trap too soon. I want them to get comfortable in here, set up their apparatus. Then we'll strike.'

After they exited, Rachel relocked the gate. Gray crossed to a nearby crumbling mausoleum, one that was open at the front. He freed the laptop from his pack and hid it inside the mausoleum, attaching a portable boost-transmitter to its USB port.

As they headed back out, he explained. 'The video cameras are not strong enough to transmit very far. The laptop will pick up the signal and boost it. It'll have enough range to reach the surface. We'll monitor it on another laptop. Once the Court is down here, trapped, we blast them with the sonic and flash charges, then sweep below with Swiss Guards—'

Explosions cut him off—muffled, like depth charges underwater. They echoed through the necropolis, followed by a louder crash of stone.

Gray crouched as small holes were punched through the roof from above. Rock and earth blasted downward. Before the debris could settle, ropes snaked through the openings, followed by one man after another.

A full assault team. They dropped into the necropolis and vanished.

Gray immediately realised what was happening. The Dragon Court was entering from the Sacred Grottoes above, accessed from inside the basilica. The Dragon Court must have come to the memorial service—then, through their Vatican contact, snuck below into the papal crypts. Their gear had probably been smuggled in earlier and hidden among the tombs. Under the cover of the service, they punched their way down here.

'Kat,' Gray whispered. 'Take Rachel to Monk. Don't engage. Get back above and find the Swiss Guard.'

'What about you?' Kat asked.

He was already moving, heading back towards St Peter's tomb. 'I'm staying here. I'll monitor from the laptop. Delay them if need be. Then signal you by radio once I spring the ambush.'

Monk came on over the radio. 'No go here. They blasted a hole right above the exit. Practically cracked my skull with a chunk of rock. The bastards are riveting the door shut. No one's going in or out this way.'

'Everyone go to ground,' Gray ordered. 'Wait for my signal.'

He crouched low and ran down the cemetery street.

They were on their own.

VIGOR ENTERED St Peter's Basilica through the sacristy door, flanked by two Swiss Guards. He entered the nave near the middle of the church.

Every pew was crowded. The space glowed with thousands of candles and hundreds of chandeliers. The Pontifical Choir sang 'Exaudi Deus', amplified and echoing as loud as any rock concert.

Vigor hurried, but forced himself not to run. Panic would kill. There were only a limited number of exits. He waved the two Swiss Guards to alert their brothers-in-arms. Vigor had to get the pope clear first and alert the presiding clerical staff to evacuate the parishioners.

On the far side of the altar, Cardinal Spera was seated with the pope. The pair sat under Bernini's *baldacchino,* a canopy of bronze that covered the altar. It rose eight storeys, supported by four massive bronze columns, and was topped by a golden sphere surmounted by a cross.

Reaching the front, Vigor edged to the left. He would circle towards the rear of the altar, where he could speak to Cardinal Spera in private.

As he pushed past a statue, a hand reached out from a shadowed doorway and gripped his elbow. He looked across. It was a lanky man his own age, someone he knew. Prefetto Alberto, the head prefect of the Archives.

'Vigor?' the prefect said. 'I heard . . .'

His words were lost to an especially loud refrain from the chorus.

Vigor leaned closer, stepping into the alcove that sheltered the doorway. It led down to the Sacred Grottoes. 'I'm sorry, Alberto. What—?'

The grip tightened. A pistol shoved hard into his ribs. It had a silencer.

'Not another word, Vigor,' Alberto warned.

INSIDE THE CRYPT, Gray lay on his belly, out of view of the opening. His pistol rested beside the laptop. He had its display turned to dark mode, glowing in UV. Two images split the screen—one feed from the camera facing St Peter's tomb, the other from the camera facing the main necropolis.

The assault team had divided into two groups. While one group patrolled the necropolis, the other had broken out flashlights to expedite their work on the tomb. They had already opened the gate, and now two men flanked the crypt, fixing two large plates to either side of the tomb.

The third man was immediately recognisable by his size. Raoul.

He carried a steel case. He opened it and removed a clear plastic cylinder, full of a familiar whitish powder. The amalgam. They must have pulverised the bone. Raoul slid the cylinder through the low opening into St Peter's tomb. Plugged in the battery . . .

Gray could wait no longer. The apparatus was set. It was their one chance to catch the Court off guard, perhaps to drive them off.

'Ready to go blackout,' Gray whispered. His hand moved to the transmitter that controlled the sonic and flash bombs. 'Take out as many as you can while they're stunned, but don't take any needless chances.'

Affirmatives answered him. Monk was holed up near the door. Kat and Rachel had found another crypt to hide in.

Gray watched the trio of men exit the tomb area, trailing wires that led to the device. Raoul closed the gate. Atop the metal platform, he pressed one hand against his ear, plainly communicating the OK to proceed.

'Blackout on the count of five,' Gray whispered. 'Earplugs in place, goggles blinkered closed. Here we go.'

Gray counted down in his head. *Five, four, three, two, one, zero.*

He hit the button on the laptop. Though protected by his earplugs, he could feel the deep *whump* of the sonic charges behind his sternum. He waited a three-count for the strobing flash grenades to expire. He blinkered open his goggles, then yanked out the earplugs. Shots echoed across the necropolis. Gray rolled to the entrance to the crypt.

Directly ahead, the metal platform was empty. No one was in sight.

Raoul and his two men were gone. Where?

The sound of gunfire intensified. A firefight waged in the dark necropolis. Gray remembered Raoul had received some communiqué just before he had ignited the sonic and flash charges. Had it been a warning?

Gray climbed the steps to the platform. He had to risk exposure to secure the apparatus and the amalgam. As he reached the top, light suddenly blazed through the window ahead. It revealed Raoul standing on the far side, a few steps from the tomb. He must have dodged back through the gate during the attack. He met Gray's eyes and lifted his arms. In his hands he held the control device to ignite the amalgam.

Gray aimed and fired. But the bulletproof glass repelled the slug.

Raoul smiled and twisted the handle on the control device.

7

The first quake threw Vigor into the air. Or maybe it was the ground that had dropped below his feet. Either way, he became airborne.

Cries rose across the basilica.

As he fell back, he took advantage of the moment to plant an elbow into the nose of the traitor Alberto, following up with a blow to his Adam's apple.

The man fell heavily. The pistol tumbled from his fingers. Vigor grabbed it, then was knocked to his knees by a second tremor. By now, screams and yells were erupting all round. But beneath it all, a deep, hollow thrum vibrated, as if a bell as large as the basilica had been struck and they were all trapped inside.

Vigor remembered the description given by the Cologne survivor. A pressure as if the walls squeezed in on themselves. It was the same here.

While he climbed to his feet, the floor continued trembling. The polished marble surface seemed to ripple and shiver. Vigor shoved the pistol under his belt, and turned to go to the aid of the pope and Cardinal Spera.

As he stepped forward, he felt it before he saw it. A sudden increase in pressure, deafening, squeezing inwards. Then it let loose. Up from the base of the four bronze columns of Bernini's *baldacchino*, fiery cascades of electrical energy spiralled upward, spitting and crackling. They rushed up the columns, across the canopy's roof, and met at the gold globe.

A crack of thunder erupted. The ground jolted again, shattering fissures in the marble floor. From the canopy's globe, a brilliant fork of lightning erupted. It blasted upwards, striking the underside of Michelangelo's dome and dancing across it. The ground bumped again, more violently.

Cracks skittered across the dome. Plates of plaster rained.

It was all coming down.

MONK PICKED HIMSELF off the floor. Blood ran into one eye. He had landed face first in the corner of a crypt, cracking his goggles, slicing his eyebrow.

He fished for his weapon. The shotgun's night scope would help him see. As he searched, the ground continued to vibrate under his fingertips.

Monk reached forward, sweeping the ground near the crypt. He felt something hard at his fingertips. Thank God.

He reached forward and realised his mistake. It was not the butt of his weapon. It was the toe of a boot.

Behind him, he felt the barrel of a rifle press against the base of his skull.

GRAY HEARD the crack of a rifle, the first shot since the quakes began. He had been thrown off the metal platform and had landed near the mausoleum where he'd hidden his laptop. He had rolled into a ball, taking a blow to his shoulder, keeping his goggles and pistol in place. But he had lost his radio.

He looked up towards the platform. Light still radiated from the tomb. He had to know what was going on in there. But he couldn't go in alone.

Making certain that no eyes were upon him, he dived back into the mausoleum and engaged the laptop. The split-screen image bloomed. The camera pointing into the main necropolis revealed nothing but darkness.

What had happened to the others?

Focusing on the opposite side of the screen, he saw two men with rifles pointed back towards the gate, Raoul's guards. But there was no sign of the big man. The tomb seemed unchanged. But the image, the *entire* image was pulsing in tune with the vibration in the stone floor, as if some emanation was being given off by the charged device, a field of energy.

Where was Raoul? Gray reached out and rewound the digital recording a full minute, stopping at the spot where Raoul stood near the tomb and twisted the control handle to his device.

On the screen, Raoul turned to watch the result. Green lights flared on the two plates fixed to either side of the tomb. Movement caught his attention. Gray used a toggle to zoom in on the tomb's small opening. The cylinder of amalgam powder vibrated—then rose off the floor.

Levitating.

Gray remembered Kat's account of how the m-state powders could levitate in a strong magnetic field, acting as superconductors. And he recalled Monk's discovery of a magnetised cross in Cologne. The plates with the green lights must be electromagnets. The Court's device simply created an electromagnetic field around the amalgam, activating the m-state superconductor.

Suddenly the image jolted with the first quake. The view fritzed completely for a second, then settled, the perspective slightly askew now as the camera shifted. On the screen, Raoul backed away from the tomb.

Gray didn't understand why. Nothing seemed to be happening.

Then he spotted it, half hidden in the glare of the flashlights. At the base of the tomb, a section of stone floor slowly tilted downwards, forming a ramp that led beneath the tomb. From below, a cobalt light flickered. Raoul stepped in front of the camera, blocking the view as he headed down the ramp.

That's where he had disappeared.

Gray sped up the video back to the present. He watched a few brilliant flashes erupt from below. Camera flashes. Raoul was recording whatever he found down there. A few seconds later, he climbed back up the ramp.

The bastard wore a grimace of satisfaction.

LYING FLAT atop the mausoleum roof, Kat had got one shot off, taking out the gunman holding a rifle to Monk's head. But another quake threw off her next shot. The remaining attacker did not hesitate. From the direction his comrade's body had fallen, he must have guessed where she hid.

He dived down and clubbed Monk with the metal hilt of a hunting knife, then pulled him up as a shield. He pressed the blade to Monk's neck.

'Come out!' the man called in heavily accented English, sounding Germanic. 'Or I will remove this one's head.'

Kat jumped lithely off the mausoleum roof and stepped out into the open, ten yards from the man who held Monk. She tossed her pistol aside. 'I surrender,' she said coldly, studying Monk's eyes as she strode forward.

The combatant relaxed. Kat noted his knife point shift away. Good.

She dived forward, pulling the dagger from her wrist sheath. She used her momentum to fling the blade. It sailed and struck the man in the eye. He fell back, carrying Monk with him.

Kat twisted, yanking a second blade from her boot. She flipped it in the direction Monk had indicated, catching the barest flicker of shadow. A short cry followed. A man fell out of the shadows, pierced through the neck.

Monk struggled to his feet. He had lost his goggles. Kat would have to guide him. She helped him up and placed his hand on her shoulder.

'Stay with me,' she whispered.

She turned as a flashlight flared. Amplified by her night-vision goggles, the sudden brightness seared into the back of her head, blinding, painful.

A fourth combatant. Someone she had missed.

GRAY HAD NOTED the bloom of light on his computer screen, deep in the necropolis. That couldn't be good. It proved not to be. On one side of the split-screen image, he watched Raoul press his radio to his ear, his smile broadening. On the other side, he watched Kat and Monk being marched out at gunpoint, arms secured behind their backs with plastic fast-ties. They were shoved up the steps to the top of the platform.

Raoul remained by the tomb, flanked by a bodyguard. 'Commander Pierce! Lieutenant Verona!' he shouted. 'Show yourselves now or these two die!'

Gray remained where he was. He didn't have the force to overpower this situation. Rescue was hopeless. And if he gave in to the demands, he would just be handing his own life over. Raoul would kill them all.

A new voice drew his attention. 'I'm coming!'

Rachel stepped into view on the second camera, her hands in the air.

Two armed gunmen collected her and drove her to join the others.

Raoul stepped forward and pointed a meaty pistol into Rachel's shoulder. 'This is a horse pistol, Commander Pierce! Fifty-six calibre! It will rip her arm off! Show yourself or I'll start removing limbs! On the count of five!'

Suppressing a groan, Gray wriggled out of his pack and grabbed an item from an inner pocket, palming it.

'Four . . .'

Gray switched the laptop into dark mode and clicked it closed. If he didn't live, the computer would serve as witness to the events down here.

'Three . . .'

Gray crawled out of the mausoleum, circling to hide his position.

'Two . . .'

He ducked back onto the main path, laced his hands on top of his head and stepped into sight. 'I'm here. Don't shoot!'

RACHEL WATCHED GRAY march up to them at gunpoint. From the hard look on his face, she recognised her error. She had hoped her surrender would buy Gray time to act, to do something to save them, or at least himself.

The Dragon Court leader shoved her aside, meeting Gray as he climbed on to the platform. Raoul raised the massive horse pistol, pointing it at Gray's chest. 'You've caused me a hell of a lot of trouble.' He cocked the gun. 'And no amount of body armour will stop this slug.'

Gray ignored him. His eyes were on Monk, Kat . . . then Rachel.

He parted his fingers over his head, revealing a matte-black egg.

'Blackout,' he shouted.

GRAY COUNTED on Raoul's full attention as the flash grenade exploded above his head. With his eyes squeezed closed against the strobing flare that still burned through his lids, he dropped and rolled to the side.

Hearing the thunderous bark of Raoul's horse pistol, Gray reached to his boot and pulled free his .40-calibre Glock. As the strobe ended, he opened his eyes. One of Raoul's men lay at the foot of the steps, a fist-sized hole through his chest, taking the slug meant for Gray.

Raoul roared and dived off the platform, shooting blindly.

'Down!' Gray yelled.

The others dropped to their knees.

Gray rolled and clipped one dazzled gunman in the ankle, toppling him off the platform. He shot another down at the foot of the steps. He searched for Raoul. The giant had landed out of sight, but still blasted at them from below, tearing holes through the meshed floor of the platform.

They were sitting ducks. They had to move.

'Get back!' Gray hissed to the others. 'Through the gate!'

He fired a volley, covering their retreat, then followed.

Shouts arose from deeper in the necropolis. Other gunmen. They were rushing to the aid of their compromised comrades.

What now? He had only one magazine of ammo.

A cry rose behind him.

Gray glanced back. He watched Rachel flailing backwards. She must have been dazzled by the flash bomb. In the darkness, she didn't see the ramp in front of the tomb and back-stepped into it. She grabbed for Kat's elbow, trying to stop her fall. But Kat was equally caught off guard.

Both women tumbled down the ramp and rolled below.

Monk met Gray's eyes. 'Shit.'

'Down,' Gray said. It was the only shelter. And besides, they had to protect whatever clue lay below.

Monk went first, and as Gray followed a new barrage began. Chunks of rock were torn from the surface of the tomb. Twisting round, Gray saw a green light glowing from one of the two plates attached to the tomb. He pointed his pistol and fired. The light winked out.

Gray ran down the ramp, noting that the trembling in the ground had stopped. Both ears popped with a sudden release of pressure.

Immediately a loud grinding sounded underfoot.

Gray dived forward and landed inside a small cavern at the foot of the ramp, a natural pocket, volcanic in origin, common in the hills of Rome.

Behind him, the ramp swung back up, closing.

Gray rolled to his feet, keeping his gun pointed up. As he had hoped, the device's activation had opened the tomb, and its deactivation was closing it. With a final grate of stone on stone, the ramp sealed above them.

Darkness settled—but it was not complete.

Gray turned. The others had gathered round a slab of metallic black rock that rested on the floor. It was lit by a tiny pyre of blue flame on its surface, rising like a small flume of electrical fire.

'Haematite,' said Kat, identifying the rock. 'An iron oxide.'

She bent down and studied the silver lines etched into its surface, tiny rivers against a black background, illuminated by the blue flames.

As Gray watched, the fire slowly faded to a flicker, then went out.

Monk drew their attention to another glowing object.

Resting in a corner of the cavern was a familiar silver cylinder, shaped like a barbell. An incendiary grenade.

A timer counted down in the dark: 04:28, 04:27.

'Looks like they intended to destroy this clue,' Monk said. He dropped to one knee, studying the device. 'Damn thing's booby-trapped.'

Gray glanced at the sealed ramp. They were trapped.

VIGOR HAD FELT the sudden release. The wash of electrical fire that had been tearing plaster from the cupola dispersed. Its energy skittered away.

Still, chaos reigned inside the basilica. Half the parishioners had managed to flee, but the logjam at the entrances had slowed the evacuation. Some people hid under pews, others had been struck by falling plaster and sat with bloody fingers pressed to scalp wounds.

The Swiss Guard had come to the rescue of the pope. But he had refused to abandon the church, acting as the captain of this sinking ship. Cardinal Spera remained at his side, in the shelter of the Clementina Chapel.

Vigor strode over to join them. The chaos was slowly subsiding. As he approached, Cardinal Spera broke through the ranks of the Swiss Guard.

'Is it over?' the cardinal asked.

'I . . . I don't know,' Vigor said honestly. He had a larger concern.

The bones had been ignited. That was plain. But what did that mean for Rachel and the others?

A new voice intruded, shouted with familiar command. Vigor turned to find a wide-shouldered, silver-haired man striding towards him. General Joseph Rende, family friend and head of the local Parioli Station.

Vigor grabbed the general's elbow. 'We have to get below. To the Scavi. Gather as many men as you can. We have to get down there. Now!'

To his credit, the general responded immediately, barking crisp commands. Black-uniformed men swiftly ran up, armed with assault weapons.

'This way!' Vigor said, heading to the sacristy door.

GRAY WATCHED the illuminated timer on the incendiary device count down in the darkness: 02:22, 02:21. He had freed both his teammates' wrists with one of Kat's hidden knives. Kat was studying the ramp mechanism with the eyes of a trained engineer.

'The mechanism is a crude pressure plate,' she said. 'Sort of like a dead man's handle. It takes weight to hold the ramp closed. But lift the weight off and the ramp opens. But it doesn't make sense.'

'What do you mean?'

'As far as I can tell, the trigger plate lies under the tomb.'

'St Peter's tomb?'

Kat nodded and directed Gray to the side. 'Here is where they pulled the stabilising pin after weighing down the plate with the tomb. Once set, the only way to open this ramp is to *move* St Peter's tomb off the plate. But that didn't happen when the Dragon Court activated their device.'

'Maybe it did. . . .' Gray pictured the cylinder containing the superconducting amalgam, how it had levitated. 'Kat, do you remember your description of the test done in Arizona on these m-state powders? How, when these superconductors were charged, they weighed *less* than zero?'

She nodded. 'Because the powder was actually *levitating* the pan it was in.'

'I think that's what happened here. I saw the amalgam cylinder levitate when the device was turned on. What if the field around the amalgam affected the tomb, too, like the pan in the experiment? While not actually lifting the massive structure, it simply made it *weigh* less.'

Kat's eyes widened. 'Triggering the pressure plate!'

'Exactly. Does that offer any clue on how to reopen the ramp?'

Kat slowly shook her head. 'Not unless we can move the tomb.'

RACHEL STARED unblinking as the timer ticked below one minute. 'There must be another way out,' she mumbled. 'There are no bones.'

Gray stared at her as if she had slipped a gear.

'Kat,' she said, 'you mentioned that someone had to pull the stabilising pin when the mechanism was first set, locking the ramp. Right?'

Kat nodded.

'Then he would have been trapped down here. So where are his bones?'

Gray clenched a fist. 'Another way out.'

'I think I just said that.' Rachel pulled a book of matches from her pocket. She struck a flame. 'All we have to do is find an opening, a secret tunnel.'

In seconds, they were all searching for a hidden exit.

Rachel tried not to glance at the timer, but failed: 00:22.

Gray squatted by the slab of haematite. He held a match low to the ground. 'Maybe it's beneath this rock.'

Monk and Gray grabbed the slab and heaved it up, legs straining.

Kat was on her knees. 'There's a narrow tunnel,' she said with relief.

'Get inside,' Gray ordered.

Kat waved Rachel down. Rachel squiggled feet first through the hole, and slid on her butt down a steep incline. Kat followed next, then Monk.

Rachel craned around, counting in her head. Four seconds remained.

Monk braced the slab with his back.

Gray dived head first between the man's planted legs. 'Now, Monk!'

Dropping, Monk let the slab's weight push him into the chute.

'Down! Down!' Gray urged. 'Get as much—'

The explosion cut out further words.

Rachel, still half turned, saw a wash of orange flames lick round the edges of the slab. She ignored caution and slid down the chute, uncontrolled.

Distantly a new noise intruded. A rumbling rush of water.

FIFTEEN MINUTES LATER, Gray helped Rachel climb out of the Tiber River. They shivered on the bank. Her teeth chattered. He hugged her close and rubbed her shoulders and back, warming her as best he could.

'I . . . I'm OK,' she said, but she leaned a bit further into him.

Monk and Kat slogged out of the river, wet and muddy.

The escape chute had dumped into an underground stream that emptied into a maze of channels. They had followed the downward flow, until at last they had reached a short stone passage that led to the Tiber.

Monk squeezed water from his shirt, glancing back at the channel. 'If they had a back door, why all the business with the Magi bones?'

Gray had considered the same question and had an answer. 'No one could find that back door by chance. These ancient alchemists hid the next clue in such a manner that the seeker not only had to solve the riddle, but have a basic understanding of the amalgam and its properties.'

'It was a test,' Rachel said, her shivering slowly subsiding. 'A trial of passage before you could move onward.'

Gray climbed the bank. He kept his arm round Rachel, helping her. At the top they saw St Peter's Basilica glowing golden against the night sky. Sirens blared and emergency lights flickered in hues of red and blue.

'Let's find out what happened,' Gray said.

AN HOUR LATER, Rachel sat wrapped in a warm, dry blanket in the offices of the Holy See's Secretary of State. Cardinal Spera, General Rende and a very relieved uncle had just listened to their preliminary account of events.

'And the Dragon Court is gone?' Gray asked.

'Even the bodies,' Vigor said. 'It took us ten minutes to break through the lower door. All we found were some discarded weapons. They must have left the way they came in . . . through the roof.'

'At least the bones of St Peter are safe,' Cardinal Spera said. 'The damage to the basilica and the necropolis can be repaired. If we had lost the relics . . .' He shook his head. 'We owe you all a large debt.'

'And no one in attendance at the memorial service died,' Rachel added.

Cardinal Spera absent-mindedly twisted his two gold rings. 'What about the cavern below the tomb?' he asked. 'What did you find?'

Rachel frowned. 'There was—'

'It was too dark to see clearly,' Gray said, cutting her off. 'There was a large slab that had some lines on it, but I suspect that the firebomb scorched the surface clean. We may never know what was there.'

Rachel understood his reluctance to speak plainly. The head prefect of the Archives had disappeared with the Dragon Court. If Prefetto Alberto worked with the Court, who else might be a part of the conspiracy?

Gray cleared his throat. 'If this debriefing is finished, I appreciate the Vatican's hospitality in offering us a suite of rooms.'

'Certainly.' The cardinal stood. 'I'll have someone show you there.'

'I'd also like to look round the Scavi myself. See if anything was missed.'

General Rende nodded. 'I can send you with one of my men.'

GRAY SEARCHED the mausoleum where he had hidden his gear. He found his pack where he had left it, unmolested. But his laptop was gone. Clearly someone had taken it. Only one person would steal the computer and leave the pack behind, someone conspicuously absent during the evening's events.

Seichan.

Gray stalked out of the necropolis and returned to the team's suite of rooms. The main room was opulent with gold leaf, embroidered furniture and rich tapestries. Kat sat in one of the chairs. Vigor in another. They had changed into thick white robes, as if this were a suite at the Ritz.

'Monk's in the bath,' Kat said, nodding to one side.

'As is Rachel,' Vigor added, pointing an arm towards the other side. All their rooms shared this common living space.

Gray felt too filthy to sit in any of the chairs, so he paced the room. 'Vigor, can you get us out of here unseen in the morning?'

'I . . . guess so. If need be. Why?'

'I want us off the map again as soon as possible. The less anyone knows of our whereabouts, the better.'

Monk entered the room. 'We going somewhere?' A butterfly bandage closed the cut over his eye. He, too, wore a white robe.

Before Gray could answer, the door on the opposite side opened. Rachel entered, barefoot and robed, her sash tied snugly. But as she strode towards the group, her robe showed calf and much of her thigh. Her hair was wet and tousled. She finger-combed it into submission, but Gray liked it better wild.

'Commander?' Monk asked, dropping heavily into a chair.

Gray took a deep swallow. *What was I saying?*

'Where are we going?' Kat prompted him.

'To find the next clue on this journey,' Gray said, clearing his throat.

Monk picked at his bandage. 'What the hell happened tonight?'

'I may have some idea.' Gray's words drew all their full attention. 'Is anyone familiar with Meissner fields?'

'I've heard that term used in reference to superconductors,' Kat said.

Gray nodded. 'When a charged superconductor is exposed to a strong electromagnetic field, a Meissner field develops. The strength of this field is proportional to the intensity of the magnetic field and the amount of power in the superconductor. It is a Meissner field that allows superconductors to levitate in a magnetic field. But other, stranger effects have been seen. Inexplicable energy bursts, true antigravity, even distortions in space.'

'Is that what happened in the basilica?' Vigor asked.

'The activation of the amalgam, both here and in Cologne, was accomplished with nothing more than a pair of large electromagnetic plates.'

Kat stirred. 'And the released energy—this Meissner field—levitated the tomb . . . or at least made it weigh less. But what about the electrical storm inside the basilica?'

'I can only guess. The bronze and gold canopy over the papal altar sits directly above St Peter's tomb. I think the metal columns of the canopy acted like giant lightning rods. They siphoned some of the energy given off below and blasted it upward.'

'But why would the ancient alchemists want to harm the basilica?'

'They wouldn't,' Vigor answered. 'Bernini's *baldacchino* was installed centuries later, in the 1600s. The electrical storm was an unfortunate accident.'

'Unlike what happened in Cologne,' Gray countered. 'The Dragon Court purposely tainted those Communion wafers with m-state gold. I think they used the parishioners as guinea pigs in some vile experiment. Their first *field* test. To judge the strength of the amalgam. The ingested m-state gold acted like the bronze canopy here. It absorbed the energy of the Meissner field, electrocuting the parishioners from the inside out.'

'We must stop them,' Vigor asserted, his voice brittle.

Gray nodded. 'But first we have to figure out where to go next. I memorised the drawing. I can sketch it out.'

Rachel glanced at him, then over to her uncle, who pulled forth a folded piece of paper. On it was a map of Europe.

'I recognised the line drawing on the rock,' Rachel said. 'The tiny river delta gave it away. Watch.'

She leaned forward and made a square box of her fingers, as if she were sizing up a photo shot. She laid it atop the eastern end of the map.

Gray stared down, frowning. The enclosed section of the coastline was a rough match to the etched line drawing on the haematite slab.

'It's a map,' he said.

'And the glowing star . . .' Rachel met his eyes.

'There must have been a tiny deposit of m-state gold embedded in the slab. It absorbed the Meissner field energy and ignited.'

'Marking a spot on the map.' Rachel placed a finger on the paper.

Gray leaned closer. A city lay at her fingertip, at the mouth of the Nile.

'Alexandria,' Gray read. 'In Egypt.'

'Once the home of the famed Library of Alexandria,' Vigor said. 'Founded by Alexander the Great himself.'

Gray straightened. 'Alexander. You mentioned he was one of the historical figures who knew about the white powder of gold. Another mage. Could he be the *fourth* mage we were instructed to seek?'

'I can't say for sure,' Vigor answered.

'I can,' Rachel replied. 'The riddle specifically refers to a *lost king*.'

Gray remembered the riddle about the fish. *Where it drowns, it floats in darkness and stares at the lost king.*

Rachel explained, 'Alexander died at thirty-three. His funeral and internment were well documented in the historical record. His body was laid in state in Alexandria.' She tapped the map. 'Only, his tomb vanished.'

Gray stared down at the map. 'Making him the lost king,' he mumbled. His gaze swept the room. 'Then we know where we have to go next.'

THE IMAGE on the laptop played through once again. From the appearance of the Dragon Court, through to the escape of the Sigma team. Whatever lay below in St Peter's tomb remained a mystery.

Disappointed, he closed the laptop and leaned back from his desk.

Commander Pierce had not been entirely forthcoming at the debriefing. His lie had been easy to read. The commander had discovered something in the tomb. But what had he found? How much did he know?

Cardinal Spera leaned back, twisting the gold ring round his finger.

It was time to end all this.

July 26

8

Aboard the private jet, Gray inventoried his pack. Director Crowe had managed to outfit them with new supplies and weapons. Even laptops. They had left before dawn, sneaking out of the Vatican City without alerting anyone to their departure. The rented Citation X plane was following a dummy flight plan to Morocco. To cover their tracks their call sign would change in midflight as they turned for Egypt. There remained only one detail to iron out.

Where to begin their search in Alexandria?

To answer this, the Citation X's cabin had been turned into a research think tank. Kat, Rachel and Vigor all hunched over workstations. Monk was in the cockpit, coordinating transportation and logistics.

Gray stood and crossed to the trio of researchers. 'Any headway?'

Kat answered. 'Mystery still surrounds Alexander. Even his parentage. His father was King Philip II of Macedonia. But Alexander came to believe his father was the god Zeus Ammon, and that he himself was a demigod.'

'Not exactly humble,' Gray said.

Vigor took over. 'It was well known that his mother and father hated each other. Some historians believe his mother, Olympias, may have had a hand in assassinating Philip. Interestingly, one writer claimed Alexander was the son not of Philip, but an Egyptian magician to the court.'

'A magician . . . as in *magi*?' Gray understood the implication.

'Whoever his parents were,' Kat said, 'he was born on July 20, 356 BC.'

Vigor shrugged. 'But even that might not be true. On that same date, the Temple of Artemis in Ephesus burned down. One of the Seven Wonders of the ancient world. The historian Plutarch wrote that Artemis herself was "too busy taking care of the birth of Alexander to send help to her threatened temple". Some scholars believe the choice of date might be propaganda, the true date of Alexander's birth moved to match this portentous event, portraying the king as a phoenix rising from the ashes.'

'And a rise it was,' Kat said. 'Alexander conquered most of the known world during his short life. He defeated King Darius of Persia, then went on to Egypt, where he founded Alexandria, then on to Babylonia.'

Vigor finished: 'Eventually he moved east into India, to conquer the Punjab. The same region where St Thomas would baptise the Magi.'

'Uniting Egypt and India,' Gray noted.

'Connecting a line of ancient knowledge,' Rachel said.

'But his life was cut short,' Kat continued, drawing back Gray's attention. 'He died in 323 BC, in mysterious circumstances. In Babylon.'

'It is said,' Vigor added, 'that upon his deathbed in the royal palace of Babylon, he gazed out upon the city's famous Hanging Gardens. Another of the Seven Wonders of the ancient world.'

'So his life began with the destruction of one and ended at another.'

'It may just be allegorical,' Vigor conceded. 'But Alexander's history seems tied to the Seven Wonders. Even the first compilation of the Seven Wonders was made by an Alexandrian librarian in the third century BC. The towering bronze statue of Colossus that spanned the harbour in Rhodes, another of the Wonders, was modelled after Alexander. Then in Olympia there's the Statue of Zeus, whom Alexander claimed as his father, a four-storey figure of gold and marble. And there can be no doubt that Alexander visited the Pyramids of Giza. He spent a decade in Egypt. So Alexander's fingerprints seem to be all over these wonders of the ancient world.'

'Can this be significant?' Gray asked.

Vigor shrugged. 'I can't say. But Alexandria itself was once home to another of the Seven Wonders, though it no longer stands. The Pharos Lighthouse. It rose from a spit of land extending into the harbour of Alexandria. At its top, a fire burned in a brazier, amplified by a gold mirror.'

'How does this connect to our search for Alexander's tomb?' Gray asked.

'I can't help but think that the lighthouse, this shining symbol of a guiding light, would be significant to the ancient Magi.'

Gray needed something more concrete. 'Let's go directly to the heart of the mystery. Alexander died in Babylon. What happened after that?'

Kat spoke up. 'There are many historical references to the parade of his body from Babylon to Alexandria. Once entombed in Alexandria, it became a shrine for visiting dignitaries, including Julius Caesar.'

'During this time,' Vigor added, 'the city was ruled by one of Alexander's generals, Ptolemy, and his descendants. They established the Library of Alexandria and turned the city into a major site of philosophical study.'

'And what happened to the tomb?'

'That's what's intriguing,' Kat said. 'The tomb was supposedly a massive sarcophagus made of gold. But in other references, including the major historian of the time, Strabo, the tomb is described as being made of *glass*.'

'Perhaps golden glass,' Gray said.

Kat nodded. 'In the early third century AD, Septimus Severus closed the tomb from viewing, placing many secret books in the vault. It was a storehouse of secret arcana that Septimus feared would be lost or stolen.'

Vigor elaborated. 'There were many attacks upon Alexandria from the first century through to the third. These attacks continued until the eventual destruction and dissolution of the library in the seventh century. I can understand why Septimus hid the most important scrolls.'

'It wasn't just military aggressors that threatened the city,' Kat added. 'Frequent earthquakes damaged significant parts of Alexandria. A whole section of the city fell into the bay in the fourth century. Some archaeologists believe that Alexander's tomb sank into a watery grave.'

Frustrated, Gray paced the narrow cabin. 'So where do we look first?'

'I may have one hint,' Rachel said, speaking for the first time in a while. She was squinting at the screen in front of her. 'There is a reference back in the ninth century, testimony from the emperor of Constantinople, that some "fabulous treasure" was hidden within or under the Pharos Lighthouse.'

Vigor nodded, eyes glowing. 'What better place to hide something you don't want dug up than under a structure too important to tear down?'

'Then it all ended in August 1303, when a massive quake shook the eastern

Mediterranean. The lighthouse was destroyed, toppling into the harbour.'

'What became of the site?' Gray asked.

'In the fifteenth century, a Mamluk sultan built a fort on the peninsula. It still stands today, the Fort of Qait Bey. Some of its construction includes the original limestone blocks that made up the lighthouse.'

'And if the treasure was never found,' Vigor continued, 'then it must still be there . . . *beneath* the fort.'

'If it ever existed,' Gray warned.

'It's a place to start looking,' Vigor said.

'And what do we do? Knock on the door and ask them if it's OK to dig under their fort?'

'Maybe there's a back entrance,' Rachel suggested. 'One under water like in Rome. Tour groups dive on the sites near Qait Bey. We could blend in and search the underwater coastline of the harbour.'

Gray nodded slowly. It was a start.

Monk pushed into the cabin from the cockpit. 'I have a van and a hotel booked under our aliases, and customs has been cleared through some cooperation with Washington. I think that should take care of everything.'

'No.' Gray turned to him. 'We're going to need a boat. Something fast.'

Monk's eyes widened. 'OK,' he dragged out. His gaze settled on Rachel. 'But she's not going to be driving the damn thing, is she?'

THE HEAT did not help Raoul's mood. It was only 9 a.m. and already the temperature spiked. His naked body gleamed with sweat as he stood at the doors out to his room's balcony. The doors were open but no breeze moved.

He hated Rome. He despised the stupefying herds of tourists, the black-draped locals smoking continually, the honking cars. And now he had learned that the bastard American and his group had somehow escaped certain doom.

At the bedside table, the phone rang. He had been expecting this call. It was what had really soured his mood.

He crossed and picked up the cellphone. 'Raoul,' he said.

'I received the report from last night's mission.' As expected, it was the Imperator of his Order. His voice was stiff with fury.

'Sir—'

He was cut off. 'I won't accept any excuse. Failure is one thing, but insubordination will not be tolerated.'

Raoul frowned at this last. 'I would never disobey.'

'Then what about the woman, Rachel Verona?'

'Sir?' He pictured the black-haired bitch. He remembered the smell of the nape of her neck as he clutched her and threatened her with a knife. He had felt her heartbeat in her throat as he squeezed and lifted her to her toes.

'You were instructed to capture her . . . not kill her. The others were to be eliminated. Those were your orders.'

'Yes, sir. Understood. But three times now, I've been restrained from using full brutal force against the American team because of this caution. I need clarification. Which is more important: the mission or the woman?'

'You do make a good point.' The edge of fury had faded from the other's voice. 'The woman is important, but the mission must not be jeopardised. The wealth and power at the end of this trail must be ours.'

And Raoul knew why. It had been drilled into him since childhood. The ultimate goal of their sect. To bring about a New World Order, one led by their Court, descendants of kings and emperors, genetically pure and superior. For generations their Court had hunted for the treasure and arcane knowledge of this lost society of mages. Whoever possessed it would hold the 'keys to the world', or so it was written in the ancient texts.

Now they were so close.

Raoul spoke. 'Then I have the go-ahead to proceed without concern for the woman's security?'

'There will be disappointment in her loss,' the Imperator answered. 'But the mission must not fail. Is that plain enough?'

'Yes, sir.'

'Good. But I will also say that if the opportunity *should* arise where the woman could be captured, all the better. The Dragon blood runs strongly through her. In fact, she had been chosen to be your mate, Raoul. The Court sees great value in strengthening our lines through such a blood tie.'

Raoul pictured the woman clutched in his arms. The smell of her fear. She *would* make a good baroness—or at least an excellent brood mare.

'Everything has been arranged in Alexandria,' the Imperator finished. 'The endgame nears. Get what we need. Slay all who stand in your way.'

RACHEL STOOD behind the wheel of the speedboat, wind whipping her hair. Once past the No Wake buoy, she gunned the throttle and shot across the bay.

Their plane had landed forty minutes ago. They had breezed through customs, greased by Monk's calls, and had found the boat and gear already waiting for them at the pier to the East Harbour.

Rachel glanced behind her. The city of Alexandria rose from the arc of the sapphire-blue bay—a massive complex of glass, steel and concrete.

But ahead rose a citadel out of the Middle Ages, the Fort of Qait Bey. It crested a spit of land that divided the bay into halves. Built of white limestone and marble, it shone starkly against the deep blue waters of the bay.

Rachel pictured the structure that had once stood here: the forty-storey-tall Pharos Lighthouse, built in tiers like a wedding cake, decorated with a giant statue of Poseidon, and tipped by a giant fiery brazier.

Nothing remained of this Wonder of the ancient world, except perhaps for a few blocks built into the citadel. Archaeologists had also discovered a tumble of blocks in the East Harbour, along with a twenty-foot section of statue, believed to be the sculpture of Poseidon. It was all that was left of the Wonder since the earthquake devastated the region.

Or was it? Could there be another treasure, one dating even further back, hidden below the foundations? The lost tomb of Alexander the Great.

Behind Rachel, the others, all certified divers, were gathered over the pile of scuba gear, checking tanks, regulators and weight belts. They had mapped out the region into quadrants for a systematic exploration of the bay around the fort. They would search in shifts, rotating one person out to rest and guard the boat.

Rachel throttled down, approaching the first dive spot. Gray stepped next to her. He rested one hand on the seat back. His fingertips brushed her shoulder.

'This is quadrant A,' he said.

She nodded. 'I'll drop anchor here and raise the orange flag warning of divers in the water.'

She noted that he kept his hand at her shoulder.

It felt good there.

GRAY FELL BACKWARDS into the sea.

Water swamped over him. Not an inch of skin was exposed to the pollution and sewage that made these waters dangerous to explore without proper protection. The seams of the full-body suit were double-taped and double-sewn. The neck and wrist seals were heavy-duty latex. Even his AGA mask completely covered his face, sealing the Viking hood over his head. The regulator was built into its faceplate.

He watched Rachel and Vigor drop into the sea on the other side of the boat. Kat was already in the water on his side.

Gray tried the radio. 'Can everyone hear me?' he asked. 'Check in.'

He got positive responses all around, even from Monk, who had insisted on the first guard shift on the boat, and was monitoring the group on an Aqua-Vu marine infrared video system.

'We'll drop to the bottom here and sweep towards shore in a wide spread. Visual contact with each other at all times. Everyone knows their positions.'

Affirmatives answered.

'Down we go,' Gray said.

He vented the air in his buoyancy vest and lowered into the water, dragged down by his weight vest. When he reached the sandy bottom, he adjusted his buoyancy to keep himself drifting just above the seabed.

Then he set out. He had a dive knife in a sheath on the back of his wrist and a flashlight on the other. With the sun directly overhead there was no need for the extra illumination, but it would come in handy to explore nooks and crannies. As he swam he pondered on whether they'd missed some clue in the map drawn on the stone in St Peter's tomb. Then, out of the silty gloom, a shape appeared ahead, jutting from the sandy bottom.

A rock? A ridge of reef? He kicked forward.

What the hell . . . ?

The stone face stared back at him, human, worn by the sea and time but its features surprisingly clear. Its upper torso rode atop the squat form of a lion.

Kat had noted his attention and swept slightly closer. 'A sphinx?'

'Another one over here,' Vigor announced. 'Broken, on its side. Divers have reported dozens of them littered around the seabed in the shadow of the fort. Some of the decorations from the original lighthouse. Fitting that these masters of riddles should be guarding this mystery.'

'What do you mean?' Gray asked.

A chuckle. 'Don't you know the story of the Sphinx? The monster terrorised the people of Thebes, eating them if they couldn't solve its riddle. "What has one voice, and is four-footed, two-footed and three-footed?"'

'And the answer?'

'Mankind,' Kat said next to him. 'We crawl on all fours as babes, then upright on two feet as adults, and lean upon a staff in old age.'

Gray pushed away from the stone statue. They had their own riddle to solve. After ten minutes of searching, they reached the rocky coastline. They had come across a tumble of giant blocks, but no passage, no opening.

'Back again,' Gray said.

They shifted down the coast twenty-five metres and set out again, swimming away from the shoreline towards the boat. They continued, back and forth, quadrant by quadrant, for another forty minutes.

'This just doesn't seem right,' Gray murmured.

The radio transmitted his voice.

'Did you find something?' Kat asked. Her shadowy form drifted closer.

'No, that's just it. The longer I'm down here, the more I'm convinced we're doing this wrong. This whole searching quadrant by quadrant . . .'

While some problems were best solved by dogged methodology, he was sure this mystery wasn't one of them.

'We've missed a clue,' he went on. 'I know it. We recognised the map in the tomb, realised it pointed to Alexander's tomb, then flew here, hoping to solve in one day a riddle that has baffled historians for more than a millennium using historical records available to anyone. The only advantage we have over all the treasure hunters of the past centuries is what was discovered under St Peter's tomb. We missed a clue down there, I'm certain.'

'Maybe we didn't miss a clue at the tomb,' Vigor said. 'Maybe we didn't look deep enough. Remember the catacombs. The riddles were multilayered, multifathomed. Could there be another layer to this riddle?'

Silence answered him, until an unexpected voice spoke up.

'That goddamn fiery star,' Monk swore. 'It wasn't just pointing down at the city of Alexandria . . . it was pointing down at the stone slab too.'

Gray felt the ring of truth in Monk's words. They had been so focused on the inscribed map, they had ignored the unusual medium of the artist.

'Haematite,' Kat said, her voice strained. 'I'm sorry, Commander. I should have thought of it. The iron in haematite is often weakly *magnetic*. Not as strongly as magnetite, but it's sometimes used as a lodestone.'

Gray realised the implication. Magnetism had also opened the first tomb. 'So the star wasn't just pointing to Alexandria, it was pointing to a magnetised stone, something we're supposed to find.'

'And what did the ancient world do with lodestones?' Vigor asked.

Gray knew the answer. 'They made compasses! Everyone topside!'

IN MINUTES, they were shedding tanks, vests and weight belts. Rachel climbed into the pilot's seat and pressed the button to raise the anchor.

'I'll watch the compass,' Gray said. 'You keep us on a slow circuit round the fort. Any twitch on the compass needle and we'll anchor and search below.'

'What if the stone isn't out here?' Rachel whispered to Gray as she eased the throttle to the barest chop of her propellers. 'What if it's inside the fort?'

'Then we'll search there next,' Gray said.

In the shade of the boat's canopy, Vigor massaged a calf muscle sore from the swim. 'I think the ultimate question of where the stone might lie—on land or in the water—depends on *when* the alchemists hid the clue. Was it before or after the Pharos Lighthouse collapsed in 1303?'

No one had an answer.

But a few minutes later, the compass needle gave a shaky twitch.

'Hold it!' Gray hissed.

The needle steadied again.

Gray placed a hand on Rachel's shoulder. 'Go back.'

Rachel tweaked the throttle into neutral and let the waves bob them back. The needle pitched again, swinging a full quarter turn.

'Drop anchor,' Gray ordered.

Everyone began to move at once, grabbing fresh tanks. Monk, who had been snoring on the portside beach, woke up with a start.

'Looks like you're on guard duty again,' Gray told him.

Once the orange flag was raised, the four divers fell back into the water.

Gray's voice reached them through the radio. 'Watch your wrist compasses. Zero in on the anomaly.'

The water was fairly shallow here. Less than ten metres. Rachel reached the sandy bottom quickly. The others dropped around her.

'Nothing's here,' Kat said.

The seabed was a flat expanse of sand.

Rachel stared at her compass. She kicked a body length away, then back again. 'The anomaly is right here.'

Gray swept his wrist over the bottom. 'She's right.'

He unsheathed his knife and began stabbing into the soft sand. The blade sank to the hilt each time. Silt stirred up, clouding the view.

On his seventh stab, the knife plainly jarred.

'Got something,' Gray said.

He sheathed the knife and began digging in the sand. The view grew quickly murky, and Rachel lost sight of him. Then she heard him gasp.

The disturbed sand dispersed and settled.

Protruding from the sand was a dark bust of a man.

'I think that's magnetite,' Kat said, studying the stone of the sculpture. She swept her wrist compass over the bust. The needle twirled. 'Lodestone.'

Rachel edged closer, staring at the face. There was no mistaking the features. She had seen the same countenance already today.

Gray recognised it too. 'It's another sphinx.' He spent ten minutes clearing the shoulders and upper torso, revealing the lion shape below.

'Hidden among the others,' Vigor said. 'I guess that answers the question of when the alchemists hid their treasure here.'

'After the lighthouse collapsed,' said Gray.

'Exactly. They must have known the location of Alexander's tomb after Septimus Severus hid it in the third century. They left it undisturbed, letting it safeguard the most valuable scrolls from the lost library. Then perhaps the quake in 1303 not only brought down the lighthouse but exposed the tomb. They took the opportunity to hide more there, to plant their next clue and allow the centuries to cover it up. And just as the clues that led to St Peter's tomb were buried in the stories of Catholicism, the clues here might be tied to Greek mythology. Why else mark the gateway with a sphinx?'

'The riddle masters of the Greeks,' Gray mumbled.

'And the monsters killed you outright if you didn't answer them correctly,' Vigor reminded them. 'Perhaps choosing this symbol is a warning.'

SEICHAN STARED out of the window as the Gulfstream IV jet tilted on a wing over the violet-blue of the Mediterranean and lined up for the final approach to the runway at Alexandria airport.

Raoul appeared to her left. 'What's the word from your contact on the ground?' he asked. He must have noted her using the jet's air-phone.

She fingered the dragon charm on her necklace. 'The others are still in the water. If you're lucky, they may solve this mystery for you.'

'We won't need them for that.' Raoul stepped back to join his men, a team of sixteen, including the Court's master adept.

Seichan had already met the esteemed Vatican bibliophile Dr Alberto Menardi, a lanky, silver-haired man with a pocked complexion, narrow eyes. He sat in the back of the plane, nursing a broken nose. She had a full dossier on him. His ties to the Sicilian Mafia ran deep. It seemed even the Vatican could not keep such weeds from taking root in their soil. Then again, she could not discount that he had a keen edge to his mind.

It had been Dr Menardi who, fifteen years ago, had discerned from the Dragon Court's library of Gnostic texts the ability of electromagnetism to unlock the energy of superconducting metals. He had overseen the research project in Lausanne, Switzerland, and tested the effects on animal, vegetable and mineral. And the occasional lone backpacker.

The plane began its final descent. Somewhere below, the Sigma team laboured. They were no threat.

It would be as easy as shooting fish in a barrel.

9

'Remember that damn fish,' Monk radioed from the boat above.

Twelve feet down, Gray frowned up at the bobbing keel over head. They had been discussing how to move a ton of stone.

'What fish are you talking about, Monk?' Gray asked.

'The painted fish in the catacombs,' Monk answered. 'I can see you guys and the statue through the Aqua-Vu camera. The sphinx is facing *towards* that big fort. Maybe it's facing towards the tunnel opening.'

'Monk could be right,' Vigor said. 'The sphinx may be nothing but a magnetic road marker.'

'There's only one way to find out,' Gray said. 'Monk, keep the boat anchored here until we're sure. We'll swim towards shore.'

Gray set off. The others trailed behind him. They stuck close together.

The shore was not far. The spit of land rose steeply. The sandy bottom ended abruptly at a tumbled maze of stone blocks. Man-made. Barnacles and anemones had taken over the area, forming their own reef.

Gray kicked off the bottom, travelling up the reefscape. He kept one arm fixed in front of him, watching the wrist compass. Passing over one block, his compass needle pitched and rolled. He was only four metres from the surface. The front of the block was nearly a metre square.

'Here,' he said, and the others joined him.

Kat took a blade and scraped off the crust of sea life. 'Haematite again.'

'Monk,' Gray said. 'Bring the boat over here and drop anchor.'

'On my way.'

Gray searched the edges of the block. It was cemented to its neighbours—by coral, sand and dense accumulations of rough-shelled mussels.

'Everyone pick a side and dig the edges clear,' he ordered.

In a couple of minutes, the block was cleared.

The beat of a propeller echoed leadenly through the water.

Monk approached the shoreline slowly. 'I can see you guys,' he said.

'Lower the anchor,' Gray said. 'Slowly.'

As the steel prong dropped from the keel, Gray swam over and guided it into a gap between the haematite block and its neighbour.

'Winch it up,' he ordered.

Monk retracted the anchor line. It grew taut. Then the chunk of stone tipped loose and rolled down the cliff face, landing heavily on the sandy floor.

When the billowing silt had cleared, Gray flicked on the flashlight on his wrist, pointing it into the opening left by the dislodged stone. The light illuminated a tunnel, angled upwards. It was a tight squeeze. No room for air tanks.

Gray took a deep breath, shimmied out of his air tank and settled it on a shelf of rock. 'I'll be right back.' He turned to face the tunnel.

He remembered the riddle of the Sphinx. How it described the first stage of man. Crawling on all fours. It was a fitting way to enter.

GRAY'S VOICE sounded excited. 'The tunnel is short,' he said. 'Take a deep breath, kick with your fins a bit and you'll pop right up here.'

'What did you find?' Vigor asked.

'Some stone tunnels. I'm going to push forward and explore.'

'I'm going with you,' Rachel blurted out.

'First let me make sure it's safe.'

Rachel shrugged out of her air tank and vest and propped them into a crevice. Gray wasn't the only bold one. 'I'm coming up.'

'Me too,' her uncle said.

In a matter of moments Rachel popped out into a small circular pool.

Gray was standing on the stone bank that lipped the pool. A drum-shaped chamber opened around her. A man-made cave. The roof was corbelled in narrowing rings. It was like being inside a tiny step pyramid.

Gray hauled her out. 'You shouldn't have come,' he said.

'And you shouldn't have gone,' she countered, eyeing the stone cave.

A moment later, Vigor appeared, splashing up into the pool. Gray sighed. He should have known better than to try to keep these two away.

Rachel shed her mask, and bent to help her uncle out of the pool.

Keeping his mask in place, Gray ducked his head under the water. The radio worked best with water contact. 'Kat, maintain a post by the tunnel exit. Once we're out of the water, we'll lose communication pretty quickly. Monk, if there's any trouble, relay it to Kat, so she can fetch us.'

Receiving affirmatives from both.

Vigor was touching the blocks that made up one wall. 'Limestone. Cut and fitted tightly, but feel . . . the blocks are cemented with lead. According to the historical record, this is the same design as the Pharos Lighthouse.'

Rachel stared around her. 'This might be part of the original lighthouse, perhaps a subfloor or basement cellar.'

Two tunnels led out from here, angled apart. One was taller than the other, but narrower. Vigor headed for the closest tunnel, the lower of the two.

'Let's see where this leads.'

Gray blocked him with an arm. 'Me first.'

He took a step forward, hunched beneath the low roof, but then froze.

Vigor bumped into him from behind.

'Back, back, back . . .' Gray urged, retreating.

'What?' Vigor asked but obeyed.

'You ever hear of the story about the man who had to choose between two doors, behind one hid a tiger, the other a lady?'

Rachel and Vigor nodded.

'I think we face a similar dilemma. Two doors.' Gray pointed to each dark tunnel. 'Remember the riddle of the Sphinx, marking the ages of man? Crawling, upright and bent over. It took crawling to get into here.' Gray recalled entering the tunnel. 'Now two ways lead forward. I'd prefer we take the other tunnel first. The one where you walk upright, the *second* stage of man.'

Vigor eyed the tunnel they had been about to enter. As an archaeologist, he knew all about booby-trapped tombs. He nodded.

Gray led the way into the other tunnel. It made a series of sharp jags, but eventually his light revealed a large space opening up ahead.

ON THE MONITOR of the Aqua-Vu camera, Monk watched Kat cooling her heels by the tunnel entrance. As he spied, she stretched a leg, turning a thigh, accentuating the long curve of her body.

He trailed a finger down the screen of the monitor. A perfect S.

He shook his head and turned away. Who was he fooling?

Squinting against the midday glare, he searched the flat expanse of blue water. Motion caught his eye. Coming round the far side of the peninsula. A sleek, midnight-blue thirty-foot Hydrofoil skimmed over the water.

Monk followed its curve round the spit of land. Maybe it was some rich Arab's private yacht. He raised a pair of binoculars.

In the bow, he spotted a pair of girls in bikinis. He had already surveyed a few of the other boats around the harbour, fixing them in place in his mental chessboard. One yacht had a party in full swing. Another houseboat-like craft had an older couple lounging about buck naked.

'Monk,' Kat called from the radio.

He wore a headset. 'What is it, Kat?'

'I'm picking up a pulsing note of static over the radio. Is that you?'

He lowered the binoculars. 'It's not me. You might be picking up someone's fish finder.' He reset the channel. 'How's that?' he asked.

Kat answered. 'Better. It's gone now. Thanks.'

Monk eyed her form on the camera screen and sighed. What was the use? He picked up his binoculars. Where were those two bikini-clad girls?

RACHEL STEPPED LAST into the chamber. The two men parted to either side in front of her. Vigor had flicked on his flashlight.

The spears of light illuminated another drum-shaped room, domed above. The ceiling plaster had been painted black, and silver stars, all metallic inlays, glowed brightly against the dark background.

The ceiling was reflected in a still pool of water that covered the entire floor. It created a mirage of a perfect sphere of stars, above and below.

But that wasn't the most amazing sight. In the middle of the chamber, rising from the water, stood a pyramid of glass, as tall as a man. It seemed to float in the centre of the phantom sphere and glinted with a familiar hue.

'Gold glass,' Gray said. 'A giant superconductor.'

They spread out along the lip of stone that surrounded the pool. Four copper pots, possibly ancient lamps, rested at the water's edge.

Rachel studied the pyramid. It was square-bottomed, four-sided, like the pyramids of Giza. 'Something's inside it,' she said, and hopped into the water. It was a little more than knee-deep.

She waded towards the pyramid, splashes behind her announcing that the others were following. When they reached the glass structure, her uncle and Gray repositioned their lamps to penetrate the pyramid.

Two shapes appeared.

One stood in the exact centre of the pyramid. It was a bronze sculpture of a giant finger, raised and pointing up.

Below the finger, a figure, crowned and masked in gold and robed in a flow of white gown, lay upon a stone altar. The arms stretched out to either side, Christlike. But the golden face was distinctly Greek.

Rachel turned to her uncle. 'Alexander the Great.'

Vigor's face glistened with tears. 'His glass tomb.'

'What's with the bronze finger?' Gray asked.

'I think it's from the Colossus of Rhodes,' Vigor said, 'the giant statue that was modelled on Alexander the Great. No part of it was thought still to exist. I think *all* of this is a testament to Alexander, and to the knowledge he helped foster. It was at the Library of Alexandria that Euclid discovered the rules of geometry. All around are triangles, pyramids, circles.'

Vigor then pointed up and down. 'The reflected sphere split by water harkens to Eratosthenes, who at Alexandria calculated the diameter of the Earth. Even the water here . . . it must be fed through small channels to keep this pool full. It was at the library that Archimedes designed the first screw-shaped water pump, which is still in use today. All of this is a monument to Alexander and the lost Library of Alexandria.'

'Weren't there supposed to be important scrolls down here?' Rachel said.

Vigor searched around. 'They must have been cleared out after the quake. When the clues were planted here.'

'Before we move on,' Gray said, 'we first must solve this riddle.'

'No,' Vigor said. 'The riddle is not even exposed yet. Remember St Peter's. We must pass a test. Prove our knowledge, like the Dragon Court did with their understanding of magnetism. Only after that was the secret revealed.'

'Then what are we supposed to do?' Gray asked.

The monsignor stepped back. 'We have to activate this pyramid.'

'And how do we go about doing that?'

Vigor turned to Gray. 'I need some soda.'

GRAY HELPED KAT climb out of the entry pool. She had ferried up the last of the cans of Coke, making a total of four six-packs.

'Would you care to explain now?' Gray asked, when they were all back at Alexander's tomb.

Vigor nodded. 'An understanding of magnetism opened the first tomb,' he said. 'It even led us here. A magnetic marker left underwater. Here, another scientific wonder must be demonstrated.'

He pointed to a copper urn at the pool's edge. There were four of them. 'Each of you take a six-pack of soda and take up a post by the jars.'

'Care to tell us what we're doing?' Gray asked as he reached his jar.

Vigor nodded. 'What we demonstrate here is the knowledge of a force the Greeks called *electrikus*. A name for the static charge of a cloth rubbed over amber. They witnessed it in the form of lightning, and along the masts of their sailing ships as St Elmo's fire.'

'Electricity,' Gray said.

Vigor nodded. 'In 1938, German archaeologist Wilhelm Koenig discovered a number of curious clay jars in the National Museum of Iraq, said to be from Persia, homeland of our biblical Magi. The odd thing about the tiny jars was that they were plugged with asphalt, and from the top protruded a copper cylinder with an iron rod inside, the exact conformation of battery cells. They were known as "the Baghdad Batteries".'

Gray shook his head. 'Ancient Duracell coppertops?'

'*Science Digest* magazine replicated these jars in 1957. They primed them with vinegar, and the jars gave off electricity.'

Gray stared down at the copper jars resting in the sea-water pool. He noted the iron rods sticking out of the top. If the monsignor was right, electricity from these batteries would flow through the water to the pyramid.

'Why don't we just jump-start the pyramid?' Kat said. 'Bring down a marine battery from the boat?'

Vigor shook his head. 'I think the activation is tied to the amount of current and the position of the batteries. We should stick to the original design.'

Gray agreed. He remembered the quake. 'So what do we do?' he asked.

Vigor popped the top to one of his Coke cans. 'On my count, we fill up the empty batteries.' He stared around the group. 'Oh, and stand well back.'

GRAY EMPTIED his third can into the cylinder core of his jar. Soon Coke was bubbling down the copper side of the battery. Full.

The others finished about the same time, and moved back.

A bit of carbonation frothed out of the tops of all the cylinders. Then a spark danced from the tip of the iron rod of Gray's jar and cascaded down the copper surface, only to fizzle out in the sea water.

Similar weak pyrotechnics drizzled from the other batteries.

'It may take a few minutes.' Vigor's voice had lost its confident edge.

Gray frowned. 'I don't think this is going to—'

Simultaneously from all four batteries, brilliant arcs of electricity crackled through the water. They struck the four sides of the pyramid.

A blast of force thumped outwards from the pyramid, throwing Gray bodily against the wall. The pressure made it feel like he was on his back, the pyramid above him, a topsy-turvy amusement ride. Yet Gray knew what held him. A Meissner field, a force that could levitate tombs.

Then the true fireworks began. From all surfaces of the pyramid, great bursts of lightning crackled to the ceiling, seeming to strike the silver stars embedded there. Jolts also lanced into the reflecting pool.

Gray felt the image burning into his retina, but he refused to close his eyes. It was worth the risk of blindness. Where the lightning struck the water, flames erupted and danced across the pool's surface.

He knew what he was witnessing. The electrolysis of water into hydrogen and oxygen. The released gas then ignited, set alight by the play of energies here. Theoretically, a superconductor could store energy, even light, within its matrix for an infinite span of time.

The energies suddenly died away. The world swung back upright as the Meissner field expired and Gray's body was released.

Vigor pointed to the ceiling. 'Look.'

Gray craned. The black paint and stars persisted, but now strange letters glowed in a fiery script across the dome of the roof.

όπως είναι ανωτέρω, έτσι είναι κατωτέρω

'It's the clue,' Rachel said.

As they stared, the letters faded rapidly. Like the fiery pyre atop the black haematite slab at St Peter's, the revelation would last only a brief time.

Gray hurried to free his underwater camera. They needed a record.

Vigor stayed his hand. 'I know what it says. It's Greek. A phrase attributed to Plato, describing how the stars affect us and are in fact a reflection of us. It became the foundation for astrology and the cornerstone of Gnostic belief: "As it is above, so it is below." '

Gray stared at the starry ceiling and at its reflection in the water. Above and below. 'But what does it mean?'

Rachel had wandered round to the other side of the pyramid. 'Look! Over here!' she shouted.

They waded round the edge of the pyramid, and Gray saw what had excited her. A section of the pyramid, six inches square, had vanished midway up one face, dissolved, consumed during the firestorm. Resting inside the hollow lay one of Alexander's outstretched hands, closed in a fist. Between the clenched fingers, a bit of gold glinted.

Rachel reached for it, but Gray motioned her away. 'Let me,' he said.

Glad he was still wearing his diving gloves, he reached out and broke off one of the fingers, earning a gasp from Vigor. It couldn't be helped.

From the fist, Gray removed a heavy, three-inch-long gold key.

'A key,' Kat said. 'But to what lock?'

Gray stepped back. 'To wherever we must go next.' His eyes wandered to the ceiling to where the letters had faded away.

'As it is above, so it is below,' Vigor repeated.

'But what is the significance?' Gray said. 'Where does it tell us to go?'

Rachel slowly turned in a circle, surveying the room. She stopped, her gaze fixed on Gray. Her eyes shone brightly. 'I know where to start.'

IN THE RAISED pilot compartment of the hydrofoil, Raoul zipped himself into his wet suit. The boat was owned by the Guild. It had cost the Dragon Court a small fortune to rent it, but there could be no mistakes today.

'Bring us in along a sweeping curve as near as possible without raising suspicion,' he ordered the captain, a swarthy Afrikaner.

Two young women, one black, one white, flanked the man. They were dressed in bikinis, but their eyes glinted with the promise of deadly force.

The captain shifted the wheel and the craft angled to the side.

Raoul clambered down to the lower deck, where his twelve-man dive team waited. His other three men would operate the strafing guns. Dr Alberto Menardi was in one of the cabins, preparing to unravel the riddles.

And there was one unwelcome addition to the team. The woman.

Seichan stood with her wet suit half-unzipped, her breasts barely concealed behind the Neoprene. She stood beside her Aquanaut sled. The tiny jet-propelled sleds could skim a diver through water at breakneck speed.

The Eurasian woman had insisted on accompanying the assault team. 'Only to observe and offer advice,' she had purred. 'Nothing more.'

They would go overboard as the hydrofoil slowed to turn round the peninsula, just sightseers getting a closer look at the old fort.

Seichan tugged her zipper up. 'Our radio man has intermittently jammed their comms. So when their radios go out, they'll be less suspicious.'

Raoul nodded. She had her uses, he'd give her that.

BACK IN THE ENTRANCE to Alexander's tomb, Rachel knelt on the stone floor and worked on her project. Kat had gone topside to check in with Monk, while Vigor finished his own inspection of the tomb chamber.

'I don't think it will fire like that again,' he said.

Gray nodded. 'The pyramid acted like a capacitor. It stored its energy in its superconducting matrix . . . until the charge was released by the shock.'

'That means,' Vigor said, 'that even if the Dragon Court discovers this chamber, they'll never be able to raise the riddle.'

'Or gain the gold key,' Gray said. 'We're finally a full step ahead of them.'

'But first we have to solve this riddle,' Rachel reminded him.

Gray came over to her. 'What are you working on?'

She had a map of the eastern Mediterranean spread on the stones. With a black felt pen, she had drawn dots on the map and assigned names to each.

She sat back. 'The phrase—"as it is above, so it is below"—was originally meant to bring the star's positions into our own lives.'

'Astrology,' Gray said.

'Not exactly,' Vigor argued. 'The stars truly ruled ancient civilisations. Constellations were the timekeepers of seasons, the guideposts for travel, the home of the gods. Civilisations honoured them by building their monuments as a reflection of the starry night. A theory about the three pyramids of Giza is that they were aligned to match the three stars of Orion's belt.'

'So we're looking for patterns,' Gray said. 'In the sky or on the Earth.'

'And the tomb is telling us what to pay attention to,' Rachel said.

Her uncle had figured it out, too. 'The bronze finger of the Colossus,' he said, staring at the tomb. 'The pyramid like the one at Giza. The remnants of the Pharos Lighthouse. Even the drum-shaped tomb might hark back to the Mausoleum of Halicarnassus.'

'I'm sorry,' Gray said with a frown. 'The mausoleum of what?'

'One of the Seven Wonders,' Rachel said. 'Alexander was tied to them all.'

'Right. His birth coinciding with one and his death another.'

Vigor nodded. 'The Temple of Artemis, and the Hanging Gardens of Babylon. They're all connected to Alexander . . . to here.'

Rachel pointed to the map she was working on. 'I've marked their locations. They're all in the region mapped out on the haematite slab.'

Gray studied the map. 'Are you saying we're supposed to be looking for a pattern among the seven of them? Where do we begin?'

'Time,' Rachel said. 'Or rather the progression of time, as hinted at by the Sphinx's riddle. Moving from birth to death.'

Gray's eyes widened. 'Chronological order. When the Wonders were built.'

Vigor knelt and took the felt pen. 'Rachel is right. The first clue to all this was hidden in a book in Cairo, near Giza. The pyramids are also the oldest of the Seven Wonders. And this tomb lies under the Pharos Lighthouse, the last of the Wonders to be built.' He placed the tip of the pen on Giza, then drew lines connecting the Seven Wonders in order of construction. 'From Giza to Babylon, then on to Olympia, where the statue of Zeus towered. From there, to Artemis's Temple at Ephesus, then Halicarnassus, then the island of Rhodes . . . until at last we reach Alexandria.' He leaned back. 'Is anyone still wondering if we're not on the right track?'

Rachel and Gray stared at his handiwork.

'It forms two triangles, like an hourglass,' Rachel said.

Vigor nodded. 'The symbol for the passage of time itself.'

'But does it point to the next location?' Rachel asked.

Gray knelt down. 'It's my turn at the map.'

'You have an idea?' Vigor said.

'You don't have to sound so shocked.'

Felt pen in hand, Gray set to work. 'That bronze finger is in the exact centre of the room, under the dome, right? Symbolically it's the axis round which the world spins. Now look at the map. What is at the centre of the hourglass?'

Rachel leaned closer. 'The island of Rhodes. Where the finger came from.'

'I think we're supposed to find the axis through the hourglass,' Gray said.

He took the felt pen and drew a line bisecting both triangles of the hourglass. Using his knife as a straight edge, he extended the line northwest.

His pen stopped at Rome. 'It must be Rome where we have to go next.'

Vigor shook his head. 'Can I borrow your knife, Commander?'

Gray handed it over, glad to let the monsignor usurp his position.

'Remember the multiple layers of riddles here. We have to look deeper.' Vigor dragged his finger along the edge of the knife blade, extending the line past Rome. 'Rome was only the first stop.' He continued the imaginary line further northwest, into France. He halted at a spot just beyond Marseilles, and smiled. 'Avignon,' he said.

Rachel gasped. 'Avignon is the place in France to which the papacy was exiled in the early fourteenth century.'

'How can we be sure?' Gray said. 'Are we reading too much into it?'

Vigor waved away his concern. 'Remember, we had already pinpointed the time when we thought the clues were planted, when the papacy left Rome. The first decade of the fourteenth century. The alchemists left us another layer to the riddle to help establish this location.' Vigor pointed to the shape on the map. 'When do you think the hourglass was invented?'

Gray shook his head. 'At least a couple of thousand years ago . . .'

'Oddly enough, the hourglass's invention matched the time of the first mechanical clocks. Only seven hundred years ago. Marking time, as all hourglasses should do, back to the founding of the French papacy.'

Gray felt a thrill chase through him. Now they knew where they needed to go next. With the gold key. To Avignon, to the French Vatican.

'Let's get out of here,' Gray said, and led them quickly down the tunnel to the entry pool. In the far chamber, he slid his mask on and ducked his head underwater, preparing to let the others know the good news.

Immediately, his radio started buzzing, irritating and loud. 'Monk . . . can anyone hear me?'

There was no answer. He listened for a moment longer, his heart thudding in his chest. That white noise wasn't static. They were being jammed.

10

Monk engaged the boat's engine while maintaining a watch for the hydrofoil through his binoculars. It had just vanished behind the tip of the peninsula. Only a few seconds ago he had watched it slow suspiciously, 200 metres away. There had been no telltale activity on deck, but he had noted a rippling line of bubbles in the craft's wake as it glided away.

Then he'd heard the whine over the radio.

A few seconds later, Kat bobbed up in the water beside the boat.

'The radio—' she started.

'Kat, something's wrong,' he shouted, cutting her off. 'Get the others.'

She reacted instantly, flipping down beneath the waves.

They needed to get out of here. Monk knew it in his gut.

'Monk!' a voice called. It was Gray surfacing to port side.

He began to lower his binoculars when he spotted an object streaking through the water. A fin cleaved through the waves. A metal fin.

Dropping the binoculars, Monk shoved the throttle to full. The boat bucked forward with a scream of the engine. He twisted the wheel to starboard, away from Gray.

'Everybody down!' he screamed, and shoved his mask over his face.

With the boat canting away under him, he ran to the stern and jumped.

RACHEL HAD SURFACED just as Monk yelled. She watched him run to the stern. Reacting to his panic, she shoved back down and twisted to dive.

Then the explosion hit.

The concussion through the water stabbed her ears, even through her Neoprene hood. The air slammed out of her. Her mask's seals broke. Sea water rushed in. She scrambled back to the surface, eyes stinging.

With her head out of water, she emptied her mask, coughing and gagging. Debris continued to rain down into the water. Smoking flotsam steamed and rocked. Flaming rivers of gasoline skimmed the waves.

To her left, a flailing shape burst out of the water. It was Monk.

She paddled over to him and grabbed an arm. His face mask had been turned half round his head. She steadied him as he gagged.

A new noise travelled over the water. Both turned. Rachel watched a hydrofoil swing round the fort, tilted up on its skids. It circled towards them.

'Down!' Monk urged.

They fled together under the water, heading in the direction of the tunnel entrance, lost in the murk stirred up by the explosion. They needed to reach the abandoned scuba tanks, a source of air.

Illumination bloomed in the gloom ahead. Rachel moved instinctively towards it, hoping to find her uncle or Gray. Out of the murk, a pair of divers swept into view, leaning on motorised sleds.

The divers swung out to trap them against the shore.

Lit by their lamps, steel arrowheads glinted. Spearguns.

Rachel held her palms up, towards the divers.

VIGOR WAS DAZED. He had knocked into Gray when the boat exploded. The monsignor had taken a chunk of Fibreglass to the side of his head, slicing through his Neoprene suit. Blood flowed from the cut.

Gray had managed to reach the abandoned air tanks and now helped hook the monsignor up. Vigor waved him off as soon as the air flowed. Gray swung to a second tank and rapidly reconnected his regulator.

He took several deep breaths. The Dragon Court would be here any second. Grabbing up his tank, Gray pointed away.

Vigor nodded, but his face searched the clouded waters.

Gray read his fear. Rachel.

They had to survive to be of any help. Gray guided Vigor along the cliff of boulders. Earlier he had noticed a sunken skiff about ten metres off. When the scuttled boat appeared he settled the monsignor in its shadow and motioned that he was going to search for the others.

Vigor nodded, trying, it seemed, to look hopeful.

Gray glided back towards the tunnel, keeping to the shadows. As he neared the tunnel entrance, a glow grew. He slowed, then moved into the darkness behind a boulder and watched.

Black-suited divers clustered round the tunnel opening. One diver ducked through the opening and vanished. After a few seconds, some confirmation must have been passed along. Another five divers swept one after the other into the tunnel.

As Gray swung away, a shape welled up in front of him, appearing from nowhere. Large. The razored tip of a speargun pressed into the flesh of his belly. Lights flared around him.

Behind the mask, Gray recognised the heavy countenance of Raoul.

THE TWO DIVERS hovered on their sleds, like surfers on broken surfboards. One motioned Rachel and Monk to the surface. Now.

As they obeyed, a dark shadow swept up behind the pair of divers.

Two flashes of silver flickered.

One diver clutched his air hose. Too late. Through the man's mask, Rachel saw his gasped breath draw in a wash of sea water. The second was ripped clean off his sled, torn away by a knife lodged in his throat.

Rachel recognised the figure in the attacker's black suit.

Kat.

She dragged a sled to Rachel and Monk and motioned to the surface.

Kicking aside the choking diver, Monk mounted the sled and grabbed the handlebar controls. He waved for Rachel to ride piggyback behind him.

She did so, throwing her arms round his shoulders.

Kat swam for the other sled, speargun in hand.

Monk twisted the throttle, and the sled dragged them up, towards fresh air.

They burst from the surf like a breaching whale, then slammed back down. Rachel was jarred, but she kept her grip. They raced across the waters, zigzagging through the flaming debris field, until they passed the overturned bulk of their speedboat—only to find the long form of the hydrofoil waiting for them on the left.

Gunfire chattered, strafing across the water, aiming right for them.

A SECOND DIVER raised a spear to the side of Gray's throat.

A knife slashed at him, wielded by Raoul.

He flinched, but the blade only cut the straps to his tank. The heavy cylinder dropped towards the bottom. Raoul pointed to the tunnel entrance.

Gray swam to the entrance. He dived through, sailed up to the entry pool and found the chamber ringed with men in wet suits.

As he climbed out of the pool he noted Seichan leaning against the wall.

At Gray's other side, a shape ploughed up into the entry pool. In a single movement, Raoul one-armed his way out of the pool and to his feet. Dragging off his mask and peeling back his hood, he strode over to Gray.

It was the first time that Gray had had a good look at the man. His features were craggy, nose long and thin, aquiline. His coal-black hair hung to his shoulders. His arms were massed with muscle, as thick as Gray's thigh.

'You're going to tell us everything you know,' Raoul said. His English was fluent, but it was accented with disdain and something Germanic.

Gray lifted an eyebrow quizzically. 'And if I don't?'

Raoul waved an arm as another form splashed up into the entry pool. Gray immediately recognised the monsignor.

'There's not much a side-scanning radar can't detect,' Raoul said.

Vigor was dragged from the pool. Blood trickled from his scalp wound. He was shoved towards them, but tripped and fell to his knees.

Gray bent down to go to his aid, but a spearhead drove him back.

Another diver surfaced in the pool. He was carrying another of those barbell-shaped charges. An incendiary grenade.

Raoul took the device, slung it over a shoulder and stepped back to them. He raised his speargun and pointed it at Vigor's crotch. 'As the monsignor has sworn off using this part of his anatomy, we'll start here. Any missteps and the monsignor will be able to join the castrato choir of his church.'

Gray straightened. 'What do you want to know?'

'Everything . . . but first, show us what you found.'

Gray lifted an arm towards the shorter of the two tunnels, the one that required one to hunch over to traverse it. 'It's that way,' he said.

Raoul waved a group of men into the tunnel. 'Check it out.'

Seichan, leaning near the tunnel entrance, stepped to follow.

'Not you,' Raoul said.

Seichan glanced over a shoulder. 'Do you and your men want to leave this harbour? The escape boat is ours,' she reminded him, and ducked away.

MONK RACED THE BULLETS as the jet sled skidded across the water. Rachel clung to him from behind, half choking his airway.

The harbour was in chaos. Other watercraft fled from the fighting, scattering like a school of fish. Monk hit the wake of a crabbing boat and sailed high into the air. Gunfire chewed into the wave below.

'Grab tight!' he cried.

He flipped the sled on its side just as they hit the water. Under they went. Straightening up, they sped through the water at a depth of three feet.

Monk had squeezed his eyes closed. But before diving under, he had caught a glimpse of an anchored sailing boat directly ahead.

If he could get under it . . . put it between him and the hydrofoil . . .

He counted in his head, estimating. Then he did an additional four-count and canted back up to the surface. They burst back into sunlight and air.

Monk craned back. They had more than cleared the sailing boat. The hydrofoil had to swing around the obstacle, losing ground.

'Monk!' Rachel yelled in his ear.

He faced forward to see a boxy wall of boat in front of him, the naked houseboat couple's. They were flying right towards its port side.

Monk slammed his weight forward and tipped the nose of the sled straight down. They dived in a steep dive . . . but was it steep enough?

The answer was no. Monk slammed into the keel with the tip of his sled. The sled flipped over. He clutched an iron grip to the handles. The sled skittered against the wood side, barnacles ripping at his shoulder. He gunned the throttle and shot deeper, finally clearing the underside of the boat.

He jetted upwards, knowing he had little time.

Rachel was gone, knocked off with the first collision.

A COMMOTION immediately sounded from down the low tunnel.

'*Eine Goldtür!*' Gray heard shouted. *A gold door.*

Raoul hurried forward, dragging Gray with him. Vigor was kept pinned at the pool's edge by a diver with a speargun.

The tunnel, lit up by the explorers' flashlights, extended only some thirty yards and was slightly curved.

'*Es wird entriegelt!*' a shout called. *Unlocked!*

From where Gray stood, he heard the click as the door was opened.

It was too loud.

Seichan spun round and leapt back towards them. She was too late.

From all walls, sharpened poles of steel shot out of crevices and shadowed nooks. They skewered across the passage, piercing through flesh and bone, and embedded into holes drilled on the opposite side. The deadly tangle started deep and swept outwards in a matter of two seconds.

Men screamed, impaled and pinned.

Seichan made it within two steps of the exit, but the tail end of the booby trap caught her. A single sharpened pole impaled her shoulder. She jerked to a stop. A pained gasp was the only sound she made, skewered on the bar.

Shocked, Raoul momentarily weakened his grip on Gray.

Taking advantage, Gray wrestled free and flung himself towards the pool. 'Go!' he shouted to Vigor.

Before he could take a second step, something struck the back of his head. Hard. The butt of a speargun. He went down on one knee.

He had underestimated the speed of the giant.

Raoul kicked Gray onto his face and pressed a boot on his neck.

'A nasty little trick,' Raoul said. 'But at least you have eliminated a problem for me, taking that bitch out of the picture.'

MONK SURFED AROUND the stern of the houseboat, searching for Rachel. Out in the harbour, a police cruiser wailed across the waters. The hydrofoil raced away, heading into international waters or some other hidden berth.

Monk spotted motion on the rear deck of the houseboat.

Rachel . . . The naked middle-aged man supported her with one arm.

Monk slowed. 'Rachel . . . are you—'

She glanced back, eyes panicked. The man raised his other arm and pointed a snub-nosed automatic rifle at Monk's face.

RAOUL KNELT on top of Gray, one knee on his back, the other on the back of his neck. One hand twisted into Gray's hair, yanking his head back. The man's other hand held the speargun towards Vigor's left eye.

The monsignor was on his knees, flanked by two divers with additional guns. A third looked on, with a knife in his hand. All eyes were narrowed with hatred. Gray's trick had slain five of their comrades.

Raoul leaned closer. 'Enough games. What did you learn in—?'

A zinging *thwack* cut off his words. The speargun clattered from Raoul's grip. A roaring howl erupted from him as he fell off Gray.

Released, Gray rolled across the floor, snatched up the abandoned speargun, and shot one of the men holding Vigor.

The other man straightened, turning his weapon on Gray, but before he could fire, a spear flashed through the air from the pool and spitted him.

Vigor slapped the unfired speargun towards Gray, then flung himself low.

Gray grabbed it and swung it towards Raoul.

The giant ran for the tunnel that led to the tomb, clutching his injured hand, pierced through by a length of steel spear. Kat's shot had been precise, disarming and disabling.

The last of the Court's men, the one with the dagger, was the first into the tunnel and led the way. Raoul followed.

Gray gained his feet, took aim at Raoul's back, and fired.

The spear struck the large man in the back and clattered harmlessly to the stone floor.

Gray cursed. He had hit the incendiary bomb slung over Raoul's shoulder.

'Let's go,' Kat said. 'I don't know how many more guards are out there.'

Vigor was already in the water. 'Rachel . . . ?'

'I sent her off with Monk on another sled.'

Tears of relief came to the monsignor's eyes.

Gray pulled down his mask. 'Let's get out of here.'

RAOUL YANKED the spear from his hand. Fire lanced from his arm to his chest, and blood poured. He pulled his glove off and tied the Neoprene round his palm, stanching and putting pressure on the wound.

He stared across the room, illuminated by his flashlight. What the hell was this place? The glass pyramid, the water, the starry dome . . .

The last surviving man, Kurt, returned from the passageway. He had gone to reconnoitre the entry pool. 'They left,' he reported.

Raoul bent to his pack on the ground. He would get a visual record for Dr Menardi, and hunt down the Americans. As Raoul dug out his camera, his foot nudged the sling holding the incendiary grenade. A fold of cloth fell away, revealing a red glow on the neighbouring wall.

He snatched the bomb and rolled it digital face forward. It read: 00:33.

He spotted the deep ding in the casing near the timer. Where the American bastard had struck it with the speargun. The impact must have shorted something, activated the timer.

Raoul retrieved his digital camera, took several rapid flash pictures, sealed the camera in a pocket, then followed Kurt to the entry room.

'Raoul!' a voice called to him.

It was Seichan. The bitch was still trapped in the other tunnel.

Raoul waved to her. 'It was nice doing business with you.'

He pulled down his mask and launched himself down the tunnel.

Then a reverberation trembled through the water, sounding like a passing freight train. The tunnel behind him flashed with a dull orange glow.

GRAY STALKED the length of the hotel suite that Monk had booked. The balcony windows overlooked Alexandria harbour.

Vigor had watched the local news station and listened as an Egyptian newsman reported on a confrontation among a group of drug smugglers.

Gray, Kat and Vigor had used air tanks and two of the abandoned sleds to flee to the far side of the harbour. Once there, they had stripped to trunks and swimsuits, and blended into the crowds of sunbathers. There was no sign of Monk and Rachel anywhere.

Gray turned to Kat. 'And you saw them leave with one of the sleds?'

She nodded, face taut with guilt. 'I should have made sure . . .'

'And we'd both be dead,' Gray said. 'You made a choice.'

'What do we do?' Vigor asked.

Gray stared out of the window. 'We have to assume they've been captured. We'll have to evacuate. We have no choice.'

RACHEL CLIMBED into the terry-cloth robe. She snugged it round her naked form while glaring at the cabin's other occupant.

The tall, muscular blonde woman ignored her and stepped to the cabin doorway. 'All finished in here!' she reported, peeling off her latex gloves. She had performed a full body-cavity search on Rachel. 'Nothing hidden.'

Rachel stared out of the tiny porthole, looking for some landmark, something to pinpoint where she was. All she saw was featureless sea.

She and Monk had been transferred, hooded and gagged, from the houseboat to a small speedboat, then whisked away to a small cove more than an hour's journey away.

Manhandled aboard the waiting hydrofoil, they were hustled below to separate cabins. The powerful craft had immediately edged out of the cove and sped away, heading straight out into the Mediterranean.

That had been more than half an hour ago.

Now Raoul came in and grabbed her arm. He dragged her to a wood-panelled cabin, which contained not only a bed and chair but also a desk, side table and bookshelves. On every flat surface, texts, magazines, even scrolls were stacked. One corner of the desk supported a laptop computer.

The room's occupant straightened and turned. He had been leaning over his desk, glasses perched on the tip of his nose. 'Rachel,' he said warmly.

She recognised the man from her visits to the Vatican Libraries. He was head prefect of the Archives, Dr Alberto Menardi.

He tapped a sheet on his desk. 'I believe this map has been embellished by your own hand.' He waved her over.

Rachel had no choice. Raoul shoved her forward.

She stared down at the map of the Mediterranean, which she had sealed in a pouch of her dry suit. The hourglass was drawn upon it, with the names of the Seven Wonders clearly written. She wished she'd burnt it.

Alberto leaned closer. He drew a fingernail along the axis line that Gray had drawn. It stopped at Rome. 'Tell me about this.'

'It's where we're supposed to go next,' Rachel lied. She was relieved her uncle had not drawn on the map in ink himself. He had simply extended the line with his finger and the straight edge of Gray's knife.

Alberto turned his head. 'Now, why is that? I'd like to hear all about what went down in that tomb. In great detail.'

Rachel kept silent. Raoul's fingers tightened on her arm. She winced.

Alberto waved Raoul away. 'There's no need for that. You have the American for that, don't you? Maybe you better show her?'

Raoul grinned, and Rachel felt a knot of terror tighten round her heart.

She was led out of the cabin and forced up the stairs to the open stern of the hydrofoil. Three men lounged on benches, carrying assault rifles. Monk was lying on his stomach, naked except for boxers, his wrists bound behind him and his legs hog-tied at the ankle. It looked like two of his fingers had been broken on his left hand, bent back at impossible angles. Blood smeared the deck. He opened one swollen eye when she stepped out.

'Untie his arms,' Raoul ordered. 'Get him on his back.'

The men responded quickly. Monk groaned as his arms were freed. He was flipped onto his back. One of the guards held a rifle at Monk's ear.

Raoul grabbed a fire-axe from a stanchion.

'What are you doing?' Rachel hurried to stand between him and Monk.

'That depends on you,' Raoul said. He hefted the axe to his shoulder.

One of the men responded to some discreet signal. Rachel's elbows were grabbed and pinned behind her. She was pulled back.

Raoul pointed his axe, one-armed, at the third man. 'Sit on his chest, hold his left arm down at the elbow.' Raoul strode forward as the man obeyed. He glanced back to Rachel. 'I believe the *professore* asked you a question.'

Alberto stepped forward. 'And don't leave out any details.'

'He has five fingers on this side,' Raoul added. 'We'll start with the broken ones. They're not of much use anyway.' He raised the axe.

'No!' Rachel choked out.

'Don't . . .' Monk groaned to her.

The guard with the rifle kicked Monk in the head.

'I'll tell you!' Rachel blurted out.

She spoke rapidly, explaining all that had happened in the tomb. She left out nothing, except for the truth. 'It all points back to Rome,' she concluded.

Alberto's eyes glowed. He turned to Raoul. 'She's lying.'

'I thought so.' He swung the axe down.

RAOUL ENJOYED HEARING the woman scream.

He pulled his axe head from where it was embedded in the deck. He had missed the captive's fingertips by the breadth of a hair.

'Next time, it's for real,' he warned the woman.

Dr Alberto stepped forward. 'Our friend here got an angled flash on the pyramid. It shows a square hole in its surface. Something you failed to mention. I know something must have been taken from the tomb. It makes no sense to point to Rome without an additional clue. What did you take?'

Tears rolled down her face.

Raoul widened his stance, hefting the axe higher over his head.

She cracked. 'A key . . . a gold key,' she whimpered. 'Gray . . . Commander Pierce has it.'

Behind her tears, Raoul heard a trace of hope in her voice.

He knew a way to squash that.

Raoul brought the axe down hard. It severed the man's hand at the wrist.

'IT'S TIME TO GO,' Gray said.

He had given Vigor and Kat an additional forty-five minutes to call all the local hospitals and medical centres, even the municipal police. Maybe they had been injured. Or were cooling their heels in a jail cell.

As Gray stood up, his satphone rang from his pack. Only a handful of people had the number: Director Crowe and his teammates.

Gray grabbed his phone and swung up its antenna. 'Commander Pierce.'

'I will keep this brief, so there's no confusion.'

Gray stiffened. It was Raoul. That could mean only one thing . . .

'We have the woman and your teammate. You'll do exactly as we say or we'll be mailing their heads to Washington and Rome.'

'How do I know they're still—?'

A shuffle sounded at the other end. A new voice gasped. He heard the tears behind the words. 'They . . . I . . . they cut off Monk's hand. He—'

The phone was taken away.

Gray's fingers clenched hard to the phone. 'What do you want?'

'The gold key from the tomb,' Raoul said. 'There is an EgyptAir flight leaving Alexandria at twenty-one hundred hours for Geneva. You will be on that flight. Alone. We will have false papers and tickets in a locker, so no computer searches will trace your flight.' Directions to the locker followed. 'You will not contact your superiors. If you do, we'll know.'

'How do I know you'll stick to your end of the bargain?'

'You don't. But as a gesture of goodwill, when you land, I'll contact you again. If you follow our directions precisely, your man will be released to a Swiss hospital. But the woman will remain in custody until you hand over the key. The others are free to go as long as they stay out of the way. If either sets foot in Italy or Switzerland, the deal is off.'

Gray understood keeping the others out of Switzerland . . . but why Italy? Then it struck him. He pictured Rachel's map. The line he had drawn. Pointing to Rome. Rachel had revealed much—but not all. Good girl.

'Agreed,' Gray said. 'I'll be on the flight.'

The connection ended. Gray repeated the conversation to the others.

Vigor's face had drained of blood. 'What shall we do?' he asked.

'I need you and Kat in Avignon. Working on the mystery there.'

'I . . . I can't,' Vigor said. 'Rachel . . .' He sank to the bed.

Gray firmed his voice. 'Rachel has bought us a slim chance in Avignon. Paid with Monk's blood. I won't let their efforts be squandered.'

Vigor looked up at him.

'You have to trust me,' Gray said. 'I'll get Rachel. You have my word.'

Whatever Vigor found in his face, he seemed to gain some resolve from it. Gray hoped it was enough.

He gathered up his pack. 'I'll contact you when I have Rachel.' He headed out. With one hope.

SEICHAN SAT IN THE DARK, still pinned to the wall. The inch-thick spear had sheared up under her collarbone and out of the top of her shoulder, missing major blood vessels and her scapula. But every movement was agony.

Still, she was alive. The firebomb Raoul had set to destroy the far chamber had barely reached this room. The heat had come close to parboiling her, though. Now she wished for that heat again. A chill had set in.

To the side, a glow grew. She turned her head. The entry pool was shining.

The water stirred. A dark shape splashed up. A diver. The flashlight blinded her as the figure climbed out.

The diver lowered the flashlight. Seichan recognised a familiar face as he yanked back his mask and approached. Commander Gray Pierce.

He stepped towards her and lifted a hacksaw. 'Let's talk.'

July 27

11

Director Painter Crowe knew he was in for another sleepless night. He had heard the reports out of Egypt of an attack at the East Harbour of Alexandria. Had Gray's team been involved? No word had arrived. The last messages had been exchanged twelve hours ago.

Painter regretted not relating his suspicions to Gray Pierce. But at that point, they had only been suspicions. And still he wasn't certain. If he proceeded more boldly, the conspirator would know he'd been discovered. It would put the team in further jeopardy. So Painter worked his end alone.

A knock on his office door drew his eyes from the computer screen.

He turned off his monitor to hide his work. He buzzed the lock. His secretary was gone for the day.

Logan Gregory entered. 'Their jet is in final approach. Due to land in Marseilles in eighteen minutes. Just after midnight local time.'

'And they're still maintaining a communication blackout?'

'The pilot will confirm their destination, but nothing else. I was able to worm out a manifest through French customs. There are two passengers, both flying anonymously under diplomatic vouchers.'

'Only two?' Painter sat up straighter, frowning.

'Yes, sir. I also have requests from Rome. The Vatican and the Carabinieri have not heard anything and are getting anxious.'

Painter had to offer them something. 'Let them know of the flight to Marseilles, and that we'll pass on further intel as we learn more.'

'Yes, sir.'

Painter stared at the blank screen. He had to work carefully. 'Once you contact them, I'll need you to run an errand for me. Out to DARPA. I have something that I need personally couriered over to Dr Sean McKnight.' Painter slid over a sealed letter in a red pouch.

Logan nodded. 'I'll take care of it.' He took the pouch, turned away, and closed the door with a click of the lock.

Painter switched his computer back on. It showed a map of the Mediterranean basin with yellow and blue lines crisscrossing it. Satellite paths. He laid his pointer over one. NRO's newest satellite, nicknamed Hawkeye. He double-clicked, and brought up trajectory details and search parameters.

He typed in Marseilles. Times came up. Painter checked his watch. The window of opportunity was narrow. He picked up the phone and spoke to security. 'Let me know when Logan Gregory has left the centre.'

'Yes, sir.'

Painter hung up and waited. Timing would be critical.

Fifteen minutes later the phone rang. Painter confirmed that Logan was gone, then stood up. The sat-recon was down one floor, neighbouring Logan's office. Painter rushed down to find a lone technician jotting in a logbook.

The man jerked to his feet. 'Director Crowe, sir . . . how can I help you?'

'I need a tap feed into NRO's HE 4 satellite.'

'Hawkeye? I'm afraid that clearance is beyond my—'

Painter placed a long alphanumeric sequence in front of him. It was valid for only the next half-hour, obtained from Sean McKnight.

The technician set to work, using GPS coordinates that Painter gave him.

After a long minute, the dark airfield bloomed onto a screen. Marseilles.

Painter directed the feed to zoom down onto a certain gate. A small plane appeared, a Citation X. It sat near the gate, door open. Was he too late?

Movement pixilated. One figure, then another stepped into view. They hurried down the stairs. Painter didn't need to magnify their faces.

Monsignor Verona and Kat Bryant.

No other passengers left the jet. Kat and the monsignor vanished through the gate. Painter waved for the feed to be cut and thanked the technician.

Where the hell was Gray?

GRAY GLANCED AROUND the small first-class cabin of the EgyptAir jet. Eight seats. Six passengers. One or more were probably spies for the Dragon Court, keeping an eye on him. It didn't matter. He was cooperating . . . for now.

He had picked up his plane tickets and false ID from a bus locker, then proceeded to the airport. The four-hour flight was interminable. He ate the gourmet meal, watched the movie, even power-napped for forty minutes.

At last they were touching down at Geneva International Airport.

They taxied to their gate, and Gray gathered up his bag. As he exited, he searched for his travelling companion.

She had been in the economy seats. She wore a blonde wig, a navy blue business suit and heavy black glasses. She carried herself with a subdued demeanour, her left arm in a sling, half hidden under her jacket.

Seichan exited ahead of him without a glance.

Once in the terminal, Gray queued for customs, showed his false papers, had them stamped, and was on his way. He hadn't checked any baggage.

He strode out to the taxi line. Seichan had vanished.

He had needed an ally. Cut off from Washington, from his own team, he had made a pact with the devil. He had freed her after exacting a promise. In return for her freedom, she would help Gray release Rachel. Afterwards, they would part ways. All debts forgiven, past and present. She had agreed.

Gray knew that her cooperation was less out of obligation than fury at Raoul. She had been left for dead, a slow agonising end. Now she wanted to make Raoul and the Court pay.

Gray's satphone finally rang. 'Commander Pierce,' he said tersely.

'Welcome to Switzerland,' Raoul said. 'There are train tickets waiting for you at the city-centre terminal, under your false name, headed to Lausanne. It leaves in thirty-five minutes. You'll be on it.'

'What about my teammate?' Gray said.

'As arranged, he's on his way to the hospital in Geneva. You'll have confirmation by the time you board the train.'

Gray climbed into a taxi. He didn't bother searching for Seichan. He had piggybacked a chip on his phone, tied to her cellphone. She had overheard the conversation. He trusted her skill to keep up with him.

'Central train station,' he told the driver.

After ten minutes the taxi offloaded him in front of the train terminal. He crossed to the ticket counter, gave his false name and showed his papers. He was given tickets to the lakeside city of Lausanne.

As he strode towards his gate, his phone rang again.

He pulled it free and adjusted the antenna. 'Commander Pierce,' he said.

'Two minutes to satisfy yourself.' Raoul again. A click and hiss then a more distant voice, echoing a bit, but familiar.

'Commander?'

'I'm here, Monk. Where are you?' Gray was sure the conversation was being eavesdropped on by more than just Seichan. He had to be careful.

'They dumped me at some hospital with this cellphone. Told me to expect your call. I'm in the emergency room. Doctors are all speaking French.'

'You're in Geneva,' Gray said. 'How are you doing?'

A long pause.

'I know about your hand,' Gray said.

'Bastards,' Monk said with fury. 'They had a doctor on board their ship. Sutured my . . . my stump. The docs here want X-rays and such, but they seem satisfied with the other doctor's umm . . . handiwork, so to speak.'

Gray's voice was hard-edged. 'Rachel?'

'I haven't seen her since they drugged me. I have no idea where she's at.'

'I'll get you out of there as soon as I can.' Gray said.

'Gray,' Monk said, voice strained. Gray recognised his tone. He wanted to communicate something, but he also knew the others were eavesdropping. 'They . . . they let me go.'

The connection fritzed again. Raoul came back on the line.

'You see, we honour our word. If you want the woman, bring the key. I'll have a car waiting for you at Lausanne.'

The connection ended.

Gray lowered the phone. *So Raoul was in Lausanne.*

He waited for the train. Finally it arrived. Gray climbed into the middle coach, then moved hurriedly towards the rear, hoping to shake any tail.

In the gap between the last two cars, Seichan waited.

She handed him a long leather jacket. Then she left by an emergency exit that opened on the opposite side of the track, away from the platform.

Gray followed, dropping down. He pulled on the jacket.

Seichan hurried across another track on to the next platform. They left the station, and Gray found himself at the edge of a parking lot.

A BMW motorcycle, black and yellow, stood a step away.

'You'll have to drive,' Seichan said. 'My shoulder . . .' She had abandoned the sling to drive from the rental office, but it was fifty miles to Lausanne.

Gray hopped on to the front and she climbed on behind him, putting her good arm round his waist. They raced out of the parking lot and zipped towards the highway that led into the mountains.

As he wound up into the heights that bordered the lake, Gray's mind drifted back to his conversation with Monk. *They let me go*. That was plain enough. But what was Monk implying?

The Court was ruthless. They had used Monk's torture to force Rachel to talk. Would they give up such an asset so readily? Monk was right. Not unless the Court had an even better hold on Rachel. But what?

RACHEL SAT in her cell, numb and exhausted.

The hydrofoil had sailed to an island in the Mediterranean, where they had transferred to a small private jet. She had been locked in a back compartment, then Raoul had blindfolded and gagged her, and she was transferred from plane to truck. A half-hour of twisty driving and she heard the wheels bumping over wooden planks. A bridge. The truck braked to a stop.

She was dragged out, and led by the elbow down steps to a small stone cell. Her hood and soggy gag were pulled off. She looked around. One wall was a solid sheet of glass, except for a rubber-sealed door and fist-sized ventilation holes. The only furniture was a steel cot with a thin mattress.

It was over an hour before Raoul appeared. He marched down the hallway and up stairs to a moonlit courtyard. Stone walls towered on all sides. An archway, sealed by a portcullis, led to a narrow bridge that spanned a gorge.

She was in a castle.

Along a wall, a row of twenty chain-link cages stretched. Low grumbles rose from that corner. Large shadows shifted.

Raoul must have noted her attention. 'Fighting dogs,' he said.

He led her towards the keep. Using a touchpad, he unlocked an oak door. It swung open, and Rachel was forced into a long hallway. A series of rooms opened off it. She glanced through an open door as she was marched past and saw banks of computers tied to rows of plates. Electromagnets, she guessed, used to experiment with the m-state compounds.

They stopped alongside a door on the opposite wall. Raoul knocked and pushed inside. It was like stepping into the turn-of-the-century parlour of a distinguished Royal Society scholar, all polished mahogany and walnut.

Bookshelves and display cabinets lined the walls, filled with neatly arranged texts. Behind glass, she noted first editions by Sir Isaac Newton. There was also an illuminated Egyptian manuscript open in one case. Rachel wondered if it was the one that had been stolen from the Cairo museum, the forged text with the encrypted stanzas.

'*Professore!*' Raoul called, closing the door behind them.

Through a back door leading to other private rooms, Dr Alberto Menardi entered. He carried a book under one arm and shook a finger at Rachel. 'You haven't been totally honest with us.'

Rachel felt her heart stop beating; her breath became trapped.

They were waved to a cluttered desk. Rachel noted her map of the Mediterranean spread out on the top. New lines had been added, circles, meridians, degree marks. Tiny arcane numbers were inscribed along one edge of the map. Plainly, Alberto had been working on the puzzle.

The prefect tapped the map. 'Rome is *not* the next place.'

Rachel forced herself not to flinch.

Alberto continued, 'The subtext to this geometric design signifies forward motion in time. The hourglass marches forward one grain at a time, to the inevitable end. For this reason, it can't be Rome. That's moving back, not forward. There is another mystery to solve here.'

Rachel shook her head. 'That's all we could calculate before we were attacked.' She waved round his room. 'We didn't have your resources.'

Alberto studied her as she spoke. 'I believe you,' he said slowly. 'Vigor is quite sharp, but this riddle is layered in mystery. Still, you kept hidden the discovery of the gold key. Maybe there's more you kept hidden.'

'I've told you everything,' she swore with mustered conviction.

Would they believe her? Would they torture her? She swallowed hard. She would never talk. Too much was at stake.

Alberto shrugged. 'There's only one way to find out if you know more. It's time we ensured we have the complete truth from you. Take her next door.'

Rachel was manhandled by Raoul back through the door and into the adjoining room. In the centre of the brightly lit space was a strange, X-shaped steel table lit by an overhead surgical lamp. She spotted a tray of surgical instruments. A figure was strapped spread-eagled to the table.

'We can stretch this interrogation all night long,' Alberto promised, stepping past to enter the room. He donned a pair of sterile latex gloves.

Raoul finally dragged her forward into the suite of surgical horrors.

Rachel finally saw who was strapped to the table.

'Someone came snooping where they shouldn't have,' Raoul said.

The captive's bloody face turned towards her. Their eyes met.

Rachel lunged forward. 'No!'

Raoul grabbed a fistful of her hair and pushed her to her knees. 'You'll watch from here.'

Alberto picked up a silver scalpel. 'We'll start with the left ear.'

'No!' Rachel screamed. 'I'll tell you! I'll tell you everything!'

Alberto lowered the blade and turned to her.

'It's Avignon,' she sobbed, staring into the terrified eyes of the prisoner.

It was her grandmother.

THE CITY OF AVIGNON glowed, shouted, sang and danced.

The Summer Theatre Festival ran each July, the world's largest showcase of music, drama and art. Youth crowded into the city. It was a round-the-clock party. Even the lowering skies did not discourage the festival-goers.

Vigor and Kat hurried through the high park to the Palace Square. The pope's castle sat on a spur of rock overlooking the river below.

'Where do we begin?' Kat asked.

Vigor had spent the flight in research, trying to answer that exact question. 'What Avignon is famous for is its Gothic architecture, which flourished during the century of the French papacy. The word "Gothic" comes from the Greek word "goetic", which translates to "magic". Such architecture was considered magical. The magnificent cathedrals and other Gothic structures, with their thin ribbing, flying buttresses, and impossible heights, were almost exclusively built by a group of masons who named themselves the Children of Solomon, a mix of Knights Templar and Cistercian monks. They retained the mathematical mysteries to build these structures, supposedly gained when the Knights Templar discovered the lost Temple of Solomon during the Crusades. It was said the temple contained King Solomon's vast treasure, possibly even the Ark of the Covenant.'

'And supposedly the Ark is where Moses stored his pots of manna,' Kat said stiffly. 'His recipe for m-state metals.'

'Don't discount that,' Vigor said. 'The Bible describes the Ark's strange powers. There are references to it levitating. And casting lightning bolts.'

'OK,' Kate said. 'Let's say these Knights Templar rediscovered the Ark and possibly these m-state superconductors. Did they understand its secrets?'

'I may have the answer, in the shape of another mysterious stone of alchemical history. The Philosopher's Stone.'

Kat frowned. 'The stone that could turn lead into gold?'

'That is a common misconception. A seventeenth-century philosopher, Eiranaeus Philalethes, a Fellow of the Royal Society, wrote that the Philosopher's Stone was "nothing but gold digested to its highest degree of purity . . . called a stone by virtue of its fixed nature . . . but its appearance is that of a fine powder." Clearly scientists at the time were experimenting with a strange form of gold, although nothing seems to have come of it.'

'What does the Philosopher's Stone have to do with Gothic architecture?'

'More than you'd think. An early-twentieth-century Frenchman named Fulcanelli wrote a best-selling treatise titled *Le Mystère des cathédrales*. It elaborated on how the Gothic cathedrals of Europe were coded with arcane messages, pointing to a vein of lost knowledge.'

'A code in stone?'

'Don't be surprised. It was what the Church was doing already. Most of the populace at the time was illiterate. The decorations of the cathedrals were both instructional and informative, biblical storytelling in stonework. And remember who I said built these massive Gothic storybooks.'

'The Knights Templar,' Kat said.

'A group known to have gained secret knowledge from the Temple of Solomon. Perhaps they incorporated some additional coded messages for their fellow Masonic alchemists. Gothic iconography is full of zodiac symbols, mathematical riddles, geometric mazes right out of alchemical texts of the time. Victor Hugo decried the Gothic art of Notre-Dame as "seditious pages" in stone.' Vigor pointed ahead, through the trees. The park ended as they neared the Palace Square. 'And Fulcanelli and Hugo weren't the only ones who detected something heretical in the Knights Templar's artwork. Do you know why Friday the thirteenth is considered unlucky?'

Kat shook her head.

'October 13, 1307. A Friday. The king of France, along with the pope, declared the Knights Templar to be heretics, sentencing them to death.

However, it is believed that the real reason the Knights were outlawed was to gain control of their riches, including the secret knowledge they possessed. The king tortured thousands of Knights, but their storehouse of riches was never discovered. Still, it marked the end of the Knights Templar.'

'Truly an unlucky day for them.'

'An interesting paper turned up in 2001,' he continued. 'It was a scroll dated a year after that bloody Friday, signed by Pope Clement V, absolving and exonerating the Knights Templar. Unfortunately, King Philippe ignored this and continued his massacre of the Knights. But why the change of heart? Why did Pope Clement build his palace here in the Gothic tradition?'

'Are you suggesting the Church took the Knights into their fold?'

'Remember how we concluded that Thomas Christians, Christians of Gnostic leanings, were already hidden inside the Church. Perhaps they convinced Pope Clement to intervene to protect the Knights.'

'To what end?'

'To hide something of great value—to the Church, to the world. During the century of the Avignon papacy, a great surge of building occurred here, much of it overseen by the Children of Solomon. They could easily have buried away something of considerable size.'

'But where do we begin looking?' Kat said.

'At the work commissioned by that wayward pope, built by the hands of the Knights, one of the largest masterworks of Gothic architecture.'

Vigor waved beyond the busy Place du Palais to a looming structure, framed by square towers, fronted by massive archways and set off by a pair of conical spires. The Palace of the Popes.

'Somewhere within its structure lies some seditious page of stone,' Vigor said, stepping closer to Kat. 'I'm sure of it. We must find it and decode it.'

'AND THAT'S HOW we calculated it was Avignon,' Rachel finished.

She had told them everything. She could not risk the prefect testing her veracity upon the flesh of her grandmother.

Monk and Rachel were soldiers. Her *nonna* was not.

Alberto turned to Raoul. 'Where are Monsignor Verona and the other American now?' he asked.

'Last I heard, they were heading to Marseilles,' Raoul said. 'In their private jet. I thought they were following orders. Staying clear of Italy.'

'Marseilles is twenty minutes from Avignon,' Alberto said, scowling.

'My grandmother . . .' Rachel said. 'Can you let her go now?'

Alberto waved a hand. One of the men stepped forward and ripped free the leather straps that held her grandmother. With tears streaming down her face, Rachel helped her *nonna* from the table.

Her grandmother shakily gained her feet. She wiped Rachel's tears. 'There, there, child . . . It was not that awful. I've been through worse.'

Rachel almost laughed. Her *nonna* was attempting to console her.

She hobbled over to the prefect and gave him a kiss on the cheek. 'Alberto, I told you Rachel was too clever for even you.'

The blood iced in Rachel's veins.

'You are right as ever, Camilla.'

Rachel could not breathe.

Her grandmother motioned for Raoul to give her his arm. 'And you, young man, maybe now you see why such strong Dragon's blood is worth protecting.' She reached up and patted the bastard's cheek. 'You and my granddaughter . . . you two will make many beautiful babies.'

Raoul turned and weighed Rachel with those cold, dead eyes.

'I will do my best,' he promised.

GRAY FOLLOWED SEICHAN up the pine-studded mountainside. They had hidden the motorbike at the bottom of a narrow gorge.

'Are you sure you can find this back entrance?' he asked.

'They had me hooded the first time I came here. But I had a GPS tracker hidden'—she glanced at Gray—'somewhere private. I recorded the approach's position and elevation. It should lead us to the entrance.'

They continued up the hillside in silence. Seichan checked her GPS device, then moved to the left. A crack in the cliff appeared, half hidden by a slab of granite, covered in moss and tiny white flowers.

She ducked under it and led the way into a narrow tunnel. Gray clicked on a penlight and checked his watch. The train from Geneva would be pulling into Lausanne in a few minutes. His absence would be noted.

Taking the lead, he sped faster up the stairs until the tunnel dumped into a domed cavity in the rock. At the back wall, a spring flowed, and in front of it stood a large slab of cut stone. An altar. Stars were painted on the ceiling.

Seichan stepped into the room behind him. 'The stairs into the castle are over there,' she said, pointing towards another tunnel leading out.

He took a step towards it, and the darkness at the mouth of the tunnel shifted. A large shape stepped into the meagre light.

Raoul. He bore a submachine gun in his hands.

Light flared to his left. Two other gunmen rose from behind the slab. Behind Gray, a steel door slammed shut across the lower passageway.

But worse, he felt the cold barrel of a gun at the base of his skull.

'He's carrying the gold key around his neck,' Seichan said.

Raoul strode forward, grabbed the chain and yanked the key free.

'Thank you for delivering this to us,' he said to Seichan. 'And Commander Pierce. We have a few questions for you before we leave for Avignon.'

Gray stared into Raoul's face. How did the Court know about Avignon?

'Rachel . . .' he gasped.

'Oh, don't worry. She's alive. Catching up with family at the moment.'

'Don't forget about his teammate at the hospital,' Seichan said. 'We don't want to leave any loose ends.'

Raoul nodded. 'That's already being taken care of.'

UNABLE TO SLEEP, Monk watched TV. A commotion outside his door drew his eye. Raised voices. He shifted higher in his bed. What was going on?

Then the door burst open.

He stared in shock as a familiar figure strode past the security guards.

Monk could not keep the shock from his voice. 'Cardinal Spera?'

RACHEL HAD BEEN returned to her cell, but she was not alone.

Her grandmother sank to the cot with a sigh. 'You may not understand now, but you will.'

Rachel shook her head. She stood against the far wall. 'How could you?'

Her grandmother stared up at her. 'I was once like you. Only sixteen when I first came to this castle from Austria, escaping as the war ended.'

Rachel remembered her grandmother's tales of her family's flight to Switzerland, then eventually Italy. 'You were escaping from the Nazis.'

'We *were* Nazis,' her *nonna* corrected. 'Papa was a party leader in Salzburg, but he also had ties to the Imperial Dragon Court of Austria. We made our escape to Switzerland through that fraternity, through the generosity of the Baron of Sauvage, Raoul's grandfather. But safe passage required payment. My father granted it. My virginity . . . to the baron. Like you, I resisted, not understanding. My father held me down the first time, for my own good. But the baron bedded me many nights while we were in hiding, until I was heavy with his bastard child. And as the child grew in my belly I grew to understand that I carried a noble traceable bloodline back to emperors and kings.'

Rachel tried to comprehend the brutality done to the young girl who would become her grandmother. Had her grandmother validated that abuse by couching it in a grander scheme? Brainwashed by her father.

'My father took me to Italy, to Castel Gandolfo. I gave birth to your mother there. I was beaten for it. A male child had been hoped for.'

Her grandmother continued relating the alternative history of their family. How she was married off to another member of the Dragon Court, one with ties to the Church. It was a marriage of convenience and deceit. Their family had been assigned to plant their children and grandchildren in the Church, as unwitting spies for the Court. To maintain secrecy, Rachel's mother and Vigor were kept unaware of their monstrous heritage.

'But you were meant for so much more,' her grandmother said proudly. 'The Imperator chose you personally to cross our family line back upon the ancient Sauvage line. Your children will be kings among kings.'

Rachel covered her face with her hands. She had revered and emulated her grandmother, respecting her no-nonsense edge. But did such solidity come from toughness or psychosis?

A shout drew her attention. She climbed to her feet.

Down the hall, a troop of guards marched past. Rachel stared in despair at the second in line. Gray, hands bound behind his back, trudged past.

He glanced into her cell and his eyes widened in surprise. 'Rachel . . .'

KAT MARCHED towards the main entrance to the Pope's Palace. Though it was 3 a.m. there was a flow of people into and out of the gateway.

'It's a tradition to hold a play inside the palace,' Vigor said. 'This year it's *Hamlet*. The play and party last well into the morning. They hold it in the Courtyard of Honour.' He pointed ahead.

They passed through the long arched gateway as a snare-beat of thunder rumbled across the sky. They came out into an open courtyard. It was dark, except for the stage on the far side. At either side, lighting towers cast spots on the actors. A crowd had gathered below the stage.

Vigor drew Kat to the side. 'I pulled down a map from the Internet. There's an entrance to the old part of the palace near the Gate of Our Lady.'

He led the way to the left. An archway opened. They ducked inside as lightning split the sky. Vigor motioned to a stout door as thunder boomed out. Kat set to work with her lockpicks. It did not take long to free the latch. She shouldered open the door and Vigor led the way.

'The private apartments of the pope lie in the Tower of Angels,' he said.

'Those rooms were always the most secured area of the palace. If something was hidden, it's probably there.'

Kat pulled out a compass and kept it fixed in front of her. A magnetic marker had led them to Alexander's tomb. It might work here, too.

They traversed several rooms and halls, their footsteps echoing through the empty, vaulted spaces. The place was a stone tomb.

They crossed the treasury, a former library, then a kitchen whose square walls narrowed down to an octagonal chimney over a central firepit.

Vigor finally led them into the Tower of Angels. Kat's compass had not twitched a beat. With no sign of a caretaker, she risked switching on a small penlight to illuminate their search.

'The pope's living room,' Vigor said at the entrance to one room.

Kat crisscrossed the length of it, studying her compass. Nothing.

It was the same in the next room. Then they climbed to another level.

'The pope's bedroom,' Vigor said, sounding disappointed and worried now, too. 'This is the last of the rooms in the apartments.'

Kat tested the empty room, from one end to the other. Still nothing.

GRAY WAS SHOVED into a stone cell. It was sealed with bulletproof glass an inch thick. The door slammed shut. He had spotted Rachel in a cell two spaces down . . . along with her grandmother. It made no sense.

Raoul moved off, leaving Seichan at the door, smiling at him.

With his hands still bound behind his back by plastic ties, he threw himself bodily at her, crashing into the glass wall. 'You goddamn bitch!'

She only smiled, kissed her fingertips, and pressed them to the glass. 'Bye, loverboy. Thanks for the ride here.'

Gray fell away from the door, turning his back, cursing, calculating. Then he overheard talk by Rachel's cell. A door was opened.

Raoul growled, 'Take Madame Camilla up to the trucks. Have all the men ready. We'll be leaving for the airport in a few minutes.'

'*Ciao*, Rachel, my *bambina*.'

No response. What was going on?

Footsteps marched away, but Gray sensed a presence by the other door.

Raoul spoke again. 'If only I had more time,' he whispered icily. 'But orders are orders. It all comes to an end in Avignon. The Imperator will return here with me. He wants to watch as I take you for the first time.'

'Fuck you,' Rachel spat back at him.

'Exactly right.' Raoul laughed. He stalked away with a final order to a guard. 'Keep a watch down here. I'll radio when I'm ready for the American. We'll have a bit of fun before we leave.'

Raoul's footsteps faded. Gray didn't wait any longer. He kicked the toe of his boot hard against the solid rock wall. A three-inch blade sprang from the heel. He crouched and sliced free the ties that bound his wrist.

He reached into the front of his pants. Had Seichan shoved something past his belt buckle when he'd thrust himself against the glass wall? Her left hand . . . it had passed through an air vent, while her other hand distracted with her feigned kiss of goodbye.

Gray pulled a canister free, stepped to the door and sprayed the hinges. The steel bolts began to dissolve. He had to give it to the Guild. They had provided Seichan with some cool toys. He waited a full minute, then yelled to the guard. 'Hey! You! Something's wrong over here.'

Footsteps approached. The guard came forward.

Gray pointed to the smoky sizzle billowing by the door. 'What the hell?' he yelled. 'Are you assholes trying to gas me?'

With a crinkled brow, the guard stepped closer to the door.

Gray hurled himself against it, popping the hinges. The plate glass slammed into the guard and he crashed against the far wall, striking his head hard. Gray shoved the door aside. Bending, he liberated the pistol from the guard's holster and a set of keys. He ran to Rachel's cell.

She was already up and at the door. 'Gray . . . !'

He keyed the lock, yanked the door open—and she was in his arms.

SEICHAN STOOD at the foot of the steps that led to the keep, watching five trucks being loaded in the courtyard. She was tracking one man among the throng. She had already appropriated a set of keys to the last vehicle.

Behind her, a door opened. Raoul stepped out, along with an old woman.

'We'll take you as far as the airport,' Raoul was saying. Then he noticed Seichan. 'I don't believe we'll be needing the Guild's services any longer.'

Seichan shrugged. 'Then I'll head out with you and be on my way.'

Raoul helped the old woman down the steps and strode towards the lead vehicle, where Dr Alberto Menardi waited. Seichan continued to track her target. Motion along one wall of the courtyard drew her eye.

A door opened. She spotted Gray. He had a pistol. Good.

Across the courtyard, Raoul lifted a radio. Most likely calling down to the cells. She could wait no longer. The man she'd been tracking wasn't as close to Raoul as she'd hoped—but he was still in the thick of things.

She fixed her eyes on the soldier who carried Gray's confiscated pack. It was easy to count on avarice among foot soldiers. The fellow was not letting his booty out of his sight. The pack was stuffed with expensive gear.

Unfortunately for him, the bottom lining of the pack also had a quarter kilo of C4 sewn into it. Seichan pressed the transmitter in her pocket.

The explosion blew out the centre of the caravan of trucks. Men and body parts flew into the dark sky. Gas tanks ignited in two of the cars. Flaming debris scattered to all corners of the courtyard.

Seichan waved to Gray, and pointed at the last truck. It was intact. Gray and the woman dashed out. The three zeroed in on the vehicle.

A pair of soldiers tried to stop them. Gray took one, Seichan the other.

As they reached the truck, the rev of an engine drew her eye towards the castle gate. The lead truck jumped forward. Raoul was making his escape. Gunfire pelted towards them as soldiers tumbled into a second vehicle.

Raoul popped up out of the sun roof of the lead truck, facing back towards them. He raised a massive horse pistol in his fist.

'Down!' Seichan barked, dropping flat.

The gun sounded like a cannon. Their truck's front headlamp exploded. A stream of oil flowed out of the engine and pooled on the stones.

One truck, then the other, shot out of the gate. Raoul's laughter carried back to them. The portcullis gate dropped behind the last vehicle, its teeth slamming into the stone notches, sealed tight.

A new sound followed. The click of a series of heavy latches.

The gates to the line of twenty kennels rose up on motorised wheels.

Monsters of muscle, leather and teeth stalked out, snarling, frothing, driven mad by the thunder and blood. Each pit dog stood chest-high, massing close to a hundred pounds.

And the dinner bell had just rung.

KAT STALKED the bedroom at the top of the Tower of Angels. 'We're looking at this the wrong way,' she said. 'Maybe there's not a magnetic marker.'

'Then what?' Vigor asked.

Lightning crackled outside the nearby window. It lit up the gardens below the tower. The rain had begun to fall harder. Another fork of lightning scintillated across the belly of the black clouds.

Kat watched the display and slowly turned to Vigor, conviction firming with insight. She pocketed her compass, knowing it was no longer needed.

'*Magnetism* opened St Peter's tomb,' she said. 'And it was magnetism that led us to Alexander's tomb. But once there, it was *electricity* that ignited the pyramid. The same might lead us to the treasure here.' She waved a hand at the dazzle of the storm. 'Lightning.'

'A flash of light that illuminates darkness.' Vigor rubbed his chin. 'I think you've struck a significant chord. Light is symbolic of knowledge. Enlightenment. It was the primary goal of Gnostic faith, to seek the primordial light mentioned in Genesis. Somewhere there must be a symbol of this, built into the design of the palace.'

Kat shook her head, at a loss.

Vigor suddenly stiffened. 'Alexander's tomb was in Egypt. The Egyptian symbol for light is a circle with a dot in the centre. Representing the sun. But sometimes it's flattened into an oval, forming an eye. The *all-seeing eye* of Masonic and Templar iconography.'

Kat had seen no such marking. 'OK, but where do we look for it?'

'It's not going to be found—but *formed*,' Vigor said. 'Why didn't I think of this before? A feature of Gothic architecture is the play of light and shadow. The Templar architects were masters of this.' He was already heading out of the door. 'We have to go back to where we already saw the potential for a flaming eye within a circle of light.'

Vigor led the way down the stairs, out of the Tower of Angels, and into a room they'd already explored.

'The kitchen?' Kat asked, surprised. She stared again at the square walls, the central raised hearth and, overhead, the octagonal chimneypiece.

Vigor reached out a hand and cupped it over her penlight. 'Wait.'

A bolt of lightning shattered outside. Enough illumination travelled down the open chimney to shine a perfect oval briefly upon the firepit.

'As it is above, so it is below,' Vigor said in a hushed voice. 'The effect is probably more evident when the sun lies at some precise angle.'

Unconvinced, Kat slipped a knife free to examine the hearth. She dug at the rock that lined the firepit, exposing an orange-hued stone. 'It's bauxite.'

Vigor grinned. 'Of course. I should have considered that another stone would point the way,' he said, joining her. 'First haematite, then magnetite, now bauxite. Bauxite has been mined right here in this area. In fact, it's named after the village of Les Baux, the seat of a medieval feudal lordship. Its castle lies only ten miles from here.'

'So?'

'The Lords of Baux were best known for their claim to be descended from Balthazar. One of the Magi.'

Kat's eyes widened. She turned back to the hearth. 'They sealed the opening with the stones of the Magi's descendants. But how do we open it?'

'You already told us. Electricity.'

Kat shed her pack. 'We don't have any of those ancient batteries.' She pulled out a larger flashlight. 'But I do have some Duracell coppertops.'

She cracked open her flashlight and used the tip of a knife to tease loose the positive and negative wires. With the power switch off, she twisted them together, then lifted her handiwork.

'You'd better stand back,' she warned.

Reaching out, she brought the flashlight's wires into contact with the bauxite stone, a weakly conductive ore. She flicked the flashlight's switch.

An arc of electricity stabbed to the stone. A deep bass tone responded, as if a large drum had been struck. Kat darted back to join Vigor as the tone faded. A fiery glow spread around the hearth, scribing the entire firepit.

'They've cemented the blocks with molten m-state glass,' Kat mumbled. 'And now the electricity is releasing the stored power in the glass.'

The hearth flared brighter, and heat washed out towards them.

Then, as the glow died down, the blocks of bauxite fell away, no longer cemented, tumbling into a pit below the hearth.

A rattling continued as the blocks tumbled deeper. No longer able to restrain her curiosity, Kat stepped forward and shone her penlight. The edges of the hearth now outlined a dark staircase leading down.

RACHEL GATHERED with Gray and Seichan on the steps to the main castle building. Though Gray had attempted to scrounge another weapon amidst the fiery carnage, all he had found were two damaged rifles. Gray carried Seichan's weapon while she was busy with her GPS unit.

The pit dogs roamed the yard, tearing at bodies, snarling and spitting at one another. A few fights broke out, savage, lightning-fast tussles.

It wouldn't be long before their pig-eyed attention turned to them.

Any noise drew the beasts. Once the first shot was fired, the entire pack would be upon them. Six bullets. Twenty dogs.

Off to the side, movement . . . Through the oily smoke, a thin figure rose among the debris, wobbly, unsteady.

Rachel recognised the shape. '*Nonna . . .*' she whispered.

A moan rose from the old woman. Blood caked her hair on the left side.

Rachel had thought her grandmother had escaped with Raoul. Had the explosion knocked her down? Rachel supposed otherwise. Raoul must have pistol-whipped her out of the way, leaving her behind, useless baggage.

A few metres away, a dark shape rose from behind a flaming tyre.

Rachel stumbled a step down.

'I see it,' Gray said, stopping her with a hand. He raised his gun and squeezed the trigger. The dog pitched over. Howls rose from it. It gnashed at its wounded back leg, attacking the pain. Other dogs swooped on it.

The old woman, startled by the beast, had fallen on her backside.

'I have to get to her,' Rachel whispered.

'I'll go with you,' Gray said.

'She's dead already,' Seichan said with a sigh, lowering her GPS unit. But she followed them down the stairs, sticking close to the only gun.

In a tight knot, they traversed the courtyard. One massive brindled beast eyed them, teeth bared. Gray covered it with his pistol.

Rachel's grandmother scooted away from the trio of dogs fighting over their injured brethren. Her movement was tracked by another two beasts, coming at her from opposite sides.

Another two shots and one beast collapsed. The other bullet only grazed the second dog. The injury seemed to pique its bloodlust. It lunged.

Rachel ran forward. Gray shot as he ran, dropping another two dogs, but the lunging dog had snatched her grandmother's arm and tugged her to the ground. Gray fired again. The impact knocked the beast off the woman, a clean head shot . . . also their last.

Dropping to her knees, Rachel cradled her grandmother's body.

The old woman stared up at her, eyes glazed. 'Mamma . . . I'm sorry . . .'

A crack of a rifle and she jerked in her granddaughter's arms, shot through the chest. Rachel looked up.

Thirty yards away, two gunmen stood beyond the iron portcullis gate. Raoul had probably sent them back to make sure no one left the castle alive.

The new blast drew off a few of the dogs.

Gray sought to use the distraction to retreat to the castle wall. Rachel followed, not letting go of her grandmother, dragging her along.

'Leave her,' Gray urged, but Rachel ignored him.

Reaching the relative shelter of the castle's wall, Rachel bent over the old woman's body and freed the bag still hooked over her *nonna*'s shoulder. She snapped the clasp, reached inside, and felt the butt of cold steel.

She pulled out her grandmother's Nazi P08 Luger. '*Grazie, Nonna.*'

Rachel aimed towards the gate and let cold anger steady her grip. She squeezed the trigger once, then fired again. Both men fell.

Seichan had her eyes on the skies. Then Gray heard it too.

The *thump-thump* of a helicopter.

It winged up over the ridge and castle walls. Lights blazed down. Rotorwash stirred a whirlwind. Dogs scattered in fear.

Seichan spoke above the roar. 'Our ride's here!'

A nylon ladder tumbled out of a door and struck the stones only yards off.

Gray raced forward, held the ladder steady and waved Rachel up. Seichan went next. Gray followed last. As the door of the helicopter was slammed behind them, Gray straightened to thank the person who had given him an arm and helped him inside.

The man wore a grin. 'Hi, boss.'

'Monk!' Gray grabbed him in a bear hug. 'How on earth—?'

'Watch the arm,' his partner said.

Gray let him loose. Monk's left arm was strapped to his body, and a leather guard sheathed the bandaged stump of his wrist.

Monk motioned him to sit and strap in as the helicopter sped away. 'We locked on to your emergency GPS signal,' he explained.

Gray pulled on his seat harness and snapped it in place. He stared at the other occupant of the cabin. 'Cardinal Spera?' he said, confused.

Seichan sat next to him and answered, 'Who do you think hired me?'

12

Kat left one of her cellphones by the firepit—to pick up any call coming in, and to leave at least one breadcrumb to follow if they became trapped—and followed Vigor below. The stone steps ended at a short tunnel. From the echo of the monsignor's footsteps, Kat sensed that a large cavern lay beyond. It was confirmed a moment later.

She stepped out onto a three-metre stone ledge. Their two lights cast wide swaths across the vaulted space. It must once have been a natural cavity in the granite, but skilled craftsmen and engineers had built a series of twelve bricked tiers, which descended towards the distant floor. Each level below was smaller than the next, like a vast circular amphitheatre . . . or an upside-down step pyramid.

She shone her light across the yawning space. Thick granite arches spanned out from the tiered footings in a corkscrew pattern, held up by giant columns. Flying buttresses. Like those that supported Gothic cathedrals.

'This had to have been built by the Knights Templar,' Vigor said, moving along the tier. 'Gothic architecture at its most perfect.'

The stone framework served only one purpose, however. To support a convoluted maze of timber scaffolding. Shelves, rooms, ladders and stairs. All held a storehouse of books, scrolls, texts, artefacts and statuary.

'It's a huge library,' Kat said.

'And museum, and storehouse, and gallery,' Vigor finished.

A stone table, like an altar, sat not far from the entry tunnel. On it, a leather-bound book was spread open under glass . . . gold glass.

Kat peered at the exposed pages. It was an illuminated manuscript. Tiny script flowed down the page. It appeared to be a list.

'I think this is the filing system for the entire library,' Vigor said. He bent over the book. 'Here it lists in Latin complete texts of forbidden gospels, not just the fragments found near the Dead Sea.' He lifted his flashlight. 'According to this ledger, somewhere out there is stored the Mandylion.'

Kat frowned. 'What's that?'

'The true burial shroud of Christ, an artefact predating the Turin Shroud. Many suspected it ended up in the treasury of the Knights Templar.' Vigor nodded. 'Out there lies the true face of Christ, perhaps.'

They headed to the narrow stairs that led from one tier to the next. A final set of stairs down led to a flat floor. All the treasure piled above was held suspended by a pair of giant arches, footed on this last tier.

Kat recognised the stone of these arches. Magnetite again. Also, directly beneath the crossing of the arches, rising from the centre of the floor, stood a waist-high column of magnetite, like a stone finger pointing upwards.

She descended the last step cautiously. A lip of natural granite surrounded a glass floor. Gold glass. She didn't step out onto it. The brick walls also had twelve mirrored plates of gold glass embedded in them.

Vigor took in these details, but both their focuses fixed to the silvery lines—probably pure platinum—that etched the floor. The image somehow fitted as an ending to this long hunt. It depicted a circular maze leading to a central rosette. The stubby pillar of magnetite rose from its centre.

Kat studied the maze. 'It looks like another mystery to solve,' she said. 'But if we already opened this storehouse, what's left to find?'

Vigor stepped closer. 'Don't forget Alexander's gold key. We didn't need it to open anything here. That means there's more than just this library.'

'WHAT IS THE VATICAN doing hiring a Guild operative?' Gray asked.

They were airborne again. The helicopter had flown them to Geneva Airport, where Cardinal Spera had a Gulfstream jet ready to fly them to Avignon. The five of them had swung their seats round to face one another.

Cardinal Spera acknowledged the question with a nod. 'It was not the Holy See itself that hired Seichan. It was a smaller group, acting independently. We heard of the Dragon Court's interest and activity. We had already used the Guild to investigate the group peripherally.'

'You hired mercenaries?' Gray accused.

'The Guild's reputation might be ruthless, but they're also efficient, honour their contracts, and get the job done.'

'Yet they didn't stop the massacre in Cologne.'

'It was an oversight on my part, I'm afraid. We were unaware of the significance of their theft of the Cairo text. Or that they would act so swiftly.' The cardinal sighed. 'So much bloodshed. After the murders, I approached the Guild again, to plant an operative among them. It was easy to do once Sigma had been called into play. The Guild offered its services, Seichan had had a run-in with you already, and the Court took the bite.'

Seichan spoke up. 'My orders were to discover what the Court knew, and thwart them however I saw fit.'

Gray studied her. Her efforts could be merely a ruse to serve the Guild. But he owed Seichan another debt. She had arranged to have Monk whisked out of hospital before Raoul's goons struck. Gray had assumed she would employ Guild operatives—not call Spera, her employer. But the cardinal had declared Monk a Vatican ambassador and shuffled him out of there.

Still, something else bothered Gray. 'Your group at the Vatican,' he said, eyeing Spera. 'What's their interest in all this?'

Spera had folded his hands on the table. Clearly he was reluctant to speak further, but Rachel reached across to him and took his hands.

'You have two gold rings with the papal seal,' she said.

The cardinal pulled his hands back, covering one hand over the other. 'One for my station as cardinal,' he explained. 'And one for my position as secretary of state. Matching rings. It's traditional.'

'But they don't match,' she said. 'I hadn't noticed until you folded your fingers together like that. They're mirror images of each other. They're *twins*.'

Gray could see she was right. 'And Thomas means "twin",' he added, staring up at the cardinal. 'You're a part of the Thomas Church. That's why you've been trying to stop the Court in secret.'

Spera slowly nodded. 'Our group has become an accepted part of the Apostolic Church. Despite beliefs to the contrary, the Church is not beyond science or research. Catholic universities, hospitals and research facilities advocate forward thinking, new concepts and ideas. And yes, a certain part is slow to respond, but it also contains members who challenge the Church and keep it malleable. That is our role.'

'And what about in the past?' Gray asked. 'This ancient society of alchemists we're hunting? The clues we've been following?'

Cardinal Spera shook his head. 'The Thomas Church of today is not the same as before. That church vanished during the French papacy, disappearing along with the Knights Templar.'

'So you're as in the dark about all this as we are,' Monk said.

'I'm afraid so.'

VIGOR WALKED around the stone lip that circled the glass floor—and its etched labyrinth. 'Notice how it's not truly a maze,' he said. 'No blind corners or dead ends. It's just one long, continuous, sinuous path. You can find this exact same maze at Chartres Cathedral outside Paris. It's called the Labyrinth of Daedalus, after the mythological architect who constructed the labyrinth for King Minos of Crete.'

'But why put such a maze down here?' Kat asked.

'The Chartres maze was based on a drawing from a second-century Greek text on alchemy. But the labyrinth at Chartres was also symbolic of journeying from this world to paradise. Worshippers would crawl on hands and knees along this tortuous path from the outside to the centre rosette, representing a pilgrimage from this world to the next.'

'Do you think it's hinting that we must make this journey ourselves?'

'Exactly. The answer is here. We need to find it before it's too late.'

Kat checked her watch. 'We should head back up right now. See if Gray has attempted to make any contact.'

AT GRAY'S EAR, the jet's air-phone's incessant ring finally stopped as the other line was picked up. 'Bryant here.'

'Kat, it's Gray. We have Rachel and Monk. How is everything?'

Kat's voice rang with relief. 'We're fine. We've found the secret entry.' She went on to explain all they'd discovered.

Once she had finished, Gray gave a short account of events in Lausanne. 'We'll be landing at Avignon Caumont airport in about thirty minutes. But we don't have much lead time on the Court. Maybe half an hour.'

Seichan had given them intel on the Court's means of transportation. Raoul had a pair of planes in a small airfield half an hour outside Lausanne.

'With all teammates secure again,' Gray told Kat, 'I'm going to break the silence with central command. I'll have Director Crowe coordinate ground support with the local authorities. I'll call again as soon as we land.'

'Roger that, Commander. We'll be waiting for you.'

Gray hung up. He dialled the access number to Sigma command. It rang through a series of scrambled switchboards and finally connected.

'Logan Gregory.'

'Dr Gregory, it's Commander Pierce.'

'Commander—' The irritation rang in the one word.

Gray cut off an official scolding for his lack of communication. 'I must speak to Painter Crowe immediately.'

'I'm afraid that's not possible, Commander. It's nearly midnight here. The director left command about five hours ago. At this time no one knows where he went.' Aggravation clipped his words again. 'But I'm still ops leader for this mission. I want a full debriefing on your whereabouts.'

Gray suddenly felt uncomfortable. Where had Crowe gone? Was he even gone? Was Gregory blocking him from reaching the director? Somewhere there was a leak at Sigma. He weighed the odds—and went with his gut.

He hung up. He had a jump on Dragon Court. He wouldn't give it away.

GRAY HURRIED with the others across the storm-swept Tarmac of Avignon Caumont airport. He had to give Cardinal Spera credit—or at least his Vatican influence. Customs was cleared in the air, and a BMW saloon waited to ferry them to the Pope's Palace. The cardinal had gone into the terminal, to raise the local authorities. It might take time as it was still only five thirty in the morning, but the Pope's Palace had to be locked down.

Drenched, they all climbed into the waiting car as a brilliant display cracked across the sky.

Rachel drove, taking the narrow streets at breakneck speeds. At this early hour there was little other traffic. A few minutes later, she wheeled them into the square before the palace. They all piled out of the vehicle, and through a gateway, to a courtyard beyond.

Gray had memorised the layout of the palace. He scouted ahead through the empty rooms, cautious but swift. When he reached the entrance to the kitchen he held the others to the hallway and eavesdropped.

Kat and Vigor. Their voices echoed up from a hole in the centre of the kitchen. A glow grew brighter, bobbling a bit.

'Kat,' Gray called out, not wanting to startle his teammate. 'It's Gray.'

The light went out. A moment later, Kat appeared. Gray waved the others into the room. Vigor emerged next from the hole.

Rachel rushed to him. He opened his arms and hugged her tight.

'The Dragon Court knows about this location,' Gray said. 'Cardinal Spera is rousing the local authorities right now. They should be here soon.'

Vigor kept one arm round his niece. 'Then we may have just enough time to unlock the true treasure below.'

Kat nodded. 'We solved the riddle here.'

'And what's the answer?' Gray asked.

Vigor's eyes brightened. 'Light.'

FROM THE TERMINAL concourse of the tiny airport, Cardinal Spera had watched the group depart. He waited five minutes as the commander had requested, giving the team time to reach the palace. He crossed to one of the armed security personnel and asked to be taken to the man's superior. He showed him his Vatican ID. 'It is a matter of utmost urgency.'

'Of course, Cardinal Spera. Right away.'

The young man led him off the concourse and through a card-coded security gate. At the end of a hall was the head of security's office. The guard knocked on the door and was gruffly called inside. He pushed the door open, and looked back at the cardinal, failing to see the pistol with a silencer raised towards the back of his head.

Cardinal Spera lifted a hand. 'No . . .'

The gunshot sounded like a firm cough. The guard's head snapped forward, followed by his body. Blood sprayed into the hallway.

A door to the side opened. Another gunman appeared. A pistol jabbed into Cardinal Spera. He was forced into the office. The door shut.

Another body already decorated the room, lying crumpled on its side.

The former security chief.

Behind his desk, a familiar figure stood.

The cardinal shook his head in disbelief. 'You're part of the Dragon Court.'

'Its leader, in fact.' A pistol rose into sight. 'Clearing the way here for the rest of my men to arrive.'

The gun lifted higher. The muzzle flashed.

Cardinal Spera felt a kick to his forehead—then nothing.

RACHEL STOOD with the other four on the granite ledge surrounding the etched glass floor. Kat stood guard up above, equipped with a radio.

They had descended the tiers to the bottom level in almost reverential silence. Her uncle had offered commentary about the massive museum housed within this subterranean cathedral, but few questions were posed.

Gray knelt to stare at the glass floor and the platinum labyrinth upon it.

'It's Daedalus's maze,' Vigor said, and briefly explained its history.

'So what are we supposed to do here? Gray asked.

'Plainly this is another riddle. Besides the maze, we have a double arch of lodestone above us. A pillar of the same in the centre. And these twelve m-state gold plates.' Vigor indicated windows of glass that pocked the wall around them. 'They are positioned along the periphery like the markings on a clock. Another timepiece. Like the hourglass that led us here.'

'So it would seem,' Gray said. 'But you mentioned light.'

Vigor nodded. 'It's always been about light. A quest for the primordial light of the Bible, the light that formed the universe. Like magnetism and electricity before, now we must prove our understanding of light . . . and not just any light. Light with *power*, or, as Kat puts it, *coherent* light.'

Gray frowned, standing up. 'You mean a laser.'

Vigor nodded. He pulled free an object from his pocket. Rachel recognised it as a laser-targeting scope from one of the Sigma weapons. 'With the power of these superconducting amalgams coupled with jewels like diamonds and rubies, the ancients might have developed some crude form of laser. I believe knowledge of that craft is necessary to open the final level.'

'How can you be sure?' Gray said.

'Kat and I measured these twelve plates of mirrored glass. They are subtly angled to reflect light from one to the other in a set pattern. But it would take a coherent light to complete the circuit. I think the energy stored in the plates will do the rest.'

'And it might not even be *energy*,' Gray said. 'If you're right about light being the base of the mystery here, superconductors not only have the capability of storing energy for an infinite period, they can also store *light*.'

Vigor's eyes widened. 'So a little coherent light might free the rest?'

'Possibly, but how do we go about starting this chain reaction?'

Vigor motioned to the lodestone pillar in the middle of the floor. 'I suspect whatever device the ancients used was meant to rest on it while aimed at one particular window. Our proverbial twelve-o'clock marker.'

'And which one's that?' Monk asked.

Vigor stepped over to the far window. 'True north,' he said. 'This is the one. I think you set the laser down, point it at this plate, then get clear.'

Gray began to step out towards the pedestal when his radio buzzed. He listened, then said 'Kat, be careful. Let them know you're not hostile. Keep silent about us until you're sure.' He ended the call.

'What's the matter?' Monk asked.

'Kat's spotted a patrol of French police. They've entered the palace. She's going to investigate.' Gray waved the group towards the stairs. 'This will have to wait till later. We'd better head back up.'

They filed out from around the glass pool. They worked their way up four tiers when a commanding voice bullhorned down to them from above.

'*TOUT LE MONDE EN BAS LÀ! SORTEZ AVEC VOS MAINS SUR LA TÊTE!*'

Everyone froze.

Rachel translated. 'They want us to exit with our hands on our heads.'

A new voice bellowed through the bullhorn in English. It was Kat. 'COMMANDER! THEY CONFISCATED MY RADIO, BUT IT IS THE FRENCH POLICE. I'VE VERIFIED THEIR LEADER'S ID.'

'Must be the guard sent by Cardinal Spera,' Monk said.

'*SORTEZ TOUTE DE SUITE! C'EST VOTRE DERNIER AVERTISSEMENT!*'

'They certainly don't sound happy,' Monk said.

'OK,' Gray ordered. 'Up we go. We need to prepare them for the arrival of Raoul and his buddies.'

They marched up the remaining tiers with their hands on their heads.

The kitchen was crowded with uniformed men. Rachel spotted Kat, back to one wall, hands on her head, too. The French police were taking no chances. Guns were raised. Gray attempted to explain in stilted French, but they were separated and made to stand against the wall.

A commotion by the hallway marked the arrival of a newcomer, someone with authority. Rachel watched a familiar family friend enter the kitchen, out of place here, but welcome. Had Cardinal Spera called him?

Her uncle brightened, too. 'General Rende! Thank God!'

It was Rachel's boss, the head of her Carabinieri unit. He cut a striking figure, even out of uniform.

Uncle Vigor tried to step forward but was forced back. 'You must get the *gendarmes* to listen. Before it's too late.'

General Rende eyed her uncle with an uncharacteristic sneer of disdain. 'It's already too late.'

Out from behind him marched Raoul.

13

Gray seethed as his wrists were secured behind his back with plastic ties. The other mercenaries, masquerading as French police, stripped them of their weapons.

Raoul stepped in front of Gray. 'You're damn tough to kill. But that's going to end now. And don't hope for a rescue call from the cardinal. He ran into an old friend at the airport.' He nodded to the general and grinned.

General Rende marched up to them, dressed in an expensive black suit and tie, polished Italian shoes. He had been in discussion with a man wearing a clerical collar. The prefect, Alberto Menardi.

'That's enough,' said the general. 'We don't have time to gloat.'

'Yes, Imperator.' Raoul backed a step.

Rende pointed down to the tunnel. 'Take them below. Find out what they've learned. Then kill them.' He stared around the room, his icy blue eyes stopping at the monsignor. Rende strode over to him. 'Fear not, my old friend. We will spare your niece. By keeping the Court abreast of archaeological and art-history treasures, you've served us well these many years.'

Vigor paled as he realised how he'd been used and manipulated.

'Now that role comes to an end,' Rende said. 'But your niece's bloodline goes back to kings and will produce kings to come.'

'By mating me with that bastard?' Rachel snapped back.

'It's not the man or the woman,' Raoul answered. 'It's always been the blood and the future. The purity of the lineage is also a treasure we seek.'

Rachel's eyes flashed with fury. She spat in his face.

He cuffed her hard across the mouth, splitting her lip.

Gray lunged forward, but a pair of rifles shoved him back.

Raoul leaned closer to her. 'I like a little fire in my bed,' he said, dragging her forward. 'And this time I'm not letting you out of my sight.'

'Get what we came here for,' Rende ordered, unperturbed by the violence. 'We'll load as much as we can. The trucks will be arriving soon.'

Gray now understood the uniforms. The masquerade would buy them time to clear a good section of the treasure below.

'Bring the axes and the drills,' Raoul said, and waved his men forward.

Gray knew the tools were not meant for heavy construction.

They were the tools of a true sadist.

Prodded by guns, the group was led back down into the tunnel. Once below, even the smirking guards grew quiet, eyes widening.

Alberto joined them. 'Simply amazing,' he said. 'And according to the *Arcadium*, these are just the dregs left at the doorstep to a greater treasure.'

Vigor stared at the prefect. 'You have Jacques de Molay's testament?'

Alberto was clutching a book tightly to his chest. 'A seventeenth-century copy. The last known to exist.'

Gray turned to Vigor, meeting his eyes questioningly.

'Jacques de Molay was the last Grand Master of the Knights Templar, tortured by the Inquisition for his refusal to reveal the location of their treasure. He was burned at the stake. But there were rumours of a Templar text, a final treatise by de Molay before he was captured.'

'The *Arcadium*,' Alberto said. 'In the possession of the Dragon Court for centuries. It hinted at a treasure. One independent of the mass of gold and jewels of Knights Templar. A greater treasure. One that would put the very keys to the world into its discoverer's hand.'

'The lost secret of the mages,' Vigor said.

They descended the tiers. Upon reaching the bottommost tier, the soldiers spread out around the granite rim. Gray and the others were forced to their knees. Alberto went down alone to the glass floor, studying its labyrinth.

Raoul stood on the steps. He waved to the guards flanking Kat to drag her forward. He bent down and picked up a power drill. He pressed the trigger. The buzz of its motor echoed across the chamber.

'We'll start with an eye,' Raoul said.

One of the guards yanked Kat's head back. She tried to fight, but the other guard kicked her hard in the belly, knocking out her breath. As they held her in place, Gray saw the tear roll from the corner of Kat's eye. Not scared. Angry. Raoul lowered the drill towards her face.

'Don't!' Gray yelled. 'There's no need. I'll tell you what we know.'

'No,' Kat said, and was punched in the face by one of the guards.

Gray understood her warning. If the Dragon Court gained the power here, it would mean Armageddon. Their own lives were not worth that price.

'I'll tell you,' Gray repeated.

But Raoul remained where he was. 'I don't recall asking any questions.'

The drill growled louder.

'Leave her alone,' Gray said. 'You're wasting time. We know how to open the gate. Harm a single one of us and you'll learn nothing.'

Raoul eyed him. 'Explain and I'll consider your offer.'

Gray searched the others, looking forlorn. 'It's light,' he said.

Kat groaned. Vigor hung his head.

'He's right,' a voice called up from the floor below. Alberto climbed a few steps. 'The glass panes on the wall are reflective and angled.'

'It takes laser light,' Gray continued, explaining what Vigor had related.

Alberto joined them. 'Yes, yes . . . it makes perfect sense.'

'Well, we'll see,' Raoul said. 'If he's wrong, we start chopping limbs.'

He ordered his men to make Rachel and the others spread out along the lower wall. Soldiers lay flat on the tier above, rifles aimed at them.

Raoul freed a laser scope and stepped towards the central pedestal. Then he seemed to think better of it. He pointed the scope at Gray.

'You,' he said. 'Set it up. Like you described.'

GENERAL RENDE checked his watch. What he had sought for so long was about to come true. Even if they failed to open whatever secret vault lay below, that storehouse alone was a treasure to dwarf all others.

He had taken a brief look. They would escape with as much as they could, and destroy the rest. His demolition expert was already going over the incendiary charges. All that was left was to wait for the trucks.

He had arranged for a caravan of three heavy-duty Peugeot lorries. They would run in shifts to a warehouse on the outskirts of town, unhooking their load, mounting an empty container, and returning. Back and forth.

The storm would serve to cover their actions, to keep any interest to a minimum. Bribes had been paid. They should have half a day.

A call came through on the radio. 'First truck is climbing the hill now.'

Thunder boomed in the distance. Now it began.

GRAY'S ARMS were cut free. He crossed to the pillar of magnetite. He placed the laser scope on the pillar, and pointed it towards the north window.

'Turn on the laser!' Raoul barked. 'Or we begin shooting out kneecaps.'

Gray reached to the power switch and thumbed it on.

A fine beam of red light shot out and struck the gold-glass plate.

He remembered the batteries at Alexander's tomb. It took a moment for whatever charge or electrical capacitance to build, then the fireworks began.

Gray had no intention of standing here when that happened. He turned and strode rapidly back to the wall.

All eyes were on the single strand of red fire that linked scope to mirror.

A deep tonal note sounded and a new ray of laser shot out from the twelve o'clock plate and struck the five o'clock one.

Then another beam of red fire blazed out, slamming into the ten-o'clock marker. It reflected immediately, springing from mirror to mirror.

Gray stared at the spread before him, forming a fiery star, waist high.

The symbolism was plain. The Star of Bethlehem. The light that had guided the Magi.

The humming note grew louder. The star's fire blazed brighter.

Then Gray felt it, some threshold crossed. Pressure slammed outwards, shoving him to the wall. The Meissner field again.

The star seemed to bow upwards from the centre as if shoved up from the floor. It reached the magnetite arches that crossed overhead.

A burst of energy crackled across the vaulted archways.

Gray felt a tug on the metal buttons of his shirt. The magnetic charge of the arches had grown tenfold.

The star's energy was repelled by the new field and slammed back down, striking the glass floor with a loud metallic chime, the strike of a giant bell.

The pillar blasted upward as if jarred by the collision. It struck the centre of the crossed arches—and stuck, two electromagnets clinging tight.

As the chime faded, Gray felt a pop in his ears as the field broke. The star winked out, though a ghost of its blaze still shone across his vision.

Overhead, the short column still clung to the intersection of the archways, pointing downward now. Gray followed the stone finger.

In the middle of the floor, where the column had stood, lay a perfect circle of solid gold. A match to the key. At its centre—*the centre of everything*—was a black slot.

'The keyhole!' Alberto said. He opened his satchel, pulled out the gold key and hurried forward onto the glass floor.

Bolts of electricity shot from the surface, piercing the man, lifting him off his feet and holding him suspended. Fire licked into him, then a final bolt of energy tossed his blackened corpse to the edge of the glass floor.

Raoul roared, swinging towards Gray. 'You knew this!'

Gray backed a step down the wall. 'How could I know he'd be fried?'

Raoul lifted his pistol and pointed it. 'Time to learn a lesson.'

But the gun was not pointed at Gray.

'No!' Rachel moaned.

The pistol blasted. Across the floor, Vigor clutched his belly with a shocked groan. His feet slid out from under him, and he sank to the floor.

Seichan moved to his side. She kept his feet from touching the glass.

But Raoul wasn't done with them. He pointed his pistol next at Kat.

'Don't!' Gray said. 'I had no idea that would happen! But I now know the mistake Alberto made! You can't just walk out to the keyhole. You have to follow the path.' He waved to the twisted maze.

Raoul's eyes narrowed. 'Makes sense,' he said. He crossed to the corpse, bent down and broke the fire-contorted fingers, still clutched round the key. He freed the length of gold and wiped away the charred flesh.

He held out the key to one of his men. 'Take this out there,' he ordered.

The soldier took the key, then crossed to the entry point of the maze. Clenching his teeth, he stepped out onto the glass floor. Nothing happened.

'Stay away from the platinum etchings,' Gray warned.

The soldier nodded. He took another step.

Without warning, a stab of crimson fire jetted out from a pair of windows. The star flickered into existence, then died again.

The soldier had frozen in place. Then his legs sagged under him. He fell back out of the maze. As he struck the ground, his body split in half, sheared across the waist by the laser.

Raoul's eyes flashed fire. He motioned Gray forward. 'I've had enough with losing my own men. *You* show me how it's done.'

Gray stooped to pick up the key from beside the corpse.

Then it struck Rachel. *Of course*.

Gray straightened up and moved to the entry point of the maze. Warily he began to step out.

'No!' Rachel called out.

'What?' Raoul barked.

Rachel spoke quickly. 'The mazes in all the cathedrals. They represented symbolic journeys. From this world to the next. To spiritual enlightenment in the centre. But to reach there, pilgrims crawled. On hands and knees.'

Gray nodded. 'Below the level of these windows.'

Even Raoul believed her. He waved for Gray to hand over the key. 'I'll take it there myself—but you're going first.'

Plainly Raoul did not have *full* trust in her idea. Gray passed him the key.

'As a matter of fact,' Raoul said, pointing his gun at Rachel, 'since it's your idea, why don't you come along, too? To help keep your man honest.'

Rachel stumbled forward. Her hands were cut free. She crouched down with Gray. He nodded to her, transmitting a silent message, *We'll be OK*.

'Let's get going,' Raoul said.

Gray went first, crawling out onto the maze without hesitation, fully trusting in Rachel's assessment. She was held back by Raoul until Gray was a full body-length away. The glass floor remained quiet.

'OK, now you,' she was ordered.

AS GRAY MADE his turns round the maze, he passed alongside neighbouring paths with Rachel and Raoul. It would only take a hip check to knock Raoul off his path. But Gray knew if he crossed the platinum lines with even a hip, he'd be killed as quickly as Raoul. And with the glass face activated, Rachel would probably be electrocuted, too. So he left Raoul unmolested.

When he crossed paths with Rachel, their eyes remained fixed upon each other. A bond had grown between them, one built on danger and trust.

Round and round they went. A droning grew inside his head, vibrating up the bones of his arms and legs. After a final turn, a straight shot led to the centre rosette. Gray hurried forward, glad to reach home base at last.

The droning grew into a murmuring just beyond the range of the audible.

Rachel crawled towards him. Staying low, he helped her into the centre. She slipped into his arms.

Raoul crawled over to them. 'The Dragon Court owes you for your generous service.' He pointed his gun. 'Stand up. Both of you.'

Gray tried to pull himself out of Rachel's arms, but she clung to him.

'Let me first,' he whispered.

'Together,' she answered. 'Trust me.'

Gray saw her determination. He took a deep breath, and the two of them stood up. Gray expected to be cut in half, but the floor remained quiet.

'A safe zone,' Rachel said. 'In the centre of the star. The lasers never crossed this part.'

'Keep back or you'll be shot,' Raoul warned. He stood up, and reached into a pocket. 'Now let's see what prize you have delivered to us.'

Raoul pulled out the key, bent down, and shoved it into the keyhole.

'A perfect fit,' he mumbled.

Gray pulled Rachel closer, fearful of what would happen next. In her ear, he whispered the secret he had been holding from everyone since Alexandria.

'The key's a fake.'

The vibration worsened. The floor pulsed with white light. With each beat, arcs of electricity raced out along the lines of platinum, crackling and flaring. In seconds, the entire labyrinth shone with an inner fire.

Gray's words echoed in Rachel's ears. *The key's a fake.*

And the labyrinth responded.

An ominous tone chimed beneath them. Pressure again built, closing and squeezing. A new Meissner field grew, strangely skewing perception.

Overhead, the whole complex seemed to vibrate. Reality bent.

Around them, the fiery star shattered back into existence, blasting forth from all the windows. Overhead the stone pedestal broke free from its magnetic attachment to the lodestone arches. It plummeted back to the ground.

Raoul looked up too late. The edge of the stone caught him in the shoulder and crushed him to the floor.

As the pillar struck, the glass shattered under them, skittering out in all directions. From the cracks, a blinding brilliance erupted.

'Hold tight,' Gray whispered.

Rachel sensed it too. A rising vibration of power, under them, around them, through them. She needed to be closer. He responded, turning her to face him, arms crushing her to his chest, leaving no space.

Something was rushing up from below. A bubble of black energy was about to strike. She closed her eyes as the world exploded with light.

ON THE FLOOR, Raoul's shoulder flamed with white-hot agony. Crushed bones ground together. He fought to escape, panicked.

A supernova exploded under and through him, so bright it penetrated to the back of his skull. It spread through his brain. He felt splayed open, every thought, action, desire bared. All his being was drawn out along a shining white thread. Stretched to the point of breaking, it left no room for anger, self-hatred, shame, loathing, fear or recrimination. Only a purity. An unadulterated essence of being. This is who he could be, who he was born to be.

He could not turn away. Time stretched towards the infinite. He was trapped, aflame in a cleansing light, far more painful than any hell.

He faced himself, his life, his possibility, his ruin, his salvation . . .

He saw the truth—and it burned. But the worst was still to come.

SEICHAN CLUTCHED the old man to her chest. Both kept their heads bowed from the blinding eruption of light, but Seichan caught glimpses from the corner of her eyes.

The fiery star blasted skywards on a fountain of light, spinning up into the dark cathedral above. Other glass mirrors, embedded in the vast library, caught the starshine and reflected it back a hundredfold. A cascade reaction spread through the entire complex. In a heartbeat, the two-dimensional star unfolded into a giant three-dimensional sphere of laser light, spinning within and around the subterranean cathedral.

Energy scintillated and crackled out from it, sweeping the tiers.

Screams bellowed and rang. Over her head, one soldier leapt from the tier above, trying to get to the floor below. But there was no sanctuary for him. Bolts struck him before he even hit the ground, burning him to bone.

But most disturbing of all, something had happened to the arched cathedral itself. The view seemed to flatten, losing all sense of depth. And even this image shimmered, as if what hung above her was merely a mirage.

GRAY HELD RACHEL. The world was pure light. He sensed the chaos beyond, but here it was just the two of them.

He remembered Vigor's words. *Primordial light.*

Rachel lifted her face. Her eyes were so bright in the reflected light that he could almost sense her thoughts. She seemed to read him, too.

Something in the character of the light, a permanence that could not be denied, an agelessness that made everything small. Except for one thing.

Gray leaned down, lips brushing hers, breaths shared.

It wasn't love. Not yet. Just a promise.

The light flared brighter as Gray deepened his kiss. What once droned, now sang. His eyes closed, but he still saw her. Her smile, the angle of her neck, the curve of her breast. He felt that permanence again, that ageless presence.

Was it the light? Was it the two of them? Only time would tell.

GENERAL RENDE fled with the first screams. He didn't need to investigate further. He had seen the sheen of energies reflected up from below. He had not got this far in the Court from being foolhardy.

He retreated out of the palace. He would commandeer one of the trucks, return to the warehouse, regroup there, and strategise a new plan.

As he exited the door, he noted that the exterior guard, still in police uniforms, maintained the gate. Good. It would hasten his retreat.

Near the truck, the driver and four uniformed guards noticed his approach and came forward to meet him.

'We must leave immediately,' Rende ordered in Italian.

'Somehow I don't see that happening,' the driver said in English. From his accent, he was clearly an American.

The general stepped back, glanced at the gateway. More French policemen, *real* French policemen, stood guard. He'd been betrayed by his own ruse.

'If you're looking for *your* men,' the American said, 'they're already secured in the back of the truck.'

General Rende stared at the driver. Black hair, blue eyes. He didn't recognise him, but he knew the voice from conversations over the phone.

'Painter Crowe,' he said.

DOWN IN THE CAVERN, the fireworks had lasted only a little over a minute. The sphere of coherent light had spun for the last time, then collapsed in on itself like a dying sun.

Gray broke the embrace with Rachel, the acuity of his senses fading with the light. But he still tasted her on his lips. That was enough. For now.

Some of the shine remained in her eyes as she searched around. The others were stirring from where they had flattened themselves against the ground. Rachel slipped out of Gray's arm to check on her uncle. Monk headed in the same direction, ready to employ his medical training.

Gray stared at the heights around him. No shots rang out. The soldiers were gone . . . along with the library. Above stretched empty space. It was as if something had cored out the centre, leaving only the amphitheatre-like rings of ascending tiers.

A moan drew his attention to the floor.

Raoul lay crumpled nearby, curled round his trapped arm, crushed under the fallen pillar. Gray stepped over and kicked his pistol aside. It skittered across the glass floor, now a cracked and scattered jigsaw. Kat came over.

'Leave him for now,' Gray said. 'We'd best collect as many weapons as we can. There's no telling how many others might be up there.'

She nodded.

Raoul rolled onto his back. His face was twisted in agony. Tears rolled down his cheeks. But Gray suspected it wasn't the crushed arm that was triggering this misery. Raoul's face had changed. The hard edge and disdain had vanished, replaced with something softer, more human.

'I didn't ask to be forgiven,' he keened out in anguish.

Gray frowned. He remembered his own sensation during that moment of exposure to the light. *Primordial light.* A sense of something greater. Something beyond comprehension.

Had something rewired the man's soul? Could there be hope for him?

Movement drew Gray's eye. He saw the danger immediately.

He moved to stop her. Ignoring him, Seichan lifted Raoul's gun.

Raoul turned to face the barrel. His expression remained anguished, but now a flicker of raw fear lit his eyes—not for the pain of death, but for what lay beyond.

'No!' Gray called.

Seichan pulled the trigger. Raoul's head snapped back with a crack almost as loud as the pistol shot.

'Why?' Gray asked, stunned, stepping forward.

Seichan rubbed her wounded shoulder. 'Payback. Remember we had a deal, Gray.' She nodded to Raoul's body. 'Besides, like the man said, he wasn't looking for forgiveness.'

PAINTER HEARD the echo of the gunshot through the palace. He motioned the French patrol to pause. 'Slowly,' he warned, waving them on. 'Be ready.'

He continued deeper into the palace. He had come to France on his own. Not even Sean McKnight knew he had undertaken this assignment, but Painter's Europol credentials had got him the field support he needed in Marseilles. It had taken the length of a transatlantic trip to track General Rende, first to a warehouse outside Avignon, then to the Pope's Palace.

Upon first hearing of a possible leak from Gray, Painter made one decision. To trust his own organisation. He had put the new Sigma together from the ground up. If there was a leak, it had to be an unintentional one.

So he had done the next logical thing: followed the trail of intel.

From Gray . . . to Sigma . . . to their Carabinieri liaison out in Rome.

General Rende had been kept abreast of every detail of the operation.

It had taken some careful prying to follow the man's tracks, which included suspicious trips to Switzerland. Eventually Painter had discovered one thin tie back to the Dragon Court. A distant relative of Rende who had been arrested two years ago for trafficking in stolen antiquities. The thief had gained his freedom from pressure by the Imperial Dragon Court.

As he'd investigated deeper, Painter had kept Logan Gregory out of the loop, so the man could continue his role as Sigma liaison. He hadn't wanted to spook Rende, not until he could be sure.

Now that his suspicions had been verified, Painter had another concern.

Was he too late?

RACHEL AND MONK secured her uncle's temporary belly wrap, using Gray's shirt. According to Monk, nothing major seemed to have been hit, but Vigor needed immediate medical attention.

Then Monk helped Vigor to his feet and half carried him.

Rachel hovered alongside them. Gray joined her, putting an arm around her waist. She leaned a bit into him, drawing strength from him.

Before they even reached the first tier, a booming voice echoed down to them, using a bullhorn again. '*SORTEZ AVEC VOS MAINS SUR LA TÊTE!*' The command echoed away, to come out with their hands up.

'*Déjà vu,*' Monk sighed. 'Pardon my French.'

Another voice boomed: 'COMMANDER PIERCE, WHAT'S YOUR STATUS?'

'Impossible!' Kat said.

'It's Director Crowe,' Gray confirmed, shock in his voice. He yelled back. 'ALL CLEAR DOWN HERE! WE'RE COMING UP!'

They began the long trek up to the kitchen. Bodies littered the tiers.

'Why were we spared?' Monk asked.

'Maybe that lower level sheltered us,' Kat said.

Gray didn't argue, but suspected it was more than that. He remembered the suffusing glow of the light. He sensed something beyond raw power.

'And what happened to the treasure house?' Seichan asked, staring out at the empty expanse. 'Was it all a hologram of some sort?'

'No,' Gray answered as they climbed. He had a theory. 'Under powerful conditions, flux tubes can be generated within a Meissner field. Affecting not only gravity, like the levitation we've already seen, but also distorting space. Einstein showed that gravity actually *curves* space. The flux tubes create such a vortex in gravity that it *bends* space, possibly even folding it in on itself, allowing movement across.' He noted the looks of disbelief. 'Research is already being done on this at NASA,' he pressed.

'Smoke and mirrors,' Monk grumbled. 'That's what I think it was.'

'But where did it all go?' Seichan asked.

Vigor coughed. 'Gone where we can't follow,' he said hoarsely. 'We were judged and found wanting.'

Gray felt Rachel begin to speak, to mention the false key. He squeezed her and nodded to her uncle, urging her to let him speak. Maybe it wasn't all the fake key. Could Vigor be right?

The monsignor continued, 'The ancients sought the source of primordial light, the spark of all existence. Maybe they finally found it, a gateway from this world into the next. They left it here for others to follow, but we came—'

'Too early,' Rachel suddenly blurted, interrupting.

'Or too late,' Gray added. The words had just popped into his head, like the flash of a camera bulb, leaving him dazed.

Rachel glanced at him. She lifted a hand to rub her forehead.

He saw a similar confusion in her eyes, as if the words had come unbidden to her, too. Perhaps Raoul was not the only one affected by the light.

'Too late . . . or too early,' Vigor continued with a shake of his head. 'Wherever the ancients fled with their treasures—into the past, into the future—they have left us with only the present.'

'To create our own heaven or hell,' Monk said.

They continued in silence, climbing tier after tier. Reaching the top level, a group of French police waited, along with a familiar face.

'Commander,' Painter said. 'It's good to see you.'

Gray shook his hand. 'You have no idea.'

'Let's get all of you topside.'

Before they could move, Vigor stirred from Monk's arm. 'Wait.'

A short distance away stood a stone table. It seemed everything had not vanished with the library. A leather-bound book rested on the table. Its glass case, though, was gone.

'The ledger,' he said, tears welling. 'They left the ledger!'

Rachel went over and picked it up. She shut it and tucked it under an arm.

'Why leave that behind?' Monk asked, helping the monsignor again.

Vigor answered, 'To let us know what awaits us.'

They hobbled towards the stairs.

Gray glanced back one more time. With the space empty, he noted the cavern's shape, a cone balanced on its tip. Or the upper half of an hourglass, pointing down towards the glass floor. But where was the lower half?

'As it is above, so it is below,' he mused.

Vigor glanced back to him, rather sharply. Gray saw the understanding and knowledge in the old man's eyes. He had already figured it out too.

The gold key was meant to open a gateway. To the lower half of the hourglass. But where? Was there a cavern directly beneath this one? Gray didn't think so. But somewhere the cathedral of knowledge waited. What had hung here was a mere reflection from another place.

Like Monk said. Smoke and mirrors.

Vigor stared at him. Gray remembered Cardinal Spera's mission: to preserve the secret of the Magi, trusting that the knowledge would reveal itself when the time was right. Maybe that's what life's journey was all about.

The quest. To seek the truth.

Gray placed a hand on Vigor's shoulder. 'Let's go home.'

With Rachel under his arm, Gray climbed the stairs.

Out of darkness and towards the light.

EPILOGUE

August 18

Gray pedalled down Cedar Street, passing by the Takoma Park Library. It seemed like the last three weeks had been spent underground at Sigma command, in meeting after meeting.

He had just come from a final debriefing with Painter Crowe. The meeting had centred on Seichan. The Guild operative had vanished like a ghost as they'd left the Pope's Palace, stepping round a corner and disappearing. But Gray had found a token from her in his pocket. Her dragon pendant.

And while the first pendant left at Fort Detrick had plainly been meant as a threat, this one felt different to Gray. A promise. Until they met again.

Kat and Monk had been at the debriefing too. Monk had sat fiddling with his new state-of-the-art prosthesis, not so much uncomfortable with his new hand as anxious about the coming evening. Kat and Monk were going out on their first real date. Kat had asked Monk out.

Gray skimmed low round the corner onto Sixth Street. His mother had asked him to come to lunch. And while he could have refused, he had been putting off something for too long.

He made a final turn, hopped the kerb and braked into the driveway of his parents' bungalow.

He called through the screen door. 'Mom, I'm home!'

He leaned the bike against the railing and opened the door.

'I'm in the kitchen!' his mother said.

Gray smelt something burning. A bit of smoke hung about the rafters.

'Is everything all right?' he asked, crossing down the short hall.

His mother wore jeans, a chequered blouse and an apron snugged around her waist. She had dropped her hours at the university to part-time, two days a week. To help care for things at home.

'I was making grilled cheese sandwiches,' she said, fluttering her hands. 'I got a phone call. Left them on the griddle too long.'

Gray eyed the pile of sandwiches on a plate. Each was charred on one side. He fingered one. The cheese hadn't even melted. How did she do that?

'Call your father,' his mother said. 'He's out back.'

Gray crossed to the open back door. 'Pop! Lunch is ready.'

'Be right there!'

His mother was setting out some plates when he returned. 'Could you pour some orange juice?' she asked. 'I need to get a fan.'

Gray stepped to the refrigerator, found the carton of juice and began filling the tumblers. With his mother gone, he set the carton down and removed a small glass vial from his back pocket.

A grey-white powder filled it halfway. The last of the amalgam.

He had done some research into the m-state powders, how the compounds stimulated endocrine systems and seemed to have a strong ameliorative affect on the brain, increasing perception, acuity . . . *and memory*.

Gray dumped the contents of the vial into one of the glasses of orange juice and used a teaspoon to stir it.

His father entered through the back door. Sawdust speckled his hair.

He wiped his boots on the rug, nodded to Gray, and dropped heavily into a chair. 'Your mother tells me you're heading back to Italy.'

'Only for five days,' Gray answered, nesting all three glasses between his palms and carrying them over. 'Another business trip.'

'Right . . .' His father eyed him. 'So who's the girl?'

Startled, Gray spilt some of the orange juice. He wasn't sure what to say.

After their rescue, he and Rachel had spent a night in Avignon together as matters were sorted out, curled in front of a small fire while the storm exhausted itself. Rachel had explained about her family's history, with tears. Finally, they had fallen asleep in each other's arms.

In the morning, circumstance and duty had pulled them apart.

Where would it lead now? He was heading back to Rome to find out.

He still called daily. Vigor was healing well. Following Cardinal Spera's funeral, he had been promoted to the position of prefect at the Archives, to oversee the repair of the damage done by the Court. Last week, Gray had received a note of thanks from Vigor, with a hidden message. Below the monsignor's signature lay two inked seals, papal insignia, mirror images of each other, the twin symbols of the Thomas Church. It seemed the secret church had found a new member to replace the lost cardinal.

Upon learning this, Gray had shipped Alexander's gold key to Vigor, the *real* gold key, from a safe-deposit box in Egypt. For safekeeping. Who better to secure it? The fake key, the one used to trick Raoul, had been fashioned at one of the many shops in Alexandria known for their skill at counterfeiting antiquities. It had taken less than an hour, performed while Gray had freed Seichan from Alexander's watery tomb.

With General Rende's testimony and confession, his sect of the Dragon

Court was slowly being rooted out. But how thoroughly or completely would never be known.

Meanwhile, Rachel continued to sort out her life. With Raoul's death, she and her family had inherited Château Sauvage, a bloody inheritance to be sure. Plans were under way to sell the château. The proceeds would go to the families of those killed in Cologne and Milan.

Gray settled the tumblers of orange juice on the table.

His father sighed and tipped back in his kitchen chair. 'Son, you've been in an awfully good mood lately. Ever since your return from that business trip last month. Only a woman puts that kind of shine on a man. I may be losing my memory, but not my eyesight. So tell me about her.'

Gray stared at his father. He heard the unspoken addendum.

While I can still remember.

His father's casual manner hid a deeper vein. Not sorrow or loss. He was reaching out for something now. In the present. Some connection to a son he'd perhaps lost in the past.

Gray froze by the table. He felt a flare of old anger, older resentment. He didn't deny it, but he let the heat wash through him.

His father must have sensed something, because he settled his chair to the floor and changed the subject. 'So, where are those sandwiches?'

Words echoed in Gray's head. *Too early . . . too late.* A last message to live in the present. To accept the past and not rush the future.

His father reached for the spiked glass of orange juice.

Gray blocked him, covering the cup with his hand. He lifted the tumbler away. 'How about a beer? I think I saw a Bud in the fridge.'

His father nodded. 'That's why I love you, son.'

Gray stepped to the sink, dumped the orange juice down the drain, and watched it swirl away.

Too early . . . too late.

It was time he lived in the present. He didn't know how much time he had with his father, but he would make the very best of what he could get.

He crossed to the fridge, grabbed two beers, popped the lids on the way back, pulled out one of the kitchen chairs, sat down, and placed a bottle in front of his father.

'Her name is Rachel.'

JAMES ROLLINS

Home: Sacramento, California
Interests: scuba diving, caving and hiking
Website: www.jamesrollins.com

RD: You once said that *Map of Bones* was the religious man's answer to *The Da Vinci Code*. Can you tell us a little more about what you meant by that?

JR: I noticed that most thrillers, when dealing with the Catholic Church or the Vatican, paint them in a disparaging light. I sought to show Catholicism, and its history, in a manner that is realistic and acknowledges some of the Vatican's corrupt past—but also stresses its role as a fundamental factor in forming Western civilisation—and how faith, whether it be the belief in God, a Higher Power, or in the substantive good in mankind, is a part of human nature.

RD: Do you have strong faith yourself?

JR: I was raised as a Roman Catholic and attended Catholic schools throughout my childhood. While I don't still adhere to many of the tenets as an adult, faith in something greater than ourselves persists as a deeply ingrained belief.

RD: How did you set about researching such a complex novel?

JR: I spent about three months reading, searching the Internet, pestering librarians, interviewing experts. I guess I can be quite annoying, but most people are very keen to help.

RD: How did you research the Vatican?

JR: I had travelled to Rome for a long vacation about ten years ago and made several friends. One of them eventually ended up at the Vatican. He was a great resource for details and secret histories.

RD: In the novel you suggest that the Vatican employs spies. Is this based on truth?

JR: Yes, it is. Like any government, the Vatican does indeed maintain a sophisticated intelligence-gathering operation, even employing full-time agents. And through its diplomatic ambassadors, charitable organisations, and its millions of parishioners and lay persons, it maintains a sophisticated global network of eyes and ears.

RD: Does the liquid body armour you describe have any basis in fact?

JR: It does indeed. It is a real material. When I wrote the book it was just undergoing testing, now it is being used in the field.

RD: Are the diving scenes in the novel based on your own experiences?

JR: I love to scuba dive but I'm not nearly as adventurous as my characters. That's one of the best things about writing—you get to go on these wild adventures, to stretch and tread where you dare not go yourself.

RD: I understand that you trained as a vet. Do you still do that job?

JR: While I don't work full-time, I still volunteer at the local animal shelter, once or twice a month.

RD: You also publish fantasy novels under the name of James Clemens. What made you start writing adventure thrillers? And which genre do you prefer?

JR: While I was trying to sell my first fantasy to a publisher, I thought I'd try my hand at writing a thriller. And, lo and behold, *both* ended up selling. As to which I prefer, it's usually whichever one I'm not currently writing! When I'm writing my thrillers, I sometimes wish I could use magic to get my characters out of a jam. When I'm writing a fantasy set in a medieval landscape, I suddenly find they need a cellphone or a fast means of transportation. So each genre has its pros and cons, challenges and joys. I wouldn't give up either of them.

RD: Are the characters of Gray and Rachel based on anyone in particular?

JR: I think a little of myself is in both characters, but ultimately they are not based on anyone particular in my life. But the villains . . . that's another story. OK, maybe not!

SACRED TREASURES

The holy relics that are stolen at the start of *Map of Bones*—the remains of the biblical Magi—are housed, just as James Rollins describes, in a gilded sarcophagus (right) in Cologne Cathedral. Canon law decrees that every Catholic altar must have an object of religious veneration beneath it. Such holy relics range from bones and mummified body parts to personal possessions and even garments of saints, apostles and martyrs. Among the more unusual are the jaw, tongue and vocal cords of St Anthony in his basilica in Padua, and the body of St Catherine of Labouré with its perfectly preserved blue eyes, on display in the Chapel of Our Lady of the Miraculous Medal in Paris.

SECRET ASSET

STELLA RIMINGTON

Why would someone hate their country so much that they would choose to work hand in hand with its sworn enemies? That's the question that faces Liz Carlyle when she learns that there is a mole working at the very heart of MI5—a sleeper who is planning a terrible revenge.

1

In the upmarket bathroom shop in Regent's Park Road in north London, the slim brown-haired woman was showing a close interest in the display of tiles. 'Do you need some help?' asked the young male assistant, who was keen to close since it was almost seven o'clock.

Liz Carlyle was killing time. In trainers and designer jeans, she looked like any of the wealthy young married women who drifted in and out of the interior-design shops and boutiques of this part of London. But Liz was neither wealthy nor married and she was certainly not drifting. She was very focused indeed. She was waiting for the device she held tightly in her left hand to vibrate once—the signal that it was safe for her to proceed to the meeting in the coffee shop farther down the road. Reflected in the mirror on the shop wall, she could see Wally Woods, the leader of the A4 team providing countersurveillance back-up, taking his time buying an *Evening Standard* from the newsvendor on the corner.

He had already sent the two pulses, which signalled that her contact, Marzipan, was inside the café waiting for her. Once his team were satisfied that no one had followed Marzipan, Wally would send the OK.

A young Asian man, dressed in jeans and a hooded top, came along from the direction of Chalk Farm. Wally and his team watched tensely as he paused to look in an estate agent's window. Moving on, he crossed the road and walked down a side street. The device in Liz's hand vibrated once.

'Thanks very much,' said Liz to the relieved shop assistant. 'I'll bring my husband in tomorrow evening and we'll decide then.' She left the shop, turned right and walked quickly towards the coffee shop.

Inside, Liz waited at the counter to order a cappuccino. She felt the familiar tension in her stomach, the quickened beating of her heart, which always accompanied work on the front line. She had missed this excitement. For the last four months or so, she had been on convalescent leave, following a counterterrorist operation in Norfolk at the end of the previous year.

She'd gone down to her mother's house in Wiltshire almost immediately after the MI5 doctor had ordered her off work. In the ensuing weeks she'd helped her mother in the garden centre she ran. On days off, they'd visited National Trust houses and occasionally socialised with neighbourhood friends. It had been pleasant, tranquil, and agonisingly uneventful. Now, on this May evening, she was happy to be back at the sharp end of operations.

She had returned to work only that week. 'Take your time. Settle in,' Charles Wetherby had told her, and back in her office in the counterterrorism agent-running section she had started with the mountain of paperwork that had accumulated in her absence. But then the message had come that afternoon from Marzipan—code name for Sohail Din—urgently requesting a meeting. Strictly speaking, Marzipan was no longer Liz's business. Her colleague Dave Armstrong had taken him over, along with the immense promise of reliable information that he represented, the minute she had left. But Dave was in Leeds on urgent business and Liz, as Marzipan's original recruiter and runner, had been the obvious choice to stand in.

She took her coffee and walked to the gloomy back of the café where Marzipan was sitting at a small corner table, reading a book.

'Hello, Sohail,' she said quietly, sitting down.

He closed his book and looked at her in surprise. 'Jane!' he exclaimed, using the name he knew her by. 'I was not expecting you, but I am so happy to see you.'

She had forgotten how young he looked, but then, he was only nineteen. When Liz had first met Sohail Din, more than a year before, he had already been accepted to read Law at Durham University and had taken a gap-year job at a small Islamic bookshop in Haringey, north London. Though it was not well paid, he had hoped it would provide an opportunity for religious discussion with other serious-minded young men like himself.

But he had soon found that the bookshop was a focal point for radical Islamist doctrine—not at all the version of Islam that Sohail had learned at home and at his local mosque. He had been shocked by the casual talk of fatwas and jihad, then still more to find that some of his fellow employees openly supported the tactics of suicide bombers. Finally, he had come to realise that some of the people who came into the shop were involved in terrorist activities. That was when he had decided to act himself, to tell his story to a Special Branch officer at a police station some distance away. He was moved quickly through a well-tried route to MI5 and his first contact there, Liz Carlyle. She had recruited him, persuading him to put off his university career one more year. In the months that followed, Marzipan had provided invaluable information.

'It's very good to see you again, Sohail,' said Liz. 'You look well.'

Marzipan put down his book, saying nothing, but gazing at her gently, solemnly. Liz could see that he was on edge.

'Are you looking forward to university?' she said, wanting to put him at ease.

'Very much,' he said earnestly.

'Good. You will do very well at Durham, you know.' Gently, she made the transition to business. 'Your message said you needed to see us urgently.'

'Two weeks ago, a man visited the bookshop,' he said. 'One of the boys in the shop told me he was an important imam visiting from Pakistan, and I thought I recognised his face from one of the videos we sell. I told this to Simon and he said that if the man came back I should contact him.'

Simon Willis was Dave Armstrong's working alias. Liz asked, 'And you've seen this man again?'

Sohail Din nodded. 'This afternoon. He did not come into the shop. He was upstairs, with three other men. Young men. All British Asians.'

'Are you sure?'

'I am certain. I heard them speak. You see, I was sent upstairs to fix the video player. Aswan—he works in the shop—had installed it, but today is his day off. He had not connected it properly to the aerial.'

'What were they watching?'

'A video the imam had brought—there was a stack of them next to the VCR. It was a video of the imam speaking in Urdu. He was saying that sometimes it was necessary to die for one's belief; he was talking about a holy war.'

She said, 'Did you see any more than that?'

Sohail shook his head. 'Not then. I didn't stay; I didn't want them to think I was paying much attention.' He paused for a moment. 'I think that the imam had come here to tutor the men. Maybe to prepare them for a mission. A suicide mission. They talk about these things in the shop.'

Liz was surprised. This seemed a very dramatic conclusion. The Marzipan she had known had been calm and level-headed; now he seemed frightened and overexcited.

Liz asked calmly, 'Why do you think that?'

Suddenly Sohail reached down and brought a small paper bag out of his knapsack. He slid it across the table. 'Here's why. I brought the video. The imam left it behind, along with the other tapes. I went upstairs and watched it just before we closed.'

Liz put the video into her bag. 'Well done, Sohail,' she said, 'but won't they notice that it's gone?'

'There were many other videos upstairs. And no one saw me go up there.'

'It will have to go back quickly,' she said firmly. 'But tell me, these three men, how old were they?'

'Two were about my age. The other one perhaps in his late twenties.'

'Would you recognise them again?'

'I can't be sure. I didn't want to look at them too carefully. But I think the older one came from the North. He had some kind of accent.'

'Do you have any idea where these three have gone now?'

'No, but I know they'll be back next week. Aswan asked if he should bring the machine down. But the owner said not to bother, as they would need it again next Thursday. That is why I think they are in training.'

Liz considered this. They had some time, then, though not very much, to put an operation in place before the group reconvened. 'Tell me, could you meet me again later this evening?' she said. 'I'd like to go and copy the video, and also collect some photographs for you to look at. Photographs of people. Can you do that?'

Sohail nodded.

'Let me tell you where to go.' She gave him an address in one of the streets north of Oxford Street. 'Take the Underground to Oxford Circus and walk west. We will make sure you aren't being followed, but if we are not happy, someone will stop you on the street and ask you for the time. They'll ask you twice—and if that happens do not go to the safe house. Walk straight on, catch a bus home. And just in case you run into anyone you know, have an excuse ready for what you're doing there.'

'That's easy,' said Sohail. 'I'll say I've been looking for CDs at the HMV shop on Oxford Street. They stay open late.'

Liz looked at her watch. 'It's now seven thirty. I'll meet you there at ten.'

'Will you be my contact again from now on?' he asked.

'We'll see,' she said mildly, for in truth she didn't know. 'It doesn't matter, you know. We all work together.'

He nodded but there was a look in his eyes that Liz at first took for simple excitement, then realised was partly fear. She smiled reassuringly at him. 'You are doing a brilliant job. Just go on being careful, Sohail.'

He smiled back at her a little bleakly, his eyes darkening. She added, 'If you ever feel you are in any danger, you must tell us at once. Use the alert procedure. We do not expect you to put yourself in unnecessary danger.'

She knew these were empty words. Of course he must be in jeopardy; in such operations risk was inevitable. Not for the first time, Liz questioned her participation in the subtle game of agent running: cautioning the agent to be careful, reassuring him that he would be protected, encouraging him to obtain the information that was needed. The only justification was the harm she was trying to prevent, but faced with a Marzipan, it was a difficult balance to preserve.

Now Sohail said resolutely, 'I will do everything I can.' Liz was moved but his words did nothing to relieve her feelings of guilt.

He was so very young, and yet so very brave. If these men in the bookshop were happy to blow themselves up, she hated to think what they would be happy to do to Sohail. Involuntarily almost, she shook her head and turned away.

LIZ HAILED A TAXI at the bottom of Primrose Hill and directed the driver to the Atrium restaurant on Millbank. From there it was a short walk to Thames House, the massive heavy-set building on the north bank of the Thames, which was the headquarters of MI5. Within twenty minutes of leaving Marzipan she was back at her desk.

There was much to do before she could get back to Sohail Din. The video had to be copied, the arrangements for the safe house confirmed, a fresh A4 team conjured up to replace Wally Woods's, now going off duty.

Reaching for the telephone, Liz dialled Judith Spratt, who was on night duty. They had both joined the Service on the same day over a decade before and were old friends. Both had worked in the counterterrorism branch now for six years, but while Liz's talents had taken her in the direction of agent running, Judith's sharp analytical skills and attention to detail had turned her into an expert investigator.

So it was to Judith that Liz now went for the portfolio of British Asians suspected of some kind of involvement in terrorism. Liz gave her a quick précis of what Marzipan had said, but none of it connected with anything Judith and her team were currently working on. Clutching the large leather portfolio Judith gave her, she took the lift down to the basement garage and collected one of the anonymous fleet vehicles housed there.

With three-quarters of an hour still to spare she drove back north, up Regent Street through Oxford Circus, eventually turning into the quiet streets of once-grand eighteenth-century houses, now the consulting rooms of the doctors, dentists and psychiatrists serving London's wealthier residents. Finally, she turned into a dark, faintly lit mews of small houses. A garage door swung up when she pressed the bleeper in the car, and she drove straight in.

Above the garage was a warm, cheerful sitting room, furnished with a couple of well-used sofas, a square dining-room table with several chairs of an unidentifiable wood, and a battered coffee table. Safe houses were one of civilisation's dead ends. Strictly utilitarian, they were kept in readiness for use, the kitchen stocked with the essentials for making coffee and tea but never any food. As Liz unpacked the portfolio of photographs onto the dining-room table, the phone rang.

'Ninety seconds,' said a voice at the other end. 'All clear.'

She opened the door immediately the bell rang and led Marzipan up the stairs. 'Would you like something to drink—tea, perhaps, or coffee?'

Sohail shook his head, saying nothing but taking in his surroundings.

'All right, then, let's get started,' she said. 'I want you to take your time looking at these, but don't think too hard about it. Usually your first instinct is accurate.'

The pictures were from a variety of sources. The best were copies of those supplied with applications for passports and driving licences. The rest mostly came from surveillance and were poorer. Sohail took his time, examining each photograph carefully before shaking his head. By eleven, when they were only halfway through, it occurred to Liz that Sohail's parents would start to worry if he were unusually late. 'I think we should call it a day,' she announced. 'Could you look at the rest tomorrow?'

He nodded, and she said, 'Then let's meet up here again. Shall we say seven thirty? Come just the same way as you did tonight.' She looked at Sohail. He seemed very tired. 'You should take a cab home. I'll call one.'

She suddenly felt an almost maternal concern for the young man. It was a pity he had yet to identify any of the three suspects. But she had long ago learned that success in her line of business took time and patience.

2

Maddie came back to Belfast when her mother Molly telephoned to tell her the news. There was nothing to be done except manage the pain. Sean Keaney would die at home.

So she had returned to the drab terraced house where her father and mother had lived for over forty years, just off the Falls Road in Belfast. Learning that death was imminent, the family had gathered like a wagon train drawing up in a circle for defence. Though it was a sparse circle, thought Maddie. One daughter had died of breast cancer two years before, and the one son—apple of his father's eye—had been shot dead fifteen years before trying to evade a British Army roadblock. Now only she and her older sister, Kate, remained.

Maddie had come only because her mother had asked her to. As a little girl, her dislike for her father had been matched by the intensity of love she'd felt for her mother, though as she grew up even this was corroded by her frustration at her mother's willingness to subordinate her own striking qualities—the musicality, the love of books, the Galway-bred sense of humour—to her husband's demand that the Struggle should always come first.

Maddie had known that her father's dedication to Irish nationalism brought him admiration of a kind. But this had only increased her own dislike of him, her anger at his callous treatment of the family. Yet she was never sure which she felt more contemptible—the man or the movement. She had got away from both as soon as she could—leaving at eighteen to study Law at University College Dublin, then staying on to work there.

There was also the violence—Maddie had been fleeing that as well. Her father had been obsessively secretive about his 'professional life', yet as the Keaney family listened to the news of each IRA 'operation'—that euphemism for bombings, shootings and death—the hush that settled over them all was knowing, not innocent. No hush could still the impact of the deaths that studded Maddie's childhood like a grotesquely crowded dartboard. Especially that of her brother, born and bred a Republican, killed before he had any idea that life might give him other choices.

Now she sat in the small sitting room with her mother and sister for hours on end, while in his bed on the floor above them her father lay, heavily sedated. Word went out, through the vast network of comrades, associates and friends, that Sean Keaney would be glad to have final visits from those who had served with him.

The visitors were all known to the family. Kieran O'Doyle, Jimmy Garrison, Seamus Ryan—even Martin McGuinness made an appearance late one night, under cover of darkness—the list was a roll call of the Republican movement.

Many had served prison terms for their part in assassinations or bombings, and were free now only because of the amnesty provisions of the Good Friday Agreement. Keaney had managed to avoid any criminal conviction, but along with most of his visitors, he had been interned in the seventies for over a year in the cell blocks of the Maze Prison.

The men were shown upstairs by Maddie, since her mother found the constant up and down exhausting. Standing by the bedside, Maddie could see that her father's shrunken form shocked his visitors. Sensing the fatigue of the man they had known as Commander, most of his old associates kept their visits short, ending them with awkward but heartfelt final farewells. Downstairs, they stopped to talk briefly with Molly and Kate.

Maddie realised that even these brief visits drained her father's dwindling energy, and she was relieved when there was no one left on the visitors' list they had drawn up. Which made her father's subsequent request, uttered after a night of such pain she thought he would not see the dawn break, all the more astonishing.

'He wants to see James Maguire!' she announced as her sister and mother gathered for breakfast in the small kitchen downstairs.

'You can't be serious,' Kate said incredulously. Even under the umbrella of Irish nationalism, Maguire and Keaney had at best co-existed edgily, their mutual antipathy held in check only by their devotion to the cause.

Yet they could not turn down a request from their dying father. Later that day, about an hour before the Keaneys had their tea, there was a knock on the door. A tall, lean man came into the house, displaying none of the modesty shown by the other former associates of Sean Keaney. When Kate took him upstairs, she later told Maddie, she found their father asleep—perhaps the bizarre meeting with a long-time enemy would not take place after all. But as she turned back to the visitor, the man said evenly, 'Hello, Keaney.'

'Come in, Maguire,' the weaker voice commanded, and Kate saw that her father's eyes had opened. He raised a bony hand to dismiss her, which he had not done with his other visitors.

Downstairs, Maddie waited in the parlour with her mother and sister, torn between curiosity and disbelief. Finally, after half an hour, they heard the bedroom door open, footsteps come down the staircase, and, without stopping for even the curtest farewell, Maguire walked out of the house.

Afterwards, Maddie found her father so exhausted that she could not bring herself to ask about the visitor, and left him to sleep. Her sister, less patiently, waited only until after tea to go upstairs, determined to discover the reason for her father's summoning Maguire. Yet she returned downstairs distraught. Some time during tea their father had died in his sleep.

CHARLES WETHERBY, Director of Counterterrorism, had been in the office since seven thirty. After Liz had briefed him by phone about her meetings with Marzipan the previous evening, he had called an emergency meeting of the Counterterrorist Committee—the joint committee of MI5, MI6, GCHQ, the Metropolitan Police and the Home Office that had been set up immediately after the Twin Towers atrocity of September 11, 2001. The CTC had accepted that, on the information available, there was a possible threat of an extreme kind. It had therefore agreed that MI5 should investigate Marzipan's information, using joint resources as necessary.

Now, at eleven o'clock, Wetherby was chairing an operations meeting of the MI5 sections involved. The operations briefing room overlooked the Thames House atrium but had no windows to the outside world. It was spacious, with several rows of chairs around a long table and at one end a screen and other technical equipment. Liz found herself sitting between Judith Spratt and Reggie Purvis, the dour Yorkshireman who headed A4, the surveillance section whose teams had been out providing counter-surveillance for Liz and Marzipan the night before.

Also present was a small army of tough-looking characters in shirt sleeves, mostly ex-military. These were members of A2, the section responsible for 'bugging and burgling'—installing covert listening devices and cameras—all experts in the skills required for their risky, nerve-stretching business. Filling the remaining seats were colleagues of Judith Spratt from Investigations: 'Technical Ted' Poyser, the chief consultant on all computer matters; Patrick Dobson, responsible for liaison with the Home Office; and Dave Armstrong, just back from Leeds.

Liz knew and liked most of her colleagues, the sole exception arriving late for the meeting. Michael Binding had returned the year before from a posting in Northern Ireland and was now head of A2. Binding treated all his female colleagues with an infuriating mix of gallantry and condescension, which Liz could deal with only by the most iron self-control.

For this morning, at least, Liz and Marzipan's video were the star turn. What shocked, as the tape played, was the malevolent concentration on brutal image and the persistence of the message, penetrating all barriers of language and culture, that it is the duty of some to hate and destroy others.

In all the clutter of blood and violence, the knives drawn across throats, the cries, the fear and the explosions, nothing in the video was more sinister, more coldly cruel than the image of a man in a white robe with a black beard, seated on a mat, speaking in a language few in the room could understand. Yet his message of hatred, didactic, unwavering, was only too clear. Finally, with a prolonged flickering the video stopped.

Wetherby ended the stunned silence. 'The man in the white robe is the imam who our agent Marzipan saw yesterday in a bookshop in Haringey. We'll have a full transcription in an hour or so, but the gist of what he was saying seemed clear enough. Judith?'

Judith had been briefed by one of the transcribers who listened in on intercepted conversations in Urdu. She glanced at her notes.

'He was issuing a call to arms—all true followers to take up the sword and so forth—the Satan America—her evil allies—death should be embraced by those who fight and they will be blessed in another world. But the interesting thing is that it wasn't just the usual diatribe. It was arranged as a kind of lesson, I thought.'

'That would chime with Marzipan's account,' Liz commented.

'What were the video clips?' someone asked.

Wetherby answered: 'The throat-cutting scene was certainly the murder of Daniel Pearl, the American reporter. The others could have been anywhere, most likely in Iraq. The text will probably help, if we need to know.'

He turned to someone at the end of the table who Liz did not recognise. He was a broad-shouldered man, smartly dressed in a well-cut suit with a face that was just short of outright handsome, she observed.

'Tom,' said Wetherby. 'What about the imam? Do we know who he is?'

'His name is Mahmood Abu Sayed. He's the head of a madrasa in Lahore. And, yes, he is a teacher, as Judith suggested. But his madrasa is known as one of the radical hotbeds. Abu Sayed himself comes from near the Afghan border. His family has strong Taliban connections. Even as radicals go, he's a hardliner.' He paused for a moment. 'I'm willing to bet he's never been in Britain before. English students have always travelled out to him in Lahore. If he's come here then I'd guess there's something pretty important in the wind.'

There was silence for a moment, then Michael Binding, chief bugger and burglar, waved his pencil to catch Wetherby's eye. 'Look, Charles, I sense we are running ahead rather fast. This imam may be a firebrand, but in his world he's presumably a distinguished kind of fellow. Is it really so remarkable that Muslim youngsters want to hear him speak or that he should get a few budding disciples together? In Northern Ireland—'

Liz interrupted, trying not to sound impatient. 'That was not Marzipan's impression and to date his instincts have proved sound. Marzipan thought that these people were preparing for a mission.'

Binding leaned back in his chair, looking cross. Wetherby smiled grimly. 'CTC have accepted that in the light of these events there may well be a specific threat,' he said. 'And I think so too. Our working assumption has to be that these three young men are preparing an atrocity of some sort and with no information to the contrary we must assume that what is in preparation is an attack in this country.' He paused. 'Of an extreme kind,' he added.

A small chill seemed to enter the room. A suicide bomber, unless detected before his mission can begin, is virtually impossible to stop. Three suicide bombers could make it three times more difficult. At least Marzipan had given them a chance, Liz reflected.

Wetherby was speaking again. 'The operation will be run by Investigations and led by Tom Dartmouth. The code word is "Foxhunt". Dave, you will continue running Marzipan.'

Liz felt her face redden with disappointment. Dave Armstrong was looking sympathetically at her but all she could conjure up was a wan smile. Her time off work hadn't been his fault. He had inherited Marzipan on fair terms, it was logical that he should continue with him. She bit her lip, said nothing. Wetherby was speaking again in a steady, confident voice.

'The aim for the moment is to find out more,' he was saying. 'There is no obvious advantage to us in moving in just yet. We have nothing to hold anyone on. Our first step must be surveillance on the shop. I'd like eavesdropping and covert cameras as soon as we can get them in. Patrick, can you see to the warrant?'

Patrick Dobson nodded. 'I'll get on to the Home Secretary's office. He's in London, I know, so it should be quick. Hopefully by six.'

Wetherby turned to Binding. 'Michael, if we get the warrant I want your chaps to go in tomorrow night. Can you do that?'

Binding nodded slowly. 'We can probably do it if Marzipan can sketch a plan of the inside of the building. We'll need prior A4 surveillance of course: who the key people are, what time they leave, who has keys.'

Tom nodded. 'We'll talk about it straight after this.'

Wetherby gathered up his papers. 'We'll reconvene tomorrow in my room. I'll want situation reports from one representative of each section. And Judith, an action note, please, through Tom and circulated.'

As the meeting began to break up, Wetherby called Liz over. 'Can I see you in my office, say at noon? I need to make a quick call first.'

As Liz left the room, Dave Armstrong came up and walked with her to the stairs. 'Thanks for standing in for me last night,' he said.

'Any time,' she said. 'How did it go up north?'

Dave shook his head. 'A lot of fuss about nothing,' he said.

They came out of the stairwell onto the fourth floor. 'Tell me,' said Liz, 'who is that man Tom? I've never seen him before. Is he new?'

'Tom Dartmouth,' said Dave. 'And, no, he's not new. He's been in Pakistan—got seconded to MI6 there after nine-eleven. He's an Arabic speaker. I should have introduced you. He's a nice bloke. Knows his onions.'

He looked at Liz for a moment, then poked her playfully with an elbow, smiling. 'Don't get excited, I'm told there's a Mrs Dartmouth.'

'Don't be ridiculous,' said Liz. 'You've got a one-track mind.'

WALKING DOWN the corridor to see Wetherby, Liz felt a mix of trepidation and anticipation. She was very disappointed, but in her heart of hearts not surprised that he had returned Marzipan to Dave Armstrong's control. She hoped that he would have something else equally important for her.

Wetherby was standing at his desk when she came into the room. As he motioned for her to sit down, she thought, not for the first time, how little she really knew about the man. With his neatly pressed suit and polished Oxfords, he would merge easily with any group of well-dressed men. But a close observer would have noticed his eyes. They had a quiet watchfulness that could turn suddenly to humour or to coldness. Liz knew from experience that a penetrating intelligence and determination lay behind the gentle appearance of the man. On her good days Liz knew she was important to him, and not just because of her skill as an investigator.

Wetherby said, 'I had an Irish nanny when I was a boy, who used to ask me, after any upset, if I was feeling "well within myself". Funny expression, but apt. How about you?'

He was smiling but watchful, and she looked him in the eye when she replied, 'You honestly don't need to worry about me.'

'I hear you've been down with your mama. She well?'

'Yes, she's fine. Worried about what the lack of rain will do to the young shrubs.' Liz paused, then asked politely. 'And how is Joanne? Any better?' Wetherby's wife suffered from a debilitating blood disease, which had made her a permanent semi-invalid.

'Not really,' said Wetherby with a frown and a slight shake of his head, as if to dismiss the unwelcome thought and move on. 'I wanted to see you because I've got an assignment for you.'

'To do with this operation?' she asked hopefully.

'Not exactly,' said Wetherby. 'Though I want you to keep involved while you work on this. Does the name Sean Keaney mean anything to you?'

Liz thought for a moment. 'The IRA man? Of course. But isn't he dead?'

'Yes, he died last month. Before he died he asked to see one of his former comrades, a man called James Maguire. That was strange because the two of them had never got on. Maguire had even suggested that Keaney might have been working for us because of his willingness to take part in the secret discussions with Willie Whitelaw in the seventies. Keaney never did work for us.' He paused, then gave a short laugh. 'But Maguire did, though he was overtly so hard line no one ever suspected it. Except Keaney. That's why when Keaney knew he was dying he asked to see Maguire. He wanted to make sure that what he said to him would get back to us. And it has.'

Wetherby paused again. 'In the early nineties, Keaney came up with the idea of trying to infiltrate the British security services. Before he died he told Maguire that he had succeeded in planting a secret asset within our ranks.'

'A secret asset? You mean a mole? Which service was it supposed to be?'

'He didn't specify. He told Maguire that this secret asset went to Oxford and it was there that he—or she—was recruited by an IRA sympathiser. Presumably by a don. The point is, according to Keaney, that more or less at the same time, the peace talks began, and the Good Friday Agreement followed. Keaney decided not to activate this agent.'

'Why did Keaney speak up now? It's been almost fifteen years.'

Wetherby pursed his lips. 'When the IRA were caught bugging Stormont, it almost derailed the peace process. Keaney said he was worried that an exposé of IRA infiltration of British Intelligence would set back the process again, this time possibly for good.'

'Do you believe that?' asked Liz.

'You mean Keaney's reason for talking now? I simply don't know.'

'Is it possible,' Liz asked tentatively, 'that Keaney might have made the whole thing up as a last blow against Her Majesty's Government?'

'Could be,' said Wetherby. 'But if there's a chance that what he said might be true, we can't ignore it. If there really is a member of one of the intelligence services who would be happy to spy for the IRA . . . someone like that might get up to anything. We've got to find out more, Liz.'

Liz saw at once that he was right. Now that they had Keaney's confession, it would have to be followed up.

'So we need to conduct an investigation, and I want you to do it.'

'Me?' said Liz, unable to contain her surprise. 'I've no experience in counterespionage and very little of Northern Ireland.'

Wetherby shook his head. 'We don't want a Northern Ireland expert on this. I need a good investigator, someone with your flair, who is not well known in Northern Ireland, but has some knowledge of the place. You had a brief posting there—a few months, wasn't it?'

Liz nodded, suddenly feeling rather flattered.

'If we don't know MI5 was the target, what about the other services?'

'I've talked with Geoffrey Fane,' he said, referring to his counterpart at MI6. 'We both agreed that it was most likely that the target service was MI5. After all, we took over Northern Ireland from MI6 in the eighties; according to Keaney, the mole joined some time in the early nineties. It would be MI5 they'd be aiming at so we'll focus here to begin with. But Fane wants to second someone to the investigation, just to keep him informed'—he looked expressionlessly at Liz, who knew that though Wetherby respected Fane's professional skills, he did not entirely trust him—'but it will be someone junior. You're in charge.

'Now, you'll need a cover story for any interviews you conduct here once you have a list of'—he paused, searching for the word he wanted—'candidates. Otherwise the mole will be alerted. I've agreed with the director general that the cover story will be this: the Parliamentary Security and Intelligence Committee is concerned that the security vetting of members of the intelligence services is not reviewed frequently enough. So, the DG has agreed, on an experimental basis, to redo the vetting of a random sample, to see if it produces anything useful. That's what you will say if anyone asks why you are making enquiries. As far as your colleagues are concerned, you are still in Counterterrorism. I think that's enough for now;

we can sort out any other details later. Do you have any questions?'

'Just one. I'd like to talk to Maguire's controller.'

Wetherby gave a sad smile. 'Not possible, I'm afraid,' he said. 'It was Ricky Perrins.'

'Oh, no.' Perrins had been tragically killed in a car accident three weeks earlier—it was one of the first things Liz learned on her return to work.

'Obviously you should look at his report. You might want to talk to Maguire—but I don't think you'll get much more out of him. I gather that having said his piece to Ricky he didn't want any more to do with us.'

3

It was the three men on the street that alarmed her. Doris Feldman was used to all sorts of comings and goings in that shop across the road with all those strange young men—how oddly they dressed; she would never get used to that—but they were as regular as clockwork, and it was always quiet by seven thirty in the evening.

Doris lived in the small flat above the ironmonger's shop she owned and ran in Haringey. Never married, Doris had inherited the shop when her parents died, and though the growth of DIY stores had almost been the death of her business, her shop attracted sufficient custom to keep her afloat.

But it didn't help her sleep. Come two o'clock she'd toss and turn, put on the light, turn on the radio, toss and turn some more, then give up—and finally get out of bed. She'd put on her dressing gown and heat up the kettle while Esther, her cat, slept in her basket by the stove like a baby.

Which was why, this Friday night—Friday? What was she thinking of? It was Saturday already, three o'clock in the morning—Doris Feldman sat in the armchair warming her hands on her mug and looking out of the window at the street. How this neighbourhood had changed. In her childhood there had been her kind, of course, immigrants from Russia and Poland, mixed with the Irish, who sometimes cut up rough, especially after too much time in the pub. Then after the war, the coloureds. Decent people many of them, but goodness they could make a noise, with their music and dancing.

Then most recently, the Asians moved in, really the strangest of them all. Quiet people, well behaved—closing time for them meant locking up their newsagent shops. They certainly seemed to pray a lot—she had long got used to seeing the men going to their mosques at all sorts of hours. Like the bookshop across the street—people in and out all day long.

Yet at night there was never any sign of life in the building. So, as she sipped her mug of tea, she sat bolt upright when she saw three men suddenly appear in the street and gather in a huddle by the front door of the bookshop. They were dressed in dark clothes, jeans and anoraks, and one man wore a leather jacket. You couldn't see their faces. One of them was right up against the door—what was he doing—fiddling with the lock? Suddenly, Doris saw the door open and the next minute all three men had slipped inside, and the door closed quickly behind them.

Doris sat there. She had never spoken to the bookshop owner, but someone was breaking into his shop. Up to no good, she was sure. Plotting, she wouldn't be surprised, like so many of these young men. It was from a sense of duty as well as concern that she got up and dialled 999.

PEGGY KINSOLVING HAD MET Geoffrey Fane only once before, when he had spoken at her induction course when she first joined MI6 a year or so ago. The second meeting was even briefer but far more memorable. He was seconding Peggy to MI5 for a month or two, he announced, on a very important confidential assignment. She would learn more when she got to Thames House. The one thing Fane wanted to stress was that she should not forget where her loyalties lay. 'Don't go native on us,' said Fane sternly.

Peggy couldn't help wondering why, if it were such an important job, they were lending MI5 someone so junior. Part of her wondered whether MI6 had already decided they did not need her particular skills and whether she was just a pawn in some personnel deal between the two services.

But no, there was a real enough job to do. The following day at Thames House, Charles Wetherby had talked to her for over half an hour. He'd been friendly, explaining that Peggy would be working with Liz Carlyle, an experienced and extremely talented investigator who had particular skills in assessing people. Liz would be leading their two-man team and they would be working direct to him. He would be keeping Geoffrey Fane informed of what they were doing. As Wetherby explained the situation, Peggy began to understand why she had been chosen. She would be following the paper trail and supporting Liz as she made her investigations. This made perfect sense to Peggy. She knew and loved the world of print, fact, data, information. It was her métier. She could disinter information which might seem meaningless and sterile to others, then, like a primitive fire-maker blowing on a spark, bring it to life. Peggy saw drama where others saw dust.

A cheerful aunt had once called her Bobbity Bookworm and this had stuck in the family, so that from the age of seven, everybody called her Bobby. She had taken her nickname with her to her school, one of the few remaining Midlands grammar schools, and then on to Oxford. At the end of three years' hard work she got a good 2:1 in English and the offer of a job as a research assistant in the British Library in London. But the clinical, subdued atmosphere of the modern reading rooms soon palled on her, and she was eternally grateful to an old acquaintance from college who had come into the library one day and told her of a specialised government department that was looking for researchers.

Which was how, at the age of twenty-five, and with round spectacles and freckles, Peggy came to be sitting in the conference room in Thames House next to Liz Carlyle, with several stacks of folders on the table before them.

Peggy had liked Liz from the start. She was straightforward, and made Peggy feel they were a team. The division of labour was clear: Liz would focus on interviews; Peggy would do the research.

She had spent her first days with B Branch, the personnel department, reading files, taking notes, organising a hunt, which her unfamiliarity with the records system made more difficult than she expected. Liz had asked Peggy to brief her on her progress so far. She handed Liz the first of what she knew were going to be many, many documents.

Liz was surprised. There were only five employees of MI5 who had attended Oxford during the first half of the nineties, and she knew most of them. She looked again at the list Peggy had handed her: Michael Binding, Patrick Dobson, Judith Spratt, Tom Dartmouth, Stephen Ogasawara.

Peggy had done well, thought Liz. She had taken very little time to get used to what must seem a very alien environment.

'I know Michael Binding,' Liz announced. 'And Judith Spratt.' A friend, she almost said, but didn't. 'Tom Dartmouth I've only just met—he's recently come back from Pakistan. He was seconded to MI6 there for a while. Like you in reverse. And Patrick Dobson was at a meeting I went to yesterday.' She handed back the list. 'What's Dobson's job exactly?'

Peggy found his file. 'His job is special liaison with the Home Office on operational matters. Degree from Pembroke College in Theology.' Liz groaned and Peggy gave an unexpectedly lively laugh. Thank God she's got a sense of humour, thought Liz.

Peggy continued: 'Married. Two children. Very active in his local church.'

Liz suppressed another groan and said, 'Right. And Stephen Ogasawara. What have you got on him?'

'He read History at Wadham. Then joined the Army, the Royal Signals. Served in Northern Ireland,' she said, pausing meaningfully. 'He's got a Japanese father, but he was born in Bath.'

'What's his job now?'

'He's not here any more. He left three years ago.'

'What did he go into? A private security firm?' With that mix of military and MI5 experience, he was probably making a fortune as a consultant in Iraq, thought Liz. Though he might not live long enough to enjoy it.

'Not quite,' said Peggy. 'He manages a dance troupe in King's Lynn.'

'How exotic,' said Liz, suppressing a smile.

Peggy asked, 'Can I take him off the list?'

'Yes,' said Liz, then thought again. 'Actually, better not. But you can certainly put him low down.' She glanced at her watch. 'You should have plenty to do while I'm in Rotterdam.' Liz gestured towards the files. 'Look out for anything on the personal front that looks unusual. And obviously, any kind of Irish connection.'

As Liz got up from the table to go, Peggy said, 'Do you mind if I ask who you're seeing in Rotterdam?'

'Not at all,' Liz said. She had already decided that if they were going to work closely together, she would need to be able to tell Peggy everything. 'I'm seeing a man called James Maguire. He was our source for the story that the IRA had put a secret asset into the security services. The officer he gave that information to is dead, so Maguire is the one person in the world, apart from us and the mole himself, who knows about it.'

'Do you think he can help us?'

Liz thought for a moment. 'Possibly. The question is whether he will. He didn't want to meet me.'

'Well good luck then,' said Peggy.

'Thanks,' said Liz, her lips pursed. 'I have a feeling I'll need it.'

THE WATER in the Old Harbour of Rotterdam was sea-green, and slopped against the sides of the canal boats and small tugs moored at one end. It was twilight, and a light rain felt soft on her face. Liz looked out across the small body of water, relic of the age when it had been the city's main port, and suddenly saw him. A tall figure, lean to the point of gauntness, walked slowly along the far edge of the harbour towards a café. He was wearing khaki trousers and a long raincoat that hung loosely from its padded shoulders, and he carried a newspaper rolled up under one arm.

Liz gave him five minutes to settle, then moved quickly round the perimeter of the harbour and into the café. Inside, wall lamps cast a rich orange glow and she spotted him at a corner table. As the man looked up and nodded, Liz walked over and sat down across from him, putting her coat on an empty chair. She said, 'Hello, Mr Maguire. I'm Jane Falconer.'

The man called Maguire didn't say hello, only remarking curtly, 'I thought I'd made it clear I told everything I know to your colleague Rob Petch,' he said, using Ricky Perrins's working alias.

'I'm sure you did,' said Liz, 'but Rob's dead, and I wanted to hear the story from you direct. Just in case Rob left something out that could help.'

'Help with what? I told him, Keaney's secret asset, whoever that might have been, was never activated.' His voice was starting to rise. Liz looked anxiously around for a waiter, and when one came over, she ordered coffee.

'White or black, madam?' the waiter asked, in flawless English.

'White, please,' she said with a smile.

Maguire still looked angry. Liz decided to use the waiter's intervention to change the subject. 'Is Rotterdam a favourite place of yours?'

Maguire shrugged to show his indifference, but then grudgingly started to talk. 'It's where I would have wanted to relocate if I ever got blown. Assuming they didn't catch me first, of course.' He looked at Liz; they both knew what he meant. In the pre-peace years every informer the IRA had unearthed and managed to get hold of had been murdered, though MI5 had never had an agent killed in Northern Ireland.

'Is that why you wanted to meet here?' She wanted to keep him talking.

'Only partly.' He stared out at the harbour with a hard look in his eyes. 'It seemed safer on the whole to meet outside Ireland.'

Liz wanted to steer him away from talk of danger. She needed to engage his curiosity instead of his fear. 'Tell me,' she said, 'what do you think happened to the person Keaney recruited?'

'What you mean is, do I think they're still there?' said Maguire almost contemptuously. 'Why does it matter? It's pretty hard to see what good it did Keaney and his pals.'

He stopped when he noticed that Liz was shaking her head. 'You're missing the point,' she said sharply. 'Keaney probably never expected his plant to help the IRA directly—after all, he couldn't be sure they'd ever do work on Northern Ireland, could he? No, I think the objective was just to screw up the Brits in some way or another.'

Maguire looked intrigued by this, but equally clearly wasn't going to say so. Instead he argued, 'I can't believe Ireland is top of the agenda these days. The war is over. So what does it matter? I'd have thought it was imams you were after, not Irish.'

Liz shrugged. 'That's the worry, of course. That it all gets ignored in a post-nine-eleven age. Then it starts up again. It's happened before.'

'You think this mole might be active? Even today?' Maguire sounded interested now despite himself.

'There's no reason to think a person like that would want a ceasefire, is there?' Liz replied.

The waiter brought Liz's coffee over, and as they waited for him to go, Maguire seemed to check himself. 'I don't believe it,' he declared. 'And, in any case, it's your problem. I've passed on Keaney's message as he asked. And that's it, as far as I'm concerned.'

Liz said quietly, 'I was hoping you might be able to help.'

'What could I possibly do?' demanded Maguire indignantly. 'Even if I wanted to.'

'Help us find out who Keaney recruited. He told you that the mole was recruited at Oxford. There must have been some link between Keaney and the university, but it's not exactly an obvious one to us.'

'Why don't you use another of your touts? Someone Keaney trusted.'

'We couldn't do that without telling the person about the mole. Too big a risk. You must see that.'

Maguire ignored her. 'Whoever this mole was, there's nothing they could do to hurt you now,' he said. 'The world's moved on. The war's over. So why do you need me? Other than to help you close the file?'

Liz took a deep breath. Instinct told her that her only chance of winning Maguire's support was to level with him.

'You know as well as I do, Mr Maguire,' she said, 'the war's not over. It's just reached a different stage. I don't need to give you a lecture on the history of the IRA. Or on the nature of treachery,' she added. She saw Maguire flinch. 'Everyone has their reasons, and treachery is nearly always also loyalty. But what matters is the nature of the cause we're loyal to. That's why we need to find this person. Their cause, whatever it is now, is not ours. Nor yours either, Mr Maguire. This is unfinished business.'

Again the shrug, superficially uninterested, but Liz could see Maguire was thinking. Finally he spoke, and now there was pathos in his voice, 'But don't you see, I'm finished business? I just want to be left alone.'

And before Liz could reply, he stood up. Without a word, he threw some euros on the table and walked away. Liz looked with despair at the money on the table. And to think she had believed she was getting somewhere.

DENNIS RUDGE was sitting at the wheel of a taxi parked at a rank in the middle of Capel Street in north London. He had a cup of coffee in one hand and a copy of the *Sun* propped on the dashboard. From where he sat he had a clear view of the bookshop and of Doris Feldman's shop front across the road. He was in eye contact with Maureen Hayes and Lebert Johnson, sitting at a table outside the Red Lion pub further down the street. In the other direction Alpha 4 and Alpha 5 were sitting in a dirty Peugeot 307, bickering noisily whenever anyone came past. Further members of A4 were parked up strategically in side roads, and a couple more cars were circling the area.

In Doris Feldman's sitting room, above her ironmonger's shop, sat Wally Woods, comfortably ensconced in Doris's armchair, with Esther the ancient cat sharing his knee with a powerful pair of binoculars.

Doris's telephone call to the police five days before at three in the morning had turned out to be a blessing in disguise. As always with A2's surreptitious entries, Special Branch had been told in advance about the operation. Hearing from uniform of Doris's 999 call, they had promptly rung in to discuss the options with A2 control. The priority was clearly to reassure the caller, and one option was simply to explain that the 'burglary' she'd seen was entirely innocent: the fuses had blown and the owner had sent in friends to replace them—something like that. But if she later mentioned the events of the weekend to the bookshop owner it *would* be disastrous, so they had decided to take a risk with the old woman, and at half past three on Saturday morning, an officer from Special Branch went to Doris Feldman's flat and explained, in the vaguest possible terms, that there were strange happenings going on across the street, which he and his colleagues were trying to find out about. A mention of 9/11 here, a reference to Islamic fundamentalism there, and Doris had readily agreed not to say a word. More important, she happily allowed the use of the flat, which was ideally situated as a static surveillance point. That was how Wally Woods came to be sitting in her armchair, with his colleague at her dining-room table manning the communications, while Reggie Purvis was coordinating the whole operation in Thames House.

Wally Woods sat on, patiently waiting. Just before three o'clock a minicab pulled up in front of the bookshop. The driver, a young Middle Eastern man, got out and walked round to open the passenger door. After a moment, a much older man dressed in a white smock with a white cap on his head, got out of the car. As he walked slowly towards the bookshop, the young man ran ahead and held the door open for him.

'Fox One has arrived and is now inside,' said Wally, and the man at the table immediately spoke into the microphone. 'All teams alert,' said Reggie Purvis in Thames House. 'Fox One is in. Repeat Fox One is in.'

Nothing obvious changed in the immediate vicinity of the shop, though A4 were ready now for whatever might happen.

In Thames House, Judith Spratt arrived in the Operations Room. A tall woman, she had fine features and always looked effortlessly elegant.

'There's been a phone call to the bookshop,' she announced to Dave Armstrong and Tom Dartmouth. 'The owner answered, and the caller asked if Rashid was there. He asked in English.'

'Who the hell is Rashid?' asked Dave.

Judith shrugged, as if to say 'you tell me'. 'The owner said there was no one by that name in the shop. Then the caller hung up.'

Tom asked, 'Do we know who made the call? Anything come up on the eavesdropping?'

'Nothing. No sound of Fox One at all. Just casual chat and cups of coffee from others in there. But the trace just came through. It's an Amsterdam number. I'll get on to it now.' She picked up the phone.

IN THE AIVD OFFICE in Amsterdam, Pieter Abbink was reaching for the phone when it rang. Picking it up quickly, he said tersely, 'Abbink.'

'Pieter, it's Judith Spratt. From London.'

Abbink laughed out loud. 'I had my hand on the telephone to call you when it rang.'

'Why was that?'

'We have a surveillance on a house here in Amsterdam. Not so good people. We've had a lot of chatter lately coming out of there. Internet, and some telephone. Somebody in the house just called a London number, and I was about to dial and ask if you could find out where it was.'

'It's an Islamic bookshop in north London, where some people we'd like to locate were meant to show up today, but they're late.'

'Do you know who they are?'

'No, and that's the problem. They've been sighted once by one of ours, but we don't have any names. Though your caller asked for Rashid.'

Abbink chuckled. 'That's like asking for Jan here in Holland. We'll check the database, but why don't I send you the photo bank?'

'You read my mind, Pieter. That's why I was calling you.'

BY THREE THIRTY, Wally Woods had told Thames House three times that the men hadn't shown, and at four o'clock, Reggie Purvis directed the arguing couple to drive round the neighbourhood, keeping close by. When at last the imam left the bookshop, his departure was greeted with relief by the A4 teams as they slotted in neatly behind him.

But the departure of the imam meant the three young men were not going to show. Purvis kept his people deployed nonetheless, waiting forlornly until six o'clock when the shop closed and the staff went home.

One hour later, Charles Wetherby, having joined the crew in the Operations Room, was dismayed (but not entirely surprised) to learn that Abu Sayed had been driven straight to Heathrow Airport, where he had checked in for a flight to Frankfurt on the first leg of his journey to Lahore.

His one piece of checked luggage, an ancient but sturdy Samsonite case, was plucked from the conveyor belt in the outgoing luggage shed, and inspected with a fine-tooth comb by no less than two veteran customs officers and an attending officer from Special Branch.

They found nothing. Indeed, the only evidence at all that the imam had even been in England lay in a Marks & Spencer bag at the bottom of his suitcase. Whatever else Abu Sayed had got up to during his stay, he had managed to find time to buy six new pairs of boxer shorts.

4

The city of dreaming spires looked wide awake to Liz. The sky was a rich enamel blue, and the temperature was moving into an almost summery seventy degrees as she and Peggy Kinsolving joined the groups of tourists thronging the pavements of Broad Street—or the Broad as Peggy called it. They had driven down together in Liz's car, and parked in a vast open car park on the western side of Oxford city centre. Now they walked past a hotel and into a shopping street indistinguishable from any other in England, then turned into a dark, narrow street of Dickensian houses, complete with overhanging shadows and protruding beams. A further turn and they were at Pembroke College, their first stop.

It was a seventeenth-century foundation with medieval bits, according to Peggy, who had swotted up diligently the day before. Numbered among its distinguished alumni were the writers Thomas Browne and Samuel Johnson and, more recently, Michael Heseltine.

They were directed by a porter through an old quad, with a small square of tended lawn. On the far wall, window boxes were filled with early geraniums. They walked on into another quad and there against the wall of the older part of the college sat a small statue of a woman, hands folded in prayer or lament. Not a good omen, thought Liz, thinking of the impending interview. She was not conventionally religious, and wondered a little nervously what role theology was going to play in the conversation.

Chaplain Hickson turned out to be an enormous man, with a vast beer belly and a thick curly beard, more Friar Tuck than the ascetic theologian Liz had expected. A Northerner, he was jolly and startlingly impious, greeting Liz and Peggy effusively before offering them coffee.

Perching on a pair of uncomfortable chairs, Liz and Peggy held mugs of Nescafé while the chaplain hunted for some biscuits. Only when he found them did their interview begin. He sat down with a happy thump on the sofa, putting a plateful of chocolate digestives within easy reach.

Liz began by explaining their visit was strictly a formality, to update the original vetting. She had been worried that a man of the cloth would be unwilling to speak freely about a former student's personal life, but the chaplain was happy to talk about the young Patrick Dobson.

'He took things very seriously and he worked extremely hard. Nothing wrong with that,' he added with a rolling laugh that suggested there was. 'But it did distance him a bit from some of the others.'

'Nothing wild about him then?' said Liz with a faint smile.

'Certainly not.' He grabbed a biscuit from the plate. 'He joined the Young Conservatives, ate all his suppers in Hall, and avoided temptation. There were no women in his life—not, I should add, because of disinclination on his part. It's just that he was hardly irresistible to the fairer sex.'

'How did you come to know him so well?' Liz asked, a little taken aback by this very personal portrait.

'He came to chapel a lot. Every week, sometimes on Wednesday.' He grimaced. 'It may sound odd coming from me, but I found him a little too religious, if you know what I mean. Pretty uncommon among lads that age.'

'Did he confide in you?'

For the first time the chaplain looked startled. 'Me? Oh no. You see, there was something of a class divide between us.'

'Really?' asked Liz. If she remembered rightly, Dobson's background was anything but patrician.

'You see, Patrick came from a working-class family. By dint of his admittedly healthy-sized brain he won a scholarship to an independent school. On arrival at Oxford he liked to wear a checked tweed suit on Sundays, which, he once told someone, was of the sort worn by "gentlemen in the country".' Hickson looked at Liz with a twinkle in his eye. 'You can imagine how much his fellow students loved that.'

'Was that the class difference you mentioned?' asked Peggy, who had stayed silent until now. She looked puzzled.

'Oh, there was no difference in our origins. We were both common as muck,' the chaplain said with a generous grin. 'The thing is, I still am.' And this time he gave such a laugh that it shook the sofa.

Leaving a few minutes later, Liz wondered whether the chaplain's mocking portrait of Dobson provided real grounds for concern. Clearly Dobson had been an earnest, slightly geeky undergraduate, so intent on erasing the traces of his humble origins that, paradoxically, it made him stand out rather than fit in. Liz was uneasy about someone who had invented a persona for himself—checked tweed suit indeed—since if they could base their life on a lie, what would keep them from basing it on more than one?

They walked on to Somerville College, where they found Judith Spratt's old tutor, an elegant bluestocking named Isabella Prideaux. In her ground-floor room, with French doors overlooking the quad, Isabella gave a brief and laudatory account of Judith's time as an undergraduate. She seemed to know where her ex-pupil had ended up. 'She keeps in touch,' she said, adding proudly, 'but then, most of my students do.'

After half an hour the ground had been covered, but they chatted on for a while longer. Then, just as Liz and Peggy were about to go, Miss Prideaux suddenly said out of the blue, 'I was awfully sorry to hear about Ravi.'

Liz's ears pricked up now. 'Yes?' she said.

'I know it sounds old-fashioned, but I do think these inter-racial alliances are always more fragile.' When Liz didn't say anything, Miss Prideaux flushed slightly, perhaps worried that she sounded racist or indiscreet, or both. She made a show of looking at her watch. 'Goodness me, here I am gossiping, and I've got a finalist in hysterics about her Anglo-Saxon paper waiting for me.'

Their last interview was in Merton College, and as they approached down a narrow alleyway running off the High, Peggy said, 'What did Miss Prideaux mean when she said she was sorry about Ravi?'

Liz shrugged. 'I'm not sure. Ravi is Judith Spratt's husband. His name is Ravi Singh; Judith uses her maiden name at work.'

'I gathered that,' said Peggy. 'Well, there's nothing in Judith's file that says her marital status has changed.'

Liz sighed. This was the inevitable downside of investigating your colleagues. 'We'd better find out for sure then. Hopefully it's nothing.'

The change in tempo from the bustle of a main street to a backwater of almost medieval calm was sudden. As they turned onto the wobbly cobblestones of Merton Street, Liz saw a small churchyard, with a path lined by several magnificent cherry trees. She imagined that this view would not have changed for five hundred years.

His name was Hilary Watts. Professor Watts to me, thought Liz, since he seemed to expect that kind of deference. He was an old-school Arabist with strong Foreign Office connections—he had played a long-time role as a talent spotter for MI6, and he had taught Tom Dartmouth and been asked for a reference by MI5 when his ex-pupil had applied. The reference had been three lines long: *Sound chap. Good languages. More than clever enough for the domestic service.*

'Domestic service'—once the prevalent MI6 view of MI5. Small surprise that Watts had not risen when she and Peggy had knocked on his door, but merely called out a peremptory 'Come in'.

Entering, the two women found the professor sitting in an ancient wing chair, its covers faded to a dull sage, gazing out at the lush grass of a playing field in Christ Church Meadow.

'Do sit down,' he said, pointing to a long settee that ran at right angles to his chair. Obeying him, they positioned themselves carefully, and Liz examined the man, who continued to look out at the meadow. It was an aged but distinguished face, with a long aquiline nose and small darting eyes of vivid blue.

He tilted his head onto one shoulder and took them both in. 'Ladies,' he said shortly. 'How can I be of assistance to you?'

Liz explained they were there to ask him about Tom Dartmouth.

'Oh, Tom,' he said. 'Gifted fellow. Came to me as a postgraduate for the lingo, though he was already good at it. Mason at Balliol said young Dartmouth took the best First in PPE the previous year.'

'Was there anything distinctive about Tom? Anything unusual?'

'All my students are unusual,' he said matter-of-factly.

'I'm sure they are,' acknowledged Liz mildly. 'But I wondered if there was anything in particular you remembered about Tom.'

Watts said sharply, 'Only that he was a disappointment. He had the makings of a very fine Arabist. He could have done a DPhil in no time—these days you've got to have one for a university post.'

Was that it? wondered Liz. Watts was cross with Tom because he'd left the land of academe. 'Was that very disappointing?'

'What?' demanded Watts, sounding annoyed. 'That he didn't want to teach? No, no, it wasn't that. God knows the world isn't short of academics.' He looked slightly miffed, as if recalling some slight. 'I arranged for him to see my friends in London.' For the first time he looked directly at Liz. 'Your counterparts.'

MI6, thought Liz. Certainly the obvious place for a high-flying Arabist.

'But the boy wasn't interested. I thought at first that meant he wanted to join the Foreign Office, have a proper diplomatic career. But no, not at all. "What is it then?" I asked him. "Money?" I could understand that—he would earn a fortune helping some bank establish itself in the Middle East. But, no, he told me he wanted to work for you people. Said he wanted to tackle the security threats direct. I asked him if he'd really worked so hard and done so well in order to become some kind of bloody policeman.' Watts paused as if revolted by the memory.

Out of nowhere, Peggy piped up. 'What did Tom say?'

Watts turned and gave Peggy a contemptuous look for her impertinence. He'd have a heart attack if he knew Peggy was from Six, thought Liz.

'He laughed, and said I didn't understand.' From Watts's expression, it was clear that this was the ultimate sin.

BACK IN LONDON early that evening, Liz dropped Peggy off at her flat in Kilburn and drove home. She took an unenthusiastic look at the sparse contents of her fridge and decided she wasn't hungry. The light on her answering machine was blinking, and reluctantly she played back the messages, hoping that it wasn't the office. She was tired: what she wanted more than anything was a deep bath, a large vodka tonic, and bed.

The first voice on the answering machine was faint and slightly hesitant. It took Liz several seconds to realise it was her mother. She was talking about the nursery—how it was suddenly busy after the long flat winter.

Then her voice changed gear, sounding almost artificially light. 'Barlow rang,' her mother said, and Liz's ears pricked up. He was her mother's GP. 'Those tests have come back and he wants me to come in. Such a bore.' There was a pause. 'Anyway, give me a ring, darling, when you can. Though I'm just off now, but I'll be in tomorrow night.'

This was not good news. Her mother was a reluctant patient, who saw her GP only when all else—stiff upper lip, hot toddies, simple stoicism—had failed. Worryingly, Barlow must be insisting she come in to see him.

Liz poured herself a stiffish vodka and listened to the second message.

It was Dave Armstrong. 'Hi, Liz, I don't know where you've been all day, but I have to see a contact in Islington this evening and I was going to offer to buy you the world's best Indian meal. The offer's still open. Call me.'

Liz went to the bathroom and turned on the taps. She always liked Dave's company but tonight she felt tired, and with the worry about her mother, she wouldn't have enjoyed herself.

Dave was a close friend in many ways, though there had never been anything more than friendship between them—and never would be. Funny that: on the surface Dave would look like an ideal candidate for a relationship. He was bright if not exactly intellectual, amusing—and, yes, good-looking.

She eased herself into the bath and for the first time that day, relaxed.

5

I hate these early starts, thought Liz. It was still only 9.15 on Monday morning and she was already halfway across the Irish Sea. The journey so far had been the usual nightmare—a packed Tube train and then the frustrating waiting around at Heathrow as the flight in from Belfast was delayed. She gazed out of the window and saw the shelf of cloud over Wales give way to blue sky and her mood lightened. Perhaps this trip was going to be more productive and enjoyable than she expected.

She was first at the Avis counter where, using her driving licence in the alias of Falconer, she rented a Renault 5. Leaving the airport behind her, she drove directly to Queen's University, where she had an appointment with Dr Liam O'Phelan, Lecturer in Irish Studies.

It felt strange returning to Belfast after ten years. Thank God I no longer have to check whether the car is being followed, or worry about whether someone has put a bomb under it, she thought. Both had been standard concerns when she was last here, back in the mid-nineties when security was precarious, but Northern Ireland was on the cusp of peace.

Driving north now on Stranmillis Road, past the lush Botanic Gardens, Liz parked on a quiet, tree-lined side street off University Road. The neighbourhood of the university was an oasis of calm respected by both sides of the sectarian divide. She walked diagonally across the lawn of a quadrangle, ringed by Victorian High Gothic buildings, looking enviously at the carefree students sprawled on the grass with their books, soaking up the sun. It was an oddly summer-like scene for May.

With a few false starts, she eventually found Liam O'Phelan in his office on the second floor of the Institute of Irish Studies.

The lavish, almost voluptuous decoration of the room took her aback. It was not what she had expected in this otherwise drab building. At one end there was a false fireplace of white marble, and covering the wooden floor, oriental rugs in reds and blues. The walls were studded with paintings, prints and drawings, and she recognised portraits of Yeats and Joyce.

'Dr O'Phelan?'

'That's right,' he said rising from his chair and extending a dry soft hand. He looked at her with sharp blue-green eyes. 'And you must be Miss Falcon. My favourite bird of prey.'

'Falconer, actually,' she said. From the file Peggy had given her, Liz knew that O'Phelan was forty-two, but his thinning hair and worry lines made him look older.

'Better still,' he said. 'I'll make us some coffee.'

O'Phelan motioned Liz to one of two old stuffed armchairs in the middle of the room. 'Please sit down,' he said formally.

While he made coffee, Liz got her papers out and looked at the notes she'd drafted. She wanted to make sure she got answers to all her questions. 'You're here to talk to me about one of my old students, I gather,' he said, placing a tray on the small table between them. His accent was cultivated, with none of the harsh burr of an Ulsterman.

'That's right. Michael Binding. You wrote a reference for him when he first applied to the MOD. You do remember him?'

'Very well,' announced O'Phelan, handing Liz one of the cups, then sitting down in the chair opposite. 'I was his thesis supervisor but not for very long. He switched supervisors when I left Oxford to come here.'

'Is that normal practice?'

'What? For me to come here?' He laughed lightly at his deliberate misunderstanding. 'Actually, it depends. In his case I think he probably wanted to change. Certainly I did.'

'You didn't get on?'

O'Phelan shrugged. 'Not particularly, but that was neither here nor there. I didn't agree with his whole approach.'

'To his thesis?' O'Phelan nodded, and she asked, 'What was it about?'

'Charles Stewart Parnell. How his political speeches reflected the politics of the age, and vice versa. Usual stuff. It was only an MLitt.'

'But you say you didn't like the line he took?'

'No, I thought it entirely wrong. Parnell to me is first and foremost an Irish nationalist. But Binding saw him only in the context of British parliamentary democracy. He seemed to believe that if Parnell had been lucky enough to be English, he would have done great things—on the other side of the Irish Sea.'

'Whereas you think Parnell was great as he was?'

As O'Phelan drank his coffee, Liz waited for his reply.

'Absolutely,' he said, and for the first time there was enthusiasm in his voice. 'But the fundamental problem I had with Binding wasn't that we held different views. I mean, if I taught only people who agreed with me I wouldn't be a very busy man. No, it was rather that he wasn't very good.'

He then elaborated on this, explaining that Binding had been poor at research, neither thought nor wrote clearly, and, in short, had possessed none of the intellectual skills expected of an Oxford postgraduate student. It was a masterpiece of denigration, couched in tones of such apparent regret that it took Liz a moment to see it for the poisonous demolition job it was. He concluded witheringly: 'I was astonished his thesis had been accepted.'

'I see,' said Liz neutrally. She picked up her pencil from the table. 'I also wanted to ask you about his private life.'

'Ask away, but I'm not sure I'll be able to help you. I didn't know him well. I was at St Antony's and he was at another college—Oriel, I think.'

'Do you know if he had many friends?'

O'Phelan shook his head. 'No I don't.'

'Or girlfriends?'

He paused and smiled slightly. 'He had girlfriends—more than one. They used to wait for him sometimes when he came to see me. There were at least two different girls. I remember thinking, "Such devotion."'

Liz smiled politely. 'What about politics? Was he interested?'

O'Phelan looked thoughtful. 'He was, as a matter of fact. He loved to argue the toss—he liked to quote the *Daily Telegraph* at me, as if that were an impartial source. Just to annoy me, probably. It usually did.'

After a few more questions, Liz reached down into her briefcase and extracted another sheet of paper from a folder. 'If you don't mind, Dr O'Phelan, I'd like to read you a list of names—they are people who were at Oxford at about the same time as Binding. I'm just wondering if you knew any of them.'

Out of the corner of her eye she watched O'Phelan's reaction as she read out the names of the others on her list of suspects. He sat still, his face impassive, until suddenly, when she was almost through, he leapt up.

'Excuse me a minute,' he said. 'I think there's someone at the door.' He went and opened it and stuck his head out. 'Ryan, I shan't be long now.'

He returned, saying, 'I beg your pardon,' and sat down again.

Liz read out the last name on the list: 'Stephen Ogasawara.'

O'Phelan shook his head. He smiled apologetically, 'I'm afraid none of them rings a bell with me, although that doesn't mean I didn't know them once. Students come and go—one simply can't remember all their names.'

'That seems entirely understandable,' said Liz, standing up. 'Well, thank you very much for your time.'

'Not at all,' said O'Phelan, getting up and walking with her to the door. 'Let me know if I can be of any further help.'

IT WAS HIS TURN to close up the shop, and since it was Thursday it was not until 7.30 that he firmly shut the front door and turned the key in the double set of Chubb locks.

It had been exactly a week since the imam had come to the shop. Then Sohail had deliberately stayed in the stockroom, counting inventory, lest his own tense nerves be obvious. To Sohail's surprise, Abu Sayed had not gone upstairs, but had stayed in the office off the main room for almost an hour. When he'd emerged, it was only to walk out to a waiting car.

What had gone wrong? Why had the three young men not shown up? Was it possible, and he felt his adrenaline stir at the thought, that the people watching—he knew they must have been there—had been detected? He himself had looked for any sign of external surveillance, on his way to and from work; but there was nothing that he could see, hard as he looked.

Yet Sohail began to feel even more jittery, wondering if somehow it was suspected that he was not simply a young man, quiet, devout, serious, working hard to help his family. He tried to be rational: this portrait was not a front; there was no reason for anyone to think he was anything else.

He waited for the bus for almost fifteen minutes, then had to stand for half the journey home. Usually, he could find a seat and read. He was in the middle of *English Torts: A Casebook*, for if he had good reason to postpone university for a year, he might as well not let all the time go to waste.

He got off the bus early so he could walk a bit before he reached home. The dark was drawing in, and he quickened his pace as he walked along the main road of his neighbourhood, then turned into a side street. At its end there was an alleyway, which ran between a warehouse on one side and the back of a row of shops on the other. It was poorly lit, and a little spooky—his little sister would not walk through it even in broad daylight—but it knocked five minutes off the way home and he turned down it without hesitation. A few moments later he thought he heard someone behind him, but turning round saw nothing. Don't be so nervous, he told himself.

As he hurried along he looked up to see a short figure approaching. He was instantly wary, until he saw the person was as dark-skinned as he was, and then he relaxed. As the man came closer Sohail thought there was something familiar about him. The man was smiling and he called out, 'Sohail!'

Reflexively Sohail smiled back, assured this was a friend after all. And sure enough his face was familiar. I know, thought Sohail, it's one of the men who didn't turn up at the bookshop. But what is he doing here?

THIS IS MORE like it, thought Liz, as she booked into the Culloden Hotel. With its gardens, spa, pool and rosetted restaurant it was a cut above her normal overnight accommodation. She had got an excellent deal on the internet and, unusually for her, she had decided to indulge herself.

Though I won't get to enjoy any of it, she thought, as she went upstairs and ordered a room-service sandwich, kicked off her shoes, and opened her laptop. As it booted, she phoned her voicemail but there were no messages.

Liz wondered if Marzipan had made any progress in identifying the photos that had come from Holland, then she forced herself to stop speculating—it's not your business now, she told herself firmly, turning her mind instead to writing up her interview with O'Phelan.

There was something not quite right about that man. He had given a polished performance, but behind the jokey front and camp demeanour she could detect there was something else going on. He was clocking the effect he was having, giving out only what he wanted her to know.

She recalled the intensity of his voice when he talked about Parnell. He was clearly a man of very strong convictions. On impressionable students, surely he must be a powerful influence. Though not, it seemed, on her colleague Michael Binding.

LIZ HAD ARRANGED to have dinner with Jimmy Fergus, an old RUC Special Branch acquaintance from her tour of duty in the nineties, and an expert in the Loyalist paramilitary groups. She had called him from London, to let him know she was coming, and the meal had been his idea.

Waiting for him in the lobby, she glanced at a copy of the local evening paper and saw that a prominent Republican had come forward claiming to have been an agent of the security forces. I wonder what's behind that? thought Liz. Ten years earlier no one would have dared to make such a claim publicly for fear of being found dead with a bag over his head.

She saw Fergus ambling across the lobby. He was a big man, with a pockmarked face and a confident grin that Liz had always found infectious.

'You've come up in the world,' he teased, indicating the hotel's ornate decor, a mix of marble columns, panelled walls and chandeliers. 'I thought of giving you dinner at your hotel,' he said, 'but when I heard which one it was, I decided we'd go somewhere with a little more local colour.'

Fergus came from Protestant farming stock in Antrim ('Honest bigots to a man', he'd once declared). A decade before, Liz had discovered that much of his bluster was a defence—part of a hard man's carapace erected around a sharp intelligence. He was also discreet, which meant that she could pick his brains and, if it seemed useful, ask for his help.

They drove in his old blue Rover to a fashionably revamped pub, with large open rooms, wood floors and a brick fireplace. In a quiet alcove at the back, over drinks, they spent time catching up. It had been four years since they'd seen each other, during a trip Fergus had made to London. Liz had been working on organised crime then.

Fergus raised an eyebrow. 'It's ironic that just as life has calmed down here, it's heated up for you.'

'So,' said Liz, 'if you're not chasing the UVF these days, what are you working on?'

'Who says I'm not chasing the UVF?' he said with a grin. 'Same people, different crimes. Murdering Catholics out, extortion, prostitution and gambling in. Standard stuff really.'

As the waiter brought their food, Fergus asked what she was doing in Northern Ireland. Liz gave him the agreed cover story about the new vetting procedures.

'I've been sent to interview a lecturer at Queen's who gave a reference for one of my colleagues fifteen years ago,' she said, hoping her tone suggested a bureaucratic interference she could have done without. 'He teaches Irish Studies and has strong views. If Ireland had only stuck with Parnell, the country would be unified today.'

Fergus gave a hollow laugh as he cut into his sirloin. 'He probably thinks Gerry Adams has sold out. What's his name?'

Liz leaned forward before she spoke. 'Liam O'Phelan.'

'I've heard of him,' he said, musing. 'Wasn't he from Dublin originally?'

'I don't know much about him,' Liz admitted. 'But I don't think he was being straight with me.'

'About his ex-pupil?'

'No, that rang true. A few other things didn't though.'

Fergus speared a chip and stared at it for a moment as he answered. 'I could check and see if we have a file on him. We may well do. At one point during the height of the violence we were very concerned about Queen's.'

'Would you mind? I'd appreciate it.'

'Sure,' said Fergus, 'use me while you can. I won't be doing this forever.'

Was Fergus going to retire? It seemed inconceivable. Liz said so, sitting back in her chair, looking at him with affectionate scepticism.

'I'm older than you think,' said Fergus. 'I'll have done twenty-five years this autumn.'

'What would you do next?' asked Liz. She couldn't envisage him back in Antrim, bringing in the wheat crop.

Fergus shrugged, a little dolefully, and Liz wished she hadn't asked. He'd already explained, regretfully, that his marriage had broken down and she knew it was a sadness that he had never had children.

Wanting to change the subject, Liz remarked, 'I saw in the paper that another former agent has gone public.'

'And I'm sure there will be more,' said Fergus seriously. 'It's hard now for some of those people who worked as secret assets, agents, whatever you like to call them, during the Troubles—for us, you lot, and particularly for the army. As politics brings old enemies together, some of them, I think, have a sort of crisis of conscience. They have a need to be understood for what they did and why. They don't see themselves as traitors. They feel they made a contribution to peace in their own way and they'd like some recognition for it.'

'They weren't all so high-minded,' said Liz. 'Some of them worked for us for the money. I don't suppose anyone will ever hear from them.'

'No, you're right. They'll just take their grievance somewhere else.'

'Anyway,' said Liz, 'it's not as though the intelligence war is over, is it? Infiltration must be easier now, for the paramilitaries.'

'There are more Catholics in Special Branch than before,' said Fergus, adding cynically, 'but that's not saying much. The new recruiting guidelines call for fifty-fifty overall in the Northern Ireland Police Force. You can imagine how popular that is with some of my colleagues. But infiltration was a worry even when there were no Catholics in the Force at all; it's just that it came from the Loyalists.

'Look, like most of Special Branch, I'm a policeman first and a Protestant second. But once in a while someone gets his priorities reversed. Of course there've been leaks to the Loyalist paramilitaries. When it happens it does a lot of damage. But the greatest damage is to the reputation of the Force. You're lucky not to have that problem.'

After dinner, Fergus drove Liz back to the Culloden. They sat in the bar on a sofa of plush red velvet while Fergus drank a large brandy and explained what had happened to his marriage. After a while, Liz called for the bill, explaining she had an early-morning flight. She kissed his cheek and said good night, adding, 'You won't forget about O'Phelan, will you?'

TWO HOURS LATER Liz was still wide awake, sitting at the desk in her room, reading the notes she had been writing.

What she had written were speculations rather than facts, but they were troubling ones, set off by Fergus's mention of infiltration in the Northern Ireland Special Branch. 'You're lucky not to have that problem,' he'd said.

But what about the mole? She wondered, not for the first time, what the IRA had expected of an infiltrator. Suppose they were posted to Counterterrorism, or the Northern Ireland desk. What exactly could they do?

Well, for one thing, they could alert the IRA to the identity of informers in its midst. That's what Philby and Blake had done in the Cold War. They could tip them off about impending arrests and, even more importantly, they could reassure them when one of their operations wasn't blown.

Yet she could imagine something even more damaging. An infiltrator in the right place might be able to feed targeting information that would help the IRA mount a damaging attack. Or they could make up false intelligence that could waste valuable resources and harm the Service's credibility. Think of the Iraq dossier and the damage that did to the reputation of the whole of British Intelligence.

But wasn't it all academic? In Sean Keaney's time frame, there hadn't been any IRA terrorist activities for the mole to assist. And MI5 hadn't lost any informers. Its reputation had not been damaged. So did that mean the mole had simply retired from business, having never been activated? Perhaps he had just quietly left the Service. Or had he simply spent the next decade loyally doing his best in MI5? Was he just one of us, no different from everyone else?

It didn't seem likely.

Time for bed, she thought. As she brushed her teeth, she contemplated how nothing in the last ten years indicated the mole had done anything—for the IRA, at least. But what if the mole had been placed in MI6? She didn't think so. Surely the original idea must have been to place him in MI5, where he could subvert the Service's work against the IRA? As it turned out, the idea had lost its value, like currency taken out of circulation.

She got into bed, lay back and thought again, uneasily, of O'Phelan. What was it that bothered her about the interview? It wasn't just a feeling that he hadn't told her the truth. There was something else . . .

She sat up again, with a start. Why hadn't she focused on it before? It was obvious. When O'Phelan had got up, gone over to the door and spoken to Ryan, the so-called student waiting in the hallway, no other voice had spoken. Because, of course, there wasn't anyone there.

O'Phelan had got up to create a diversion, to disguise his reaction to something she'd said.

What had they been discussing that made him do that? Nothing . . . she had been reciting the names on her list: Patrick Dobson, Judith Spratt, Tom Dartmouth . . .

That was what had bothered O'Phelan.

He knew one of the names.

She closed her eyes but she was too tired to focus. She would start again in the morning.

And only then did she remember. She had forgotten to ring her mother.

THE NEXT MORNING, as Liz was checking out of the Culloden Hotel, the watcher in Doris Feldman's flat rang Dave Armstrong in Thames House.

'Marzipan hasn't shown up,' the watcher said. 'It's nine eighteen.'

'Perhaps he's running late,' said Dave.

'He's never been late before. We thought you'd want to know.'

'OK,' said Dave, suddenly attentive, for he realised that what they said was right. 'Ring me in ten minutes and let me know if he's shown.'

By ten o'clock there was still no sign of Marzipan. Very worried now, Dave decided, reluctantly, to ring Sohail's mobile.

The number rang and a man said, 'Hello?'

An Englishman, Dave noted, with an Estuary accent. He asked quietly, 'Is Sohail there?'

'This is the Metropolitan Police. Please identify yourself.'

LANDING AT HEATHROW, Liz bought a copy of the *Evening Standard* before taking the Underground into central London.

She had been thinking on and off about O'Phelan. Lying to her, if that's what he had done, didn't mean he was necessarily an IRA recruiter, and she couldn't believe it was Michael Binding he would have wanted to recruit. His contempt for his former pupil had been the one part of her interview she had found authentic.

She picked up her copy of the *Standard* and looked through the news pages. The stories seemed wearyingly familiar: protests from retailers about the effects of the congestion charge, delays in the construction of the new Wembley Stadium, an MP arrested for driving under the influence of alcohol. Then on page five she saw an item that riveted her:

TOTTENHAM RACE KILLING

> A man discovered dead in a Tottenham alley this morning was the victim of a brutal attack. The body, said to be that of a young Asian man, was found by a passer-by early this morning in an alley off Cresswell Crescent, in an area where racial tension has been high. The British National Party (BNP) has been particularly active in the local community. Police said the victim, in his early twenties, was wearing a blue anorak, jeans and hiking boots. His name has been withheld until relatives have been informed.

Liz stared at the same page, glassy-eyed, for several minutes. When she had last seen Sohail Din, in the safe house at Devonshire Place, he had been wearing a blue anorak, jeans and a pair of hiking boots.

6

Wetherby was sitting at his desk gazing out of the window at the sun sparkling on the Thames, but his face showed no pleasure in the view. The death of an agent was the worst nightmare for any intelligence service. Agents were recruited by persuasion, cajolery and sometimes by the promise of payment. Some agents, and Marzipan was one, offered their services out of loyalty to the country. In return they were promised protection. That was the deal. For the Service to break its side of the bargain was a professional failure of the worst kind.

Wetherby turned to Tom Dartmouth. 'Do we know when it happened?'

'Apparently it was sometime last night,' Dartmouth replied.

'I see,' said Wetherby, standing up, and walking to the window. The spring sunshine had given way to a sudden shower. 'How did it happen?'

'At first glance, it looks like a racist attack,' said Dartmouth. 'Could be a lunatic member of the BNP—they're strong in that area.' He hesitated. 'But slitting someone's throat is an uncommon method of murder in this country. I think we have to assume that this murder is tied to our investigation.'

Wetherby turned back from the window. 'I want maximum effort put on this, Tom. We've got to find out what's happened.' Tom nodded. 'And keep me closely in touch.' Wetherby paused. 'Has anyone spoken to Liz Carlyle?'

'I gather she's expected in just after lunch.'

Wetherby looked at Dartmouth. He was a clever man, but he was also hard to read. Wetherby had yet to see him show any feelings. 'Someone has to tell Liz that Marzipan is dead, Tom. It should be me, but I'm due to see the Home Secretary. I need to explain the background to Marzipan's death.'

Dartmouth said quietly, 'I'll tell her, Charles. After all, it's my operation.'

Wetherby nodded. He turned back to the window again, seemingly lost in thought. Then the moment of contemplation passed and he walked back to his desk. 'I suppose you'll have to,' he said conclusively.

Dartmouth's eyes narrowed slightly and Wetherby continued, speaking at a rapid clip, dictating orders. 'This is now a police case: a murder has been committed. Get them to pull in the bookshop people. Maybe one of them will talk, though if Abu Sayed is driving this from Pakistan, they may have let him use the shop as a courtesy and not have a clue who the three young men are. You said that Six were watching Abu Sayed in Pakistan. Let them know what's happened. Any contact with the UK should be reported to us. Get on to the Dutch and see if they've got anything from their operation.'

He stopped for a moment, thinking hard, his brow furrowed in concentration. 'I want a meeting with you, Dave and Judith before close of play.' He thought for a second, then added, 'I think Liz should be there as well. As Marzipan's controller before Dave, she may have useful ideas to contribute.'

He sighed and stood up. 'I'm going to walk around.' After news of Marzipan's death, Wetherby knew the mood among the agent runners would be black. It was important for him to show his support.

'The problem remains,' he added as he walked towards the door, 'that we have lost our link to the bookshop group.'

'I know,' said Dartmouth calmly, standing up to leave.

For once, Wetherby found his cool imperturbability not entirely helpful.

LIZ HAD PHONED Peggy Kinsolving from Belfast shortly after seeing O'Phelan, and by 8.30 the following morning Peggy was on the coach from Victoria heading towards Oxford, mentally reviewing what she'd discovered so far.

O'Phelan was born in 1964 in Liverpool to an Irish mother, and an English father who left the family when Liam was ten years old. Liam and his mother moved back to Ireland, to a suburb of Dublin. He had won a scholarship to University College Dublin, where he achieved a starred First in History. His doctoral dissertation, *Parnell and the English Establishment*, had been published by Oxford University Press. Awarded a Junior Research Fellowship at St Antony's College, Oxford, he had left after two years to work at the Institute of Irish Studies at Queen's University Belfast. He was unmarried.

That was the skeleton; now Peggy hoped Oxford would put meat on the bones. When she arrived at Oxford she would have liked a coffee, but she had a huge task to get through and she wanted to get back to London that evening, so she went straight to the New Bodleian library, a square monstrosity of yellow stone next to Blackwell's bookshop.

By one o'clock she had gone through the five-year tranche of the *Oxford Gazette*, *Oxford Today* and the *Oxford Magazine*, looking for any reference to O'Phelan, but her trained eye had found none.

So much for the official publications. She knew that often it was the nooks and crannies of the ephemeral that held the most interesting finds. So she had requested archive issues of *Cherwell*, the student newspaper, which appeared every two weeks in term time. It didn't take her long. At 1.40 p.m. she saw, in the issue dated April 4, 1991, under the listing headed LECTURES, a weekly series of talks at the Old Firehouse, labelled 'Fighting Talk'. Four pounds per head, wine and beer available afterwards, all welcome. Three forthcoming talks were listed: 'The Miners' Struggle' by a Labour MP; 'Sexuality and Sexism' by a former editor of *Spare Rib*; 'To Be Announced' by Liam O'Phelan, lecturer at St Antony's.

Great title, thought Peggy sourly, the small elation at finding O'Phelan's name evaporating in the face of 'To Be Announced'. It probably wasn't important anyway. Given his CV, he had doubtless talked about Parnell.

She explained her problem to the assistant, a helpful woman in glasses and a black T-shirt who looked about Peggy's age. 'You say you've checked *Cherwell*. What about the *Gazette*?'

'There's nothing there.'

'There's always *Daily Doings*, I suppose,' the woman said, as an afterthought. 'But it's not really a publication. I doubt anyone keeps back issues.'

Peggy remembered it: an enormous single-page broadsheet that appeared every day, listing everything from rooms to let to poetry readings. 'Are they still on Warnborough Road?'

'I think so. That weird house.'

Twenty minutes later, after a brisk walk up Woodstock Road, Peggy was entering the basement door of a tall Victorian house of yellow and orange brick. She stepped into a large low-ceilinged room in the middle of which were two pine kitchen tables, covered with a jumble of papers and used coffee cups. A laser printer was churning out pages onto the floor.

'Hello?' said Peggy tentatively, then when no one replied, she called out again more vigorously.

After a moment, a door opened and a young man appeared, so tall that his head almost brushed the ceiling. 'Don't worry, you've got lots of time. The deadline's not till five,' he said in an American accent.

Peggy explained she didn't want to place an ad, then told him what she was looking for.

'Hmm,' he said, 'how far back are you looking?'

Peggy swallowed. 'Actually, it was fifteen years ago.'

The American laughed out loud. 'Sorry,' he said, waving an arm at the clutter. 'No chance. Space, space everywhere and not a drop to use. We only have two rooms,' he added.

'I see,' said Peggy, slowly. 'I don't suppose you have a digital copy.'

He shook his head reflexively, but suddenly stopped, and his mouth opened, in a pantomime of revelation. 'Hang on a minute. The guy who started this place loved computers. He told me he'd bought his first machine in 1979. It was probably the first word processor at the university.'

'Did he keep the disks from then?'

'That's just it. He did. They're next door. Come and see.'

In the adjoining room he dug around in a cupboard and brought out a big taped-up cardboard box. He cut it open with a Stanley knife to reveal a jumble of disks and reels of magnetic tape. 'It's all labelled quite carefully,' said the American as he looked at some of the disks. 'Here,' he said, holding one up. 'This is 1990.' He fumbled some more. 'And '91 and . . . '92.'

'That's brilliant,' said Peggy, astonished by her stroke of luck.

'There's just one problem,' he said, putting the disks back. 'You wouldn't be able to read them. They're incompatible with today's machines. Sorry.'

Her heart sank, but then she thought of 'Technical Ted' Poyser, MI5's specialist on all matters electronic. 'Listen,' said Peggy, 'could I borrow one of them anyway? I've got a friend who's a real computer whiz. He's got lots of old machines. He might be able to help me.'

The American had not expected this. 'Well, it's not really my property to lend,' he said hesitantly.

'Please,' pleaded Peggy. 'If they're no good to anyone, couldn't I just borrow one? I promise I'll bring it back.' She could see he was wavering. 'I'll leave a deposit if it helps.'

He thought about this for a moment, then made up his mind. 'Nah,' he said. Then he added, 'It's cool. You don't have to leave a deposit.'

BY FIVE O'CLOCK Peggy was on the third floor of Thames House, consulting 'Technical Ted' Poyser.

Ted's office was more of a cubbyhole than an office. The walls were piled high with hardware devices, wires draped everywhere, and in the middle was Ted, crouched on a stool like a spider in a complicated web. He looked at Peggy without enthusiasm until he saw the disk she held in her hand.

'What have we here?' he asked. 'A blast from the past?'

Peggy handed him the disk. 'Can you read it?' she asked.

He examined it, admiringly. Eventually he murmured, 'Why don't you get yourself a cup of tea from the canteen? I'm going to be a minute.'

When she came back a quarter of an hour later Ted was seated in front of a terminal that seemed to be attached to half a dozen different CPUs on a table. 'What you've got here is a disk from a North Star computer, *circa* 1980. Where on earth did you find it?' he asked.

'It's a long story. But I'm hoping there's something on it I'm looking for.'

'I doubt there is a single machine in the UK today that can read this disk.' He made a face. 'Formats change twice a decade, at least. Two decades and you're lost.'

'Really,' she said edgily. She was happy to share Ted's delight with the disk, but she wanted to know what was on it. And fast.

'I suppose you want to know if I can actually read the bloody thing.'

'Yes,' she said emphatically.

'The short answer is, no, I can't.' When Peggy's face fell he smiled and pointed a commanding finger at her. 'But I will.'

LIZ COULD HARDLY sit still. Tom Dartmouth had been talking on and on about Marzipan, but after the first few minutes she'd stopped listening. He hadn't even known Sohail. Marzipan was her agent—she'd recruited him, she'd run him, and almost as soon as she'd handed him over, they'd got him killed. She'd promised to look after him and she hadn't. She needed to talk to Charles. Somehow, somebody hadn't looked after Sohail.

Tom was seated behind his desk, droning on in a calm, reasonable voice that Liz was finding more and more infuriating.

'But why wasn't there countersurveillance on him?' she cut in. 'Especially after the three men didn't show.'

'We certainly thought of it,' said Dartmouth, 'but there was no reason to think that there was any link between their failure to show and Marzipan. Believe me, Dave went through it with him very carefully the next day.'

Liz conceded the logic of this. Countersurveillance might have increased the risk, since there was always the danger of it being spotted.

But then what had they missed? Or was he suggesting there was nothing there to miss? 'Are you telling me you believe this was a race murder?'

'No, of course not. And we've made it clear to the Met that we have an interest in this. Special Branch have arranged for all the CCTV within a square mile of the murder site to be collected. If any of those three was in the area, I hope we'll spot them.'

Liz nodded, then asked, 'Did Sohail look at the Dutch pictures before he was killed?'

Tom shook his head. 'No. Dave was meeting him at the safe house tonight.'

'Oh God,' said Liz, not far from tears.

Sohail Din's murder was such a personal blow to Liz that it was only as the shock subsided that she saw the full extent of the disaster. His death had cut their one link to the bookshop three, and unless they could be found, many more people than Sohail might be destined to die. Finding Sohail's killers was essential to help them unravel whatever was being planned.

LIZ DECIDED TO GO home once it was clear there was nothing useful she could do by staying. It seemed incredible that she had started the day in Belfast with her mind focused on Liam O'Phelan and since she had arrived back in London she had thought about nothing but Sohail. She was looking forward to getting back to her flat and trying to get the day's events in some sort of order.

As the lift doors on the fourth floor started to close, a hand intervened and they slid open again. Tom Dartmouth entered, and gave Liz a weary smile. 'What a day,' he said, loosening his tie with one hand. 'Especially for you. Fancy a drink?'

It was said casually, but warmly. She was still angry, but no longer with Tom—in fact she felt badly for having been so aggressive with him that afternoon. 'Why not?' she said.

He took her to the bar in a new steel and glass hotel near Thames House, a venue far slicker than the pubs that were the usual watering holes for MI5 staff. 'I thought it would be a little quieter here,' he explained.

It was the first time she had been with Tom other than in meetings and she noticed for the first time how attractive he was. He was a tall man, six feet one or two, rangy and square-shouldered. In his lightweight blue suit, and with the remains of a tan, he was turning a few female heads.

Liz ordered dry white wine, and when she found herself crunching her way through a bowl of rice crackers on the table in front of them, she realised she had not eaten since breakfast in the Culloden Hotel.

'I wanted to ask you about Marzipan,' Tom said as soon as their drinks arrived. 'You knew him longer than Dave did. If there was anything in Marzipan's history that was worth pursuing, you'd be the one to know. I was just wondering about his friends—you know, that perhaps he'd said something to one of them he shouldn't have.'

'He was a genuine loner,' said Liz. She took a sip of her wine. 'It's one of the things we established when he was first recruited. He didn't have any really close pals, and most of his schoolmates are at university now.'

She faltered slightly. 'As Marzipan was supposed to be . . .'

'I know this has been hard for you,' he said sympathetically.

'It's hard for Dave too,' she said a little curtly, then reminded herself that Tom was trying to be nice and, besides, none of it was his fault. She added, 'Did you ever have this sort of thing happen to you in Pakistan?'

'Yes, I did once,' he admitted. 'There was a Pakistani named Fahdi. He was extremely westernised, but he worked in Lahore and had relatives on the Afghan border. He was certain that his rural cousins had been helping Bin Laden after the Yanks failed to capture him in the caves at the end of the Afghan war. I have to say I was sceptical—we were getting about twenty sightings a day, none of which came to anything—but Fahdi was absolutely positive. So we packed him off, with a GPS transponder sewn into his rucksack.'

Tom stopped and took a long swallow of his drink.

'What happened?' asked Liz.

'Two weeks later we got notification of the signal. It was just over the Pakistani border in Afghanistan. We sent in a small group of SAS with American back-up from Special Forces. They went in at night expecting a firefight—the area was full of Taliban and Al Qaeda—but when they moved in on the rendezvous there was no one there.'

'What about the signal?'

'I should have said there was no one there alive. They found the body of Fahdi. In his mouth they found the transponder, popped in like a sweet, still working.'

'How horrible,' said Liz.

'What bothered me most was that I thought it was far too dangerous, but I let him talk me round.' He looked up at Liz. 'So I think I know what you're going through.'

She shrugged. 'I'm all right.'

He signalled for the bill, and when it came insisted on paying, despite Liz's offer to go halves. 'Nonsense,' he said. 'I asked you, remember?'

As they walked out of the hotel Liz stopped and pointed in the opposite direction from Thames House. 'I'm going that way to the Tube. Thanks for the drink.'

'Would you like a lift?' asked Tom. 'I've got my car today.'

'You don't even know where I live,' said Liz firmly. 'I might be taking you miles out of your way.'

'Kentish Town, right? Dave Armstrong mentioned it the other day.'

Why was Dave Armstrong talking about her to Tom Dartmouth? She didn't know whether to feel flattered or annoyed. But drinks had been pleasant, and a lift would save her time.

'If it's really not inconvenient,' she said, 'that would be great.'

In the car both were quiet at first, as Tom navigated around the evening traffic near Victoria.

'Did you grow up in London?' she asked. She didn't really know a lot about Tom other than a collection of facts from his CV: the schools he'd gone to, the subjects he'd studied at Oxford, the maiden name of his mother.

'Yes. In Kensington.' He glanced over at her. 'Back then the middle class could still live there.'

'Then Oxford,' she said quietly.

He seemed taken unawares, then nodded. 'That's right. I did a BA, then another degree. In Arabic Studies.'

'You must have done well to be able to stay on.'

'I scraped a First. My tutor was as surprised as I was.'

'You could have landed a plum job in the City.'

He mused on this. 'Perhaps. But banking never really appealed.'

'So why did you apply to MI5? I'd have thought that if you studied Arabic you'd have been natural Six material.'

'Oh, I don't know. Five does the real business,' he said, with a small deprecating laugh she found appealing. He seemed so self-confident at work that it was refreshing to find he didn't take himself altogether seriously. 'Anyway, it's your turn,' he said 'How long have you been in the Service?'

'Almost fifteen years.'

'Never,' he said. 'You're far too young.'

'Flattery will get you nowhere,' Liz declared.

'Well, it certainly won't get me to Kentish Town,' said Tom as they stopped at a traffic light, and he looked around, puzzled.

For the next ten minutes Liz concentrated on giving directions, until suddenly she realised they were about to turn into her street and the evening, at least as far as it concerned Tom Dartmouth, was about to end.

In front of her house he pulled into an empty parking space, and kept the engine running. Hesitantly, Liz said, 'It's kind of you to drive me home. Your family must be waiting for you.'

He looked puzzled. 'Family?'

'I thought you were married.' Liz saw no point being coy.

'Who told you that?'

'Dave Armstrong, naturally,' she said. 'Who else?'

He shook his head with a degree of wonderment. 'He was right about Kentish Town, but wrong about me.'

He said this dispassionately, showing none of the emotional baggage so often carried by divorced men—some bitter, some still in love with their ex-wives, a few jubilant as schoolboys at their liberation. What a relief to hear just cut-and-dried acknowledgment of a fact.

Partly because of this, and partly because she had enjoyed his company, Liz was on the verge of asking if he'd like to come in for coffee when he looked at his watch. 'Listen, I'd better go and leave you to your beauty sleep. And, actually, I could use some myself. I've been working flat out for the last two weeks.'

She nodded, feeling slightly disappointed. Then he added cheerfully, 'Now that I know how to get here, maybe we could do it again some time.'

'What?' she asked teasingly. 'Another lift home?'

'Why not?' he said. 'One of my uncles was a chauffeur. I'm sure I've inherited some of his genes.'

Liz was a little surprised, having pegged Tom as middle class through and through. He said, 'Do you ever go up to the Heath?'

'Sometimes in summer,' she said. 'Why?'

'I used to go there as a boy with my father. He was mad about kites, but hopeless at flying them. We'd spend hours trying to get them off the ground.' He gave a little laugh, as if visualising his father's ineptitude.

'Then, one autumn morning, my father brought home a new kite he claimed was extra special. We went to Hampstead Heath right away because the light went early in the afternoons. The wind was blowing incredibly hard and the kite was about twice as tall as I was, but somehow we managed to get it into the air. And then it flew for hours.' For a while he seemed lost in memory. Then he turned and gave Liz a quick smile.

'What were you doing in north London?' she asked. 'I thought you said you grew up in Kensington?'

He nodded. 'I did, but that was after my father died.' He smiled wistfully. 'He got knocked down by a car on his way to work. When my mother remarried, we moved to Kensington. I suppose you could say she did rather better for herself second time round.' He said this lightly as well, but Liz sensed genuine hostility underneath his mild mockery.

They said good night, and Tom waited until Liz had unlocked the door to her building and waved before driving off. She entered her flat and kicked her shoes off, poured a glass of Sauvignon from an open bottle in the fridge, then sat down on her one comfortable chair. She realised how much she had liked Tom Dartmouth this evening.

Yes, he was good-looking; yes, he was excellent at his job, sophisticated and highly educated; but on a personal level what had struck her had nothing to do with credentials. It was Tom's wry, levelling sense of humour that had first appealed—especially the fact that he didn't hesitate to poke gentle fun at himself. And she liked the way he said he'd 'scraped' a First, though she knew he'd gained the best degree in his year.

But the modesty and the sense of humour weren't really what struck Liz now. Underneath Tom's easy-going manner, she sensed a deep, lurking sadness. He is carrying a wound, thought Liz, the way a war veteran might carry shrapnel deep inside. Somehow she doubted Tom often talked about his father—she felt flattered that he had with her.

Don't get carried away, she told herself. Still, she was intrigued by Tom Dartmouth, and wondered how long it would be before he offered to chauffeur her again. I hope it's soon, she decided.

THREE DAYS LATER, Rose Love, a junior member of Investigations, came to see Judith Spratt in the Operations Room. Judith liked the first-year recruit, and she tried to encourage her. For although Rose had a First from York University and was also a strikingly pretty young woman, she seemed very unsure of herself. Now she spoke to Judith in little more than a whisper. 'Sorry to bother you, but it's about the CCTV footage.'

'Yes,' said Judith, struggling to suppress her impatience. Doubtless there was another hitch—a disk wiped by a shop owner, or undated material supplied by the supermarket security men.

'It's just I think that possibly we may have found something.'

'Let me see,' Judith said, getting up from her seat.

Ten minutes later she called Tom Dartmouth to the room downstairs, and together they looked at a monitor while Rose moved through the footage screen by screen. 'There!' called Judith sharply, and the screen froze. It was not a very clear picture, but three figures were discernible at the front of the shop by the till. They were male, Asian, and seemed to be young. None of them looked at the camera, or for that matter at Irwin Patel, the owner of the shop, who was serving them. The time meter said 20:24.

'Sorry,' said Tom apologetically, 'but you better talk me through it. It all looks like ultrasound scans to me.'

'The man at the till. We think he may be a match with one of the Dutch photos.' Judith passed him a print-out. The face that stared out from it was of a personable-looking youth of Asian appearance, who was struggling to grow a moustache and had a slight overbite and a broad smile.

'They've identified him as Rashid Khan. He's nineteen years old and comes from Wolverhampton.'

'OK,' said Tom, giving a self-deprecating laugh. 'But for the life of me I couldn't tell you which of these three he's meant to be.'

'Look again,' said Judith. 'The man at the till. See anything unusual?'

Tom peered closely at the screen. 'He's not very tall, is he?'

Judith nodded. 'Five foot one-and-a-half inches, to be precise. At least according to the passport application of Rashid Khan. But that's not all—look closely at the face.' Tom did so obediently. 'Same moustache, or effort at one. Same slight prominence of the upper teeth.'

'Can't say I see that,' said Tom. He held up his hands in a gesture of mock surrender. 'But you're the experts. If you say it's a match then I have to accept that.'

'We think it's a match,' said Judith. 'No guarantees.'

Tom nodded. 'But assuming you're right, who the hell is Rashid Khan?'

'We've got no trace under that name,' said Judith. 'I'm seeing Dave Armstrong right after you,' she added, since identifying a suspect might be her responsibility, but finding them was someone else's.

AT FIRST, IRWIN PATEL thought the policeman was returning the CCTV footage he had taken away the week before, but this time he was accompanied by a man in a grey parka jacket. 'Could we have a word,' asked the policeman, 'in the back of the shop?'

'Oscar,' called Irwin, and gestured for his son to man the till, then led the two men to the small storeroom which doubled as an office.

'Yes, gentlemen?' said Irwin politely but a little nervously.

The man in the parka spoke. 'We found pictures on the footage you gave us of someone we are interested in.' He handed a still photo captured from the CCTV video footage to Irwin, who studied it carefully.

'Do you remember serving this man?'

Irwin thought hard. He wanted to help, but the fact was that probably fifty per cent of his business was passing trade—one-off visitors to his shop he would never see again. 'No,' he said at last.

'Or the men behind him?'

Irwin peered at the photograph for some time. The beat policeman said impatiently, 'Can't you remember a group of three like this? It was probably last Monday, if that's any help.'

'If I had to guess,' Irwin remarked, 'I would say I serve over fifty Asian men under the age of thirty every day. Some come in alone, some with a friend, and some with two friends. I do not recognise any of these men.'

The constable groaned, but the man in the parka seemed unperturbed. 'How about this man?' he asked, handing another photograph to Irwin. It was the photo Judith Spratt had extracted from the five hundred or so sent by her Dutch counterparts only days before.

Irwin's face lit up. 'I've seen this man!' he exclaimed. 'Here in the shop. He bought rolling papers—you know, for cigarettes. I remember that because he was very short. Not much more than five feet tall,' he added. 'I remember wanting to tell him that smoking stunts your growth.'

And at this even the po-faced policeman laughed. He looked towards the man by his side. He was probably Special Branch, but he wasn't a bad bloke—he'd said to call him Dave. And Dave was happy now.

7

Miss Prideaux's remark that she was 'awfully sorry to hear about Ravi' had been nagging at Liz, ever since her trip to Oxford. Judith had said nothing to her about any problem with her husband, Ravi Singh, a handsome westernised Sikh who was a successful investment banker. Their marriage always seemed so happy that Liz wondered if perhaps Ravi was ill.

Normally, Liz wouldn't have thought of prying into a colleague's matrimonial affairs, but Judith was on the list of suspects. When she had asked B Branch if Judith had recently mentioned anything about Ravi—any change of circumstances in her private life, as she was required to do—the answer came back that she had not. Liz's heart sank. She would have to say something herself.

She was already feeling low. The previous evening she'd phoned her mother, who had seen Dr Barlow about her test results that afternoon.

The phone seemed to ring for ever. 'Hello, darling,' her mother said when she finally picked up and heard the anxiety in her daughter's voice. 'I'm so sorry. I was in the garden picking some flowers.'

How typical of her mother's priorities, thought Liz, with a daughter's mixed affection and annoyance. 'What did Barlow say?'

Her mother paused, her normal reaction to her daughter's directness. 'It's nothing too terrible, Liz.'

'Good,' she said, trying to sound cheerful rather than impatient. 'Tell me what he said.'

'Well, it seems they've found something growing and I guess they want to see what it is. A biopsy?' She said it hesitantly.

Only my mother, thought Liz, can make a tumour sound like the Latin name for a species of rose. 'When is this?'

'Saturday week. It shouldn't take long.'

Liz said immediately that she would go down that Friday. Her mother's protestations did not last for long, and Liz could tell that she was relieved.

Now, as she sat at her desk, she felt tears in her eyes. She had woken in the night thinking about Marzipan, the mole hunt that didn't seem to be getting anywhere, the terrorists on the loose, and finally her mother's tests. And, to top it all off, Liz knew she would have to talk to Judith.

Her thoughts were interrupted by the ringing of her phone. 'We've cracked it,' Peggy announced excitedly.

'Sorry?' said Liz.

'Technical Ted. He's managed to decipher the disk. The talk Liam O'Phelan gave in Oxford was entitled "From Boston to Belfast: Britain's Dirty War in Northern Ireland and Abroad".'

Liz's pulse began to race. O'Phelan's topic suggested an interest in contemporary Irish political affairs which his high-flown historical chatter about Charles Stewart Parnell did not. It also indicated a strongly Republican and anti-British position.

'Well done,' Liz said to Peggy, and she meant it.

DAVE ARMSTRONG WAS SITTING in a Wolverhampton McDonald's with the Special Branch officer who had phoned him the night before.

'Do we know who's in the house?' Dave asked, watching, fascinated, as the officer tucked into a Big Mac.

'Not precisely. It's a family residence. People named Khan. Respectable couple—the man is a sales rep for a restaurant supply business. His wife works part-time in a laundry. Three kids—all teenagers. Two boys and a girl. Your guy's the eldest but hasn't—as far as we know—left home yet.'

Dave had already planned his approach. He had no intention of risking his life or the life of any officer entering the house of Rashid Khan. He was also well aware how much ill will a heavy-handed approach might cause.

'I'd like to start with just a knock on the door. I want concealed back-up that's armed and ready and expecting trouble, but they're not to do anything until they see what the initial response is.'

'And who's going to be the man at the door?'

'I am,' said Dave.

Two hours later he rang the bell of the Khans' house. Unarmed, he knew how helpless he would be if someone answered the door with a gun. He was surprised when a teenaged girl, still in school uniform, opened the door.

'Yes?' she ventured timidly.

'I'm from the Benefits Office,' said Dave, 'and I wanted a word with Rashid Khan. It's just a routine check about his claim. Is he in?'

Her astonishment seemed genuine. 'No, but why? Is he in trouble?'

'Are your mother and father at home?'

Ten minutes later Rashid's father's bewilderment was growing. 'Are you sure it is our son you are looking for?' he asked yet again. 'It doesn't make sense. He shares everything with us.'

'Everything?' asked Dave, who had learned nothing from the man that would explain his son's disaffection—Mr Khan thought Rashid had been in Holland for work experience before taking up his place at university.

'Everything,' repeated the father defiantly.

'Then why don't you know where he is now?'

HE DROVE TO WOKINGHAM with unusual caution and parked in a Pay-and-Display car park in the centre of town. From there he took a taxi to an address on an estate on the fringes of the city.

The address was not the passenger's final destination. He waited until the taxi had pulled away, then walked to the end of the street of small houses and turned in sharply at number 48. He was about to ring the bell when the door opened. Without a greeting, he slid inside and stood in the hallway.

'Where are the other two?'

'Upstairs, watching television. Do you want to see them?'

'No. Leave them.'

The visitor sat down on the sofa and motioned for Bashir Siddiqui to sit down across from him on the room's one chair. 'They've had a breakthrough.

They checked the CCTV coverage for the area around the alley where the fellow from the bookshop was disposed of, and they've recognised one of you in a newsagent's store. Rashid.'

Bashir groaned. He had not wanted to go into any shop that evening, but Rashid had insisted. 'How did they know who he was?' he asked. Rashid had been picked partly because he had no UK record of any kind.

'One of Abu Sayed's associates rang from Holland on the day you were supposed to be at the bookshop. The call was traced, and the Dutch security people sent photographs over. One of them was of Rashid; when they compared the CCTV footage they made a match.' He paused. 'There's no point going into who's to blame for what. What's important now is that you listen very carefully to me and do what I say.'

Bashir nodded in submission.

'There is no reason to think they are on to you,' the man continued. 'They know about Rashid, yes, but they don't have any idea where he is. Provided you don't make any more stupid mistakes, there is no way for them to find out. But, from now on, there is to be no external communication with anyone. No mobile phone, no text messages, not even an internet café. Is that clear?'

Bashir nodded again, for he was comfortable following the orders of the Englishman. It was the Englishman, after all, who had initially recruited him. He asked hesitantly, 'Can we leave the house?'

The man thought for a moment. 'Yes. It would seem odd to the neighbours if none of you were seen coming in and out. But not all three of you together. And keep Rashid out of the town centre.'

'Shall I tell him he's been identified?'

The Englishman shook his head. 'I think it might frighten him. He might get panicky.' He got up and shook hands with Bashir. 'If you can just keep your cool, all will be well. There isn't that much longer to wait.'

PATRICK DOBSON had fractured his wrist and was spending a few days at home. Liz decided that she and Peggy would call on him there. In her experience, there was a lot to be picked up about a person from their home.

The Dobson residence was a large, thirties mock-Tudor house of brown brick, with white plaster gables and beams, set in a leafy suburban garden. Peggy said, 'I hadn't realised MI5 paid so well.' Sometimes with Peggy it was difficult to distinguish innocence from irony, but this time there was no mistaking her tartness.

Liz laughed. 'I think you'll find,' she said, 'that there's been another source of funds into the Dobson household.'

Patrick Dobson was not even forty years old, but his home seemed middle-aged with its panelled oak, mock Elizabethan fireplaces and leaded windows. On the walls hung a mix of family portraits and watercolours of nineteenth-century colonial scenes—a procession of elephants in Delhi under the Raj, and an antique map of the Imperial City of Beijing.

'What a beautiful room,' said Peggy admiringly, when they were shown into what Dobson grandly called his drawing room.

If you like that sort of thing, thought Liz caustically.

Now Dobson thanked Peggy for her compliment, adding, 'This was my wife's parents' house. Her father was in the Colonial Service. My wife inherited the house after they died.'

That explains it, thought Liz. She knew about his father-in-law from the file. He had been a district officer in Uganda.

Dobson sat, neat and upright, in a comfortable armchair across from the chintz sofa she and Peggy were sitting on. He was a short, pie-faced man, with blond hair combed straight back. Wearing a blue blazer and grey flannels he was a model of stiff politeness.

'This shouldn't take long, Patrick,' Liz said cheerfully, in an effort to make things less formal.

They reviewed the bare facts of his CV—his boyhood in south London, his schooling (a scholarship to Alleyn's School in Dulwich), his time at Oxford, followed by entry into MI5. Dobson spoke so animatedly about his current job in the DG's office that Liz was unable to ask a single question.

She was about to interrupt when a knock at the door did the job for her. A woman came in with a tray—a pot of coffee, cups and saucers.

'Ah, Teresa. These are the colleagues I told you about.'

She nodded politely, and came forward with the tray. Liz and Peggy rose to their feet and Dobson made introductions, but it was obvious his wife did not want to linger. 'I won't intrude,' she said with a forced smile, looking only at her husband. 'I'm just off to the church to do the flowers.'

'Of course, darling. See you later.'

Liz sat back down with her coffee, discomfited. If she didn't take charge, she felt she would soon be lost in this safe suburban world. 'If I could just go back to your time at Oxford, Patrick,' she said. 'You were very religious as an undergraduate, I gather.'

'Only by the standards of the other students,' he said defensively. 'I went to chapel every week. I still do. I don't think there's anything peculiar about it. Do you?'

Liz said mildly, 'Of course not.'

He relaxed slightly. 'I imagine you've seen the chaplain at Pembroke. How is he these days?'

'Fine. At least he seemed that way to me.' However caustic Hickson had been about his ex-pupil, Liz was happy to admit she'd seen him. 'He said you were a Young Conservative at Oxford.'

'I was interested,' said Dobson with a shrug. 'Don't tell me that's unusual, too?' For the first time there was an edge to his voice.

Liz shrugged. 'It's probably me who was unusual.' She said, half confidingly, 'I was a bit of a leftie at university. I'm surprised I got through the vetting.' She laughed. 'It was quite a political time. Everyone was worked up about the Palestinians.' She paused. 'And Ireland, of course.'

But Dobson didn't bite. 'The big issue in my day was rent increases.'

Peggy had been a non-participant in the interview so far, studiously taking notes. Now she looked up for the first time. 'But you've got Irish blood, haven't you?' she asked brightly.

Dobson stared at her coldly. 'I believe one of my grandmothers was Irish,' he said slowly.

'Did she emigrate here?'

'Emigrate? What a grand word—I imagine she'd have said she came here for work. The story was that she was "in service" in Galway for an Anglo-Irish family. When they moved back to London she came with them. She met my grandfather, and married him.' He added pointedly, 'He was English. Owned a string of garages in south London.'

'She must have had quite a story to tell,' gushed Peggy. Liz, who was beginning to admire Peggy's skill at drawing people out, sat back and watched. 'Did you know your grandmother?' Peggy asked.

'A bit,' he said reluctantly. 'She died when I was a boy.'

'She must have missed Ireland,' said Peggy sympathetically. 'Did she ever go back?'

'I imagine she went back sometimes.' He hesitated, almost imperceptibly. Liz imagined he was calculating what they already knew, and what they could find out. He'd be surprised, thought Liz, thinking of the day before, when Peggy had proudly shown her a complex genealogical chart of the Dobson maternal line. That's when Liz had suggested Peggy ask the questions about the family.

'Actually,' Dobson admitted, 'I went with her once. To Connemara. That's where she was from.'

'Family still there?' asked Liz as casually as she could.

Dobson shrugged. 'I would think so. It was a typically Irish set-up—my grandmother was one of seven children.'

'Your grandmother's maiden name was O'Hare, wasn't it?' Peggy said.

Dobson began to nod, then stopped suddenly. 'How did you know that?'

Peggy ignored him, and looking at her notes continued: 'And her eldest brother was named Sean, yes?' She didn't wait for an answer. 'He moved north to Londonderry, before the War—and had two sons, the eldest named Kieran, and Kieran himself had one son—Patrick. Same name as yours. And he was—is, I should say—your second cousin.'

Dobson stayed completely silent until Peggy finished. Then ignoring her, he stared at Liz. She couldn't tell if it was fear or anger in his eyes. 'Yes?' he asked neutrally.

'Well,' said Liz, matter-of-factly, 'Patrick was detained and spent twelve months in the Maze. Applicants to MI5 are asked to declare any relative who has been convicted of a crime, or been charged with subversive activity. Yet Patrick O'Hare was not on your form. Can you tell me why?'

Outwardly Dobson stayed impressively calm. 'Is there a point to this?'

'We have to be thorough,' she said firmly.

Dobson looked irritated. 'I knew nothing about this cousin of mine. How could I? For goodness sake, I was five years old when it happened.'

'Of course,' said Liz, and she moved quickly on to another topic, to Peggy's mystification.

'So what do you think?' asked Liz, as they joined the M3.

'I don't believe he didn't know about his cousin,' Peggy replied.

'Why not?'

Peggy pondered this. Dobson hadn't liked any of the questions about his mother's Irish roots. Initially she had put this down to snobbery—presumably a pig farm in Galway didn't sit easily for a man now accustomed to a wing chair in Surrey. Yet though he had acknowledged his background, he'd flatly denied any knowledge of his IRA relative.

And Liz had backed off. Why? Peggy said tentatively, 'Weren't you surprised he didn't know his second cousin?'

'It seems a pretty remote connection,' said Liz. 'Anyway, on the application it's immediate family they're interested in. He didn't have to declare his second cousin even if he knew about him.'

'Doesn't matter,' said Peggy, sticking to her guns. 'I still think he was being economical with the truth.'

Liz smiled, checking the rear-view mirror, before changing lanes. 'Actually, so do I,' she said. 'But it's nothing to do with his family tree.'

'What then?' Peggy was surprised.

'Dobson said he was only five when his cousin was interned.'

Peggy did a mental calculation. Patrick Dobson had been born in 1968; his namesake cousin had been interned in 1973. 'But Dobson *was* only five,' she said.

'I'm sure he was,' said Liz crisply. 'But Internment lasted four years. So how did Dobson know which year his cousin was put in the Maze? I didn't tell him; you didn't either. And yet think of his exact words: "I was five years old when it happened."' She flashed a sideways smile at Peggy. 'So no, I don't believe him either. But what we don't know is whether he lied for a purpose, or just because he's got a hang-up about his forebears.'

8

Rashid knew nothing of the Englishman's warning that his identity had been uncovered, and Bashir had conveyed none of his own alarm, though he had stressed to Rashid and the other conspirator that they were not to be in contact with anyone.

And Rashid would have obeyed this unquestioningly had he not been worried about his sister Yasmina. He had tried in the last two years, since his own increasing involvement with Islam, to watch over her, growing concerned as she turned sixteen and began to make friends with boys, especially English boys. Rashid knew, even if his parents had not realised, that Yasmina was a pretty girl and she was vulnerable.

So when, in the early afternoon, Bashir had said he could go out, he ignored the older man's command to stay out of shops and within five minutes he was catching the bus into Wokingham. Here he bought a mobile phone, the simplest model, pay as you go, and a ten-pound voucher for it.

When he looked at his watch he realised he had been gone almost an hour. Bashir would soon be worried. Back at the bus stop, he waited impatiently;

he did not want to use his phone there as several people were standing in the queue.

At last the bus came. He got off one stop early and walked quickly, then broke into a run when he came within a street of Somerset Drive. He stopped by some railings and dialled Yasmina's mobile phone. He felt perfectly safe, since his throwaway phone was untraceable.

'Yasmina?'

'Rashid, are you all right? Where are you?'

'It doesn't matter—I'm not allowed to tell you. But I am fine. I should be home in just a few weeks.'

'Is it safe to phone?' Yasmina said.

'Why wouldn't it be?' asked Rashid, surprised.

'It's just—' she began, then stopped.

'Tell me, Yasmina.'

'All right, but you mustn't let Papa know. Not even that we talked. A man came here looking for you. He said he was from the Benefits—but I don't think he was. Papa was very upset afterwards.'

Rashid's pulse began to race, and his right hand, holding the phone, shook so much that he had to steady it with his left. A passing woman looked at him oddly, and he turned to face the railing away from her gaze.

He knew his parents would never understand; they had lost all sense of their origins and their faith. He pitied them, for they would never be truly welcome in this new 'home' either. But they had probably helped the police as much as they could, he concluded bitterly. He tried to calm his agitation. 'Yasmina, do you know what this man wanted?'

'Yes, Rashid. He wanted you.'

IN THAMES HOUSE the trace came through to the monitors and the phone on Judith Spratt's desk rang. 'We've got a call to the Khans that we're tracking now. Think you'll want to hear this one,' said Lawrence, a junior transcriber, to Judith. 'It's to the sister's mobile. We think it's her brother.'

'Fast as you can then,' said Judith.

Five minutes later, Lawrence came back with a transcript of the conversation, which Judith, now joined by Tom Dartmouth, scanned quickly. 'Where was the call made from?' asked Tom.

'We're working on it. It was a mobile phone, probably a throwaway.'

Tom looked at Lawrence. 'How close a fix can we get on him?'

Lawrence shrugged. 'Can't say at the moment. Two, maybe three miles?'

Tom swore softly. 'That's a hell of a big urban area.'

'Thanks, Lawrence,' said Judith, and the junior withdrew. She and Tom needed to determine what to do next. She said, 'Apparently the Khan parents were totally bewildered when Dave explained what their son was up to. They promised to cooperate completely. Now, thanks to the sister, this Rashid bloke knows we're looking for him.'

'No bad thing,' said Tom calmly. 'If he can screw up this badly when he thinks he's safe, let's hope he screws up even more now he feels hunted.'

DAVE ARMSTRONG had volunteered to work with Special Branch checking the letting agencies in Wokingham and he was now regretting it. He could have been back in London, working at his desk, or chatting up Rose Love, the pretty new girl in Investigations who was a younger, prettier version of Liz Carlyle, but who might prove more susceptible to his charms.

Looking at his list, Dave saw with relief that there was only one more agency to visit. Lanky, with long legs, and hair that was shaggy by the standards of Thames House, Dave stood out among the more staid Service personnel, but he fitted in with the people on the streets where he spent so much of his time.

At 5.15 p.m. the small tidy office of Hummingbird Lettings was winding down for the day. The receptionist had left, and Dave found himself alone in a large room with four empty desks. Then a thin and bony-faced man with greying hair and black NHS spectacles came out, holding a cup of tea. Starting at the sight of the man in a parka, he sloshed tea from his cup. 'We're shut,' he said automatically.

Dave smiled broadly. 'I'm Simon Willis,' he said. 'I rang before.'

'Oh, yes,' the man said, 'the gentleman from the . . . police.'

'That's it,' said Dave brightly, 'won't take a minute.'

They sat down at the desk and the man introduced himself as Richard Penbury. 'So how can I help?' Penbury asked.

'I am making a discreet enquiry,' said Dave, trying his best to sound official, 'into the rental of a property to one, possibly two or even three, young Asian males. It might be a small house, or a medium or largish flat.'

The man was shaking his head even before Dave finished his sentence.

'No, most of my rentals this year have been repeaters, or long-term lets for properties people have bought for investment.'

'Think for a minute please, Mr Penbury, about any new rentals. Are you sure none were to Asians? It doesn't matter if they weren't male.'

Mr Penbury took no time to dismiss this as well. 'No Asians. I'm certain. We've rented properties for and to them, but not recently.'

'Then let me ask you this: think back to all the rentals you've made in the past six months. Was there anything unusual about any of them? Anything that comes to mind? This is important or I wouldn't be bothering you.'

And slowly, if unwillingly, Mr Penbury seemed to do this. 'There was one property that was a bit unusual. A house on Somerset Drive. The owner moved to Devon and we look after it for her. Someone took it on a six-month winter let.'

'And?' asked Dave, since this didn't sound so memorable.

'Well, he paid all six months in advance. That's not unheard of, but I wouldn't say it was normal, and the thing is it hasn't been used. The last time I checked the property, no one had been in the house at all. I even asked the neighbours, and they said they hadn't seen anyone there since the owner moved out.'

'When did you speak to them?'

Mr Penbury thought for a moment. 'About three weeks ago.'

'Could I see the information for the tenant, please?'

Mr Penbury hesitated, then nodded and went to a filing cabinet in the corner. He came back a minute later with a file. Dave scanned it quickly, knowing that if this turned out to be a link to the bombers, then the name used, Edward Larrabee, would not be real. 'Tell me,' he asked, 'do you know the name of the neighbours?'

'I do as a matter of fact,' said Mr Penbury, 'I do. The wife plays badminton with my wife. They're called Dawnton; I think he's Trevor.'

AFTER DROPPING her daughter at school, Maddie Keaney drove her small Ford into the heart of Dublin and left it in the garage near the Liffey, where she and the other law-firm partners had their own parking spaces. She was a slight figure, neatly dressed in a conservative black skirt and white blouse.

As she entered the Victorian building of grey stone that housed the offices of Gallagher & O'Donnell, she realised she had been at the firm for exactly fifteen years. She wasn't a native of Dublin, and it was not so much the city's virtues that kept her here, but the simple fact that it wasn't Belfast.

She had come south to read Law at University College Dublin as soon as she was able, and after taking her degree (a good one; she had worked hard) and qualifying, she had been offered what was supposed to be a short-term placement with Gallagher & O'Donnell, and there she had stayed.

What had made her flee Belfast at the earliest opportunity? Her father—even Sean Keaney's recent death had failed to dent the unalloyed hostility she had felt for as long as she could remember.

Maddie took the lift to the third floor. She stopped in the outer office where Caitlin, the unhelpful secretary she shared with another partner, sat. 'Good morning,' Maddie said. 'What have I got today?'

Caitlin pursed her lips, and looked reluctantly at the desk diary. 'There's a Mr Murphy coming to see you in a quarter of an hour.'

'What does he want?' Maddie specialised in conveyancing, working mainly with a few large developers. It was rare to have a new client.

'I don't know,' said Caitlin. 'He said you'd been highly recommended.'

'By whom?'

'I didn't think to ask,' said Caitlin.

Vaguely irritated, Maddie occupied the next ten minutes in phone calls—to her ex-husband about his maintenance payments (late again), and another to the owner of a Georgian town house who was seeking planning permission to convert it into flats. Then Maddie's phone purred and Caitlin informed her that her appointment was waiting in reception. When Maddie came out, she found a tall, shambling figure of a man, putting down a copy of the *Irish Times* and slowly getting up from his chair.

He looked to be in his late sixties, possibly older, and was wearing a long raincoat over a thick sweater and shirt.

Maddie found her palm engulfed by a hand the size of a large animal's paw. She looked up into a doughy, weather-beaten face that looked as if it had seen too much of life. There was something familiar about the man, but she couldn't place it.

She ushered him into her office. 'Will you have tea or coffee?'

'I will not,' he said as he sat down. His voice was low and soft.

From behind her desk, Maddie glanced at the man and lined up her notepad and pencil. 'So how can I help you, Mr Murphy?'

'It's Maguire,' the man said slowly. 'James Maguire.'

Then Maddie understood why he seemed familiar. It had only been a glimpse or two—the tall figure climbing the stairs behind her sister the night her father died, then later leaving the Belfast house without a word of goodbye. It was the raincoat she remembered.

She felt a chill as she looked at her father's enemy across the desk. What was he doing here now, and under a false name? Was this to be the visitation that had haunted her childhood: the masked men bursting in, the gun drawn and fired as she and her parents sat in front of the television? She thought of her daughter, and fear began to shake her, like a rattle in an empty box. Sweet Jesus, she thought, this is not the way I want to die.

Suddenly the man's face creased into a gentle smile. 'Don't be alarmed,' he said, for he must have seen the fear in her eyes. 'I wasn't sure you'd agree to see me if I used my real name.'

Maddie gathered herself. 'Well, then, Mr Maguire, what do you want with me?'

'It's about your father,' he said. 'On the day he died, he made certain requests of me. But I'm hampered, you see, by not knowing enough.'

'I doubt I can help you,' she said. 'I kept well out of my father's affairs.'

Maguire gazed at her, as though summing her up. 'He wanted me to get in touch with some professor he knew. A sympathiser to the cause, you understand. He was Irish, this man, but I believe he spent some time teaching at Oxford. It was your father's dying wish that I get hold of this man. I'd hardly be bothering you otherwise, now would I, Miss Keaney?'

Maddie felt irritation overcome her sense of alarm. Why was this man dragging her into whatever mucky errand he'd agreed to carry out for her father? 'Why didn't you ask my father when you saw him?' she demanded.

'My dear,' said Maguire, oblivious to how this made Maddie bristle. 'Your father was barely conscious when I saw him. The only thing he said to me was "Ask Kirsty Brien." You know her, don't you?'

'She used to be my best friend,' said Maddie dully, her heart sinking. She tried to think of her former best friend with equanimity, but it was difficult.

They'd met at University College Dublin and had been inseparable, despite all manner of differences. Kirsty was tall where Maddie was short, Kirsty was blonde where Maddie had mouse-coloured hair, and most of all Kirsty was political where Maddie hated even the word. The bedrock of all Kirsty's left-wing beliefs had been a vision of a united Ireland. She worked tirelessly to achieve it—demonstrating, writing letters, organising boycotts. Kirsty was called the new Bernadette Devlin so often that she seemed to believe it herself.

None of this would have mattered at all to their friendship, if Maddie had not taken her best friend home one spring break to stay with her family.

Sean Keaney had taken to her at once, and she to him. They shared a commitment to the Struggle, of course, but it was more than that. There was nothing unsavoury about the closeness between her father and Kirsty—not even in her sourest moments had Maddie thought so. It was worse than that. Sean

Keaney was an admired father figure for Kirsty, thought Maddie bitterly. Her best friend had unforgivably occupied the space she did not want herself.

'Why aren't you talking to Kirsty Brien instead of me? She'll tell you what you need to know.'

Maguire shook his head, as if she'd missed the point. 'She won't see me.'

That made sense. Kirsty would be rock solid in her loyalties, just like Sean Keaney had been.

'So what do you want to know?' she asked, already dreading the prospect of contacting her former closest friend. She had last seen her across the grave at Sean Keaney's funeral.

'I want to know who this academic man is.'

She said nothing.

'Look,' he said, 'you know your father and I didn't see eye to eye over many things. But one thing we would have agreed on is that the battle's over now. The fighting's done. Your father knew that; so do I. What he wanted me to do for him is meant to keep the war shut down for good.'

Maddie looked sceptical. 'How do I know you're telling the truth?'

'You don't,' he said simply. 'All you can do is look this old man in the face; then I think you'll be able to tell.'

And she did as he said, and found his gaze unflinching.

'Give me a minute,' she said, standing up. 'I'll get us some coffee.' She needed time to marshal her thoughts.

That last spring at university in Dublin, she had seen very little of Kirsty. Part of it was her own doing—she was already determined to get a good degree and then to stay in the Republic.

But Kirsty was busy, too. She had taken up with a postgraduate student, older, good-looking but flamboyant. Maddie thought it strange. He didn't look the type to be interested in girls, but he and Kirsty had become inseparable. The man was brilliant, everyone said, though arrogant with it. He had just won a Junior Research Fellowship at Oxford, which he was taking up the following year. Maddie wondered if their relationship would survive.

Then one Saturday night, Maddie had run into Kirsty by herself at the Students' Union. Spontaneously they had gone out, just like old times, to a new wine bar in the Golden Mile. Maddie had drunk three Tom Collins, and had plucked up courage to ask Kirsty about her new friend. 'So are you?'

'Am I what?' Kirsty had demanded, her indignation inflamed by alcohol.

'Are you sleeping with him or not?'

And Kirsty had laughed so loudly that the neighbouring table of students stopped talking to look. 'Don't be ridiculous,' Kirsty finally said. 'I'm only seeing him for your father's sake.'

'What?' Maddie had wanted an explanation. But Kirsty had seemed to regret her admission and had stood up abruptly. 'Come on,' she said. 'There's Danny Mills and his mates. Let's join them.'

The memory dissolved now as she handed Maguire his coffee. 'Will you ring her for me then?' he asked, entreatingly.

She shook her head. 'There's no need. I know the man you're looking for.'

THELMA DAWNTON was just about to leave for the badminton club when a man who said he was from the letting agency phoned to ask about the house next door. She was in a hurry, so the conversation was brief.

She played doubles in the mixed competition, alongside Evan Dewhart, unattached but dull. They lost to a young married couple in the final set. Afterwards Thelma and Evan bought the drinks.

When she got home Trevor was in front of the telly. As his programme ended, she mentioned the call from the letting agency earlier that evening. 'He was asking about the house next door. He said they were trying to get in touch with the person who'd signed the lease. He wanted to know if he might be living there now.'

'Why's he asking you? Why couldn't he ask the lot next door direct?'

'That's just it. When I said there had been three Asians next door for the last couple of weeks, he sounded surprised. He said it might be a police matter, so please could I not mention our conversation to any of them until he'd had time to call the authorities. Do you think something funny's going on over there?' She jerked her head in the direction of their neighbours. 'Could we have terrorists living next door to us or something?'

'Not any more,' said Trevor. 'I saw them packing up their car when I got home. You'd better ring the agent in the morning.'

BUT THELMA NEVER RANG. At 5.30 a.m. she was woken by the sound of someone knocking on a door. At first she thought it was her front door, but then she realised it was coming from the house next door. Curious, she got up and looked out of the window.

What she saw was astonishing.

There was a group of men at her neighbour's front door. Three of them wore helmets and held rifles of the kind she'd seen policemen carrying at Heathrow. One of them, in a policeman's uniform, was pounding on the door, shouting. 'Open up,' he roared. 'The house is surrounded. At the count of ten, we will force our way in. One . . . two . . . three . . .'

From her vantage point, Thelma could see into the strip of garden at the back of the house, and she saw three other men, weapons at the ready.

'Four . . . five . . . six . . .'

In the street lined up were a white police van and two Range Rovers.

'Seven . . . eight . . . nine . . . ten.'

There was a pause, and then she heard a splintering noise followed by a thud, and the men disappeared from view into the house.

'Jesus Christ!' Trevor was now standing next to her in his pyjamas. 'Didn't you tell them they've all gone?'

'How could I?' she asked plaintively. 'You only told me last night. I was going to call the agency when they opened this morning.'

Trevor snorted and pointed at the armed policemen in front of the neighbouring house. 'Do they look like letting agents to you?' He opened the window and bellowed, 'Officer, they've all gone!'

A man with a megaphone detached himself from the tense group. Pointing it right at Trevor and Thelma, his voice was astonishingly clear in the morning air. '*Stay inside! Move back from the windows. I repeat: move back from the windows.*'

They retreated at once to the spare bedroom on the far side of the house, where they huddled together until there was more knocking. This time it *was* their door.

'I'd better answer it,' said Trevor.

'I'm coming with you,' declared Thelma, frightened at the prospect of being left alone.

A man in a parka was standing there with a policeman cradling an automatic weapon behind him. 'Mrs Dawnton?' the man in the parka said. 'We spoke last night.'

'You're the gentleman who rang?' He didn't look like a letting agent, especially with that policeman behind him.

Dave nodded impatiently. 'You told me there were three Asian men staying next door.' His tone was mildly accusing.

'That's right,' said Thelma.

'There were, Officer,' said Trevor, insinuating himself between Thelma and the man. 'But they left last night.'

'After we spoke,' explained Thelma anxiously. 'I was going to ring—'

Dave cut her off. 'What time did they go?' he asked Trevor.

'Half-seven, quarter to eight.'

'Did they have a car?'

Trevor nodded. 'I think it was a Golf. They didn't have much gear.'

A policeman came up to Dave and whispered in his ear. 'Excuse me,' said Dave. 'I'd like to come back. Say in half an hour?'

'I don't know,' said Trevor, 'I've got work to go to.'

'I'd be very grateful if you went in late today,' said Dave. 'I'd be happy to ring your boss if you like, and explain we need to talk to you first.'

Trevor looked slightly miffed. 'No need for that. I'll tell him.'

'Right then,' said Dave. 'See you a little later on.'

It was almost ninety minutes before he came back. In the meantime the Dawntons had watched the dogs go in—an Alsatian and two spaniels, their tails wagging wildly. Out of sight of the watchers, all three dogs had become very excited when they sniffed the carpeted floor of the wardrobe in one of the bedrooms, leading the white-suited forensics officers to conclude that fertiliser had been stored in the house. Stored recently, in fact.

The euphoria of the forensics team after this discovery was not shared by Dave Armstrong, who drove back to London late that night in an unusual state of alarm. It was not simply that he knew he and his colleagues could now proceed in the certainty that the men they sought were bombers. Even more worrying was the fact that they had left in a rush—according to Trevor Dawnton, 'they looked like they were two steps in front of the bailiffs'. It was true Rashid's sister had told Rashid the 'Benefits' were looking for him, but that would not have triggered such a panicked departure, since the sister had no idea of his whereabouts. Dave had spent another hour with the Dawntons, long enough to persuade himself that it was inconceivable that either of the couple, or indeed Mr Penbury from the letting agency, would have tipped off the suspects.

So why then had the men fled in the nick of time? Was it just coincidence?

Perhaps, but Dave Armstrong wasn't paid to believe in coincidence. Ruling out Penbury, the Dawntons and Rashid's sister left him with possible sources for the tip-off that did nothing but worry him, and which prompted him to make a call to Charles Wetherby's voicemail.

DAVE GAVE HIMSELF plenty of time to get to Thames House by eight the next morning for the meeting he had requested with Wetherby.

Wetherby wore a light grey summer suit and was standing by the window, watching the antics of a large heron on a mudflat below, when

Dave entered the office. He listened without comment as Dave briefed him on the events in Wokingham, including the discovery of traces of fertiliser. 'So we almost had them,' he said. 'What bad luck.' He sighed morosely.

Dave took a deep breath. 'That's just it, Charles. I'm not convinced luck had anything to do with it.'

Wetherby turned round. 'What are you trying to say?' he asked sharply.

'According to the neighbours, the suspects left suddenly. In a big hurry. As if they'd had advance warning we were coming.'

'You mean they'd been tipped off? Who would have done that?'

'That's the problem. I'm confident it wasn't the letting agent, and I very much doubt it was the neighbours.'

'Then who?'

'Thames House,' he said quietly.

Wetherby's gaze did not shift. 'So someone inside the Service?'

'I realise it may sound bizarre,' said Dave, trying to make it clear he wasn't happy to broach the idea, 'but the fact is, our suspects seem to have known we were coming—twice. It's too much of a coincidence. After all, there was no explanation for their no-show at the bookshop.'

'That could have been for a number of reasons,' Wetherby declared. 'I don't really see how that and their departure from Wokingham are related. It may be normal practice for these suspects to stay on the move.'

What had seemed an airtight argument to Dave, now seemed flimsy. 'Charles, I'm not trying to make a legal case,' he said, floundering. 'I just wanted to say my piece.'

'I don't want to get involved in a wild-goose chase,' Wetherby said forcefully. 'It would only distract us from the real task, which is to catch these suspects before they do anything.'

Dave nodded unhappily. Wetherby sat back in his chair, easing off slightly. 'Does the name Peter Wright mean anything to you?' he asked.

Dave gave a hollow laugh. 'Yes, of course.'

Wetherby picked up a pencil and thumped its end on the desk. 'Peter Wright and his cronies investigated the Director General, Roger Hollis, for years. On no hard evidence at all. It did a huge amount of damage.'

Dave was mortified that Wetherby seemed to be putting him in the same category as Peter Wright. 'I don't think I'm being paranoid, Charles,' he said, aggrieved.

'Nor do I, actually,' replied Wetherby. 'But without any hard facts, I can't afford to worry about your hunch. I'm glad you shared your concerns with me, but it's evidence we need.' He smiled benevolently, which only made Dave feel worse as their meeting ended.

Yet sitting over a coffee in the cafeteria downstairs, Dave was troubled by the vehemence of Wetherby's reaction. It was as if Wetherby had had the same idea himself, then rejected it. He isn't going to follow it up at all, Dave thought sourly, cheering up a bit when he realised that Wetherby had not actually forbidden him from doing so.

9

Liam O'Phelan was notoriously impatient with students who dithered or didn't know what they thought, and now it made him impatient with himself. In the wake of 'Miss Falconer's' visit he didn't know what to do.

Part of him was tempted to let sleeping dragons lie, as he sensed that stirring them might be dangerous. He even wondered, fleetingly, if he could be prosecuted for recruiting the man in London. Then he reminded himself that they had never called on the fellow to do anything.

Yet part of him—the greater part, he recognised as days turned into a week, a week turned into two—wanted to stir things up, if only for his own curiosity. What would have happened to his recruit after all these years? Would he still share O'Phelan's disgust with the state of affairs in Northern Ireland, this wretched phony peace that was no more than a sell-out?

Curiosity won out, and with an energy he hadn't felt in years he went to work in a half-exhilarated, half-anxious state. It took a dozen phone calls, but finally he had the number he wanted. It was a mobile phone number.

'Hello, there,' he said, when his call was answered. 'Do you know who this is?'

He waited, and what he heard seemed to please him. 'No flies on you, even after all these years. Now, listen, a woman came to see me, asking questions . . . I thought that might get your attention. What's that . . .? I'd say she was in her mid-thirties. Light brown hair, shoulder length, green eyes, average height. Attractive in a brisk kind of way, well spoken. She said her name was Falconer, and that she was from the Ministry of Defence. I did my best to look as though I believed her. We know better, now, don't we?'

'STILL SCEPTICAL?' asked Charles Wetherby, looking up from the menu.

'About the mole? No,' said Liz, giving a small smile to acknowledge that her views had changed. 'I think we may have a problem after all.'

'Let's order first,' said Wetherby, signalling to a waitress. 'Then we won't be interrupted while you tell me about it.'

Keyed up as she was, it was frustrating to have to wait to tell him her news. She had asked to see him that morning, immediately after the phone call from Ireland. He had suggested lunch well away from Thames House at Café Bagatelle, a chic restaurant in the sculpture garden of the Wallace Collection, in Manchester Square.

The waitress came up at last and they ordered from the set menu. 'I'm going to have a glass of wine,' said Wetherby, and Liz followed suit.

When the waitress finally left them, Wetherby unfolded his napkin and turned to Liz. 'So what have you found out?' He seemed relaxed.

'I had a call this morning from James Maguire.'

Wetherby looked surprised. 'Will he help us after all?'

'He has already. He went to see Sean Keaney's daughter in Dublin. It turns out that one of her great pals at university was an acolyte of her father's. An IRA sympathiser named Kirsty Brien.' Liz paused, and lowered her voice, though there was no one at the two tables nearest them. 'Kirsty had a male friend who was an academic. First at Oxford, now at Queen's Belfast. What's more, she told Maddie Keaney that she was only seeing the man for old man Keaney's sake.'

Wetherby's eyebrows rose in surprise. 'So you've closed the circle,' he said. 'Well done. I was sure you were right to have misgivings about O'Phelan—you don't often get it wrong. What's your next step?'

'I'll interview him again. I'll go early next week,' Liz said. 'I don't want to alarm him by making it sound too urgent. We still can't prove anything.'

'No, that sounds right to me.'

Their starters arrived, and Liz cut into her goat's cheese galette. 'Charles, have you thought about what you're going to do if we do find a mole? I mean, especially if he or she was never activated?'

'I'll do whatever it takes to get him or her out of the Service.' Wetherby laid down his fork. 'Anything else I'll happily leave to the attorney general. That assumes, of course, that they weren't activated—Keaney may not have told the truth about that.'

'But supposing the IRA didn't activate the mole,' Liz pressed. 'I wonder how they would have felt about that. Badly let down, I would think.'

Charles paused as the waitress cleared the table for their main courses. 'So you've had that thought too. I must admit that it's been haunting me.' Wetherby's tone expressed obvious concern. 'At first I was thinking it's unlikely an IRA plant is going to do us active harm at present, so this may not be top priority. But now I'm not so sure.'

He hesitated and Liz thought he was about to say something else. But the waitress came to put down their plates and the moment passed.

'I'll be leaving work early on Friday,' Liz said. 'I have to go and see my mother.'

'Is she all right?' asked Wetherby. His enquiry sounded genuine.

'I'm not sure that she is,' admitted Liz. 'They've found a growth, and she has to go into hospital for a biopsy. I want to go down and take her in.'

'Of course,' said Wetherby. He sighed, fingering the knot in his tie.

'I'm sure it will be fine,' said Liz, putting on a brave front she didn't really feel.

Wetherby must have sensed this, for he reached across the table, and gave Liz's arm an affectionate squeeze. 'I know how badly the whole Marzipan business hit you. It was terrible for us all, but much worse for you. I thought you behaved superbly—but I knew you would. I do hope your mother's news is good.'

And then, looking stern, after this unusual display of emotion, he picked up his knife and fork and returned to his meal.

IN THESE POST-9/11 days identification was needed even on a UK flight. Inside his combination-locked cupboard in Thames House, there was an operational passport, in an alias identity, but he did not want to risk that name appearing on a flight manifest. He had another passport. It too was in an alias, but not one countenanced by any British government authority. Procuring it had been complicated—he'd used a Czech forger, now retired, who'd done work for Mossad—and very expensive. It was his insurance policy and it was proving its worth now.

Like the professional he was, he assumed his false identity as soon as he left his house. He was Sherwood, a businessman with interests in Northern Ireland. He had scheduled the day tightly, catching the seven o'clock flight from Heathrow and, with any luck, he would be back in London by two o'clock. His absence was covered by a few days off work. He had told his secretary that he had some medical appointments and would work from home. That sort of excuse deterred all but the most tactless questioner.

Sherwood thought about the don, as he had done virtually nonstop since receiving his phone call. He was probably a professor by now. There was no doubting his intellect. His judgment was a different matter. That was why he had to go on this quick visit.

What an impressive man the don had seemed—articulate, passionate, charismatic—when they'd first met, especially to a fresh-faced undergraduate. Did the don have a 'personal life', that euphemism for sex? Possibly. There was that girl he spoke about so often, the firebrand back in Dublin.

There were other ambiguities. The don spent his days in a cloistered world of history and ideas, but was entranced by the world of action. Yet, as Sherwood knew from experience, the don lived vicariously. Like one of those armchair Irish-Americans, happy to send money to his IRA cousins from the safety of a Boston bar room, though he'd be insulted by the comparison.

How strange to think of America now, for it was America that had brought him into touch with the don in the first place. He had travelled to the States during his gap year before university to try to find out as much as he could about the father he had last seen ten years before, six months before his sudden death.

He had learned more than he'd bargained for, once he unearthed his father's closest friend. Harry Quinn, retired features writer on the New York *Daily News*, was happy to meet up with his former pal's son at his old watering hole, Costello's Bar on 44th Street. They had sat in a booth, surrounded by hard-drinking hacks, while Quinn explained what had really happened. It was not the heart attack described by his mother. Instead, his father had jumped off the 59th Street Bridge. A suicide, prompted by disgrace.

Visiting the New York Public Library's newspaper holdings on East 40th Street, the son had discovered the whole seamy story, recounted in the newspapers of the time.

It had begun altogether differently. In a series of three articles for the New York *Daily News*, his father had recounted the confessions of one Samuel Lightfoot, a former member of the SAS who had served four tours of duty in Northern Ireland.

As retold by his father, Lightfoot described a history of brutality and violence by the SAS in Northern Ireland which surprised even its most vigorous detractors. Put simply, Lightfoot and his fellow SAS members had operated a policy of shoot to kill that was premeditated and sometimes indiscriminate. A wealth of documentary detail was produced, specifying times, locations and people involved.

The effect of the exposé had been explosive. In the House of Representatives, the Speaker Tip O'Neill, often attacked by his fellow Irish-Americans for his criticism of the IRA, now lent his name to a resolution demanding an end to all British undercover activity in Northern Ireland. Even the august *New York Times*, usually sniffy about its plebeian counterpart the *Daily News*, acknowledged the impact of the articles, and one of its columnists suggested their author would be a shoe-in for a Pulitzer prize.

Briefly, his father enjoyed a success most journalists dare not even dream about. This was indisputably one of the major stories of the decade.

And then the roof had caved in. Four days after his first article appeared, the *Sunday Times* of London had run its own bombshell on the front page. The Lightfoot articles, it declared unequivocally, were built upon a mountain of sand; their source, Samuel Lightfoot, was a con man of the first order, whose military career had consisted of a brief part-time membership of the Territorial Army. His sole contact with the SAS had been a solitary weekend outing to their training facilities in Herefordshire. To add insult to ignominy, Lightfoot had been convicted of fraud in the sixties and had served three years in prison.

The uproar had dwarfed even the initial reaction to the articles themselves, making the national evening television news. The *Daily News* ran an unprecedented front-page retraction, published an editorial remarkable for its supine contrition, and summarily fired his father. All of which the *New York Times* gleefully reported, with an exhaustiveness missing from its earlier account of the original articles.

Two months later, his father's death merited a one-inch story in the Metropolitan section of that newspaper. The *Daily News* did not report it.

The young man had returned to England, where he said nothing about what he had found to his mother or his odious stepfather. They merely thought him uncommunicative, reluctant to describe his travels in America.

Inside he was in turmoil, feeling a mixture of bewilderment and shame. How had his father been fooled by such an obvious charlatan, whose real name, it had emerged, wasn't even Lightfoot? Was the duped author of these discredited articles really the man of his memory? A gallant, confident, carefree figure, eliciting admiration and devotion from his son?

The young man felt only misery now. A state that lasted throughout his first year at Oxford. He did his coursework diligently, but kept himself to himself, brooding about what he now saw as an irredeemably tainted kind of inheritance.

It was O'Phelan who saved him, though any gratitude on his own part had long evaporated in the face of the tutor's own ultimate betrayal.

In his second year he'd met a girl at a dance in St Hilda's. She had been very left wing, and had asked him to a political talk, one of a series given at the Old Firehouse, entitled: 'From Boston to Belfast: Britain's Dirty War in Northern Ireland and Abroad'. The thesis was familiar to anyone who had ever listened to an IRA spokesman on TV: far from acting as peacekeepers, the British wanted to retain the status quo of imperialist occupation and would do anything (anything, the lecturer had stressed) to keep it that way.

But the effect of his talk on his undergraduate listener soon became absolutely hypnotic, for after these prefatory nationalist pieties, Liam O'Phelan (that was the speaker's name) had begun to talk with passion about an undeclared policy of shoot to kill which he said was being conducted by the SAS in Northern Ireland. O'Phelan even mentioned the murder of an innocent Armagh farmer that had appeared in one of his father's articles, too.

Afterwards he had gone up to the young don, and asked whether it wasn't true that many of his accusations had long ago been discredited.

'What do you mean?' O'Phelan had asked sharply. 'Discredited how?'

Well, he had explained, hadn't there been that scandal in New York, where a reporter, making accusations not dissimilar to those made by O'Phelan tonight, had either colluded with or been duped by a con man?

O'Phelan looked at him witheringly. 'Honestly, you Brits,' he said. 'You'll believe anything your tame press wants you to. The whole thing was a set-up. The source of the story, the man calling himself Lightfoot, was a plant of British Intelligence. The poor journalist never stood a chance, even though most of what he wrote was true. Bloody clever of the Secret Service,' he said, but without admiration, adding with a shrug, 'Not that you'll believe me.'

Perhaps he was surprised to see the student nodding, the hint of a smile on his face. 'Oh, I believe you. That poor journalist was my father.'

O'Phelan had taken him under his wing, and he had resided there quite willingly, even affecting an interest in Irish history and Irish nationalism to please the tutor. If O'Phelan ever suspected the sincerity of his attachment to his own cause, he never said so, for by then they had hatched their plot. Anyway, who in the IRA would care about his deepest motives, if they managed to insert him into the very heart of their enemy?

And they shared that enemy. The young man fully accepted O'Phelan's assertion that his father had been the victim of a conspiracy. Who were the conspirators? Probably the British Consulate in New York, its 'cultural attaché'—the usual slot for the MI6 resident—briefing hard to a sympathetic reporter, and presto: one life destroyed. His father may technically have killed himself, but by any humane standard he had been killed.

Thanks to O'Phelan he saw his father's killers in the raw—the members of the English Establishment that people claimed no longer existed. What nonsense, thought Sherwood, as the plane climbed to its cruising level. The Establishment not only survived, it prospered. He was part of it himself.

He remembered how O'Phelan had seen his manifest Englishness as an advantage from the start. 'No one will ever suspect,' the don had told him. 'They'll think you're English through and through. Trust me, they never turn on their own. Look at Philby; they believed him when he said he wasn't a mole. Or Blunt. Even when they knew he was a spy, they let him go on working for the Queen.'

His plane landed in Belfast in light drizzle with a hard bump that threw spray up under the wing. Disembarking, he moved through the terminal quickly, pulling up the collar of his coat while he joined the taxi queue, on his way to a day meeting in Northern Ireland.

'How punctual,' said O'Phelan, with a thin-lipped smile. As he turned back into the room, his visitor entered and closed the door behind him.

'Have a seat and I'll make some tea. Or would you prefer coffee? There's whisky, if you'd like a drink. No? It is a bit early.'

O'Phelan was excited, finding it hard to stand still, gripping the back of his chair with both hands, then taking a step back to inspect his visitor. 'You haven't aged much, I have to say.' He ran a hand through his thinning hair, and smiled. 'Would that time had been so kind to me.

'I want to hear what you've been up to all these years. Tell me all. Oh, but first the coffee, or will you have tea?'

And in his excitement he darted back to the small alcove in the far corner of the room, where he turned on the kettle and busied himself extracting china cups and saucers from the cupboard.

'How do you like it, black or white?' he called back over his shoulder. There was no reply, which puzzled O'Phelan only momentarily. For suddenly he was choking, and something was blocking his windpipe. By the time the kettle boiled O'Phelan was dead.

10

When Liz arrived for work she went straight to her desk to check her mail. She found a message from Jimmy Fergus in Belfast, asking her to ring him urgently. He sounded uncharacteristically subdued when he answered her call. 'I've got some bad news,' he said.

'What's the matter?'

'This man O'Phelan . . .'

'Yes?' There must be nothing on him in the database, she thought. A pity.

'He's been murdered in his room at Queen's.'

'You're joking,' said Liz. 'What happened?'

'He was found last night, but the pathologist says he was killed in the morning. Somebody strangled him.'

'Any idea who or why?'

'Not yet. We're looking into his personal life. He was unmarried, but so far nothing's come up on the sexual front.'

'Why did it take so long to find him? Where were his students?'

'He'd cancelled his afternoon class. He told one of his students an old friend was coming to see him. We're trying to locate this old friend.'

'Keep me posted, please. We have an interest in this one.'

Liz put the phone down, her mind racing. Another death on her watch. Get a hold of yourself, she said half aloud, then saw Dave Armstrong at his nearby desk staring at her. 'You OK?' he asked.

She nodded, but she knew she wasn't. She stood up and walked down the corridor to the conference room she and Peggy were using. Peggy was out of the room, and Liz closed the door and sat down to think things through.

Was she somehow responsible for this one? She wondered if inadvertently she had made a slip and put O'Phelan at risk. She had better tell Wetherby right away, she thought, just as the door opened and, as if on cue, Wetherby himself came in. 'I thought you might be here,' he said with a thin smile, but then he saw her face. 'What's wrong, Liz?' He pulled back a chair and sat down at the conference table next to her.

'I've just spoken with Belfast Special Branch. Liam O'Phelan, that lecturer, has been murdered.'

Wetherby looked stunned. 'Did anyone know you'd been to see him?'

'Only Peggy and Jimmy Fergus—I had dinner with him the same night. I wanted to know if O'Phelan was in the Special Branch database over there.' She paused and saw that Wetherby was looking reflective. She said, a little bitterly, 'I feel as if I'm back to square one.'

'Not at all,' said Wetherby. 'You know there was a link between O'Phelan and Keaney. And you were sure there was one between O'Phelan and someone on your list. Now you're just going to have to find that link some other way. There was never any guarantee O'Phelan was going to help you.'

'That's true,' Liz acknowledged, though she felt confident she would have got more out of him second time round, especially now she knew about his ties to Sean Keaney.

She realised Charles was looking at her appraisingly. He said, 'You had a bit of a knock last year. Then Marzipan, and now this.' He stood up, tugging at his tie thoughtfully. 'You're a strong person, Liz, and I'm not worried about you. Provided you don't start worrying about yourself.'

'OK,' she said quietly, taking his point. There was sometimes self-indulgence in feeling guilty. It was certainly possible that if she had never gone to see O'Phelan he would not have been murdered, but with that kind of reasoning, she might as well give up her job. Her real regret was that she hadn't gone back to see him sooner.

'I need to talk to Michael Binding urgently,' she said. 'O'Phelan was his referee—that's why I went to see him in the first place.'

'Michael's got a few days' holiday, Liz. If I call him back it might set off all sorts of alarm bells prematurely.'

Liz was nodding her head. 'No, it can wait. For all my reservations about O'Phelan, I don't think he was holding anything back about Michael Binding. It was something else he wasn't coming clean about.'

'Perhaps you should focus on O'Phelan's time at Oxford.'

She nodded. 'I'll ask Peggy to have another look.'

THE BOOKSHOP OWNER, when called in for questioning, turned out to be Jamaican, an ex-Rasta with a string of narcotics convictions. Now a Muslim, he brought to his new creed the fervour of the converted. And a new name—the Kingston-born Otis Quarrie now went under the exotic soubriquet Jamil Abdul-Hakim. Gone were the dreadlocks and the Rasta hat; now he wore a white caftan and sandals. However, Abdul-Hakim had seemed sincerely sorry about Sohail's death; equally, he seemed authentically to believe it had been a racist murder.

'If we could just get back to this imam, Abu Sayed,' Dave said. 'My understanding is that he was supposed to meet certain followers here but the meeting never came off.' He handed over the photographs of Rashid Khan and the other two men. 'Were these the men the imam was supposed to meet?'

The Jamaican glanced casually at them, then shrugged.

'But you recognise them, don't you?'

'They were here, man, sure. So?'

'What happened? Why didn't they show?'

'You'd have to ask them di question,' Abdul-Hakim said with a smirk.

IN THE LIVING ROOM of her house in Wokingham, Thelma Dawnton was distinctly miffed. Trevor had insisted on being present when Simon came back for another chat. Thelma would never have dreamed of being anything but a loyal wife (well, she might have dreamed, but reality was different), but glancing over at Trevor she resented his unnecessary chaperoning.

Still, she had to admit that Trevor knew about some things she didn't. Like cars—which Simon seemed very keen on.

At first, they had talked about the men next door, and Thelma knew she had been helpful there—more than Trevor, for sure, since, as he would be the first to admit, he couldn't tell a Pakistani from a Zulu. But when Simon changed the subject to cars he focused his attention solely on her husband. 'You said it was a Golf these men drove. Black—or was it dark blue?'

'Black.' Trevor was adamant.

'Can you remember anything else about it? Anything unusual?'

And Trevor had sat there and thought. 'It was a T-reg.'

She wanted to say what did that matter, but then she looked at Simon's excited face and decided not to say anything at all. Men, she thought with disgust. Men and cars.

SARAH MANPINI SAT on her own in the control room outside Reading, finding the viewing room a relief after yet another session with the late-shift patrolmen, who even after two years still seemed to find her surname hilarious. She was on her third hour of CCTV analysis and she felt like a couch potato, so little had happened: twenty-seven VW Golfs had triggered the M4 traffic cameras in the Reading area for one reason or another in the forty-eight hour period she was reviewing, but only three had been black or dark enough to pass as black.

Two of those had been heading east and she duly recorded their number plates. The third had been going west like the clappers—the speed had triggered the camera—but its numbers had not come out on the screen. She replayed the segment of the tape and peered at it closely. Luminescent paint had been applied to the plastic strip of numerals. Clever, she thought—that must be the car. She called in further tapes, now that she knew the time the Golf had triggered the camera west of Reading. And bingo: at the Newbury exit thirty minutes later the Golf had left the M4. From the secondary camera she knew only that it had then headed north.

LIZ HADN'T BEEN in Tom Dartmouth's office since the day of Marzipan's death, and then she had not taken in how clinical the room seemed. Today she was attending a meeting Tom was chairing of the Operation Foxhunt team, and there was an air of anxiety and gloom. They were not making much progress in finding the bookshop group or their target. In fact, Operation Foxhunt did not seem to be getting anywhere.

Tom was chairing the meeting, the first Liz had attended for two weeks. He did it competently, but lacked Wetherby's ability to bind people into a team. Reggie Purvis, from A4, had given his report: there had been no significant visitors to the bookshop or to Rashid Khan's home in Wolverhampton. Surveillance of his sister had produced nothing of interest.

Michael Binding for A2 was more long-winded but equally downbeat: there had been no more phone calls to the bookshop or to Rashid's home from Amsterdam, and no more calls of interest to his sister.

Now Judith Spratt was finishing up her side of things. 'I've just heard from Reading Control Room that they've got a possible dark-coloured Golf exiting the M4 at Newbury on the night the men left the Wokingham house. It was heading north. They're working on it now.'

Tom turned to Dave. 'Anything else?' he asked, sounding keen to wind things up.

Dave gave a short account of his disappointing interview with Jamil Abdul-Hakim. As he paused for a moment, Liz noticed Michael Binding collecting his papers for a quick exit. Judith was busy looking in her bag.

'Then I had a call this morning,' Dave said. Something in his voice made everyone stop and pay attention. 'When I interviewed the neighbours yesterday, all the husband told me about was the car. But his wife rang me this morning to say she had remembered something else.'

He paused again, and Liz wondered what he was up to. Dave was milking this audience like an actor keen to take another bow. That wasn't like him at all. Who was he trying to impress?

'Mrs Dawnton says she saw someone visiting the terrorists a few weeks ago. A white male. He came at night, but she got a good view of him because he triggered their security light. She thinks she could identify him if she saw him again. I'm going down this afternoon to talk to her.'

Nobody said a word. In the silence Liz noticed the hum from a strip light. 'Good,' said Tom at last. 'Keep us posted.'

WHY DIDN'T I BRING my sunglasses? thought Liz, then realised that two days of nonstop rain had made the prospect of decent weather seem remote. Yet, in its hesitant English way, summer was approaching, and as she left London on the M3, the dipping sun shone straight into her eyes.

She was feeling gloomy. Her mother's brave front on the phone had been automatic cause for alarm, since with her mother's generation, Liz knew that the more blithe the denial the more serious the problem must be.

Half an hour later, Liz was parking outside the octagonal gatehouse in Bowerbridge where she had grown up and where her mother still lived. The house was set back from the road, inside the russet brick wall that ran round the perimeter of what had once been a large estate.

Her father had been the estate manager for over thirty years and after his death, Liz's mother had stayed on. Last year she had bought the freehold—unnecessarily in a sense, since she was allowed to live there rent-free for the rest of her days. But behind this acquisition was her unspoken hope that some day Liz would move there, too. Join her in the garden centre, meet a man, get married, have children, settle down.

The rest of the estate had been sold, and the 'big house'—a Georgian pile of cream stone—had been converted into flats and ground-floor offices for the garden centre, which now occupied the old kitchen garden. At first, Liz's mother had taken a part-time job there, but now she managed the business. Emerging from the crushing impact of her husband's death, she had made a new kind of life—one she was obviously enjoying. Which made the prospect of serious illness seem to Liz an especially cruel blow.

Her mother was in the kitchen, waiting for the kettle to boil. 'Hello, darling,' she said. 'I wasn't expecting you this soon.'

'Traffic wasn't bad at all,' said Liz breezily. She didn't want to tell her mother that with Wetherby's blessing she had knocked off early to make sure she got down at a reasonable hour.

'I was just thinking about our supper,' her mother said, pointing vaguely to the Aga.

'Let me do it,' said Liz. Unusually, her mother let her take over, and sat down at the kitchen table while Liz made scrambled eggs and toast. As they ate, Liz avoided all talk of the next day's hospital procedure, sensing her mother preferred it that way. Keep it light, Liz told herself. For the first time, her mother seemed frail and vulnerable.

LIZ TOOK HER MOTHER to the hospital after lunch the next day. The doctors planned to keep her in overnight.

The procedure took place at three o'clock and by four her mother was back in the ward, though drowsy from the anaesthetic. Liz stayed for half an hour, then returned to the gatehouse to feed Purdey, her mother's white long-haired cat. She was opening a tin in her mother's kitchen, when she heard a car pull onto the gravel. Looking up, she saw a tall, wide-shouldered man slowly getting out of a low-slung sporty model.

To her surprise she saw that it was Tom Dartmouth.

She had completely forgotten that she'd told him she'd be at her mother's that weekend, and equally that he was, coincidentally, staying with friends nearby. Why hadn't he rung first? she thought crossly, only too aware that in trainers and a grey T-shirt she hardly looked her best. Then she realised he probably had phoned, while she was with her mother at the hospital.

She went out to greet him. 'Tom,' she said, 'I've just got back.'

'Good timing then,' he said, as he crossed the drive.

She steered him into the house and through the hall to the sitting room. 'Can I get you something? Cup of tea?'

Tom made a show of consulting his watch. 'After six,' he declared. 'Something stronger wouldn't go amiss.'

Liz looked with alarm at the drinks tray—her mother was hopeless about keeping her supplies replenished. 'There's some whisky,' she said, pointing to a half-drunk bottle of Famous Grouse.

'Any gin?' asked Tom hopefully.

'I'll just see,' she said without optimism.

In the larder she found an ancient bottle of Gordon's with just enough left in it for a large G&T. She found ice and tonic water in the fridge, though no lemon, picked up two glasses and brought everything out on a tray to the sitting room. Tom was standing by the French windows. 'Pretty garden,' he announced. 'Does she get someone in to do it?'

'Perish the thought,' said Liz. 'My mother doesn't even let me help her.'

'How is she?' he asked. 'When does she get out?'

'Tomorrow. That's when we'll know.'

Tom seemed to sense, rightly, that she didn't want to talk about it, for he pointed outside, saying, 'It's a lovely spot. Has she been here long?'

'Thirty years,' said Liz, handing over the drink. She poured herself a glass of tonic. 'I grew up here. My father looked after the estate.'

Tom came and sat down in the large easy chair where Liz's mother spent her evenings, knitting, reading or watching the television. 'Cheers,' he said, lifting his glass. He drank, then sat back comfortably in the chair.

'Cheers,' replied Liz from the sofa. 'Where are you staying?'

'My friends are about ten miles west of here. Off the road to Blandford.'

'What's the name of their village?'

Tom shrugged his shoulders. 'They've got a farm, and I'm afraid I haven't taken much notice of my surroundings. I think they said the village was walkable, but I didn't catch its name.' He chuckled. 'I've just been so glad to be in a place where the telephone doesn't ring all the time.'

'You must have been frantic these last few weeks.'

'You could say that,' said Tom, taking another long pull on his drink. 'Still am. I've left Judith in charge this weekend. How about you? You're doing something for Wetherby, aren't you?' When she only nodded in reply, he said, 'Sorry, not meaning to pry.'

She shrugged. It occurred to her that if they were going to talk about work, she might as well use the opportunity. 'Tell me,' she said, 'when you were at Oxford did you ever come across an Irish lecturer named O'Phelan?'

Tom picked up his glass and looked at her with interest. 'You mean the guy who was murdered? I saw it in the papers.'

'That's the one. I was supposed to see him about something. But now . . .' She left the conclusion unspoken.

'As a matter of fact, I did,' said Tom. 'Well, I didn't know him; it's more I knew of him. He was a fairly notorious character.'

'Really? Why was that?'

Tom smiled a little awkwardly. 'O'Phelan was what the obituarists like to call a confirmed bachelor. Each to his own, of course, but he was sometimes a bit predatory with his students. A great pal of mine was taught by him, and one day, right in the middle of a supervision, O'Phelan pounced. My friend literally had to fight his way out of the man's rooms.' At the memory, Tom gave a knowing grin. 'Fortunately, he was the fly-half in the

College XV so he didn't have much trouble staying out of his clutches. But he did need to find a new supervisor.'

'What was your friend's name?'

Tom looked surprised by her question. It didn't matter, of course, but she liked having names. It helped her remember people's stories.

'Clapton,' he said slowly. 'Philip Clapton. Why do you ask?'

Liz gave an innocent shrug. 'I don't know. Just curious, I guess.' She smiled winningly. 'Anyway, you've opened up a whole new side to O'Phelan. I'd heard he was a staunch Republican.'

Tom looked blankly at Liz. 'Maybe he was. It wasn't something I ever came across. What's this stuff?' he suddenly demanded, brushing at his dark blue cord trousers, which were covered from the knees down in white hair.

'Sorry,' said Liz. 'Purdey must have rubbed against you. She likes men.'

'Wretched cat,' said Tom, still picking off the hairs. He looked up brightly. 'Listen, I've got an idea. Why don't you let me give you supper? There's a hotel in Salisbury that's supposed to have a very good restaurant.'

She knew it was thoughtful, but it was the last thing she wanted right now. 'It's really kind of you,' she said, 'but I'm going to have to pass. I wouldn't be good company. Anyway, I need to be near the phone. Just in case.'

Tom was unwilling to take no for an answer. 'Bring your mobile. You need to relax. Take your mind off things.'

She forced a smile but shook her head. 'Perhaps some other time.'

Tom seemed to get the message at last. 'I'll hold you to that,' he said. He looked at his watch. 'It's getting on,' he declared. 'I'd better be going.'

After he'd gone, Liz mulled over their conversation. I'd better call Jimmy Fergus, she thought, and point him in the right direction. Though if 'rough trade' was the reason for O'Phelan's death, then why had he been killed in his college room, rather than at his home?

She went into the kitchen and put some soup on the stove and a slice of bread in the toaster. She wished Tom had not been so insistent; it made her feel impolite. She would be happy to have dinner with him—but in London, she thought, not when I'm here worrying about my mother.

She had never gone out with a colleague; mixing business and pleasure seemed to invite trouble. Not that dating men outside the Service had proved any easier. Either they were married, thought Liz, or too inquisitive about her job—or both.

Was the prospect of a date with Tom the solution? At least they could talk freely about their work. Perhaps this explained the Service's view of intra-Service romances. They weren't exactly encouraged, but weren't forbidden, either. But she wasn't sure whether the prospect of Tom Dartmouth as a suitor was alluring or mildly alarming.

Suddenly Liz laughed at herself—she'd let her imagination carry her away, expanding a tentative dinner invitation into a full-blown romance. Yet Tom's intentions seemed pretty clear, now didn't they?

'I'VE SPOKEN TO YOUR mother already, so she knows the situation,' announced the consultant brusquely. 'The growth she has is malignant.'

I hope you were gentler with her, thought Liz, feeling furious, though she knew it was the news rather than his method of imparting it which was most upsetting her. 'What happens next?' she asked, knowing her mother would have been in too much shock to take it all in.

She forced herself to concentrate as the consultant began to speak dispassionately about the programme that lay ahead. An operation to remove the growth; chemotherapy if they discovered it had spread; radiation after that. All this, thought Liz despairingly, for a woman who resisted taking so much as an aspirin.

PEGGY WAS POSITIVELY fizzing when Liz met her for coffee in the conference room late on Monday morning. 'I think I've found out why Ravi is no longer living at home. I had a Google Alert tied to his name and I got a flash this morning. There's an article in this morning's *Financial Times*.'

She pushed a newspaper clipping across the table. Liz had been dreading talking to Judith about her domestic situation. She was, after all, a friend.

'Apparently Ravi Singh and an associate were being investigated by the Office of Fair Trading for insider share dealing,' Peggy continued. 'But that's not all. The Serious Fraud Office has been called in, because they think Ravi and this other chap may have been involved in an identity-fraud scam using other people's credit-card numbers.'

'This is terrible,' Liz declared, handing the clipping back. Silently she asked herself, What on earth am I going to say to Judith?

It wasn't simply that they were friends. Liz had been to Judith's house in Fulham for dinner several times over the years. They were happy occasions, low-key and relaxed. In Liz's eyes, Judith had always seemed to be the epitome of a woman who had it all—a successful career, a happy marriage, a much-loved daughter, Daisy. It was a tough balancing act, yet Judith seemed to manage it with elegance and grace.

Liz walked back to her office and dialled Judith's extension but there was no reply. Later on, though, Liz saw her eating lunch alone at a table in the far corner of the Thames House cafeteria. Her expression made it clear that she did not want company. She slid her tray along the table and sat down opposite her.

'I see you didn't fancy the bolognese either,' said Liz lightly, pointing to their respective salads. Judith managed a wan smile. She looks terrible, thought Liz. 'I've been looking for you,' she said.

Judith raised a mild, uninterested eye. She had her hair tied back, which usually complimented her sharp, strong features. Today, despite a lot of make-up, it only highlighted her drawn face.

'I haven't said anything, because there hasn't been a need to. But you know the vetting updates the Security Committee ordered?'

'Yes,' said Judith. Liz thought she sounded slightly wary.

'Well, I've had to do some of them. It's meant to be largely a paper exercise and I don't need to interview people . . .'

'Unless,' said Judith impassively.

'Unless,' said Liz, wishing her friend would make this easier for them both, 'there is some discrepancy. Something that needs explaining.'

'And you want to know about Ravi?' Judith said tonelessly.

Liz felt as if she was persecuting her friend, but she knew she had no choice. 'Well, it *is* in the papers. Is he still living with you?'

'No, he left before Christmas.' And she never said a word, thought Liz. 'I'm still living in the house,' said Judith a little defensively.

'I know,' said Liz. 'But we're supposed to inform B Branch if our circumstances change. You know that, Judith,' she said, as gently as she could.

For the first time Judith's voice showed animation. '"Circumstances change"?' she said sarcastically. 'You can say that again. How many other people are you vetting?'

'I'm doing Oxbridge people first. There were several up with you.' Judith didn't reply, so Liz went on. 'Were you friends with any of them?'

'Like who?' she said.

'Patrick Dobson was there.'

'Was he?'

One down, thought Liz. 'Doesn't matter. Michael Binding was there, too.'

'As he never ceases to tell me,' said Judith sourly. Liz knew she shared her own irritation with Binding's condescending treatment of his female colleagues. 'If you have to interview him, please do me a favour.'

'What's that?'

'Pretend you think his college was St Hilda's. It's the only all-women's college. He'll be mortified.'

Liz smiled at the thought of Binding's sense of outrage. Then she asked, 'What about Tom Dartmouth? He was there at the same time.'

Judith nodded. 'I didn't know him, though I knew who he was.'

'Why was that?'

Judith gave a small conspiratorial grin. 'Didn't you know the names of the best-looking boys at college?'

Liz laughed. 'By heart,' she said, but came back to her question. 'But you didn't know him?'

'No,' said Judith simply. 'Not that I could say I really know him now. Funnily enough, I saw his wife a few months ago.'

'Aren't they divorced?'

'Yes.' She sighed, seemingly at the comparison with her own shattered ménage. 'I saw her in Harrods Food Hall, of all places. I waved but she didn't wave back. She may not have recognised me. I only met her once or twice.'

Time to get back to the point, thought Liz. Slightly hesitantly she asked, 'Have you spoken to Ravi?'

Judith shook her head. 'Not for weeks. We communicate through lawyers now. He hasn't even come to see Daisy. It's been incredibly hurtful, but in the light of today's news, perhaps he's just been trying to spare us.'

'So you've only just found out about his problems?' Liz had assumed it was his 'problems' that had led Judith to throw him out.

'Yes,' said Judith. She looked at Liz, at first quizzically, then with outright disbelief. 'You don't think I had anything to do with them, do you?'

'No, I don't.' She knew Judith too well to doubt her sincerity.

Judith nodded with her chin down and Liz was afraid she was going to cry, but instead she put her fork down and demanded, 'What happens now? Do I get disciplined?'

'It's not up to me,' Liz said, very grateful that it wasn't. 'I can't see it as a very big deal. With any luck, they'll just put a note on your file.'

Judith smiled faintly. 'The thing is, Liz, I know how it looks. People will think either "Why didn't she stand by her husband when he got in trouble?", or "No wonder she threw him out—the man's a crook."'

'Possibly,' said Liz, not sure what Judith was trying to say.

'But don't you see?' and for the first time there was passion in Judith's voice. 'I didn't throw him out. He left me.' Liz tried not to show her surprise, as Judith controlled her emotions. 'Look, Liz, I'm married to someone who doesn't love me any more. And today I've discovered he's a crook. But do you know the most terrible thing about it all?'

Her voice faltered and this time Liz thought she really would break down. But again Judith seemed to catch hold of herself. 'It's that I'd have him back tomorrow, crook or not. Isn't that pathetic?'

11

Michael Binding was a tall man, dressed today in a check flannel shirt, dark grey trousers and clunky brown brogues. He sat uncomfortably on the front edge of his steel-framed chair, across the conference table from Liz, a hostile expression on his face. She was grateful for Peggy Kinsolving's presence beside her.

Liz had begun with what was by now her standard explanation of what she was doing and why she needed to see him. But Binding wasn't buying any of it. 'News to me,' he'd said. 'When did these new guidelines come down? And why weren't we told?'

Liz tried to seem nonchalant. 'You'd have to ask B Branch for the details.'

'Ah, I see,' said Binding, 'you're only following orders.'

She decided patience with his rudeness was only going to encourage it. 'That's right,' she said snappily, 'like we all do.' Binding's pale blue eyes widened as she continued, 'And one of those orders was that if anyone was obstructive I should report the fact right away.' She noticed that Peggy was sinking even further down into her chair. 'It's up to you,' Liz declared. 'We can take this higher, or you can answer my questions. Either way we're going to end up back here doing the same thing. So which is it going to be?'

Binding stared defiantly at Liz while he considered this. Sighing audibly for dramatic effect, he said, 'Very well. What do you want to ask me?'

'I want to talk to you about Liam O'Phelan.'

'The late Liam O'Phelan? Why on earth do you want to talk about him?'

'He wrote a reference for you when you initially applied to the Service.'

Binding seemed surprised by this. 'What did it say?'

'I have to say he was not very flattering. Thankfully for you, your other referees were. I went to see him last week, just before he was murdered.'

Binding frowned, his eyes narrowing. 'What did he say about me?'

'He said you didn't see eye to eye about your thesis.'

Binding laughed out loud. 'If only.' He shook his head dismissively. 'It wasn't that at all. But what is your point, Liz? I fell out with my supervisor fifteen years ago, so I decided to strangle him?' His tone was scathing. 'Am I a suspect?'

'I shouldn't have thought so, though obviously it's a police matter. So far their view seems to be that O'Phelan probably picked up somebody who turned nasty.'

'Picked up? As in rough trade?' Binding looked horrified. 'I think not.'

What? thought Liz. 'So he had lots of girlfriends?' she asked.

'I didn't say that,' Binding retorted. 'Listen to what I'm saying.'

Liz gritted her teeth. God, how I pity his wife, she thought. 'I am listening. But I'm not sure I get your drift.'

Binding sighed again, then said with exaggerated patience, 'O'Phelan wasn't homosexual.'

'How do you know that?' Liz said challengingly.

'Because for a time I knew him rather well.' And suddenly, as if tired of sparring with her, Binding sat back in his chair and began to talk.

THERE HAD BEEN a party that spring, one Saturday in St Antony's College in north Oxford. He'd been invited by his supervisor O'Phelan, who was a Fellow there, though Binding's own college was Oriel.

He'd hesitated before going all the way to St Antony's, which was at the other end of town, for what promised to be a free glass of plonk and some cheese titbits. But he decided it would be prudent to go—his supervisor had made a point of inviting him.

O'Phelan was young, not much older than Binding himself. He was an Irishman who'd only been in Oxford for a couple of years. He had a Junior Research Fellowship, but he'd already got his DPhil, and was considered brilliant. Binding wouldn't have disputed this. For the first two terms he thought Liam O'Phelan was the most stimulating teacher he'd ever had.

Not that he always agreed with him, especially not about Ireland, where even in the early 1990s O'Phelan continued to see the British presence in the North as a colonial occupation. But there was humour to their exchanges, and O'Phelan seemed positively to relish their jousting.

Binding was confident he'd earned O'Phelan's respect for his work, which was on his tutor's own particular passion: Charles Parnell. O'Phelan had been especially encouraging about the draft of a chapter of his thesis, and Binding thought then that he might have a chance of an academic career. Anyway, continued Binding, that afternoon he'd hurried up the Banbury Road, little realising that the next hour would change his life.

The party was quite a large affair—all the postgrads and all the Fellows had been invited—and because it was warm for late April, it was held in the college grounds, on the lawn down from the main building. He didn't know many people, but he spotted O'Phelan in the crowd and, taking a glass of wine, started working his way over to him to say hello.

Then he'd noticed a girl he'd never seen before. She was tall, with blonde hair and a strikingly pixie-pretty face. She wore a short pink skirt that was just within the bounds of decorum, and looked very sure of herself. Running into a postgrad he knew named Fergusson, Binding asked him about the girl, and learned that she was visiting O'Phelan from Dublin. 'Rather lively,' Fergusson added, and watching her Binding saw at once what he meant. She was talking to another student, a handsome sporty guy, and she was making the kind of eye and body contact that looked destined to head past mere flirtation and into the realm of serious intent.

It was then that he noticed O'Phelan's reaction. The lecturer was standing slightly further up the slope of lawn, stuck with the warden and his chatty wife. But every few seconds O'Phelan's gaze moved round to the girl, and her seductive performance with the postgraduate student. 'Liam doesn't look too happy,' Fergusson noted drily.

There was only one conclusion: O'Phelan was besotted with this girl.

Binding decided to try and do him a favour.

'I suppose I was sucking up,' he admitted to Liz. 'But I was young then, and keen to get on.'

So he had gone up to the girl and introduced himself, ignoring the obvious irritation of the sporty student at this interruption. The girl had seemed happy enough to turn her attentions onto Binding, and within seconds she was flirting with him. She had lively green eyes and a saucy smile, and if she had been anybody's guest but O'Phelan's, he would have reciprocated.

She made no bones about being Irish: she seemed to find the very Englishness of the party amusing, and she teased him about it. He began to tease her back, assuming she would take it in good part. She might mouth the platitudes of the need for a united Ireland, he told the girl, but surely the last thing she and her countrymen wanted was to regain the burden of the six counties of Ulster. Wasn't it ironic, he continued, warming to his theme, that so many IRA members, sworn enemies of the British state, actually lived off that state? None of them could bite off their nose to spite their face, he added, because their noses were stuck, feeding in a British trough.

The girl had launched into a furious tirade, her tone no longer light, her green eyes suddenly narrowed into mean slits. Her target was the English: their elitism, their racism, even the way their youth were educated, typified by the awful man she was currently talking to. This meant him.

Binding was completely taken aback by her reaction to what was meant to be a joke, and he tried to calm her down. But she wasn't having any of it. He'd started to feel slightly panicky, afraid they were making a scene, and he'd looked wildly around for help, but no one came to his rescue—O'Phelan was still taken up with the warden and the sporty student had fled the minute the girl had turned on Binding.

And then something in Binding had snapped. He'd tried placating, he'd tried apologising, so finally he too lost his temper.

Binding stared ruefully at the expanse of table between himself and Liz. 'I said something like, "Why don't you go back to your peat bog?"' Enraged, the girl suddenly lifted her glass and tossed it right at his face. Then she stormed out of the party, followed by a clearly agitated O'Phelan.

The next day Binding had written to the don to apologise, but he didn't receive an answer. Then some days later O'Phelan left a message at the Oriel lodge, cancelling their next supervision; ten days later, he cancelled again. With his deadline looming, Binding submitted his thesis chapter to O'Phelan for formal approval, which brought forth the tersest of notes:

> Dear Binding,
>
> I am writing to inform you that I will be leaving Oxford to take up a position at Queen's University Belfast in Michaelmas Term. I am afraid therefore that it will no longer be possible for me to supervise your thesis, though after reading your sample chapter I cannot in any case advise the faculty to give you leave to continue.
>
> Yours sincerely,
> L. K. O'Phelan

'I never saw or heard from him again,' said Binding with a shake of his head. 'Not that I wanted to. I was too busy at first trying to keep my place. O'Phelan had written to the faculty saying I'd failed the first year chapter requirement. At the last minute I found someone in my own college willing to take me on, but he knew far less about my subject than I did.

'Anyway,' he continued, looking relieved to be finishing his story, 'I was sorry to hear O'Phelan had been killed, but don't expect a lengthy mourning period from me. As for why he died, all I can say is he wasn't gay.'

Liz had only one question. 'What was the name of the student this girl was chatting up before you interrupted?'

Binding looked at her with half a smile. Something of his arrogance had come back. 'This has to be the strangest vetting interview in history. Honestly Liz, what are you after?' He raised a hand as if to ward off any reply. 'I know, I know. You'll ask the questions around here, thank you very much. The bloke's name was Clapton.'

'Was he a rugby player?'

'How on earth did you know that?' asked Binding, with unfeigned astonishment. But Liz wasn't listening any more to anything but her own furious thoughts. She was trying to reconcile three completely contradictory stories. If I can do that, she thought, I'll know who the mole is.

JUDITH SPRATT WAS off work ill, so it was Rose Love who came to find Dave. Something had changed in Rose, he thought. She looked older, for one thing, in smart trousers and a crimson blouse. She'd tied her hair back, too. He decided he wasn't going to let her forget their dinner date, postponed since the discovery of the safe house in Wokingham.

'Wantage police have contacted us with the chassis number of a T-reg VW Golf found burnt-out on the Downs,' she announced. 'I've been on to the German manufacturers and they've promised to get back to me today to tell me which dealer it got shipped to. The rest will be up to DVLA.'

'How long?' he said anxiously.

'Have you got a piece of string?' she asked with a laugh. Gone was the shy girl of a month before, he realised.

'What happened to our date?' he asked.

'Too busy,' she said, but there was a playfulness behind the primness.

'You are?'

Rose nodded sagely. 'And so are you.' But her smile was sly enough to give him hope.

SHE COULDN'T EXACTLY say why, but she thought someone was there. In a doorway, or in the shadows, or behind a car—but there.

Peggy felt it first just after she left Thames House, as she walked along the river towards the Tube station. Thinking she had dropped something from her bag she stopped abruptly, and would not have thought twice about the dark figure fifty yards or so behind her had it not stopped abruptly too. It was a man—she was somehow certain it was a man.

Don't get paranoid, Peggy told herself, but she wished she'd been on a countersurveillance course. She felt ill-prepared for sharp-end operational work, but then her job was research and analysis. She'd been told when she joined MI6 that after a few years she might well be posted abroad. That would be when she'd get the operational training. In a small station abroad they said everyone had to get involved. She looked forward to it.

Meanwhile, working with Liz Carlyle in MI5, Peggy had discovered an urgency that drew everyone in. She liked the recognition that everyone in their different ways had a part to play in what was going on, but she had no confidence in her ability to spot a tail.

So when the sense of being followed wouldn't go away, she decided to put it to the test. Turning right onto Vauxhall Bridge Road she stopped under the portico of one of the stucco Regency mansions, long ago divided into offices, and waited there. No one came round the corner.

Stop fantasising, she told herself, relieved she had been wrong. She entered Pimlico Underground Station, virtually deserted in the mid morning, and took the escalator down without a single person behind her or on the opposite side, coming up.

At Victoria, she switched to the Circle Line, heading for her first appointment. This shouldn't take long, thought Peggy; it was her second meeting, the meeting in Kilburn, from which she was anticipating some excitement.

She'd dug further into Patrick Dobson's extended Irish family, and discovered a branch that had moved to London thirty years before. She wanted to find out if these cousins knew Dobson—he had vociferously denied any contact with the Irish side of his family. Peggy was posing as a sociology student at UCL, writing a dissertation on the Irish in London, a topic she found interesting enough that it shouldn't be difficult to play the part.

She checked her notes for her first meeting. It should be routine, she thought. She was going at Liz's prompting: Tom Dartmouth's wife had recently been seen in London, which was unusual, since the woman was supposed to live in Haifa. 'She was probably just visiting,' Liz said, 'but please check it out.' Peggy didn't have a lot to go on from the file:

> Margarita Levy, b. 1967 Tel Aviv, d. of Major-General Ariel Levy and Jessica Finegold. Educated at the Tel Aviv Conservatory and the Juilliard School (NY). Member of the Tel Aviv Symphony Orchestra 1991–5. M. Thomas Dartmouth 1995, div. 2001. No children.

And Margarita had not been easy to locate. At the Haifa address, now inhabited by rehoused settlers from Gaza, no one knew who had lived there before them. The Tel Aviv Symphony Orchestra could unearth no forwarding address. A painstaking trawl through online music sites proved more productive. A casual reference in a music student's blog, a check in the telephone directory, and Peggy found Margarita Levy at last, giving private violin lessons. Though not in Haifa, or anywhere in Israel for that matter.

THE FLAT WAS in a Victorian mansion block off Kensington High Street. Opening the door, Margarita Levy smiled shyly at Peggy and shook hands. She was a tall, striking woman, with lush black hair neatly swept back. 'Come in,' she said and pointed to the sitting room. 'Make yourself comfortable. I will be right with you.' And she disappeared into another room from which came the sound of voices.

A few minutes later she heard the front door close and Margarita came back into the sitting room. She was dressed simply but elegantly in a sleeveless black dress and Peggy noticed that she did not wear a wedding ring. 'I'm going to make some tea,' she announced. 'Would you like some?'

'I'd love some.'

When Margarita moved into the kitchen next door, Peggy followed her as far as the doorway.

'How long have you been back in England?' asked Peggy.

'Back?' asked Margarita. She was filling a milk jug. 'What do you mean?'

'We had you down as living in Israel. That's why I'm here.'

'I haven't lived in Israel for over ten years. Not since I married Tom.' Margarita put tea things on a tray and carried it into the sitting room. She hesitated before pouring the tea. 'Tell me something, is Tom all right?'

'He's fine, I believe.'

She looked only slightly reassured. 'I was worried when you asked to see me about him. Pakistan is so dangerous these days.'

Peggy realised the woman didn't know Tom was back in London. 'When did you last speak to Tom?'

Margarita grimaced and shook her head. 'Not since he went to Pakistan.' But then she added, 'I did see him, at a concert two or three years ago. I assumed he was back on leave. He had someone with him,' she smiled ruefully. 'So I just waved at him during the interval.'

Peggy had come here expecting anger, bitterness, or even complete indifference. Not this sense of sad bewilderment. 'It must have been quite a change for you. To get married and leave your family and friends like that.'

'Of course,' Margarita said simply.

'Though at least there was Tom's family over here.'

Margarita shook her head. 'Not really. His mother died before I knew Tom. His stepfather was friendly, but I only met him once. Tom didn't want anything to do with him.'

'Was Tom close to his natural father?'

Margarita shook her head again. 'He died when Tom was only a boy. His stepfather raised him, and Tom took his name. He resented that, I know—it was at his mother's insistence. Tom idolised his own father, though he never knew him as an adult.' She paused. 'You do know he killed himself?'

'Well, yes,' lied Peggy, trying to stifle her astonishment. 'How old was Tom when it happened?'

'He couldn't have been more than seven or eight. Poor thing,' she added. 'He didn't find out about it until he was almost grown up.'

'Why did Tom's father kill himself? Was he depressed?' ventured Peggy.

'He had made a mess of things, so possibly. At the time, he was a journalist in New York. I believe he got into trouble writing about Ireland. Tom didn't talk about it. He only mentioned it once, when we first started seeing each other.'

At the memory, her melancholy seemed to return. She looked at Peggy. 'It is odd, isn't it,' she said, 'how sometimes people talk less, not more as the years pass.'

AS PEGGY LEFT the flat, she rang the Dobson relations in Kilburn and postponed her visit. She needed to see Liz Carlyle right away. It was one thing to find Tom had misled the Service about his wife's whereabouts—you could argue Judith Spratt had done the same thing—it was quite another to find a possible link between Tom and Liam O'Phelan.

It's the American connection, thought Peggy, as she walked back up Kensington High Street to the Underground. She recalled the talk the don had given in Oxford. 'From Boston to Belfast: Britain's Dirty War in Northern Ireland and Abroad'. At the Underground she was surprised to find the eastbound platform unusually crowded for the late-morning hour.

At last, the board signalled one minute before the next Circle Line train was due, and Peggy worked her way towards the front of the platform, ending up close to the yellow line. Too close, she decided, and tried to take a step back, but the crowd was simply too dense for her to move.

Thank God the train's coming, she thought, as she saw the train's yellow headlight in the tunnel.

Suddenly as the train broke out of the tunnel Peggy felt a pressure in the small of her back, nudging at first, then more insistent. Her feet started to inch well over the yellow line, moving irresistibly towards the platform's edge. Panic seized her, and suddenly she screamed, involuntarily, the noise like the drawn-out pitch of a locomotive's whistle. Then all went dark.

THE MAN SEEMED to be wearing a uniform, and on her face she felt something wet and cold. The blur suddenly resolved itself and she saw with snapshot clarity a man in front of her, extending an arm as he dabbed at her cheeks with a damp tissue. She was sitting on a plastic chair in what looked to be a large broom cupboard under the stairs of the Underground station.

'What happened?' she asked.

'You fainted, Miss,' the station attendant said. 'There was a bit of a crush on the platform.' He straightened up and looked down solicitously at Peggy. 'Lucky for you the woman next to you saw you starting to drop. She managed to grab you in time—and a bloke helped her haul you back.'

'I am sorry,' said Peggy, trying to pull herself together. Then she recalled the pressure on her back. 'Did the woman leave her name?'

'No, once I arrived on the scene she took the next train.'

And Peggy suddenly remembered her own sense of urgency. She stood up, a little wobbly. 'I'm all right now,' she declared, then smiled at the attendant. 'Thank you for your help.'

She walked along the platform towards the stairs. She'd decided that, in the circumstances, she deserved a taxi.

12

Westminster Green, a small patch of grass opposite the Houses of Parliament, is a favourite spot for TV journalists to interview MPs. Today, in the June sunshine, a small crowd was gathered to watch the BBC's political correspondent interviewing a member of the Cabinet.

Liz was sitting on a bench in Victoria Tower Gardens, across the road, waiting for Charles Wetherby. When she had rung to ask to see him urgently, to her surprise he had insisted that they meet outside Thames House. She had made the ten-minute walk to the little park, and was now enjoying the warm afternoon, trying to catch some sun on her face.

When Wetherby joined her on the bench a quarter of an hour later, Liz plunged straight in with a description of Peggy's interview with Tom Dartmouth's ex-wife. Then she summarised her recent interviews, setting out their contradictions which she now thought she had resolved. Through a mix of intuition, logic and Peggy's finds, Liz had come to a conclusion.

'Let's go through it all again slowly,' said Wetherby. 'You believe O'Phelan was the recruiter for the mole, at the instigation of Sean Keaney. Just explain again why?'

Liz thought carefully for a moment. 'Because O'Phelan was at Oxford; he held strong nationalist views; and he had a connection to Sean Keaney through this woman Kirsty, who befriended O'Phelan at Keaney's instigation.'

Wetherby nodded. 'All right, let's agree that O'Phelan was the recruiter. How do we know it wasn't Michael Binding he recruited?'

'We don't for sure, but it seems improbable. There can't be any question that the two of them fell out, although it's true that their accounts of why it happened differ: O'Phelan said it was because Binding's work was second-rate; Binding says it was because he had a row at a party with Kirsty.'

'And who do you believe?'

'Binding,' Liz said without hesitation.

Wetherby gave an ironic smile. He knew Liz's opinion of her patronising colleague. 'Why's that?' he said, not challengingly, but to try and set out the sequence of argument.

'Binding had a First from Manchester, and he'd worked too hard to get to Oxford simply to down tools when he was there. In any case, Binding's story may make O'Phelan look vengeful and malicious, but it doesn't cast Binding himself in a very good light.'

'The "go back to your peat bog" remark?' When Liz nodded, Wetherby asked, 'If you ruled out Binding as our mole, how did it lead you to Tom?'

'It didn't, until he added his own ingredient, which was an account of O'Phelan that didn't square with what anybody else has told me. Tom claimed O'Phelan was a sexual predator with his male students, yet none of the evidence from Binding and Maguire, or the police investigation into his murder, backs that up.'

'But why would Tom invent this story about O'Phelan?'

For the first time Liz felt a slight chill, as their discussion moved from motivation to murder. 'To divert attention from the real reason O'Phelan was killed. Which was to shut him up.' Liz didn't need to wait for the next question. 'And, yes, that means in my view Tom murdered O'Phelan. Just as I think Tom is the mole. There's another thing too,' added Liz, almost as an afterthought. 'Tom told me his father was killed in a road accident, but Margarita told Peggy that he committed suicide in New York.'

Wetherby was staring across the street, apparently distracted by the television interview. The lack of attention was unlike him.

'The problem is that we can't prove any of this,' she continued. 'If Tom was recruited by O'Phelan for the IRA, he was never activated. He will never admit it. So unless we can tie him to O'Phelan's murder, I don't see what we could charge him with.'

Charles still didn't seem to be listening. She said, with a trace of impatience, 'We'll have to do something, Charles, won't we? I mean I know it may not seem urgent, but—'

Wetherby interrupted her. He said softly, 'It is urgent, Liz. That's what's bothering me.' He sighed and leaned forward. 'I didn't tell you before, because it wasn't relevant to your investigation, but after Dave Armstrong missed the terrorists in Wokingham, he came to see me. What is not widely known—because we've kept it secret—is that the terrorists vacated the house only after Dave had requested Special Branch go in. Dave decided there must have been a leak: the terrorists' departure was too hasty and too well timed. The leak could have come from anywhere—the local police, the estate agent who let the house . . . except Dave thinks the same thing happened at Marzipan's bookshop, when the three men didn't show up. Someone tipped them off there as well.'

Wetherby sighed, then continued. 'The only people who knew about both operations were in Thames House. If there was a leak, and I believe there were two of them, we have to think they came from within the Service.'

'You think there's another mole?' asked Liz. No wonder Charles looks preoccupied, she thought. Compared to this immediate threat, an IRA informer who never went to work must seem small beer.

Wetherby's expression grew even more serious. 'I should think the odds of there being two moles in MI5 are at least several million to one.'

Liz felt a sudden sense of alarm. 'You mean, that if Tom's the IRA mole, he also tipped off the terrorists?'

'Yes. That's exactly what I mean. And there's something else I should tell you. I think you were at the last Foxhunt operational meeting. You may remember that Dave said that the Dawnton woman, the neighbour, had told him that a white man had called at the suspects' house. He said that she'd seen this man clearly and thought she could identify him. That wasn't true. Dave made it up to see if it flushed anyone out. It did. After the meeting, Tom went to see Dave to find out more. He was clearly worried.'

'I wondered what Dave was doing when he said all that.'

Liz's mobile rang, and she looked at the number on the screen. 'Excuse me, Charles, it's Peggy.' She pressed the green button and said a quiet 'Hi.'

'I can't find him, Liz,' Peggy said at once. 'He's not in the building and he's not answering his mobile. No one knows where he is.'

'Hold on a minute,' said Liz, and turned to Wetherby. 'I sent Peggy to look for Tom, but he's nowhere to be found. And no one's heard from him all day.' He's gone AWOL, thought Liz.

'I see,' Wetherby said grimly. 'Please ask Peggy to find Dave Armstrong and have him meet me in my office in fifteen minutes.'

When she'd rung off, Wetherby stood up. 'I had better get back,' he declared, adding easily, 'Why don't you walk with me? If Tom's done a runner, it doesn't matter if we're seen talking together.'

Liz said, 'When Peggy went to see Tom's ex-wife this morning she was convinced she was being followed. Afterwards, on her way here, she thought someone tried to push her off the platform—just as the train was approaching. It sounds unlikely to me, but I thought it best to send her to find Tom on a pretext, so he'd realise she'd already briefed me on her meeting. That way, if he had any idea of silencing her, he'd know it was too late.'

'You were right to try and protect her,' Wetherby said, 'though I'm sure you're right to think Peggy was imagining it. Still, for her own peace of mind she must have protection at home tonight. I'm going to ask Dave to start looking for Tom, but my hunch is, he's gone.

'What we have to work out is what Tom's next move will be. I have a terrible feeling we haven't much time. We know the nature of his IRA link, but not what his connection is with the terrorists.'

'Could it have started in Pakistan?'

'Possibly,' said Wetherby pensively. 'I think you should go and talk to Geoffrey Fane. I'll ring him as soon as we get back.'

IMPRESSIVE, THOUGHT LIZ, as she entered Geoffrey Fane's office later that day. It was a large eyrie, beautifully appointed, high up in the postmodern colossus on the south bank of the Thames that is the headquarters of MI6.

Fane was on the phone but when he saw Liz in his outer office, he waved her in. She sat down in a padded leather chair in front of his old-fashioned partner's desk, mentally reviewing what she was going to tell him. He'll be surprised, she thought, though I bet he won't show it.

'Forgive me,' said Fane, putting down the phone and standing up to shake hands. 'Our man in Bogota is a little verbose.'

He wore a blue pinstripe suit, which accentuated his height, and an Honourable Artillery Company tie. With his high cheekbones and aquiline nose, he cut a dashing figure, though, as Liz already knew, he was hard to warm to. His manner of talking was articulate and often amusing, but he could suddenly, capriciously, turn on people. In their few encounters, Liz had never sensed him to be entirely trustworthy.

They sat down again, and Liz went straight to the point. 'I wanted to see you about this Irish business.'

'Ah, yes, the peculiar legacy of Sean Keaney.'

'Yes. We've come to the conclusion that there actually is a mole.'

'Really? In place? Planted by the IRA?' Fane sounded incredulous.

'Originally,' said Liz. 'But we think he's moved on.'

Fane shot both cuffs rather carefully, and Liz suppressed a smile. For all his patrician air, he had a dandy's showman instincts.

'Left the Service, you mean? Do you know who he was?'

'No. I don't mean that. He's still here. We think it's Tom Dartmouth.'

'Tom Dartmouth?' Fane could not disguise his surprise. 'Does Charles share this view?' he said with sharp scepticism.

'He does,' she said coolly. She was not going to be bullied by Fane.

Fane sat up straight. He looked ready to challenge her, so she continued quickly. 'It's likely to remain that way too, because Tom has vanished.'

'Vanished?' said Fane, his aggression suddenly deflated.

'Obviously we wanted to let you know right away,' said Liz. 'Particularly because of Tom's secondment to Six. But I'm also here to find out more about his time in Pakistan. We're concerned that he may have moved on from the IRA and that he is helping a small Islamic terrorist group we're trying to find—Operation Foxhunt—we think it's possible he first made contact with them in Pakistan.'

'Yes, of course I know about Foxhunt, but what has that to do with the IRA?' By the time Liz had explained her thesis, Fane's expression had turned from scepticism to gravity. 'Well, as it happens, our station chief in Islamabad is with us this week.'

A few telephone calls later, and Miles Pennington, MI6's head of station in Pakistan, walked into Fane's office. According to Fane, Pennington was an 'old Asia hand' and with his deep tan and lightweight khaki suit he certainly looked the part. Extending a firm, dry hand for Liz to shake, he sat down and listened while Fane explained why they needed his help.

'We want to talk about Tom Dartmouth,' said Fane, all languor gone. 'Elizabeth will explain what we're looking for.'

Liz and Fane had agreed that Pennington did not need to know about the IRA angle and so she focused only on the immediate problem. 'We are urgently trying to locate three suspected terrorists here in the UK. They are all British, but of Asian origin. There's one we have identified and he's from a Pakistani family in the Midlands. The other two are unknown to us.'

She paused, aware that Pennington must be wondering what this had to do with Tom Dartmouth, whom he knew only as a junior colleague. Taking a deep breath Liz said, 'We have reason to believe that Tom Dartmouth is actively helping the terrorists.' She ignored Pennington's stunned expression. 'Unfortunately, he's gone to ground. So we're trying to understand what's behind all this. One of the problems we're having is that he's only been back here in London for four months and before that he'd been with you for four years. So we'd like your view of him.'

Pennington took some time to respond. At last, choosing his words with care, he said, 'Intelligent, fluent Arabic speaker, worked very hard.'

'What about life outside work?' Liz asked. 'Did you see much of him?'

'Yes. We are all pretty close, given the circumstances in Pakistan. Though of course he was in Lahore and I'm mainly in Islamabad. He seemed to fit in pretty well.'

'Was there anything strange about him, anything remarkable?'

'Not really,' said Pennington. 'He wasn't the most outgoing of colleagues. But he wasn't mysterious or anything like that.' He gave a low sigh, half regretful, half resigned. 'I suppose the right word to describe him would be "detached". Thinking about it, he was always keeping something in reserve.'

'Can you tell me about his work?'

Pennington looked relieved to move to less psychological ground. 'Tom kept a sharp eye on the madrasas, in particular, ones that were trying to recruit any young British Asians coming out to study. Contrary to what the papers say, many of these students coming from the UK only get radicalised once they're in Pakistan, and fall under the sway of extremist imams.'

Pennington scratched his cheek, comfortable again. 'He was liaising with Pakistan Intelligence much of the time.'

'How did Tom report to you?'

'Directly,' said Pennington. 'We spoke almost every day, and once a fortnight he'd come in for our station meeting.'

'Did you see his reports to MI5?'

Pennington looked startled. 'Not all of them personally, but they would have been duplicates of written reports he gave us, plus anything else he thought would be of specific interest to your lot. You see, part of his job was to try to turn anyone we thought either had been or might be recruited—by the extremists. It's always a long shot, but worth a go.'

'And did he have any success?'

'Ultimately no. But for a while he was working on one boy in particular.'

'Do you remember his name?'

'No,' said Pennington. 'But it will be in the file.' He turned to Fane, 'You'll have a copy here, won't you?'

'Yes,' said Fane. 'I'll get it dug out for you.'

LIZ WALKED OVER the bridge and went back to Thames House. You had to hand it to Tom, she thought, with grudging admiration. He had played things perfectly, merging chameleon-like into his environment.

'Is Judith about?' Liz asked Rose Love, who was halfway through a mug of tea and a chocolate biscuit at her desk.

'She's at home, Liz. She wasn't feeling very well.'

Damn, thought Liz. She needed help right away. She'd returned from Vauxhall Cross with three names, each the target of an approach from Tom Dartmouth. They included the boy Pennington had mentioned, whose name was Bashir Siddiqui.

'Can I help?' asked Rose.

Liz looked at her appraisingly. She seemed a nice girl, very pretty, but Liz didn't want rumours flying around about her pulling the files of a colleague. Still, she didn't see any alternative; Judith might be out for days.

'Would you do a look-up for me on these names? You'll find them in reports from Six's Pakistan station. Probably sent by Tom Dartmouth when he was seconded over there. Tom's away at present, so I can't ask him.'

'OK,' said Rose, cheerfully.

Liz went back to her desk, answered some emails, then went to the conference room she and Peggy were using, intent on looking through Tom's personnel file again. She was surprised to find Rose Love there, chatting to Peggy. 'I was just about to come and find you,' said Rose. 'I've got the answer you wanted.'

'You have? That was quick.'

'I just did a look-up on the names. Two of them are there in the reports, but not the third.' She handed a piece of paper to Liz. The missing name was Bashir Siddiqui. Protected by Tom, by the simple expedient of omitting his name from his reports to MI5.

'Thanks, Rose. Now I just have to figure out how to find him.'

Rose looked puzzled. 'Oh I've done that too.' Seeing Liz's surprise, she turned shy about her show of initiative. 'I cross-checked his name against the list of British Asians travelling to Pakistan for long periods of time.' She added proudly, 'He's from Wolverhampton.'

EDDIE MORGAN DIDN'T WANT to get fired, but since it would be the fourth time in five years he was at least used to it. 'Anyone can sell,' his boss Jack Symonson liked to declaim. Then with a sarcastic sideways glance at Eddie, 'Well, almost anyone.'

His wife Gloria would be upset, Eddie knew, but she should know by now that there was always another job in the used-car business. He knew cars—that wasn't the issue—and customers liked him (even his bosses conceded that).

Why can't I sell? he asked himself for the third time that week, as a blonde woman, recently divorced and looking for something sporty, said, 'I'll think about it,' and left the forecourt after forty minutes of his time.

Someone whistled, and he looked and saw Gillian, the receptionist, beckoning him from the showroom door. 'Boss wants to see you, Eddie.'

Here we go, thought Eddie as he went inside, doing up his tie like a man tidying up on his way to the firing squad.

He was surprised, after entering Symonson's office, to find him with another man. 'Eddie, come in. This is Simon Willis, from DVLA. He wants to ask you about a car.' Willis was young and informally dressed—he wore a parka and chinos—and as Eddie sat down, he grinned.

What was DVLA doing here? wondered Eddie. Or was this guy a cop? Whatever his weaknesses, Eddie had always been straight.

Willis said, 'I'm looking for a Golf, T-reg, that our records say was sold here about two months ago.'

'By me?'

Symonson laughed derisively. 'Miracles do happen, Eddie.'

Hilarious, thought Eddie sourly. As Symonson continued to chortle, Willis said, 'The car was bought by a man named Siddiqui. Here's his picture.'

He handed a photograph to Eddie. It was an enlarged passport shot of a young Asian man with dark mournful eyes and a wispy attempt at a goatee.

'Do you remember him?' asked Willis.

'I'll say,' said Eddie. How could he forget him? It was his first sale in almost two weeks. That morning the young Asian man had come in and started looking around, curtly rejecting the offers of two of the other salesmen for help. Eddie had therefore approached him tentatively, but the man had been receptive enough to let Eddie escort him around the cars in the forecourt, until suddenly he had stopped in front of the black Golf.

Eddie had begun the spiel, but the young man had cut him off. 'Spare me the bullshit,' he'd said. 'What'll you take for it?'

Eddie said to Willis now, 'Yes, that's the one. Why? Is there a problem?'

'Not with the car,' said Willis. Eddie looked at him more closely. Eddie had seen enough policemen over the years to know that, whatever Willis said, this was not your average copper.

Eddie said, 'If he had a problem with the van, that's his lookout. I warned him it was pretty iffy.'

There was silence as Willis seemed to digest this. 'What van?' he asked.

'The one he bought two days later. When I saw him come in I reckoned he'd had a problem with the Golf. But no, he wanted a van as well.'

'What make?'

'I think it was a Ford I sold him. It'll be in the books.' He gestured towards Symonson. 'It was six years old, I remember that. White, of course. He insisted on climbing into the back to see how big it was. I warned him about the transmission, but he didn't seem to care.'

'Did he say what he wanted it for or where he might be going?'

Eddie shook his head. 'He didn't say much at all. No small talk.'

Willis nodded but Eddie could tell he wasn't happy. 'Thanks for your help,' Willis said. 'If there's anything at all you remember about this man, please give me a ring.' He took out his wallet and extracted a card.

'OK,' said Eddie, looking at the card. I'll be damned, he thought, he is from DVLA after all.

As Eddie got up to go, Symonson said, 'Will you be around later, Eddie? I need to talk to you.'

'Yes, Jack,' he said, knowing full well what they would be talking about.

13

Liz was surprised to learn that Tom lived in Fulham. When he had given her a lift back to her flat in Kentish Town, she'd thought that he lived in north London and that she wasn't taking him out of his way. Now she walked the two or three streets from the Underground station to Tom's address in a quiet, leafy backwater of uniform, semidetached Edwardian houses, mostly divided into flats.

As she approached the front door, two A2 officers emerged as if by magic from a van parked further down the street. Liz recognised the tall broad figure of Bernie, an affable ex-Army sergeant she had worked with before. With him was Dom, his sidekick, a short, wiry man, fit from running marathons. Dom's expertise was locks—he loved them; he studied them; he brooded over them, like an enthusiast with his stamp collection.

But Dom's skills were not needed at first as the front door to the house was open and a cleaning lady, who had been mopping the tiled floor in the hall, was just leaving. She took no notice as they walked up the stairs to the first floor where Tom lived. Bernie rapped on the front door.

Though they were confident he wasn't there, they waited a full minute before Dom set to work. No one wanted any surprises. He picked the first lock in fifteen seconds, the Chubb took a little longer.

Liz hadn't known what to expect, and her first impression was of overpowering neatness and cleanliness. The white walls were hung with a few large bland prints, and the furniture was modern and looked new.

'Nice place,' said Bernie as he led them into the other rooms: an alcove kitchen and dining area, two bedrooms in the back. Tom slept in the larger one; the spare bedroom was clearly used as a study. There was a small desk along one wall and a filing cabinet in the corner. 'Do you reckon he was always this tidy, or did he clean up before he did a bunk?' Bernie asked.

Liz ran a finger under the desk top and, raising it into the air, found no dust. 'I think it's always like this.'

'It'll take about an hour,' said Bernie. He and Dom left Liz to it while they went to work, looking for hiding places. This was just a preliminary search. Later, if necessary, the whole place would be taken to pieces.

Liz focused on what was visible. She went first to inspect Tom's bedroom.

There were a couple of good suits and some jackets hanging from a rail in the cupboard. A chest of drawers held boxer shorts and socks, and a dozen crisp, cotton shirts, neatly folded. So he dresses well, thought Liz. Well, I already knew that.

She looked at the books in the tall oak bookcase set against one wall. The reading was a mix of light fiction and heavier stuff—history and politics. Tom obviously liked thrillers, with a soft spot for the works of Frederick Forsyth. There were almost two shelves on terrorism, and several recent volumes on Al Qaeda. So what? thought Liz. I've got some of these myself. These were the tools of his trade. She noted that there were only a couple of books about Ireland. Nothing political; no accounts of the recent history of the IRA.

Then she saw it. Tucked into the end of one shelf, a thin blue volume: *Parnell and the English Establishment*. She didn't need to open it to know the author's name. Liam O'Phelan, Queen's University Belfast.

Liz was growing frustrated by the absence, throughout the flat, of anything personal—correspondence, mementoes, photographs. It seemed likely that Tom had scoured the flat and removed anything that might indicate what sort of man he was—and what he was planning to do. Though he had forgotten O'Phelan's book.

In the study, Liz was surprised to find the filing cabinet unlocked, but less so when she browsed through what it held: bills, tax statements and correspondence with the Inland Revenue, bank statements.

As she took out the pile of credit card statements, she noticed an entry on the most recent one: the Lucky Pheasant Hotel, Salisbury: £212.83. Looking at it in surprise, she realised its date was the weekend of her mother's biopsy. So much for those friends with the farm off the Blandford road, thought Liz. No wonder Tom had been so vague about the location—the farm probably didn't exist, any more than his friends did. Tom had been staying all along in the Lucky Pheasant. Why? What was he doing there?

Seeing me, thought Liz. Popping by, popping in, then after a long candle-lit supper in the restaurant of the Lucky Pheasant, popping the 'How about it?' question. What was she meant to have done? Fall into his arms, and then the feather pillows of his four-poster bed?

That must have been the plan, thought Liz, designed to put her off the path she'd been investigating. He had hoped she would be distracted by a new passion for him. The arrogant bastard, thought Liz. Thank God I said no. Now I better go and talk to the woman who didn't.

IT WAS ALL very civilised. The Delft cups and the small Viennese biscuits on a china plate, the strong coffee, and in the background classical music playing softly. It was so genteel that Liz wanted to scream.

Sipping her coffee, Margarita looked at her searchingly. 'It's Tom again, isn't it? The young woman who came to see me before—she said it was just a formality. But it can't be. Not if you've come as well. Is he in trouble?'

'Yes, I think he is. Have you heard from him?'

'No. I told the woman before I haven't spoken to Tom since he went to Pakistan. What has he done?'

'Disappeared, for one thing. We think he may be helping some people. People who want to cause harm.'

'What kind of harm?'

'That's what we don't know—and why we need to find him. I've been to his flat, but there weren't many clues.'

'He didn't like possessions. He called them clutter,' said Margarita with a hint of a smile. 'We couldn't have been more different.'

Liz looked round the room and a photograph in a silver frame on one of the side tables caught her eye. It had been taken in front of the Marylebone Register Office—Liz recognised the place from the newspaper photographs of celebrity weddings. Tom and Margarita stood on the steps, arm in arm, facing the camera. What was immediately striking was the difference in their expressions: Margarita, stunning in a pale ivory silk jacket, beamed, her delight quite apparent; Tom, on the other hand, stood in a dark suit with a buttonhole carnation, looking as if he'd just been sentenced to six months. 'You look very happy,' she said diplomatically. 'Who was best man?'

'He didn't have one,' said Margarita, and the words spoke for themselves. She added drily, 'Our driver that day was the only witness. He took the photograph, too.'

'Weren't your parents there?'

'No. Tom made it clear he didn't want them. Naturally my mother was very upset. She wanted us to get married in Israel. But Tom insisted.'

Margarita stood up and moved to the window where she stared out at the rooftops. She wore a grey woollen sweater which emphasised her full figure; she was tall, Liz realised, and must have caused quite a stir in the orchestra world. She seemed to be suffused by a haunting sadness.

'So Tom didn't get on with your parents?'

'He only met them a few times, but it was all right. I'd worried, since he was an Arabist—I thought my father might think he was anti-Semitic.'

'Was he right about that? Is Tom anti-Semitic?'

Margarita deliberated for a moment. 'It's certainly true that Tom had little time for Israel. But I was sympathetic to the Palestinians myself—many Israelis are. So we did not really disagree. That wasn't the problem.'

'What was the problem?'

Margarita turned her head and stared at Liz. 'He never loved me,' she said without a trace of self-pity. 'At the beginning he was charming. Relaxed, funny, irreverent. But I realise now that it was never really about me. Does that make sense?'

She looked so imploringly at Liz that she felt compelled to nod sympathetically. Liz had seen something of that mix of charm and ruthless self-absorption in Tom's overtures to her.

Struggling for control, Margarita continued. 'I thought for a while that he did love me. Probably because I so much wanted him to. But he didn't.' She shook her head regretfully, then with a strained voice, half raw from emotion, she said, 'Love never entered into it.'

'Was there anyone he did love?'

'His father,' she said without hesitation. 'I mean his real father, of course. And that was only because he never really knew him.'

'Did Tom talk about his father?'

'Almost never. And when he did, it wasn't about his father so much, as the people who had ruined him. That was the word he used—"ruined".'

'Who were these people?'

Margarita smiled bitterly. 'You may well ask. I did, but he wouldn't answer me.'

Liz said, 'You know, at work Tom was very unemotional, very controlled. You have to be in our business. Emotion just gets in the way. But he must have felt strongly about something.'

'You mean other than his father?' said Margarita, turning her back to Liz and staring silently at the photograph on the table.

'I wasn't thinking about what he loved so much as what he didn't love. Did he get angry about anything?'

'He never showed anger,' said Margarita flatly, adding wistfully, 'It would have been better if he had.' She sat down again. 'He did hate being sent to boarding school. He was made to go to his stepfather's old school. I know he resented that, but the odd thing is that one would expect him to have loved Oxford.'

'Didn't he?' asked Liz.

'Quite the contrary. I kept asking him to show me round. I'd have liked to see his old college with him, all his old haunts. But he refused.'

'Did he say why?'

'Not really. He was like that: he decided and that was that. Once I tried teasing him: I said, "What if our children want to go to university there?" He told me that the Empire had been built on power and hypocrisy, and that Oxford still was. I thought he was joking. Then he said he'd sooner not have children than send them to Oxford.'

'Perhaps he was saying it for effect.'

Margarita looked intently at Liz. 'Tom didn't say things for effect.'

Liz decided it was time to go. There was little more to be gained from the interview. 'Thank you for the coffee and the chat,' she said, standing up. 'It's been very helpful.' As she moved to the door, she stopped for a final question. 'If you had to guess where Tom had gone, where would it be?'

Margarita gave a weary shrug. 'Who knows? He had no home of homes, not even in his heart. That's what I've been trying to tell you.'

HAD SHE LEARNED anything about Tom? Liz wondered as she walked to the Underground. He seemed to be a man with no cause. A man who could not—did not—love anything or anyone. How else to explain an IRA recruit who seemed to have lost interest in Ireland? An IRA recruit enlisting British Muslims in Pakistan to commit who knows what atrocity against his own country? Tom seemed to possess a psychology that Liz had never encountered before.

What is this all about? thought Liz, and for some reason she kept returning to her question to Margarita. 'Was there anyone he did love?' And the answer had been, 'His father. I mean his real father, of course.' But how could his love for his father, a disgraced hack who'd killed himself over thirty years before, be a motive now?

Suddenly Liz thought, I am only looking at this from one end. What if instead of loving, Tom hated, really hated? Who had he blamed for his father's downfall?

She remembered the details from Peggy's account. Unsurprisingly, Tom's father had protested his innocence of the charge that he'd faked his story, claiming he'd been the victim of an elaborate sting. According to him, the source for his exposé had been a plant, dangled like bait in front of his nose by . . . by whom?

The British, of course. Some unspecified cabal of the Army, the Secret

Service, and no doubt the British Consulate in New York. Tom's father had blamed his downfall on the British.

Liz stood stock-still on the pavement outside High Street Kensington station. What had he said to Margarita—a country 'built on power and hypocrisy'? And he'd been serious. Deadly serious.

How stupid I've been, thought Liz. There was only one trail to follow, she told herself. Follow the hate.

PEGGY KINSOLVING had enlarged a map of the Home Counties and it sat in front of them on the conference-room table. Wetherby was trying to look upbeat, but she sensed his concern. She was glad he was there, though, because all afternoon an idea had been brewing in her mind—far-fetched perhaps, but it wouldn't go away. She was counting on Wetherby to decide whether she was being foolish or inspired.

She looked across the table at Dave Armstrong, who was reporting on what he'd found out in Wolverhampton. 'Bashir bought this van a few days after he bought the Golf. I've circulated the licence numbers, but I'm sure he would have changed them—he did on the Golf.'

Wetherby spoke up, sounding tired. 'They'll probably keep the van locked up anyway until they need it. That suggests that, unless they've got yet another car, they're staying in a town with good public transport.'

Liz looked at the Xs marked on the map in Biro. 'London,' she announced, then pointed slightly west, 'then Wokingham.' She moved her hand up, west and north, and jabbed at another spot. 'And most recently, up on the Downs.'

'What's near there?' asked Wetherby. 'Wantage?'

Liz shook her head. 'I don't think that could be the target. It's a market town. No military installation. And Peggy's checked for public events. There's a market every Saturday.'

'Doesn't seem likely,' said Wetherby.

'What about Didcot?' asked Peggy, who had discussed this with Liz before the two men arrived. She pointed a few miles east from the dumped car's position on the map. 'Its population is twenty-five thousand and growing fast. There are enough Asians among the population for our suspects to blend in. And, most important, it's got the power station. It's coal fired, though people often think it is nuclear because it's near Harwell. Those cooling towers would be quite a target. You can see them from miles away.'

'Hold on,' said Wetherby. 'If they're down there, shouldn't we be worrying about Aldermaston? That's where the nuclear bombs are made.'

'But they'd never get near a place like that,' said Dave. 'And how would they know what to attack without inside information? There's no reason to think Tom has any.'

'What do you think, Liz?' Wetherby seemed to sense her scepticism.

'I can see them staying in Didcot, but I can't really see the power station or Aldermaston as the target. There's no symbolic value in either. And, anyway, you'd need a much bigger operation than Tom seems to have.'

'You're confident that Tom is leading these men, not just helping them?'

'Yes,' said Liz firmly. 'Tom likes to control things, even if it's behind the scenes. Everything his ex-wife Margarita said confirms that. This is a mission of some sort, and he's leading it. In his mind there's a reason for it.'

'Do you think he's working with Al Qaeda?' Dave asked.

'No. I think he recruited Bashir on his own account in Pakistan. He had plenty of access to him—he was meant to be recruiting him for Six.'

Wetherby tapped the end of his pencil on the table. 'All right, if not Didcot or Aldermaston, then where?' There was impatience in his voice. 'I have a feeling that we don't have much time. Burning the car suggests to me that they are on the verge of doing whatever they're planning to do.'

He stared at Liz as if somehow she might hold the answer, and seemed grateful when she spoke up.

'I think it's Oxford,' she said.

'Oxford? Why Oxford? I've known people to be unhappy at the place,' he said. 'But not hate it with passion.'

'I just don't know,' Liz replied. 'I don't actually think it's the place, so much as what it represents to Tom. Somehow, for him, it's become the Establishment incarnate. Peggy's been trying to find out if something special's going on there.'

'I'll try again,' Peggy said. 'I got on to the secretary in the Registrar's office, but she's been out all afternoon.' She got up and left the room.

'Was this the influence of O'Phelan?'

'To an extent. But I think it has more to do with Tom's own feelings. He's carried a deep hatred for England ever since his father killed himself. He believes his father was set up, by the intelligence services and the Government and the Establishment—whatever that's supposed to be.'

'Was he?' asked Dave.

'No. I think his father was just the victim of a con man trying to make money out of a sensational story that wasn't true. The tragedy in a sense is that his father didn't think he was writing anti-British propaganda; he actually thought he was writing the truth.'

'But then why isn't Tom trying to blow up Thames House? Or Vauxhall Cross?' asked Dave.

'If he wants to strike symbolically at the Establishment—as well as do a lot of damage—we are the wrong target,' Wetherby said emphatically.

'So he blows up a High Table at Oxford instead?' said Dave. Liz could understand his scepticism, but she was working on gut feeling now—more and more certain that Oxford would be Tom's target.

Peggy re-entered the room, looking ashen-faced. 'I haven't been able to reach the Registrar's secretary because she's been terribly busy with preparations for Encaenia.'

'That must be it!' exclaimed Wetherby.

'What's Encaenia?' asked Dave.

'It's a ceremony held in the Sheldonian Theatre on a Wednesday during the summer term, where they give out honorary degrees,' Wetherby explained. 'There are usually a foreign dignitary or two—I think last year it was President Chirac.'

'It's not just Encaenia,' Peggy said. 'They're installing the new Chancellor as well.'

'Lord Rackton?' asked Wetherby and Peggy nodded.

Dave's mouth made a small moue. Rackton had been a senior Tory minister, often described as the best Prime Minister the country never had.

Peggy was looking at her notes. 'The Chancellor's ceremony is at 11.30 in the Sheldonian. That's followed by Encaenia at 12.30. In between, the recipients of honorary degrees and university officials meet in one of the nearby colleges for Lord Crewe's Benefaction.'

'Which is?' asked Liz.

Peggy quoted out loud: '"Peaches, strawberries and champagne." They're refreshments paid for by a legacy of Lord Crewe in the eighteenth century. This year the Benefaction is in Lincoln College, so they only have to go round the corner.'

'It's quite an event,' said Wetherby. 'A sort of showpiece of the university. Very colourful—eminent people, very public, very accessible.' He finished quietly, 'I'm afraid it does make sense.' No one had to ask what 'it' was.

'When is this Encaenia?' Dave asked Peggy. Please, prayed Liz, let it be weeks away.

Peggy looked at him wide-eyed. 'It's tomorrow.'

14

Tom had found a small hotel in Witney, west of Oxford. He paid in advance for a week's stay, booking in the name of Sherwood. He used the same name to hire the car and buy the plane ticket.

He rang Bashir once, after driving carefully to the outskirts of Burford, taking back roads that had no cameras. Bashir sounded calm, but then he was of a different calibre—and commitment—from that stupid boy Rashid, who thankfully was destined only for a supporting role. So far, Rashid had been the only mistake. But it was too late to do anything about him.

Part of Tom was relieved about that, for he had got no joy from killing his old tutor O'Phelan, or from ordering the killing of Marzipan. Not that he felt any guilt—they had been necessary murders. Nor did he find it troubling that Bashir and Khaled were eager to die. He had no interest in their motives or their cause. The point was they would serve his purpose.

And now it was Wednesday morning. D-Day, Tom told himself, as he packed, amused by how English that sounded. Later this day he would drive to Bristol where he had booked another hotel room for the night. An early-morning flight to Shannon, and then on to New York. There he would decide what the second stage of his long-term campaign should be. Long term—he had no intention of being anything but a permanent thorn in the side of his father's persecutors.

LIZ DROVE DOWN to Oxford with Wetherby very early in the morning. As they came down through the chalk cut at Stokenchurch, and the Thames Valley opened up ahead of them, Wetherby broke the silence to say, 'Part of me is hoping we're wrong.'

'I know,' said Liz.

'On the other hand, if we are, it may be somewhere else.'

They took the Oxford exit off the M40, then got held up for several minutes queuing at the roundabout on the eastern outskirts of the city. Liz pulled out into the roundabout and overtook a lumbering lorry, then slipped neatly into the road towards Headington and stopped at the traffic lights.

'Do you feel you understand him now?' Wetherby asked.

'Given the resentment he must have felt about his father's death, I suppose

I can understand the IRA's appeal, especially when their approach was made by a charismatic figure like O'Phelan. What I don't get is how it could be switched to another set of terrorists and another cause. Especially since I don't think Tom has any particular sympathy for Islam.'

'Does he believe in anything?'

'Not in the sense of a credo. That's why I don't understand what he's trying to do today—assuming we're right. An old Tory is becoming Chancellor; some ambassadors are getting degrees. What on earth would be the point of killing them?'

'Don't forget, he's already murdered O'Phelan,' said Wetherby. 'And caused Marzipan's death, even if he didn't kill him.'

'They both threatened to get in the way of his plans.' Liz shrugged. 'Though to want to kill all these people today . . . I simply can't fathom it.'

'Neither can I,' said Wetherby. 'It doesn't sound right somehow.'

AT SIX FOOT FOUR INCHES in his stocking feet, Constable Winston was at least an inch taller when he wore the regulation black shoes. He stood out, and he thought of this as an attribute—especially at public gatherings where he became a focal point for colleagues lost in the crowd.

Normally he liked working on public occasions. This morning, however, PC Winston was unhappy to be on duty. He usually had Wednesday off, and took the kids to school. The shift briefing at 6.45 that morning had not adequately explained the urgency. 'We have been alerted to the possibility of an incident at today's university ceremonies,' the duty sergeant had proclaimed. 'We will keep you posted as more information becomes available.'

What on earth did that mean? wondered PC Winston, as he approached the corner of Turl Street, or the Turl, as it was better known. He stood there for a moment, admiring the still-misty view down the quaint street, with the ice-cream-cone spire of Lincoln College Library towering above the college wall. He had been on duty when President Clinton had received an honorary degree, almost a decade before, and remembered the stony brusqueness of the Secret Service men, the way they had insisted that even policemen like himself be vetted for that day.

He walked on into Broad Street, which was bordered at this end by a line of pastel-coloured shops on one side and by the Victorian gables of Balliol on the other. It funnelled down to a narrow strait by the Sheldonian, where the elaborate Encaenia ceremony would take place. Now, while the sun struggled to emerge, the street was virtually empty of pedestrians and cars.

He passed the 'Roman Emperors', a line of grim-faced busts perched on stone pedestals that punctuated the length of iron railing in front of the Sheldonian. Noticing a van parked on a double-yellow line ahead, he picked up his pace. Then two men, each with a sniffer dog on a lead, suddenly came out of the back of the van.

The dog handler nodded as he approached. 'Is this a problem?' he said with a gesture towards the double yellow.

'Not this early,' said Winston. 'What's up?'

'Beats me,' said the man. 'I've come from Reading for this job.'

And though PC Winston was himself puzzled, pride in his own force made him declare with a certainty he didn't feel, 'It's the Animal Liberation lot. Very unpredictable.'

It was then that another PC, a recruit named Jacobs, appeared, moving towards them. 'Here you are,' he said breezily to PC Winston, and handed him an A4 sheet on which mugshots had been enlarged and photocopied. They showed three Asian men, young, entirely innocent-looking. Winston scanned the faces thinking, they don't look like animal lovers to me.

AT 9.15 A.M. LIZ listened intently as the briefing began. She was sitting on one of a row of uncomfortable plastic chairs in the Operations Room of the Thames Valley Headquarters in St Aldates, facing a projector screen. Next to Liz on one side sat Dave Armstrong, who had come down the night before, and looked tense and exhausted. On her other side were Wetherby and the Chief Constable, a hawk-like man named Ferris. Further along sat other senior police officers, including the head of Special Branch.

The Deputy Chief Constable, Colin Matheson, in charge of the operation, was addressing them. He was a trim man in his late thirties with jet-black hair and a line in dry wit. His manner was brisk and professional.

Matheson raised his pointer to signal to someone at the back of the room, and at once a map of the city centre appeared on the screen. 'From what you've told us,' he said, looking at Wetherby, and moving his pointer along Broad Street to the Sheldonian, 'this is the focal point.'

'We think so,' said Wetherby. 'The Installation of the Chancellor is going to be there, and then Encaenia. It's difficult to predict the target but I think a single assassination would not be the first choice of the three men in question. They are Islamic extremists who probably hope to do as much damage as possible in the most visible way.'

Chief Constable Ferris asked Wetherby 'Do we know if they're armed?'

Wetherby shook his head. 'No, we don't. I think it's unlikely they would carry weapons, but we can't rule it out. We do know they possess explosives—we found traces of fertiliser in a safe house they were using.'

'So which ceremony are they likely to attack?'

'I'd say Encaenia, where there will be a lot of dignitaries.'

'Any sense of how they'll do it?' the Chief Constable asked, unable to mask his anxiety.

'I think there are two possibilities,' said Wetherby. 'It could be a suicide bombing on foot, in which case at least one of them will have to get close to the procession, wearing some sort of apparatus. Or they'll use a vehicle, which we think is more likely. We know they have a white Transit van and that the buyer, who is one of the three main suspects, was particularly interested in its load capacity.'

Matheson nodded and pointed to the blank monitors on the wall. 'We're rigging some temporary video to cover the target area as well as we can. We expect to have them working in the next half-hour. Sniffer dogs have come in from Reading and are checking the building for explosives now.'

The head of Oxford's Special Branch spoke up. 'Photographs of the three suspects are being distributed to all officers in the area.'

He passed copies to Wetherby, who looked at them, then passed them on to Dave and Liz. Rashid looked terribly young, thought Liz.

'Every armed response unit in the Thames Valley has been called in,' said Ferris. 'And there will be armed officers all along the route.'

'We're also placing four snipers up high as well,' Matheson said, putting the pointer directly on the Sheldonian. 'One here in the cupola. Another here,' he said pointing to the Bodleian, 'to cover the courtyard between the Clarendon Building and the Sheldonian. And two on Broad Street, one facing east from the top of the Blackwell's music shop, the other facing west from the same position. We'll also have a dozen armed Special Branch officers in plain clothes mingling with the spectators.'

He went on. 'We are looking for any van in the middle of town. We've got extra shifts of uniformed officers walking the streets. White vans are not exactly uncommon, and of course they may have painted the van a different colour. But we're doing everything we can.'

After this recital of preventive measures, a silence filled the room. No one seemed eager to break it.

'So,' concluded Matheson at last, his face grim, 'let's hope that we're fully prepared.'

WAKING EARLY, they ate a simple breakfast, then said prayers. Rashid watched Bashir and Khaled closely. He admired them for what they were about to do, and part of him wished he too was going to become a martyr that day in the struggle against the enemies of Islam. But he knew that he would one day face death himself in another operation. He would have liked to go home first, before joining the imam at his madrasa in Pakistan, but he knew that was not possible. The police were looking for him.

As the three of them squeezed into the front seat of the van, Bashir reluctantly gave Rashid a new pay-as-you-go mobile he had bought in Didcot, walking the mile to the new shopping centre on the main road, up from the station. 'You are to use this once, and only once,' he instructed the small, younger man. 'To ring me as we have planned.'

Bashir drove into Oxford on smaller roads, approaching the city from the west. He followed the one-way system and parked in the quiet neighbourhood of Jericho, once home to the printers of the University Press.

Bashir found himself remembering where it had all begun, many thousands of miles away. He had met the Englishman in the marketplace in Lahore—the man had popped his head out of a shop as Bashir passed and said casually, 'Do you speak Urdu? Can you help translate for me?' Bashir was fluent in Urdu—his parents had spoken it at home in Wolverhampton—and he helped the man negotiate the purchase of one hundred embroidered rugs from Kashmir.

Afterwards they had had coffee together, and the Englishman explained that he worked for an import-export firm in Dubai and was in Lahore on a three-month buying trip. Unfamiliarity with the language was making his task harder; would Bashir by any chance be willing to help? He would be paid of course—a figure was mentioned that made Bashir's eyes blink. Flattered and intrigued, Bashir had agreed.

On the surface their relationship had been strictly professional, though when the haggling in the market was done each day and they retreated to a café for refreshment, their conversation ranged through politics and religion. Bashir was not naive, and more than once it crossed his mind that this man, who was often outspoken to the point of indiscretion, was not what he said he was. But in their conversations the Englishman was never probing or intrusive; indeed, his views seemed oddly un-Western, for he was very knowledgeable about Islam. He was also vehemently anti-American, dismissing 9/11 blithely as a case of 'chickens coming home to roost'.

The imam had been encouraging Bashir to attend a training camp, to equip him to join his Muslim brethren fighting in Afghanistan or even Iraq. But he had been resistant. Why? He was not sure himself, until at one of their meetings the Englishman had put a new idea in his head. What would he achieve by dying anonymously in an alien land? So what if the US and UK armies lost a few soldiers? What those powers really dreaded was warfare conducted on their own turf.

The Englishman said all this in a series of random remarks, but for Bashir they crystallised his own thinking—and his own reluctance to volunteer to fight alongside Al Qaeda recruits. Why not go ahead and be trained, he thought, but take the battle home?

But what could he do on his own? At their next meeting, somewhat rashly he said as much to the Englishman. And that was when their fateful bargain had been reached. For the Englishman had offered to help.

It was an offer Bashir was initially suspicious of, assuming the Englishman was leading him into a trap. Perhaps he made that clear, for the Englishman now made his own confession. He said he understood if Bashir didn't trust him, and Bashir had good reason not to, since the import-export business was not the full extent of his professional activities. Yes, he had ties with intelligence services, but he also had agendas of his own, which happened to coincide with Bashir's desire to strike against the West.

The rest was . . . history in the making, thought Bashir now. He had met Rashid and Khaled at a mosque in Wolverhampton and found them eager to wage jihad. They were young, and eager to be led. The Englishman had agreed to their enlistment because of these characteristics and also, he had explained to Bashir, because they were both virgins in security terms.

A mistake, perhaps, since Rashid had proved nervy and prone to ill-judgment. Still, on this day Rashid would have little enough to do—just a phone call. So it should be possible to ensure he kept his nerve.

It was 11.30 a.m.

TOM LEFT HIS RENTAL car at the Park and Ride on the northern edge of town. The first step was almost over.

Now he took the commuter bus like any weekday shopper and got off opposite the Radcliffe Infirmary. It was an extraordinarily beautiful day now, the sun out in full force, a breeze keeping it from becoming too warm.

Turning into the Broad he walked along to Blackwell's bookshop. There he went to the coffee shop on the first floor, ordered a double espresso, and took it over to a seat by the window. A ringside seat, he thought, looking across the street at the Sheldonian, curved on this side, its yellowed stone topped by the bright white paint of its wooden cupola.

There were no cars parked in the middle of the Broad; it had been cordoned off. He wondered about this, but only momentarily, for it made sense—the cars would mar the beauty of the procession as it moved along.

He skimmed the copy of the *Guardian* he'd picked up, but kept a constant eye on the street. Students and the occasional don came down the steps of the Clarendon Building opposite, carrying briefcases and rucksacks. At the corner of the Turl, he saw a uniformed policeman, giving directions. The policeman looked entirely unruffled. Good, thought Tom.

At exactly noon, he finished his coffee and stood up to go. Had he stayed by the window two minutes longer, he would have seen the policeman joined by four colleagues, two of whom wore bulletproof vests and were carrying Heckler & Koch carbines.

On the ground floor, he browsed through children's books at the back of the shop, then at exactly five minutes past twelve he walked across the floor to the inconspicuous recess of the shop's one lift. He pressed the button, and waited; he had allowed sixty extra seconds in case there was a hitch.

The lift door opened, and a woman emerged. He smiled pleasantly, then moved in and quickly selected the top floor before anyone could join him in the lift. As it ascended he keyed the pre-set number on his mobile. The signal was strong. On the third floor he put his finger on the DOORS CLOSE button—he didn't want any interruptions.

Then he spoke: 'Listen carefully. I will not repeat this message . . .'

IT WAS TIME to move. Bashir started the van and drove up to Walton Street, where he passed the imposing façade of Oxford University Press. At the traffic lights he went left and drove carefully for 200 yards, then pulled over in front of the Ashmolean Museum. Rashid prepared to climb out. Bashir reached across Khaled in the middle and extended his hand.

Rashid shook it nervously. 'May Allah be with you,' he offered tentatively. He shook hands with Khaled too and uttered the same blessing.

Bashir gravely repeated his instructions for a final time. 'Take your time walking there. Don't rush or it will draw attention to yourself. I'll expect your call in twenty minutes. But don't forget: ring only as the procession comes into view.' He looked at Rashid solemnly. 'May Allah be with you,' he intoned, and motioned for Rashid to get out of the van.

There was no time to waste. Bashir turned left onto St Giles, noting the policeman on the far side of the street. He drove towards north Oxford, only to loop back towards the centre of town. About half a mile north of the Sheldonian, he pulled into a quiet side street next to the red-brick walls of Keble College and parked the van. In silence, he and Khaled waited for Rashid to call.

At last, as the moment neared, Bashir felt a slow wave of calm settle over him. He turned and reached carefully into the back of the van until his hand found the length of rope. He pulled it gently until the free end was in the front seat with him, where he laid it carefully on Khaled's side of the gearbox. One sharp tug by Khaled in ten minutes, a half-second delay, and he and Bashir would be in their future.

LIZ STARED INTENTLY at the monitors surveying Broad Street. She barely noticed when Dave stuck a plastic cup of white coffee in front of her. 'Six sugars, right?' he teased, noting her preoccupation, and she gave a fleeting smile before resuming her watch. The Chancellor had left the Sheldonian a few minutes before, now 'installed', and had walked to Lincoln College under the watchful eye of a sharpshooter on the library's roof and with the full attention of several plain-clothes policemen on the ground.

Suddenly a young policewoman rushed into the room. 'Sir,' she said, seeming to address both Matheson and the Chief Constable, 'we've just had a warning call. It said there's about to be a major incident on Broad Street.'

'What were the exact words?' demanded Wetherby.

'I can play it back for you,' the policewoman said. She went to a console at the back of the room and hit a switch.

'Listen carefully,' said an English male voice. 'I will not repeat this message. In fifteen minutes, a bomb will go off in the middle of the procession on Broad Street. Look out for a young Pakistani man. You need to act fast.'

Liz and Wetherby looked at each other tensely.

Ferris the Chief Constable interjected. 'It's not a hoax, is it?'

'No,' said Wetherby. 'It is not a hoax. We recognise the voice.'

'Why did Tom call?' asked Dave, bewildered.

Wetherby was shaking his head. He looked mystified. 'If Tom knows what he's doing, I certainly don't.'

PC WINSTON'S RADIO had crackled barely two or three minutes before with its urgent message, and he was positioned in front of the gates of Trinity quad, helping to redirect the flow of foot traffic. The normal robust number of pedestrians was augmented today by visitors wanting to witness the Encaenia procession, and they were slow to clear, despite the urgency of the policemen ordering them away from the Sheldonian.

The little man might have gone unnoticed if he had not been dressed so unlike a student, wearing a proper shirt instead of a T-shirt, and holding—somehow awkwardly—a mobile phone. And this sense that he was different was confirmed for PC Winston when the man peeled off from the crowd, moving back against the college gates. He's waiting for something, thought Winston, watching him closely as he fingered his phone.

PC Winston could move fast when he had to. The phone had just got to the little man's ear, when Winston's long arm took hold of his hand. 'Excuse me, sir,' he said, 'could I have a look at your phone, please?'

Looking up at him, the Asian seemed absolutely petrified. 'Of course,' he said nervously, smiling weakly as he let go of the phone. Then he suddenly turned and took off down Broad Street towards the centre of the town.

Clutching the phone, PC Winston ran after him, shouting, 'Stop him!'

As Rashid ran towards the corner of the Magdalen Street churchyard, he was suddenly thrown against the outer wall of Balliol, then pinned there by the firm hands of another uniformed policeman. Got him! thought Winston.

WHERE WAS HE? Why hadn't Rashid rung? Bashir disobeyed the Englishman's instructions and dialled Rashid's mobile, only to find it was switched off. Damn! He checked his watch—the procession would be reaching Broad Street at any moment. What had the Englishman said? 'If there's any hiccup, just go. Whatever happens, you must not be late.'

He would wait another thirty seconds, he decided. Next to him Khaled suddenly stirred, and pointed through the windscreen. Looking out towards the end of the street, where the lush green lawns of University Parks were visible in the background, Bashir saw them.

One was in uniform, two were in plain clothes, checking each parked car, then moving on quickly. They were coming this way.

Please ring, please ring, Rashid. Bashir knew it was almost a prayer. He saw one of the plain-clothes men point towards his end of the street, and then Bashir realised that he was pointing at him. The uniformed policeman broke into a sprint, grabbing his helmet with one hand while he shouted into a radio held by the other. The two plain-clothes men were behind him, and all three ran at full speed down the middle of the road.

He couldn't wait any longer. He turned on the ignition and pulled out sharply, intending to accelerate towards Parks Road, where he would turn onto the half-mile street that would lead them to their target. Seeing him start up the van, the man in uniform veered off onto the pavement, and one of the plain-clothes policemen drew a gun from inside his coat and crouched behind the rear of a parked car.

Then Bashir saw a large van—the kind used to ferry policemen back and forth from football matches—stop directly across the far end of the side street, blocking his exit. He braked sharply just in time to swerve into a small road that circled behind the back of Keble College. Racing along behind the modern extensions at the back of the college, he negotiated the ninety-degree left turn with a small screech of his tyres. But he cursed out loud when he saw another police van pulling up to block off this side road as well. There was nothing for it: Bashir floored the accelerator, driving straight towards the police vehicle, then just short of it he threw the steering wheel abruptly right. His front tyre hit the high corner of the pavement and the van shot into the air, landing with a heavy thump on Parks Road.

Bashir regained control and accelerated down the tree-lined street towards the Encaenia procession. It must have reached the Broad, he told himself. *Mustn't be late, mustn't be late.* Out of the corner of his eye he saw Khaled grip the free end of the rope tightly.

The traffic light ahead was turning amber but he ignored it, turning sharply right. He scraped inside the far pavement, just in front of the lower steps of the Clarendon Building, and struggled to aim the van towards the procession that should be heading straight towards him. When Khaled pulled the rope the explosion would kill anyone within a hundred yards.

But the Broad was absolutely empty. No procession, no pedestrians, not even a student on a bicycle. It was like a ghost town.

Bashir began to panic as he felt a heavy thump against his front left tyre. What had he hit? Then almost simultaneously he felt the heavy whoomph of another tyre blowing. Suddenly he lost control of the steering.

The van skewed left, in a curving skid that propelled him towards the wall in front of the Sheldonian. Bashir knew that Khaled didn't need to pull the rope. The impact alone would trigger the detonators, he thought.

LIZ CROUCHED with Charles Wetherby behind one of the police cars, waiting for the explosion. Beside her, Wetherby spontaneously threw a protective arm round her shoulders.

There was a harsh, grating sound of metal hitting an immovable object, and a muffled thump. Then there was silence. Liz peered cautiously over the bonnet of the police car.

The van had hit the wall and been thrown upwards, where it lay against the tall iron railings, pointing towards the sky, its front tyres spinning.

Matheson moved out from the protection of the cars and began shouting orders. A fire engine appeared behind them. Avoiding the forbidding bollards at that end of the Broad, it trundled heavily up along the pavement by the shops towards the van.

As it arrived, armed policemen emerged from the crannies and doorways and moved towards the crashed vehicle. A Special Branch officer in plain clothes got to the van first, and tugged at the driver's door, fruitlessly. He's brave, thought Liz, since there was a petrol tank that could still detonate.

She came out from behind the car and began to walk with Wetherby towards the van. Dave joined them, looking stunned. 'What was that about?' he asked. Neither Liz nor Wetherby responded.

As they moved down the Broad, firemen were shooting powerful jets of foam over the van.

Liz said, 'I don't understand why Tom made the phone call.'

'Well he didn't warn us about the van,' said Dave sharply.

Wetherby shrugged. 'Perhaps he felt he didn't need to.'

Liz looked at him enquiringly, just as Matheson intercepted them. 'There were two men in the van. They're both dead,' he announced.

'Killed by the crash?' asked Wetherby.

Matheson nodded. 'They had a fertiliser bomb in the back of the van, but it didn't go off. It looks as if the detonators didn't work.'

'I'm not sure they were meant to,' said Wetherby slowly.

'You think they knew there wasn't going to be an explosion?' Liz asked.

'No, but I think Tom did,' said Wetherby. 'You said yourself that you couldn't understand why he'd want to kill so many innocent people. He wanted the van to get through, but he knew it wasn't going to blow up.'

'Why would he do that?' asked Liz. 'What would the point be?'

Wetherby shrugged. 'Perhaps to demonstrate it could be done. To show us up as dangerously incompetent.' He pointed up the street, where Liz could see a television crew advancing. 'You can be confident their footage is going to make the national news this evening. None of us is going to look good.'

'So that's what he wants?' asked Liz. 'To destroy the Service's reputation?'

'Something like that.'

'Hang on,' interrupted Dave. 'He didn't care if the two blokes died, did he?' he asked impatiently, gesturing towards the crashed van.

'Of course he didn't,' said Wetherby. He gave a mirthless laugh. 'I'm not defending Tom. I'm just saying I think his objective was more subtle than we gave him credit for. And thank God. Think how many people could have been killed if he hadn't phoned . . .'

They were standing in the middle of the Broad, only yards from the van. Along the high railings above the wall the van had hit, Liz saw that two stone pedestals were empty—their 'Roman Emperor' heads had gone.

Wetherby pointed at some smashed fragments and said wryly, 'Somehow I don't think those are the only heads that are going to roll.'

15

The policeman was moving everyone away from the windows, though Tom knew it wasn't necessary. They were all led to the vast basement room of the bookshop, where he kept a careful eye on his watch. After eight minutes he smiled involuntarily as the countdown finally ended. Three years, he told himself, I planned this for three years—and now at last the moment's come.

He felt absolutely jubilant. He knew that the police would be reeling with confusion as they discovered that the crashed van contained fertiliser that had not exploded: the detonators he had given Bashir were useless—they wouldn't light a cigarette, thought Tom, much less set off a bomb.

The local reaction, as news spread like wildfire about this near-disaster, would be relief. But further away, at Thames House, the reaction would be altogether different. In Thames House, he reckoned, the inhabitants would be having a collective heart attack. Their embarrassment at this close call would rapidly give way to anxious post-mortems, internal enquiries, a media storm, questions in the House, the fear that he might strike again.

Now a policeman let them out at last, and they all trooped up the staircase that led directly out onto the Broad. Twenty feet short of the exit, Tom looked out at the street from the top stair and saw the familiar figure of Liz Carlyle standing in the road, talking to Charles Wetherby.

At first, he didn't believe his eyes. How had they got onto him here? How had they known his target? It didn't make any sense.

Could they have turned one of the bombers? No, for only Bashir had known the exact target—and he would never betray a cause he was so willing to die for. Had O'Phelan talked before Tom had got to him in Belfast? It seemed inconceivable—why would the lecturer have rung Tom to warn him that Liz had been asking nosy questions?

There seemed no obvious answer to what had gone wrong, but he had no time to think it through. He had to get out of here fast. This was just stage one, after all. He mustn't be stopped now.

THE MARKSMAN in the Sheldonian's cupola was still there. Turning round, Liz noticed another sniper, on the roof of Blackwell's music shop.

Something about the scene was bothering her. She looked at Charles, and suddenly a thought came from nowhere. 'I think Tom is here,' she suddenly said. 'He'll want to see all this.'

Wetherby looked startled. 'Really?' he said doubtfully. Then he seemed to think about it. 'Maybe you're right.'

Matheson came back to them again. 'We've got about thirty people still in Blackwell's, downstairs in the Norrington Room. We put them there for their own safety. I'm about to let them out, unless you have any objection.'

'No, that's fine,' said Wetherby, and Matheson was on his way to the bookshop when Liz called after him. 'Excuse me,' she said. 'Could we just check everyone as they leave?'

He looked at her, surprised, then turned to Wetherby, who nodded approval and said, 'We could have a quick look.'

They walked over, and stood at the Trinity College end of the shop front, watching as the customers emerged. There was no one they recognised.

'I need to find out what they've done with the suspect they arrested,' declared Wetherby. He turned to Dave and Liz. 'Have a final look inside.'

Dave watched the retreating figure of Wetherby, shaking his head. 'If Tom had been anywhere near here, he'd be long gone by now. But if he *was* in the bookshop, wouldn't he have just gone out of the back door?'

Liz nodded and they went together through the shop's main entrance. 'Let's split up,' she said. 'You start downstairs. I'll go to the top floor and work down. We can meet in the middle.'

'OK,' said Dave. 'Watch yourself,' he added, but Liz had already started up the staircase.

The first floor was eerily empty. The café was deserted, though its tables still held coffee cups and half-eaten pastries—clearly people had been moved out at speed. She moved on to the second floor and kept climbing—she would cover these lower floors on her way down. Reaching the top floor, she found a swing door on her left and a sign for the toilets. Slightly hesitantly, she went into the men's room. The single stall was empty, but the window was open at the bottom. Sticking her head out, she saw a small, inner courtyard below. From the window to the paving stones was a straight drop of almost fifty feet. Tom wouldn't have survived that, thought Liz.

As she came out again into the main corridor, Liz heard a noise—a long low gliding sound, as if something were being dragged along. She stood still, listening hard, but didn't hear it again.

Suspicious, she walked cautiously round the corner into a room full of second-hand books. There was a faint aroma of old leather and dust. At the end of the room a door was marked 'Staff Only', and Liz was walking towards it when she saw the window in the corner. It was wide open.

Moving quickly, she looked out. Immediately below her was the low roofline of a modern annexe to Trinity College that adjoined the shop.

An easy way out, Liz thought. And then she saw him.

Leaning against the slanted line of tiles, holding onto the frame of a wooden skylight cut into the roof.

It was Tom.

He was trying to open the skylight, and Liz realised that if he succeeded, he would jump down and disappear into the building.

She had her mobile phone in her bag—she could call and make sure the building was surrounded by police. But by the time she got through—and to whom? Dave was downstairs, Charles at St Aldates checking on the surviving terrorist—Tom might have escaped.

'Tom!' she shouted, leaning out of the window. Her voice rang out, echoing in the tiny courtyard below.

He paused, but only momentarily. He didn't look back but, clearly deciding to give up on the skylight, began to edge his way along the roof. He was heading towards the line of older buildings. There he could move at greater speed along the gabled roofs stretching to the gardens at the back of the college. Then he'd be off.

'Tom! There's no point. They're waiting for you on the ground.'

This time he did react. He hauled himself up onto the roof ridge. Crouching there, he looked almost boyish, like an undergraduate, climbing in after the gates were locked at night. Slowly he turned round, and his eyes swept across until they reached the window where Liz stood.

There was nothing playful in his steady stare. His eyes were steely, and his face looked filled with determination.

'Tom,' Liz said again, mildly this time, trying to keep her voice under control. But before she could say anything else, he shook his head emphatically. And then, swinging nimbly down the far side of the slanted roof, he disappeared out of view.

IN CONTRAST to the morning, the drive back to London seemed to take for ever. As they left Oxford, scudding banks of cloud moved in from the south, dispelling the sun and turning the sky a dull hazy grey. Rain began to fall, first in fierce short-lived downbursts, then in a steady monotonous drizzle.

Numbed by the events of the day, Liz and Charles barely spoke to each other at first. Then, as if by mutual consent, they talked almost compulsively about anything and everything. Except what had happened. Favourite holidays, favourite restaurants, favourite parts of the country, even *The Da Vinci Code*, which neither she nor Wetherby had read. It was an almost manic defence against the sheer unbelievability of what they had just witnessed. The low wailing sound, like the painful keening of an animal, that pierced the silence after Tom slipped from view, kept replaying in her mind. Then came the haunting suspicion that he may possibly have allowed himself to fall. They would never know.

Being realists, both knew the avoidance strategy couldn't last. As they swept down into the large bowl at High Wycombe, Wetherby sighed, cutting short his account of a particularly happy holiday spent sailing around The Needles. 'How did you know Tom would be there?' he asked.

'I can't say I knew,' said Liz. 'It was just a hunch.'

Wetherby gave a small snort. 'I have to say your hunches are better than most of the rational analysis I receive.'

It was a compliment, but Liz couldn't help feeling that luck had played as large a role as prescience. And what if Tom hadn't slipped?

Wetherby seemed to read her thoughts. 'Where do you think Tom was going to go?'

Liz gazed at a golf course carved out of the side of a hill, and thought about this. Presumably Tom was planning to leave the country, and go on the run abroad. But where?

'Tom spoke fluent Arabic,' she said at last, 'so conceivably he would have tried to slip into one of the Middle Eastern countries, and carve out some sort of new career for himself with a new identity.'

'He'd have run the risk of being spotted. It's a small world—Westerners in the Arab world.'

'Perhaps he'd have gone to New York,' said Liz. 'You know, following his father's footsteps. I think there was certainly more he wanted to do.'

'More of the same?' asked Wetherby mildly.

'Who knows? But revenge on some other institution, I think. The newspaper who fired his father. MI6, possibly.'

They were nearing the junction with the M25, and the road signs listed Heathrow, which somehow seemed appropriate for this talk of Tom's plans. 'But why did he run in the first place?' she asked rhetorically. 'I mean, what could we have pinned on him? O'Phelan's death wasn't solved—no witness, no fingerprints, no trace of Tom in Belfast. The same with Marzipan. The forensic investigation found nothing to point to his killer.'

Wetherby smiled wistfully. 'I think you are missing the point. Tom fled because Tom wanted us to know.'

'But why? What difference would that make?'

'To Tom,' said Wetherby patiently, 'all the difference in the world. For Tom, the point was to humiliate us, to make us feel powerless and small.'

'Like his father must have felt,' murmured Liz.

'I suppose,' said Wetherby. 'But my point is, Tom's motives weren't political. If they had been, the detonators would have worked.'

'And he wouldn't have made the phone call.'

'Quite.'

'So was he simply mad?' asked Liz.

'We'll never know now,' said Wetherby. 'What we do know is that he wasn't who we thought he was.'

THE MEETING WAS ENDING, but the long grim process had only just begun.

The press coverage of the aborted bomb attempt in Oxford had been sensational. TEN SECONDS FROM DEATH announced the *Daily Mail*, with a split front page showing the crashed van on one side and a picture of the new Chancellor on the other, looking shocked in his academic gown. IT'S A DUD! proclaimed the *Sun*, which managed to get a picture of Rashid Khan being led out to a prison van. The broadsheets were more circumspect. *The Times* account—BOMBERS' PLOT FOILED IN OXFORD—was followed by its other upmarket colleagues in emphasising the fact that the conspiracy had been detected rather than how close it had come to success.

All of course mentioned the deaths of the van driver and his passenger, and also the death of a Security Service officer—though as a 'D' notice had landed within hours on the desk of every newspaper editor in the UK, Tom's death was merely described as a 'tragic accident'.

However events were described, the facts were undeniable: two terrorists had been within a whisker of blowing up a symbol of one of Britain's oldest institutions along with a host of dignitaries. Though some of the papers credited the security services with foiling the plot, none suggested it had been anything but a very narrow squeak.

Fortunately for Liz and her colleagues, the media's shrill attention proved short-lived—displaced by a particularly horrific attack in Baghdad. Yet within MI5 and MI6 the impact of the Oxford Plot was anything but temporary. Analysis of what happened and why was just beginning. This initial meeting was going to be the first of many. Already the various sections were starting their own damage assessments.

As people gathered their papers and started to leave the room, Dave Armstrong caught Liz's eye. 'Got time for a coffee?' he asked.

'Maybe later,' she said, for something made her want to stay behind.

As the room emptied she found herself alone at the table with Wetherby, who was looking tired and subdued even by his undemonstrative standards. He managed a rueful smile. 'I've chaired happier meetings in my time.'

'At least everyone knows what they've got to do.'

'Yes. It's obviously important to track right back through all this. Everything. Right back to Tom's recruitment,' said Wetherby, lifting a hand in acknowledgment of the detail they had all just waded through. 'We need to understand why we didn't pick up that there was something wrong about him. There'll be an enquiry,' he said, with a tone of resignation.

'Is Peggy going straight back to Vauxhall Cross?' she asked.

'Not yet. I've asked Fane to let her stay on for a bit to help with the damage assessment.'

'I need to speak to you about her, actually. She's making noises about staying here. It seems she likes MI5.'

Wetherby raised his eyebrows. 'That will really help things with Fane. He's already suggested we were a little careless, seconding a traitor to MI6.' He paused and glanced tensely at his watch, then relaxed. He had time to talk, and Liz sensed he wanted to. 'About halfway through the meeting I began to have the oddest feeling. As if something were missing. You know that sensation when you've left your wallet at home? You don't know what you've lost; you just know something should be there that isn't.' Wetherby looked at Liz. Then, all vagueness gone, his expression hardened. 'And then I realised it wasn't any thing that was missing. It was a person.'

'Tom.'

'Exactly,' he said, his eyes now focused on her.

It was true, Liz realised. Around the table minutes before had sat Michael Binding, with a couple of his men from A2; Patrick Dobson; Reggie Purvis and his deputy from A4; Judith Spratt, still looking shaky but at least present; Liz, Dave, Charles . . . all the usual attendees. Except one.

Wetherby said, 'He hadn't been back long, but he felt like one of us.'

'That's why he was so hard to catch. He fitted in perfectly.'

'That was part of the plan,' said Wetherby, looking thoughtful. 'As it turns out,' he said sadly, 'he was never with us right from the beginning. But his hatred, it seems to me, was for the Service, not for its officers. Somehow I find it hard to take that personally. Don't you?'

Liz thought of the weekend Tom had 'dropped by' her mother's house, his lies about his friends on a farm, the hotel receipt. He had tried to use her for his own twisted reasons.

'No, Charles,' she said, 'I do take it personally. He was never loyal to the Service or to any of us. He was using us as a means to an end. He was loyal only to his own warped sense of mission to destroy everything we work for. In the wilderness of mirrors he was the wrong way round.'

'Of course you're right,' conceded Charles, with a smile. 'It's meaningless to make a distinction between the Service and its officers. What was it E. M. Forster said? "If I had to choose between betraying my country and betraying my friend, I hope I should have the guts to betray my country." I've always felt our duty was precisely the opposite.'

'Me too,' said Liz simply. They sat in silence for a moment.

'How's your mother?' Wetherby asked quietly.

He is a nice man, thought Liz. Here he is, with his career in the balance, and he manages to remember my mother. 'OK, I think,' she said gratefully. 'She's had the operation and it seems to have gone well.'

'Good,' said Wetherby encouragingly.

'Yes, they think they've got it all,' said Liz. And for some reason she thought of Tom and the damage he had caused. 'At least it seems that way,' she said, adding carefully, 'though you can never be sure.'

STELLA RIMINGTON

Born: London, 1935
Former profession: Director General of MI5
Autobiography: *Open Secret*, 2001

RD: How did you first start working for MI5?
SR: Quite by chance. I had trained to be a historical archivist and worked at that profession for several years. Then my husband got a diplomatic posting to the British High Commission in New Delhi, so I gave up my job to go out to India as a diplomatic wife. There I was, doing what diplomats' wives did in the sixties, which was not very much except running jumble sales, going to coffee mornings and amateur dramatics, when I was offered a job as a part-time clerk typist in the MI5 office at the High Commission. It was the tap-on-the-shoulder method of recruitment that British Intelligence was practising in those days. When we came back home I joined up as a full-time member of the Service, thinking it would be a more interesting profession than Archives—and that's what it turned out to be.
RD: What would you have done with your life, do you think, if you hadn't worked for British Intelligence?
SR: I would probably have continued as an archivist and, when my first daughter was born, I might well have become a full-time mother.
RD: Is the job of head of MI5 as glamorous as it seems in James Bond films?
SR: Though the James Bond films are great entertainment, they have nothing at all to do with the real intelligence profession. After all, James Bond is really no more than a licensed killer. The work of MI5 is about intelligence gathering and analysis. They certainly don't kill people, and very often the action that is taken as a result of the intelligence they gather is taken by others, for example the police.
RD: Was it difficult to write about terrorism in the wake of the recent attacks?
SR: It is a subject I feel the need to treat quite carefully. It would not be very realistic to write novels about MI5 nowadays without mentioning terrorism, as unfortunately it is such a major part of their work. But, in my books the terrorists will never win. In both *At Risk* and in *Secret Asset*, the terrorist plot has a special angle and it does not work out as the would-be terrorists intend.
RD: Does the character of Liz Carlyle owe anything to you, or to your own experiences in the service?

SR: Yes, it does, although Liz Carlyle is definitely a fictional character. She is not me or anyone else I have ever met. But the things she has to deal with at work and in her private life are situations based on reality—her relationship with her colleagues, for example, the difficulty she finds in balancing her life and a job that requires both secrecy and one hundred per cent commitment. The way she approaches her work, though, with a blend of rational analysis and intuition, and her particular combination of common sense and emotion, are unique to her, I think.

RD: What was the starting point for *Secret Asset*?

SR: The inspiration for the mole came from my work in MI5 in the early seventies, when I was part of a team investigating whether there were any more people who had been recruited by the KGB in the 1930s, like Philby, Burgess and Maclean, who might still be active as moles in the public service. When I was thinking of a plot for *Secret Asset* I started to wonder what would have happened if the IRA had tried to do something similar. The terrorist part of the story came from the various recent cases we have all read about in the newspapers, and also from my own experience of working against terrorism in the eighties and nineties.

RD: Apart from writing, how do you spend your time now that you've retired from the service?

SR: I do a little mentoring—helping executives in companies and other organisations to address the different issues they face as they move up in their careers—and I do some speaking, largely at conferences, on leadership. Also, from time to time I help my daughters by looking after my grandchildren: both girls, one aged seven and the other ten months. I want to concentrate most of my time on writing from now on, and am well on with the planning of the next Liz Carlyle book.

RD: Are you enjoying being a grandmother?

SR: It's the great joy of my life. I love seeing them and, so far, they love seeing me, which is perfect.

RD: What do your friends and family think of your new, successful career as a writer?

SR: They love it and they enjoy offering advice on the plots and reading the books when they are finished. They are pleased that it has worked out well because they know that it's been a long-held ambition of mine to write thrillers.

RD: What do you do to relax?

SR: I read other people's books, talk to friends and family, and I just like to sit in the garden and listen to the birds and reflect about nothing and everything.

RD: And, finally, what three adjectives would you use to describe yourself?

SR: Energetic, conscientious, family-orientated.

Illustrations and Photos:
Page 4–5: Joseph Finder © Joel Benjamin; Alan Titchmarsh © Frank Noon; James Rollins © David Sylvian; Stella Rimington © Jamie Hughes.
Killer Instinct: 6–8:image: Getty/Digital Vision; page 150 © Joel Benjamin; page 151 © Universal/The Kobal Collection.
Love & Dr Devon: 152–4: illustration: Marion Hill; page 272 © Frank Noon.
Map of Bones: 274–6: illustration: David Ricketts@velvet tamarind; images: Corbis; page 442: © David Sylvian; page 443 © The Bridgeman Art Library.
Secret Asset: 444–5: images: Getty/Photonica; page 574 © Jamie Hughes.
Dustjacket spine: Corbis; Getty/Digital Vision.

Printed and bound by GGP Media GmbH, Pössneck, Germany

020-245 DJ0000-1